JANE AUSTEN was born at Steventon Parsonage, Hampshire, England, on December 16, 1775, the seventh of eight children. She was educated, in the main, by her minister-father, and began her literary career by writing parodies and sketches for the amusement of her family. Though her life was uneventful, placid, and circumscribed, Jane Austen was highly sensitive to what went on around her. Her observations on the manners of her time and of her class were incorporated in her novels, which include *Sense and Sensibility* (1811), *Pride and Prejudice* (1813), *Mansfield Park* (1814), and *Emma* (1816). The author died on July 18, 1817.

EMILY BRONTË was born July 30, 1818, the second of the three famous Brontë sisters, two years younger than Charlotte and a year and a half older than Anne. Her mother died when she was three, and Emily and her sisters and brother grew up in the isolated Yorkshire village of Haworth with no real schooling and little care. Sensitive, shy, fiercely reserved and absolutely unable to bear any regimentation, Emily Brontë poured the secret thoughts of her tormented soul into her one prose creation, *Wuthering Heights* (1847), the book which established her as a major figure in English literature. She died in 1848.

GEORGE ELIOT (Mary Ann Evans Cross) was born on November 22, 1819, at Arbury Farm, Warwickshire, England. Upon leaving school at the age of sixteen, she embarked on a program of independent study to further her intellectual growth. In 1841 she moved to Coventry, where the influence of "skeptics and rationalists" swayed her from an intense religious devoutness to an eventual break with the church. In 1854 came the fateful meeting with George Henry Lewes, the gifted editor of *The Leader*, who was to become her advisor and companion for the next twenty-four years. Her first book, *Scenes of Clerical Life* (1857), was followed by *Adam Bede* (1859), *Mill on the Floss* (1860), and *Silas Marner* (1861). The death of Lewes, in 1878, left her stricken and lonely. After a brief illness she died on December 22, 1880, in London.

THREE NINETEENTH-CENTURY NOVELS

PRIDE AND PREJUDICE
by Jane Austen

WUTHERING HEIGHTS
by Emily Brontë

SILAS MARNER
by George Eliot

WITH AN INTRODUCTION BY
Victoria Glendinning

A SIGNET CLASSIC
NEW AMERICAN LIBRARY

TIMES MIRROR
NEW YORK AND SCARBOROUGH, ONTARIO
THE NEW ENGLISH LIBRARY LIMITED, LONDON

NAL BOOKS ARE ALSO AVAILABLE AT DISCOUNTS IN BULK
QUANTITY FOR INDUSTRIAL OR SALES-PROMOTIONAL USE.
FOR DETAILS, WRITE TO PREMIUM MARKETING DIVISION,
NEW AMERICAN LIBRARY, INC., 1301 AVENUE OF THE
AMERICAS, NEW YORK, NEW YORK 10019.

> *Pride and Prejudice, Wuthering Heights,* and *Silas Marner* are
> also available as separate volumes published in paperback by
> The New American Library.

SIGNET CLASSIC TRADEMARK REG. U.S. PAT. OFF. AND FOREIGN COUNTRIES
REGISTERED TRADEMARK—MARCA REGISTRADA
HECHO EN CHICAGO, U.S.A.

SIGNET, SIGNET CLASSICS, MENTOR, PLUME AND MERIDIAN BOOKS
are published *in the United States* by
The New American Library, Inc.,
1301 Avenue of the Americas, New York, New York 10019,
in Canada by The New American Library of Canada Limited,
81 Mack Avenue, Scarborough, Ontario M1L 1M8,
in the United Kingdom by The New English Library Limited,
Barnard's Inn, Holborn, London, EC1N 2JR, England

First Signet Classic Printing, October, 1979

1 2 3 4 5 6 7 8 9

PRINTED IN THE UNITED STATES OF AMERICA

INTRODUCTION

Introductions would be more use coming at the end, as epilogues, in the same way as it is more interesting to read a guidebook when one is home again. Description, then, can be checked against memory; and one had the pleasure of disagreeing with the author's opinions. And if it appears that we have missed something particularly delightful or significant, why, then, we must go back again and see.

These three novels are all well worth a second visit, and a third. Thousands of novels were published in England during the nineteenth century, but *Pride and Prejudice, Wuthering Heights,* and *Silas Marner* are among those that have survived, to be read by people whose behavior and experience would seem to be quite different from the behavior and experience of the characters in the books, or of their authors. They must, therefore, still give people pleasure; they are all three very readable—and they must have something to say about human nature, and therefore about our own natures, which transcends historical period. This is part of what is meant by the label "classic."

With the raising of women's consciousness and the rise of Women's Studies in colleges, there is a temptation to see women writers in a class together, united and to some extent predetermined by the historical peculiarities of women's role in society. In thinking about Jane Austen, Emily Brontë, and George Eliot, this is helpful in only a limited way. There are some experiences they had in common, but these were the very reverse of the traditional female fate. For example, none of them had children, and only one of them married: George Eliot in her middle age established a liaison with a man which lasted until his death and was closer than many "real marriages"; then after his death, at the age of sixty, she married a man much younger than herself. All three novels were written with tremendous force and pressure; this is part of what has made them immortal. But the drive that powered each of these extraordinary women was totally different. In their minds, they inhabited different worlds.

Jane Austen, the furthest away from us in time, is the closest to us in spirit, if only because the tone of her writing and its subject matter is more accessible to us. Born in 1775, she was the daughter of a country clergyman, the seventh child in a family of eight. She lived surrounded by cousins, nephews, and nieces; it was this world of minor landed gentry and clergy, set in the pleasant villages and towns of the south of England, that she wrote about in her six novels, published between 1811 and 1817. Her "civilized" domestic comedy, which continues in a thousand forms into our own day, was then unfamiliar.

All her novels are based on one theme: the self-discovery of a young girl, ending in marriage. But Jane Austen is not conventionally romantic about marriage. A spinster herself, she wrote to a niece that "anything is to be preferred or endured rather than marrying without Affection." Marriage in her day, however, was the only respectable future for a girl, and the discreet hooking of a rich young husband was the covert purpose of all those pleasant balls, morning calls, and long visits to country houses. The ironic first sentence of *Pride and Prejudice* says it all: "It is a truth universally acknowledged, that a single man in possession of a good fortune must be in want of a wife." Social pressure, and family pressure from mothers not necessarily as terrible as Mrs. Bennet, saw to it that a girl needed considerable independence of mind to hold out against what was expected of her.

Three especially unworthy marriages stand out in *Pride and Prejudice*. The first is that between our heroine Elizabeth's own parents: Mrs. Bennet, garrulous, calculating, and in the true sense vulgar, is clearly "a woman of weak understanding and illiberal mind" even in the eyes of her daughters—or at least of her elder daughters, since the younger ones are as shallow as she. Mr. Bennet—here Jane Austen gives an affectionate but clear-sighted picture of an ineffectual male—having lost all "respect, esteem and confidence" where his wife is concerned, simply opts out. Shrewd Elizabeth "had never been blind to the impropriety of her father's behaviour as a husband."

The second unworthy marriage is that between the unspeakably silly and snobbish Mr. Collins and nice Charlotte Lucas, who clearly married him just to "be married," to the great disappointment of her friend Elizabeth. And the third is the featherbrained Lydia's marriage to the unreliable Mr. Wickham; this is a union between two lightweight people, neither of whom is capable of a serious commitment, and which is bound, the reader knows, to end squalidly.

But the center of the story belongs to Elizabeth Bennet, in whose "lively, playful disposition, which delighted in anything ridiculous," we get as near as we may to the personality of the author. Jane Austen must have been a formidable girl (she wrote the first draft of *Pride and Prejudice* when she was twenty-one, though it was not published until 1813, when she was in her late thirties), for she—and Elizabeth—see through so much that is pretentious, dishonest, or just plain silly. Lady Catherine de Bourgh is a caricature, and like all good caricatures immediately recognizable; her claims for her mute and obviously deficient daughter add a *frisson* of human pathos. Miss Bingham's idiotic playing-up to Mr. Darcy in her efforts to win his attention is also something we have all seen. Though values and costume and idioms change, a foolish girl's attempts to get herself noticed by an attractive man do not.

The case of Elizabeth and Mr. Darcy is something else. The "pride" of the title is his: an arrogant, saturnine man, he is in love with Elizabeth but finds her family and background appalling. He condescends to let her know both these facts, and is amazed at her spirited reaction. The "prejudice" is hers: she believes, without verification, damaging things she has heard about Mr. Darcy; she is, too, unable to modify the original bad impression she received of him. Yet we know they are made for one another. Their relationship, and the character of Mr. Darcy, point up two perennial truths: how close the tension of hostility is to the tension of love, and how compellingly attractive to some women are "difficult," apparently inaccessible, uncompromising men. (Emily Brontë takes this to a far wilder extreme with Heathcliff in *Wuthering Heights*.)

But Mr. Darcy is a gentleman. Jane Austen could never have conceived of a Heathcliff; and the Brontë sisters had no time for Jane Austen, whose books they saw as passionless, superficial, and overloaded with worldly concerns. Yet in her merciless analysis of the precise quality of the feeling between people, Jane Austen is the very opposite of trivial.

Emily Brontë's personality and environment was far

stranger than Jane Austen's, even though both were the daughters of clergymen. Emily was born in 1818; she came between her two famous sisters, Charlotte (the author of *Jane Eyre*) and Anne. Their mother died young, and their two elder sisters died in childhood from tuberculosis; their brother, Branwell, was a perpetual anxiety, an alcoholic, and a failure. The family lived in almost complete social isolation in the tiny parsonage at Haworth, on the edge of the graveyard. The Yorkshire moors, wild, windswept, and barren, surround the steep-streeted village, and the winters there are long and hard. This is the landscape and climate which pervade *Wuthering Heights*. The girls as children had abnormally vivid imaginations and built up among themselves elaborate daydreams and written histories and romances, which they continued well beyond the age when most girls have given up such things. *Wuthering Heights* probably had its roots in the "Gondal saga" composed over many years by Emily and Anne. Emily's book was finished in 1846 and published the next year under the pseudonym "Ellis Bell." The following year, at the age of thirty, she died.

Apart from a short stay in Belgium, Emily hardly left the parsonage in all her short life. She had no sexual experience, and very little experience of any kind. Charlotte wrote of her: "My sister's disposition was not naturally gregarious . . . except to go to church or take a walk on the hills, she rarely crossed the threshold of home. Though her feeling for the people round was benevolent, intercourse with them she never sought; nor, with very few exceptions, ever experienced." She knew about local happenings by hearsay; and what is reported in gossip tends to be the scandalous and the tragic. As the narrator Mr. Lockwood in her novel says, the people "in these regions . . . *do* live more in earnest, more in themselves, and less in surface, change, and frivolous external things."

Wuthering Heights is probably the most purely passionate novel in English. It is absolutely amoral. Emily Brontë has been called a pagan, a mystic, an earth-worshipper; whatever she is, the moral problem never entered her head. She is writing from a point of view beyond right and wrong. Her heroine, Catherine Earnshaw, is spiteful (she slaps kind Nelly in the face, she shakes the child Hareton cruelly), vindictive, vain, and irrational. She marries Edgar Linton without love. She is prepared to die for a revenge, "to break their hearts by breaking my own." Heathcliff, whom she loves, is even more

viii

black-hearted. Isabella, after being married to him for a short time, asks whether he is a man: "If so, is he mad? And if not, is he a devil?" The question has never been answered. Yet the passionate attachment of Catherine and Heathcliff has a depth and strength that defy comment and criticism. "I *am* Heathcliff," Cathy says, and Heathcliff tells her "I could as soon forget you as my existence." There is no sentimentality, no tenderness, in their relation; it is as hard and immovable as "the eternal rock," a fact of life. It transcends sexuality.

Catherine dies halfway through the book; we read the other half for her sake, haunted, like Heathcliff, by her memory and the power of her personality. While he is still in the story, so is she.

It is not a well-constructed book. The device of having the story told at various times at second-hand through Mr. Lockwood is awkward; the relationships between the Earnshaws and Lintons in the third generation become confusing; we cannot care for Catherine Linton as we cared for her mother. But the power of the whole makes such complaints uninteresting. Charlotte Brontë said that the book was "moorish, and wild, and knotty as a root of heath," as was its author. The poet D. G. Rossetti wrote to a friend after reading it that "the action is laid in Hell—only it seems places and people have English names there."

Fair enough; but there are glimpses of a pagan heaven, as well. There is a sweet moment when young Catherine Linton, sitting close to Hareton whom she loves, beguiles him by "sticking primroses in his porridge." This is charming; perhaps one of Emily's sisters, on her birthday, stuck primroses in her porridge. I feel sure it happened; for Emily's sake, I hope so. More important is the tranquil, lyrical beauty of the last paragraph of the book (read it aloud). It must be one of the finest last paragraphs ever written; it is all the more heartbreaking coming after the storms and sorrows that terminate here, and because it takes an act of faith in "that quiet earth" to believe that Catherine and Heathcliff may really be at peace at last.

George Eliot was born in 1819, only a year after Emily Brontë, but she lived to the age of sixty, and was just over forty when she wrote *Silas Marner*. George Eliot was the pen name of Mary Ann (or Mary Anne, or Marian) Evans, brought up in Warwickshire in the then leafy Midlands of

England. She was a plain, passionate, earnest woman; an autodidact, an intellectual, and a moralist. She was brought up in a strict Evangelical religion, but lost her faith; moral problems, however, continued to absorb her. In London, she studied philosophy, translated, and wrote for and edited a magazine—became a "woman of letters." This highminded existence was transformed when she began to live with the scholar and critic George Henry Lewes; it was he who encouraged her to write fiction. Her liaison with Lewes, which began when she was about thirty-five, brought her great happiness, even though she had to bear insults and some social ostracism on account of their "living in sin" (he was not free to marry her). The redeeming quality of loving relationships is the main theme of *Silas Marner;* she wrote to her publisher, Blackwood, that she hoped he would not find it "at all a sad story, as a whole, since it sets—or is intended to set—in a strong light the remedial influences of pure, natural human relations."

What one remembers after a first reading of *Silas Marner* is precisely what she intended: the lonely old miser to whom happiness comes in the form of a motherless child to be cared for. In fact he was not old—only forty at the crisis of the story—and Eppie does not appear on his hearth until well over halfway through the book. The study of Silas's gradual deterioration, his "narrowing and hardening," the long drama of his guineas, and the subplot of Godfrey and Nancy, take up the lion's share. Most of Eppie's childhood is glided over with astonishing swiftness; we have to take on trust most of "the new things that would come with the coming years" as a result of Silas's enlarged affections and horizons. The story is, as one contemporary critic of this novel said, "huddled up at the end."

Yet the point that is made is made beautifully. Silas has been living cut off from "a life of belief and love." He survived by an arid obsession with his money; once it is stolen, he is left with a hole in the middle of his life. Eppie, whose fair curls he first mistakes for his lost money, is soft gold, living gold, the gold of life; she melts his heart and through her he is brought back into humanity.

Silas's previous isolation is highlighted by our familiarity with the tightly knit community around him. With the group at the Rainbow, George Eliot gives her sympathetic, humorous version of the comforting continuity of village life. The essence of conversation at the Rainbow is repetitiveness; the customers pay each other "old-established compliments in sound traditional phrases." Mr. Macey's story is "listened to as if it had been a favourite tune" which everyone has heard a hundred times but likes to hear again; he tells his story in the "expected words," punctuated by expected pauses and expected questions. Yet George Eliot has these rustics discussing in their own terms weighty questions which exercised the "modern" philosophers she studied: Mr. Macey, to take one example, is talking about the difference between "objective" and "subjective" perceptions when he refers to "the 'pinion a man has of himsen" and "the 'pinion other folks have on him."

George Eliot's touch is not always so deft. Jane Austen's comments about people's behavior are light, ironic, succinct; she does not go in for generalizations or moral-pointing. Emily Brontë is fiercely involved in the particular case; her characters are what obsess her, not any general application of principles. George Eliot is, even in a simple story like *Silas Marner*, much readier to make a general point or teach a lesson, and it is at these moments that she is at her least inspired. Take this sentence from *Silas Marner:* "The lapse of time during which a given event has not happened, is, in this logic of habit, constantly alleged as a reason why the event should never happen, even when the lapse of time is precisely the added condition which makes the event imminent." It is not too hard to work out what she means; but it could have been put less academically.

George Eliot is by no means all head; she has a warm heart and a vivid perception of feelings and personalities. Think only, in *Silas Marner*, of Nancy's musings about her childlessness; the character of jolly, homely Priscilla; and Mrs. Winthrop's untutored spiritual certainties. Nor is *Silas Marner* her greatest or most representative novel. *The Mill on the Floss*, which came earlier, has more of herself in it; and *Middlemarch*, which came later, is a great novel, and in its insights into the failure of two marriages conveys a great deal about women's disappointed expectations of men and men's of women. *Middlemarch*, said the novelist Virginia Woolf, "is one of the few English novels written for grown-up people," and it is the one by which George Eliot's stature should be measured.

The three novels in this volume each make a different appeal. A close reading of all three makes considerable, even gymnastic, demands on the responses. Enjoying *Pride and*

Prejudice is a matter of appreciating the comedy of social behavior and the way in which people—especially women—accommodate their needs and longings to the dictates of their social circle. *Wuthering Heights* requires a surrender to the world of dream, fantasy, and violent emotions which transcend the everyday; a bad trip for some, a good one for others, but few people can remain indifferent in the face of Emily Brontë's imaginative energy. And *Silas Marner* appeals to the humane intelligence, to the logic of human affection, and brings us back from the heights to the problems of the individual finding his place, and his peace, in the community.

Which of the three you prefer will be a private matter, depending on taste and temperament, for as Jane Austen wrote in another novel, *Emma,* "One half of the world cannot understand the pleasures of the other."

VICTORIA GLENDINNING

London
January 1979.

xii

PRIDE
AND PREJUDICE

———— ◆ ————

by Jane Austen

V o l u m e   I

❦

CHAPTER ONE

It is a truth universally acknowledged that a single man
in possession of a good fortune must be in want of a wife.

However little known the feelings or views of such a
man may be on his first entering a neighbourhood, this
truth is so well fixed in the minds of the surrounding
families that he is considered as
some one or other of their daug

"My dear Mr. Bennet," said l
"have you heard that Netherfield

Mr. Bennet replied that he ha

"But it is," returned she; "f
been here, and she told me all a

Mr. Bennet made no answer.

"Do not you want to know w
his wife impatiently.

"*You* want to tell me, and I
hearing it."

This was invitation enough.

"Why, my dear, you must know, Mrs. Long says that
Netherfield is taken by a young man of large fortune
from the north of England; that he came down on Monday in a chaise and four to see the place, and was so
much delighted with it that he agreed with Mr. Morris
immediately; that he is to take possession before
aelmas, and some of his servants are to be in
by the end of next week."

"What is his name?"

"Bingley."

"Is he married or single?"

"Oh! single, my dear, to be sure! A single man of large fortune; four or five thousand a year. What a fine thing for our girls!"

"How so? how can it affect them?"

"My dear Mr. Bennet," replied his wife, "how can you be so tiresome! You must know that I am thinking of his marrying one of them."

"Is that his design in settling here?"

"Design! nonsense, how can you talk so! But it is very likely that he *may* fall in love with one of them, and therefore you must visit him as soon as he comes."

"I see no occasion for that. You and the girls may go, or you may send them by themselves, which perhaps will be still better, for as you are as handsome as any of them, Mr. Bingley might like you the best of the party."

"My dear, you flatter me. I certainly *have* had my share of beauty, but I do not pretend to be anything extraordinary now. When a woman has five grown up daughters, she ought to give over thinking of her own beauty."

"In such cases, a woman has not often much beauty to think of."

"But, my dear, you must indeed go and see Mr. Bingley when he comes into the neighbourhood."

"It is more than I engage for, I assure you."

"But consider your daughters. Only think what an establishment it would be for one of them. Sir William and Lady Lucas are determined to go, merely on that account, for in general you know they visit no newcomers. Indeed you must go, for it will be impossible for *us* to visit him if you do not."

"You are over scrupulous surely. I dare say Mr. Bingley will be very glad to see you; and I will send a few lines by you to assure him of my hearty consent to his marrying whichever he chooses of the girls; though I must throw in a good word for my little Lizzy."

"I desire you will do no such thing. Lizzy is not a bit ___ than the others; and I am sure she is not half so ___ Jane, nor half so good-humoured as Lydia. ___ lways giving *her* the preference."

"___ne of them much to recommend them," ___ are all silly and ignorant like other girls; but Lizzy has something more of quickness than her sisters."

"Mr. Bennet, how can you abuse your own children in such a way? You take delight in vexing me. You have no compassion on my poor nerves."

"You mistake me, my dear. I have a high respect for your nerves. They are my old friends. I have heard you mention them with consideration these twenty years at least."

"Ah! you do not know what I suffer."

"But I hope you will get over it, and live to see many young men of four thousand a year come into the neighbourhood."

"It will be no use to us if twenty such should come since you will not visit them."

"Depend upon it, my dear, that when there are twenty, I will visit them all."

Mr. Bennet was so odd a mixture of quick parts, sarcastic humour, reserve, and caprice, that the experience of three and twenty years had been insufficient to make his wife understand his character. *Her* mind was less difficult to develop. She was a woman of mean understanding, little information, and uncertain temper. When she was discontented she fancied herself nervous. The business of her life was to get her daughters married; its solace was visiting and news.

CHAPTER TWO

MR. Bennet was among the earliest of those who waited on Mr. Bingley. He had always intended to visit him, though to the last always assuring his wife that he should not go; and till the evening after the visit was paid, she had no knowledge of it. It was then disclosed in the following manner. Observing his second daughter employed in trimming a hat, he suddenly addressed her with,

"I hope Mr. Bingley will like it, Lizzy."

"We are not in a way to know *what* Mr. Bingley likes," said her mother resentfully, "since we are not to visit."

"But you forget, Mama," said Elizabeth, "that we shall

meet him at the assemblies, and that Mrs. Long has promised to introduce him."

"I do not believe Mrs. Long will do any such thing. She has two nieces of her own. She is a selfish, hypocritical woman, and I have no opinion of her."

"No more have I," said Mr. Bennet; "and I am glad to find that you do not depend on her serving you."

Mrs. Bennet deigned not to make any reply; but unable to contain herself, began scolding one of her daughters.

"Don't keep coughing so, Kitty, for heaven's sake! Have a little compassion on my nerves. You tear them to pieces."

"Kitty has no discretion in her coughs," said her father; "she times them ill."

"I do not cough for my own amusement," replied Kitty fretfully.

"When is your next ball to be, Lizzy?"

"To-morrow fortnight."

"Aye, so it is," cried her mother, "and Mrs. Long does not come back till the day before; so, it will be impossible for her to introduce him, for she will not know him herself."

"Then, my dear, you may have the advantage of your friend, and introduce Mr. Bingley to *her*."

"Impossible, Mr. Bennet, impossible, when I am not acquainted with him myself; how can you be so teasing?"

"I honour your circumspection. A fortnight's acquaintance is certainly very little. One cannot know what a man really is by the end of a fortnight. But if *we* do not venture, somebody else will; and after all, Mrs. Long and her nieces must stand their chance; and therefore, as she will think it an act of kindness, if you decline the office, I will take it on myself."

The girls stared at their father. Mrs. Bennet said only, "Nonsense, nonsense!"

"What can be the meaning of that emphatic exclamation?" cried he. "Do you consider the forms of introduction, and the stress that is laid on them, as nonsense? I cannot quite agree with you *there*. What say you, Mary? for you are a young lady of deep reflection, I know, and read great books, and make extracts."

Mary wished to say something very sensible, but knew not how.

"While Mary is adjusting her ideas," he continued, "let us return to Mr. Bingley."

"I am sick of Mr. Bingley," cried his wife.

"I am sorry to hear *that*; but why did not you tell me so before? If I had known as much this morning, I certainly would not have called on him. It is very unlucky; but as I have actually paid the visit, we cannot escape the acquaintance now."

The astonishment of the ladies was just what he wished—that of Mrs. Bennet perhaps surpassing the rest—though when the first tumult of joy was over, she began to declare that it was what she had expected all the while.

"How good it was in you, my dear Mr. Bennet! But I knew I should persuade you at last. I was sure you loved your girls too well to neglect such an acquaintance. Well, how pleased I am! and it is such a good joke, too, that you should have gone this morning, and never said a word about it till now."

"Now, Kitty, you may cough as much as you choose," said Mr. Bennet; and, as he spoke, he left the room, fatigued with the raptures of his wife.

"What an excellent father you have, girls," said she, when the door was shut. "I do not know how you will ever make him amends for his kindness; or me either, for that matter. At our time of life it is not so pleasant, I can tell you, to be making new acquaintance every-day; but for your sakes, we would do anything. Lydia, my love, though you *are* the youngest, I dare say Mr. Bingley will dance with you at the next ball."

"Oh!" said Lydia stoutly, "I am not afraid; for though I *am* the youngest, I'm the tallest."

The rest of the evening was spent in conjecturing how soon he would return Mr. Bennet's visit, and determining when they should ask him to dinner.

CHAPTER THREE

NOT all that Mrs. Bennet, however, with the assistance of her five daughters, could ask on the subject was sufficient to draw from her husband any satisfactory description of Mr. Bingley. They attacked him in various ways —with barefaced questions, ingenious suppositions, and distant surmises—but he eluded the skill of them all; and they were at last obliged to accept the second-hand intelligence of their neighbour Lady Lucas. Her report was highly favourable. Sir William had been delighted with him. He was quite young, wonderfully handsome, extremely agreeable, and to crown the whole, he meant to be at the next assembly with a large party. Nothing could be more delightful! To be fond of dancing was a certain step towards falling in love; and very lively hopes of Mr. Bingley's heart were entertained.

"If I can but see one of my daughters happily settled at Netherfield," said Mrs. Bennet to her husband, "and all the others equally well married, I shall have nothing to wish for."

In a few days Mr. Bingley returned Mr. Bennet's visit, and sat about ten minutes with him in his library. He had entertained hopes of being admitted to a sight of the young ladies, of whose beauty he had heard much; but he saw only the father. The ladies were somewhat more fortunate, for they had the advantage of ascertaining from an upper window that he wore a blue coat and rode a black horse.

An invitation to dinner was soon afterwards dispatched; and already had Mrs. Bennet planned the courses that were to do credit to her housekeeping, when an answer arrived which deferred it all. Mr. Bingley was obliged to be in town the following day, and consequently unable to accept the honour of their invitation, etc. Mrs. Bennet was quite disconcerted. She could not imagine what business he could have in town so soon after his arrival in Hertfordshire; and she began to fear that he might be always flying about from one place to another, and never settled at Netherfield as he ought to be. Lady Lucas quieted her fears a little by starting the idea of his being gone to London only to get a large party for the ball, and a report soon followed that Mr. Bingley was to bring twelve ladies and seven gentlemen with him to the assembly. The girls grieved over such a number of ladies; but were comforted the day before the ball by hearing that, instead of twelve, he had brought only six with him from London, his five sisters and a cousin. And when the party entered the assembly room, it consisted of only five altogether; Mr. Bingley, his two sisters, the husband of the eldest, and another young man.

Mr. Bingley was good-looking and gentlemanlike; he had a pleasant countenance, and easy, unaffected manners. His sisters were fine women, with an air of decided fashion. His brother-in-law, Mr. Hurst, merely looked the gentleman; but his friend Mr. Darcy soon drew the attention of the room by his fine, tall person, handsome features, noble mien—and the report which was in general circulation within five minutes after his entrance of his having ten thousand a year. The gentlemen pronounced him to be a fine figure of a man, the ladies declared he was much handsomer than Mr. Bingley, and he was looked at with great admiration for about half the evening, till his manners gave a disgust which turned the tide of his popularity; for he was discovered to be proud, to be above his company, and above being pleased; and not all his large estate in Derbyshire could then save him from having a most forbidding, disagreeable countenance, and being unworthy to be compared with his friend.

Mr. Bingley had soon made himself acquainted with all the principal people in the room; he was lively and unreserved, danced every dance, was angry that the ball closed so early, and talked of giving one himself at Netherfield. Such amiable qualities must speak for themselves. What a contrast between him and his friend! Mr. Darcy danced only once with Mrs. Hurst and once with Miss Bingley, declined being introduced to any other lady, and spent the rest of the evening in walking about the room, speaking occasionally to one of his own party. His character was decided. He was the proudest, most disagreeable man in the world, and everybody hoped that he would never come there again. Amongst the most violent against him was Mrs. Bennet, whose dislike of his general behaviour was sharpened into particular resentment by his having slighted one of her daughters.

Elizabeth Bennet had been obliged by the scarcity of gentlemen to sit down for two dances; and during part of that time, Mr. Darcy had been standing near enough for her to overhear a conversation between him and Mr. Bingley, who came from the dance for a few minutes to press his friend to join it.

"Come, Darcy," said he, "I must have you dance. I hate to see you standing about by yourself in this stupid manner. You had much better dance."

"I certainly shall not. You know how I detest it, unless I am particularly acquainted with my partner. At such an assembly as this, it would be insupportable. Your sisters are engaged, and there is not another woman in the room whom it would not be a punishment to me to stand up with."

"I would not be so fastidious as you are," cried Bingley, "for a kingdom! Upon my honour, I never met with so many pleasant girls in my life as I have this evening; and there are several of them you see uncommonly pretty."

"*You* are dancing with the only handsome girl in the room," said Mr. Darcy, looking at the eldest Miss Bennet.

"Oh! she is the most beautiful creature I ever beheld! But there is one of her sisters sitting down just behind you, who is very pretty, and I dare say, very agreeable. Do let me ask my partner to introduce you."

"Which do you mean?" and turning round, he looked for a moment at Elizabeth, till catching her eye, he withdrew his own and coldly said, "She is tolerable; but not handsome enough to tempt *me;* and I am in no humour at present to give consequence to young ladies who are slighted by other men. You had better return to your partner and enjoy her smiles, for you are wasting your time with me."

Mr. Bingley followed his advice. Mr. Darcy walked off; and Elizabeth remained with no very cordial feelings towards him. She told the story however with great spirit among her friends; for she had a lively, playful disposition, which delighted in anything ridiculous.

The evening altogether passed off pleasantly to the whole family. Mrs. Bennet had seen her eldest daughter much admired by the Netherfield party. Mr. Bingley had danced with her twice, and she had been distinguished by his sisters. Jane was as much gratified by this as her mother could be, though in a quieter way. Elizabeth felt

Jane's pleasure. Mary had heard herself mentioned to Miss Bingley as the most accomplished girl in the neighbourhood; and Catherine and Lydia had been fortunate enough to be never without partners, which was all that they had yet learnt to care for at a ball. They returned therefore in good spirits to Longbourn, the village where they lived, and of which they were the principal inhabitants. They found Mr. Bennet still up. With a book he was regardless of time, and on the present occasion he had a good deal of curiosity as to the event of an evening which had raised such splendid expectations. He had rather hoped that all his wife's views on the stranger would be disappointed, but he soon found that he had a very different story to hear.

"Oh! my dear Mr. Bennet," as she entered the room, "we have had a most delightful evening, a most excellent ball. I wish you had been there. Jane was so admired, nothing could be like it. Everybody said how well she looked; and Mr. Bingley thought her quite beautiful, and danced with her twice. Only think of *that* my dear; he actually danced with her twice; and she was the only creature in the room that he asked a second time. First of all, he asked Miss Lucas. I was so vexed to see him stand up with her; but, however, he did not admire her at all: indeed, nobody can, you know; and he seemed quite struck with Jane as she was going down the dance. So, he inquired who she was, and got introduced, and asked her for the two next. Then, the two third he danced with Miss King, and the two fourth with Maria Lucas, and the two fifth with Jane again, and the two sixth with Lizzy, and the Boulanger——"

"If he had had any compassion for *me*," cried her husband impatiently, "he would not have danced half so much! For God's sake, say no more of his partners. Oh! that he had sprained his ankle in the first dance!"

"Oh! my dear," continued Mrs. Bennet, "I am quite delighted with him. He is so excessively handsome! and his sisters are charming women. I never in my life saw anything more elegant than their dresses. I dare say the lace upon Mrs. Hurst's gown——"

Here she was interrupted again. Mr. Bennet protested against any description of finery. She was therefore obliged to seek another branch of the subject, and related,

13

with much bitterness of spirit and some exaggeration, the shocking rudeness of Mr. Darcy.

"But I can assure you," she added, "that Lizzy does not lose much by not suiting *his* fancy; for he is a most disagreeable, horrid man, not at all worth pleasing. So high and so conceited that there was no enduring him! He walked here, and he walked there, fancying himself so very great! Not handsome enough to dance with! I wish you had been there, my dear, to have given him one of your set-downs. I quite detest the man."

CHAPTER FOUR

WHEN Jane and Elizabeth were alone, the former, who had been cautious in her praise of Mr. Bingley before, expressed to her sister how very much she admired him.

"He is just what a young man ought to be," said she, "sensible, good-humoured, lively; and I never saw such happy manners!—so much ease, with such perfect good breeding!"

"He is also handsome," replied Elizabeth, "which a young man ought likewise to be, if he possibly can. His character is thereby complete."

"I was very much flattered by his asking me to dance a second time. I did not expect such a compliment."

"Did not you? *I* did for you. But that is one great difference between us. Compliments always take *you* by surprise, and *me* never. What could be more natural than his asking you again? He could not help seeing that you were about five times as pretty as every other woman in the room. No thanks to his gallantry for that. Well, he certainly is very agreeable, and I give you leave to like him. You have liked many a stupider person."

"Dear Lizzy!"

"Oh! you are a great deal too apt, you know, to like people in general. You never see a fault in anybody. All the world are good and agreeable in your eyes. I never heard you speak ill of a human being in my life."

"I would wish not to be hasty in censuring any one; but I always speak what I think."

"I know you do; and it is *that* which makes the wonder. With *your* good sense, to be so honestly blind to the follies and nonsense of others! Affectation of candour is common enough; one meets it everywhere. But to be candid without ostentation or design—to take the good of everybody's character and make it still better, and say nothing of the bad—belongs to you alone. And so, you like this man's sisters too, do you? Their manners are not equal to his."

"Certainly not—at first. But they are very pleasing women when you converse with them. Miss Bingley is to live with her brother and keep his house; and I am much mistaken if we shall not find a very charming neighbour in her."

Elizabeth listened in silence, but was not convinced; their behaviour at the assembly had not been calculated to please in general; and with more quickness of observation and less pliancy of temper than her sister, and with a judgment too unassailed by any attention to herself, she was very little disposed to approve them. They were in fact very fine ladies; not deficient in good humour when they were pleased, nor in the power of being agreeable where they chose it; but proud and conceited. They were rather handsome, had been educated in one of the first private seminaries in town, had a fortune of twenty thousand pounds, were in the habit of spending more than they ought, and of associating with people of rank; and were therefore in every respect entitled to think well of themselves, and meanly of others. They were of a respectable family in the north of England, a circumstance more deeply impressed on their memories than that their brother's fortune and their own had been acquired by trade.

Mr. Bingley inherited property to the amount of nearly an hundred thousand pounds from his father, who had intended to purchase an estate, but did not live to do it. Mr. Bingley intended it likewise, and sometimes made choice of his county; but as he was now provided with a good house and the liberty of a manor, it was doubtful to many of those who best knew the easiness of his temper whether he might not spend the remainder of his days at Netherfield, and leave the next generation to purchase.

His sisters were very anxious for his having an estate of his own; but though he was now established only as a tenant, Miss Bingley was by no means unwilling to preside at his table, nor was Mrs. Hurst, who had married a man of more fashion than fortune, less disposed to consider his house as her home when it suited her. Mr. Bingley had not been of age two years, when he was tempted by an accidental recommendation to look at Netherfield House. He did look at it and into it for half an hour, was pleased with the situation and the principal rooms, satisfied with what the owner said in its praise, and took it immediately.

Between him and Darcy there was a very steady friendship, in spite of a great opposition of character. Bingley was endeared to Darcy by the easiness, openness, ductility of his temper, though no disposition could offer a greater contrast to his own, and though with his own he never appeared dissatisfied. On the strength of Darcy's regard Bingley had the firmest reliance, and of his judgment the highest opinion. In understanding, Darcy was the superior. Bingley was by no means deficient, but Darcy was clever. He was at the same time haughty, reserved, and fastidious, and his manners, though well bred, were not inviting. In that respect his friend had greatly the advantage. Bingley was sure of being liked wherever he appeared, Darcy was continually giving offence.

The manner in which they spoke of the Meryton assembly was sufficiently characteristic. Bingley had never met with pleasanter people or prettier girls in his life; everybody had been most kind and attentive to him, there had been no formality, no stiffness, he had soon felt acquainted with all the room; and as to Miss Bennet, he could not conceive an angel more beautiful. Darcy, on the contrary, had seen a collection of people in whom there was little beauty and no fashion, for none of whom he had felt the smallest interest, and from none received either attention or pleasure. Miss Bennet he acknowledged to be pretty, but she smiled too much.

Mrs. Hurst and her sister allowed it to be so—but still they admired her and liked her, and pronounced her to be a sweet girl, and one whom they should not object to know more of. Miss Bennet was therefore established as a sweet girl, and their brother felt authorized by such commendation to think of her as he chose.

WITHIN a short walk of Longbourn lived a family with whom the Bennets were particularly intimate. Sir William Lucas had been formerly in trade in Meryton, where he had made a tolerable fortune and risen to the honour of knighthood by an address to the King, during his mayoralty. The distinction had perhaps been felt too strongly. It had given him a disgust to his business and to his residence in a small market town; and quitting them both, he had removed with his family to a house about a mile from Meryton, denominated from that period Lucas Lodge, where he could think with pleasure of his own importance, and unshackled by business, occupy himself solely in being civil to all the world. For though elated by his rank, it did not render him supercilious; on the contrary, he was all attention to everybody. By nature inoffensive, friendly and obliging, his presentation at St. James's had made him courteous.

Lady Lucas was a very good kind of woman, not too clever to be a valuable neighbour to Mrs. Bennet.—They had several children. The eldest of them, a sensible, intelligent young woman, about twenty-seven, was Elizabeth's intimate friend.

That the Miss Lucases and the Miss Bennets should meet to talk over a ball was absolutely necessary; and the morning after the assembly brought the former to Longbourn to hear and to communicate.

"*You* began the evening well, Charlotte," said Mrs. Bennet with civil self-command to Miss Lucas. "*You* were Mr. Bingley's first choice."

"Yes; but he seemed to like his second better."

"Oh!—you mean Jane, I suppose—because he danced with her twice. To be sure that *did* seem as if he admired her—indeed I rather believe he *did*—I heard something about it—but I hardly know what—something about Mr. Robinson."

"Perhaps you mean what I overheard between him and Mr. Robinson; did not I mention it to you? Mr. Robinson's asking him how he liked our Meryton assemblies, and whether he did not think there were a great many pretty women in the room, and *which* he thought the prettiest? and his answering immediately to the last question—Oh! the eldest Miss Bennet beyond a doubt, there cannot be two opinions on that point."

"Upon my word! Well, that was very decided indeed —that does seem as if——but however, it may all come to nothing you know."

"*My* overhearings were more to the purpose than *yours*, Eliza," said Charlotte. "Mr. Darcy is not so well worth listening to as his friend, is he? Poor Eliza!—to be only just *tolerable.*"

"I beg you would not put it into Lizzy's head to be vexed by his ill-treatment; for he is such a disagreeable man that it would be quite a misfortune to be liked by him. Mrs. Long told me last night that he sat close to her for half an hour without once opening his lips."

"Are you quite sure, Ma'am?—is not there a little mistake?" said Jane. "I certainly saw Mr. Darcy speaking to her."

"Aye—because she asked him at last how he liked Netherfield, and he could not help answering her; but she said he seemed very angry at being spoke to."

"Miss Bingley told me," said Jane, "that he never speaks much unless among his intimate acquaintance. With *them* he is remarkably agreeable."

"I do not believe a word of it, my dear. If he had been so very agreeable he would have talked to Mrs. Long. But I can guess how it was; everybody says that he is ate up with pride, and I dare say he had heard somehow that Mrs. Long does not keep a carriage, and had come to the ball in a hack chaise."

"I do not mind his not talking to Mrs. Long," said Miss Lucas, "but I wish he had danced with Eliza."

"Another time, Lizzy," said her mother, "I would not dance with *him,* if I were you."

"I believe, Ma'am, I may safely promise you *never* to dance with him."

"His pride," said Miss Lucas, "does not offend *me* so much as pride often does, because there is an excuse for it. One cannot wonder that so very fine a young man, with family, fortune, everything in his favour, should think highly of himself. If I may so express it, he has a *right* to be proud."

"That is very true," replied Elizabeth, "and I could easily forgive *his* pride, if he had not mortified *mine*."

"Pride," observed Mary, who piqued herself upon the solidity of her reflections, "is a very common failing I believe. By all that I have ever read, I am convinced that it is very common indeed, that human nature is particularly prone to it, and that there are very few of us who do not cherish a feeling of self-complacency on the score of some quality or other, real or imaginary. Vanity and pride are different things, though the words are often used synonymously. A person may be proud without being vain. Pride relates more to our opinion of ourselves, vanity to what we would have others think of us."

"If I were as rich as Mr. Darcy," cried a young Lucas who came with his sisters, "I should not care how proud I was. I would keep a pack of foxhounds, and drink a bottle of wine everyday."

"Then you would drink a great deal more than you ought," said Mrs. Bennet; "and if I were to see you at it I should take away your bottle directly."

The boy protested that she should not; she continued to declare that she would, and the argument ended only with the visit.

CHAPTER SIX

THE ladies of Longbourn soon waited on those of Netherfield. The visit was returned in due form. Miss Bennet's pleasing manners grew on the goodwill of Mrs. Hurst and Miss Bingley; and though the mother was found to be intolerable and the younger sisters not worth speaking to, a wish of being better acquainted with *them* was expressed towards the two eldest. By Jane this attention was received with the greatest pleasure; but Elizabeth still saw superciliousness in their treatment of everybody, hardly excepting even her sister, and could not like them; though their kindness to Jane, such as it was, had a value as arising in all probability from the influence of their brother's admiration. It was generally evident whenever they met that he *did* admire her; and to *her* it was equally evident that Jane was yielding to the preference which she had begun to entertain for him from the first, and was in a way to be very much in love; but she considered with pleasure that it was not likely to be discovered by the world in general, since Jane united with great strength of feeling a composure of temper and a uniform cheerfulness of manner, which would guard her from the suspicions of the impertinent. She mentioned this to her friend Miss Lucas.

"It may perhaps be pleasant," replied Charlotte, "to be able to impose on the public in such a case; but it is sometimes a disadvantage to be so very guarded. If a woman conceals her affection with the same skill from the object of it, she may lose the opportunity of fixing him; and it will then be but poor consolation to believe the world equally in the dark. There is so much of gratitude or vanity in almost every attachment that it is not safe to leave any to itself. We can all *begin* freely—a slight preference is natural enough; but there are very few of us who have heart enough to be really in love without encouragement. In nine cases out of ten, a woman had better show *more* affection than she feels. Bingley likes your sister undoubtedly; but he may never do more than like her, if she does not help him on."

"But she does help him on, as much as her nature will allow. If *I* can perceive her regard for him, he must be a simpleton indeed not to discover it too."

"Remember, Eliza, that he does not know Jane's disposition as you do."

"But if a woman is partial to a man, and does not endeavour to conceal it, he must find it out."

"Perhaps he must, if he sees enough of her. But though Bingley and Jane meet tolerably often, it is never for many hours together; and as they always see each other in large mixed parties, it is impossible that every moment should be employed in conversing together. Jane should therefore make the most of every half hour in which she can command his attention. When she is secure of him, there will be leisure for falling in love as much as she chooses."

"Your plan is a good one," replied Elizabeth, "where nothing is in question but the desire of being well married; and if I were determined to get a rich husband, or any husband, I dare say I should adopt it. But these are not Jane's feelings; she is not acting by design. As yet, she cannot even be certain of the degree of her own regard, nor of its reasonableness. She has known him only a fortnight. She danced four dances with him at Meryton; she saw him one morning at his own house, and has since dined in company with him four times. This is not quite enough to make her understand his character."

"Not as you represent it. Had she merely *dined* with him, she might only have discovered whether he had a good appetite; but you must remember that four evenings have been also spent together—and four evenings may do a great deal."

"Yes; these four evenings have enabled them to ascertain that they both like *vingt-et-un* better than commerce; but with respect to any other leading characteristic, I do not imagine that much has been unfolded."

"Well," said Charlotte, "I wish Jane success with all my heart; and if she were married to him to-morrow, I should think she had as good a chance of happiness as if she were to be studying his character for a twelvemonth. Happiness in marriage is entirely a matter of chance. If the dispositions of the parties are ever so well known to each other, or ever so similar beforehand, it does not advance their felicity in the least. They always continue to grow sufficiently unlike afterwards to have their share of vexation, and it is better to know as little as possible of the defects of the person with whom you are to pass your life."

"You make me laugh, Charlotte; but it is not sound. You know it is not sound, and that you would never act in this way yourself."

Occupied in observing Mr. Bingley's attentions to her sister, Elizabeth was far from suspecting that she was herself becoming an object of some interest in the eyes of his friend. Mr. Darcy had at first scarcely allowed her to be pretty; he had looked at her without admiration at the ball; and when they next met, he looked at her only to criticize. But no sooner had he made it clear to himself and his friends that she had hardly a good feature in her face, than he began to find it was rendered uncommonly intelligent by the beautiful expression of her dark eyes. To this discovery succeeded some others equally mortifying. Though he had detected with a critical eye more than one failure of perfect symmetry in her form, he was forced to acknowledge her figure to be light and pleasing; and in spite of his asserting that her manners were not those of the fashionable world, he was caught by their easy playfulness. Of this she was perfectly unaware; to her he was only the man who made himself agreeable nowhere, and who had not thought her handsome enough to dance with.

He began to wish to know more of her, and as a step towards conversing with her himself, attended to her conversation with others. His doing so drew her notice. It was at Sir William Lucas's, where a large party were assembled.

"What does Mr. Darcy mean," said she to Charlotte, "by listening to my conversation with Colonel Forster?"

"That is a question which Mr. Darcy only can answer."

"But if he does it any more I shall certainly let him know that I see what he is about. He has a very satirical eye, and if I do not begin by being impertinent myself, I shall soon grow afraid of him."

On his approaching them soon afterwards, though without seeming to have any intention of speaking, Miss Lucas defied her friend to mention such a subject to him, which immediately provoking Elizabeth to do it, she turned to him and said,

"Did not you think, Mr. Darcy, that I expressed myself uncommonly well just now, when I was teasing Colonel Forster to give us a ball at Meryton?"

"With great energy—but it is a subject which always makes a lady energetic."

"You are severe on us."

"It will be *her* turn soon to be teased," said Miss Lucas. "I am going to open the instrument, Eliza, and you know what follows."

"You are a very strange creature by way of a friend! —always wanting me to play and sing before anybody and everybody! If my vanity had taken a musical turn, you would have been invaluable, but as it is, I would really rather not sit down before those who must be in the habit of hearing the very best performers." On Miss Lucas's persevering, however, she added, "Very well; if it must be so, it must." And gravely glancing at Mr.

Darcy, "There is a fine old saying, which everybody here is of course familiar with—'Keep your breath to cool your porridge'—and I shall keep mine to swell my song."

Her performance was pleasing, though by no means capital. After a song or two, and before she could reply to the entreaties of several that she would sing again, she was eagerly succeeded at the instrument by her sister Mary, who having, in consequence of being the only plain one in the family, worked hard for knowledge and accomplishments, was always impatient for display.

Mary had neither genius nor taste; and though vanity had given her application, it had given her likewise a pedantic air and conceited manner, which would have injured a higher degree of excellence than she had reached. Elizabeth, easy and unaffected, had been listened to with much more pleasure, though not playing half so well; and Mary, at the end of a long concerto, was glad to purchase praise and gratitude by Scotch and Irish airs at the request of her younger sisters, who with some of the Lucases and two or three officers joined eagerly in dancing at one end of the room.

Mr. Darcy stood near them in silent indignation at such a mode of passing the evening, to the exclusion of all conversation, and was too much engrossed by his own thoughts to perceive that Sir William Lucas was his neighbour, till Sir William thus began.

"What a charming amusement for young people this is, Mr. Darcy! There is nothing like dancing after all. I consider it as one of the first refinements of polished societies."

"Certainly, sir; and it has the advantage also of being in vogue amongst the less polished societies of the world. Every savage can dance."

Sir William only smiled. "Your friend performs delightfully," he continued after a pause, on seeing Bingley join the group; "and I doubt not that you are an adept in the science yourself, Mr. Darcy."

"You saw me dance at Meryton, I believe, sir."

"Yes, indeed, and received no inconsiderable pleasure from the sight. Do you often dance at St. James's?"

"Never, sir."

"Do you not think it would be a proper compliment to the place?"

"It is a compliment which I never pay to any place if I can avoid it."

"You have a house in town, I conclude?"

Mr. Darcy bowed.

"I had once some thoughts of fixing in town myself—for I am fond of superior society; but I did not feel quite certain that the air of London would agree with Lady Lucas."

He paused in hopes of an answer; but his companion was not disposed to make any; and Elizabeth at that instant moving towards them, he was struck with the notion of doing a very gallant thing, and called out to her,

"My dear Miss Eliza, why are not you dancing?—Mr. Darcy, you must allow me to present this young lady to you as a very desirable partner. You cannot refuse to dance, I am sure, when so much beauty is before you." And taking her hand, he would have given it to Mr. Darcy, who, though extremely surprised, was not unwilling to receive it, when she instantly drew back, and said with some discomposure to Sir William,

"Indeed, sir, I have not the least intention of dancing. I entreat you not to suppose that I moved this way in order to beg for a partner."

Mr. Darcy with grave propriety requested to be allowed the honour of her hand; but in vain. Elizabeth was determined; nor did Sir William at all shake her purpose by his attempt at persuasion.

"You excel so much in the dance, Miss Eliza, that it is cruel to deny me the happiness of seeing you; and though this gentleman dislikes the amusement in general, he can have no objection, I am sure, to oblige us for one half hour."

"Mr. Darcy is all politeness," said Elizabeth, smiling.

"He is indeed—but considering the inducement, my dear Miss Eliza, we cannot wonder at his complaisance; for who would object to such a partner?"

Elizabeth looked archly, and turned away. Her resistance had not injured her with the gentleman, and he was thinking of her with some complacency, when thus accosted by Miss Bingley,

"I can guess the subject of your reverie."

"I should imagine not."

"You are considering how insupportable it would be to pass many evenings in this manner—in such society; and indeed I am quite of your opinion. I was never more annoyed! The insipidity and yet the noise; the nothingness and yet the self-importance of all these people! What would I give to hear your strictures on them!"

"Your conjecture is totally wrong, I assure you. My mind was more agreeably engaged. I have been meditating on the very great pleasure which a pair of fine eyes in the face of a pretty woman can bestow."

Miss Bingley immediately fixed her eyes on his face, and desired he would tell her what lady had the credit of inspiring such reflections. Mr. Darcy replied with great intrepidity,

"Miss Elizabeth Bennett."

"Miss Elizabeth Bennet!" repeated Miss Bingley. "I am all astonishment. How long has she been such a favourite?—and pray when am I to wish you joy?"

"That is exactly the question which I expected you to ask. A lady's imagination is very rapid; it jumps from admiration to love, from love to matrimony in a moment. I knew you would be wishing me joy."

"Nay, if you are so serious about it, I shall consider the matter as absolutely settled. You will have a charming mother-in-law, indeed, and of course she will be always at Pemberley with you."

He listened to her with perfect indifference, while she chose to entertain herself in this manner, and as his composure convinced her that all was safe, her wit flowed long.

CHAPTER SEVEN

MR. Bennet's property consisted almost entirely in an estate of two thousand a year, which, unfortunately for his daughters, was entailed in default of heirs male, on a distant relation; and their mother's fortune, though ample for her situation in life, could but ill supply the deficiency of his. Her father had been an attorney in Meryton, and had left her four thousand pounds.

She had a sister married to a Mr. Philips, who had been a clerk to their father, and succeeded him in the business, and a brother settled in London in a respectable line of trade.

The village of Longbourn was only one mile from Meryton; a most convenient distance for the young ladies, who were usually tempted thither three or four times a week to pay their duty to their aunt and to a milliner's shop just over the way. The two youngest of the family, Catherine and Lydia, were particularly frequent in these attentions; their minds were more vacant than their sisters', and when nothing better offered, a walk to Meryton was necessary to amuse their morning hours and furnish conversation for the evening; and however bare of news the country in general might be, they always contrived to learn some from their aunt. At present, indeed, they were well supplied both with news and happiness by the recent arrival of a militia regiment in the neighbourhood; it was to remain the whole winter, and Meryton was the head-quarters.

Their visits to Mrs. Philips were now productive of the most interesting intelligence. Everyday added something to their knowledge of the officers' names and connections. Their lodgings were not long a secret, and at length they began to know the officers themselves. Mr. Philips visited them all, and this opened to his nieces a source of felicity unknown before. They could talk of nothing but officers; and Mr. Bingley's large fortune, the mention of which gave animation to their mother, was worthless in their eyes when opposed to the regimentals of an ensign.

After listening one morning to their effusions on this subject, Mr. Bennet coolly observed,

"From all that I can collect by your manner of talking, you must be two of the silliest girls in the country. I have suspected it some time, but I am now convinced."

Catherine was disconcerted, and made no answer; but Lydia, with perfect indifference, continued to express her admiration of Captain Carter, and her hope of seeing him in the course of the day, as he was going the next morning to London.

"I am astonished, my dear," said Mrs. Bennet, "that you should be so ready to think your own children silly.

If I wished to think slightingly of anybody's children, it should not be of my own however."

"If my children are silly I must hope to be always sensible of it."

"Yes—but as it happens, they are all of them very clever."

"This is the only point, I flatter myself, on which we do not agree. I had hoped that our sentiments coincided in every particular, but I must so far differ from you as to think our two youngest daughters uncommonly foolish."

"My dear Mr. Bennet, you must not expect such girls to have the sense of their father and mother. When they get to our age I dare say they will not think about officers any more than we do. I remember the time when I liked a redcoat myself very well—and indeed so I do still at my heart; and if a smart young colonel, with five or six thousand a year, should want one of my girls, I shall not say nay to him; and I thought Colonel Forster looked very becoming the other night at Sir William's in his regimentals."

"Mama," cried Lydia, "my aunt says that Colonel Forster and Captain Carter do not go so often to Miss Watson's as they did when they first came; she sees them now very often standing in Clarke's library."

Mrs. Bennet was prevented replying by the entrance of the footman with a note for Miss Bennet; it came from Netherfield, and the servant waited for an answer. Mrs. Bennet's eyes sparkled with pleasure, and she was eagerly calling out, while her daughter read,

"Well, Jane, who is it from? what is it about? what does he say? Well, Jane, make haste and tell us; make haste, my love."

"It is from Miss Bingley," said Jane, and then read it aloud.

My dear Friend,

If you are not so compassionate as to dine to-day with Louisa and me, we shall be in danger of hating each other for the rest of our lives, for a whole day's *tête-à-tête* between two women can never end without a quarrel. Come as soon as you can on the receipt of this.

My brother and the gentlemen are to dine with the officers. Yours ever.

CAROLINE BINGLEY

"With the officers!" cried Lydia. "I wonder my aunt did not tell us of *that*."

"Dining out," said Mrs. Bennet, "that is very unlucky."

"Can I have the carriage?" said Jane.

"No, my dear, you had better go on horseback, because it seems likely to rain, and then you must stay all night."

"That would be a good scheme," said Elizabeth, "if you were sure that they would not offer to send her home."

"Oh! but the gentlemen will have Mr. Bingley's chaise to go to Meryton; and the Hursts have no horses to theirs."

"I had much rather go in the coach."

"But, my dear, your father cannot spare the horses, I am sure. They are wanted in the farm, Mr. Bennet, are not they?"

"They are wanted in the farm much oftener than I can get them."

"But if you have got them to-day," said Elizabeth, "my mother's purpose will be answered."

She did at last extort from her father an acknowledgment that the horses were engaged. Jane was therefore obliged to go on horseback, and her mother attended her to the door with many cheerful prognostics of a bad day. Her hopes were answered; Jane had not been gone long before it rained hard. Her sisters were uneasy for her, but her mother was delighted. The rain continued the whole evening without intermission; Jane certainly could not come back.

"This was a lucky idea of mine, indeed!" said Mrs. Bennet, more than once, as if the credit of making it rain were all her own. Till the next morning, however, she was not aware of all the felicity of her contrivance. Breakfast was scarcely over when a servant from Netherfield brought the following note for Elizabeth:

MY DEAREST LIZZY,

I find myself very unwell this morning, which, I

suppose, is to be imputed to my getting wet through yesterday. My kind friends will not hear of my returning home till I am better. They insist also on my seeing Mr. Jones—therefore do not be alarmed if you should hear of his having been to me—and excepting a sore throat and headache there is not much the matter with me.

YOURS, ETC.

"Well, my dear," said Mr. Bennet, when Elizabeth had read the note aloud, "if your daughter should have a dangerous fit of illness, if she should die, it would be a comfort to know that it was all in pursuit of Mr. Bingley, and under your orders."

"Oh! I am not at all afraid of her dying. People do not die of little trifling colds. She will be taken good care of. As long as she stays there, it is all very well. I would go and see her, if I could have the carriage."

Elizabeth, feeling really anxious, was determined to go to her, though the carriage was not to be had; and as she was no horsewoman, walking was her only alternative. She declared her resolution.

"How can you be so silly," cried her mother, "as to think of such a thing in all this dirt! You will not be fit to be seen when you get there."

"I shall be very fit to see Jane—which is all I want."

"Is this a hint to me, Lizzy," said her father, "to send for the horses?"

"No, indeed. I do not wish to avoid the walk. The distance is nothing, when one has a motive; only three miles. I shall be back by dinner."

"I admire the activity of your benevolence," observed Mary, "but every impulse of feeling should be guided by reason; and, in my opinion, exertion should always be in proportion to what is required."

"We will go as far as Meryton with you," said Catherine and Lydia. Elizabeth accepted their company, and the three young ladies set off together.

"If we make haste," said Lydia, as they walked along, "perhaps we may see something of Captain Carter before he goes."

In Meryton they parted; the two youngest repaired to the lodgings of one of the officers' wives, and Elizabeth continued her walk alone, crossing field after field at a quick pace, jumping over stiles and springing over puddles with impatient activity, and finding herself at last within view of the house, with weary ankles, dirty stockings, and a face glowing with the warmth of exercise.

She was shown into the breakfast-parlour, where all but Jane were assembled, and where her appearance created a great deal of surprise. That she should have walked three miles so early in the day, in such dirty weather, and by herself, was almost incredible to Mrs. Hurst and Miss Bingley; and Elizabeth was convinced that they held her in contempt for it. She was received, however, very politely by them; and in their brother's manners there was something better than politeness; there was good humour and kindness. Mr. Darcy said very little, and Mr. Hurst nothing at all. The former was divided between admiration of the brilliancy which exercise had given to her complexion, and doubt as to the occasion's justifying her coming so far alone. The latter was thinking only of his breakfast.

Her inquiries after her sister were not very favourably answered. Miss Bennet had slept ill, and though up, was very feverish and not well enough to leave her room. Elizabeth was glad to be taken to her immediately; and Jane, who had only been withheld by the fear of giving alarm or inconvenience from expressing in her note how much she longed for such a visit, was delighted at her entrance. She was not equal, however, to much conversation, and when Miss Bingley left them together, could attempt little beside expressions of gratitude for the extraordinary kindness she was treated with. Elizabeth silently attended her.

When breakfast was over, they were joined by the sisters; and Elizabeth began to like them herself, when she saw how much affection and solicitude they showed for Jane. The apothecary came, and having examined his patient, said, as might be supposed, that she had caught a violent cold, and that they must endeavour to get the better of it; advised her to return to bed, and promised her some draughts. The advice was followed readily, for the feverish symptoms increased, and her head ached acutely. Elizabeth did not quit her room for a moment, nor were the other ladies often absent; the gentlemen being out, they had in fact nothing to do elsewhere.

When the clock struck three, Elizabeth felt that she must go; and very unwillingly said so. Miss Bingley offered her the carriage, and she only wanted a little pressing to accept it, when Jane testified such concern in parting with her that Miss Bingley was obliged to convert the offer of the chaise into an invitation to remain at Netherfield for the present. Elizabeth most thankfully consented, and a servant was dispatched to Longbourn to acquaint the family with her stay, and bring back a supply of clothes.

CHAPTER EIGHT

At five o'clock the two ladies retired to dress, and at half past six Elizabeth was summoned to dinner. To the civil inquiries which then poured in, and amongst which she had the pleasure of distinguishing the much superior solicitude of Mr. Bingley's, she could not make a very favourable answer. Jane was by no means better. The sisters, on hearing this, repeated three or four times how much they were grieved, how shocking it was to have a bad cold, and how excessively they disliked being ill themselves; and then thought no more of the matter: and their indifference towards Jane when not immediately before them, restored Elizabeth to the enjoyment of all her original dislike.

Their brother, indeed, was the only one of the party whom she could regard with any complacency. His anxiety for Jane was evident, and his attentions to herself most pleasing, and they prevented her feeling herself so much an intruder as she believed she was considered by the others. She had very little notice from any but him. Miss Bingley was engrossed by Mr. Darcy, her sister scarcely less so; and as for Mr. Hurst, by whom Elizabeth sat, he was an indolent man, who lived only to eat, drink, and play at cards, who when he found her prefer a plain dish to a ragout, had nothing to say to her.

When dinner was over she returned directly to Jane, and Miss Bingley began abusing her as soon as she was out of the room. Her manners were pronounced to be very bad indeed, a mixture of pride and impertinence; she had no conversation, no style, no taste, no beauty. Mrs. Hurst thought the same, and added,

"She has nothing, in short, to recommend her, but being an excellent walker. I shall never forget her appearance this morning. She really looked almost wild."

"She did indeed, Louisa. I could hardly keep my countenance. Very nonsensical to come at all! Why must *she* be scampering about the country because her sister had a cold? Her hair so untidy, so blowsy!"

"Yes, and her petticoat; I hope you saw her petticoat, six inches deep in mud, I am absolutely certain; and the gown which had been let down to hide it, not doing its office."

"Your picture may be very exact, Louisa," said Bingley; "but this was all lost upon me. I thought Miss Elizabeth Bennet looked remarkably well when she came into the room this morning. Her dirty petticoat quite escaped my notice."

"*You* observed it, Mr. Darcy, I am sure," said Miss Bingley; "and I am inclined to think that you would not wish to see *your sister* make such an exhibition."

"Certainly not."

"To walk three miles, or four miles, or five miles, or whatever it is, above her ankles in dirt, and alone, quite alone! what could she mean by it? It seems to me to show an abominable sort of conceited independence, a most country town indifference to decorum."

"It shows an affection for her sister that is very pleasing," said Bingley.

"I am afraid, Mr. Darcy," observed Miss Bingley, in a half whisper, "that this adventure has rather affected your admiration of her fine eyes."

"Not at all," he replied; "they were brightened by the exercise."—A short pause followed this speech, and Mrs. Hurst began again.

"I have an excessive regard for Jane Bennet, she is really a very sweet girl, and I wish with all my heart she were well settled. But with such a father and mother, and such low connections, I am afraid there is no chance of it."

"I think I have heard you say that their uncle is an attorney in Meryton."

"Yes; and they have another, who lives somewhere near Cheapside."

"That is capital," added her sister, and they both laughed heartily.

"If they had uncles enough to fill *all* Cheapside," cried Bingley, "it would not make them one jot less agreeable."

"But it must very materially lessen their chance of marrying men of any consideration in the world," replied Darcy.

To this speech Bingley made no answer; but his sisters gave it their hearty assent, and indulged their mirth for some time at the expense of their dear friend's vulgar relations.

With a renewal of tenderness, however, they repaired to her room on leaving the dining-parlour, and sat with her till summoned to coffee. She was still very poorly, and Elizabeth would not quit her at all, till late in the evening when she had the comfort of seeing her asleep, and when it appeared to her rather right than pleasant that she should go downstairs herself. On entering the drawing-room she found the whole party at loo, and was immediately invited to join them; but suspecting them to be playing high she declined it, and making her sister the excuse, said she would amuse herself for the short time she could stay below with a book. Mr. Hurst looked at her with astonishment.

"Do you prefer reading to cards?" said he; "that is rather singular."

"Miss Eliza Bennet," said Miss Bingley, "despises cards. She is a great reader and has no pleasure in anything else."

"I deserve neither such praise nor such censure," cried Elizabeth; "I am *not* a great reader, and I have pleasure in many things."

"In nursing your sister I am sure you have pleasure," said Bingley; "and I hope it will soon be increased by seeing her quite well."

Elizabeth thanked him from her heart, and then walked towards a table where a few books were lying. He immediately offered to fetch her others; all that his library afforded.

33

"And I wish my collection were larger for your benefit and my own credit; but I am an idle fellow, and though I have not many, I have more than I ever look into."

Elizabeth assured him that she could suit herself perfectly with those in the room.

"I am astonished," said Miss Bingley, "that my father should have left so small a collection of books. What a delightful library you have at Pemberley, Mr. Darcy!"

"It ought to be good," he replied, "it has been the work of many generations."

"And then you have added so much to it yourself, you are always buying books."

"I cannot comprehend the neglect of a family library in such days as these."

"Neglect! I am sure you neglect nothing that can add to the beauties of that noble place. Charles, when you build your house, I wish it may be half as delightful as Pemberley."

"I wish it may."

"But I would really advise you to make your purchase in that neighbourhood, and take Pemberley for a kind of model. There is not a finer county in England than Derbyshire."

"With all my heart; I will buy Pemberley itself if Darcy will sell it."

"I am talking of possibilities, Charles."

"Upon my word, Caroline, I should think it more possible to get Pemberley by purchase than by imitation."

Elizabeth was so much caught by what passed as to leave her very little attention for her book; and soon laying it wholly aside, she drew near the card-table, and stationed herself between Mr. Bingley and his eldest sister to observe the game.

"Is Miss Darcy much grown since the spring?" said Miss Bingley; "will she be as tall as I am?"

"I think she will. She is now about Miss Elizabeth Bennet's height, or rather taller."

"How I long to see her again! I never met with anybody who delighted me so much. Such a countenance, such manners! and so extremely accomplished for her age! Her performance on the pianoforte is exquisite."

"It is amazing to me," said Bingley, "how young

ladies can have patience to be so very accomplished as they all are."

"All young ladies accomplished! My dear Charles, what do you mean?"

"Yes, all of them, I think. They all paint tables, cover screens, and net purses. I scarcely know any one who cannot do all this, and I am sure I never heard a young lady spoken of for the first time without being informed that she was very accomplished."

"Your list of the common extent of accomplishments," said Darcy, "has too much truth. The word is applied to many a woman who deserves it no otherwise than by netting a purse, or covering a screen. But I am very far from agreeing with you in your estimation of ladies in general. I cannot boast of knowing more than half a dozen, in the whole range of my acquaintance, that are really accomplished."

"Nor I, I am sure," said Miss Bingley.

"Then," observed Elizabeth, "you must comprehend a great deal in your idea of an accomplished woman."

"Yes; I do comprehend a great deal in it."

"Oh! certainly," cried his faithful assistant, "no one can be really esteemed accomplished who does not greatly surpass what is usually met with. A woman must have a thorough knowledge of music, singing, drawing, dancing, all the modern languages, to deserve the word; and besides all this, she must possess a certain something in her air and manner of walking, the tone of her voice, her address and expressions, or the word will be but half deserved."

"All this she must possess," added Darcy, "and to all this she must yet add something more substantial, in the improvement of her mind by extensive reading."

"I am no longer surprised at your knowing *only* six accomplished women. I rather wonder now at your knowing *any.*"

"Are you so severe upon your own sex as to doubt the possibility of all this?"

"*I* never saw such a woman. *I* never saw such capacity, and taste, and application, and elegance, as you describe, united."

Mrs. Hurst and Miss Bingley both cried out against the injustice of her implied doubt, and were both protesting that they knew many women who answered this description, when Mr. Hurst called them to order with bitter complaints of their inattention to what was going forward. As all conversation was thereby at an end, Elizabeth soon afterwards left the room.

"Eliza Bennet," said Miss Bingley, when the door was closed on her, "is one of those young ladies who seek to recommend themselves to the other sex by undervaluing their own; and with many men, I dare say, it succeeds. But, in my opinion, it is a paltry device, a very mean art."

"Undoubtedly," replied Darcy, to whom this remark was chiefly addressed, "there is meanness in *all* the arts which ladies sometimes condescend to employ for captivation. Whatever bears affinity to cunning is despicable."

Miss Bingley was not so entirely satisfied with this reply as to continue the subject.

Elizabeth joined them again only to say that her sister was worse, and that she could not leave her. Bingley urged Mr. Jones's being sent for immediately; while his sisters, convinced that no country advice could be of any service, recommended an express to town for one of the most eminent physicians. This she would not hear of; but she was not so unwilling to comply with their brother's proposal; and it was settled that Mr. Jones should be sent for early in the morning, if Miss Bennet were not decidedly better. Bingley was quite uncomfortable; his sisters declared that they were miserable. They solaced their wretchedness, however, by duets after supper, while he could find no better relief to his feelings than by giving his housekeeper directions that every possible attention might be paid to the sick lady and her sister.

CHAPTER NINE

ELIZABETH passed the chief of the night in her sister's room, and in the morning had the pleasure of being able to send a tolerable answer to the inquiries which she very early received from Mr. Bingley by a housemaid, and some time afterwards from the two elegant ladies who waited on his sisters. In spite of this amendment, however, she requested to have a note sent to Longbourn, desiring her mother to visit Jane and form her own judgment of her situation. The note was immediately dispatched, and its contents as quickly complied with. Mrs. Bennet, accompanied by her two youngest girls, reached Netherfield soon after the family breakfast.

Had she found Jane in any apparent danger, Mrs. Bennet would have been very miserable; but being satisfied on seeing her that her illness was not alarming, she had no wish of her recovering immediately, as her restoration to health would probably remove her from Netherfield. She would not listen therefore to her daughter's proposal of being carried home; neither did the apothecary, who arrived about the same time, think it at all advisable. After sitting a little while with Jane, on Miss Bingley's appearance and invitation, the mother and three daughters all attended her into the breakfast parlour. Bingley met them with hopes that Mrs. Bennet had not found Miss Bennet worse than she expected.

"Indeed I have, sir," was her answer. "She is a great deal too ill to be moved. Mr. Jones says we must not think of moving her. We must trespass a little longer on your kindness."

"Removed!" cried Bingley. "It must not be thought of. My sister, I am sure, will not hear of her removal."

"You may depend upon it, madam," said Miss Bingley, with cold civility, "that Miss Bennet shall receive every possible attention while she remains with us."

Mrs. Bennet was profuse in her acknowledgments.

"I am sure," she added, "if it was not for such good friends I do not know what would become of her, for she is very ill indeed, and suffers a vast deal, though with the greatest patience in the world, which is always the way with her, for she has without exception the sweetest temper I ever met with. I often tell my other girls they are nothing to *her*. You have a sweet room here, Mr. Bingley, and a charming prospect over that gravel walk. I do not know a place in the country that is equal to Netherfield. You will not think of quitting it in a hurry, I hope, though you have but a short lease."

"Whatever I do is done in a hurry," replied he; "and therefore if I should resolve to quit Netherfield, I should probably be off in five minutes. At present, however, I consider myself as quite fixed here."

"That is exactly what I should have supposed of you," said Elizabeth.

"You begin to comprehend me, do you?" cried he, turning towards her.

"Oh! yes—I understand you perfectly."

"I wish I might take this for a compliment; but to be so easily seen through I am afraid is pitiful."

"That is as it happens. It does not necessarily follow that a deep, intricate character is more or less estimable than such a one as yours."

"Lizzy," cried her mother, "remember where you are, and do not run on in the wild manner that you are suffered to do at home."

"I did not know before," continued Bingley immediately, "that you were a studier of character. It must be an amusing study."

"Yes; but intricate characters are the *most* amusing. They have at least that advantage."

"The country," said Darcy, "can in general supply but few subjects for such a study. In a country neighbourhood you move in a very confined and unvarying society."

"But people themselves alter so much that there is something new to be observed in them forever."

"Yes, indeed," cried Mrs. Bennet, offended by his manner of mentioning a country neighbourhood. "I assure you there is quite as much of *that* going on in the country as in town."

Everybody was surprised; and Darcy, after looking at her for a moment, turned silently away. Mrs. Bennet, who fancied she had gained a complete victory over him, continued her triumph.

"I cannot see that London has any great advantage over the country for my part, except the shops and public places. The country is a vast deal pleasanter, is not it, Mr. Bingley?"

"When I am in the country," he replied, "I never wish to leave it; and when I am in town it is pretty much the same. They have each their advantages, and I can be equally happy in either."

"Aye—that is because you have the right disposition.

But that gentleman," looking at Darcy, "seemed to think the country was nothing at all."

"Indeed, Mama, you are mistaken," said Elizabeth, blushing for her mother. "You quite mistook Mr. Darcy. He only meant that there were not such a variety of people to be met with in the country as in town, which you must acknowledge to be true."

"Certainly, my dear, nobody said there were; but as to not meeting with many people in this neighbourhood, I believe there are few neighbourhoods larger. I know we dine with four and twenty families."

Nothing but concern for Elizabeth could enable Bingley to keep his countenance. His sister was less delicate, and directed her eye towards Mr. Darcy with a very expressive smile. Elizabeth, for the sake of saying something that might turn her mother's thoughts, now asked her if Charlotte Lucas had been at Longbourn since *her* coming away.

"Yes, she called yesterday with her father. What an agreeable man Sir William is, Mr. Bingley—is not he? So much the man of fashion! So genteel and so easy! He has always something to say to everybody. *That* is my idea of good breeding; and those persons who fancy themselves very important and never open their mouths quite mistake the matter."

"Did Charlotte dine with you?"

"No, she would go home. I fancy she was wanted about the mince pies. For my part, Mr. Bingley, *I* always keep servants that can do their own work; *my* daughters are brought up differently. But everybody is to judge for themselves, and the Lucases are very good sort of girls, I assure you. It is a pity they are not handsome! Not that *I* think Charlotte so *very* plain— but then she is our particular friend."

"She seems a very pleasant young woman," said Bingley.

"Oh! dear, yes; but you must own she is very plain. Lady Lucas herself has often said so, and envied me Jane's beauty. I do not like to boast of my own child, but to be sure, Jane—one does not often see anybody better looking. It is what everybody says. I do not trust my own partiality. When she was only fifteen, there was a gentleman at my brother Gardiner's in town so much in love with her that my sister-in-law was sure he would make her an offer before we came away. But, however, he did not. Perhaps he thought her too young. However, he wrote some verses on her, and very pretty they were."

"And so ended his affection," said Elizabeth impatiently. "There has been many a one, I fancy, overcome in the same way. I wonder who first discovered the efficacy of poetry in driving away love!"

"I have been used to consider poetry as the *food* of love," said Darcy.

"Of a fine, stout, healthy love it may. Everything nourishes what is strong already. But if it be only a slight, thin sort of inclination, I am convinced that one good sonnet will starve it entirely away."

Darcy only smiled; and the general pause which ensued made Elizabeth tremble lest her mother should be exposing herself again. She longed to speak, but could think of nothing to say; and after a short silence Mrs. Bennet began repeating her thanks to Mr. Bingley for his kindness to Jane, with an apology for troubling him also with Lizzy. Mr. Bingley was unaffectedly civil in his answer, and forced his younger sister to be civil also, and say what the occasion required. She performed her part indeed without much graciousness, but Mrs. Bennet was satisfied, and soon afterwards ordered her carriage. Upon this signal, the youngest of her daughters put herself forward. The two girls had been whispering to each other during the whole visit, and the result of it was that the youngest should tax Mr. Bingley with having promised on his first coming into the country to give a ball at Netherfield.

Lydia was a stout, well-grown girl of fifteen, with a fine complexion and good-humoured countenance; a favourite with her mother, whose affection had brought her into public at an early age. She had high animal spirits, and a sort of natural self-consequence, which the attentions of the officers, to whom her uncle's good dinners and her own easy manners recommended her, had increased into assurance. She was very equal therefore to address Mr. Bingley on the subject of the ball, and abruptly reminded him of his promise, adding that it would be the most shameful thing in the world if he did not keep it. His answer to this sudden attack was delightful to their mother's ear.

"I am perfectly ready, I assure you, to keep my engagement; and when your sister is recovered, you shall if you please name the very day of the ball. But you would not wish to be dancing while she is ill."

Lydia declared herself satisfied. "Oh! yes—it would be much better to wait till Jane was well, and by that time most likely Captain Carter would be at Meryton again. And when you have given *your* ball," she added, "I shall insist on their giving one also. I shall tell Colonel Forster it will be quite a shame if he does not."

Mrs. Bennet and her daughters then departed, and Elizabeth returned instantly to Jane, leaving her own and her relations' behaviour to the remarks of the two ladies and Mr. Darcy; the latter of whom, however, could not be prevailed on to join in their censure of *her,* in spite of all Miss Bingley's witticisms on *fine eyes.*

CHAPTER TEN

THE day passed much as the day before had done. Mrs. Hurst and Miss Bingley had spent some hours of the morning with the invalid, who continued, though slowly, to mend; and in the evening Elizabeth joined their party in the drawing-room. The loo table, however, did not appear. Mr. Darcy was writing, and Miss Bingley, seated near him, was watching the progress of his letter, and repeatedly calling off his attention by messages to his sister. Mr. Hurst and Mr. Bingley were at piquet, and Mrs. Hurst was observing their game.

Elizabeth took up some needlework, and was sufficiently amused in attending to what passed between Darcy and his companion. The perpetual commendations of the lady either on his handwriting, or on the evenness of his lines, or on the length of his letter, with the perfect unconcern with which her praises were received, formed a curious dialogue, and was exactly in unison with her opinion of each.

"How delighted Miss Darcy will be to receive such a letter!"

He made no answer.

"You write uncommonly fast."

"You are mistaken. I write rather slowly."

"How many letters you must have occasion to write in the course of the year! Letters of business too! How odious I should think them!"

"It is fortunate, then, that they fall to my lot instead of to yours."

"Pray tell your sister that I long to see her."

"I have already told her so once, by your desire."

"I am afraid you do not like your pen. Let me mend it for you. I mend pens remarkably well."

"Thank you—but I always mend my own."

"How can you contrive to write so even?"

He was silent.

"Tell your sister I am delighted to hear of her improvement on the harp, and pray let her know that I am quite in raptures with her beautiful little design for a table, and I think it infinitely superior to Miss Grantley's."

"Will you give me leave to defer your raptures till I write again?—At present I have not room to do them justice."

"Oh! it is of no consequence. I shall see her in January. But do you always write such charming long letters to her, Mr. Darcy?"

"They are generally long; but whether always charming, it is not for me to determine."

"It is a rule with me that a person who can write a long letter with ease cannot write ill."

"That will not do for a compliment to Darcy, Caroline," cried her brother, "because he does *not* write with ease. He studies too much for words of four syllables. Do not you, Darcy?"

"My style of writing is very different from yours."

"Oh!" cried Miss Bingley, "Charles writes in the most careless way imaginable. He leaves out half his words, and blots the rest."

"My ideas flow so rapidly that I have not time to express them—by which means my letters sometimes convey no ideas at all to my correspondents."

"Your humility, Mr. Bingley," said Elizabeth, "must disarm reproof."

"Nothing is more deceitful," said Darcy, "than the

42

appearance of humility. It is often only carelessness of opinion, and sometimes an indirect boast."

"And which of the two do you call *my* little recent piece of modesty?"

"The indirect boast—for you are really proud of your defects in writing, because you consider them as proceeding from a rapidity of thought and carelessness of execution, which if not estimable, you think at least highly interesting. The power of doing anything with quickness is always much prized by the possessor, and often without any attention to the imperfection of the performance. When you told Mrs. Bennet this morning that if you ever resolved on quitting Netherfield you should be gone in five minutes, you meant it to be a sort of panegyric, of compliment to yourself—and yet what is there so very laudable in a pecipitance which must leave very necessary business undone, and can be of no real advantage to yourself or any one else?"

"Nay," cried Bingley, "this is too much, to remember at night all the foolish things that were said in the morning. And yet, upon my honour, I believed what I said of myself to be true, and I believe it at this moment. At least, therefore, I did not assume the character of needless precipitance merely to show off before the ladies."

"I dare say you believed it; but I am by no means convinced that you would be gone with such celerity. Your conduct would be quite as dependant on chance as that of any man I know; and if, as you were mounting your horse, a friend were to say, 'Bingley, you had better stay till next week,' you would probably do it, you would probably not go—and, at another word, might stay a month."

"You have only proved by this," cried Elizabeth, "that Mr. Bingley did not do justice to his own disposition. You have shown him off now much more than he did himself."

"I am exceedingly gratified," said Bingley, "by your converting what my friend says into a compliment on the sweetness of my temper. But I am afraid you are giving it a turn which that gentleman did by no means intend; for he would certainly think the better of me if under such a circumstance I were to give a flat denial, and ride off as fast as I could."

"Would Mr. Darcy then consider the rashness of your original intention as atoned for by your obstinacy in adhering to it?"

"Upon my word I cannot exactly explain the matter, Darcy must speak for himself."

"You expect me to account for opinions which you choose to call mine, but which I have never acknowledged. Allowing the case, however, to stand according to your representation, you must remember, Miss Bennet, that the friend who is supposed to desire his return to the house, and the delay of his plan, has merely desired it, asked it without offering one argument in favour of its propriety."

"To yield readily—easily—to the *persuasion* of a friend is no merit with you."

"To yield without conviction is no compliment to the understanding of either."

"You appear to me, Mr. Darcy, to allow nothing for the influence of friendship and affection. A regard for the requester would often make one readily yield to a request, without waiting for arguments to reason one into it. I am not particularly speaking of such a case as you have supposed about Mr. Bingley. We may as well wait, perhaps, till the circumstance occurs, before we discuss the discretion of his behaviour thereupon. But in general and ordinary cases between friend and friend, where one of them is desired by the other to change a resolution of no very great moment, should you think ill of that person for complying with the desire, without waiting to be argued into it?"

"Will it not be advisable before we proceed on this subject to arrange with rather more precision the degree of importance which is to appertain to this request, as well as the degree of intimacy subsisting between the parties?"

"By all means," cried Bingley; "let us hear all the particulars, not forgetting their comparative height and size; for that will have more weight in the argument, Miss Bennet, than you may be aware of. I assure you that if Darcy were not such a great tall fellow, in comparison with myself, I should not pay him half so much deference. I declare I do not know a more awful object than Darcy, on particular occasions and in particular places; at his own house especially, and of a Sunday evening when he has nothing to do."

Mr. Darcy smiled; but Elizabeth thought she could perceive that he was rather offended; and therefore checked her laugh. Miss Bingley warmly resented the indignity he had received, in an expostulation with her brother for talking such nonsense.

"I see your design, Bingley," said his friend. "You dislike an argument, and want to silence this."

"Perhaps I do. Arguments are too much like disputes. If you and Miss Bennet will defer yours till I am out of the room, I shall be very thankful; and then you may say whatever you like of me."

"What you ask," said Elizabeth, "is no sacrifice on my side; and Mr. Darcy had much better finish his letter."

Mr. Darcy took her advice, and did finish his letter.

When that business was over, he applied to Miss Bingley and Elizabeth for the indulgence of some music. Miss Bingley moved with alacrity to the pianoforte, and after a polite request that Elizabeth would lead the way, which the other as politely and more earnestly negatived, she seated herself.

Mrs. Hurst sang with her sister, and while they were thus employed Elizabeth could not help observing as she turned over some music books that lay on the instrument how frequently Mr. Darcy's eyes were fixed on her. She hardly knew how to suppose that she could be an object of admiration to so great a man; and yet that he should look at her because he disliked her was still more strange. She could only imagine however, at last, that she drew his notice because there was a something about her more wrong and reprehensible, according to his ideas of right, than in any other person present. The supposition did not pain her. She liked him too little to care for his approbation.

After playing some Italian songs, Miss Bingley varied the charm by a lively Scotch air; and soon afterwards Mr. Darcy, drawing near Elizabeth, said to her—

"Do not you feel a great inclination, Miss Bennet, to seize such an opportunity of dancing a reel?"

She smiled, but made no answer. He repeated the question, with some surprise at her silence.

"Oh!" said she, "I heard you before; but I could not

45

immediately determine what to say in reply. You wanted me, I know, to say 'Yes' that you might have the pleasure of despising my taste; but I always delight in overthrowing those kind of schemes, and cheating a person of their premeditated contempt. I have therefore made up my mind to tell you that I do not want to dance a reel at all—and now despise me if you dare."

"Indeed I do not dare."

Elizabeth, having rather expected to affront him, was amazed at his gallantry; but there was a mixture of sweetness and archness in her manner which made it difficult for her to affront anybody; and Darcy had never been so bewitched by any woman as he was by her. He really believed that were it not for the inferiority of her connections he should be in some danger.

Miss Bingley saw, or suspected enough to be jealous; and her great anxiety for the recovery of her dear friend Jane received some assistance from her desire of getting rid of Elizabeth.

She often tried to provoke Darcy into disliking her guest by talking of their supposed marriage, and planning his happiness in such an alliance.

"I hope," said she, as they were walking together in the shrubbery the next day, "you will give your mother-in-law a few hints, when this desirable event takes place, as to the advantage of holding her tongue; and if you can compass it, do cure the younger girls of running after the officers.—And, if I may mention so delicate a subject, endeavour to check that little something, bordering on conceit and impertinence, which your lady possesses."

"Have you anything else to propose for my domestic felicity?"

"Oh! yes.—Do let the portraits of your uncle and aunt Philips be placed in the gallery at Pemberley. Put them next to your great uncle the judge. They are in the same profession, you know; only in different lines. As for your Elizabeth's picture, you must not attempt to have it taken, for what painter could do justice to those beautiful eyes?"

"It would not be easy, indeed, to catch their expression, but their colour and shape, and the eye-lashes, so remarkably fine, might be copied."

At that moment they were met from another walk by Mrs. Hurst and Elizabeth herself.

"I did not know that you intended to walk," said Miss Bingley, in some confusion, lest they had been overheard.

"You used us abominably ill," answered Mrs. Hurst, "in running away without telling us that you were coming out."

Then taking the disengaged arm of Mr. Darcy, she left Elizabeth to walk by herself. The path just admitted three. Mr. Darcy felt their rudeness and immediately said,

"This walk is not wide enough for our party. We had better go into the avenue."

But Elizabeth, who had not the least inclination to remain with them, laughingly answered,

"No, no; stay where you are. You are charmingly group'd, and appear to uncommon advantage. The picturesque would be spoiled by admitting a fourth. Goodbye."

She then ran gaily off, rejoicing as she rambled about, in the hope of being at home again in a day or two. Jane was already so much recovered as to intend leaving her room for a couple of hours that evening.

CHAPTER ELEVEN

WHEN the ladies removed after dinner, Elizabeth ran up to her sister, and seeing her well guarded from cold, attended her into the drawing-room, where she was welcomed by her two friends with many professions of pleasure; and Elizabeth had never seen them so agreeable as they were during the hour which passed before the gentlemen appeared. Their powers of conversation were considerable. They could describe an entertainment with accuracy, relate an anecdote with humour, and laugh at their acquaintance with spirit.

But when the gentlemen entered, Jane was no longer the first object. Miss Bingley's eyes were instantly turned towards Darcy, and she had something to say to him before he had advanced many steps. He addressed himself directly to Miss Bennet, with a polite congratulation;

Mr. Hurst also made her a slight bow, and said he was "very glad"; but diffuseness and warmth remained for Bingley's salutation. He was full of joy and attention. The first half hour was spent in piling up the fire, lest she should suffer from the change of room; and she removed at his desire to the other side of the fire-place, that she might be farther from the door. He then sat down by her, and talked scarcely to any one else. Elizabeth, at work in the opposite corner, saw it all with great delight.

When tea was over, Mr. Hurst reminded his sister-in-law of the card-table—but in vain. She had obtained private intelligence that Mr. Darcy did not wish for cards; and Mr. Hurst soon found even his open petition rejected. She assured him that no one intended to play, and the silence of the whole party on the subject seemed to justify her. Mr. Hurst had therefore nothing to do, but to stretch himself on one of the sofas and go to sleep. Darcy took up a book; Miss Bingley did the same; and Mrs. Hurst, principally occupied in playing with her bracelets and rings, joined now and then in her brother's conversation with Miss Bennet.

Miss Bingley's attention was quite as much engaged in watching Mr. Darcy's progress through *his* book, as in reading her own; and she was perpetually either making some inquiry, or looking at his page. She could not win him, however, to any conversation; he merely answered her question, and read on. At length, quite exhausted by the attempt to be amused with her own book, which she had only chosen because it was the second volume of his, she gave a great yawn and said, "How pleasant it is to spend an evening in this way! I declare after all there is no enjoyment like reading! How much sooner one tires of anything than of a book! When I have a house of my own, I shall be miserable if I have not an excellent library."

No one made any reply. She then yawned again, threw aside her book, and cast her eyes round the room in quest of some amusement; when hearing her brother mentioning a ball to Miss Bennet, she turned suddenly towards him and said,

"By the bye, Charles, are you really serious in meditating a dance at Netherfield? I would advise you, before you determine on it, to consult the wishes of the present party; I am much mistaken if there are not some among us to whom a ball would be rather a punishment than a pleasure."

"If you mean Darcy," cried her brother, "he may go to bed, if he chooses, before it begins—but as for the ball, it is quite a settled thing; and as soon as Nicholls has made white soup enough I shall send round my cards."

"I should like balls infinitely better," she replied, "if they were carried on in a different manner; but there is something insufferably tedious in the usual process of such a meeting. It would surely be much more rational if conversation instead of dancing made the order of the day."

"Much more rational, my dear Caroline, I dare say; but it would not be near so much like a ball."

Miss Bingley made no answer; and soon afterwards got up and walked about the room. Her figure was elegant, and she walked well; but Darcy, at whom it was all aimed, was still inflexibly studious. In the desperation of her feelings she resolved on one effort more; and, turning to Elizabeth, said,

"Miss Eliza Bennet, let me persuade you to follow my example, and take a turn about the room.—I assure you it is very refreshing after sitting so long in one attitude."

Elizabeth was surprised, but agreed to it immediately. Miss Bingley succeeded no less in the real object of her civility; Mr. Darcy looked up. He was as much awake to the novelty of attention in that quarter as Elizabeth herself could be, and unconsciously closed his book. He was directly invited to join their party, but he declined it, observing that he could imagine but two motives for their choosing to walk up and down the room together, with either of which motives his joining them would interfere. "What could he mean? she was dying to know what could be his meaning"—and asked Elizabeth whether she could at all understand him?

"Not at all," was her answer; "but depend upon it, he means to be severe on us, and our surest way of disappointing him will be to ask nothing about it."

Miss Bingley, however, was incapable of disappointing Mr. Darcy in anything, and persevered therefore in requiring an explanation of his two motives.

"I have not the smallest objection to explaining them," said he, as soon as she allowed him to speak. "You either choose this method of passing the evening because you are in each other's confidence and have secret affairs to discuss, or because you are conscious that your figures appear to the greatest advantage in walking—if the first, I should be completely in your way; and if the second, I can admire you much better as I sit by the fire."

"Oh! shocking!" cried Miss Bingley. "I never heard anything so abominable. How shall we punish him for such a speech?"

"Nothing so easy, if you have but the inclination," said Elizabeth. "We can all plague and punish one another. Tease him—laugh at him. Intimate as you are, you must know how it is to be done."

"But upon my honour I do *not*. I do assure you that my intimacy has not yet taught me *that*. Tease calmness of temper and presence of mind! No, no—I feel he may defy us there. And as to laughter, we will not expose ourselves, if you please, by attempting to laugh without a subject. Mr. Darcy may hug himself."

"Mr. Darcy is not to be laughed at!" cried Elizabeth. "That is an uncommon advantage, and uncommon I hope it will continue, for it would be a great loss to *me* to have many such acquaintance. I dearly love a laugh."

"Miss Bingley," said he, "has given me credit for more than can be. The wisest and the best of men, nay, the wisest and best of their actions, may be rendered ridiculous by a person whose first object in life is a joke."

"Certainly," replied Elizabeth—"there are such people, but I hope I am not one of *them*. I hope I never ridicule what is wise or good. Follies and nonsense, whims and inconsistencies *do* divert me, I own, and I laugh at them whenever I can.—But these, I suppose, are precisely what you are without."

"Perhaps that is not possible for any one. But it has been the study of my life to avoid those weaknesses which often expose a strong understanding to ridicule."

"Such as vanity and pride."

"Yes, vanity is a weakness indeed. But pride—where

there is a real superiority of mind, pride will be always under good regulation."

Elizabeth turned away to hide a smile.

"Your examination of Mr. Darcy is over, I presume," said Miss Bingley; "and pray what is the result?"

"I am perfectly convinced by it that Mr. Darcy has no defect. He owns it himself without disguise."

"No"—said Darcy, "I have made no such pretension. I have faults enough, but they are not, I hope, of understanding. My temper I dare not vouch for. It is, I believe, too little yielding—certainly too little for the convenience of the world. I cannot forget the follies and vices of others as soon as I ought, nor their offenses against myself. My feelings are not puffed about with every attempt to move them. My temper would perhaps be called resentful. My good opinion once lost is lost for ever."

"*That* is a failing indeed!" cried Elizabeth. "Implacable resentment *is* a shade in a character. But you have chosen your fault well. I really cannot *laugh* at it. You are safe from me."

"There is, I believe, in every disposition a tendency to some particular evil, a natural defect, which not even the best education can overcome."

"And *your* defect is a propensity to hate everybody."

"And yours," he replied with a smile, "is wilfully to misunderstand them."

"Do let us have a little music," cried Miss Bingley, tired of a conversation in which she had no share. "Louisa, you will not mind my waking Mr. Hurst."

Her sister made not the smallest objection, and the pianoforte was opened, and Darcy, after a few moments recollection, was not sorry for it. He began to feel the danger of paying Elizabeth too much attention.

CHAPTER TWELVE

In consequence of an agreement between the sisters, Elizabeth wrote the next morning to her mother to beg that the carriage might be sent for them in the course of the day. But Mrs. Bennet, who had calculated on her daughters remaining at Netherfield till the following Tuesday, which would exactly finish Jane's week, could not bring herself to receive them with pleasure before. Her answer, therefore, was not propitious, at least not to Elizabeth's wishes, for she was impatient to get home. Mrs. Bennet sent them word that they could not possibly have the carriage before Tuesday; and in her postscript it was added that if Mr. Bingley and his sister pressed them to stay longer, she could spare them very well.— Against staying longer, however, Elizabeth was positively resolved—nor did she much expect it would be asked; and fearful, on the contrary, as being considered as intruding themselves needlessly long, she urged Jane to borrow Mr. Bingley's carriage immediately, and at length it was settled that their original design of leaving Netherfield that morning should be mentioned, and the request made.

The communication excited many professions of concern; and enough was said of wishing them to stay at least till the following day to work on Jane; and till the morrow, their going was deferred. Miss Bingley was then sorry that she had proposed the delay, for her jealousy and dislike of one sister much exceeded her affection for the other.

The master of the house heard with real sorrow that they were to go so soon, and repeatedly tried to persuade Miss Bennet that it would not be safe for her—that she was not enough recovered; but Jane was firm where she felt herself to be right.

To Mr. Darcy it was welcome intelligence—Elizabeth had been at Netherfield long enough. She attracted him more than he liked—and Miss Bingley was uncivil to *her*, and more teasing than usual to himself. He wisely resolved to be particularly careful that no sign of admiration should *now* escape him, nothing that could elevate her with the hope of influencing his felicity, sensible that if such an idea had been suggested his behaviour during the last day must have material weight in confirming or crushing it. Steady to his purpose, he scarcely spoke ten words to her through the whole of Saturday, and though they were at one time left by themselves for half an hour, he adhered most conscientiously to his book, and would not even look at her.

On Sunday, after morning service, the separation, so agreeable to almost all, took place. Miss Bingley's civility to Elizabeth increased at last very rapidly, as well as her affection for Jane; and when they parted, after assuring the latter of the pleasure it would always give her to see her either at Longbourn or Netherfield and embracing her most tenderly, she even shook hands with the former. Elizabeth took leave of the whole party in the liveliest spirits.

They were not welcomed home very cordially by their mother. Mrs. Bennet wondered at their coming, and thought them very wrong to give so much trouble, and was sure Jane would have caught cold again.—But their father, though very laconic in his expressions of pleasure, was really glad to see them; he had felt their importance in the family circle. The evening conversation, when they were all assembled, had lost much of its animation, and almost all its sense, by the absence of Jane and Elizabeth.

They found Mary, as usual, deep in the study of thorough bass and human nature; and had some new extracts to admire, and some new observations of threadbare morality to listen to. Catherine and Lydia had information for them of a different sort. Much had been done, and much had been said in the regiment since the preceding Wednesday; several of the officers had dined lately with their uncle, a private had been flogged, and it had actually been hinted that Colonel Forster was going to be married.

CHAPTER THIRTEEN

"I HOPE, my dear," said Mr. Bennet to his wife, as they were at breakfast the next morning, "that you have ordered a good dinner to-day, because I have reason to expect an addition to our family party."

"Who do you mean, my dear? I know of nobody that is coming, I am sure, unless Charlotte Lucas should happen to call in, and I hope *my* dinners are good enough for her. I do not believe she often sees such at home."

"The person of whom I speak is a gentleman and a stranger." Mrs. Bennet's eyes sparkled. "A gentleman and a stranger! It is Mr. Bingley, I am sure. Why, Jane —you never dropped a word of this; you sly thing! Well, I am sure I shall be extremely glad to see Mr. Bingley. But—good lord! how unlucky! there is not a bit of fish to be got to-day. Lydia, my love, ring the bell. I must speak to Hill, this moment."

"It is *not* Mr. Bingley," said her husband; "it is a person whom I never saw in the whole course of my life."

This roused a general astonishment; and he had the pleasure of being eagerly questioned by his wife and five daughters at once.

After amusing himself some time with their curiosity, he thus explained. "About a month ago I received this letter, and about a fortnight ago I answered it, for I thought it a case of some delicacy, and requiring early attention. It is from my cousin, Mr. Collins, who, when I am dead, may turn you all out of this house as soon as he pleases."

"Oh! my dear," cried his wife, "I cannot bear to hear that mentioned. Pray do not talk of that odious man. I do think it is the hardest thing in the world that your estate should be entailed away from your own children; and I am sure if I had been you, I should have tried long ago to do something or other about it."

Jane and Elizabeth attempted to explain to her the nature of an entail. They had often attempted it before, but it was a subject on which Mrs. Bennet was beyond the reach of reason; and she continued to rail bitterly against the cruelty of settling an estate away from a family of five daughters, in favour of a man whom nobody cared anything about.

"It certainly is a most iniquitous affair," said Mr. Bennet, "and nothing can clear Mr. Collins from the guilt of inheriting Longbourn. But if you will listen to his letter, you may perhaps be a little softened by his manner of expressing himself."

"No, that I am sure I shall not; and I think it was very impertinent of him to write to you at all, and very hypocritical. I hate such false friends. Why could not he keep on quarrelling with you, as his father did before him?"

"Why, indeed, he does seem to have had some filial scruples on that head, as you will hear."

Hunsford, near Westerham, Kent,
15*th October.*

DEAR SIR,

THE disagreement subsisting between yourself and
my late honoured father always gave me much uneasiness, and since I have had the misfortune to lose him,
I have frequently wished to heal the breach; but for
some time I was kept back by my own doubts, fearing
lest it might seem disrespectful to his memory for me
to be on good terms with any one with whom it had always pleased him to be at variance.—"There, Mrs.
Bennet."—My mind however is now made up on the
subject, for having received ordination at Easter, I have
been so fortunate as to be distinguished by the patronage of the Right Honourable Lady Catherine de Bourgh,
widow of Sir Lewis de Bourgh, whose bounty and bene-
ficence has preferred me to the valuable rectory of this
parish, where it shall be my earnest endeavour to demean
myself with grateful respect towards her Ladyship, and
be very ready to perform those rites and cere-
monies which are instituted by the Church of England.
As a clergyman, moreover, I feel it my duty to promote
and establish the blessing of peace in all families
within the reach of my influence; and on these grounds
I flatter myself that my present overtures of goodwill
are highly commendable, and that the circumstance of
my being next in the entail of Longbourn estate will be
kindly overlooked on your side, and not lead you to reject the offered olive branch. I cannot be otherwise than
concerned at being the means of injuring your amiable
daughters, and beg leave to apologize for it, as well as to
assure you of my readiness to make them every possible
amends—but of this hereafter. If you should have no
objection to receive me into your house, I propose myself the satisfaction of waiting on you and your family,
Monday, November 18th, by four o'clock, and shall
probably trespass on your hospitality till the Saturday
sennight following, which I can do without any inconvenience, as Lady Catherine is far from objecting to
my occasional absence on a Sunday, provided that some
other clergyman is engaged to do the duty of the day.
I remain, dear sir, with respectful compliments to your
lady and daughters, your well-wisher and friend,

WILLIAM COLLINS

"At four o'clock, therefore, we may expect this peace-making gentleman," said Mr. Bennet, as he folded up the letter. "He seems to be a most conscientious and polite young man, upon my word; and I doubt not will prove a valuable acquaintance, especially if Lady Catherine should be so indulgent as to let him come to us again."

"There is some sense in what he says about the girls, however; and if he is disposed to make them any amends, I shall not be the person to discourage him."

"Though it is difficult," said Jane, "to guess in what way he can mean to make us the atonement he thinks our due, the wish is certainly to his credit."

Elizabeth was chiefly struck with his extraordinary deference for Lady Catherine, and his kind intention of christening, marrying, and burying his parishioners whenever it were required.

"He must be an oddity, I think," said she. "I cannot make him out.—There is something very pompous in his style.—And what can he mean by apologizing for being next in the entail?—We cannot suppose he would help it, if he could.—Can he be a sensible man, sir?"

"No, my dear; I think not. I have great hopes of finding him quite the reverse. There is a mixture of servility and self-importance in his letter, which promises well. I am impatient to see him."

"In point of composition," said Mary, "his letter does not seem defective. The idea of the olive branch perhaps is not wholly new, yet I think it is well expressed."

To Catherine and Lydia neither the letter nor its writer were in any degree interesting. It was next to impossible that their cousin should come in a scarlet coat, and it was now some weeks since they had received pleasure from the society of a man in any other colour. As for their mother, Mr. Collins's letter had done away much of her ill will, and she was preparing to see him with a degree of composure, which astonished her husband and daughters.

Mr. Collins was punctual to his time, and was received with great politeness by the whole family. Mr. Bennet indeed said little; but the ladies were ready enough to talk, and Mr. Collins seemed neither in need of encouragement, nor inclined to be silent himself. He was a tall, heavy looking young man of five and twenty. His air was grave and stately, and his manners were very formal. He had not been long seated before he complimented Mrs. Bennet on having so fine a family of daughters; said he had heard much of their beauty, but that, in this instance, fame had fallen short of the truth; and added that he did not doubt her seeing them all in due time well disposed of in marriage. This gallantry was not much to the taste of some of his hearers, but Mrs. Bennet, who quarrelled with no compliments, answered most readily,

"You are very kind, sir, I am sure; and I wish with all my heart it may prove so; for else they will be destitute enough. Things are settled so oddly."

"You allude perhaps to the entail of this estate."

"Ah! sir, I do indeed. It is a grievous affair to my poor girls, you must confess. Not that I mean to find fault with *you*, for such things I know are all chance in this world. There is no knowing how estates will go when once they come to be entailed."

"I am very sensible, madam, of the hardship to my fair cousins—and could say much on the subject, but that I am cautious of appearing forward and precipitate. But I can assure the young ladies that I come prepared to admire them. At present I will not say more, but perhaps when we are better acquainted——"

He was interrupted by a summons to dinner; and the girls smiled on each other. They were not the only objects of Mr. Collins's admiration. The hall, the dining-room, and all its furniture were examined and praised; and his commendation of everything would have touched Mrs. Bennet's heart, but for the mortifying supposition of his viewing it all as his own future property. The dinner too in its turn was highly admired; and he begged to know to which of his fair cousins the excellence of its cookery was owing. But here he was set right by Mrs. Bennet, who assured him with some asperity that they were very well able to keep a good cook, and that her daughters had nothing to do in the kitchen. He begged pardon for having displeased her. In a softened tone she declared herself not at all offended; but he continued to apologize for about a quarter of an hour.

CHAPTER FOURTEEN

During dinner Mr. Bennet scarcely spoke at all; but when the servants were withdrawn, he thought it time to have some conversation with his guest, and therefore started a subject in which he expected him to shine, by observing that he seemed very fortunate in his patroness. Lady Catherine de Bourgh's attention to his wishes and consideration for his comfort appeared very remarkable. Mr. Bennet could not have chosen better. Mr. Collins was eloquent in her praise. The subject elevated him to more than usual solemnity of manner, and with a most important aspect he protested that he had never in his life witnessed such behaviour in a person of rank—such affability and condescension as he had himself experienced from Lady Catherine. She had been graciously pleased to approve of both the discourses, which he had already had the honour of preaching before her. She had also asked him twice to dine at Rosings, and had sent for him only the Saturday before to make up her pool of quadrille in the evening. Lady Catherine was reckoned proud by many people he knew, but *he* had never seen anything but affability in her. She had always spoken to him as she would to any other gentleman; she made not the smallest objection to his joining in the society of the neighbourhood, nor to his leaving his parish occasionally for a week or two to visit his relations. She had even condescended to advise him to marry as soon as he could, provided he chose with discretion; and had once paid him a visit in his humble parsonage, where she had perfectly approved all the alterations he had been making, and had even vouchsafed to suggest some herself—some shelves in the closets upstairs."

"That is all very proper and civil, I am sure," said Mrs. Bennet, "and I dare say she is a very agreeable woman. It is a pity that great ladies in general are not more like her. Does she live near you, sir?"

"The garden in which stands my humble abode is separated only by a lane from Rosings Park, her ladyship's residence."

"I think you said she was a widow, sir? has she any family?"

"She has one only daughter, the heiress of Rosings, and of very extensive property."

"Ah!" cried Mrs. Bennet, shaking her head, "then she is better off than many girls. And what sort of young lady is she? Is she handsome?"

"She is a most charming young lady indeed. Lady Catherine herself says that in point of true beauty, Miss De Bourgh is far superior to the handsomest of her sex, because there is that in her features which marks the young woman of distinguished birth. She is unfortunately of a sickly constitution, which has prevented her making that progress in many accomplishments, which she could not otherwise have failed of, as I am informed by the lady who superintended her education, and who still resides with them. But she is perfectly amiable, and often condescends to drive by my humble abode in her little phaeton and ponies."

"Has she been presented? I do not remember her name among the ladies at court."

"Her indifferent state of health unhappily prevents her being in town; and by that means, as I told Lady Catherine myself one day, has deprived the British court of its brightest ornament. Her ladyship seemed pleased with the idea, and you may imagine that I am happy on every occasion to offer those little delicate compliments which are always acceptable to ladies. I have more than once observed to Lady Catherine that her charming daughter seemed born to be a duchess, and that the most elevated rank, instead of giving her consequence, would be adorned by her. These are the kind of little things which please her ladyship, and it is a sort of attention which I conceive myself peculiarly bound to pay."

"You judge very properly," said Mr. Bennet, "and it is happy for you that you possess the talent of flattering with delicacy. May I ask whether these pleasing attentions proceed from the impulse of the moment, or are the result of previous study?"

"They arise chiefly from what is passing at the time, and though I sometimes amuse myself with suggesting and arranging such little elegant compliments as may be adapted to ordinary occasions, I always wish to give them as unstudied an air as possible."

Mr. Bennet's expectations were fully answered. His cousin was as absurd as he had hoped, and he listened to him with the keenest enjoyment, maintaining at the same time the most resolute composure of countenance, and except in an occasional glance at Elizabeth, requiring no partner in his pleasure.

By tea-time however the dose had been enough, and Mr. Bennet was glad to take his guest into the drawing-room again; and when tea was over, glad to invite him to read aloud to the ladies. Mr. Collins readily assented, and a book was produced; but on beholding it (for everything announced it to be from a circulating library) he started back, and begging pardon, protested that he never read novels.—Kitty stared at him, and Lydia exclaimed.—Other books were produced, and after some deliberation he chose Fordyce's *Sermons*. Lydia gaped as he opened the volume, and before he had, with very monotonous solemnity, read three pages, she interrupted him with,

"Do you know, Mama, that my uncle Philips talks of turning away Richard, and if he does, Colonel Forster will hire him. My aunt told me so herself on Saturday. I shall walk to Meryton to-morrow to hear more about it, and to ask when Mr. Denny comes back from town."

Lydia was bid by her two eldest sisters to hold her tongue; but Mr. Collins, much offended, laid aside his book, and said,

"I have often observed how little young ladies are interested by books of a serious stamp, though written solely for their benefit. It amazes me, I confess—for certainly, there can be nothing so advantageous to them as instruction. But I will no longer importune my young cousin."

Then turning to Mr. Bennet, he offered himself as his antagonist at backgammon. Mr. Bennet accepted the challenge, observing that he acted very wisely in leaving the girls to their own trifling amusements. Mrs. Bennet and her daughters apologized most civilly for Lydia's interruption, and promised that it should not occur again, if he would resume his book; but Mr. Collins, after assuring them that he bore his young cousin no ill will, and should never resent her behaviour as any affront, seated himself at another table with Mr. Bennet, and prepared for backgammon.

CHAPTER FIFTEEN

MR. COLLINS was not a sensible man, and the deficiency of nature had been but little assisted by education or society—the greatest part of his life having been spent under the guidance of an illiterate and miserly father—and though he belonged to one of the universities, he had merely kept the necessary terms, without forming at it any useful acquaintance. The subjection in which his father had brought him up had given him originally great humility of manner, but it was now a good deal counteracted by the self-conceit of a weak head, living in retirement, and the consequential feelings of early and unexpected prosperity. A fortunate chance had recommended him to Lady Catherine de Bourgh when the living of Hunsford was vacant; and the respect which he felt for her high rank, and his veneration for her as his patroness, mingling with a very good opinion of himself, of his authority as a clergyman, and his rights as a rector, made him altogether a mixture of pride and obsequiousness, self-importance and humility.

Having now a good house and very sufficient income, he intended to marry; and in seeking a reconciliation with the Longbourn family he had a wife in view, as he meant to choose one of the daughters, if he found them as handsome and amiable as they were represented by common report. This was his plan of amends—of atonement—for inheriting their father's estate; and he thought it an excellent one, full of eligibility and suitableness, and excessively generous and disinterested on his own part.

His plan did not vary on seeing them. Miss Bennet's lovely face confirmed his views, and established all his strictest notions of what was due to seniority; and for the first evening *she* was his settled choice. The next morning, however, made an alteration; for in a quarter of an hour's *tête-à-tête* with Mrs. Bennet before break-

61

fast, a conversation beginning with his parsonage-house, and leading naturally to the avowal of his hopes that a mistress for it might be found at Longbourn, produced from her, amid very complaisant smiles and general encouragement, a caution against the very Jane he had fixed on.—"As to her *younger* daughters she could not take upon her to say—she could not positively answer—but she did not *know* of any prepossession; her *eldest* daughter, she must mention—she felt it incumbent on her to hint—was likely to be very soon engaged."

Mr. Collins had only to change from Jane to Elizabeth —and it was soon done—done while Mrs. Bennet was stirring the fire. Elizabeth, equally next to Jane in birth and beauty, succeeded her of course.

Mrs. Bennet treasured up the hint, and trusted that she might soon have two daughters married; and the man whom she could not bear to speak of the day before was now high in her good graces.

Lydia's intention of walking to Meryton was not forgotten; every sister except Mary agreed to go with her; and Mr. Collins was to attend them, at the request of Mr. Bennet, who was most anxious to get rid of him and have his library to himself; for thither Mr. Collins had followed him after breakfast, and there he would continue, nominally engaged with one of the largest folios in the collection, but really talking to Mr. Bennet, with little cessation, of his house and garden at Hunsford. Such doings discomposed Mr. Bennet exceedingly. In his library he had been always sure of leisure and tranquillity; and though prepared, as he told Elizabeth, to meet with folly and conceit in every other room in the house, he was used to be free from them there; his civility, therefore, was most prompt in inviting Mr. Collins to join his daughters in their walk; and Mr. Collins, being in fact much better fitted for a walker than a reader, was extremely well pleased to close his large book, and go.

In pompous nothings on his side, and civil assents on that of his cousins, their time passed till they entered Meryton. The attention of the younger ones was then no longer to be gained by *him*. Their eyes were immediately wandering up in the street in quest of the officers, and nothing less than a very smart bonnet indeed, or a really new muslin in a shop window, could recall them.

But the attention of every lady was soon caught by a young man, whom they had never seen before, of most gentlemanlike appearance, walking with an officer on the other side of the way. The officer was the very Mr. Denny, concerning whose return from London Lydia came to inquire, and he bowed as they passed. All were struck with the stranger's air, all wondered who he could be, and Kitty and Lydia, determined if possible to find out, led the way across the street, under pretence of wanting something in an opposite shop, and fortunately had just gained the pavement when the two gentlemen turning back had reached the same spot. Mr. Denny addressed them directly, and entreated permission to introduce his friend, Mr. Wickham, who had returned with him the day before from town, and he was happy to say had accepted a commission in their corps. This was exactly as it should be; for the young man wanted only regimentals to make him completely charming. His appearance was greatly in his favour; he had all the best part of beauty, a fine countenance, a good figure, and very pleasing address. The introduction was followed up on his side by a happy readiness of conversation—a readiness at the same time perfectly correct and unassuming; and the whole party were still standing and talking together very agreeably when the sound of horses drew their notice, and Darcy and Bingley were seen riding down the street. On distinguishing the ladies of the group, the two gentlemen came directly towards them, and began the usual civilities. Bingley was the principal spokesman, and Miss Bennet the principal object. He was then, he said, on his way to Longbourn on purpose to inquire after her. Mr. Darcy corroborated it with a bow, and was beginning to determine not to fix his eyes on Elizabeth, when they were suddenly arrested by the sight of the stranger, and Elizabeth happening to see the countenance of both as they looked at each other, was all astonishment at the effect of the meeting. Both changed colour, one looked white, the other red. Mr. Wickham, after a few moments, touched his hat—a salutation which Mr. Darcy just deigned to return. What could be the meaning of it? It was impossible to imagine; it was impossible not to long to know.

In another minute Mr. Bingley, but without seeming to have noticed what passed, took leave and rode on with his friend.

Mr. Denny and Mr. Wickham walked with the young ladies to the door of Mr. Philips' house, and then made their bows, in spite of Miss Lydia's pressing entreaties that they would come in, and even in spite of Mrs. Philips' throwing up the parlour window and loudly seconding the invitation.

Mrs. Philips was always glad to see her nieces; and the two eldest, from their recent absence, were particularly welcome, and she was eagerly expressing her surprise at their sudden return home, which, as their own carriage had not fetched them, she should have known nothing about, if she had not happened to see Mr. Jones's shop boy in the street, who had told her that they were not to send any more draughts to Netherfield because the Miss Bennets were come away, when her civility was claimed towards Mr. Collins by Jane's introduction of him. She received him with her very best politeness, which he returned with as much more, apologizing for his intrusion, without any previous acquaintance with her, which he could not help flattering himself however might be justified by his relationship to the young ladies who introduced him to her notice. Mrs. Philips was quite awed by such an excess of good breeding; but her contemplation of one stranger was soon put an end to by exclamations and inquiries about the other, of whom, however, she could only tell her nieces what they already knew, that Mr. Denny had brought him from London, and that he was to have a lieutenant's commission in the ——shire. She had been watching him the last hour, she said, as he walked up and down the street; and had Mr. Wickham appeared, Kitty and Lydia would certainly have continued the occupation; but unluckily no one passed the windows now except a few of the officers, who in comparison with the stranger were become "stupid, disagreeable fellows." Some of them were to dine with the Philipses the next day, and their aunt promised to make her husband call on Mr. Wickham, and give him an invitation also, if the family from Longbourn would come in the evening. This was agreed to, and Mrs. Philips protested that they would have a nice comfortable noisy game of lottery tickets and a little bit of hot supper afterwards. The prospect of such delights was very cheering, and they parted in mutual good spirits. Mr. Collins repeated his apologies in quitting the room, and was assured with unwearying civility that they were perfectly needless.

As they walked home, Elizabeth related to Jane what she had seen pass between the two gentlemen; but though Jane would have defended either or both, had they appeared to be wrong, she could no more explain such behaviour than her sister.

Mr. Collins on his return highly gratified Mrs. Bennet by admiring Mrs. Philips's manners and politeness. He protested that except Lady Catherine and her daughter, he had never seen a more elegant woman; for she had not only received him with the utmost civility, but had even pointedly included him in her invitation for the next evening, although utterly unknown to her before. Something he supposed might be attributed to his connection with them, but yet he had never met with so much attention in the whole course of his life.

CHAPTER SIXTEEN

As no objection was made to the young people's engagement with their aunt, and all Mr. Collins's scruples of leaving Mr. and Mrs. Bennet for a single evening during his visit were most steadily resisted, the coach conveyed him and his five cousins at a suitable hour to Meryton; and the girls had the pleasure of hearing, as they entered the drawing-room, that Mr. Wickham had accepted their uncle's invitation, and was then in the house.

When this information was given, and they had all taken their seats, Mr. Collins was at leisure to look around him and admire, and he was so much struck with the size and furniture of the apartment that he declared he might almost have supposed himself in the small summer breakfast parlour at Rosings, a comparison that did not at first convey much gratification;

but when Mrs. Philips understood from him what Rosings was, and who was its proprietor, when she had listened to the description of only one of Lady Catherine's drawing-rooms, and found that the chimney-piece alone had cost eight hundred pounds, she felt all the force of the compliment, and would hardly have resented a comparison with the housekeeper's room.

In describing to her all the grandeur of Lady Catherine and her mansion, with occasional digressions in praise of his own humble abode and the improvements it was receiving, he was happily employed until the gentlemen joined them; and he found in Mrs. Philips a very attentive listener, whose opinion of his consequence increased with what she heard, and who was resolving to retail it all among her neighbours as soon as she could. To the girls, who could not listen to their cousin, and who had nothing to do but to wish for an instrument, and examine their own indifferent imitations of china on the mantlepiece, the interval of waiting appeared very long. It was over at last however. The gentlemen did approach; and when Mr. Wickham walked into the room, Elizabeth felt that she had neither been seeing him before, nor thinking of him since, with the smallest degree of unreasonable admiration. The officers of the—— shire were in general a very creditable, gentlemanlike set, and the best of them were of the present party; but Mr. Wickham was as far beyond them all in person, countenance, air, and walk, as *they* were superior to the broad-faced stuffy uncle Philips, breathing port wine, who followed them into the room.

Mr. Wickham was the happy man towards whom almost every female eye was turned, and Elizabeth was the happy woman by whom he finally seated himself; and the agreeable manner in which he immediately fell into conversation, though it was only on its being a wet night and on the probability of a rainy season, made her feel that the commonest, dullest, most threadbare topic might be rendered interesting by the skill of the speaker.

With such rivals for the notice of the fair as Mr. Wickham and the officers, Mr. Collins seemed likely to sink into insignificance; to the young ladies he certainly was nothing; but he had still at intervals a kind listener in

66

Mrs. Philips, and was, by her watchfulness, most abundantly supplied with coffee and muffin.

When the card-tables were placed, he had an opportunity of obliging her in return by sitting down to whist.

"I know little of the game, at present," said he, "but I shall be glad to improve myself, for in my situation of life——" Mrs. Philips was very thankful for his compliance, but could not wait for his reason.

Mr. Wickham did not play at whist, and with ready delight was he received at the other table between Elizabeth and Lydia. At first there seemed danger of Lydia's engrossing him entirely, for she was a most determined talker; but being likewise extremely fond of lottery tickets, she soon grew too much interested in the game, too eager to make bets and exclaiming after prizes, to have attention for any one in particular. Allowing for the common demands of the game, Mr. Wickham was therefore at leisure to talk to Elizabeth, and she was very willing to hear him, though what she chiefly wished to hear she could not hope to be told, the history of his acquaintance with Mr. Darcy. She dared not even mention that gentleman. Her curiosity however was unexpectedly relieved. Mr. Wickham began the subject himself. He inquired how far Netherfield was from Meryton; and after receiving her answer, asked in an hesitating manner how long Mr. Darcy had been staying there.

"About a month," said Elizabeth; and then, unwilling to let the subject drop, added, "He is a man of very large property in Derbyshire, I understand."

"Yes," replied Wickham; "his estate there is a noble one. A clear ten thousand per annum. You could not have met with a person more capable of giving you certain information on that head than myself—for I have been connected with his family in a particular manner from my infancy."

Elizabeth could not but look surprised.

"You may well be surprised, Miss Bennet, at such an assertion, after seeing, as you probably might, the very cold manner of our meeting yesterday. Are you much acquainted with Mr. Darcy?"

"As much as I ever wish to be," cried Elizabeth

warmly—"I have spent four days in the same house with him, and I think him very disagreeable."

"I have no right to give *my* opinion," said Wickham, "as to his being agreeable or otherwise. I am not qualified to form one. I have known him too long and too well to be a fair judge. It is impossible for *me* to be impartial. But I believe your opinion of him would in general astonish—and perhaps you would not express it quite so strongly anywhere else.—Here you are in your own family."

"Upon my word I say no more *here* than I might say in any house in the neighbourhood, except Netherfield. He is not at all liked in Hertfordshire. Everybody is disgusted with his pride. You will not find him more favourably spoken of by any one."

"I cannot pretend to be sorry," said Wickham, after a short interruption, "that he or that any man should not be estimated beyond their deserts; but with *him* I believe it does not often happen. The world is blinded by his fortune and consequence, or frightened by his high and imposing manners, and sees him only as he chooses to be seen."

"I should take him, even on *my* slight acquaintance, to be an ill-tempered man." Wickham only shook his head.

"I wonder," said he, at the next opportunity of speaking, "whether he is likely to be in this country much longer."

"I do not at all know; but I *heard* nothing of his going away when I was at Netherfield. I hope your plans in favour of the——shire will not be affected by his being in the neighbourhood."

"Oh! no—it is not for *me* to be driven away by Mr. Darcy. If *he* wishes to avoid seeing *me*, he must go. We are not on friendly terms, and it always gives me pain to meet him, but I have no reason for avoiding *him* but what I might proclaim to all the world: a sense of very great ill usage, and most painful regrets at his being what he is. His father, Miss Bennet, the late Mr. Darcy, was one of the best men that ever breathed, and the truest friend I ever had; and I can never be in company with this Mr. Darcy without being grieved to the soul by a thousand tender recollections. His behaviour to myself has been scandalous; but I verily believe I could forgive him anything and everything, rather than his disappointing the hopes and disgracing the memory of his father."

Elizabeth found the interest of the subject increase, and listened with all her heart; but the delicacy of it prevented farther inquiry.

Mr. Wickham began to speak on more general topics, Meryton, the neighbourhood, the society, appearing highly pleased with all that he had yet seen, and speaking of the latter especially, with gentle but very intelligible gallantry.

"It was the prospect of constant society, and good society," he added, "which was my chief inducement to enter the——shire. I knew it to be a most respectable, agreeable corps, and my friend Denny tempted me farther by his account of their present quarters, and the very great attentions and excellent acquaintance Meryton had procured them. Society, I own, is necessary to me. I have been a disappointed man, and my spirits will not bear solitude. I *must* have employment and society. A military life is not what I was intended for, but circumstances have now made it eligible. The church *ought* to have been my profession—I was brought up for the church, and I should at this time have been in possession of a most valuable living, had it pleased the gentleman we were speaking of just now."

"Indeed!"

"Yes—the late Mr. Darcy bequeathed me the next presentation of the best living in his gift. He was my godfather, and excessively attached to me. I cannot do justice to his kindness. He meant to provide for me amply, and thought he had done it; but when the living fell, it was given elsewhere."

"Good heavens!" cried Elizabeth; "but how could *that* be?—How could his will be disregarded?—Why did not you seek legal redress?"

"There was just such an informality in the terms of the bequest as to give me no hope from law. A man of honour could not have doubted the intention, but Mr. Darcy chose to doubt it—or to treat it as a merely conditional recommendation, and to assert that I had forfeited all claim to it by extravagance, imprudence, in short anything or nothing. Certain it is that the living became vacant two years ago, exactly as I was of an age to hold it, and that it was given to another man; and no less certain is it, that I cannot accuse myself of having really done anything to deserve to lose it. I have a warm, unguarded temper, and I may perhaps have sometimes spoken my opinion *of* him, and *to* him, too freely. I can recall nothing worse. But the fact is that we are very different sort of men, and that he hates me."

"This is quite shocking!—He deserves to be publicly disgraced."

"Sometime or other he *will* be—but it shall not be by *me*. Till I can forget his father, I can never defy or expose *him*."

Elizabeth honoured him for such feelings, and thought him handsomer than ever as he expressed them.

"But what," said she, after a pause, "can have been his motive? What can have induced him to behave so cruelly?"

"A thorough, determined dislike of me—a dislike which I cannot but attribute in some measure to jealousy. Had the late Mr. Darcy liked me less, his son might have borne with me better; but his father's uncommon attachment to me irritated him, I believe, very early in life. He had not a temper to bear the sort of competition in which we stood—the sort of preference which was often given me."

"I had not thought Mr. Darcy so bad as this—though I have never liked him, I had not thought so very ill of him—I had supposed him to be despising his fellow-creatures in general, but did not suspect him of descending to such malicious revenge, such injustice, such inhumanity as this!"

After a few minutes reflection, however, she continued, "I *do* remember his boasting one day, at Netherfield, of the implacability of his resentments, of his having an unforgiving temper. His disposition must be dreadful."

"I will not trust myself on the subject," replied Wickham, "*I* can hardly be just to him."

Elizabeth was again deep in thought, and after a time exclaimed, "To treat in such a manner the godson, the friend, the favourite of his father!"—She could have

70

added, "A young man too, like *you*, whose very countenance may vouch for your being amiable"—but she contented herself with "And one, too, who had probably been his own companion from childhood, connected together, as I think you said, in the closest manner!"

"We were born in the same parish, within the same park, the greatest part of our youth was passed together; inmates of the same house, sharing the same amusements, objects of the same parental care. *My* father began life in the profession which your uncle, Mr. Philips, appears to do so much credit to—but he gave up everything to be of use to the late Mr. Darcy, and devoted all his time to the care of the Pemberley property. He was most highly esteemed by Mr. Darcy, a most intimate, confidential friend. Mr. Darcy often acknowledged himself to be under the greatest obligations to my father's active superintendence, and when immediately before my father's death, Mr. Darcy gave him a voluntary promise of providing for me, I am convinced that he felt it to be as much a debt of gratitude to *him*, as of affection to myself."

"How strange!" cried Elizabeth. "How abominable!—I wonder that the very pride of this Mr. Darcy has not made him just to you!—If from no better motive that he should not have been too proud to be dishonest, for dishonesty I must call it."

"It *is* wonderful," replied Wickham, "for almost all his actions may be traced to pride; and pride has often been his best friend. It has connected him nearer with virtue than any other feeling. But we are none of us consistent; and in his behaviour to me there were stronger impulses even than pride."

"Can such abominable pride as his have ever done him good?"

"Yes. It has often led him to be liberal and generous—to give his money freely, to display hospitality, to assist his tenants, and relieve the poor. Family pride, and *filial* pride, for he is very proud of what his father was, have done this. Not to appear to disgrace his family, to degenerate from the popular qualities, or lose the influence of the Pemberley House, is a powerful motive. He has also *brotherly* pride, which with *some* brotherly affection makes him a very kind and careful guardian of his sister; and you will hear him generally cried up as the most attentive and best of brothers."

"What sort of a girl is Miss Darcy?"

He shook his head.—"I wish I could call her amiable. It gives me pain to speak ill of a Darcy. But she is too much like her brother—very, very proud. As a child she was affectionate and pleasing, and extremely fond of me; and I have devoted hours and hours to her amusement. But she is nothing to me now. She is a handsome girl, about fifteen or sixteen, and I understand highly accomplished. Since her father's death, her home has been London, where a lady lives with her and superintends her education."

After many pauses and many trials of other subjects, Elizabeth could not help reverting once more to the first, and saying,

"I am astonished at his intimacy with Mr. Bingley! How can Mr. Bingley, who seems good humour itself and is, I really believe, truly amiable, be in friendship with such a man? How can they suit each other?—Do you know Mr. Bingley?"

"Not at all."

"He is a sweet tempered, amiable, charming man. He cannot know what Mr. Darcy is."

"Probably not; but Mr. Darcy can please where he chooses. He does not want abilities. He can be a conversible companion if he thinks it worth his while. Among those who are at all his equals in consequence, he is a very different man from what he is to the less prosperous. His pride never deserts him; but with the rich, he is liberal-minded, just, sincere, rational, honourable, and perhaps agreeable—allowing something for fortune and figure."

The whist party soon afterwards breaking up, the players gathered round the other table, and Mr. Collins took his station between his cousin Elizabeth and Mrs. Philips. The usual inquiries as to his success were made by the latter. It had not been very great; he had lost every point; but when Mrs. Philips began to express her concern thereupon, he assured her with much earnest gravity that it was not of the least importance, that he considered the money as a mere trifle, and begged she would not make herself uneasy.

"I know very well, madam," said he, "that when

persons sit down to a card-table, they must take their chance of these things; and happily I am not in such circumstances as to make five shillings any object. There are undoubtedly many who could not say the same, but thanks to Lady Catherine de Bourgh, I am removed far beyond the necessity of regarding little matters."

Mr. Wickham's attention was caught; and after observing Mr. Collins for a few moments, he asked Elizabeth in a low voice whether her relation were very intimately acquainted with the family of De Bourgh.

"Lady Catherine de Bourgh," she replied, "has very lately given him a living. I hardly know how Mr. Collins was first introduced to her notice, but he certainly has not known her long."

"You know of course that Lady Catherine de Bourgh and Lady Anne Darcy were sisters, consequently that she is aunt to the present Mr. Darcy."

"No, indeed, I did not. I knew nothing at all of Lady Catherine's connections. I never heard of her existence till the day before yesterday."

"Her daughter, Miss De Bourgh, will have a very large fortune, and it is believed that she and her cousin will unite the two estates."

This information made Elizabeth smile, as she thought of poor Miss Bingley. Vain indeed must be all her attentions, vain and useless her affection for his sister and her praise of himself, if he were already self-destined to another.

"Mr. Collins," said she, "speaks highly both of Lady Catherine and her daughter; but from some particulars that he has related of her ladyship, I suspect his gratitude misleads him, and that in spite of her being his patroness, she is an arrogant, conceited woman."

"I believe her to be both in a great degree," replied Wickham; "I have not seen her for many years, but I very well remember that I never liked her, and that her manners were dictatorial and insolent. She has the reputation of being remarkably sensible and clever: but I rather believe she derives part of her abilities from her rank and fortune, part from her authoritative manner, and the rest from the pride of her nephew, who chooses that everyone connected with him should have an understanding of the first class."

Elizabeth allowed that he had given a very rational account of it, and they continued talking together with mutual satisfaction till supper put an end to cards; and gave the rest of the ladies their share of Mr. Wickham's attentions. There could be no conversation in the noise of Mrs. Philips's supper party, but his manners recommended him to everybody. Whatever he said was said well; and whatever he did, done gracefully. Elizabeth went away with her head full of him. She could think of nothing but of Mr. Wickham, and of what he had told her, all the way home; but there was not time for her even to mention his name as they went, for neither Lydia nor Mr. Collins were once silent. Lydia talked incessantly of lottery tickets, of the fish she had lost and the fish she had won; and Mr. Collins—in describing the civility of Mr. and Mrs. Philips, protesting that he did not in the least regard his losses at whist, enumerating all the dishes at supper, and repeatedly fearing that he crowded his cousins—had more to say than he could well manage before the carriage stopped at Longbourn House.

CHAPTER SEVENTEEN

Elizabeth related to Jane the next day what had passed between Mr. Wickham and herself. Jane listened with astonishment and concern; she knew not how to believe that Mr. Darcy could be so unworthy of Mr. Bingley's regard; and yet, it was not in her nature to question the veracity of a young man of such amiable appearance as Wickham. The possibility of his having really endured such unkindness was enough to interest all her tender feelings; and nothing therefore remained to be done, but to think well of them both, to defend the conduct of each, and throw into the account of accident or mistake, whatever could not be otherwise explained.

"They have both," said she, "been deceived, I dare say, in some way or other of which we can form no idea. Interested people have perhaps misrepresented each to the other. It is, in short, impossible for us to conjecture the causes or circumstances which may have alienated them, without actual blame on either side."

"Very true, indeed; and now, my dear Jane, what

74

have you got to say in behalf of the interested people who have probably been concerned in the business? Do clear *them* too, or we shall be obliged to think ill of somebody."

"Laugh as much as you choose, but you will not laugh me out of my opinion. My dearest Lizzy, do but consider in what a disgraceful light it places Mr. Darcy to be treating his father's favourite in such a manner —one whom his father had promised to provide for. It is impossible. No man of common humanity, no man who had any value for his character, could be capable of it. Can his most intimate friends be so excessively deceived in him? Oh! no."

"I can much more easily believe Mr. Bingley's being imposed on than that Mr. Wickham should invent such a history of himself as he gave me last night; names, facts, everything mentioned without ceremony. If it be not so, let Mr. Darcy contradict it. Besides, there was truth in his looks."

"It is difficult indeed—it is distressing. One does not know what to think."

"I beg your pardon; one knows exactly what to think."

But Jane could think with certainty on only one point— that Mr. Bingley, if he *had been* imposed on, would have much to suffer when the affair became public.

The two young ladies were summoned from the shrubbery where this conversation passed by the arrival of some of the very persons of whom they had been speaking; Mr. Bingley and his sisters came to give their personal invitation for the long expected ball at Netherfield, which was fixed for the following Tuesday. The two ladies were delighted to see their dear friend again, called it an age since they had met, and repeatedly asked what she had been doing with herself since their separation. To the rest of the family they paid little attention; avoiding Mrs. Bennet as much as possible, saying not much to Elizabeth, and nothing at all to the others. They were soon gone again, rising from their seats with an activity which took their brother by surprise, and hurrying off as if eager to escape from Mrs. Bennet's civilities.

The prospect of the Netherfield ball was extremely agreeable to every female of the family. Mrs. Bennet chose to consider it as given in compliment to her eldest daughter, and was particularly flattered by receiving the invitation from Mr. Bingley himself, instead of a ceremonious card. Jane pictured to herself a happy evening in the society of her two friends, and the attentions of their brother; and Elizabeth thought with pleasure of dancing a great deal with Mr. Wickham, and of seeing a confirmation of everything in Mr. Darcy's looks and behaviour. The happiness anticipated by Catherine and Lydia depended less on any single event, or any particular person, for though they each, like Elizabeth, meant to dance half the evening with Mr. Wickham, he was by no means the only partner who could satisfy them, and a ball was, at any rate, a ball. And even Mary could assure her family that she had no disinclination for it.

"While I can have my mornings to myself," said she, "it is enough. I think it no sacrifice to join occasionally in evening engagements. Society has claims on us all; and I profess myself one of those who consider intervals of recreation and amusement as desirable for everybody."

Elizabeth's spirits were so high on the occasion that though she did not often speak unnecessarily to Mr. Collins, she could not help asking him whether he intended to accept Mr. Bingley's invitation, and if he did, whether he would think it proper to join in the evening's amusement; and she was rather surprised to find that he entertained no scruple whatever on that head, and was very far from dreading a rebuke either from the Archbishop, or Lady Catherine de Bourgh, by venturing to dance.

"I am by no means of opinion, I assure you," said he, "that a ball of this kind, given by a young man of character, to respectable people, can have any evil tendency; and I am so far from objecting to dancing myself that I shall hope to be honoured with the hands of all my fair cousins in the course of the evening, and I take this opportunity of soliciting yours, Miss Elizabeth, for the two first dances especially—a preference which I trust my cousin Jane will attribute to the right cause, and not to any disrespect for her."

Elizabeth felt herself completely taken in. She had

fully proposed being engaged by Wickham for those very dances: and to have Mr. Collins instead! Her liveliness had been never worse timed. There was no help for it, however. Mr. Wickham's happiness and her own was perforce delayed a little longer, and Mr. Collins's proposal accepted with as good a grace as she could. She was not the better pleased with his gallantry from the idea it suggested of something more. It now first struck her that *she* was selected from among her sisters as worthy of being the mistress of Hunsford Parsonage, and of assisting to form a quadrille table at Rosings, in the absence of more eligible visitors. The idea soon reached to conviction, as she observed his increasing civilities toward herself and heard his frequent attempt at a compliment on her wit and vivacity; and though more astonished than gratified herself by this effect of her charms, it was not long before her mother gave her to understand that the probability of their marriage was exceedingly agreeable to *her*. Elizabeth however did not choose to take the hint, being well aware that a serious dispute must be the consequence of any reply. Mr. Collins might never make the offer, and till he did, it was useless to quarrel about him.

If there had not been a Netherfield ball to prepare for and talk of, the younger Miss Bennets would have been in a pitiable state at this time, for from the day of the invitation to the day of the ball, there was such a succession of rain as prevented their walking to Meryton once. No aunt, no officers, no news could be sought after; the very shoe-roses for Netherfield were got by proxy. Even Elizabeth might have found some trial of her patience in weather, which totally suspended the improvement of her acquaintance with Mr. Wickham; and nothing less than a dance on Tuesday could have made such a Friday, Saturday, Sunday, and Monday endurable to Kitty and Lydia.

CHAPTER EIGHTEEN

TILL Elizabeth entered the drawing-room at Netherfield and looked in vain for Mr. Wickham among the cluster of redcoats there assembled, a doubt of his being present had never occurred to her. The certainty of meeting him had not been checked by any of those recollections that might not unreasonably have alarmed her. She had dressed with more than usual care, and prepared in the highest spirits for the conquest of all that remained unsubdued of his heart, trusting that it was not more than might be won in the course of the evening. But in an instant arose the dreadful suspicion of his being purposely omitted for Mr. Darcy's pleasure in the Bingleys' invitation to the officers; and though this was not exactly the case, the absolute fact of his absence was pronounced by his friend Mr. Denny, to whom Lydia eagerly applied, and who told them that Wickham had been obliged to go to town on business the day before, and was not yet returned; adding, with a significant smile,

"I do not imagine his business would have called him away just now, if he had not wished to avoid a certain gentleman here."

This part of his intelligence, though unheard by Lydia, was caught by Elizabeth, and as it assured her that Darcy was not less answerable for Wickham's absence than if her first surmise had been just, every feeling of displeasure against the former was so sharpened by immediate disappointment that she could hardly reply with tolerable civility to the polite inquiries which he directly afterwards approached to make.—Attention, forbearance, patience with Darcy was injury to Wickham. She was resolved against any sort of conversation with him, and turned away with a degree of ill humour, which she could not wholly surmount even in speaking to Mr. Bingley, whose blind partiality provoked her.

But Elizabeth was not formed for ill-humour; and though every prospect of her own was destroyed for the evening, it could not dwell long on her spirits; and having told all her griefs to Charlotte Lucas, whom she had not seen for a week, she was soon able to make a voluntary transition to the oddities of her cousin, and to point him out to her particular notice. The two first dances, however, brought a return of distress; they were dances of mortification. Mr. Collins, awkward and solemn, apologizing instead of attending, and often moving wrong without being aware of it, gave her all the shame and misery which a disagreeable partner for a couple of dances can give. The moment of her release from him was ecstacy.

She danced next with an officer, and had the refreshment of talking of Wickham, and of hearing that he was universally liked. When those dances were over she returned to Charlotte Lucas, and was in conversation with her when she found herself suddenly addressed by Mr. Darcy, who took her so much by surprise in his application for her hand that, without knowing what she did, she accepted him. He walked away again immediately, and she was left to fret over her own want of presence of mind; Charlotte tried to console her.

"I dare say you will find him very agreeable."

"Heaven forbid!—*That* would be the greatest misfortune of all!—To find a man agreeable whom one is determined to hate!—Do not wish me such an evil."

When the dancing recommenced, however, and Darcy approached to claim her hand, Charlotte could not help cautioning her in a whisper not to be a simpleton and allow her fancy for Wickham to make her appear unpleasant in the eyes of a man often times his consequence. Elizabeth made no answer, and took her place in the set, amazed at the dignity to which she was arrived in being allowed to stand opposite to Mr. Darcy, and reading in her neighbours' looks their equal amazement in beholding it. They stood for some time without speaking a word; and she began to imagine that their silence was to last through the two dances, and at first was resolved not to break it; till suddenly fancying that it would be the greater punishment to her partner to oblige him to talk, she made some slight observation on the dance. He replied, and was again silent. After a pause of some minutes she addressed him a second time with,

"It is *your* turn to say something now, Mr. Darcy. *I* talked about the dance, and *you* ought to make some kind of remark on the size of the room, or the number of couples."

He smiled, and assured her that whatever she wished him to say should be said.

"Very well.—That reply will do for the present.—Perhaps by and by I may observe that private balls are much pleasanter than public ones.—But *now* we may be silent."

"Do you talk by rule, then, while you are dancing?"

"Sometimes. One must speak a little, you know. It would look odd to be entirely silent for half an hour together, and yet for the advantage of *some*, conversation ought to be so arranged as that they may have the trouble of saying as little as possible."

"Are you consulting your own feelings in the present case, or do you imagine that you are gratifying mine?"

"Both," replied Elizabeth archly; "for I have always seen a great similarity in the turn of our minds.—We are each of an unsocial, taciturn disposition, unwilling to speak, unless we expect to say something that will amaze the whole room, and be handed down to posterity with all the *éclat* of a proverb."

"This is no very striking resemblance of your own character, I am sure," said he. "How near it may be to *mine*, I cannot pretend to say.—*You* think it is a faithful portrait undoubtedly."

"I must not decide on my own performance."

He made no answer, and they were again silent till they had gone down the dance, when he asked her if she and her sisters did not very often walk to Meryton. She answered in the affirmative, and unable to resist the temptation, added, "When you met us there the other day, we had just been forming a new acquaintance."

The effect was immediate. A deeper shade of *hauteur* overspread his features, but he said not a word, and Elizabeth, though blaming herself for her own weakness, could not go on. At length Darcy spoke, and in a constrained manner said,

"Mr. Wickham is blessed with such happy manners as may insure his *making* friends—whether he may be equally capable of *retaining* them is less certain."

"He has been so unlucky as to lose *your* friendship," replied Elizabeth with emphasis, "and in a manner which he is likely to suffer from all his life."

Darcy made no answer, and seemed desirous of changing the subject. At that moment Sir William Lucas appeared close to them, meaning to pass through the set to the other side of the room; but on perceiving

Mr. Darcy he stopped with a bow of superior courtesy to compliment him on his dancing and his partner.

"I have been most highly gratified indeed, my dear Sir. Such very superior dancing is not often seen. It is evident that you belong to the first circles. Allow me to say, however, that your fair partner does not disgrace you, and that I must hope to have this pleasure often repeated, especially when a certain desirable event, my dear Miss Eliza (glancing at her sister and Bingley), shall take place. What congratulations will then flow in! I appeal to Mr. Darcy: but let me not interrupt you, Sir.—You will not thank me for detaining you from the bewitching converse of that young lady, whose bright eyes are also upbraiding me."

The latter part of this address was scarcely heard by Darcy; but Sir William's allusion to his friend seemed to strike him forcibly, and his eyes were directed with a very serious expression towards Bingley and Jane, who were dancing together. Recovering himself, however, shortly, he turned to his partner, and said,

"Sir William's interruption has made me forget what we were talking of."

"I do not think we were speaking at all. Sir William could not have interrupted any two people in the room who had less to say for themselves.—We have tried two or three subjects already without success, and what we are to talk of next I cannot imagine."

"What think you of books?" said he, smiling.

"Books—Oh! no.—I am sure we never read the same, or not with the same feelings."

"I am sorry you think so; but if that be the case, there can at least be no want of subject.—We may compare our different opinions."

"No—I cannot talk of books in a ballroom; my head is always full of something else."

"The *present* always occupies you in such scenes,—does it?" said he, with a look of doubt.

"Yes, always," she replied, without knowing what she said, for her thoughts had wandered far from the subject, as soon afterwards appeared by her suddenly exclaiming, "I remember hearing you once say, Mr. Darcy, that you hardly ever forgave, that your resentment once created was unappeasable. You are very cautious, I suppose, as to its *being created*."

"I am," said he, with a firm voice.

"And never allow yourself to be blinded by prejudice?"

"I hope not."

"It is particularly incumbent on those who never change their opinion to be secure of judging properly at first."

"May I ask to what these questions tend?"

"Merely to the illustration of *your* character," said she, endeavouring to shake off her gravity. "I am trying to make it out."

"And what is your success?"

She shook her head. "I do not get on at all. I hear such different accounts of you as puzzle me exceedingly."

"I can readily believe," answered he gravely, "that report may vary greatly with respect to me; and I could wish, Miss Bennet, that you were not to sketch my character at the present moment, as there is reason to fear that the performance would reflect no credit on either."

"But if I do not take your likeness now, I may never have another opportunity."

"I would by no means suspend any pleasure of yours," he coldly replied. She said no more, and they went down the other dance and parted in silence; on each side dissatisfied, though not to an equal degree, for in Darcy's breast there was a tolerable powerful feeling towards her, which soon procured her pardon, and directed all his anger against another.

They had not long separated when Miss Bingley came towards her, and with an expression of civil disdain thus accosted her,

"So, Miss Eliza, I hear you are quite delighted with George Wickham! Your sister has been talking to me about him, and asking me a thousand questions; and I find that the young man forgot to tell you, among his other communications, that he was the son of old Wickham, the late Mr. Darcy's steward. Let me recommend you, however, as a friend, not to give implicit confidence to all his assertions; for as to Mr. Darcy's using him ill, it is perfectly false; for on the contrary, he has been always remarkably kind to him, though George Wickham has treated Mr. Darcy in a most infamous manner. I do not know the particulars, but I know very well that Mr. Darcy is not in the least to blame, that he cannot bear to hear George Wickham mentioned, and that though my brother thought he could not well avoid including him in his invitation to the officers, he was excessively glad to find that he had taken himself out of the way. His coming into the country at all is a most insolent thing indeed, and I wonder how he could presume to do it. I pity you, Miss Eliza, for this discovery of your favourite's guilt; but really considering his descent, one could not expect much better."

"His guilt and his descent appear by your account to be the same," said Elizabeth angrily; "for I have heard you accuse him of nothing worse than of being the son of Mr. Darcy's steward, and of *that,* I can assure you, he informed me himself."

"I beg your pardon," replied Miss Bingley, turning away with a sneer. "Excuse my interference. It was kindly meant."

"Insolent girl!" said Elizabeth to herself. "You are much mistaken if you expect to influence me by such a paltry attack as this. I see nothing in it but your own wilful ignorance and the malice of Mr. Darcy." She then sought her eldest sister, who had undertaken to make inquiries on the same subject of Bingley. Jane met her with a smile of such sweet complacency, a glow of such happy expression, as sufficiently marked how well she was satisfied with the occurrences of the evening. Elizabeth instantly read her feelings, and at that moment solicitude for Wickham, resentment against his enemies, and everything else gave way before the hope of Jane's being in the fairest way for happiness.

"I want to know," said she, with a countenance no less smiling than her sister's, "what you have learned about Mr. Wickham. But perhaps you have been too pleasantly engaged to think of any third person, in which case you may be sure of my pardon."

"No," replied Jane, "I have not forgotten him; but I have nothing satisfactory to tell you. Mr. Bingley does not know the whole of his history, and is quite ignorant of the circumstances which have principally offended Mr. Darcy; but he will vouch for the good conduct, the probity and honour of his friend, and is perfectly convinced that Mr. Wickham has deserved much less attention from Mr. Darcy than he has received; and I am sorry to say that by his account as well as his sister's, Mr. Wickham is by no means a respectable young man. I am afraid he has been very imprudent, and has deserved to lose Mr. Darcy's regard."

"Mr. Bingley does not know Mr. Wickham himself?"

"No; he never saw him till the other morning at Meryton."

"This account then is what he has received from Mr. Darcy. I am perfectly satisfied. But what does he say of the living?"

"He does not exactly recollect the circumstances, though he has heard them from Mr. Darcy more than once, but he believes that it was left to him *conditionally* only."

"I have not a doubt of Mr. Bingley's sincerity," said Elizabeth warmly; "but you must excuse my not being convinced by assurances only. Mr. Bingley's defence of his friend was a very able one, I dare say, but since he is unacquainted with several parts of the story, and has learned the rest from that friend himself, I shall venture still to think of both gentlemen as I did before."

She then changed the discourse to one more gratifying to each, and on which there could be no difference of sentiment. Elizabeth listened with delight to the happy, though modest hopes which Jane entertained of Bingley's regard, and said all in her power to heighten her confidence in it. On their being joined by Mr. Bingley himself, Elizabeth withdrew to Miss Lucas, to whose inquiry after the pleasantness of her last partner she had scarcely replied before Mr. Collins came up to them and told her with great exultation that he had just been so fortunate as to make a most important discovery.

"I have found out," said he, "by a singular accident, that there is now in the room a near relation of my patroness. I happened to overhear the gentleman himself mentioning to the young lady who does the honours of this house the names of his cousin Miss De Bourgh, and of her mother Lady Catherine. How wonderfully these sort of things occur! Who would have thought of my meeting with—perhaps—a nephew of Lady Catherine de Bourgh in this assembly!—I am most thankful that the discovery is made in time for me to pay my respects to him, which I am now going to do, and trust he will excuse my not having done it before. My total ignorance of the connection must plead my apology."

"You are not going to introduce yourself to Mr. Darcy?"

"Indeed I am. I shall entreat his pardon for not having done it earlier. I believe him to be Lady Catherine's *nephew*. It will be in my power to assure him that her ladyship was quite well yesterday sennight."

Elizabeth tried hard to dissuade him from such a scheme; assuring him that Mr. Darcy would consider his addressing him without introduction as an impertinent freedom, rather than a compliment to his aunt; that it was not in the least necessary there should be any notice on either side, and that if it were, it must belong to Mr. Darcy, the superior in consequence, to begin the acquaintance.—Mr. Collins listened to her with the determined air of following his own inclination, and when she ceased speaking, replied thus,

"My dear Miss Elizabeth, I have the highest opinion in the world of your excellent judgment in all matters within the scope of your understanding, but permit me to say that there must be a wide difference between the established forms of ceremony amongst the laity, and those which regulate the clergy; for give me leave to observe that I consider the clerical office as equal in point of dignity with the highest rank in the kingdom—provided that a proper humility of behaviour is at the same time maintained. You must therefore allow me to follow the dictates of my conscience on this occasion, which leads me to perform what I look on as a point of duty. Pardon me for neglecting to profit by your advice, which on every other subject shall be my constant guide, though in the case before us I consider myself more fitted by education and habitual study to decide on what is right than a young lady like yourself." And with a low bow he left her to attack Mr. Darcy, whose reception of his advances she eagerly watched, and whose astonishment at being so addressed was very evident. Her cousin prefaced his speech with a solemn bow, and though she could not hear a word of it, she felt as if hearing it all, and saw in the motion of his lips the words "apology," "Hunsford," and "Lady Catherine de Bourgh."—It vexed her to see him expose himself to such a man. Mr. Darcy was eyeing him with unrestrained wonder, and when at last Mr. Collins allowed him time to speak, replied with an air of distant civility. Mr. Collins, however, was not discouraged from speaking again, and Mr. Darcy's contempt seemed abundantly increasing with the length of his second speech, and at the end of it he only made him a slight bow, and moved another way. Mr. Collins then returned to Elizabeth.

"I have no reason, I assure you," said he, "to be dissatisfied with my reception. Mr. Darcy seemed much pleased with the attention. He answered me with the utmost civility, and even paid me the compliment of saying that he was so well convinced of Lady Catherine's discernment as to be certain she could never bestow a favour unworthily. It was really a very handsome thought. Upon the whole, I am much pleased with him."

As Elizabeth had no longer any interest of her own to pursue, she turned her attention almost entirely on her sister and Mr. Bingley, and the train of agreeable reflections which her observations gave birth to made her perhaps almost as happy as Jane. She saw her in idea settled in that very house in all the felicity which a marriage of true affection could bestow; and she felt capable under such circumstances of endeavouring even to like Bingley's two sisters. Her mother's thoughts she plainly saw were bent the same way, and she determined not to venture near her, lest she might hear too much. When they sat down to supper, therefore, she considered it a most unlucky perverseness which placed them within one of each other; and deeply was she vexed to find that her mother was talking to that one person (Lady Lucas) freely, openly, and of nothing else but of her expectation that Jane would be soon married to Mr. Bingley.—It was an animating subject, and Mrs. Bennet seemed incapable of fatigue while enumerating the advantages of the match. His being such a charming young man, and so rich, and living but three miles from them, were the first points of self-gratulation; and then it was such a comfort to think how fond the two sisters were of Jane, and to be certain that they must desire the connection as much as she could do. It was, moreover, such a promising thing for her younger daughters, as Jane's marrying so greatly must throw them in the way of other rich men; and lastly, it was so pleasant at her time of life to be able to consign her single daughters to the care of their sister that she might not be obliged to go into company more than she liked. It was necessary to make this circumstance a matter of pleasure, because on such occasions it is the etiquette; but no one was less likely than Mrs. Bennet to find comfort in staying at home at any period of her life. She concluded with many good wishes that Lady Lucas might soon be equally fortunate, though evidently and triumphantly believing there was no chance of it.

In vain did Elizabeth endeavour to check the rapidity of her mother's words, or persuade her to describe her felicity in a less audible whisper; for to her inexpressible vexation, she could perceive that the chief of it was overheard by Mr. Darcy, who sat opposite to them. Her mother only scolded her for being nonsensical.

"What is Mr. Darcy to me, pray, that I should be afraid of him? I am sure we owe him no such particular civility as to be obliged to say nothing *he* may not like to hear."

"For heaven's sake, madam, speak lower.—What advantage can it be to you to offend Mr. Darcy?—You will never recommend yourself to his friend by so doing."

Nothing that she could say, however, had any influence. Her mother would talk of her views in the same intelligible tone. Elizabeth blushed and blushed again with shame and vexation. She could not help frequently glancing her eye at Mr. Darcy, though every glance convinced her of what she dreaded; for though he was not always looking at her mother, she was convinced that his attention was invariably fixed by her. The expression of his face changed gradually from indignant contempt to a composed and steady gravity.

At length, however, Mrs. Bennet had no more to say; and Lady Lucas, who had been long yawning at the reception of delights which she saw no likelihood of sharing, was left to the comforts of cold ham and chicken. Elizabeth now began to revive. But not long was the interval of tranquillity; for when supper was over, singing was talked of, and she had the mortification of seeing Mary, after very little entreaty, preparing to oblige the company. By many significant looks and silent entreaties did she endeavour to prevent such a proof of complaisance—but in vain; Mary would not understand them; such an opportunity of exhibiting was delightful to her, and she began her song. Elizabeth's eyes were fixed on her with most painful sensations; and she watched her progress through the several stanzas with an impatience which was very ill rewarded at their close; for Mary, on receiving amongst the thanks of the table the hint of a hope that she might be prevailed on to favour them again, after the pause of half a minute began another. Mary's powers were by no means fitted for such a display; her voice was weak, and her manner affected. Elizabeth was in agonies. She looked at Jane to see how she bore it; but Jane was very composedly talking to Bingley. She looked at his two sisters, and saw them making signs of derision at each other, and at Darcy, who continued however impenetrably grave. She looked at her father to entreat his interference, lest Mary should be singing all night. He took the hint, and when Mary had finished her second song, said aloud,

"That will do extremely well, child. You have delighted us long enough. Let the other young ladies have time to exhibit."

Mary, though pretending not to hear, was somewhat disconcerted; and Elizabeth sorry for her, and sorry for her father's speech, was afraid her anxiety had done no good.—Others of the party were now applied to.

"If I," said Mr. Collins, "were so fortunate as to be able to sing, I should have great pleasure, I am sure, in obliging the company with an air; for I consider music as a very innocent diversion, and perfectly compatible with the profession of a clergyman. I do not mean however to assert that we can be justified in devoting too much of our time to music, for there are certainly other things to be attended to. The rector of a parish has much to do. In the first place, he must make such an agreement for tithes as may be beneficial to himself and not offensive to his patron. He must write his own sermons; and the time that remains will not be too much for his parish duties and the care and improvement of his dwelling, which he cannot be excused from making as comfortable as possible. And I do not think it of light importance that he should have attentive and conciliatory manners towards everybody, especially towards those to whom he owes his preferment. I cannot acquit him of that duty; nor could I think well of the man who should omit an occasion of testifying his respect towards anybody connected with the family." And with a bow to Mr. Darcy, he concluded his speech, which had been spoken so loud as to be heard by half the room.—Many stared.—Many smiled; but no one looked more amused than Mr. Bennet himself, while his wife seriously commended Mr. Collins for having spoken so sensibly, and observed in a half-whisper to Lady Lucas that he was a remarkably clever, good kind of young man.

To Elizabeth it appeared that had her family made an agreement to expose themselves as much as they could during the evening, it would have been impossible for them to play their parts with more spirit or finer success; and happy did she think it for Bingley and her sister that some of the exhibition had escaped his notice, and that his feelings were not of a sort to be much distressed by the folly which he must have witnessed. That his two sisters and Mr. Darcy, however, should have such an opportunity of ridiculing her relations was bad enough, and she could not determine whether the silent contempt of the gentleman, or the insolent smiles of the ladies, were more intolerable.

The rest of the evening brought her little amusement. She was teased by Mr. Collins, who continued most perseveringly by her side, and though he could not prevail with her to dance with him again, put it out of her power to dance with others. In vain did she entreat him to stand up with somebody else, and offer to introduce him to any young lady in the room. He assured her that as to dancing he was perfectly indifferent to it; that his chief object was by delicate attentions to recommend himself to her, and that he should therefore make a point of remaining close to her the whole evening. There was no arguing upon such a project. She owed her greatest relief to her friend Miss Lucas, who often joined them, and good-naturedly engaged Mr. Collins's conversation to herself.

She was at least free from the offence of Mr. Darcy's farther notice; though often standing within a very short distance of her, quite disengaged, he never came near enough to speak. She felt it to be the probable consequence of her allusions to Mr. Wickham, and rejoiced in it.

The Longbourn party were the last of all the company to depart; and by a manœuvre of Mrs. Bennet had to wait for their carriages a quarter of an hour after everybody else was gone, which gave them time to see how heartily they were wished away by some of the family. Mrs. Hurst and her sister scarcely opened their mouths except to complain of fatgiue, and were evidently impatient to have the house to themselves. They repulsed every attempt of Mrs. Bennet at conversation, and by so doing threw a languor over the whole party, which was very little relieved by the long speeches of Mr. Collins, who was complimenting Mr. Bingley and his sisters on the elegance of their entertainment, and the hospitality and politeness which had marked their behaviour to their guests. Darcy said nothing at all. Mr. Bennet, in equal silence, was enjoying the scene. Mr. Bingley and Jane were standing together, a little detached from the rest, and talked only to each other. Elizabeth preserved as steady a silence as either Mrs. Hurst or Miss Bingley; and even Lydia was too much fatigued to utter more than the occasional exclamation of "Lord, how tired I am!" accompanied by a violent yawn.

When at length they arose to take leave, Mrs. Bennet was most pressingly civil in her hope of seeing the whole family soon at Longbourn; and addressed herself particularly to Mr. Bingley, to assure him how happy he would make them by eating a family dinner with them at any time, without the ceremony of a formal invitation. Bingley was all grateful pleasure, and he readily engaged for taking the earliest opportunity of waiting on her, after his return from London, whither he was obliged to go the next day for a short time.

Mrs. Bennet was perfectly satisfied; and quitted the

90

house under the delightful persuasion that, allowing for the necessary preparations of settlements, new carriages and wedding clothes, she should undoubtedly see her daughter settled at Netherfield in the course of three or four months. Of having another daughter married to Mr. Collins, she thought with equal certainty, and with considerable, though not equal, pleasure. Elizabeth was the least dear to her of all her children; and though the man and the match were quite good enough for *her,* the worth of each was eclipsed by Mr. Bingley and Netherfield.

CHAPTER NINETEEN

THE next day opened a new scene at Longbourn. Mr. Collins made his declaration in form. Having resolved to do it without loss of time, as his leave of absence extended only to the following Saturday, and having no feelings of diffidence to make it distressing to himself even at the moment, he set about it in a very orderly manner, with all the observances which he supposed a regular part of the business. On finding Mrs. Bennet, Elizabeth and one of the younger girls together soon after breakfast, he addressed the mother in these words,

"May I hope, madam, for your interest with your fair daughter Elizabeth, when I solicit for the honour of a private audience with her in the course of this morning?"

Before Elizabeth had time for anything but a blush of surprise, Mrs. Bennet instantly answered,

"Oh dear!—Yes—certainly.—I am sure Lizzy will be very happy—I am sure she can have no objection.—Come Kitty, I want you upstairs." And gathering her work together, she was hastening away, when Elizabeth called out,

"Dear Ma'am, do not go.—I beg you will not go.—Mr. Collins must excuse me.—He can have nothing to say to me that anybody need not hear. I am going away myself."

"No, no, nonsense, Lizzy. I desire you will stay where you are."—And upon Elizabeth's seeming really, with vexed and embarrassed looks, about to escape, she added, "Lizzy, I *insist* upon your staying and hearing Mr. Collins."

Elizabeth would not oppose such an injunction—and a moment's consideration making her also sensible that it would be wisest to get it over as soon and as quietly as possible, she sat down again, and tried to conceal by incessant employment the feelings which were divided between distress and diversion. Mrs. Bennet and Kitty walked off, and as soon as they were gone Mr. Collins began.

"Believe me, my dear Miss Elizabeth, that your modesty, so far from doing you any disservice, rather adds to your other perfections. You would have been less amiable in my eyes had there *not* been this little unwillingness; but allow me to assure you that I have your respected mother's permission for this address. You can hardly doubt the purport of my discourse, however your natural delicacy may lead you to dissemble; my attentions have been too marked to be mistaken. Almost as soon as I entered the house I singled you out as the companion of my future life. But before I am run away with by my feelings on this subject, perhaps it will be advisable for me to state my reasons for marrying—and moreover for coming into Hertfordshire with the design of selecting a wife, as I certainly did."

The idea of Mr. Collins, with all his solemn composure, being run away with by his feelings, made Elizabeth so near laughing that she could not use the short pause he allowed in any attempt to stop him farther, and he continued:

"My reasons for marrying are, first, that I think it a right thing for every clergyman in easy circumstances (like myself) to set the example of matrimony in his parish. Secondly, that I am convinced it will add very greatly to my happiness; and thirdly, which perhaps I ought to have mentioned earlier, that it is the particular advice and recommendation of the very noble lady whom I have the honour of calling patroness. Twice has she condescended to give me her opinion (unasked too!) on this subject; and it was but the very Saturday night before I left Hunsford—between our pools at quadrille, while Mrs. Jenkinson was arranging Miss De Bourgh's footstool, that she said, 'Mr. Collins, you must marry. A clergyman like you must marry. Choose properly, choose a gentlewoman for *my* sake; and for your *own*, let her be an active, useful sort of person, not brought up high, but able to make a small income go a good way. This is my advice. Find such a woman as soon as you can, bring her to Hunsford, and I will visit her.' Allow me, by the way, to observe, my fair cousin, that I do not reckon the notice and kindness of Lady Catherine de Bourgh as among the least of the advantages in my power to offer. You will find her manners beyond anything I can describe; and your wit and vivacity I think must be acceptable to her, especially when tempered with the silence and respect which her rank will inevitably excite. Thus much for my general intention in favour of matrimony; it remains to be told why my views were directed to Longbourn instead of my own neighbourhood, where I assure you there are many amiable young women. But the fact is that being, as I am, to inherit this estate after the death of your honoured father (who, however, may live many years longer), I could not satisfy myself without resolving to choose a wife from among his daughters, that the loss to them might be as little as possible, when the melancholy event takes place—which, however, as I have already said, may not be for several years. This has been my motive, my fair cousin, and I flatter myself it will not sink me in your esteem. And now nothing remains for me but to assure you in the most animated language of the violence of my affection. To fortune I am perfectly indifferent, and shall make no demand of that nature on your father, since I am well aware that it could not be complied with; and that one thousand pounds in the 4 per cents, which will not be yours till after your mother's decease, is all that you may ever be entitled to. On that head, therefore, I shall be uniformly silent; and you may assure yourself that no ungenerous reproach shall ever pass my lips when we are married."

It was absolutely necessary to interrupt him now.

"You are too hasty, sir," she cried. "You forget that I have made no answer. Let me do it without farther loss of time. Accept my thanks for the compliment you are paying me. I am very sensible of the honour of your proposals, but it is impossible for me to do otherwise than decline them."

"I am not now to learn," replied Mr. Collins, with a

formal wave of the hand, "that it is usual with young ladies to reject the addresses of the man whom they secretly mean to accept, when he first applies for their favour; and that sometimes the refusal is repeated a second or even a third time. I am therefore by no means discouraged by what you have just said, and shall hope to lead you to the altar ere long."

"Upon my word, sir," cried Elizabeth, "your hope is rather an extraordinary one after my declaration. I do assure you that I am not one of those young ladies (if such young ladies there are) who are so daring as to risk their happiness on the chance of being asked a second time. I am perfectly serious in my refusal.—You could not make *me* happy, and I am convinced that I am the last woman in the world who would make *you* so.— Nay, were your friend Lady Catherine to know me, I am persuaded she would find me in every respect ill qualified for the situation."

"Were it certain that Lady Catherine would think so," said Mr. Collins very gravely—"but I cannot imagine that her ladyship would at all disapprove of you. And you may be certain that when I have the honour of seeing her again I shall speak in the highest terms of your modesty, economy, and other amiable qualifications."

"Indeed, Mr. Collins, all praise of me will be unnecessary. You must give me leave to judge for myself, and pay me the compliment of believing what I say. I wish you very happy and very rich, and by refusing your hand, do all in my power to prevent your being otherwise. In making me the offer, you must have satisfied the delicacy of your feelings with regard to my family, and may take possession of Longbourn estate whenever it falls, without any self-reproach. This matter may be considered, therefore, as finally settled." And rising as she thus spoke, she would have quitted the room had not Mr. Collins thus addressed her,

"When I do myself the honour of speaking to you next on this subject I shall hope to receive a more favourable answer than you have now given me; though I am far from accusing you of cruelty at present, because I know it to be the established custom of your sex to reject a man on the first application, and perhaps you have even now said as much to encourage my suit as would be consistent with the true delicacy of the female character."

"Really, Mr. Collins," cried Elizabeth with some warmth, "you puzzle me exceedingly. If what I have hitherto said can appear to you in the form of encouragement, I know not how to express my refusal in such a way as may convince you of its being one."

"You must give me leave to flatter myself, my dear cousin, that your refusal of my addresses is merely words of course. My reasons for believing it are briefly these: it does not appear to me that my hand is unworthy your acceptance, or that the establishment I can offer would be any other than highly desirable. My situation in life, my connections with the family of De Bourgh, and my relationship to your own, are circumstances highly in my favour; and you should take it into farther consideration that in spite of your manifold attractions, it is by no means certain that another offer of marriage may ever be made you. Your portion is unhappily so small that it will in all likelihood undo the effects of your loveliness and amiable qualifications. As I must therefore conclude that you are not serious in your rejection of me, I shall choose to attribute it to your wish of increasing my love by suspense, according to the usual practice of elegant females."

"I do assure you, sir, that I have no pretension whatever to that kind of elegance which consists in tormenting a respectable man. I would rather be paid the compliment of being believed sincere. I thank you again and again for the honour you have done me in your proposals, but to accept them is absolutely impossible. My feelings in every respect forbid it. Can I speak plainer? Do not consider me now as an elegant female intending to plague you, but as a rational creature speaking the truth from her heart."

"You are uniformly charming!" cried he, with an air of awkward gallantry; "and I am persuaded that when sanctioned by the express authority of both your excellent parents, my proposals will not fail of being acceptable."

To such perserverance in wilful self-deception Elizabeth would make no reply, and immediately and in silence withdrew; determined, that if he persisted in considering her repeated refusals as flattering encouragement, to apply to her father, whose negative might be uttered in such a manner as must be decisive, and whose behaviour at least could not be mistaken for the affectation and coquetry of an elegant female.

CHAPTER TWENTY

MR. COLLINS was not left long to the silent contemplation of his successful love; for Mrs. Bennet, having dawdled about in the vestibule to watch for the end of the conference, no sooner saw Elizabeth open the door and with quick step pass her towards the staircase, than she entered the breakfast-room and congratulated both him and herself in warm terms on the happy prospect of their nearer connection. Mr. Collins received and returned these felicitations with equal pleasure, and then proceeded to relate the particulars of their interview, with the result of which he trusted he had every reason to be satisfied, since the refusal which his cousin had steadfastly given him would naturally flow from her bashful modesty and the genuine delicacy of her character.

This information, however, startled Mrs. Bennet; she would have been glad to be equally satisfied that her daughter had meant to encourage him by protesting against his proposals, but she dared not to believe it, and could not help saying so.

"But depend upon it, Mr. Collins," she added, "that Lizzy shall be brought to reason. I will speak to her about it myself directly. She is a very headstrong foolish girl, and does not know her own interest; but I will *make* her know it."

"Pardon me for interrupting you, madam," cried Mr. Collins; "but if she is really headstrong and foolish, I know not whether she would altogether be a very desirable wife to a man in my situation, who naturally looks for happiness in the marriage state. If therefore she actually persists in rejecting my suit, perhaps it were better not to force her into accepting me, because if liable to such defects of temper, she could not contribute much to my felicity."

96

"Sir, you quite misunderstand me," said Mrs. Bennet, alarmed. "Lizzy is only headstrong in such matters as these. In everything else she is as good natured a girl as ever lived. I will go directly to Mr. Bennet, and we shall very soon settle it with her, I am sure."

She would not give him time to reply, but hurrying instantly to her husband, called out as she entered the library,

"Oh! Mr. Bennet, you are wanted immediately; we are all in an uproar. You must come and make Lizzy marry Mr. Collins, for she vows she will not have him, and if you do not make haste he will change his mind and not have *her*."

Mr. Bennet raised his eyes from his book as she entered, and fixed them on her face with a calm unconcern which was not in the least altered by her communication.

"I have not the pleasure of understanding you," said he, when she had finished her speech. "Of what are you talking?"

"Of Mr. Collins and Lizzy. Lizzy declares she will not have Mr. Collins, and Mr. Collins begins to say that he will not have Lizzy."

"And what am I to do on the occasion?—It seems an hopeless business."

"Speak to Lizzy about it yourself. Tell her that you insist upon her marrying him."

"Let her be called down. She shall hear my opinion."

Mrs. Bennet rang the bell, and Miss Elizabeth was summoned to the library.

"Come here, child," cried her father as she appeared. "I have sent for you on an affair of importance. I understand that Mr. Collins has made you an offer of marriage. Is it true?" Elizabeth replied that it was. "Very well—and this offer of marriage you have refused?"

"I have, Sir."

"Very well. We now come to the point. Your mother insists upon your accepting it. Is it not so, Mrs. Bennet?"

"Yes, or I will never see her again."

"An unhappy alternative is before you, Elizabeth. From this day you must be a stranger to one of your parents.—Your mother will never see you again if you do *not* marry Mr. Collins, and I will never see you again if you *do*."

Elizabeth could not but smile at such a conclusion of such a beginning; but Mrs. Bennet, who had persuaded herself that her husband regarded the affair as she wished, was excessively disappointed.

"What do you mean, Mr. Bennet, by talking in this way? You promised me to *insist* upon her marrying him."

"My dear," replied her husband, "I have two small favours to request. First, that you will allow me the free use of my understanding on the present occasion; and secondly, of my room. I shall be glad to have the library to myself as soon as may be."

Not yet, however, in spite of her disappointment in her husband, did Mrs. Bennet give up the point. She talked to Elizabeth again and again; coaxed and threatened her by turns. She endeavoured to secure Jane in her interest, but Jane with all possible mildness declined interfering; and Elizabeth sometimes with real earnestness and sometimes with playful gaiety replied to her attacks. Though her manner varied; however, her determination never did.

Mr. Collins, meanwhile, was meditating in solitude on what had passed. He thought too well of himself to comprehend on what motive his cousin could refuse him; and though his pride was hurt, he suffered in no other way. His regard for her was quite imaginary; and the possibility of her deserving her mother's reproach prevented his feeling any regret.

While the family were in this confusion, Charlotte Lucas came to spend the day with them. She was met in the vestibule by Lydia, who, flying to her, cried in a half whisper, "I am glad you are come, for there is such fun here!—What do you think has happened this morning?—Mr. Collins has made an offer to Lizzy, and she will not have him."

Charlotte had hardly time to answer before they were joined by Kitty, who came to tell the same news, and no sooner had they entered the breakfast-room, where Mrs. Bennet was alone, than she likewise began on the subject, calling on Miss Lucas for her compassion, and entreating her to persuade her friend Lizzy to comply with the wishes of all her family. "Pray do, my dear Miss Lucas," she added in a melancholy tone, "for nobody is on my side, nobody takes part with me, I am cruelly used, nobody feels for my poor nerves."

Charlotte's reply was spared by the entrance of Jane and Elizabeth.

"Aye, there she comes," continued Mrs. Bennet, "looking as unconcerned as may be, and caring no more for us than if we were at York, provided she can have her own way.—But I tell you what, Miss Lizzy, if you take it into your head to go on refusing every offer of marriage in this way, you will never get a husband at all—and I am sure I do not know who is to maintain you when your father is dead. *I* shall not be able to keep you —and so I warn you. I have done with you from this very day. I told you in the library, you know, that I should never speak to you again, and you will find me as good as my word. I have no pleasure in talking to undutiful children. Not that I have much pleasure indeed in talking to anybody. People who suffer as I do from nervous complaints can have no great inclination for talking. Nobody can tell what I suffer!—But it is always so. Those who do not complain are never pitied."

Her daughters listened in silence to this effusion, sensible that any attempt to reason with or soothe her would only increase the irritation. She talked on, therefore, without interruption from any of them till they were joined by Mr. Collins, who entered with an air more stately than usual, and on perceiving whom, she said to the girls,

"Now, I do insist upon it, that you, all of you, hold your tongues, and let Mr. Collins and me have a little conversation together."

Elizabeth passed quietly out of the room, Jane and Kitty followed, but Lydia stood her ground, determined to hear all she could; and Charlotte, detained first by the civility of Mr. Collins, whose inquiries after herself and all her family were very minute, and then by a little curiosity, satisfied herself with walking to the window and pretending not to hear. In a doleful voice Mrs. Bennet thus began the projected conversation.— "Oh! Mr. Collins!"—

"My dear madam," replied he, "let us be forever silent on this point. Far be it from me," he presently continued in a voice that marked his displeasure, "to resent the behaviour of your daughter. Resignation to inevitable evils is the duty of us all; the peculiar duty of a young man who has been so fortunate as I have been in early preferment; and I trust I am resigned. Perhaps not the less so from feeling a doubt of my positive happiness had my fair cousin honoured me with her hand; for I have often observed that resignation is never so perfect as when the blessing denied begins to lose somewhat of its value in our estimation. You will not, I hope, consider me as showing any disrespect to your family, my dear madam, by thus withdrawing my pretensions to your daughter's favour, without having paid yourself and Mr. Bennet the compliment of requesting you to interpose your authority in my behalf. My conduct may, I fear, be objectionable in having accepted my dismission from your daughter's lips instead of your own. But we are all liable to error. I have certainly meant well through the whole affair. My object has been to secure an amiable companion for myself, with due consideration for the advantage of all your family, and if my *manner* has been at all reprehensible, I here beg leave to apologize."

CHAPTER TWENTY-ONE

THE discussion of Mr. Collins's offer was now nearly at an end, and Elizabeth had only to suffer from the uncomfortable feelings necessarily attending it, and occasionally from some peevish allusion of her mother. As for the gentleman himself, *his* feelings were chiefly expressed, not by embarrassment or dejection, or by trying to avoid her, but by stiffness of manner and resentful silence. He scarcely ever spoke to her, and the assiduous attentions which he had been so sensible of himself were transferred for the rest of the day to Miss Lucas, whose civility in listening to him was a seasonable relief to them all, and especially to her friend.

The morrow produced no abatement of Mrs. Bennet's ill humour or ill health. Mr. Collins was also in the same state of angry pride. Elizabeth had hoped that his resentment might shorten his visit, but his plan did not appear in the least affected by it. He was always to have gone on Saturday, and to Saturday he still meant to stay.

After breakfast, the girls walked to Meryton to inquire if Mr. Wickham were returned, and to lament over his absence from the Netherfield ball. He joined them on their entering the town and attended them to their aunt's, where his regret and vexation, and the concern of everybody was well talked over. To Elizabeth, however, he voluntarily acknowledged that the necessity of his absence *had* been self imposed.

"I found," said he, "as the time drew near that I had better not meet Mr. Darcy; that to be in the same room, the same party with him for so many hours together, might be more than I could bear, and that scenes might arise unpleasant to more than myself."

She highly approved his forbearance, and they had leisure for a full discussion of it, and for all the commendation which they civilly bestowed on each other, as Wickham and another officer walked back with them to Longbourn, and during the walk he particularly attended to her. His accompanying them was a double advantage; she felt all the compliment it offered to herself, and it was most acceptable as an occasion of introducing him to her father and mother.

Soon after their return, a letter was delivered to Miss Bennet; it came from Netherfield, and was opened immediately. The envelope contained a sheet of elegant, little, hot pressed paper, well covered with a lady's fair, flowing hand; and Elizabeth saw her sister's countenance change as she read it, and saw her dwelling intently on some particular passages. Jane recollected herself soon, and putting the letter away, tried to join with her usual cheerfulness in the general conversation; but Elizabeth felt an anxiety on the subject which drew off her attention even from Wickham; and no sooner had he and his companion taken leave than a glance from Jane invited her to follow her upstairs. When they had gained their own room, Jane taking out the letter, said,

"This is from Caroline Bingley; what it contains has surprised me a good deal. The whole party have left Netherfield by this time, and are on their way to town;

and without any intention of coming back again. You shall hear what she says."

She then read the first sentence aloud, which comprised the information of their having just resolved to follow their brother to town directly, and of their meaning to dine that day in Grosvenor street, where Mr. Hurst had a house. The next was in these words. "I do not pretend to regret anything I shall leave in Hertfordshire, except your society, my dearest friend; but we will hope at some future period to enjoy many returns to the delightful intercourse we have known, and in the meanwhile may lessen the pain of separation by a very frequent and most unreserved correspondence. I depend on you for that." To these high flown expressions, Elizabeth listened with all the insensibility of distrust; and though the suddenness of their removal surprised her, she saw nothing in it really to lament; it was not to be supposed that their absence from Netherfield would prevent Mr. Bingley's being there; and as to the loss of their society, she was persuaded that Jane must soon cease to regard it, in the enjoyment of his.

"It is unlucky," said she, after a short pause, "that you should not be able to see your friends before they leave the country. But may we not hope that the period of future happiness to which Miss Bingley looks forward may arrive earlier than she is aware, and that the delightful intercourse you have known as friends will be renewed with yet greater satisfaction as sisters?—Mr. Bingley will not be detained in London by them."

"Caroline decidedly says that none of the party will return into Hertfordshire this winter. I will read it to you—

"When my brother left us yesterday, he imagined that the business which took him to London might be concluded in three or four days, but as we are certain it cannot be so, and at the same time convinced that when Charles gets to town, he will be in no hurry to leave it again, we have determined on following him thither, that he may not be obliged to spend his vacant hours in a comfortless hotel. Many of my acquaintance are already there for the winter; I wish I could hear that you, my dearest friend, had any intention of making one in the crowd, but of that I despair. I sincerely hope your Christmas in Hertfordshire may abound in the gaieties which that season generally brings, and that your beaux will be so numerous as to prevent your feeling the loss of the three of whom we shall deprive you."

"It is evident by this," added Jane, "that he comes back no more this winter."

"It is only evident that Miss Bingley does not mean he *should*."

"Why will you think so? It must be his own doing. He is his own master. But you do not know *all*. I *will* read you the passage which particularly hurts me. I will have no reserves from *you*: 'Mr. Darcy is impatient to see his sister and to confess the truth, *we* are scarcely less eager to meet her again. I really do not think Georgiana Darcy has her equal for beauty, elegance, and accomplishments; and the affection she inspires in Louisa and myself is heightened into something still more interesting from the hope we dare to entertain of her being hereafter our sister. I do not know whether I ever before mentioned to you my feelings on this subject, but I will not leave the country without confiding them, and I trust you will not esteem them unreasonable. My brother admires her greatly already, he will have frequent opportunity now of seeing her on the most intimate footing, her relations all wish the connection as much as his own, and a sister's partiality is not misleading me, I think, when I call Charles most capable of engaging any woman's heart. With all these circumstances to favour an attachment and nothing to prevent it, am I wrong, my dearest Jane, in indulging the hope of an event which will secure the happiness of so many?' "

"What think you of *this* sentence, my dear Lizzy?" said Jane as she finished it. "Is it not clear enough? Does it not expressly declare that Caroline neither expects nor wishes me to be her sister; that she is perfectly convinced of her brother's indifference, and that if she suspects the nature of my feelings for him, she means (most kindly!) to put me on my guard? Can there be any other opinion on the subject?"

"Yes, there can; for mine is totally different.—Will you hear it?"

"Most willingly."

"You shall have it in few words. Miss Bingley sees that her brother is in love with you, and wants him to marry Miss Darcy. She follows him to town in the hope of keeping him there, and tries to persuade you that he does not care about you."

Jane shook her head.

"Indeed, Jane, you ought to believe me. No one who has ever seen you together can doubt his affection. Miss Bingley I am sure cannot. She is not such a simpleton. Could she have seen half as much love in Mr. Darcy for herself, she would have ordered her wedding clothes. But the case is this. We are not rich enough, or grand enough for them; and she is the more anxious to get Miss Darcy for her brother, from the notion that when there has been *one* intermarriage, she may have less trouble in achieving a second; in which there is certainly some ingenuity, and I dare say it would succeed, if Miss de Bourgh were out of the way. But, my dearest Jane, you cannot seriously imagine that because Miss Bingley tells you her brother greatly admires Miss Darcy he is in the smallest degree less sensible of *your* merit than when he took leave of you on Tuesday, or that it will be in her power to persuade him that instead of being in love with you, he is very much in love with her friend."

"If we thought alike of Miss Bingley," replied Jane, "your representation of all this might make me quite easy. But I know the foundation is unjust. Caroline is incapable of wilfully deceiving any one; and all that I can hope in this case is that she is deceived herself."

"That is right. You could not have started a more happy idea, since you will not take comfort in mine. Believe her to be deceived by all means. You have now done your duty by her, and must fret no longer."

"But, my dear sister, can I be happy, even supposing the best, in accepting a man whose sisters and friends are all wishing him to marry elsewhere?"

"You must decide for yourself," said Elizabeth, "and if upon mature deliberation, you find that the misery of disobliging his two sisters is more than equivalent to the happiness of being his wife, I advise you by all means to refuse him."

"How can you talk so?"—said Jane faintly smiling—"You must know that though I should be exceedingly grieved at their disapprobation, I could not hesitate."

"I did not think you would; and that being the case, I cannot consider your situation with much compassion."

"But if he returns no more this winter, my choice will never be required. A thousand things may arise in six months!"

The idea of his returning no more Elizabeth treated with the utmost contempt. It appeared to her merely the suggestion of Caroline's interested wishes, and she could not for a moment suppose that those wishes, however openly or artfully spoken, could influence a young man so totally independent of everyone.

She represented to her sister as forcibly as possible what she felt on the subject, and had soon the pleasure of seeing its happy effect. Jane's temper was not desponding, and she was gradually led to hope, though the diffidence of affection sometimes overcame the hope, that Bingley would return to Netherfield and answer every wish of her heart.

They agreed that Mrs. Bennet should only hear of the departure of the family, without being alarmed on the score of the gentleman's conduct; but even this partial communication gave her a great deal of concern, and she bewailed it as exceedingly unlucky that the ladies should happen to go away just as they were all getting so intimate together. After lamenting it, however, at some length, she had the consolation of thinking that Mr. Bingley would be soon down again and soon dining at Longbourn, and the conclusion of all was the comfortable declaration that, though he had been invited only to a family dinner, she would take care to have two full courses.

CHAPTER TWENTY-TWO

The Bennets were engaged to dine with the Lucases, and again during the chief of the day was Miss Lucas so kind as to listen to Mr. Collins. Elizabeth took an opportunity of thanking her. "It keeps him in good humour," said she, "and I am more obliged to you than I can express." Charlotte assured her friend of her satisfaction in being useful, and that it amply repaid her for the little sacrifice of her time. This was very amiable, but Charlotte's kindness extended farther than Elizabeth had any conception of; its object was nothing less than to secure her from any return of Mr. Collins's addresses by engaging them towards herself. Such was Miss Lucas's scheme; and appearances were so favourable that when they parted at night, she would have felt almost sure of success if he had not been to leave Hertfordshire so very soon. But here she did injustice to the fire and independence of his character, for it led him to escape out of Longbourn House the next morning with admirable slyness, and hasten to Lucas Lodge to throw himself at her feet. He was anxious to avoid the notice of his cousins, from a conviction that if they saw him depart they could not fail to conjecture his design, and he was not willing to have the attempt known till its success could be known likewise; for though feeling almost secure, and with reason, for Charlotte had been tolerably encouraging, he was comparatively diffident since the adventure of Wednesday. His reception however was of the most flattering kind. Miss Lucas perceived him from an upper window as he walked towards the house, and instantly set out to meet him accidentally in the lane. But little had she dared to hope that so much love and eloquence awaited her there.

In as short a time as Mr. Collins's long speeches would allow, everything was settled between them to the satisfaction of both; and as they entered the house, he earnestly entreated her to name the day that was to make him the happiest of men; and though such a solicitation must be waved for the present, the lady felt no inclination to trifle with his happiness. The stupidity with which he was favoured by nature must guard his courtship from any charm that could make a woman wish for its continuance; and Miss Lucas, who accepted him solely from the pure and disinterested desire of an establishment, cared not how soon that establishment were gained.

Sir William and Lady Lucas were speedily applied to for their consent; and it was bestowed with a most joyful alacrity. Mr. Collins's present circumstances made it a most eligible match for their daughter, to whom they could give little fortune; and his prospects of future wealth were exceedingly fair. Lady Lucas began directly to calculate with more interest than the matter had ever excited before how many years longer Mr. Bennet was likely to live; and Sir William gave it as his decided opinion that whenever Mr. Collins should be in possession of the Longbourn estate, it would be highly expedient that both he and his wife should make their appearance at St. James's. The whole family in short were properly overjoyed on the occasion. The younger girls formed hopes of *coming out* a year or two sooner than they might otherwise have done; and the boys were relieved from their apprehension of Charlotte's dying an old maid. Charlotte herself was tolerably composed. She had gained her point, and had time to consider of it. Her reflections were in general satisfactory. Mr. Collins to be sure was neither sensible nor agreeable; his society was irksome, and his attachment to her must be imaginary. But still he would be her husband. Without thinking highly either of men or of matrimony, marriage had always been her object; it was the only honourable provision for well-educated young women of small fortune, and however uncertain of giving happiness, must be their pleasantest preservative from want. This preservative she had now obtained; and at the age of twenty-seven, without having ever been handsome, she felt all the good luck of it. The least agreeable circumstance in the business was the surprise it must occasion to Elizabeth Bennet, whose friendship she valued beyond that of any other person. Elizabeth would wonder, and probably would blame her; and though her resolution was not to be shaken, her feelings must be hurt by such disapprobation. She resolved to give her the information herself, and therefore charged Mr. Collins when he returned to Longbourn to dinner to drop no hint of what had passed before any of the family. A promise of secrecy was of course very dutifully given, but it could not be kept without difficulty; for the curiosity excited by his long absence burst forth in such very direct questions on his return as required some ingenuity to evade, and he was at the same time exercising great self-denial, for he was longing to publish his prosperous love.

As he was to begin his journey too early on the morrow to see any of the family, the ceremony of leave-taking was performed when the ladies moved for the night; and Mrs. Bennet with great politeness and cordiality said how happy they should be to see him at Longbourn again, whenever his other engagements might allow him to visit them.

"My dear madam," he replied, "this invitation is particularly gratifying, because it is what I have been hoping to receive; and you may be very certain that I shall avail myself of it as soon as possible."

They were all astonished; and Mr. Bennet, who could by no means wish for so speedy a return, immediately said,

"But is there not danger of Lady Catherine's disapprobation here, my good sir? You had better neglect your relations than run the risk of offending your patroness."

"My dear sir," replied Mr. Collins, "I am particularly obliged to you for this friendly caution, and you may depend upon my not taking so material a step without her ladyship's concurrence."

"You cannot be too much on your guard. Risk anything rather than her displeasure; and if you find it likely to be raised by your coming to us again, which I should think exceedingly probable, stay quietly at home, and be satisfied that *we* shall take no offence."

"Believe me, my dear sir, my gratitude is warmly excited by such affectionate attention; and depend upon it, you will speedily receive from me a letter of thanks for this, as well as for every other mark of your regard during my stay in Hertfordshire. As for my fair cousins, though my absence may not be long enough to render it necessary, I shall now take the liberty of wishing them health and happiness, not excepting my cousin Elizabeth."

With proper civilities the ladies then withdrew, all of

them equally surprised to find that he meditated a quick return. Mrs. Bennet wished to understand by it that he thought of paying his addresses to one of her younger girls, and Mary might have been prevailed on to accept him. She rated his abilities much higher than any of the others; there was a solidity in his reflections which often struck her, and though by no means so clever as herself, she thought that if encouraged to read and improve himself by such an example as hers, he might become a very agreeable companion. But on the following morning, every hope of this kind was done away. Miss Lucas called soon after breakfast, and in a private conference with Elizabeth related the event of the day before.

The possibility of Mr. Collins's fancying himself in love with her friend had once occurred to Elizabeth within the last day or two; but that Charlotte could encourage him seemed almost as far from possibility as that she could encourage him herself, and her astonishment was consequently so great as to overcome at first the bounds of decorum, and she could not help crying out,

"Engaged to Mr. Collins! my dear Charlotte—impossible!"

The steady countenance which Miss Lucas had commanded in telling her story gave way to a momentary confusion here on receiving so direct a reproach; though, as it was no more than she expected, she soon regained her composure, and calmly replied,

"Why should you be surprised, my dear Eliza? Do you think it incredible that Mr. Collins should be able to procure any woman's good opinion, because he was not so happy as to succeed with you?"

But Elizabeth had now recollected herself, and making a strong effort for it was able to assure her with tolerable firmness that the prospect of their relationship was highly grateful to her, and that she wished her all imaginable happiness.

"I see what you are feeling," replied Charlotte, "you must be surprised, very much surprised—so lately as Mr. Collins was wishing to marry you. But when you have had time to think it over, I hope you will be satisfied with what I have done. I am not romantic, you know. I never was. I ask only a comfortable home; and considering Mr. Collins's character, connections, and situation in life, I am convinced that my chance of happiness with him is as fair as most people can boast on entering the marriage state."

Elizabeth quietly answered, "Undoubtedly"—and after an awkward pause, they returned to the rest of the family. Charlotte did not stay much longer, and Elizabeth was then left to reflect on what she had heard. It was a long time before she became at all reconciled to the idea of so unsuitable a match. The strangeness of Mr. Collins's making two offers of marriage within three days was nothing in comparison of his being now accepted. She had always felt that Charlotte's opinion of matrimony was not exactly like her own, but she could not have supposed it possible that when called into action, she would have sacrificed every better feeling to worldly advantage. Charlotte the wife of Mr. Collins was a most humiliating picture!—And to the pang of a friend disgracing herself and sunk in her esteem was added the distressing conviction that it was impossible for that friend to be tolerably happy in the lot she had chosen.

CHAPTER TWENTY-THREE

ELIZABETH was sitting with her mother and sisters, reflecting on what she had heard, and doubting whether she were authorized to mention it, when Sir William Lucas himself appeared, sent by his daughter to announce her engagement to the family. With many compliments to them, and much self-gratulation on the prospect of a connection between the houses, he unfolded the matter—to an audience not merely wondering, but incredulous; for Mrs. Bennet, with more perseverance than politeness, protested he must be entirely mistaken, and Lydia, always unguarded and often uncivil, boisterously exclaimed,

"Good Lord! Sir William, how can you tell such a story? Do not you know that Mr. Collins wants to marry Lizzy?"

Nothing less than the complaisance of a courtier could have borne without anger such treatment; but Sir William's good breeding carried him through it all, and though he begged leave to be positive as to the truth of his information, he listened to all their impertinence with the most forbearing courtesy.

Elizabeth, feeling it incumbent on her to relieve him from so unpleasant a situation, now put herself forward to confirm his account by mentioning her prior knowledge of it from Charlotte herself; and endeavoured to put a stop to the exclamations of her mother and sisters by the earnestness of her congratulations to Sir William, in which she was readily joined by Jane, and by making a variety of remarks on the happiness that might be expected from the match, the excellent character of Mr. Collins, and the convenient distance of Hunsford from London.

Mrs. Bennet was in fact too much overpowered to say a great deal while Sir William remained; but no sooner had he left them than her feelings found a rapid vent. In the first place, she persisted in disbelieving the whole of the matter; secondly, she was very sure that Mr. Collins had been taken in; thirdly, she trusted that they would never be happy together; and fourthly, that the match might be broken off. Two inferences, however, were plainly deduced from the whole; one, that Elizabeth was the real cause of all the mischief; and the other, that she herself had been barbarously used by them all; and on these two points she principally dwelt during the rest of the day. Nothing could console and nothing appease her. Nor did that day wear out her resentment. A week elapsed before she could see Elizabeth without scolding her, a month passed away before she could speak to Sir William or Lady Lucas without being rude, and many months were gone before she could at all forgive their daughter.

Mr. Bennet's emotions were much more tranquil on the occasion, and such as he did experience he pronounced to be of a most agreeable sort; for it gratified him, he said, to discover that Charlotte Lucas, whom he had been used to think tolerably sensible, was as foolish as his wife, and more foolish than his daughter!

Jane confessed herself a little surprised at the match;

but she said less of her astonishment than of her earnest desire for their happiness; nor could Elizabeth persuade her to consider it as improbable. Kitty and Lydia were far from envying Miss Lucas, for Mr. Collins was only a clergyman; and it affected them in no other way than as a piece of news to spread at Meryton.

Lady Lucas could not be insensible of triumph on being able to retort on Mrs. Bennet the comfort of having a daughter well married; and she called at Longbourn rather oftener than usual to say how happy she was, though Mrs. Bennet's sour looks and ill-natured remarks might have been enough to drive happiness away.

Between Elizabeth and Charlotte there was a restraint which kept them mutually silent on the subject; and Elizabeth felt persuaded that no real confidence could ever subsist between them again. Her disappointment in Charlotte made her turn with fonder regard to her sister, of whose rectitude and delicacy she was sure her opinion could never be shaken, and for whose happiness she grew daily more anxious, as Bingley had now been gone a week, and nothing was heard of his return.

Jane had sent Caroline an early answer to her letter, and was counting the days till she might reasonably hope to hear again. The promised letter of thanks from Mr. Collins arrived on Tuesday, addressed to their father, and written with all the solemnity of gratitude which a twelvemonth's abode in the family might have prompted. After discharging his conscience on that head, he proceeded to inform them, with many rapturous expressions, of his happiness in having obtained the affection of their amiable neighbour, Miss Lucas, and then explained that it was merely with the view of enjoying her society that he had been so ready to close with their kind wish of seeing him again at Longbourn, whither he hoped to be able to return on Monday fortnight; for Lady Catherine, he added, so heartily approved his marriage that she wished it to take place as soon as possible, which he trusted would be an unanswerable argument with his amiable Charlotte to name an early day for making him the happiest of men.

Mr. Collins's return into Hertfordshire was no longer

a matter of pleasure to Mrs. Bennet. On the contrary she was as much disposed to complain of it as her husband.—It was very strange that he should come to Longbourn instead of to Lucas Lodge; it was also very inconvenient and exceedingly troublesome.—She hated having visitors in the house while her health was so indifferent, and lovers were of all people the most disagreeable. Such were the gentle murmurs of Mrs. Bennet, and they gave way only to the greater distress of Mr. Bingley's continued absence.

Neither Jane nor Elizabeth were comfortable on this subject. Day after day passed away without bringing any other tidings of him than the report which shortly prevailed in Meryton of his coming no more to Netherfield the whole winter, a report which highly incensed Mrs. Bennet and which she never failed to contradict as a most scandalous falsehood.

Even Elizabeth began to fear—not that Bingley was indifferent—but that his sisters would be successful in keeping him away. Unwilling as she was to admit an idea so destructive of Jane's happiness, and so dishonourable to the stability of her lover, she could not prevent its frequently recurring. The united efforts of his two unfeeling sisters and of his overpowering friend, assisted by the attractions of Miss Darcy and the amusements of London, might be too much, she feared, for the strength of his attachment.

As for Jane, *her* anxiety under this suspense was, of course, more painful than Elizabeth's; but whatever she felt she was desirous of concealing, and between herself and Elizabeth, therefore, the subject was never alluded to. But as no such delicacy restrained her mother, an hour seldom passed in which she did not talk of Bingley, express her impatience for his arrival, or even require Jane to confess that if he did not come back, she should think herself very ill used. It needed all Jane's steady mildness to bear these attacks with tolerable tranquillity.

Mr. Collins returned most punctually on the Monday fortnight, but his reception at Longbourn was not quite so gracious as it had been on his first introduction. He was too happy, however, to need much attention; and luckily for the others, the business of love-making relieved them from a great deal of his company. The chief of every day was spent by him at Lucas Lodge, and he sometimes returned to Longbourn only in time to make an apology for his absence before the family went to bed.

Mrs. Bennet was really in a most pitiable state. The very mention of anything concerning the match threw her into an agony of ill humour, and wherever she went she was sure of hearing it talked of. The sight of Miss Lucas was odious to her. As her successor in that house, she regarded her with jealous abhorrence. Whenever Charlotte came to see them she concluded her to be anticipating the hour of possession; and whenever she spoke in a low voice to Mr. Collins, was convinced that they were talking of the Longbourn estate, and resolving to turn herself and her daughters out of the house as soon as Mr. Bennet were dead. She complained bitterly of all this to her husband.

"Indeed, Mr. Bennet," said she, "it is very hard to think that Charlotte Lucas should ever be mistress of this house, that *I* should be forced to make way for *her,* and live to see her take my place in it!"

"My dear, do not give way to such gloomy thoughts. Let us hope for better things. Let us flatter ourselves that *I* may be the survivor."

This was not very consoling to Mrs. Bennet, and therefore, instead of making any answer, she went on as before,

"I cannot bear to think that they should have all this estate. If it was not for the entail I should not mind it."

"What should you not mind?"

"I should not mind anything at all."

"Let us be thankful that you are preserved from a state of such insensibility."

"I never can be thankful, Mr. Bennet, for anything about the entail. How any one could have the conscience to entail away an estate from one's own daughters I cannot understand; and all for the sake of Mr. Collins too! Why should *he* have it more than anybody else?"

"I leave it to yourself to determine," said Mr. Bennet.

V o l u m e   I I

⁎

CHAPTER ONE

MISS BINGLEY's letter arrived, and put an end to doubt. The very first sentence conveyed the assurance of their being all settled in London for the winter, and concluded with her brother's regret at not having had time to pay his respects to his friends in Hertfordshire before he left the country.

Hope was over, entirely over; and when Jane could attend to the rest of the letter, she found little, except the professed affection of the writer, that could give her any comfort. Miss Darcy's praise occupied the chief of it. Her many attractions were again dwelt on, and Caroline boasted joyfully of their increasing intimacy, and ventured to predict the accomplishment of the wishes which had been unfolded in her former letter. She wrote also with great pleasure of her brother's being an inmate of Mr. Darcy's house, and mentioned with raptures some plans of the latter with regard to new furniture.

Elizabeth, to whom Jane very soon communicated the chief of all this, heard it in silent indignation. Her heart was divided between concern for her sister, and resentment against all the others. To Caroline's assertion of her brother's being partial to Miss Darcy she paid no credit. That he was really fond of Jane, she doubted no more than she had ever done; and much as she had always been disposed to like him, she could not think without anger, hardly without contempt, on that easiness of temper, that want of proper resolution which now made him the slave of his designing friends, and led him to sacrifice his own happiness to the caprice of their inclinations. Had his own happiness, however, been the only sacrifice, he might have been allowed to sport with it in whatever manner he thought best; but her sister's was involved in it, as she thought he must be sensible himself. It was a subject, in short, on which reflection would be long indulged, and must be unavailing. She could think of nothing else, and yet whether Bingley's regard had really died away, or were suppressed by his friends' interference; whether he had been aware of Jane's attachment, or whether it had escaped his observation; whichever were the case, though her opinion of him must be materially affected by the difference, her sister's situation remained the same, her peace equally wounded.

A day or two passed before Jane had courage to speak of her feelings to Elizabeth; but at last on Mrs. Bennet's leaving them together, after a longer irritation than usual about Netherfield and its master, she could not help saying,

"Oh! that my dear mother had more command over herself; she can have no idea of the pain she gives me by her continual reflections on him. But I will not repine. It cannot last long. He will be forgot, and we shall all be as we were before."

Elizabeth looked at her sister with incredulous solicitude, but said nothing.

"You doubt me," cried Jane, slightly colouring; "indeed you have no reason. He may live in my memory as the most amiable man of my acquaintance, but that is all. I have nothing either to hope or fear, and nothing to reproach him with. Thank God! I have not *that* pain. A little time therefore. I shall certainly try to get the better."

With a stronger voice she soon added, "I have this comfort immediately, that it has not been more than an error of fancy on my side, and that it has done no harm to any one but myself."

"My dear Jane!" exclaimed Elizabeth, "you are too good. Your sweetness and disinterestedness are really angelic; I do not know what to say to you. I feel as if I had never done you justice, or loved you as you deserve."

Miss Bennet eagerly disclaimed all extraordinary merit, and threw back the praise on her sister's warm affection.

"Nay," said Elizabeth, "this is not fair. *You* wish to think all the world respectable, and are hurt if I speak ill of anybody. *I* only want to think *you* perfect, and you set yourself against it. Do not be afraid of my running into any excess, of my encroaching on your privilege of universal goodwill. You need not. There are few people whom I really love, and still fewer of whom I think well. The more I see of the world, the more am I dissatisfied with it; and everyday confirms my belief of the inconsistency of all human characters, and of the little dependence that can be placed on the appearance of either merit or sense. I have met with two instances lately; one I will not mention; the other is Charlotte's marriage. It is unaccountable! in every view it is unaccountable!"

"My dear Lizzy, do not give way to such feelings as these. They will ruin your happiness. You do not make allowance enough for difference of situation and temper. Consider Mr. Collins's respectability, and Charlotte's prudent, steady character. Remember that she is one of a large family; that as to fortune, it is a most eligible match; and be ready to believe, for everybody's sake, that she may feel something like regard and esteem for our cousin."

"To oblige you, I would try to believe almost anything, but no one else could be benefited by such a belief as this; for were I persuaded that Charlotte had any regard for him, I should only think worse of her understanding than I now do of her heart. My dear Jane, Mr. Collins is a conceited, pompous, narrow-minded, silly man; you know he is, as well as I do; and you must feel, as well as I do, that the woman who marries him cannot have a proper way of thinking. You shall not defend her, though it is Charlotte Lucas. You shall not, for the sake of one individual, change the meaning of principle and integrity, nor endeavour to persuade yourself or me that selfishness is prudence, and insensibility of danger, security for happiness."

"I must think your language too strong in speaking of both," replied Jane, "and I hope you will be convinced of it by seeing them happy together. But enough of this. You alluded to something else. You mentioned *two* instances. I cannot misunderstand you, but I en-

117

treat you, dear Lizzy, not to pain me by thinking *that person* to blame, and saying your opinion of him is sunk. We must not be so ready to fancy ourselves intentionally injured. We must not expect a lively young man to be always so guarded and circumspect. It is very often nothing but our own vanity that deceives us. Women fancy admiration means more than it does."

"And men take care that they should."

"If it is designedly done, they cannot be justified; but I have no idea of there being so much design in the world as some persons imagine."

"I am far from attributing any part of Mr. Bingley's conduct to design," said Elizabeth; "but without scheming to do wrong, or to make others unhappy, there may be error, and there may be misery. Thoughtlessness, want of attention to other people's feelings, and want of resolution, will do the business."

"And do you impute it to either of those?"

"Yes; to the last. But if I go on, I shall displease you by saying what I think of persons you esteem. Stop me whilst you can."

"You persist, then, in supposing his sisters influence him."

"Yes, in conjunction with his friend."

"I cannot believe it. Why should they try to influence him? They can only wish for his happiness, and if he is attached to me, no other woman can secure it."

"Your first position is false. They may wish many things besides his happiness; they may wish his increase of wealth and consequence; they may wish him to marry a girl who has all the importance of money, great connections, and pride."

"Beyond a doubt, they *do* wish him to choose Miss Darcy," replied Jane; "but this may be from better feelings than you are supposing. They have known her much longer than they have known me; no wonder if they love her better. But, whatever may be their own wishes, it is very unlikely they should have opposed their brother's. What sister would think herself at liberty to do it, unless there were something very objectionable? If they believed him attached to me, they would not try to part us; if he were so, they could not succeed. By supposing such an affection, you make everybody acting unnaturally and wrong, and me most unhappy. Do not distress me by the idea. I am not ashamed of having been mistaken—or, at least, it is slight, it is nothing in comparison of what I should feel in thinking ill of him or his sisters. Let me take it in the best light, in the light in which it may be understood."

Elizabeth could not oppose such a wish; and from this time Mr. Bingley's name was scarcely ever mentioned between them.

Mrs. Bennet still continued to wonder and repine at his returning no more, and though a day seldom passed in which Elizabeth did not account for it clearly, there seemed little chance of her ever considering it with less preplexity. Her daughter endeavoured to convince her of what she did not believe herself, that his attentions to Jane had been merely the effect of a common and transient liking, which ceased when he saw her no more; but though the probability of the statement was admitted at the time, she had the same story to repeat everyday. Mrs. Bennet's best comfort was that Mr. Bingley must be down again in the summer.

Mr. Bennet treated the matter differently. "So, Lizzy," said he one day, "your sister is crossed in love, I find. I congratulate her. Next to being married, a girl likes to be crossed in love a little now and then. It is something to think of, and gives her a sort of distinction among her companions. When is your turn to come? You will hardly bear to be long outdone by Jane. Now is your time. Here are officers enough at Meryton to disappoint all the young ladies in the country. Let Wickham be *your* man. He is a pleasant fellow, and would jilt you creditably."

"Thank you, sir, but a less agreeable man would satisfy me. We must not all expect Jane's good fortune."

"True," said Mr. Bennet, "but it is a comfort to think that whatever of that kind may befall you, you have an affectionate mother who will always make the most of it."

Mr. Wickham's society was of material service in dispelling the gloom, which the late perverse occurrences had thrown on many of the Longbourn family. They saw him often, and to his other recommendations was now added that of general unreserve. The whole of what

Elizabeth had already heard, his claims on Mr. Darcy, and all that he had suffered from him, was now openly acknowledged and publicly canvassed; and everybody was pleased to think how much they had always disliked Mr. Darcy before they had known anything of the matter.

Miss Bennet was the only creature who could suppose there might be any extenuating circumstances in the case, unknown to the society of Hertfordshire; her mild and steady candour always pleaded for allowances, and urged the possibility of mistakes—but by everybody else Mr. Darcy was condemned as the worst of men.

CHAPTER TWO

AFTER a week spent in professions of love and schemes of felicity, Mr. Collins was called from his amiable Charlotte by the arrival of Saturday. The pain of separation, however, might be alleviated on his side by preparations for the reception of his bride, as he had reason to hope that shortly after his next return into Hertfordshire, the day would be fixed that was to make him the happiest of men. He took leave of his relations at Longbourn with as much solemnity as before, wished his fair cousins health and happiness again, and promised their father another letter of thanks.

On the following Monday, Mrs. Bennet had the pleasure of receiving her brother and his wife, who came as usual to spend the Christmas at Longbourn. Mr. Gardiner was a sensible, gentlemanlike man, greatly superior to his sister as well by nature as education. The Netherfield ladies would have had difficulty in believing that a man who lived by trade, and within view of his own warehouses, could have been so well bred and agreeable. Mrs. Gardiner, who was several years younger than Mrs. Bennet and Mrs. Philips, was an amiable, intelligent, elegant woman, and a great favourite with all her Longbourn nieces. Between the two eldest and herself especially there subsisted a very particular regard. They had frequently been staying with her in town.

The first part of Mrs. Gardiner's business on her arrival was to distribute her presents and describe the newest fashions. When this was done, she had a less active part to play. It became her turn to listen. Mrs. Bennet had many grievances to relate, and much to complain of. They had all been very ill-used since she last saw her sister. Two of her girls had been on the point of marriage, and after all there was nothing in it.

"I do not blame Jane," she continued, "for Jane would have got Mr. Bingley, if she could. But, Lizzy! Oh, sister! it is very hard to think that she might have been Mr. Collins's wife by this time, had not it been for her own perverseness. He made her an offer in this very room, and she refused him. The consequence of it is that Lady Lucas will have a daughter married before I have, and that Longbourn estate is just as much entailed as ever. The Lucases are very artful people indeed, sister. They are all for what they can get. I am sorry to say it of them, but so it is. It makes me very nervous and poorly to be thwarted so in my own family, and to have neighbours who think of themselves before anybody else. However, your coming just at this time is the greatest of comforts, and I am very glad to hear what you tell us of long sleeves."

Mrs. Gardiner, to whom the chief of this news had been given before, in the course of Jane and Elizabeth's correspondence with her, made her sister a slight answer, and in compassion to her nieces turned the conversation.

When alone with Elizabeth afterwards, she spoke more on the subject. "It seems likely to have been a desirable match for Jane," said she. "I am sorry it went off. But these things happen so often! A young man, such as you describe Mr. Bingley so easily falls in love with a pretty girl for a few weeks, and when accident separates them, so easily forgets her that these sort of inconstancies are very frequent."

"An excellent consolation in its way," said Elizabeth, "but it will not do for *us*. We do not suffer by *accident*. It does not often happen that the interference of friends will persuade a young man of independent fortune to think no more of a girl, whom he was violently in love with only a few days before."

"But that expression of 'violently in love' is so hackneyed, so doubtful, so indefinite, that it gives me very little idea. It is as often applied to feelings which arise from an half-hour's acquaintance as to a real, strong attachment. Pray, how *violent was* Mr. Bingley's love?"

"I never saw a more promising inclination. He was growing quite inattentive to other people, and wholly engrossed by her. Every time they met, it was more decided and remarkable. At his own ball he offended two or three young ladies by not asking them to dance, and I spoke to him twice myself, without receiving an answer. Could there be finer symptoms? Is not general incivility the very essence of love?"

"Oh, yes!—of that kind of love which I suppose him to have felt. Poor Jane! I am sorry for her, because, with her disposition, she may not get over it immediately. It had better have happened to *you,* Lizzy; you would have laughed yourself out of it sooner. But do you think she would be prevailed on to go back with us? Change of scene might be of service—and perhaps a little relief from home may be as useful as anything."

Elizabeth was exceedingly pleased with this proposal, and felt persuaded of her sister's ready acquiescence.

"I hope," added Mrs. Gardiner, "that no consideration with regard to this young man will influence her. We live in so different a part of town, all our connections are so different, and as you well know, we go out so little that it is very improbable they should meet at all, unless he really comes to see her."

"And *that* is quite impossible; for he is now in the custody of his friend, and Mr. Darcy would no more suffer him to call on Jane in such a part of London! My dear aunt, how could you think of it? Mr. Darcy may perhaps have *heard* of such a place as Gracechurch Street, but he would hardly think a month's ablution enough to cleanse him from its impurities, were he once to enter it; and depend upon it, Mr. Bingley never stirs without him."

"So much the better. I hope they will not meet at all. But does not Jane correspond with the sister? *She* will not be able to help calling."

"She will drop the acquaintance entirely."

But in spite of the certainty in which Elizabeth affected to place this point, as well as the still more interesting one of Bingley's being withheld from seeing Jane, she felt a solicitude on the subject which convinced her, on examination, that she did not consider it entirely hopeless. It was possible, and sometimes she thought it probable, that his affection might be reanimated, and the influence of his friends successfully combated by the more natural influence of Jane's attractions.

Miss Bennet accepted her aunt's invitation with pleasure, and the Bingleys were no otherwise in her thoughts at the time, than as she hoped that by Caroline's not living in the same house with her brother, she might occasionally spend a morning with her, without any danger of seeing him.

The Gardiners stayed a week at Longbourn; and what with the Philipses, the Lucases, and the officers, there was not a day without its engagement. Mrs. Bennet had so carefully provided for the entertainment of her brother and sister that they did not once sit down to a family dinner. When the engagement was for home, some of the officers always made part of it, of which officers Mr. Wickham was sure to be one; and on these occasions, Mrs. Gardiner, rendered suspicious by Elizabeth's warm commendation of him, narrowly observed them both. Without supposing them, from what she saw, to be very seriously in love, their preference of each other was plain enough to make her a little uneasy; and she resolved to speak to Elizabeth on the subject before she left Hertfordshire, and represent to her the imprudence of encouraging such an attachment.

To Mrs. Gardiner, Wickham had one means of affording pleasure, unconnected with his general powers. About ten or a dozen years ago, before her marriage, she had spent a considerable time in that very part of Derbyshire to which he belonged. They had, therefore, many acquaintance in common; and though Wickham had been little there since the death of Darcy's father five years before, it was yet in his power to give her fresher intelligence of her former friends than she had been in the way of procuring.

Mrs. Gardiner had seen Pemberley, and known the late Mr. Darcy by character perfectly well. Here consequently was an inexhaustible subject of discourse. In comparing her recollection of Pemberley with the minute description which Wickham could give, and in bestowing her tribute of praise on the character of its late possessor, she was delighting both him and herself. On being made acquainted with the present Mr. Darcy's treatment of him, she tried to remember something of that gentleman's reputed disposition when quite a lad which might agree with it, and was confident at last that she recollected having heard Mr. Fitzwilliam Darcy formerly spoken of as a very proud, ill-natured boy.

CHAPTER THREE

Mrs. Gardiner's caution to Elizabeth was punctually and kindly given on the first favourable opportunity of speaking to her alone; after honestly telling her what she thought, she thus went on:

"You are too sensible a girl, Lizzy, to fall in love merely because you are warned against it; and, therefore, I am not afraid of speaking openly. Seriously, I would have you be on your guard. Do not involve yourself, or endeavour to involve him in an affection which the want of fortune would make so very imprudent. I have nothing to say against *him;* he is a most interesting young man; and if he had the fortune he ought to have, I should think you could not do better. But as it is— you must not let your fancy run away with you. You have sense, and we all expect you to use it. Your father would depend on *your* resolution and good conduct, I am sure. You must not disappoint your father."

"My dear aunt, this is being serious indeed."

"Yes, and I hope to engage you to be serious likewise."

"Well, then, you need not be under any alarm. I will take care of myself, and of Mr. Wickham too. He shall not be in love with me, if I can prevent it."

"Elizabeth, you are not serious now."

"I beg your pardon. I will try again. At present I am not in love with Mr. Wickham; no, I certainly am not. But he is, beyond all comparison, the most agreeable man I ever saw—and if he becomes really attached to me—I believe it will be better that he should not. I see the imprudence of it.—Oh! *that* abominable Mr. Darcy!—My father's opinion of me does me the greatest honour; and I should be miserable to forfeit it. My father, however, is partial to Mr. Wickham. In short, my dear aunt, I should be very sorry to be the means of making any of you unhappy; but since we see everyday that where there is affection, young people are seldom withheld by immediate want of fortune from entering into engagements with each other, how can I promise to be wiser than so many of my fellow creatures if I am tempted, or how am I even to know that it would be wisdom to resist? All that I can promise you, therefore, is not to be in a hurry. I will not be in a hurry to believe myself his first object. When I am in company with him, I will not be wishing. In short, I will do my best."

"Perhaps it will be as well if you discourage his coming here so very often. At least, you should not *remind* your mother of inviting him."

"As I did the other day," said Elizabeth, with a conscious smile; "very true, it will be wise in me to refrain from *that*. But do not imagine that he is always here so often. It is on your account that he has been so frequently invited this week. You know my mother's ideas as to the necessity of constant company for her friends. But really, and upon my honour, I will try to do what I think to be wisest; and now, I hope you are satisfied."

Her aunt assured her that she was; and Elizabeth having thanked her for the kindness of her hints, they parted; a wonderful instance of advice being given on such a point, without being resented.

Mr. Collins returned into Hertfordshire soon after it had been quitted by the Gardiners and Jane; but as he took up his abode with the Lucases, his arrival was no great inconvenience to Mrs. Bennet. His marriage was now fast approaching, and she was at length so far resigned as to think it inevitable, and even repeatedly to say in an ill-natured tone that she "*wished* they might be happy." Thursday was to be the wedding day, and on Wednesday Miss Lucas paid her farewell visit; and when she rose to take leave, Elizabeth, ashamed of her mother's ungracious and reluctant good wishes, and sincerely affected herself, accompanied her out of the room. As they went downstairs together, Charlotte said,

"I shall depend on hearing from you very often, Eliza."

"*That* you certainly shall."

125

"And I have another favour to ask. Will you come and see me?"

"We shall often meet, I hope, in Hertfordshire."

"I am not likely to leave Kent for some time. Promise me, therefore, to come to Hunsford."

Elizabeth could not refuse, though she foresaw little pleasure in the visit.

"My father and Maria are to come to me in March," added Charlotte, "and I hope you will consent to be of the party. Indeed, Eliza, you will be as welcome to me as either of them."

The wedding took place; the bride and bridegroom set off for Kent from the church door, and everybody had as much to say or to hear on the subject as usual. Elizabeth soon heard from her friend; and their correspondence was as regular and frequent as it had ever been; that it should be equally unreserved was impossible. Elizabeth could never address her without feeling that all the comfort of intimacy was over and though determined not to slacken as a correspondent, it was for the sake of what had been, rather than what was. Charlotte's first letters were received with a good deal of eagerness; there could not but be curiosity to know how she would speak of her new home, how she would like Lady Catherine, and how happy she would dare pronounce herself to be; though, when the letters were read, Elizabeth felt that Charlotte expressed herself on every point exactly as she might have foreseen. She wrote cheerfully, seemed surrounded with comforts, and mentioned nothing which she could not praise. The house, furniture, neighbourhood, and roads, were all to her taste, and Lady Catherine's behaviour was most friendly and obliging. It was Mr. Collins's picture of Hunsford and Rosings rationally softened; and Elizabeth perceived that she must wait for her own visit there to know the rest.

Jane had already written a few lines to her sister to announce their safe arrival in London; and when she wrote again, Elizabeth hoped it would be in her power to say something of the Bingleys.

Her impatience for this second letter was as well rewarded as impatience generally is. Jane had been a week in town, without either seeing or hearing from Caroline.

She accounted for it, however, by supposing that her last letter to her friend from Longbourn had by some accident been lost.

"My aunt," she continued, "is going to-morrow into that part of the town, and I shall take the opportunity of calling in Grosvenor Street."

She wrote again when the visit was paid, and she had seen Miss Bingley. "I did not think Caroline in spirits," were her words, "but she was very glad to see me, and reproached me for giving her no notice of my coming to London. I was right, therefore; my last letter had never reached her. I inquired after their brother, of course. He was well, but so much engaged with Mr. Darcy that they scarcely ever saw him. I found that Miss Darcy was expected to dinner. I wish I could see her. My visit was not long, as Caroline and Mrs. Hurst were going out. I dare say I shall soon see them here."

Elizabeth shook her head over this letter. It convinced her that accident only could discover to Mr. Bingley her sister's being in town.

Four weeks passed away, and Jane saw nothing of him. She endeavoured to persuade herself that she did not regret it; but she could no longer be blind to Miss Bingley's inattention. After waiting at home every morning for a fortnight, and inventing every evening a fresh excuse for her, the visitor did at last appear; but the shortness of her stay, and yet more, the alteration of her manner, would allow Jane to deceive herself no longer. The letter which she wrote on this occasion to her sister will prove what she felt.

"My dearest Lizzy will, I am sure, be incapable of triumphing in her better judgment, at my expense, when I confess myself to have been entirely deceived in Miss Bingley's regard for me. But, my dear sister, though the event has proved you right, do not think me obstinate if I still assert that, considering what her behaviour was, my confidence was as natural as your suspicion. I do not at all comprehend her reason for wishing to be intimate with me, but if the same circumstances were to happen again, I am sure I should be deceived again. Caroline did not return my visit till yesterday; and not a note, not a line, did I receive in the meantime. When she did

127

come, it was very evident that she had no pleasure in it; she made a slight, formal apology for not calling before, said not a word of wishing to see me again, and was in every respect so altered a creature that when she went away, I was perfectly resolved to continue the acquaintance no longer. I pity, though, I cannot help blaming her. She was very wrong in singling me out as she did; I can safely say that every advance to intimacy began on her side. But I pity her, because she must feel that she has been acting wrong, and because I am very sure that anxiety for her brother is the cause of it. I need not explain myself farther; and though *we* know this anxiety to be quite needless, yet if she feels it, it will easily account for her behaviour to me; and so deservedly dear as he is to his sister, whatever anxiety she may feel on his behalf is natural and amiable. I cannot but wonder, however, at her having any such fears now, because, if he had at all cared about me, we must have met long, long ago. He knows of my being in town, I am certain, from something she said herself; and yet it should seem by her manner of talking as if she wanted to persuade herself that he is really partial to Miss Darcy. I cannot understand it. If I were not afraid of judging harshly, I should be almost tempted to say that there is a strong appearance of duplicity in all this. But I will endeavour to banish every painful thought, and think only of what will make me happy, your affection and the invariable kindness of my dear uncle and aunt. Let me hear from you very soon. Miss Bingley said something of his never returning to Netherfield again, of giving up the house, but not with any certainty. We had better not mention it. I am extremely glad that you have such pleasant accounts from our friends at Hunsford. Pray go to see them with Sir William and Maria. I am sure you will be very comfortable there.

"Yours, etc."

This letter gave Elizabeth some pain; but her spirits returned as she considered that Jane would no longer be duped—by the sister at least. All expectation from the brother was now absolutely over. She would not even wish for any renewal of his attentions. His character sunk on every review of it; and as a punishment for him, as well as a possible advantage to Jane, she seriously hoped he might really soon marry Mr. Darcy's sister, as, by Wickham's account, she would make him abundantly regret what he had thrown away.

Mrs. Gardiner about this time reminded Elizabeth of her promise concerning that gentleman, and required information; and Elizabeth had such to send as might rather give contentment to her aunt than to herself. His apparent partiality had subsided, his attentions were over, he was the admirer of someone else. Elizabeth was watchful enough to see it all, but she could see it and write of it without material pain. Her heart had been but slightly touched, and her vanity was satisfied with believing that *she* would have been his only choice, had fortune permitted it. The sudden acquisition of ten thousand pounds was the most remarkable charm of the young lady, to whom he was now rendering himself agreeable; but Elizabeth, less clear-sighted perhaps in his case than in Charlotte's, did not quarrel with him for his wish of independence. Nothing, on the contrary, could be more natural; and while able to suppose that it cost him a few struggles to relinquish her, she was ready to allow it a wise and desirable measure for both, and could very sincerely wish him happy.

All this was acknowledged to Mrs. Gardiner; and after relating the circumstances, she thus went on: "I am now convinced, my dear aunt, that I have never been much in love; for had I really experienced that pure and elevating passion, I should at present detest his very name, and wish him all manner of evil. But my feelings are not only cordial towards *him;* they are even impartial towards Miss King. I cannot find out that I hate her at all, or that I am in the least unwilling to think her a very good sort of girl. There can be no love in all this. My watchfulness has been effectual; and though I should certainly be a more interesting object to all my acquaintance, were I distractedly in love with him, I cannot say that I regret my comparative insignificance. Importance may sometimes be purchased too dearly. Kitty and Lydia take his defection much more to heart than I do. They are young in the ways of the world, and not yet open to the mortifying conviction that handsome young men must have something to live on, as well as the plain."

CHAPTER FOUR

WITH no greater events than these in the Longbourn family, and otherwise diversified by little beyond the walks to Meryton, sometimes dirty and sometimes cold, did January and February pass away. March was to take Elizabeth to Hunsford. She had not at first thought very seriously of going thither; but Charlotte, she soon found, was depending on the plan, and she gradually learned to consider it herself with greater pleasure as well as greater certainty. Absence had increased her desire of seeing Charlotte again, and weakened her disgust of Mr. Collins. There was novelty in the scheme, and as, with such a mother and such uncompanionable sisters, home could not be faultless, a little change was not unwelcome for its own sake. The journey would moreover give her a peep at Jane; and, in short, as the time drew near, she would have been very sorry for any delay. Everything, however, went on smoothly, and was finally settled according to Charlotte's first sketch. She was to accompany Sir William and his second daughter. The improvement of spending a night in London was added in time, and the plan became perfect as plan could be.

The only pain was in leaving her father, who would certainly miss her, and who, when it came to the point, so little liked her going that he told her to write to him, and almost promised to answer her letter.

The farewell between herself and Mr. Wickham was perfectly friendly; on his side even more. His present pursuit could not make him forget that Elizabeth had been the first to excite and to deserve his attention, the first to listen and to pity, the first to be admired; and in his manner of bidding her adieu, wishing her every enjoyment, reminding her of what she was to expect in Lady Catherine de Bourgh, and trusting their opinion of her—their opinion of everybody—would always coincide, there was a solicitude, an interest which she felt must ever attach her to him with a most sincere regard; and she parted from him convinced that whether married or single, he must always be her model of the amiable and pleasing.

Her fellow-travelers the next day were not of a kind to make her think him less agreeable. Sir William Lucas, and his daughter Maria, a good-humoured girl, but as empty-headed as himself, had nothing to say that could be worth hearing, and were listened to with about as much delight as the rattle of the chaise. Elizabeth loved absurdities, but she had known Sir William's too long. He could tell her nothing new of the wonders of his presentation and knighthood; and his civilities were worn out like his information.

It was a journey of only twenty-four miles, and they began it so early as to be in Gracechurch Street by noon. As they drove to Mr. Gardiner's door, Jane was at a drawing-room window watching their arrival; when they entered the passage she was there to welcome them, and Elizabeth, looking earnestly in her face, was pleased to see it healthful and lovely as ever. On the stairs were a troop of little boys and girls, whose eagerness for their cousin's appearance would not allow them to wait in the drawing-room, and whose shyness, as they had not seen her for a twelvemonth, prevented their coming lower. All was joy and kindness. The day passed most pleasantly away; the morning in bustle and shopping, and the evening at one of the theatres.

Elizabeth then contrived to sit by her aunt. Their first subject was her sister; and she was more grieved than astonished to hear, in reply to her minute inquiries, that though Jane always struggled to support her spirits, there were periods of dejection. It was reasonable, however, to hope that they would not continue long. Mrs. Gardiner gave her the particulars also of Miss Bingley's visit in Gracechurch Street, and repeated conversations occurring at different times between Jane and herself, which proved that the former had, from her heart, given up the acquaintance.

Mrs. Gardiner then rallied her niece on Wickham's desertion, and complimented her on bearing it so well.

"But, my dear Elizabeth," she added, "what sort of girl is Miss King? I should be sorry to think our friend mercenary."

"Pray, my dear aunt, what is the difference in matrimonial affairs between the mercenary and the prudent motive? Where does discretion end, and avarice begin? Last Christmas you were afraid of his marrying me, because it would be imprudent; and now, because he is trying to get a girl with only ten thousand pounds, you want to find out that he is mercenary."

"If you will only tell me what sort of girl Miss King is, I shall know what to think."

"She is a very good kind of girl, I believe. I know no harm of her."

"But he paid her not the smallest attention, till her grandfather's death made her mistress of this fortune."

"No—why should he? If it was not allowable for him to gain *my* affections because I had no money, what occasion could there be for making love to a girl whom he did not care about, and who was equally poor?"

"But there seems indelicacy in directing his attentions towards her so soon after this event."

"A man in distressed circumstances has not time for all those elegant decorums which other people may observe. If *she* does not object to it, why should *we?*"

"*Her* not objecting, does not justify *him*. It only shows her being deficient in something herself—sense or feeling."

"Well," cried Elizabeth, "have it as you choose. He shall be mercenary, and *she* shall be foolish."

"No, Lizzy, that is what I do *not* choose. I should be sorry, you know, to think ill of a young man who has lived so long in Derbyshire."

"Oh! if that is all, I have a very poor opinion of young men who live in Derbyshire; and their intimate friends who live in Hertfordshire are not much better. I am sick of them all. Thank Heaven! I am going tomorrow where I shall find a man who has not one agreeable quality, who has neither manner nor sense to recommend him. Stupid men are the only ones worth knowing, after all."

"Take care, Lizzy; that speech savours strongly of disappointment."

Before they were separated by the conclusion of the play, she had the unexpected happiness of an invitation to accompany her uncle and aunt in a tour of pleasure which they proposed taking in the summer.

"We have not quite determined how far it shall carry us," said Mrs. Gardiner, "but perhaps to the lakes."

No scheme could have been more agreeable to Elizabeth, and her acceptance of the invitation was most ready and grateful. "My dear, dear aunt," she rapturously cried, "what delight! what felicity! You give me fresh life and vigour. Adieu to disappointment and spleen. What are men to rocks and mountains? Oh! what hours of transport we shall spend! And when we *do* return, it shall not be like other travellers, without being able to give one accurate idea of anything. We *will* know where we have gone—we *will* recollect what we have seen. Lakes, mountains, and rivers shall not be jumbled together in our imaginations; nor, when we attempt to describe any particular scene, will we begin quarrelling about its relative situation. Let *our* first effusions be less insupportable than those of the generality of travellers."

CHAPTER FIVE

EVERY object in the next day's journey was new and interesting to Elizabeth; and her spirits were in a state for enjoyment; for she had seen her sister looking so well as to banish all fear for her health, and the prospect of her northern tour was a constant source of delight.

When they left the high road for the lane to Hunsford, every eye was in search of the parsonage, and every turning expected to bring it in view. The paling of Rosings Park was their boundary on one side. Elizabeth smiled at the recollection of all that she had heard of its inhabitants.

At length the parsonage was discernible. The garden sloping to the road, the house standing in it, the green pales and the laurel hedge, everything declared they were arriving. Mr. Collins and Charlotte appeared at the door, and the carriage stopped at the small gate, which led by a short gravel walk to the house, amidst the nods and smiles of the whole party. In a moment they were all out of the chaise, rejoicing at the sight of each other. Mrs. Collins welcomed her friend with the liveliest pleasure, and Elizabeth was more and more satisfied with coming, when she found herself so affectionately received. She saw instantly that her cousin's manners were not altered by his marriage; his formal civility was just what it had been, and he detained her some minutes at the gate to hear and satisfy his inquiries after all her family. They were then, with no other delay than his pointing out the neatness of the entrance, taken into the house; and as soon as they were in the parlour, he welcomed them a second time with ostentatious formality to his humble abode, and punctually repeated all his wife's offers of refreshment.

Elizabeth was prepared to see him in his glory; and she could not help fancying that in displaying the good proportion of the room, its aspect and its furniture, he addressed himself particularly to her, as if wishing to make her feel what she had lost in refusing him. But though everything seemed neat and comfortable, she was not able to gratify him by any sigh of repentance; and rather looked with wonder at her friend that she could have so cheerful an air, with such a companion. When Mr. Collins said anything of which his wife might reasonably be ashamed, which certainly was not unseldom, she involuntarily turned her eye on Charlotte. Once or twice she could discern a faint blush; but in general Charlotte wisely did not hear. After sitting long enough to admire every article of furniture in the room, from the sideboard to the fender, to give an account of their journey and of all that had happened in London, Mr. Collins invited them to take a stroll in the garden, which was large and well laid out, and to the cultivation of which he attended himself. To work in his garden was one of his most respectable pleasures; and Elizabeth admired the command of countenance with which Charlotte talked of the healthfulness of the exercise, and owned she encouraged it as much as possible. Here, leading the way through every walk and cross-walk, and scarcely allowing them an interval to utter the praises he asked for, every view was pointed out with a minuteness which left beauty entirely behind. He could number the fields in every direction, and could tell how many trees there were in the most distant clump. But of all the views which his garden, or which the country, or the kingdom could boast, none were to be compared with the prospect of Rosings, afforded by an opening in the trees that bordered the park nearly opposite the front of his house. It was a handsome modern building, well situated on rising ground.

From his garden, Mr. Collins would have led them round his two meadows, but the ladies not having shoes to encounter the remains of a white frost, turned back; and while Sir William accompanied him, Charlotte took her sister and friend over the house, extremely well pleased, probably, to have the opportunity of showing it without her husband's help. It was rather small, but well built and convenient; and everything was fitted up and arranged with a neatness and consistency of which Elizabeth gave Charlotte all the credit. When Mr. Collins could be forgotten, there was really a great air of comfort throughout, and by Charlotte's evident enjoyment of it, Elizabeth supposed he must be often forgotten.

She had already learned that Lady Catherine was still in the country. It was spoken of again while they were at dinner, when Mr. Collins joining in, observed,

"Yes, Miss Elizabeth, you will have the honour of seeing Lady Catherine de Bourgh on the ensuing Sunday at church, and I need not say you will be delighted with her. She is all affability and condescension, and I doubt not but you will be honoured with some portion of her notice when service is over. I have scarcely any hesitation in saying that she will include you and my sister Maria in every invitation with which she honours us during your stay here. Her behaviour to my dear Charlotte is charming. We dine at Rosings twice every week, and are never allowed to walk home. Her ladyship's carriage is regularly ordered for us. I *should* say, one of her ladyship's carriages, for she has several."

"Lady Catherine is a very respectable, sensible woman indeed," added Charlotte, "and a most attentive neighbour."

"Very true, my dear, that is exactly what I say. She is the sort of woman whom one cannot regard with too much deference."

The evening was spent chiefly in talking over Hertfordshire news, and telling again what had been already written; and when it closed, Elizabeth in the solitude of her chamber had to meditate upon Charlotte's degree of contentment, to understand her address in guiding, and composure in bearing with her husband, and to acknowledge that it was all done very well. She had also to anticipate how her visit would pass, the quiet tenor of their usual employments, the vexatious interruptions of Mr. Collins, and the gaieties of their intercourse with Rosings. A lively imagination soon settled it all.

About the middle of the next day, as she was in her room getting ready for a walk, a sudden noise below seemed to speak the whole house in confusion; and after listening a moment, she heard somebody running upstairs in a violent hurry, and calling loudly after her. She opened the door, and met Maria in the landing place, who, breathless with agitation, cried out,

"Oh, my dear Eliza! pray make haste and come into the dining-room, for there is such a sight to be seen! I will not tell you what it is. Make haste and come down this moment."

Elizabeth asked questions in vain; Maria would tell her nothing more, and down they ran into the dining-room, which fronted the lane, in quest of this wonder; it was two ladies stopping in a low phaeton at the garden gate.

"And is this all?" cried Elizabeth. "I expected at least that the pigs were got into the garden, and here is nothing but Lady Catherine and her daughter!"

"La! my dear," said Maria, quite shocked at the mistake, "it is not Lady Catherine. The old lady is Mrs. Jenkinson, who lives with them. The other is Miss De Bourgh. Only look at her. She is quite a little creature. Who would have thought she could be so thin and small."

"She is abominably rude to keep Charlotte out-of-doors in all this wind. Why does she not come in?"

"Oh! Charlotte says she hardly ever does. It is the greatest of favours when Miss De Bourgh comes in."

"I like her appearance," said Elizabeth, struck with other ideas. "She looks sickly and cross. Yes, she will do for him very well. She will make him a very proper wife."

Mr. Collins and Charlotte were both standing at the gate in conversation with the ladies; and Sir William, to Elizabeth's high diversion, was stationed in the doorway in earnest contemplation of the greatness before him, and constantly bowing whenever Miss De Bourgh looked that way.

At length there was nothing more to be said; the ladies drove on, and the others returned into the house. Mr. Collins no sooner saw the two girls than he began to congratulate them on their good fortune, which Charlotte explained by letting them know that the whole party was asked to dine at Rosings the next day.

CHAPTER SIX

MR. Collins's triumph in consequence of this invitation was complete. The power of displaying the grandeur of his patroness to his wondering visitors, and of letting them see her civility towards himself and his wife, was exactly what he had wished for; and that an opportunity of doing it should be given so soon was such an instance of Lady Catherine's condescension as he knew not how to admire enough.

"I confess," said he, "that I should not have been at all surprised by her ladyship's asking us on Sunday to drink tea and spend the evening at Rosings. I rather expected, from my knowledge of her affability, that it would happen. But who could have foreseen such an attention as this? Who could have imagined that we should receive an invitation to dine there (an invitation moreover including the whole party) so immediately after your arrival!"

"I am the less surprised at what has happened," replied Sir William, "from that knowledge of what the manners of the great really are, which my situation in life has allowed me to acquire. About the court, such instances of elegant breeding are not uncommon."

Scarcely anything was talked of the whole day or next morning but their visit to Rosings. Mr. Collins was carefully instructing them in what they were to expect, that the sight of such rooms, so many servants, and so splendid a dinner might not wholly overpower them.

When the ladies were separating for the toilette, he said to Elizabeth,

"Do not make yourself uneasy, my dear cousin, about your apparel. Lady Catherine is far from requiring that elegance of dress in us which becomes herself and daughter. I would advise you merely to put on whatever of your clothes is superior to the rest, there is no occasion for anything more. Lady Catherine will not think the worse of you for being simply dressed. She likes to have the distinction of rank preserved."

While they were dressing, he came two or three times to their different doors to recommend their being quick, as Lady Catherine very much objected to be kept waiting for her dinner. Such formidable accounts of her ladyship, and her manner of living, quite frightened Maria Lucas, who had been little used to company, and she looked forward to her introduction at Rosings with as much apprehension as her father had done to his presentation at St. James's.

As the weather was fine, they had a pleasant walk of about half a mile across the park. Every park has its beauty and its prospects; and Elizabeth saw much to be pleased with, though she could not be in such raptures as Mr. Collins expected the scene to inspire, and was but slightly affected by his enumeration of the windows in front of the house, and his relation of what the glazing altogether had originally cost Sir Lewis de Bourgh.

When they ascended the steps to the hall, Maria's alarm was every moment increasing, and even Sir William did not look perfectly calm. Elizabeth's courage did not fail her. She had heard nothing of Lady Catherine that spoke her awful from any extraordinary talents or miraculous virtue, and the mere stateliness of money and rank she thought she could witness without trepidation.

From the entrance hall, of which Mr. Collins pointed out, with a rapturous air, the fine proportion and finished ornaments, they followed the servants through an ante-chamber, to the room where Lady Catherine, her daughter, and Mrs. Jenkinson were sitting. Her ladyship, with great condescension, arose to receive them; and as Mrs. Collins had settled it with her husband that the office of introduction should be hers, it was performed in a proper manner, without any of those apologies and thanks which he would have thought necessary.

In spite of having been at St. James's, Sir William was so completely awed by the grandeur surrounding him that he had but just courage enough to make a very low bow, and take his seat without saying a word; and his daughter, frightened almost out of her senses, sat on the edge of her chair, not knowing which way to look. Elizabeth found herself quite equal to the scene, and could observe the three ladies before her composedly. Lady Catherine was a tall, large woman, with strongly-marked features, which might once have been handsome. Her air was not conciliating, nor was her manner of receiving them, such as to make her visitors forget their inferior rank. She was not rendered formidable by silence; but whatever she said was spoken in so authoritative a tone as marked her self-importance, and brought Mr. Wickham immediately to Elizabeth's mind; and from the observation of the day altogether, she believed Lady Catherine to be exactly what he had represented.

When, after examining the mother, in whose countenance and deportment she soon found some resemblance of Mr. Darcy, she turned her eyes on the daughter; she could almost have joined in Maria's astonishment at her being so thin and so small. There was neither in figure nor face any likeness between the ladies. Miss De Bourgh was pale and sickly; her features, though not plain, were insignificant; and she spoke very little, except in a low voice, to Mrs. Jenkinson, in whose appearance there was nothing remarkable, and who was entirely engaged in listening to what she said, and placing a screen in the proper direction before her eyes.

After sitting a few minutes, they were all sent to one of the windows to admire the view, Mr. Collins attending them to point out its beauties, and Lady Catherine kindly informing them that it was much better worth looking at in the summer.

The dinner was exceedingly handsome, and there were all the servants and all the articles of plate which Mr. Collins had promised; and as he had likewise foretold, he took his seat at the bottom of the table, by her ladyship's desire, and looked as if he felt that life could furnish nothing greater. He carved, and ate, and praised with delighted alacrity; and every dish was commended, first by him, and then by Sir William, who was now enough recovered to echo whatever his son-in-law said, in a manner which Elizabeth wondered Lady Catherine could bear. But Lady Catherine seemed gratified by their excessive admiration, and gave most gracious smiles especially when any dish on the table proved a novelty to them. The party did not supply much conversation. Elizabeth was ready to speak whenever there was an opening, but she was seated between Charlotte and Miss De Bourgh—the former of whom was engaged in listening to Lady Catherine, and the latter said not a word to her all dinner time. Mrs. Jenkinson was chiefly employed in watching how little Miss De Bourgh ate, pressing her to try some other dish, and fearing she was indisposed. Maria thought speaking out of the question, and the gentlemen did nothing but eat and admire.

When the ladies returned to the drawing-room, there was little to be done but to hear Lady Catherine talk, which she did without any intermission till coffee came in, delivering her opinion on every subject in so decisive a manner as proved that she was not used to have her judgment controverted. She inquired into Charlotte's domestic concerns familiarly and minutely, and gave her a great deal of advice as to the management of them all; told her how everything ought to be regulated in so small a family as hers, and instructed her as to the care of her cows and her poultry. Elizabeth found that nothing was beneath this great lady's attention which could furnish her with an occasion of dictating to others. In the intervals of her discourse with Mrs. Collins, she addressed a variety of questions to Maria and Elizabeth, but especially to the latter, of whose connections she knew the least, and who she observed to Mrs. Collins was a very genteel, pretty kind of girl. She asked her at different times how many sisters she had, whether they were older or younger than herself, whether any of them were likely to be married, whether they were handsome, where they had been educated, what carriage her father kept, and what had been her mother's maiden name?— Elizabeth felt all the impertinence of her questions, but answered them very composedly.—Lady Catherine then observed,

"Your father's estate is entailed on Mr. Collins, I think. For your sake," turning to Charlotte, "I am glad of it; but otherwise I see no occasion for entailing estates from the female line.—It was not thought necessary in Sir Lewis de Bourgh's family.—Do you play and sing, Miss Bennet?"

"A little."

"Oh! then—sometime or other we shall be happy to hear you. Our instrument is a capital one, probably superior to—— You shall try it someday.—Do your sisters play and sing?"

"One of them does."

"Why did not you all learn?—You ought all to have learned. The Miss Webbs all play, and their father has not so good an income as your's.—Do you draw?"

"No, not at all."

"What, none of you?"

"Not one."

"That is very strange. But I suppose you had no opportunity. Your mother should have taken you to town every spring for the benefit of masters."

"My mother would have had no objection, but my father hates London."

"Has your governess left you?"

"We never had any governess."

"No governess! How was that possible? Five daughters brought up at home without a governess! I never heard of such a thing. Your mother must have been quite a slave to your education."

Elizabeth could hardly help smiling, as she assured her that had not been the case.

"Then, who taught you? Who attended to you? Without a governess you must have been neglected."

"Compared with some families, I believe we were; but such of us as wished to learn never wanted the means. We were always encouraged to read, and had all the masters that were necessary. Those who chose to be idle, certainly might."

"Aye, no doubt; but that is what a governess will prevent, and if I had known your mother, I should have advised her most strenuously to engage one. I always say that nothing is to be done in education without steady and regular instruction, and nobody but a governess can give it. It is wonderful how many families I have been the means of supplying in that way. I am always glad to get a young person well placed out. Four nieces of Mrs. Jenkinson are most delightfully situated through my means; and it was but the other day that I recommended another young person, who was merely accidentally mentioned to me, and the family are quite delighted with her. Mrs. Collins, did I tell you of Lady Metcalfe's calling yesterday to thank me? She finds Miss Pope a treasure. 'Lady Catherine,' said she, 'you have given me a treasure.' Are any of your younger sisters out, Miss Bennet?"

"Yes, ma'am, all."

"All!—What, all five out at once? Very odd!—And you only the second.—The younger ones out before the elder are married!—Your younger sisters must be very young?"

"Yes, my youngest is not sixteen. Perhaps *she* is full young to be much in company. But really, ma'am, I think it would be very hard upon younger sisters that they should not have their share of society and amusement because the elder may not have the means or inclination to marry early. The last born has as good a right to the pleasures of youth as the first. And to be kept back on *such* a motive! I think it would not be very likely to promote sisterly affection or delicacy of mind."

"Upon my word," said her ladyship, "you give your opinion very decidedly for so young a person. Pray, what is your age?"

"With three younger sisters grown up," replied Elizabeth smiling, "your ladyship can hardly expect me to own it."

Lady Catherine seemed quite astonished at not receiving a direct answer; and Elizabeth suspected herself to be the first creature who had ever dared to trifle with so much dignified impertinence.

"You cannot be more than twenty, I am sure—therefore you need not conceal your age."

"I am not one and twenty."

When the gentlemen had joined them, and tea was over, the card-tables were placed. Lady Catherine, Sir William, and Mr. and Mrs. Collins sat down to quadrille; and as Miss De Bourgh chose to play at cassino, the two girls had the honour of assisting Mrs. Jenkinson to make up her party. Their table was superlatively stupid. Scarcely a syllable was uttered that did not relate to the game, except when Mrs. Jenkinson expressed her fears of Miss De Bourgh's being too hot or too cold, or having too much or too little light. A great deal more passed at the other table. Lady Catherine was generally speaking—stating the mistakes of the three others, or relating some anecdote of herself. Mr. Collins was employed in agreeing to everything her ladyship said, thanking her for every fish he won, and apologizing if he thought he won too many. Sir William did not say much. He was storing his memory with anecdotes and noble names.

When Lady Catherine and her daughter had played as long as they chose, the tables were broke up, the carriage was offered to Mrs. Collins, gratefully accepted, and immediately ordered. The party then gathered round the fire to hear Lady Catherine determine what weather they were to have on the morrow. From these instructions they were summoned by the arrival of the coach, and with many speeches of thankfulness on Mr. Collins's side, and as many bows on Sir William's, they departed. As soon as they had driven from the door, Elizabeth was called on by her cousin to give her opinion of all that she had seen at Rosings, which, for Charlotte's sake, she made more favourable than it really was. But her commendation, though costing her some trouble, could by no means satisfy Mr. Collins, and he was very soon obliged to take her ladyship's praise into his own hands.

CHAPTER SEVEN

SIR William stayed only a week at Hunsford; but his visit was long enough to convince him of his daughter's being most comfortably settled, and of her possessing such a husband and such a neighbour as were not often met with. While Sir William was with them, Mr. Collins devoted his mornings to driving him out in his gig, and showing him the country; but when he went away, the whole family returned to their usual employments, and Elizabeth was thankful to find that they did not see more of her cousin by the alteration, for the chief of the time between breakfast and dinner was now passed by him either at work in the garden, or in reading and writing, and looking out of window in his own book room, which fronted the road. The room in which the ladies sat was backwards. Elizabeth at first had rather wondered that Charlotte should not prefer the dining-parlour for common use; it was a better sized room, and had a pleasanter aspect; but she soon saw that her friend had an excellent reason for what she did, for Mr. Collins would undoubtedly have been much less in his own apartment had they sat in one equally lively; and she gave Charlotte credit for the arrangement.

From the drawing-room they could distinguish nothing in the lane, and were indebted to Mr. Collins for the knowledge of what carriages went along, and how often especially Miss De Bourgh drove by in her phaeton, which he never failed coming to inform them of, though it happened almost everyday. She not unfrequently stopped at the parsonage, and had a few minutes' conversation with Charlotte, but was scarcely ever prevailed on to get out.

Very few days passed in which Mr. Collins did not walk to Rosings, and not many in which his wife did not think it necessary to go likewise; and till Elizabeth recollected that there might be other family livings to be disposed of, she could not understand the sacrifice of so many hours. Now and then, they were honoured with a call from her ladyship, and nothing escaped her observation that was passing in the room during these visits. She examined into their employments, looked at their work, and advised them to do it differently; found fault with the arrangement of the furniture, or detected the housemaid in negligence; and if she accepted any refreshment, seemed to do it only for the sake of finding out that Mrs. Collins's joints of meat were too large for her family.

Elizabeth soon perceived that though this great lady was not in the commission of the peace for the county, she was a most active magistrate in her own parish, the minutest concerns of which were carried to her by Mr. Collins; and whenever any of the cottagers were disposed to be quarrelsome, discontented, or too poor, she sallied forth into the village to settle their differences, silence their complaints, and scold them into harmony and plenty.

The entertainment of dining at Rosings was repeated about twice a week; and allowing for the loss of Sir William, and there being only one card-table in the evening, every such entertainment was the counterpart of the first. Their other engagements were few, as the style of living of the neighbourhood in general was beyond the Collinses' reach. This however was no evil to Elizabeth, and upon the whole she spent her time comfortably enough; there were half hours of pleasant conversation with Charlotte, and the weather was so fine for the time of year that she had often great enjoyment out-of-doors. Her favourite walk, and where she frequently went while the others were calling on Lady Catherine, was along the open grove which edged that side of the park, where there was a nice sheltered path, which no one seemed to value but herself, and where she felt beyond the reach of Lady Catherine's curiosity.

In this quiet way, the first fortnight of her visit soon passed away. Easter was approaching, and the week preceding it was to bring an addition to the family at Rosings, which in so small a circle must be important. Elizabeth had heard soon after her arrival that Mr. Darcy was expected there in the course of a few weeks, and though there were not many of her acquaintance whom she did not prefer, his coming would furnish one comparatively new to look at in their Rosings parties, and she might be amused in seeing how hopeless Miss Bingley's designs on him were by his behaviour to his cousin, for whom he was evidently destined by Lady Catherine, who talked of his coming with the greatest satisfaction, spoke of him in terms of the highest admiration, and seemed almost angry to find that he had already been frequently seen by Miss Lucas and herself.

His arrival was soon known at the parsonage, for Mr. Collins was walking the whole morning within view of the lodges opening into Hunsford Lane in order to have the earliest assurance of it; and after making his bow as the carriage turned into the park, hurried home with the great intelligence. On the following morning he hastened to Rosings to pay his respects. There were two nephews of Lady Catherine to require them, for Mr. Darcy had brought with him a Colonel Fitzwilliam, the younger son of his uncle, Lord——, and to the great surprise of all the party, when Mr. Collins returned the gentlemen accompanied him. Charlotte had seen them from her husband's room crossing the road, and immediately running into the other, told the girls what an honour they might expect, adding,

"I may thank you, Eliza, for this piece of civility. Mr. Darcy would never have come so soon to wait upon me."

Elizabeth had scarcely time to disclaim all right to the compliment before their approach was announced by the doorbell, and shortly afterwards the three gentlemen entered the room. Colonel Fitzwilliam, who led the way, was about thirty, not handsome, but in person and address most truly the gentleman. Mr. Darcy looked just as he had been used to look in Hertfordshire, paid his compliments, with his usual reserve, to Mrs. Collins; and whatever might be his feelings towards her friend, met her with every appearance of composure. Elizabeth merely curtsyed to him, without saying a word.

Colonel Fitzwilliam entered into conversation directly with the readiness and ease of a well-bred man, and talked very pleasantly; but his cousin, after having addressed a slight observation on the house and garden to Mrs. Collins, sat for sometime without speaking to anybody. At length, however, his civility was so far awakened as to inquire of Elizabeth after the health of her family. She answered him in the usual way, and after a moment's pause, added,

"My eldest sister has been in town these three months. Have you never happened to see her there?"

She was perfectly sensible that he never had; but she wished to see whether he would betray any consciousness of what had passed between the Bingleys and Jane; and she thought he looked a little confused as he answered that he had never been so fortunate as to meet Miss Bennet. The subject was pursued no farther, and the gentlemen soon afterwards went away.

CHAPTER EIGHT

COLONEL Fitzwilliam's manners were very much admired at the parsonage, and the ladies all felt that he must add considerably to the pleasure of their engagements at Rosings. It was some days, however, before they received any invitation thither, for while there were visitors in the house, they could not be necessary; and it was not till Easter-day, almost a week after the gentlemen's arrival, that they were honoured by such an attention, and then they were merely asked on leaving church to come there in the evening. For the last week they had seen very little of either Lady Catherine or her daughter. Colonel Fitzwilliam had called at the parsonage more than once during the time, but Mr. Darcy they had only seen at church.

The invitation was accepted of course, and at a proper hour they joined the party in Lady Catherine's drawing-room. Her ladyship received them civilly, but it was plain that their company was by no means so acceptable as when she could get nobody else; and she was, in fact, almost engrossed by her nephews, speaking to them, especially to Darcy, much more than to any other person in the room.

Colonel Fitzwilliam seemed really glad to see them; anything was a welcome relief to him at Rosings; and Mrs. Collins's pretty friend had moreover caught his fancy very much. He now seated himself by her, and talked so agreeably of Kent and Hertfordshire, of travelling and staying at home, of new books and music, that Elizabeth had never been half so well entertained in that room before; and they conversed with so much spirit and flow as to draw the attention of Lady Catherine herself, as well as of Mr. Darcy. *His* eyes had been soon and repeatedly turned towards them with a look of curiosity; and that her ladyship after a while shared the feeling was more openly acknowledged, for she did not scruple to call out,

"What is that you are saying, Fitzwilliam? What is it you are talking of? What are you telling Miss Bennet? Let me hear what it is."

"We are speaking of music, madam," said he, when no longer able to avoid a reply.

"Of music! Then pray speak aloud. It is of all subjects my delight. I must have my share in the conversation, if you are speaking of music. There are few people in England, I suppose, who have more true enjoyment of music than myself, or a better natural taste. If I had ever learned, I should have been a great proficient. And so would Anne, if her health had allowed her to apply. I am confident that she would have performed delightfully. How does Georgiana get on, Darcy?"

Mr. Darcy spoke with affectionate praise of his sister's proficiency.

"I am very glad to hear such a good account of her," said Lady Catherine; "and pray tell her from me that she cannot expect to excel, if she does not practise a great deal."

"I assure you, madam," he replied, "that she does not need such advice. She practises very constantly."

"So much the better. It cannot be done too much; and when I next write to her, I shall charge her not to neglect it on any account. I often tell young ladies that no excellence in music is to be acquired, without constant practise. I have told Miss Bennet several times, that she will never play really well, unless she practises more; and though Mrs. Collins has no instrument, she is very welcome, as I have often told her, to come to Rosings everyday and play on the pianoforte in Mrs. Jenkinson's room. She would be in nobody's way, you know, in that part of the house."

Mr. Darcy looked a little ashamed of his aunt's ill breeding, and made no answer.

When coffee was over, Colonel Fitzwilliam reminded Elizabeth of having promised to play to him; and she sat down directly to the instrument. He drew a chair near her. Lady Catherine listened to half a song and then talked, as before, to her other nephew, till the latter walked away from her, and moving with his usual deliberation towards the pianoforte, stationed himself so as to command a full view of the fair performer's countenance. Elizabeth saw what he was doing, and at the first convenient pause, turned to him with an arch smile, and said,

"You mean to frighten me, Mr. Darcy, by coming in all this state to hear me? But I will not be alarmed, though your sister *does* play so well. There is a stubbornness about me that never can bear to be frightened at the will of others. My courage always rises with every attempt to intimidate me."

"I shall not say that you are mistaken," he replied, "because you could not really believe me to entertain any design of alarming you; and I have had the pleasure of your acquaintance long enough to know that you find great enjoyment in occasionally professing opinions which in fact are not your own."

Elizabeth laughed heartily at this picture of herself, and said to Colonel Fitzwilliam, "Your cousin will give you a very pretty notion of me, and teach you not to believe a word I say. I am particularly unlucky in meeting with a person so well able to expose my real character, in a part of the world where I had hoped to pass myself off with some degree of credit. Indeed, Mr. Darcy, it is very ungenerous in you to mention all that you knew to my disadvantage in Hertfordshire—and, give me leave to say, very impolitic too—for it is provoking me to retaliate, and such things may come out as will shock your relations to hear."

"I am not afraid of you," said he smilingly.

"Pray let me hear what you have to accuse him of," cried Colonel Fitzwilliam. "I should like to know how he behaves among strangers."

"You shall hear then—but prepare yourself for something very dreadful. The first time of my ever seeing him in Hertfordshire, you must know, was at a ball—and at this ball, what do you think he did? He danced only four dances! I am sorry to pain you—but so it was. He danced only four dances, though gentlemen were scarce; and, to my certain knowledge, more than one young lady was sitting down in want of a partner. Mr. Darcy, you cannot deny the fact."

"I had not at that time the honour of knowing any lady in the assembly beyond my own party."

"True; and nobody can ever be introduced in a ballroom. Well, Colonel Fitzwilliam, what do I play next? My fingers wait your orders."

"Perhaps," said Darcy, "I should have judged better, had I sought an introduction, but I am ill qualified to recommend myself to strangers."

"Shall we ask your cousin the reason of this?" said Elizabeth, still addressing Colonel Fitzwilliam. "Shall we ask him why a man of sense and education, and who has lived in the world, is ill qualified to recommend himself to strangers?"

"I can answer your question," said Fitzwilliam, "without applying to him. It is because he will not give himself the trouble."

"I certainly have not the talent which some people possess," said Darcy, "of conversing easily with those I have never seen before. I cannot catch their tone of conversation, or appear interested in their concerns, as I often see done."

"My fingers," said Elizabeth, "do not move over this instrument in the masterly manner which I see so many women's do. They have not the same force or rapidity, and do not produce the same expression. But then I have always supposed it to be my own fault—because I would not take the trouble of practising. It is not that I do not believe *my* fingers as capable as any other woman's of superior execution."

Darcy smiled and said, "You are perfectly right. You have employed your time much better. No one admitted to the privilege of hearing you can think anything wanting. We neither of us perform to strangers."

Here they were interrupted by Lady Catherine, who called out to know what they were talking of. Elizabeth immediately began playing again. Lady Catherine approached, and after listening for a few minutes, said to Darcy,

"Miss Bennet would not play at all amiss, if she practised more, and could have the advantage of a London master. She has a very good notion of fingering, though her taste is not equal to Anne's. Anne would have been a delightful performer, had her health allowed her to learn."

Elizabeth looked at Darcy to see how cordially he assented to his cousin's praise; but neither at that moment nor at any other could she discern any symptom of love; and from the whole of his behaviour to Miss De Bourgh she derived this comfort for Miss Bingley that he might have been just as likely to marry *her,* had she been his relation.

Lady Catherine continued her remarks on Elizabeth's performance, mixing with them many instructions on execution and taste. Elizabeth received them with all the forbearance of civility; and at the request of the gentlemen remained at the instrument till her ladyship's carriage was ready to take them all home.

CHAPTER NINE

ELIZABETH was sitting by herself the next morning and writing to Jane, while Mrs. Collins and Maria were gone on business into the village, when she was startled by a ring at the door, the certain signal of a visitor. As she had heard no carriage, she thought it not unlikely to be Lady Catherine, and under that apprehension was putting away her half-finished letter that she might escape all impertinent questions, when the door opened, and to her very great surprise, Mr. Darcy, and Mr. Darcy only, entered the room.

He seemed astonished too on finding her alone, and apologized for his intrusion by letting her know that he had understood all the ladies to be within.

They then sat down, and when her inquiries after Rosings were made, seemed in danger of sinking into total silence. It was absolutely necessary, therefore, to think of something, and in this emergence recollecting *when* she had seen him last in Hertfordshire, and feeling curious to know what he would say on the subject of their hasty departure, she observed,

"How very suddenly you all quitted Netherfield last November, Mr. Darcy! It must have been a most agreeable surprise to Mr. Bingley to see you all after him so soon; for if I recollect right, he went but the day before. He and his sisters were well, I hope, when you left London."

"Perfectly so—I thank you."

She found that she was to receive no other answer—and after a short pause, added,

"I think I have understood that Mr. Bingley has not much idea of ever returning to Netherfield again?"

"I have never heard him say so; but it is probable that he may spend very little of his time there in future. He has many friends, and he is at a time of life when friends and engagements are continually increasing."

"If he means to be but little at Netherfield, it would

151

be better for the neighbourhood that he should give up the place entirely, for then we might possibly get a settled family there. But perhaps Mr. Bingley did not take the house so much for the convenience of the neighbourhood as for his own, and we must expect him to keep or quit it on the same principle."

"I should not be surprised," said Darcy, "if he were to give it up, as soon as any eligible purchase offers."

Elizabeth made no answer. She was afraid of talking longer of his friend; and having nothing else to say, was now determined to leave the trouble of finding a subject to him.

He took the hint, and soon began with, "This seems a very comfortable house. Lady Catherine, I believe, did a great deal to it when Mr. Collins came to Hunsford."

"I believe she did—and I am sure she could not have bestowed her kindness on a more grateful object."

"Mr. Collins appears very fortunate in his choice of a wife."

"Yes, indeed; his friends may well rejoice in his having met with one of the very few sensible women who would have accepted him, or have made him happy if they had. My friend has an excellent understanding—though I am not certain that I consider her marrying Mr. Collins as the wisest thing she ever did. She seems perfectly happy, however, and in a prudential light, it is certainly a very good match for her."

"It must be very agreeable to her to be settled within so easy a distance of her own family and friends."

"An easy distance do you call it? It is nearly fifty miles."

"And what is fifty miles of good road? Little more than half a day's journey. Yes, I call it a *very* easy distance."

"I should never have considered the distance as one of the *advantages* of the match," cried Elizabeth. "I should never have said Mrs. Collins was settled *near* her family."

"It is a proof of your own attachment to Hertfordshire. Anything beyond the very neighbourhood of Longbourn, I suppose, would appear far."

As he spoke there was a sort of smile, which Elizabeth fancied she understood; he must be supposing her to be thinking of Jane and Netherfield, and she blushed as she answered,

"I do not mean to say that a woman may not be settled too near her family. The far and the near must be relative, and depend on many varying circumstances. Where there is fortune to make the expense of travelling unimportant, distance becomes no evil. But that is not the case *here*. Mr. and Mrs. Collins have a comfortable income, but not such a one as will allow of frequent journeys—and I am persuaded my friend would not call herself *near* her family under less than *half* the present distance."

Mr. Darcy drew his chair a little towards her, and said, "*You* cannot have a right to such very strong local attachment. *You* cannot have been always at Longbourn."

Elizabeth looked surprised. The gentleman experienced some change of feeling; he drew back his chair, took a newspaper from the table, and glancing over it, said, in a colder voice,

"Are you pleased with Kent?"

A short dialogue on the subject of the country ensued, on either side calm and concise—and soon put an end to by the entrance of Charlotte and her sister, just returned from their walk. The *tête-à-tête* surprised them. Mr. Darcy related the mistake which had occasioned his intruding on Miss Bennet, and after sitting a few minutes longer without saying much to anybody, went away.

"What can be the meaning of this!" said Charlotte, as soon as he was gone. "My dear Eliza he must be in love with you, or he would never have called on us in this familiar way."

But when Elizabeth told of his silence, it did not seem very likely, even to Charlotte's wishes, to be the case; and after various conjectures, they could at last only suppose his visit to proceed from the difficulty of finding anything to do, which was the more probable from the time of year. All field sports were over. Within doors there was Lady Catherine, books, and a billiard table, but gentlemen cannot be always within doors; and in the nearness of the parsonage, or the pleasantness of the walk to it, or of the people who lived in it, the two cousins found a temptation from this period of walking thither almost everyday. They called at various times of the morning, sometimes separately, sometimes together, and now and then accompanied by their aunt. It was plain to them all that Colonel Fitzwilliam came because he had pleasure in their society, a persuasion which of course recommended him still more; and Elizabeth was reminded by her own satisfaction in being with him, as well as by his evident admiration of her, of her former favourite George Wickham; and though, in comparing them, she saw there was less captivating softness in Colonel Fitzwilliam's manners, she believed he might have the best informed mind.

But why Mr. Darcy came so often to the parsonage it was more difficult to understand. It could not be for society, as he frequently sat there ten minutes together without opening his lips; and when he did speak, it seemed the effect of necessity rather than of choice—a sacrifice to propriety, not a pleasure to himself. He seldom appeared really animated. Mrs. Collins knew not what to make of him. Colonel Fitzwilliam's occasionally laughing at his stupidity proved that he was generally different, which her own knowledge of him could not have told her; and as she would have liked to believe this change the effect of love, and the object of that love, her friend Eliza, she set herself seriously to work to find it out.—She watched him whenever they were at Rosings, and whenever he came to Hunsford; but without much success. He certainly looked at her friend a great deal, but the expression of that look was disputable. It was an earnest, steadfast gaze, but she often doubted whether there were much admiration in it, and sometimes it seemed nothing but absence of mind.

She had once or twice suggested to Elizabeth the possibility of his being partial to her, but Elizabeth always laughed at the idea; and Mrs. Collins did not think it right to press the subject, from the danger of raising expectations which might only end in disappointment; for in her opinion it admitted not of a doubt that all her friend's dislike would vanish, if she could suppose him to be in her power.

In her kind schemes for Elizabeth, she sometimes planned her marrying Colonel Fitzwilliam. He was beyond comparison the pleasantest man; he certainly admired her, and his situation in life was most eligible; but, to counterbalance these advantages, Mr. Darcy had considerable patronage in the church, and his cousin could have none at all.

CHAPTER TEN

MORE than once did Elizabeth in her ramble within the park unexpectedly meet Mr. Darcy. She felt all the perverseness of the mischance that should bring him where no one else was brought; and to prevent its ever happening again, took care to inform him at first that it was a favourite haunt of hers. How it could occur a second time therefore was very odd! Yet it did, and even a third. It seemed like wilful ill nature, or a voluntary penance, for on these occasions it was not merely a few formal inquiries and an awkward pause and then away, but he actually thought it necessary to turn back and walk with her. He never said a great deal, nor did she give herself the trouble of talking or of listening much; but it struck her in the course of their third rencontre that he was asking some odd unconnected questions—about her pleasure in being at Hunsford, her love of solitary walks, and her opinion of Mr. and Mrs. Collins's happiness; and that in speaking of Rosings and her not perfectly understanding the house he seemed to expect that whenever she came into Kent again she would be staying *there* too. His words seemed to imply it. Could he have Colonel Fitzwilliam in his thoughts? She supposed, if he meant anything, he must mean an allusion to what might arise in that quarter. It distressed her a little, and she was quite glad to find herself at the gate in the pales opposite the parsonage.

She was engaged one day as she walked, in re-perusing Jane's last letter and dwelling on some passages which proved that Jane had not written in spirits, when, instead of being again surprised by Mr. Darcy, she saw on looking up that Colonel Fitzwilliam was meeting her. Putting away the letter immediately and forcing a smile, she said,

"I did not know before that you ever walked this way."

"I have been making the tour of the park," he replied, "as I generally do every year, and intend to close it with a call at the parsonage. Are you going much farther?"

"No, I should have turned in a moment."

And accordingly she did turn, and they walked towards the parsonage together.

"Do you certainly leave Kent on Saturday?" said she.

"Yes—if Darcy does not put it off again. But I am at his disposal. He arranges the business just as he pleases."

"And if not able to please himself in the arrangement, he has at least great pleasure in the power of choice. I do not know anybody who seems more to enjoy the power of doing what he likes than Mr. Darcy."

"He likes to have his own way very well," replied Colonel Fitzwilliam. "But so we all do. It is only that he has better means of having it than many others, because he is rich, and many others are poor. I speak feelingly. A younger son, you know, must be inured to self-denial and dependence."

"In my opinion, the younger son of an earl can know very little of either. Now, seriously, what have you ever known of self-denial and dependence? When have you been prevented by want of money from going wherever you chose, or procuring anything you had a fancy for?"

"These are home questions—and perhaps I cannot say that I have experienced many hardships of that nature. But in matters of greater weight, I may suffer from the want of money. Younger sons cannot marry where they like."

"Unless where they like women of fortune, which I think they very often do."

"Our habits of expense make us too dependent, and there are not many in my rank of life who can afford to marry without some attention to money."

"Is this," thought Elizabeth, "meant for me?" and she coloured at the idea; but recovering herself, said in a lively tone, "And pray, what is the usual price of an earl's younger son? Unless the elder brother is very sickly, I suppose you would not ask above fifty thousand pounds."

He answered her in the same style, and the subject

dropped. To interrupt a silence which might make him fancy her affected with what had passed, she soon afterwards said,

"I imagine your cousin brought you down with him chiefly for the sake of having somebody at his disposal. I wonder he does not marry to secure a lasting convenience of that kind. But, perhaps his sister does as well for the present, and as she is under his sole care, he may do what he likes with her."

"No," said Colonel Fitzwilliam, "that is an advantage which he must divide with me. I am joined with him in the guardianship of Miss Darcy."

"Are you, indeed?" And pray what sort of guardians do you make? Does your charge give you much trouble? Young ladies of her age are sometimes a little difficult to manage, and if she has the true Darcy spirit, she may like to have her own way."

As she spoke, she observed him looking at her earnestly, and the manner in which he immediately asked her why she supposed Miss Darcy likely to give them any uneasiness convinced her that she had somehow or other got pretty near the truth. She directly replied,

"You need not be frightened. I never heard any harm of her; and I dare say she is one of the most tractable creatures in the world. She is a very great favourite with some ladies of my acquaintance, Mrs. Hurst and Miss Bingley. I think I have heard you say that you know them."

"I know them a little. Their brother is a pleasant gentlemanlike man—he is a great friend of Darcy's."

"Oh! yes," said Elizabeth dryly—"Mr. Darcy is uncommonly kind to Mr. Bingley, and takes a prodigious deal of care of him."

"Care of him!—Yes, I really believe Darcy does take care of him in those points where he most wants care. From something that he told me in our journey hither, I have reason to think Bingley very much indebted to him. But I ought to beg his pardon, for I have no right to suppose that Bingley was the person meant. It was all conjecture."

"What is it you mean?"

"It is a circumstance which Darcy of course would not wish to be generally known, because if it were to

157

get round to the lady's family, it would be an unpleasant thing."

"You may depend upon my not mentioning it."

"And remember that I have not much reason for supposing it to be Bingley. What he told me was merely this: that he congratulated himself on having lately saved a friend from the inconveniences of a most imprudent marriage, but without mentioning names or any other particulars, and I only suspected it to be Bingley from believing him the kind of young man to get into a scrape of that sort, and from knowing them to have been together the whole of last summer."

"Did Mr. Darcy give you his reasons for this interference?"

"I understood that there were some very strong objections against the lady."

"And what arts did he use to separate them?"

"He did not talk to me of his own arts," said Fitzwilliam smiling. "He only told me what I have now told you."

Elizabeth made no answer, and walked on, her heart swelling with indignation. After watching her a little, Fitzwilliam asked her why she was so thoughtful.

"I am thinking of what you have been telling me," said she. "Your cousin's conduct does not suit my feelings. Why was he to be the judge?"

"You are rather disposed to call his interference officious?"

"I do not see what right Mr. Darcy had to decide on the propriety of his friend's inclination, or why, upon his own judgment alone, he was to determine and direct in what manner that friend was to be happy. But," she continued, recollecting herself, "as we know none of the particulars it is not fair to condemn him. It is not to be supposed that there was much affection in the case."

"That is not an unnatural surmise," said Fitzwilliam, "but it is lessening the honour of my cousin's triumph very sadly."

This was spoken jestingly, but it appeared to her so just a picture of Mr. Darcy that she would not trust herself with an answer; and, therefore, abruptly changing the conversation, talked on indifferent matters till they reached the parsonage. There, shut into her own room, as soon as their visitor left them, she could think without interruption of all that she had heard. It was not to be supposed that any other people could be meant than those with whom she was connected. There could not exist in the world *two* men over whom Mr. Darcy could have such boundless influence. That he had been concerned in the measures taken to separate Mr. Bingley and Jane she had never doubted; but she had always attributed to Miss Bingley the principal design and arrangement of them. If his own vanity, however, did not mislead him, *he* was the cause, his pride and caprice were the cause of all that Jane had suffered, and still continued to suffer. He had ruined for awhile every hope of happiness for the most affectionate, generous heart in the world; and no one could say how lasting an evil he might have inflicted.

"There were some very strong objections against the lady," were Colonel Fitzwilliam's words, and these strong objections probably were her having one uncle who was a country attorney, and another who was in business in London.

"To Jane herself," she exclaimed, "there could be no possibility of objection. All loveliness and goodness as she is! Her understanding excellent, her mind improved, and her manners captivating. Neither could anything be urged against my father, who, though with some peculiarities, has abilities which Mr. Darcy himself need not disdain, and respectability which he will probably never reach." When she thought of her mother indeed, her confidence gave way a little, but she would not allow that any objections *there* had material weight with Mr. Darcy, whose pride, she was convinced, would receive a deeper wound from the want of importance in his friend's connections than from their want of sense; and she was quite decided at last that he had been partly governed by this worst kind of pride, and partly by the wish of retaining Mr. Bingley for his sister.

The agitation and tears which the subject occasioned brought on a headache; and it grew so much worse towards the evening that added to her unwillingness to see Mr. Darcy, it determined her not to attend her cousins to Rosings, where they were engaged to drink tea. Mrs. Collins, seeing that she was really unwell, did not press her to go, and as much as possible prevented her husband from pressing her, but Mr. Collins could not conceal his apprehension of Lady Catherine's being rather displeased by her staying at home.

CHAPTER ELEVEN

WHEN they were gone, Elizabeth, as if intending to exasperate herself as much as possible against Mr. Darcy, chose for her employment the examination of all the letters which Jane had written to her since her being in Kent. They contained no actual complaint, nor was there any revival of past occurrences, or any communication of present suffering. But in all, and in almost every line of each, there was a want of that cheerfulness which had been used to characterize her style, and which, proceeding from the serenity of a mind at ease with itself, and kindly disposed towards everyone, had been scarcely ever clouded. Elizabeth noticed every sentence conveying the idea of uneasiness, with an attention which it had hardly received on the first perusal. Mr. Darcy's shameful boast of what misery he had been able to inflict gave her a keener sense of her sister's sufferings. It was some consolation to think that his visit to Rosings was to end on the day after the next, and a still greater that in less than a fortnight she should herself be with Jane again, and enabled to contribute to the recovery of her spirits by all that affection could do.

She could not think of Darcy's leaving Kent, without remembering that his cousin was to go with him; but Colonel Fitzwilliam had made it clear that he had no intentions at all, and agreeable as he was, she did not mean to be unhappy about him.

While settling this point, she was suddenly roused by the sound of the doorbell, and her spirits were a little fluttered by the idea of its being Colonel Fitzwilliam himself, who had once before called late in the evening, and might now come to inquire particularly after her. But this idea was soon banished, and her spirits were very differently affected, when, to her utter amazement, she saw Mr. Darcy walk into the room. In an hurried manner he immediately began an inquiry after her health, imputing his visit to a wish of hearing that she were better. She answered him with cold civility. He sat down for a few moments, and then getting up walked about the room. Elizabeth was surprised, but said not a word. After a silence of several minutes he came towards her in an agitated manner, and thus began,

"In vain have I struggled. It will not do. My feelings will not be repressed. You must allow me to tell you how ardently I admire and love you."

Elizabeth's astonishment was beyond expression. She stared, coloured, doubted, and was silent. This he considered sufficient encouragement, and the avowal of all that he felt and had long felt for her immediately followed. He spoke well, but there were feelings besides those of the heart to be detailed, and he was not more eloquent on the subject of tenderness than of pride. His sense of her inferiority—of its being a degradation—of the family obstacles which judgment had always opposed to inclination were dwelt on with a warmth which seemed due to the consequence he was wounding, but was very unlikely to recommend his suit.

In spite of her deeply-rooted dislike, she could not be insensible to the compliment of such a man's affection, and though her intentions did not vary for an instant, she was at first sorry for the pain he was to receive; till, roused to resentment by his subsequent language, she lost all compassion in anger. She tried, however, to compose herself to answer him with patience, when he should have done. He concluded with representing to her the strength of that attachment which, in spite of all his endeavours, he had found impossible to conquer; and with expressing his hope that it would now be rewarded by her acceptance of his hand. As he said this, she could easily see that he had no doubt of a favourable answer. He *spoke* of apprehension and anxiety, but his countenance expressed real security. Such a circumstance could only exasperate farther, and when he ceased, the colour rose into her cheeks, and she said,

"In such cases as this, it is, I believe, the established mode to express a sense of obligation for the sentiments avowed, however unequally they may be returned. It is natural that obligation should be felt, and if I could *feel* gratitude, I would now thank you. But I cannot—I have

161

never desired your good opinion, and you have certainly bestowed it most unwillingly. I am sorry to have occasioned pain to anyone. It has been most unconsciously done, however, and I hope will be of short duration. The feelings which, you tell me, have long prevented the acknowledgment of your regard can have little difficulty in overcoming it after this explanation."

Mr. Darcy, who was leaning against the mantlepiece with his eyes fixed on her face, seemed to catch her words with no less resentment than surprise. His complexion became pale with anger, and the disturbance of his mind was visible in every feature. He was struggling for the appearance of composure, and would not open his lips till he believed himself to have attained it. The pause was to Elizabeth's feelings dreadful. At length, in a voice of forced calmness, he said,

"And this is all the reply which I am to have the honour of expecting! I might, perhaps, wish to be informed why, with so little *endeavour* at civility, I am thus rejected. But it is of small importance."

"I might as well inquire," replied she, "why with so evident a design of offending and insulting me you chose to tell me that you liked me against your will, against your reason, and even against your character? Was not this some excuse for incivility, if I *was* uncivil? But I have other provocations. You know I have. Had not my own feelings decided against you, had they been indifferent, or had they even been favourable, do you think that any consideration would tempt me to accept the man who has been the means of ruining, perhaps forever, the happiness of a most beloved sister?"

As she pronounced these words, Mr. Darcy changed colour; but the emotion was short, and he listened without attempting to interrupt her while she continued.

"I have every reason in the world to think ill of you. No motive can excuse the unjust and ungenerous part you acted *there*. You dare not, you cannot deny that you have been the principal, if not the only means, of dividing them from each other, of exposing one to the censure of the world for caprice and instability, the other to its derision for disappointed hopes, and involving them both in misery of the acutest kind."

She paused, and saw with no slight indignation that he

was listening with an air which proved him wholly unmoved by any feeling of remorse. He even looked at her with a smile of affected incredulity.

"Can you deny that you have done it?" she repeated.

With assumed tranquility, he then replied, "I have no wish of denying that I did everything in my power to separate my friend from your sister, or that I rejoice in my success. Towards *him* I have been kinder than towards myself."

Elizabeth disdained the appearance of noticing this civil reflection, but its meaning did not escape, nor was it likely to conciliate her.

"But it is not merely this affair," she continued, "on which my dislike is founded. Long before it had taken place, my opinion of you was decided. Your character was unfolded in the recital which I received many months ago from Mr. Wickham. On this subject, what can you have to say? In what imaginary act of friendship can you here defend yourself? Or under what misrepresentation can you here impose upon others?"

"You take an eager interest in that gentleman's concerns," said Darcy in a less tranquil tone, and with a heightened colour.

"Who that knows what his misfortunes have been can help feeling an interest in him?"

"His misfortunes!" repeated Darcy contemptuously; "yes, his misfortunes have been great indeed."

"And of your infliction," cried Elizabeth with energy. "You have reduced him to his present state of poverty, comparative poverty. You have withheld the advantages, which you must know to have been designed for him. You have deprived the best years of his life of that independence which was no less his due than his desert. You have done all this! and yet you can treat the mention of his misfortunes with contempt and ridicule."

"And this," cried Darcy, as he walked with quick steps across the room, "is your opinion of me! This is the estimation in which you hold me! I thank you for explaining it so fully. My faults, according to this calculation, are heavy indeed! But perhaps," added he, stopping in his walk, and turning towards her, "these offences might have been overlooked, had not your pride been hurt by my honest confession of the scruples that had long prevented my forming any serious design. These bitter accusations might have been suppressed, had I with greater policy concealed my struggles, and flattered you into the belief of my being impelled by unqualified, unalloyed inclination; by reason, by reflection, by everything. But disguise of every sort is my abhorrence. Nor am I ashamed of the feelings I related. They were natural and just. Could you expect me to rejoice in the inferiority of your connections? To congratulate myself on the hope of relations whose condition in life is so decidedly beneath my own?"

Elizabeth felt herself growing more angry every moment; yet she tried to the utmost to speak with composure when she said,

"You are mistaken, Mr. Darcy, if you suppose that the mode of your declaration affected me in any other way than as it spared me the concern which I might have felt in refusing you, had you behaved in a more gentlemanlike manner."

She saw him start at this, but he said nothing, and she continued,

"You could not have made me the offer of your hand in any possible way that would have tempted me to accept it."

Again his astonishment was obvious; and he looked at her with an expression of mingled incredulity and mortification. She went on.

"From the very beginning, from the first moment, I may almost say, of my acquaintance with you, your manners impressing me with the fullest belief of your arrogance, your conceit, and your selfish disdain of the feelings of others, were such as to form that groundwork of disapprobation on which succeeding events have built so immovable a dislike; and I had not known you a month before I felt that you were the last man in the world whom I could ever be prevailed on to marry."

"You have said quite enough, madam. I perfectly comprehend your feelings, and have now only to be ashamed of what my own have been. Forgive me for having taken up so much of your time, and accept my best wishes for your health and happiness."

And with these words he hastily left the room, and

Elizabeth heard him the next moment open the front door and quit the house.

The tumult of her mind was now painfully great. She knew not how to support herself, and from actual weakness sat down and cried for half an hour. Her astonishment, as she reflected on what had passed, was increased by every review of it. That she should receive an offer of marriage from Mr. Darcy! that he should have been in love with her for so many months! so much in love as to wish to marry her in spite of all the objections which had made him prevent his friend's marrying her sister, and which must appear at least with equal force in his own case, was almost incredible! it was gratifying to have inspired unconsciously so strong an affection. But his pride, his abominable pride, his shameless avowal of what he had done with respect to Jane, his unpardonable assurance in acknowledging, though he could not justify it, and the unfeeling manner in which he had mentioned Mr. Wickham, his cruelty towards whom he had not attempted to deny, soon overcame the pity which the consideration of his attachment had for a moment excited.

She continued in very agitating reflections till the sound of Lady Catherine's carriage made her feel how unequal she was to encounter Charlotte's observation, and hurried away to her room.

CHAPTER TWELVE

ELIZABETH awoke the next morning to the same thoughts and meditations which had at length closed her eyes. She could not yet recover from the surprise of what had happened; it was impossible to think of anything else and totally indisposed for employment, she resolved soon after breakfast to indulge herself in air and exercise. She was proceeding directly to her favourite walk, when the recollection of Mr. Darcy's sometimes coming there stopped her, and instead of entering the park, she turned up the lane, which led her farther from the turnpike road. The park paling was still the boundary on one side, and she soon passed one of the gates into the ground.

After walking two or three times along that part of the lane, she was tempted, by the pleasantness of the morning, to stop at the gates and look into the park. The five weeks which she had now passed in Kent had made a great difference in the country, and everyday was adding to the verdure of the early trees. She was on the point of continuing her walk, when she caught a glimpse of a gentleman within the sort of grove which edged the park; he was moving that way; and fearful of its being Mr. Darcy, she was directly retreating. But the person who advanced was now near enough to see her, and stepping forward with eagerness, pronounced her name. She had turned away, but on hearing herself called, though in a voice which proved it to be Mr. Darcy, she moved again towards the gate. He had by that time reached it also, and holding out a letter, which she instinctively took, said with a look of haughty composure, "I have been walking in the grove sometime in the hope of meeting you. Will you do me the honour of reading that letter?" And then, with a slight bow, turned again into the plantation, and was soon out of sight.

With no expectation of pleasure, but with the strongest curiosity, Elizabeth opened the letter, and to her still increasing wonder, perceived an envelope containing two sheets of letter paper, written quite through, in a very close hand.—The envelope itself was likewise full.—Pursuing her way along the lane, she then began it. It was dated from Rosings, at eight o'clock in the morning, and was as follows:

"Be not alarmed, madam, on receiving this letter by the apprehension of its containing any repetition of those sentiments, or renewal of those offers, which were last night so disgusting to you. I write without any intention of paining you, or humbling myself, by dwelling on wishes, which, for the happiness of both, cannot be too soon forgotten; and the effort which the formation and the perusal of this letter must occasion should have been spared, had not my character required it to be written and read. You must, therefore, pardon the freedom with which I demand your attention; your feelings, I know, will bestow it unwillingly, but I demand it of your justice.

"Two offences of a very different nature, and by no

166

means of equal magnitude, you last night laid to my charge. The first mentioned was that regardless of the sentiments of either, I had detached Mr. Bingley from your sister—and the other, that I had, in defiance of various claims, in defiance of honour and humanity, ruined the immediate prosperity, and blasted the prospects of Mr. Wickham. Wilfully and wantonly to have thrown off the companion of my youth, the acknowledged favourite of my father, a young man who had scarcely any other dependence than on our patronage, and who had been brought up to expect its exertion, would be a depravity, to which the separation of two young persons, whose affection could be the growth of only a few weeks, could bear no comparison. But from the severity of that blame which was last night so liberally bestowed, respecting each circumstance, I shall hope to be in future secured, when the following account of my actions and their motives has been read. If, in the explanation of them which is due to myself, I am under the necessity of relating feelings which may be offensive to yours, I can only say that I am sorry.—The necessity must be obeyed—and farther apology would be absurd.—I had not been long in Hertfordshire before I saw, in common with others, that Bingley preferred your eldest sister to any other young woman in the country.—But it was not till the evening of the dance at Netherfield that I had any apprehension of his feeling a serious attachment.—I had often seen him in love before. At that ball, while I had the honour of dancing with you, I was first made acquainted, by Sir William Lucas's accidental information, that Bingley's attentions to your sister had given rise to a general expectation of their marriage. He spoke of it as a certain event, of which the time alone could be undecided. From that moment I observed my friend's behaviour attentively; and I could then perceive that his partiality for Miss Bennet was beyond what I had ever witnessed in him. Your sister I also watched.—Her look and manners were open, cheerful and engaging as ever, but without any symptom of peculiar regard, and I remained convinced from the evening's scrutiny that though she received his attentions with pleasure, she did not invite them by any participation of sentiment.—If *you* have not been mistaken here,

I must have been in an error. Your superior knowledge of your sister must make the latter probable.—If it be so, if I have been misled by such error to inflict pain on her, your resentment has not been unreasonable. But I shall not scruple to assert that the serenity of your sister's countenance and air was such as might have given the most acute observer a conviction that, however amiable her temper, her heart was not likely to be easily touched. That I was desirous of believing her indifferent is certain—but I will venture to say that my investigations and decisions are not usually influenced by my hopes or fears. I did not believe her to be indifferent because I wished it; I believed it on impartial conviction, as truly as I wished it in reason. My objections to the marriage were not merely those, which I last night acknowledged to have required the utmost force of passion to put aside in my own case; the want of connection could not be so great an evil to my friend as to me. But there were other causes of repugnance—causes which, though still existing, and existing to an equal degree in both instances, I had myself endeavoured to forget, because they were not immediately before me.—These causes must be stated, though briefly. —The situation of your mother's family, though objectionable, was nothing in comparison of that total want of propriety so frequently, so almost uniformly betrayed by herself, by your three younger sisters, and occasionally even by your father.—Pardon me.—It pains me to offend you. But amidst your concern for the defects of your nearest relations, and your displeasure at this representation of them, let it give you consolation to consider that to have conducted yourselves so as to avoid any share of the like censure is praise no less generally bestowed on you and your eldest sister than it is honourable to the sense and disposition of both. I will only say farther that from what passed that evening, my opinion of all parties was confirmed, and every inducement heightened, which could have led me before to preserve my friend from what I esteemed a most unhappy connection. He left Netherfield for London on the day following, as you, I am certain, remember, with the design of soon returning. The part which I acted is now to be explained. His sisters' uneasiness had been equally excited with my own; our coincidence of feeling was soon discovered; and, alike sensible that no time was to be lost in detaching their brother, we shortly resolved on joining him directly in London. We accordingly went—and there I readily engaged in the office of pointing out to my friend the certain evils of such a choice. I described and enforced them earnestly. But, however this remonstrance might have staggered or delayed his determination, I do not suppose that it would ultimately have prevented the marriage, had it not been seconded by the assurance, which I hesitated not in giving, of your sister's indifference. He had before believed her to return his affection with sincere, if not with equal regard. But Bingley has great natural modesty, with a stronger dependence on my judgment than on his own. To convince him, therefore, that he had deceived himself, was no very difficult point. To persuade him against returning into Hertfordshire, when that conviction had been given, was scarcely the work of a moment. I cannot blame myself for having done thus much. There is but one part of my conduct in the whole affair on which I do not reflect with satisfaction; it is that I condescended to adopt the measures of art so far as to conceal from him your sister's being in town. I knew it myself, as it was known to Miss Bingley, but her brother is even yet ignorant of it. That they might have met without ill consequence is perhaps probable; but his regard did not appear to me enough extinguished for him to see her without some danger. Perhaps this concealment, this disguise, was beneath me. It is done, however, and it was done for the best. On this subject I have nothing more to say, no other apology to offer. If I have wounded your sister's feelings, it was unknowingly done; and though the motives which governed me may to you very naturally appear insufficient, I have not yet learned to condemn them. With respect to that other, more weighty accusation, of having injured Mr. Wickham, I can only refute it by laying before you the whole of his connection with my family. Of what he has *particularly* accused me I am ignorant; but of the truth of what I shall relate, I can summon more than one witness of undoubted veracity. Mr. Wickham is the son of a very respectable man, who had for many years the management of all the Pemberley estates; and whose good conduct in the discharge of his trust naturally inclined my father to be of service to him, and on George Wickham, who was his godson, his kindness was therefore liberally bestowed. My father supported him at school, and afterwards at Cambridge—most important assistance, as his own father, always poor from the extravagance of his wife, would have been unable to give him a gentleman's education. My father was not only fond of this young man's society, whose manners were always engaging; he had also the highest opinion of him, and hoping the church would be his profession, intended to provide for him in it. As for myself, it is many, many years since I first began to think of him in a very different manner. The vicious propensities—the want of principle which he was careful to guard from the knowledge of his best friend could not escape the observation of a young man of nearly the same age with himself, and who had opportunities of seeing him in unguarded moments, which Mr. Darcy could not have. Here again I shall give you pain—to what degree you only can tell. But whatever may be the sentiments which Mr. Wickham has created, a suspicion of their nature shall not prevent me from unfolding his real character. It adds even another motive. My excellent father died about five years ago; and his attachment to Mr. Wickham was to the last so steady that in his will he particularly recommended it to me to promote his advancement in the best manner that his profession might allow, and if he took orders, desired that a valuable family living might be his as soon as it became vacant. There was also a legacy of one thousand pounds. His own father did not long survive mine, and within half a year from these events, Mr. Wickham wrote to inform me that, having finally resolved against taking orders, he hoped I should not think it unreasonable for him to expect some more immediate pecuniary advantage, in lieu of the preferment by which he could not be benefited. He had some intention, he added, of studying the law, and I must be aware that the interest of one thousand pounds would be a very insufficient support therein. I rather wished, than believed him to be sincere; but at any rate, was perfectly ready to accede to his proposal. I knew that Mr. Wickham ought not to be a clergyman. The business was therefore soon settled. He resigned all claim to assistance in the church, were it possible that he could ever be in a situation to receive it, and accepted in return three thousand pounds. All connection between us seemed now dissolved. I thought too ill of him to invite him to Pemberley, or admit his society in town. In town I believe he chiefly lived, but his studying the law was a mere pretence, and being now free from all restraint, his life was a life of idleness and dissipation. For about three years I heard little of him; but on the decease of the incumbent of the living which had been designed for him, he applied to me again by letter for the presentation. His circumstances, he assured me, and I had no difficulty in believing it, were exceedingly bad. He had found the law a most unprofitable study, and was now absolutely resolved on being ordained, if I would present him to the living in question—of which he trusted there could be little doubt, as he was well assured that I had no other person to provide for, and I could not have forgotten my revered father's intentions. You will hardly blame me for refusing to comply with this entreaty, or for resisting every repetition of it. His resentment was in proportion to the distress of his circumstances—and he was doubtless as violent in his abuse of me to others as in his reproaches to myself. After this period, every appearance of acquaintance was dropped. How he lived I know not. But last summer he was again most painfully obtruded on my notice. I must now mention a circumstance which I would wish to forget myself, and which no obligation less than the present should induce me to unfold to any human being. Having said thus much, I feel no doubt of your secrecy. My sister, who is more than ten years my junior, was left to the guardianship of my mother's nephew, Colonel Fitzwilliam, and myself. About a year ago, she was taken from school, and an establishment formed for her in London; and last summer she went with the lady who presided over it to Ramsgate; and thither also went Mr. Wickham, undoubtedly by design; for there proved to have been a prior acquaintance between him and Mrs. Younge, in whose character we were most unhappily deceived; and by her connivance and aid, he so far recommended himself to Georgiana, whose affectionate heart retained a strong impression of his kindness to her as a child, that she was persuaded to believe herself in love, and to consent to an elopement. She was then but fifteen, which must be her excuse; and after stating her imprudence, I am happy to add that I owed the knowledge of it to herself. I joined them unexpectedly a day or two before the intended elopement, and then Georgiana, unable to support the idea of grieving and offending a brother whom she almost looked up to as a father, acknowledged the whole to me. You may imagine what I felt and how I acted. Regard for my sister's credit and feelings prevented any public exposure, but I wrote to Mr. Wickham, who left the place immediately, and Mrs. Younge was of course removed from her charge. Mr. Wickham's chief object was unquestionably my sister's fortune, which is thirty thousand pounds; but I cannot help supposing that the hope of revenging himself on me was a strong inducement. His revenge would have been complete indeed. This, madam, is a faithful narrative of every event in which we have been concerned together; and if you do not absolutely reject it as false, you will, I hope, acquit me henceforth of cruelty towards Mr. Wickham. I know not in what manner, under what form of falsehood he has imposed on you; but his success is not perhaps to be wondered at. Ignorant as you previously were of everything concerning either, detection could not be in your power, and suspicion certainly not in your inclination. You may possibly wonder why all this was not told you last night. But I was not then master enough of myself to know what could or ought to be revealed. For the truth of everything here related, I can appeal more particularly to the testimony of Colonel Fitzwilliam, who from our near relationship and constant intimacy, and still more as one of the executors of my father's will, has been unavoidably acquainted with every particular of these transactions. If your abhorrence of *me* should make *my* assertions valueless, you cannot be prevented by the same cause from confiding in my cousin; and that there may be the possibility of consulting him, I shall endeavour to find some opportunity of putting this letter in your hands in the course of the morning. I will only add, God bless you.

"FITZWILLIAM DARCY."

CHAPTER THIRTEEN

IF Elizabeth, when Mr. Darcy gave her the letter, did not expect it to contain a renewal of his offers, she had formed no expectation at all of its contents. But such as they were, it may be well supposed how eagerly she went through them, and what a contrariety of emotion they excited. Her feelings as she read were scarcely to be defined. With amazement did she first understand that he believed any apology to be in his power; and steadfastly was she persuaded that he could have no explanation to give, which a just sense of shame would not conceal. With a strong prejudice against everything he might say, she began his account of what had happened at Netherfield. She read, with an eagerness which hardly left her power of comprehension, and from impatience of knowing what the next sentence might bring, was incapable of attending to the sense of the one before her eyes. His belief of her sister's insensibility she instantly resolved to be false, and his account of the real, the worst objections to the match, made her too angry to have any wish of doing him justice. He expressed no regret for what he had done which satisfied her; his style was not penitent, but haughty. It was all pride and insolence.

But when this subject was succeeded by his account of Mr. Wickham, when she read with somewhat clearer attention, a relation of events, which, if true, must overthrow every cherished opinion of his worth, and which bore so alarming an affinity to his own history of himself, her feelings were yet more acutely painful and more difficult of definition. Astonishment, apprehension, and even horror oppressed her. She wished to discredit it entirely, repeatedly exclaiming, "This must be false! This cannot be! This must be the grossest falsehood!"—and when she had gone through the whole letter, though scarcely knowing anything of the last page or two, put it hastily away, protesting that she would not regard it, that she would never look at it again.

In this perturbed state of mind, with thoughts that could rest on nothing, she walked on; but it would not do; in half a minute the letter was unfolded again, and collecting herself as well as she could, she again began the mortifying perusal of all that related to Wickham, and commanded herself so far as to examine the meaning of every sentence. The account of his connection with the Pemberley family was exactly what he had related himself; and the kindness of the late Mr. Darcy, though she had not before known its extent, agreed equally well with his own words. So far each recital confirmed the other: but when she came to the will, the difference was great. What Wickham had said of the living was fresh in her memory, and as she recalled his very words, it was impossible not to feel that there was gross duplicity on one side or the other; and, for a few moments, she flattered herself that her wishes did not err. But when she read, and reread with the closest attention, the particulars immediately following of Wickham's resigning all pretensions to the living, of his receiving in lieu so considerable a sum as three thousand pounds, again was she forced to hesitate. She put down the letter, weighed every circumstance with what she meant to be impartiality—deliberated on the probability of each statement—but with little success. On both sides it was only assertion. Again she read on. But every line proved more clearly that the affair, which she had believed it impossible that any contrivance could so represent as to render Mr. Darcy's conduct in it less than infamous, was capable of a turn which must make him entirely blameless throughout the whole.

The extravagance and general profligacy which he scrupled not to lay to Mr. Wickham's charge exceedingly shocked her; the more so as she could bring no proof of its injustice. She had never heard of him before his entrance into the ——shire Militia, in which he had engaged at the persuasion of the young man, who, on meeting him accidentally in town, had there renewed a slight acquaintance. Of his former way of life, nothing had been known in Hertfordshire but what he told himself. As to his real character, had information been in her power, she had never felt a wish of inquiring. His countenance, voice, and manner, had established him at once in the possession of every virtue. She tried to recollect some instance of goodness, some distinguished trait of integrity or benevolence, that might rescue him from the attacks of Mr. Darcy; or at least, by the predominance of virtue, atone for those casual errors under which she would endeavour to class what Mr. Darcy had described as the idleness and vice of many years continuance. But no such recollection befriended her. She could see him instantly before her in every charm of air and address; but she could remember no more substantial good than the general approbation of the neighbourhood, and the regard which his social powers had gained him in the mess. After pausing on this point a considerable while, she once more continued to read. But, alas! the story which followed of his designs on Miss Darcy received some confirmation from what had passed between Colonel Fitzwilliam and herself only the morning before; and at last she was referred for the truth of every particular to Colonel Fitzwilliam himself—from whom she had previously received the information of his near concern in all his cousin's affairs, and whose character she had no reason to question. At one time she had almost resolved on applying to him, but the idea was checked by the awkwardness of the application, and at length wholly banished by the conviction that Mr. Darcy would never have hazarded such a proposal, if he had not been well assured of his cousin's corroboration.

She perfectly remembered everything that had passed in conversation between Wickham and herself in their first evening at Mr. Philips's. Many of his expressions were still fresh in her memory. She was *now* struck with the impropriety of such communications to a stranger, and wondered it had escaped her before. She saw the indelicacy of putting himself forward as he had done, and the inconsistency of his professions with his conduct. She remembered that he had boasted of having no fear of seeing Mr. Darcy—that Mr. Darcy might leave the country, but that *he* should stand his ground; yet he had avoided the Netherfield ball the very next week. She remembered also that till the Netherfield family had quitted the country, he had told his story to no one but herself; but that after their removal, it had been everywhere discussed; that he had then no reserves, no scruples in sinking Mr. Darcy's character, though he had assured her that respect for the father would always prevent his exposing the son.

How differently did everything now appear in which he was concerned! His attentions to Miss King were now the consequence of views solely and hatefully mercenary; and the mediocrity of her fortune proved no longer the moderation of his wishes, but his eagerness to grasp at anything. His behaviour to herself could now have had no tolerable motive; he had either been deceived with regard to her fortune, or had been gratifying his vanity by encouraging the preference which she believed she had most incautiously shown. Every lingering struggle in his favour grew fainter and fainter; and in farther justification of Mr. Darcy, she could not but allow that Mr. Bingley, when questioned by Jane, had long ago asserted his blamelessness in the affair; that proud and repulsive as were his manners, she had never, in the whole course of their acquaintance, an acquaintance which had latterly brought them much together and given her a sort of intimacy with his ways, seen anything that betrayed him to be unprincipled or unjust—anything that spoke him of irreligious or immoral habits. That among his own connections he was esteemed and valued—that even Wickham had allowed him merit as a brother, and that she had often heard him speak so affectionately of his sister as to prove him capable of *some* amiable feeling. That had his actions been what Wickham represented them, so gross a violation of everything right could hardly have been concealed from the world; and that friendship between a person capable of it, and such an amiable man as Mr. Bingley, was incomprehensible.

She grew absolutely ashamed of herself. Of neither Darcy nor Wickham could she think without feeling that she had been blind, partial, prejudiced, absurd.

"How despicably have I acted!" she cried. "I, who have prided myself on my discernment!—I, who have valued myself on my abilities! who have often disdained the generous candour of my sister, and gratified my vanity in useless or blameable distrust.—How humiliating is this discovery!—Yet, how just a humiliation!—Had I been in love, I could not have been more wretchedly blind. But vanity, not love, has been my folly. Pleased with the preference of one, and offended by the neglect of the other, on the very beginning of our acquaintance I have courted prepossession and ignorance, and driven reason away, where either were concerned. Till this moment I never knew myself.

From herself to Jane—from Jane to Bingley, her thoughts were in a line which soon brought to her recollection that Mr. Darcy's explanation *there* had appeared very insufficient; and she read it again. Widely different was the effect of a second perusal.—How could she deny that credit to his assertions, in one instance, which she had been obliged to give in the other?—He declared himself to have been totally unsuspicious of her sister's attachment; and she could not help remembering what Charlotte's opinion had always been. Neither could she deny the justice of his description of Jane. She felt that Jane's feelings, though fervent, were little displayed, and that there was a constant complacency in her air and manner, not often united with great sensibility.

When she came to that part of the letter in which her family were mentioned, in terms of such mortifying, yet merited reproach, her sense of shame was severe. The justice of the charge struck her too forcibly for denial, and the circumstances to which he particularly alluded, as having passed at the Netherfield ball, and as confirming all his first disapprobation, could not have made a stronger impression on his mind than on hers.

The compliment to herself and her sister was not unfelt. It soothed, but it could not console her for the contempt which had been thus self-attracted by the rest of her family; and as she considered that Jane's disappointment had in fact been the work of her nearest relations, and reflected how materially the credit of both must be hurt by such impropriety of conduct, she felt depressed beyond anything she had ever known before.

After wandering along the lane for two hours, giving way to every variety of thought, reconsidering events, determining probabilities, and reconciling herself as well as she could, to a change so sudden and so important, fatigue, and a recollection of her long absence, made her at length return home; and she entered the house with the wish of appearing cheerful as usual, and the resolution of repressing such reflections as must make her unfit for conversation.

She was immediately told that the two gentlemen from Rosings had each called during her absence; Mr. Darcy, only for a few minutes to take leave, but that Colonel Fitzwilliam had been sitting with them at least an hour, hoping for her return, and almost resolving to walk after her till she could be found.—Elizabeth could but just *affect* concern in missing him; she really rejoiced at it. Colonel Fitzwilliam was no longer an object. She could think only of her letter.

CHAPTER FOURTEEN

THE two gentlemen left Rosings the next morning; and Mr. Collins having been in waiting near the lodges to make them his parting obeisance was able to bring home the pleasing intelligence of their appearing in very good health, and in as tolerable spirits as could be expected, after the melancholy scene so lately gone through at Rosings. To Rosings he then hastened to console Lady Catherine and her daughter; and on his return brought back, with great satisfaction, a message from her ladyship, importing that she felt herself so dull as to make her very desirous of having them all to dine with her.

Elizabeth could not see Lady Catherine without recollecting that had she chosen it, she might by this time have been presented to her as her future niece; nor could she think, without a smile, of what her ladyship's indignation would have been. "What would she have said?—how would she have behaved?" were questions with which she amused herself.

Their first subject was the diminution of the Rosings party.—"I assure you, I feel it exceedingly," said Lady Catherine; "I believe nobody feels the loss of friends so much as I do. But I am particularly attached to these young men; and know them to be so much attached to me!—They were excessively sorry to go! But so they always are. The dear colonel rallied his spirits tolerably till just at last; but Darcy seemed to feel it most acutely, more I think than last year. His attachment to Rosings certainly increases."

Mr. Collins had a compliment, and an allusion to throw in here, which were kindly smiled on by the mother and daughter.

Lady Catherine observed after dinner that Miss Bennet seemed out of spirits, and immediately accounting for it herself by supposing that she did not like to go home again so soon, she added,

"But if that is the case, you must write to your mother to beg that you may stay a little longer. Mrs. Collins will be very glad of your company, I am sure."

"I am much obliged to your ladyship for your kind invitation," replied Elizabeth, "but it is not in my power to accept it. I must be in town next Saturday."

"Why, at that rate, you will have been here only six weeks. I expected you to stay two months. I told Mrs. Collins so before you came. There can be no occasion for your going so soon. Mrs. Bennet could certainly spare you for another fortnight."

"But my father cannot. He wrote last week to hurry my return."

"Oh! your father of course may spare you, if your mother can. Daughters are never of so much consequence to a father. And if you will stay another *month* complete, it will be in my power to take one of you as far as London, for I am going there early in June for a week; and as Dawson does not object to the barouche box, there will be very good room for one of you—and indeed, if the weather should happen to be cool, I should not object to taking you both, as you are neither of you large."

"You are all kindness, madam; but I believe we must abide by our original plan."

Lady Catherine seemed resigned.

"Mrs. Collins, you must send a servant with them. You know I always speak my mind, and I cannot bear the idea of two young women travelling post by themselves. It is highly improper. You must contrive to send somebody. I have the greatest dislike in the world to that sort of thing. Young women should always be properly guarded and attended, according to their situation in life. When my niece Georgiana went to Ramsgate last summer, I made a point of having two men servants go with her. Miss Darcy, the daughter of Mr. Darcy of Pemberley, and Lady Anne could not have appeared with propriety in a different manner. I am excessively attentive to all those things. You must send John with the young ladies, Mrs. Collins. I am glad it occurred to me to mention it; for it would really be discreditable to *you* to let them go alone."

"My uncle is to send a servant for us."

"Oh!—Your uncle!—He keeps a man-servant, does he?—I am very glad you have somebody who thinks of those things. Where shall you change horses?—Oh! Bromley, of course.—If you mention my name at the Bell, you will be attended to."

Lady Catherine had many other questions to ask respecting their journey, and as she did not answer them all herself, attention was necessary, which Elizabeth believed to be lucky for her; or, with a mind so occupied, she might have forgotten where she was. Reflection must be reserved for solitary hours; whenever she was alone, she gave way to it as the greatest relief; and not a day went by without a solitary walk, in which she might indulge in all the delight of unpleasant recollections.

Mr. Darcy's letter she was in a fair way of soon knowing by heart. She studied every sentence: and her feelings towards its writer were at times widely different. When she remembered the style of his address, she was still full of indignation; but when she considered how unjustly she had condemned and upbraided him, her anger was turned against herself; and his disappointed feelings became the object of compassion. His attachment excited gratitude, his general character respect; but she could not approve him; nor could she for a moment repent her refusal, or feel the slightest inclination ever to see him again. In her own past behaviour, there was a constant source of vexation and regret; and in the unhappy defects of her family a subject of yet heavier chagrin. They were hopeless of remedy. Her father, contented with laughing at them, would never exert himself to restrain the wild giddiness of his youngest daughters; and her mother, with manners so far from right herself, was entirely insensible of the evil. Elizabeth had frequently united with Jane in an endeavour to check the imprudence of Catherine and Lydia; but while they were supported by their mother's indulgence, what chance could there be of improvement? Catherine, weak-spirited, irritable, and completely under Lydia's guidance, had been always affronted by their advice; and Lydia, self-willed and careless, would scarcely give them a hearing. They were ignorant, idle, and vain. While there was an officer in Meryton, they would flirt with him; and while Meryton was within a walk of Longbourn, they would be going there forever.

Anxiety on Jane's behalf was another prevailing concern, and Mr. Darcy's explanation, by restoring Bingley to all her former good opinion, heightened the sense of what Jane had lost. His affection was proved to have been sincere, and his conduct cleared of all blame, unless any could attach to the implicitness of his confidence in his friend. How grievous then was the thought that of a situation so desirable in every respect, so replete with advantage, so promising for happiness, Jane had been deprived by the folly and indecorum of her own family!

When to these recollections was added the development of Wickham's character, it may be easily believed that the happy spirits which had seldom been depressed before were now so much affected as to make it almost impossible for her to appear tolerably cheerful.

Their engagements at Rosings were as frequent during the last week of her stay as they had been at first. The very last evening was spent there; and her ladyship again inquired minutely into the particulars of their journey, gave them directions as to the best method of packing, and was so urgent on the necessity of placing gowns in the only right way, that Maria thought herself obliged, on her return, to undo all the work of the morning, and pack her trunk afresh.

When they parted, Lady Catherine, with great condescension, wished them a good journey, and invited them to come to Hunsford again next year; and Miss De Bourgh exerted herself so far as to curtsy and hold out her hand to both.

CHAPTER FIFTEEN

On Saturday morning Elizabeth and Mr. Collins met for breakfast a few minutes before the others appeared; and he took the opportunity of paying the parting civilities which he deemed indispensably necessary.

"I know not, Miss Elizabeth," said he, "whether Mrs. Collins has yet expressed her sense of your kindness in coming to us, but I am very certain you will not leave the house without receiving her thanks for it. The favour of your company has been much felt, I assure you. We know how little there is to tempt any one to our humble abode. Our plain manner of living, our small rooms, and few domestics, and the little we see of the world, must make Hunsford extremely dull to a young lady like yourself; but I hope you will believe us grateful for the condescension, and that we have done everything in our power to prevent your spending your time unpleasantly."

Elizabeth was eager with her thanks and assurances of happiness. She had spent six weeks with great enjoyment; and the pleasure of being with Charlotte, and the kind attentions she had received, must make *her* feel the obliged. Mr. Collins was gratified; and with a more smiling solemnity replied,

"It gives me the greatest pleasure to hear that you have passed your time not disagreeably. We have certainly done our best; and most fortunately having it in our power to introduce you to very superior society, and from our connection with Rosings, the frequent means of varying the humble home scene, I think we may flatter ourselves that your Hunsford visit cannot have been entirely irksome. Our situation with regard to Lady Catherine's family is indeed the sort of extraordinary advantage and blessing which few can boast. You see on what a footing we are. You see how continually we are engaged there. In truth I must acknowledge that, with all the disadvantages of this humble parsonage, I should not think any one abiding in it an object of compassion, while they are sharers of our intimacy at Rosings."

Words were insufficient for the elevation of his feelings; and he was obliged to walk about the room, while Elizabeth tried to unite civility and truth in a few short sentences.

"You may, in fact, carry a very favourable report of us into Hertfordshire, my dear cousin. I flatter myself at least that you will be able to do so. Lady Catherine's great attentions to Mrs. Collins you have been a daily witness of; and altogether I trust it does not appear that your friend has drawn an unfortunate—but on this point it will be as well to be silent. Only let me assure you, my dear Miss Elizabeth, that I can from my heart most cordially wish you equal felicity in marriage. My dear Charlotte and I have but one mind and one way of thinking. There is in everything a most remarkable resemblance of character and ideas between us. We seem to have been designed for each other."

Elizabeth could safely say that it was a great happiness where that was the case, and with equal sincerity could add that she firmly believed and rejoiced in his domestic comforts. She was not sorry, however, to have the recital of them interrupted by the entrance of the lady from whom they sprung. Poor Charlotte!—it was melancholy to leave her to such society! But she had chosen it with her eyes open; and though evidently regretting that her visitors were to go, she did not seem to ask for compassion. Her home and her housekeeping, her parish and her poultry, and all their dependent concerns, had not yet lost their charms.

At length the chaise arrived, the trunks were fastened on, the parcels placed within, and it was pronounced to be ready. After an affectionate parting between the friends, Elizabeth was attended to the carriage by Mr. Collins, and as they walked down the garden, he was commissioning her with his best respects to all her family, not forgetting his thanks for the kindness he had received at Longbourn in the winter, and his compliments to Mr. and Mrs. Gardiner, though unknown. He then handed her in, Maria followed, and the door was on the point of being closed, when he suddenly reminded them, with some consternation, that they had hitherto forgotten to leave any message for the ladies of Rosings.

"But," he added, "you will of course wish to have your humble respects delivered to them, with your grateful thanks for their kindness to you while you have been here."

Elizabeth made no objection; the door was then allowed to be shut, and the carriage drove off.

"Good gracious!" cried Maria, after a few minutes silence, "it seems but a day or two since we first came! —and yet how many things have happened!"

"A great many indeed," said her companion with a sigh.

"We have dined nine times at Rosings, besides drinking tea there twice! How much I shall have to tell!"

Elizabeth privately added, "And how much I shall have to conceal."

Their journey was performed without much conversation, or any alarm; and within four hours of their leaving Hunsford, they reached Mr. Gardiner's house, where they were to remain a few days.

Jane looked well, and Elizabeth had little opportunity of studying her spirits, amidst the various engagements which the kindness of her aunt had reserved for them. But Jane was to go home with her, and at Longbourn there would be leisure enough for observation.

It was not without an effort meanwhile that she could wait even for Longbourn, before she told her sister of Mr. Darcy's proposals. To know that she had the power of revealing what would so exceedingly astonish Jane, and must, at the same time, so highly gratify whatever of her own vanity she had not yet been able to reason away, was such a temptation to openness as nothing could have conquered, but the state of indecision in which she remained, as to the extent of what she should communicate; and her fear, if she once entered on the subject, of being hurried into repeating something of Bingley, which might only grieve her sister farther.

CHAPTER SIXTEEN

IT was the second week in May in which the three young ladies set out together from Gracechurch Street for the town of———in Hertfordshire; and, as they drew near the appointed inn where Mr. Bennet's carriage was to meet them, they quickly perceived, in token of the coachman's punctuality, both Kitty and Lydia looking out of a dining-room upstairs. These two girls had been above an hour in the place, happily employed in visiting an opposite milliner, watching the sentinel on guard, and dressing a salad and cucumber.

After welcoming their sisters, they triumphantly displayed a table set out with such cold meat as an inn larder usually affords, exclaiming, "Is not this nice? is not this an agreeable surprise?"

"And we mean to treat you all," added Lydia; "but you must lend us the money, for we have just spent ours at the shop out there." Then showing her purchases: "Look here, I have bought this bonnet. I do not think it is very pretty; but I thought I might as well buy it as not. I shall pull it to pieces as soon as I get home, and see if I can make it up any better."

And when her sisters abused it as ugly, she added, with perfect unconcern, "Oh! but there were two or three much uglier in the shop; and when I have bought some prettier-coloured satin to trim it with fresh, I think it will be very tolerable. Besides, it will not much signify what one wears this summer, after the———shire have left Meryton, and they are going in a fortnight."

"Are they indeed?" cried Elizabeth, with the greatest satisfaction.

"They are going to be encamped near Brighton; and I do so want papa to take us all there for the summer! It would be such a delicious scheme, and I dare say would hardly cost anything at all. Mamma would like to go too of all things! Only think what a miserable summer else we shall have!"

"Yes," thought Elizabeth, *"that* would be a delightful scheme, indeed, and completely do for us at once. Good Heaven! Brighton, and a whole campful of soldiers, to us, who have been overset already by one poor regiment of militia, and the monthly balls of Meryton."

"Now I have got some news for you," said Lydia, as they sat down to table. "What do you think? It is excellent news, capital news, and about a certain person that we all like."

Jane and Elizabeth looked at each other, and the waiter was told that he need not stay. Lydia laughed, and said,

"Aye, that is just like your formality and discretion. You thought the waiter must not hear, as if he cared! I dare say he often hears worse things said than I am going to say. But he is an ugly fellow! I am glad he is gone. I never saw such a long chin in my life. Well, but now for my news: it is about dear Wickham; too good for the waiter, is not it? There is no danger of Wickham's marrying Mary King. There's for you! She is gone down to her uncle at Liverpool; gone to stay. Wickham is safe."

"And Mary King is safe!" added Elizabeth, "safe from a connection imprudent as to fortune."

"She is a great fool for going away, if she liked him."

"But I hope there is no strong attachment on either side," said Jane.

"I am sure there is not on *his*. I will answer for it, he never cared three straws about her. Who *could* about such a nasty little freckled thing?"

Elizabeth was shocked to think that, however incapable of such coarseness of *expression* herself, the coarseness of the *sentiment* was little other than her own breast had formerly harboured and fancied liberal!

As soon as all had ate, and the elder ones paid, the carriage was ordered; and after some contrivance, the whole party, with all their boxes, workbags, and parcels, and the unwelcome addition of Kitty's and Lydia's purchases, were seated in it.

"How nicely we are crammed in!" cried Lydia. "I am glad I bought my bonnet, if it is only for the fun of having another bandbox! Well, now let us be quite comfortable and snug, and talk and laugh all the way home. And in the first place, let us hear what has happened to you all since you went away. Have you seen any pleasant men? Have you had any flirting? I was in great hopes that one of you would have got a husband before you came back. Jane will be quite an old maid soon, I declare. She is almost three and twenty! Lord, how ashamed I should be of not being married before three and twenty! My aunt Philips wants you so to get husbands, you can't think. She says Lizzy had better have taken Mr. Collins; but *I* do not think there would have been any fun in it. Lord! how I should like to be married before any of you; and then I would chaperon you about to all the balls. Dear me! we had such a good piece of fun the other day at Colonel Forster's. Kitty and me were to spend the day there, and Mrs. Forster promised to have a little dance in the evening (by the by, Mrs. Forster and me are *such* friends!); and so she asked the two Harringtons to come, but Harriet was ill, and so Pen was forced to come by herself; and then, what do you think we did? We dressed up Chamberlayne in woman's clothes, on purpose to pass for a lady—only think what fun! Not a soul knew it, but Colonel and Mrs. Forster, and Kitty and me, except for my aunt, for we were forced to borrow one of her gowns; and you cannot imagine how well he looked! When Denny, and Wickham, and Pratt, and two or three more of the men came in, they did not know him in the least. Lord! how I laughed! and so did Mrs. Forster. I thought I should have died. And *that* made the men suspect something, and then they soon found out what was the matter."

With such kind of histories of their parties and good jokes did Lydia, assisted by Kitty's hints and additions, endeavour to amuse her companions all the way to Longbourn. Elizabeth listened as little as she could, but there was no escaping the frequent mention of Wickham's name.

Their reception at home was most kind. Mrs. Bennet rejoiced to see Jane in undiminished beauty; and more than once during dinner did Mr. Bennet say voluntarily to Elizabeth,

"I am glad you are come back, Lizzy."

Their party in the dining-room was large, for almost all the Lucases came to meet Maria and hear the news: and various were the subjects which occupied them; Lady Lucas was inquiring of Maria across the table after the welfare and poultry of her eldest daughter; Mrs. Bennet was doubly engaged, on one hand collecting an account of the present fashions from Jane, who sat some way below her, and on the other hand, retailing them all to the younger Miss Lucases; and Lydia, in a voice rather louder than any other person's, was enumerating the various pleasures of the morning to anybody who would hear her.

"Oh! Mary," said she, "I wish you had gone with us, for we had such fun! As we went along, Kitty and me drew up all the blinds, and pretended there was nobody in the coach; and I should have gone so all the way, if Kitty had not been sick; and when we got to the George, I do think we behaved very handsomely, for we treated the other three with the nicest cold luncheon in the world, and if you would have gone, we would have treated you too. And then when we came away it was such fun! I thought we never should have got into the coach. I was ready to die of laughter. And then we were so merry all the way home! We talked and laughed so loud that anybody might have heard us ten miles off!"

To this, Mary very gravely replied, "Far be it from me, my dear sister, to depreciate such pleasures. They would doubtless be congenial with the generality of female minds. But I confess they would have no charms for *me*. I should infinitely prefer a book."

But of this answer Lydia heard not a word. She seldom listened to anybody for more than half a minute, and never attended to Mary at all.

In the afternoon Lydia was urgent with the rest of the girls to walk to Meryton and see how everybody went on; but Elizabeth steadily opposed the scheme. It should not be said that the Miss Bennets could not be at home half a day before they were in pursuit of the officers. There was another reason for her opposition. She dreaded seeing Wickham again, and was resolved to avoid it as long as possible. The comfort to *her* of the regiment's approaching removal was indeed beyond expression. In a fortnight they were to go, and once gone, she hoped there could be nothing more to plague her on his account.

She had not been many hours at home before she found that the Brighton scheme, of which Lydia had given them a hint at the inn, was under frequent discussion between her parents. Elizabeth saw directly that her father had not the smallest intention of yielding; but his answers were at the same time so vague and equivocal that her mother, though often disheartened, had never yet despaired of succeeding at last.

CHAPTER SEVENTEEN

ELIZABETH'S impatience to acquaint Jane with what had happened could no longer be overcome; and at length resolving to suppress every particular in which her sister was concerned, and preparing her to be surprised, she related to her the next morning the chief of the scene between Mr. Darcy and herself.

Miss Bennet's astonishment was soon lessened by the strong sisterly partiality which made any admiration of Elizabeth appear perfectly natural; and all surprise was shortly lost in other feelings. She was sorry that Mr. Darcy should have delivered his sentiments in a manner so little suited to recommend them; but still more was she grieved for the unhappiness which her sister's refusal must have given him.

"His being so sure of succeeding was wrong," said she; "and certainly ought not to have appeared; but consider how much it must increase his disappointment."

"Indeed," replied Elizabeth, "I am heartily sorry for him; but he has other feelings which will probably soon drive away his regard for me. You do not blame me, however, for refusing him?"

"Blame you! Oh, no."

"But you blame me for having spoken so warmly of Wickham."

"No—I do not know that you were wrong in saying what you did."

"But you *will* know it, when I have told you what happened the very next day."

She then spoke of the letter, repeating the whole of its contents as far as they concerned George Wickham. What a stroke was this for poor Jane! who would willingly have gone through the world without believing that so much wickedness existed in the whole race of mankind as was here collected in one individual. Nor was Darcy's vindication, though grateful to her feelings, capable of consoling her for such discovery. Most earnestly did she labour to prove the probability of error, and seek to clear one, without involving the other.

"This will not do," said Elizabeth. "You never will

be able to make both of them good for anything. Take your choice, but you must be satisfied with only one. There is but such a quantity of merit between them; just enough to make one good sort of man; and of late it has been shifting about pretty much. For my part, I am inclined to believe it all Mr. Darcy's, but you shall do as you choose."

It was sometime, however, before a smile could be extorted from Jane.

"I do not know when I have been more shocked," said she. "Wickham so very bad! It is almost past belief. And poor Mr. Darcy! dear Lizzy, only consider what he must have suffered. Such a disappointment! and with the knowledge of your ill opinion too! and having to relate such a thing of his sister! It is really too distressing. I am sure you must feel it so."

"Oh! no, my regret and compassion are all done away by seeing you so full of both. I know you will do him such ample justice that I am growing every moment more unconcerned and indifferent. Your profusion makes me saving; and if you lament over him much longer, my heart will be as light as a feather."

"Poor Wickham; there is such an expression of goodness in his countenance! such an openness and gentleness in his manner."

"There certainly was some great mismanagement in the education of those two young men. One has got all the goodness, and the other all the appearance of it."

"I never thought Mr. Darcy so deficient in the *appearance* of it as you used to do."

"And yet I meant to be uncommonly clever in taking so decided a dislike to him, without any reason. It is such a spur to one's genius, such an opening for wit to have a dislike of that kind. One may be continually abusive without saying anything just; but one cannot be always laughing at a man without now and then stumbling on something witty."

"Lizzy, when you first read that letter, I am sure you could not treat the matter as you do now."

"Indeed I could not. I was uncomfortable enough. I was very uncomfortable, I may say unhappy. And with no one to speak to of what I felt, no Jane to comfort me and say that I had not been so very weak and vain and nonsensical as I knew I had! Oh! how I wanted you!"

"How unfortunate that you should have used such very strong expressions in speaking of Wickham to Mr. Darcy, for now they *do* appear wholly undeserved."

"Certainly. But the misfortune of speaking with bitterness is a most natural consequence of the prejudices I had been encouraging. There is one point on which I want your advice. I want to be told whether I ought, or ought not, to make our acquaintance in general understand Wickham's character."

Miss Bennet paused a little and then replied, "Surely there can be no occasion for exposing him so dreadfully. What is your own opinion?"

"That it ought not to be attempted. Mr. Darcy has not authorized me to make his communication public. On the contrary, every particular relative to his sister was meant to be kept as much as possible to myself; and if I endeavour to undeceive people as to the rest of his conduct, who will believe me? The general prejudice against Mr. Darcy is so violent that it would be the death of half the good people in Meryton to attempt to place him in an amiable light. I am not equal to it. Wickham will soon be gone; and therefore it will not signify to anybody here what he really is. Sometime hence it will be all found out, and then we may laugh at their stupidity in not knowing it before. At present I will say nothing about it."

"You are quite right. To have his errors made public might ruin him forever. He is now perhaps sorry for what he has done, and anxious to re-establish a character. We must not make him desperate."

The tumult of Elizabeth's mind was allayed by this conversation. She had got rid of two of the secrets which had weighed on her for a fortnight, and was certain of a willing listener in Jane whenever she might wish to talk again of either. But there was still something lurking behind, of which prudence forbad the disclosure. She dared not relate the other half of Mr. Darcy's letter, nor explain to her sister how sincerely she had been valued by his friend. Here was knowledge in which no one could partake; and she was sensible that nothing less than a perfect understanding between the parties could justify her in throwing off this last incumbrance of mystery. "And then," said she, "if that very improbable event should ever take place, I shall merely be able to tell what Bingley may tell in a much more agreeable manner himself. The liberty of communication cannot be mine till it has lost all its value!"

She was now, on being settled at home, at leisure to observe the real state of her sister's spirits. Jane was not happy. She still cherished a very tender affection for Bingley. Having never even fancied herself in love before, her regard had all the warmth of first attachment, and from her age and disposition, greater steadiness than first attachments often boast; and so fervently did she value his remembrance, and prefer him to every other man, that all her good sense, and all her attention to the feelings of her friends, were requisite to check the indulgence of those regrets, which must have been injurious to her own health and their tranquillity.

"Well, Lizzy," said Mrs. Bennet one day, "what is your opinon *now* of this sad business of Jane's? For my part, I am determined never to speak of it again to anybody. I told my sister Philips so the other day. But I cannot find out that Jane saw anything of him in London. Well, he is a very undeserving young man—and I do not suppose there is the least chance in the world of her ever getting him now. There is no talk of his coming to Netherfield again in the summer; and I have inquired of everybody, too, who is likely to know."

"I do not believe that he will ever live at Netherfield any more."

"Oh, well! it is just as he chooses. Nobody wants him to come. Though I shall always say that he used my daughter extremely ill; and if I was her, I would not have put up with it. Well, my comfort is I am sure Jane will die of a broken heart, and then he will be sorry for what he has done."

But as Elizabeth could not receive comfort from any such expectation, she made no answer.

"Well, Lizzy," continued her mother soon afterwards, "and so the Collinses live very comfortable, do they? Well, well, I only hope it will last. And what sort of table do they keep? Charlotte is an excellent manager, I dare say. If she is half as sharp as her mother, she is saving enough. There is nothing extravagant in *their* housekeeping, I dare say."

"No, nothing at all."

"A great deal of good management, depend upon it. Yes, yes. *They* will take care not to outrun their income. *They* will never be distressed for money. Well, much good may it do them! And so, I suppose, they often talk of having Longbourn when your father is dead. They look upon it quite as their own, I dare say, whenever that happens."

"It was a subject which they could not mention before me."

"No. It would have been strange if they had. But I make no doubt, they often talk of it between themselves. Well, if they can be easy with an estate that is not lawfully their own, so much the better. *I* should be ashamed of having one that was only entailed on me."

CHAPTER EIGHTEEN

THE first week of their return was soon gone. The second began. It was the last of the regiment's stay in Meryton, and all the young ladies in the neighbourhood were drooping apace. The dejection was almost universal. The elder Miss Bennets alone were still able to eat, drink, and sleep, and pursue the usual course of their employments. Very frequently were they reproached for this insensibility by Kitty and Lydia, whose own misery was extreme, and who could not comprehend such hard-heartedness in any of the family.

"Good Heaven! What is to become of us! What are we to do!" would they often exclaim in the bitterness of woe. "How can you be smiling so, Lizzy?"

Their affectionate mother shared all their grief; she remembered what she had herself endured on a similar occasion five and twenty years ago.

"I am sure," said she, "I cried for two days together when Colonel Millar's regiment went away. I thought I should have broke my heart."

"I am sure I shall break *mine*," said Lydia.

"If one could but go to Brighton!" observed Mrs. Bennet.

"Oh, yes!—if one could but go to Brighton! But Papa is so disagreeable."

"A little sea-bathing would set me up forever."

"And my aunt Philips is sure it would do *me* a great deal of good," added Kitty.

Such were the kind of lamentations resounding perpetually through Longbourn house. Elizabeth tried to be diverted by them; but all sense of pleasure was lost in shame. She felt anew the justice of Mr. Darcy's objections; and never had she before been so much disposed to pardon his interference in the views of his friend.

But the gloom of Lydia's prospect was shortly cleared away; for she received an invitation from Mrs. Forster, the wife of the colonel of the regiment, to accompany her to Brighton. This invaluable friend was a very young woman, and very lately married. A resemblance in good humour and good spirits had recommended her and Lydia to each other, and out of their *three* months' acquaintance they had been intimate *two*.

The rapture of Lydia on this occasion, her adoration of Mrs. Forster, the delight of Mrs. Bennet, and the mortification of Kitty, are scarcely to be described. Wholly inattentive to her sister's feelings, Lydia flew about the house in restless ecstasy, calling for everyone's congratulations and laughing and talking with more violence than ever, whilst the luckless Kitty continued in the parlour repining at her fate in terms as unreasonable as her accent was peevish.

"I cannot see why Mrs. Forster should not ask *me* as well as Lydia," said she, "though I am *not* her particular friend. I have just as much right to be asked as she has, and more too, for I am two years older."

In vain did Elizabeth attempt to make her reasonable, and Jane to make her resigned. As for Elizabeth herself, this invitation was so far from exciting in her the same feelings as in her mother and Lydia that she considered it as the death-warrant of all possibility of common sense for the latter; and detestable as such a step must make her were it known, she could not help secretly advising her father not to let her go. She represented to him all the improprieties of Lydia's general behaviour, the little advantage she could derive from the friendship of such a woman as Mrs. Forster, and the probability of her being yet more imprudent with such a companion at Brighton, where the temptations must be greater than at home. He heard her attentively, and then said,

"Lydia will never be easy till she has exposed herself in some public place or other, and we can never expect her to do it with so little expense or inconvenience to her family as under the present circumstances."

"If you were aware," said Elizabeth, "of the very great disadvantage to us all which must arise from the public notice of Lydia's unguarded and imprudent manner; nay, which has already arisen from it, I am sure you would judge differently in the affair."

"Already arisen!" repeated Mr. Bennet. "What, has she frightened away some of your lovers? Poor little Lizzy! But do not be cast down. Such squeamish youths as cannot bear to be connected with a little absurdity are not worth a regret. Come, let me see the list of the pitiful fellows who have been kept aloof by Lydia's folly."

"Indeed you are mistaken. I have no such injuries to resent. It is not of peculiar, but of general evils, which I am now complaining. Our importance, our respectability in the world, must be affected by the wild volatility, the assurance and disdain of all restraint which mark Lydia's character. Excuse me—for I must speak plainly. If you, my dear father, will not take the trouble of checking her exuberant spirits, and of teaching her that her present pursuits are not to be the business of her life, she will soon be beyond the reach of amendment. Her character will be fixed, and she will, at sixteen, be the most determined flirt that ever made herself and her family ridiculous. A flirt, too, in the worst and meanest degree of flirtation; without any attraction beyond youth and a tolerable person; and from the ignorance and emptiness of her mind, wholly unable to ward off any portion of that universal contempt which her rage for admiration will excite. In this danger Kitty is also comprehended. She will follow wherever Lydia leads. Vain, ignorant, idle, and absolutely uncontrolled! Oh! my dear father, can you suppose it possible that they will not be censured and despised wherever they are known, and that their sisters will not be often involved in the disgrace?"

Mr. Bennet saw that her whole heart was in the subject; and affectionately taking her hand, said in reply,

"Do not make yourself uneasy, my love. Wherever you and Jane are known, you must be respected and valued; and you will not appear to less advantage for having a couple of—or I may say, three very silly sisters. We shall have no peace at Longbourn if Lydia does not go to Brighton. Let her go then. Colonel Forster is a sensible man, and will keep her out of any real mischief; and she is luckily too poor to be an object of prey to anybody. At Brighton she will be of less importance even as a common flirt than she has been here. The officers will find women better worth their notice. Let us hope, therefore, that her being there may teach her her own insignificance. At any rate, she cannot grow many degrees worse, without authorizing us to lock her up for the rest of her life."

With this answer Elizabeth was forced to be content; but her own opinion continued the same, and she left him disappointed and sorry. It was not in her nature, however, to increase her vexations by dwelling on them. She was confident of having performed her duty, and to fret over unavoidable evils, or augment them by anxiety, was no part of her disposition.

Had Lydia and her mother known the substance of her conference with her father, their indignation would hardly have found expression in their united volubility. In Lydia's imagination, a visit to Brighton comprised every possibility of earthly happiness. She saw with the creative eye of fancy, the streets of that gay bathing place covered with officers. She saw herself the object of attention to tens and to scores of them at present unknown. She saw all the glories of the camp; its tents stretched forth in beauteous uniformity of lines, crowded with the young and the gay, and dazzling with scarlet; and to complete the view, she saw herself seated beneath a tent, tenderly flirting with at least six officers at once.

Had she known that her sister sought to tear her from such prospects and such realities as these, what would have been her sensations? They could have been understood only by her mother, who might have felt nearly the same. Lydia's going to Brighton was all that consoled her for the melancholy conviction of her husband's never intending to go there himself.

But they were entirely ignorant of what had passed; and their raptures continued with little intermission to the very day of Lydia's leaving home.

Elizabeth was now to see Mr. Wickham for the last time. Having been frequently in company with him since her return, agitation was pretty well over, the agitations of former partiality entirely so. She had even learned to detect, in the very gentleness which had first delighted her, an affectation and a sameness to disgust and weary. In his present behaviour to herself, moreover, she had a fresh source of displeasure, for the inclination he soon testified of renewing those attentions which had marked the early part of their acquaintance could only serve, after what had since passed, to provoke her. She lost all concern for him in finding herself thus selected as the object of such idle and frivolous gallantry; and while she steadily repressed it, could not but feel the reproof contained in his believing that however long, and for whatever cause, his attentions had been withdrawn, her vanity would be gratified and her preference secured at any time by their renewal.

On the very last day of the regiment's remaining in Meryton, he dined with others of the officers at Longbourn; and so little was Elizabeth disposed to part from him in good humour that on his making some inquiry as to the manner in which her time had passed at Hunsford, she mentioned Colonel Fitzwilliam's and Mr. Darcy's having both spent three weeks at Rosings, and asked him if he were acquainted with the former.

He looked surprised, displeased, alarmed; but with a moment's recollection and a returning smile, replied that he had formerly seen him often; and after observing that he was a very gentlemanlike man, asked her how she had liked him. Her answer was warmly in his favour. With an air of indifference he soon afterwards added, "How long did you say he was at Rosings?"

"Nearly three weeks."

"And you saw him frequently?"

"Yes, almost everyday."

"His manners are very different from his cousin's."

"Yes, very different. But I think Mr. Darcy improves on acquaintance."

"Indeed!" cried Wickham with a look which did not escape her. "And pray may I ask?" but checking himself, he added in a gayer tone, "Is it in address that he improves? Has he deigned to add ought of civility to his ordinary style? for I dare not hope," he continued in a lower and more serious tone, "that he is improved in essentials."

"Oh, no!" said Elizabeth. "In essentials, I believe, he is very much what he ever was."

While she spoke, Wickham looked as if scarcely knowing whether to rejoice over her words, or to distrust their meaning. There was a something in her countenance which made him listen with an apprehensive and anxious attention, while she added,

"When I said that he improved on acquaintance, I did not mean that either his mind or manners were in a state of improvement, but that from knowing him better, his disposition was better understood."

Wickham's alarm now appeared in a heightened complexion and agitated look; for a few minutes he was silent; till, shaking off his embarrassment, he turned to her again, and said in the gentlest of accents,

"You who so well know my feelings towards Mr. Darcy, will readily comprehend how sincerely I must rejoice that he is wise enough to assume even the *appearance* of what is right. His pride in that direction may be of service, if not to himself, to many others, for it must deter him from such foul misconduct as I have suffered by. I only fear that the sort of cautiousness to which you, I imagine, have been alluding is merely adopted on his visits to his aunt, of whose good opinion and judgment he stands much in awe. His fear of her has always operated, I know, when they were together; and a good deal is to be imputed to his wish of forwarding the match with Miss De Bourgh, which I am certain he has very much at heart."

Elizabeth could not repress a smile at this, but she answered only by a slight inclination of the head. She saw that he wanted to engage her on the old subject of his grievances, and she was in no humour to indulge him. The rest of the evening passed with the *appearance*, on his side, of usual cheerfulness, but with no farther attempt to distinguish Elizabeth; and they parted at last with mutual civility, and possibly a mutual desire of never meeting again.

When the party broke up, Lydia returned with Mrs. Forster to Meryton, from whence they were to set out early the next morning. The separation between her and her family was rather noisy than pathetic. Kitty was the only one who shed tears; but she did weep from vexation and envy. Mrs. Bennet was diffuse in her good wishes for the felicity of her daughter, and impressive in her injunctions that she would not miss the opportunity of enjoying herself as much as possible, advice which there was every reason to believe would be attended to; and in the clamourous happiness of Lydia herself in bidding farewell, the more gentle adieus of her sisters were uttered without being heard.

CHAPTER NINETEEN

HAD Elizabeth's opinion been all drawn from her own family, she could not have formed a very pleasing picture of conjugal felicity or domestic comfort. Her father, captivated by youth and beauty, and that appearance of good humour which youth and beauty generally give, had married a woman whose weak understanding and illiberal mind had very early in their marriage put an end to all real affection for her. Respect, esteem, and confidence, had vanished forever; and all his views of domestic happiness were overthrown. But Mr. Bennet was not of a disposition to seek comfort for the disappointment which his own imprudence had brought on in any of those pleasures which too often console the unfortunate for their folly or their vice. He was fond of the country and of books; and from these tastes had arisen his principal enjoyments. To his wife he was very little otherwise indebted than as her ignorance and folly had contributed to his amusement. This is not the sort of happiness which a man would in general wish to owe to his wife; but where other powers of entertainment are wanting, the true philosopher will derive benefit from such as are given.

Elizabeth, however, had never been blind to the impropriety of her father's behaviour as a husband. She had always seen it with pain; but respecting his abilities, and grateful for his affectionate treatment of herself, she endeavoured to forget what she could not overlook, and to banish from her thoughts that continual breach of conjugal obligation and decorum which, in exposing his wife to the contempt of her own children, was so highly reprehensible. But she had never felt so strongly as now the disadvantages which must attend the children of so unsuitable a marriage, nor ever been so fully aware of the evils arising from so ill-judged a direction of talents, talents which rightly used might at least have preserved the respectability of his daughters, even if incapable of enlarging the mind of his wife.

When Elizabeth had rejoiced over Wickham's departure, she found little other cause for satisfaction in the loss of the regiment. Their parties abroad were less varied than before; and at home she had a mother and sister whose constant repinings at the dullness of everything around them threw a real gloom over their domestic circle; and though Kitty might in time regain her natural degree of sense, since the disturbers of her brain were removed, her other sister, from whose disposition greater evil might be apprehended, was likely to be hardened in all her folly and assurance by a situation of such double danger as a watering place and a camp. Upon the whole, therefore, she found what has been sometimes found before, that an event to which she had looked forward with impatient desire did not in taking place bring all the satisfaction she had promised herself. It was consequently necessary to name some other period for the commencement of actual felicity; to have some other point on which her wishes and hopes might be fixed, and by again enjoying the pleasure of anticipation, console herself for the present and prepare for another disappointment. Her tour to the lakes was now the object of her happiest thoughts; it was her best consolation for all the uncomfortable hours which the discontentedness of her mother and Kitty made inevitable; and could she have included Jane in the scheme, every part of it would have been perfect.

"But it is fortunate," thought she, "that I have something to wish for. Were the whole arrangement complete, my disappointment would be certain. But here, my carrying with me one ceaseless source of regret in my sister's absence, I may reasonably hope to have all my expectations of pleasure realized. A scheme of which every part promises delight can never be successful; and general disappointment is only warded off by the defence of some little peculiar vexation."

When Lydia went away, she promised to write very often and very minutely to her mother and Kitty; but her letters were always long expected, and always very short. Those to her mother contained little else than that they were just returned from the library, where such and such officers had attended them, and where she had seen such beautiful ornaments as made her quite wild, that she had a new gown, or a new parasol, which she would have described more fully, but was obliged to leave off in a violent hurry, as Mrs. Forster called her, and they were going to the camp; and from her correspondence with her sister, there was still less to be learned, for her letters to Kitty, though rather longer, were much too full of lines under the words to be made public.

After the first fortnight or three weeks of her absence, health, good humour, and cheerfulness began to reappear at Longbourn. Everything wore a happier aspect. The families who had been in town for the winter came back again, and summer finery and summer engagements arose. Mrs. Bennet was restored to her usual querulous serenity, and by the middle of June Kitty was so much recovered as to be able to enter Meryton without tears, an event of such happy promise as to make Elizabeth hope that by the following Christmas she might be so tolerably reasonable as not to mention an officer above once a day, unless by some cruel and malicious arrangement at the War Office, another regiment should be quartered in Meryton.

The time fixed for the beginning of their northern tour was now fast approaching; and a fortnight only was wanting of it, when a letter arrived from Mrs. Gardiner, which at once delayed its commencement and curtailed its extent. Mr. Gardiner would be prevented by business from setting out till a fortnight later in July and must be in London again within a month; and as that left too short a period for them to go so far and see so much as they had proposed, or at least to see it with the leisure and comfort they had built on, they were obliged to give up the lakes, and substitute a more contracted tour; and according to the present plan, were to go no farther northward than Derbyshire. In that county there was enough to be seen to occupy the chief of their three weeks; and to Mrs. Gardiner it had a peculiarly strong attraction. The town where she had formerly passed some years of her life, and where they were now to spend a few days, was probably as great an object of her curiosity as all the celebrated beauties of Matlock, Chatsworth, Dovedale, or the Peak.

Elizabeth was excessively disappointed; she had set her heart on seeing the lakes; and still thought there might have been time enough. But it was her business to be satisfied—and certainly her temper to be happy; and all was soon right again.

With the mention of Derbyshire, there were many ideas connected. It was impossible for her to see the word without thinking of Pemberley and its owner. "But surely," said she, "I may enter his county with impunity, and rob it of a few petrified spars without his perceiving me."

The period of expectation was now doubled. Four weeks were to pass away before her uncle and aunt's arrival. But they did pass away, and Mr. and Mrs. Gardiner, with their four children, did at length appear at Longbourn. The children, two girls of six and eight years old, and two younger boys, were to be left under the particular care of their cousin Jane, who was the general favourite, and whose steady sense and sweetness of temper exactly adapted her for attending to them in every way—teaching them, playing with them, and loving them.

The Gardiners stayed only one night at Longbourn, and set off the next morning with Elizabeth in pursuit of novelty and amusement. One enjoyment was certain—that of suitableness as companions; a suitableness which comprehended health and temper to bear inconveniences —cheerfulness to enhance every pleasure—and affection and intelligence, which might supply it among themselves if there were disappointments abroad.

It is not the object of this work to give a description of Derbyshire, nor of any of the remarkable places through which their route thither lay: Oxford, Blenheim, Warwick, Kenelworth, Birmingham, etc., are sufficiently known. A small part of Derbyshire is all the present concern. To the little town of Lambton, the scene of Mrs.

Gardiner's former residence, and where she had lately learned that some acquaintance still remained, they bent their steps, after having seen all the principal wonders of the country; and within five miles of Lambton, Elizabeth found from her aunt, that Pemberley was situated. It was not in their direct road, nor more than a mile or two out of it. In talking over their route the evening before, Mrs. Gardiner expressed an inclination to see the place again. Mr. Gardiner declared his willingness, and Elizabeth was applied to for her approbation.

"My love, should not you like to see a place of which you have heard so much?" said her aunt. "A place, too, with which so many of your acquaintance are connected. Wickham passed all his youth there, you know."

Elizabeth was distressed. She felt that she had no business at Pemberley, and was obliged to assume a disinclination for seeing it. She must own that she was tired of great houses; after going over so many, she really had no pleasure in fine carpets or satin curtains.

Mrs. Gardiner abused her stupidity. "If it were merely a fine house richly furnished," said she, "I should not care about it myself; but the grounds are delightful. They have some of the finest woods in the country."

Elizabeth said no more—but her mind could not acquiesce. The possibility of meeting Mr. Darcy while viewing the place instantly occurred. It would be dreadful! She blushed at the very idea; and thought it would be better to speak openly to her aunt than to run such a risk. But against this there were objections; and she finally resolved that it could be the last resource, if her private inquiries as to the absence of the family were unfavourably answered.

Accordingly, when she retired at night, she asked the chambermaid whether Pemberley were not a very fine place, what was the name of its proprietor, and with no little alarm, whether the family were down for the summer. A most welcome negative followed the last question —and her alarms being now removed, she was at leisure to feel a great deal of curiosity to see the house herself; and when the subject was revived the next morning, and she was again applied to, could readily answer, and with a proper air of indifference, that she had not really any dislike to the scheme.

To Pemberley, therefore, they were to go.

Volume III

❖

CHAPTER ONE

ELIZABETH, as they drove along, watched for the first appearance of Pemberley Woods with some perturbation; and when at length they turned in at the lodge, her spirits were in a high flutter.

The park was very large, and contained great variety of ground. They entered it in one of its lowest points, and drove for some time through a beautiful wood, stretching over a wide extent.

Elizabeth's mind was too full for conversation, but she saw and admired every remarkable spot and point of view. They gradually ascended for half a mile, and then found themselves at the top of a considerable eminence, where the wood ceased, and the eye was instantly caught by Pemberley House, situated on the opposite side of a valley into which the road with some abruptness wound. It was a large, handsome, stone building, standing well on rising ground, and backed by a ridge of high woody hills; and in front, a stream of some natural importance was swelled into greater, but without any artificial appearance. Its banks were neither formal nor falsely adorned. Elizabeth was delighted. She had never seen a place for which nature had done more, or where natural beauty had been so little counteracted by an awkward taste. They were all of them warm in their admiration; and at that moment she felt that to be mistress of Pemberley might be something!

They descended the hill, crossed the bridge, and drove to the door; and while examining the nearest aspect of the house, all her apprehensions of meeting its owner returned. She dreaded lest the chambermaid had been mistaken. On applying to see the place, they were admitted into the hall; and Elizabeth, as they waited for the housekeeper, had leisure to wonder at her being where she was.

The housekeeper came—a respectable-looking, elderly woman, much less fine, and more civil, than she had any notion of finding her. They followed her into the dining-parlour. It was a large, well-proportioned room, handsomely fitted up. Elizabeth, after slightly surveying it, went to a window to enjoy its prospect. The hill, crowned with wood, from which they had descended, receiving increased abruptness from the distance, was a beautiful object. Every disposition of the ground was good; and she looked on the whole scene, the river, the trees scattered on its banks, and the winding of the valley, as far as she could trace it, with delight. As they passed into other rooms, these objects were taking different positions; but from every window there were beauties to be seen. The rooms were lofty and handsome, and their furniture suitable to the fortune of their proprietor; but Elizabeth saw, with admiration of his taste, that it was neither gaudy nor uselessly fine; with less of splendor, and more real elegance, than the furniture of Rosings.

"And of this place," thought she, "I might have been mistress! With these rooms I might now have been familiarly acquainted! Instead of viewing them as a stranger, I might have rejoiced in them as my own, and welcomed to them as visitors my uncle and aunt.—But no"—recollecting herself—"that could never be: my uncle and aunt would have been lost to me: I should not have been allowed to invite them."

This was a lucky recollection—it saved her from something like regret.

She longed to inquire of the housekeeper whether her master were really absent, but had not courage for it. At length, however, the question was asked by her uncle; and she turned away with alarm, while Mrs. Reynolds replied that he was, adding, "but we expect him to-morrow with a large party of friends." How rejoiced was Elizabeth that their own journey had not by any circumstance been delayed a day!

Her aunt now called her to look at a picture. She approached, and saw the likeness of Mr. Wickham suspended amongst several other miniatures over the mantlepiece. Her aunt asked her, smilingly, how she liked it. The housekeeper came forward, and told them it was the picture of a young gentleman, the son of her late master's steward, who had been brought up by him at his own expense.—"He is now gone into the army," she added, "but I am afraid he has turned out very wild."

Mrs. Gardiner looked at her niece with a smile, but Elizabeth could not return it.

"And that," said Mrs. Reynolds, pointing to another of the miniatures, "is my master—and very like him. It was drawn at the same time as the other—about eight years ago."

"I have heard much of your master's fine person," said Mrs. Gardiner, looking at the picture; "it is a handsome face. But, Lizzy, you can tell us whether it is like or not."

Mrs. Reynolds's respect for Elizabeth seemed to increase on this intimation of her knowing her master.

"Does that young lady know Mr. Darcy?"

Elizabeth coloured, and said—"A little."

"And do not you think him a very handsome gentleman, ma'am?"

"Yes, very handsome."

"I am sure *I* know none so handsome; but in the gallery upstairs you will see a finer, larger picture of him than this. This room was my late master's favourite room, and these miniatures are just as they used to be then. He was very fond of them."

This accounted to Elizabeth for Mr. Wickham's being among them.

Mrs. Reynolds then directed their attention to one of Miss Darcy, drawn when she was only eight years old.

"And is Miss Darcy as handsome as her brother?" said Mr. Gardiner.

"Oh! yes—the handsomest young lady that ever was seen; and so accomplished! She plays and sings all day long. In the next room is a new instrument just come down for her—a present from my master; she comes here to-morrow with him."

Mr. Gardiner, whose manners were easy and pleasant, encouraged her communicativeness by his questions and remarks; Mrs. Reynolds, either from pride or attachment, had evidently great pleasure in talking of her master and his sister.

"Is your master much at Pemberley in the course of the year?"

"Not so much as I could wish, sir; but I dare say he may spend half his time here; and Miss Darcy is always down for the summer months."

"Except," thought Elizabeth, "when she goes to Ramsgate."

"If your master would marry, you might see more of him."

"Yes, sir; but I do not know when *that* will be. I do not know who is good enough for him."

Mr. and Mrs. Gardiner smiled. Elizabeth could not help saying, "It is very much to his credit, I am sure, that you should think so."

"I say no more than the truth, and what everybody will say that knows him," replied the other. Elizabeth thought this was going pretty far; and she listened with increasing astonishment as the housekeeper added, "I have never had a cross word from him in my life, and I have known him ever since he was four years old."

This was praise of all others most extraordinary, most opposite to her ideas. That he was not a good-tempered man had been her firmest opinion. Her keenest attention was awakened; she longed to hear more, and was grateful to her uncle for saying,

"There are very few people of whom so much can be said. You are lucky in having such a master."

"Yes, sir, I know I am. If I was to go through the world, I could not meet with a better. But I have always observed that they who are good-natured when children, are good-natured when they grow up; and he was always the sweetest-tempered, most generous-hearted boy in the world."

Elizabeth almost stared at her.—"Can this be Mr. Darcy!" thought she.

"His father was an excellent man," said Mrs. Gardiner.

"Yes, ma'am, that he was indeed; and his son will be just like him—just as affable to the poor."

Elizabeth listened, wondered, doubted, and was impatient for more. Mrs. Reynolds could interest her on no other point. She related the subject of the pictures, the dimensions of the rooms, and the price of the furniture, in vain. Mr. Gardiner, highly amused by the kind of family prejudice to which he attributed her excessive commendation of her master, soon led again to the subject; and she dwelt with energy on his many merits, as they proceeded together up the great staircase.

"He is the best landlord and the best master," said she, "that ever lived. Not like the wild young men now-a-days who think of nothing but themselves. There is not one of his tenants or servants but what will give him a good name. Some people call him proud; but I am sure I never saw anything of it. To my fancy, it is only because he does not rattle away like other young men."

"In what an amiable light does this place him!" thought Elizabeth.

"This fine account of him," whispered her aunt, as they walked, "is not quite consistent with his behaviour to our poor friend."

"Perhaps we might be deceived."

"That is not very likely; our authority was too good."

On reaching the spacious lobby above, they were shown into a very pretty sitting-room, lately fitted up with greater elegance and lightness than the apartments below; and were informed that it was but just done to give pleasure to Miss Darcy, who had taken a liking to the room when last at Pemberley.

"He is certainly a good brother," said Elizabeth, as she walked towards one of the windows.

Mrs. Reynolds anticipated Miss Darcy's delight when she should enter the room. "And this is always the way with him," she added. "Whatever can give his sister any pleasure is sure to be done in a moment. There is nothing he would not do for her."

The picture gallery, and two or three of the principal bedrooms, were all that remained to be shown. In the former were many good paintings; but Elizabeth knew nothing of the art; and from such as had been already visible below, she had willingly turned to look at some drawings of Miss Darcy's, in crayons, whose subjects were usually more interesting, and also more intelligible.

In the gallery there were many family portraits, but

they could have little to fix the attention of a stranger. Elizabeth walked on in quest of the only face whose features would be known to her. At last it arrested her —and she beheld a striking resemblance of Mr. Darcy, with such a smile over the face, as she remembered to have sometimes seen when he looked at her. She stood several minutes before the picture in earnest contemplation, and returned to it again before they quitted the gallery. Mrs. Reynolds informed them that it had been taken in his father's lifetime.

There was certainly at this moment in Elizabeth's mind a more gentle sensation towards the original than she had ever felt in the height of their acquaintance. The commendation bestowed on him by Mrs. Reynolds was of no trifling nature. What praise is more valuable than the praise of an intelligent servant? As a brother, a landlord, a master, she considered how many people's happiness were in his guardianship!—How much of pleasure or pain it was in his power to bestow!—How much of good or evil must be done by him! Every idea that had been brought forward by the housekeeper was favourable to his character, and as she stood before the canvas on which he was represented, and fixed his eyes upon herself, she thought of his regard with a deeper sentiment of gratitude than it had ever raised before; she remembered its warmth, and softened its impropriety of expression.

When all of the house that was open to general inspection had been seen, they returned downstairs, and taking leave of the housekeeper, were consigned over to the gardener, who met them at the hall door.

As they walked across the lawn towards the river, Elizabeth turned back to look again; her uncle and aunt stopped also, and while the former was conjecturing as to the date of the building, the owner of it himself suddenly came forward from the road, which led behind it to the stables.

They were within twenty yards of each other, and so abrupt was his appearance that it was impossible to avoid his sight. Their eyes instantly met, and the cheeks of each were overspread with the deepest blush. He absolutely started, and for a moment seemed immovable from surprise; but shortly recovering himself, advanced towards the party, and spoke to Elizabeth, if not in terms of perfect composure, at least of perfect civility.

She had instinctively turned away; but stopping on his approach, received his compliments with an embarrassment impossible to be overcome. Had his first appearance, or his resemblance to the picture they had just been examining, been insufficient to assure the other two that they now saw Mr. Darcy, the gardener's expression of surprise on beholding his master, must immediately have told it. They stood a little aloof while he was talking to their niece, who, astonished and confused, scarcely dared lift her eyes to his face, and knew not what answer she returned to his civil inquiries after her family. Amazed at the alteration in his manner since they last parted, every sentence that he uttered was increasing her embarrassment; and every idea of the impropriety of her being found there, recurring to her mind the few minutes in which they continued together, were some of the most uncomfortable of her life. Nor did he seem much more at ease; when he spoke, his accent had none of its usual sedateness; and he repeated his inquiries as to the time of her having left Longbourn, and of her stay in Derbyshire, so often and in so hurried a way as plainly spoke the distraction of his thoughts.

At length, every idea seemed to fail him; and after standing a few moments without saying a word, he suddenly recollected himself, and took leave.

The others then joined her, and expressed their admiration of his figure; but Elizabeth heard not a word, and wholly engrossed by her own feelings, followed them in silence. She was overpowered by shame and vexation. Her coming there was the most unfortunate, the most ill-judged thing in the world! How strange must it appear to him! In what a disgraceful light might it not strike so vain a man! It might seem as if she had purposely thrown herself in his way again! Oh! why did she come? or, why did he thus come a day before he was expected? Had they been only ten minutes sooner, they should have been beyond the reach of his discrimination, for it was plain that he was that moment arrived, that moment alighted from his horse or his carriage. She blushed again and again over the perverseness of the meeting. And his behaviour, so strikingly altered—what could it mean? That he should even speak to her was amazing!—but to speak with such civility, to inquire after her family! Never in her life had she seen his manners so little dignified, never had he spoken with such gentleness as on this unexpected meeting. What a contrast did it offer to his last address in Rosings Park, when he put his letter into her hand! She knew not what to think, nor how to account for it.

They had now entered a beautiful walk by the side of the water, and every step was bringing forward a nobler fall of ground, or a finer reach of the woods to which they were approaching; but it was some time before Elizabeth was sensible of any of it; and, though she answered mechanically to the repeated appeals of her uncle and aunt, and seemed to direct her eyes to such objects as they pointed out, she distinguished no part of the scene. Her thoughts were all fixed on that one spot of Pemberley House, whichever it might be, where Mr. Darcy then was. She longed to know what at that moment was passing in his mind, in what manner he thought of her, and whether, in defiance of everything, she was still dear to him. Perhaps he had been civil only because he felt himself at ease; yet there had been *that* in his voice which was not like ease. Whether he had felt more of pain or of pleasure in seeing her she could not tell, but he certainly had not seen her with composure.

At length, however, the remarks of her companions on her absence of mind roused her, and she felt the necessity of appearing more like herself.

They entered the woods, and bidding adieu to the river for awhile, ascended some of the higher grounds; whence, in spots where the opening of the trees gave the eye power to wander, were many charming views of the valley, the opposite hills, with the long range of woods overspreading many, and occasionally part of the stream. Mr. Gardiner expressed a wish of going round the whole park, but feared it might be beyond a walk. With a triumphant smile, they were told that it was ten miles round. It settled the matter; and they pursued the accustomed circuit; which brought them again, after some time, in a descent among hanging woods, to the edge of the water, in one of its narrowest parts. They crossed it by a simple bridge, in character with the general air of the scene; it was a spot less adorned than any they had yet visited; and the valley, here contracted into a glen, allowed room only for the stream, and a narrow walk amidst the rough coppice-wood which bordered it. Elizabeth longed to explore its windings; but when they had crossed the bridge and perceived their distance from the house, Mrs. Gardiner, who was not a great walker, could go no farther, and thought only of returning to the carriage as quickly as possible. Her niece was, therefore, obliged to submit, and they took their way towards the house on the opposite side of the river in the nearest direction; but their progress was slow, for Mr. Gardiner, though seldom able to indulge the taste, was very fond of fishing, and was so much engaged in watching the occasional appearance of some trout in the water, and talking to the man about them, that he advanced but little. Whilst wandering on in this slow manner, they were again surprised, and Elizabeth's astonishment was quite equal to what it had been at first, by the sight of Mr. Darcy approaching them, and at no great distance. The walk being here less sheltered than on the other side allowed them to see him before they met. Elizabeth, however astonished, was at least more prepared for an interview than before, and resolved to appear and to speak with calmness, if he really intended to meet them. For a few moments, indeed, she felt that he would probably strike into some other path. This idea lasted while a turning in the walk concealed him from their view; the turning past, he was immediately before them. With a glance she saw that he had lost none of his recent civility; and to imitate his politeness, she began, as they met, to admire the beauty of the place; but she had not got beyond the words "delightful" and "charming," when some unlucky recollections obtruded, and she fancied that praise of Pemberley from her might be mischievously construed. Her colour changed, and she said no more.

Mrs. Gardiner was standing a little behind; and on her pausing, he asked her if she would do him the honour of introducing him to her friends. This was a stroke of civility for which she was quite unprepared; and she could hardly suppress a smile at his being now seeking the acquaintance of some of those very people against whom his pride had revolted in his offer to herself. "What will be his surprise," thought she, "when he knows who they are! He takes them now for people of fashion."

The introduction, however, was immediately made; and as she named their relationship to herself, she stole a sly look at him to see how he bore it; and was not without the expectation of his decamping as fast as he could from such disgraceful companions. That he was *surprised* by the connexion was evident; he sustained it however with fortitude, and so far from going away, turned back with them and entered into conversation with Mr. Gardiner. Elizabeth could not but be pleased, could not but triumph. It was consoling that he should know she had some relations for whom there was no need to blush. She listened most attentively to all that passed between them, and gloried in every expression, every sentence of her uncle, which marked his intelligence, his taste or his good manners.

The conversation soon turned upon fishing, and she heard Mr. Darcy invite him, with the greatest civility, to fish there as often as he chose, while he continued in the neighbourhood, offering at the same time to supply him with fishing tackle, and pointing out those parts of the stream where there was usually most sport. Mrs. Gardiner, who was walking arm in arm with Elizabeth, gave her a look expressive of her wonder. Elizabeth said nothing, but it gratified her exceedingly; the compliment must be all for herself. Her astonishment, however, was extreme; and continually was she repeating, "Why is he so altered? From what can it proceed? It cannot be for *me*, it cannot be for *my* sake that his manners are thus softened. My reproofs at Hunsford could not work such a change as this. It is impossible that he should still love me."

After walking some time in this way, the two ladies in front, the two gentlemen behind, on resuming their places, after descending to the brink of the river for the better inspection of some curious water-plant, there chanced to be a little alteration. It originated in Mrs. Gardiner, who, fatigued by the exercise of the morning, found Elizabeth's arm inadequate to her support, and consequently preferred her husband's. Mr. Darcy took her place by her niece, and they walked on together. After a short silence, the lady first spoke. She wished him to know that she had been assured of his absence before she came to the place, and accordingly began by observing that his arrival had been very unexpected—"for your housekeeper," she added, "informed us that you would certainly not be here till to-morrow; and indeed, before we left Bakewell, we understood that you were not immediately expected in the country." He acknowledged the truth of it all; and said that business with his steward had occasioned his coming forward a few hours before the rest of the party with whom he had been travelling. "They will join me early to-morrow," he continued, "and among them are some who will claim an acquaintance with you—Mr. Bingley and his sisters."

Elizabeth answered only by a slight bow. Her thoughts were instantly driven back to the time when Mr. Bingley's name had been last mentioned between them; and if she might judge from his complexion, *his* mind was not very differently engaged.

"There is also one other person in the party," he continued after a pause, "who more particularly wishes to be known to you—will you allow me, or do I ask too much, to introduce my sister to your acquaintance during your stay at Lambton?"

The surprise of such an application was great indeed; it was too great for her to know in what manner she acceded to it. She immediately felt that whatever desire Miss Darcy might have of being acquainted with her must be the work of her brother, and without looking farther, it was satisfactory; it was gratifying to know that his resentment had not made him think really ill of her.

They now walked on in silence, each of them deep in thought. Elizabeth was not comfortable; that was impossible; but she was flattered and pleased. His wish of introducing his sister to her was a compliment of the highest kind. They soon outstripped the others, and when they had reached the carriage, Mr. and Mrs. Gardiner were half a quarter of a mile behind.

He then asked her to walk into the house—but she declared herself not tired, and they stood together on the lawn. At such a time, much might have been said,

214

and silence was very awkward. She wanted to talk, but there seemed an embargo on every subject. At last she recollected that she had been travelling, and they talked of Matlock and Dove Dale with great perseverance. Yet time and her aunt moved slowly—and her patience and her ideas were nearly worn out before the *tête-à-tête* was over. On Mr. and Mrs. Gardiner's coming up, they were all pressed to go into the house and take some refreshment; but this was declined, and they parted on each side with the utmost politeness. Mr. Darcy handed the ladies into the carriage, and when it drove off, Elizabeth saw him walking slowly towards the house.

The observations of her uncle and aunt now began; and each of them pronounced him to be infinitely superior to anything they had expected. "He is perfectly well behaved, polite, and unassuming," said her uncle.

"There *is* something a little stately in him to be sure," replied her aunt, "but it is confined to his air, and is not unbecoming. I can now say with the housekeeper that though some people may call him proud, *I* have seen nothing of it."

"I was never more surprised than by his behaviour to us. It was more than civil; it was really attentive; and there was no necessity for such attention. His acquaintance with Elizabeth was very trifling."

"To be sure, Lizzy," said her aunt, "he is not so handsome as Wickham; or rather he has not Wickham's countenance, for his features are perfectly good. But how came you to tell us that he was so disagreeable?"

Elizabeth excused herself as well as she could; said that she had liked him better when they met in Kent than before, and that she had never seen him so pleasant as this morning.

"But perhaps he may be a little whimsical in his civilities," replied her uncle. "Your great men often are; and therefore I shall not take him at his word about fishing, as he might change his mind another day, and warn me off his grounds."

Elizabeth felt that they had entirely mistaken his character, but said nothing.

"From what we have seen of him," continued Mrs. Gardiner, "I really should not have thought that he could have behaved in so cruel a way by anybody, as he has done by poor Wickham. He has not an ill-natured look. On the contrary, there is something pleasing about his mouth when he speaks. And there is something of dignity in his countenance that would not give one an unfavourable idea of his heart. But, to be sure, the good lady who showed us the house did give him a most flaming character! I could hardly help laughing aloud sometimes. But he is a liberal master, I suppose, and *that* in the eye of a servant comprehends every virtue."

Elizabeth here felt herself called on to say something in vindication of his behaviour to Wickham; and therefore gave them to understand, in as guarded a manner as she could, that by what she had heard from his relations in Kent, his actions were capable of a very different construction; and that his character was by no means so faulty, nor Wickham's so amiable, as they had been considered in Hertfordshire. In confirmation of this, she related the particulars of all the pecuniary transactions in which they had been connected, without actually naming her authority, but stating it to be such as might be relied on.

Mrs. Gardiner was surprised and concerned; but as they were now approaching the scene of her former pleasures, every idea gave way to the charm of recollection; and she was too much engaged in pointing out to her husband all the interesting spots in its environs to think of anything else. Fatigued as she had been by the morning's walk, they had no sooner dined than she set off again in quest of her former acquaintance, and the evening was spent in the satisfactions of an intercourse renewed after many years discontinuance.

The occurrences of the day were too full of interest to leave Elizabeth much attention for any of these new friends; and she could do nothing but think, and think with wonder, of Mr. Darcy's civility, and above all, of his wishing her to be acquainted with his sister.

CHAPTER TWO

ELIZABETH had settled it that Mr. Darcy would bring his sister to visit her the very day after her reaching

Pemberley; and was consequently resolved not to be out of sight of the inn the whole of that morning. But her conclusion was false; for on the very morning after their own arrival at Lambton, these visitors came. They had been walking about the place with some of their new friends, and were just returned to the inn to dress themselves for dining with the same family, when the sound of a carriage drew them to a window, and they saw a gentleman and lady in a curricle driving up the street. Elizabeth immediately recognizing the livery, guessed what it meant, and imparted no small degree of surprise to her relations by acquainting them with the honour which she expected. Her uncle and aunt were all amazement; and the embarrassment of her manner as she spoke, joined to the circumstance itself, and many of the circumstances of the preceding day, opened to them a new idea on the business. Nothing had ever suggested it before, but they now felt that there was no other way of accounting for such attentions from such a quarter than by supposing a partiality for their niece. While these newly-born notions were passing in their heads, the perturbation of Elizabeth's feelings was every moment increasing. She was quite amazed at her own discomposure; but amongst other causes of disquiet, she dreaded lest the partiality of the brother should have said too much in her favour; and more than commonly anxious to please, she naturally suspected that every power of pleasing would fail her.

She retreated from the window, fearful of being seen; and as she walked up and down the room, endeavouring to compose herself, saw such looks of inquiring surprise in her uncle and aunt, as made everything worse.

Miss Darcy and her brother appeared, and this formidable introduction took place. With astonishment did Elizabeth see that her new acquaintance was at least as much embarrassed as herself. Since her being at Lambton, she had heard that Miss Darcy was exceedingly proud; but the observation of a very few minutes convinced her that she was only exceedingly shy. She found it difficult to obtain even a word from her beyond a monosyllable.

Miss Darcy was tall and on a larger scale than Elizabeth; and though little more than sixteen, her figure was formed, and her appearance womanly and graceful. She was less handsome than her brother, but there was sense and good humour in her face, and her manners were perfectly unassuming and gentle. Elizabeth, who had expected to find in her as acute and unembarrassed an observer as ever Mr. Darcy had been, was much relieved by discerning such different feelings.

They had not been long together before Darcy told her that Bingley was also coming to wait on her; and she had barely time to express her satisfaction, and prepare for such a visitor, when Bingley's quick step was heard on the stairs, and in a moment he entered the room. All Elizabeth's anger against him had been long done away; but had she still felt any, it could hardly have stood its ground against the unaffected cordiality with which he expressed himself, on seeing her again. He inquired in a friendly, though general way, after her family, and looked and spoke with the same good-humoured ease that he had ever done.

To Mr. and Mrs. Gardiner he was scarcely a less interesting personage than to herself. They had long wished to see him. The whole party before them, indeed, excited a lively attention. The suspicions which had just arisen of Mr. Darcy and their niece directed their observation towards each with an earnest, though guarded, inquiry; and they soon drew from those inquiries the full conviction that one of them at least knew what it was to love. Of the lady's sensations they remained a little in doubt; but that the gentleman was overflowing with admiration was evident enough.

Elizabeth, on her side, had much to do. She wanted to ascertain the feelings of each of her visitors, she wanted to compose her own, and to make herself agreeable to all; and in the latter object, where she feared most to fail, she was most sure of success, for those to whom she endeavoured to give pleasure were prepossessed in her favour. Bingley was ready, Georgiana was eager, and Darcy determined to be pleased.

In seeing Bingley, her thoughts naturally flew to her sister; and oh! how ardently did she long to know whether any of his were directed in a like manner. Sometimes she could fancy that he talked less than on former occasions, and once or twice pleased herself with the notion that as he looked at her, he was trying to trace a resemblance. But, though this might be imaginary, she could not be deceived as to his behaviour to Miss Darcy, who had been set up as a rival of Jane. No look appeared on either side that spoke particular regard. Nothing occurred between them that could justify the hopes of his sister. On this point she was soon satisfied; and two or three little circumstances occurred ere they parted, which, in her anxious interpretation, denoted a recollection of Jane, not untinctured by tenderness, and a wish of saying more that might lead to the mention of her, had he dared. He observed to her, at a moment when the others were talking together, and in a tone which had something of real regret, that it "was a very long time since he had had the pleasure of seeing her"; and before she could reply, he added, "It is above eight months. We have not met since the 26th of November, when we were all dancing together at Netherfield."

Elizabeth was pleased to find his memory so exact; and he afterwards took occasion to ask her, when unattended to by any of the rest, whether *all* her sisters were at Longbourn. There was not much in the question, nor in the preceding remark, but there was a look and a manner which gave them meaning.

It was not often that she could turn her eyes on Mr. Darcy himself; but whenever she did catch a glimpse, she saw an expression of general complaisance, and in all that he said, she heard an accent so far removed from *hauteur* or disdain of his companions, as convinced her that the improvement of manners which she had yesterday witnessed, however temporary its existence might prove, had at least outlived one day. When she saw him thus seeking the acquaintance, and courting the good opinion, of people with whom any intercourse a few months ago would have been a disgrace; when she saw him thus civil, not only to herself, but to the very relations whom he had openly disdained; and recollected their last lively scene in Hunsford Parsonage, the difference, the change was so great, and struck so forcibly on her mind, that she could hardly restrain her astonishment from being visible. Never, even in the company of his dear friends at Netherfield, or his dignified relations at Rosings, had she seen him so desirous to please, so free from self-consequence or unbending reserve as now, when no importance could result from the success of his endeavours, and when even the acquaintance of those to whom his attentions were addressed would draw down the ridicule and censure of the ladies both of Netherfield and Rosings.

Their visitors stayed with them above half an hour, and when they arose to depart, Mr. Darcy called on his sister to join him in expressing their wish of seeing Mr. and Mrs. Gardiner and Miss Bennet to dinner at Pemberley before they left the country. Miss Darcy, though with a diffidence which marked her little in the habit of giving invitations, readily obeyed. Mrs. Gardiner looked at her niece, desirous of knowing how *she*, whom the invitation most concerned, felt disposed as to its acceptance, but Elizabeth had turned away her head. Presuming, however, that this studied avoidance spoke rather a momentary embarrassment than any dislike of the proposal, and seeing in her husband, who was fond of society, a perfect willingness to accept it, she ventured to engage for her attendance, and the day after the next was fixed on.

Bingley expressed great pleasure in the certainty of seeing Elizabeth again, having still a great deal to say to her, and many inquiries to make after all their Hertfordshire friends. Elizabeth, construing all this into a wish of hearing her speak of her sister, was pleased; and on this account, as well as some others, found herself, when their visitors left them, capable of considering the last half hour with some satisfaction, though while it was passing, the enjoyment of it had been little. Eager to be alone, and fearful of inquiries or hints from her uncle and aunt, she stayed with them only long enough to hear their favourable opinion of Bingley, and then hurried away to dress.

But she had no reason to fear Mr. and Mrs. Gardiner's curiosity; it was not their wish to force her communication. It was evident that she was much better acquainted with Mr. Darcy than they had before any idea of; it was evident that he was very much in love with her. They saw much to interest, but nothing to justify inquiry.

Of Mr. Darcy it was now a matter of anxiety to think well; and as far as their acquaintance reached, there was no fault to find. They could not be untouched by his politeness, and had they drawn his character from their own feelings, and his servant's report, without any reference to any other account, the circle in Hertfordshire to which he was known would not have recognized it for Mr. Darcy. There was now an interest, however, in believing the housekeeper; and they soon became sensible that the authority of a servant who had known him since he was four years old, and whose own manners indicated respectability, was not to be hastily rejected. Neither had anything occurred in the intelligence of their Lambton friends that could materially lessen its weight. They had nothing to accuse him of but pride; pride he probably had, and if not, it would certainly be imputed by the inhabitants of a small market town, where the family did not visit. It was acknowledged, however, that he was a liberal man, and did much good among the poor.

With respect to Wickham, the travellers soon found that he was not held there in much estimation; for though the chief of his concerns with the son of his patron were imperfectly understood, it was yet a well-known fact that on his quitting Derbyshire he had left many debts behind him, which Mr. Darcy afterwards discharged.

As for Elizabeth, her thoughts were at Pemberley this evening more than the last; and the evening, though as it passed it seemed long, was not long enough to determine her feelings towards *one* in that mansion; and she lay awake two whole hours, endeavouring to make them out. She certainly did not hate him. No; hatred had vanished long ago, and she had almost as long been ashamed of ever feeling a dislike against him that could be so called. The respect created by the conviction of his valuable qualities, though at first unwillingly admitted, had for some time ceased to be repugnant to her feelings; and it was now heightened into somewhat of a friendlier nature by the testimony so highly in his favour, and bringing forward his disposition in so amiable a light, which yesterday had produced. But above all, above respect and esteem, there was a motive within her of goodwill which could not be overlooked. It was gratitude. Gratitude not merely for having once loved her, but for loving her still well enough to forgive all the petulance and acrimony of her manner in rejecting him, and all the unjust accusations accompanying her rejection. He who, she had been persuaded, would avoid her as his greatest enemy seemed, on this accidental meeting, most eager to preserve the acquaintance, and without any indelicate display of regard, or any peculiarity of manner, where their two selves only were concerned, was soliciting the good opinion of her friends, and bent on making her known to his sister. Such a change in a man of so much pride excited not only astonishment but gratitude—for to love, ardent love, it must be attributed; and as such its impression on her was of a sort to be encouraged, as by no means unpleasing, though it could not be exactly defined. She respected, she esteemed, she was grateful to him, she felt a real interest in his welfare; and she only wanted to know how far she wished that welfare to depend upon herself, and how far it would be for the happiness of both that she should employ the power, which her fancy told her she still possessed, of bringing on the renewal of his addresses.

It had been settled in the evening, between the aunt and niece that such a striking civility as Miss Darcy's, in coming to them on the very day of her arrival at Pemberley, for she had reached it only to a late breakfast, ought to be imitated, though it could not be equalled, by some exertion of politeness on their side; and consequently, that it would be highly expedient to wait on her at Pemberley the following morning. They were, therefore, to go. Elizabeth was pleased; though when she asked herself the reason, she had very little to say in reply.

Mr. Gardiner left them soon after breakfast. The fishing scheme had been renewed the day before, and a positive engagement made of his meeting some of the gentlemen at Pemberley by noon.

CHAPTER THREE

CONVINCED as Elizabeth now was that Miss Bingley's dislike of her had originated in jealousy, she could not help feeling how very unwelcome her appearance at Pemberley must be to her, and was curious to know with how much civility on that lady's side the acquaintance would now be renewed.

On reaching the house, they were shown through the hall into the saloon, whose northern aspect rendered it delightful for summer. Its windows opening to the ground admitted a most refreshing view of the high woody hills behind the house, and of the beautiful oaks and Spanish chestnuts which were scattered over the intermediate lawn.

In this room they were received by Miss Darcy, who was sitting there with Mrs. Hurst and Miss Bingley and the lady with whom she lived in London. Georgiana's reception of them was very civil; but attended with all that embarrassment which, though proceeding from shyness and the fear of doing wrong, would easily give to those who felt themselves inferior the belief of her being proud and reserved. Mrs. Gardiner and her niece, however, did her justice, and pitied her.

By Mrs. Hurst and Miss Bingley, they were noticed only by a curtsy; and on their being seated, a pause, awkward as such pauses must always be, succeeded for a few moments. It was first broken by Mrs. Annesley, a genteel, agreeable-looking woman, whose endeavour to introduce some kind of discourse proved her to be more truly well-bred than either of the others; and between her and Mrs. Gardiner, with occasional help from Elizabeth, the conversation was carried on. Miss Darcy looked as if she wished for courage enough to join in it; and sometimes did venture a short sentence, when there was least danger of its being heard.

Elizabeth soon saw that she was herself closely watched by Miss Bingley, and that she could not speak a word, especially to Miss Darcy, without calling her attention. This observation would not have prevented her from trying to talk to the latter, had they not been seated at an inconvenient distance; but she was not sorry to be spared the necessity of saying much. Her own thoughts were employing her. She expected every moment that some of the gentlemen would enter the room. She wished, she feared that the master of the house might be amongst them; and whether she wished or feared it most she could scarcely determine. After sitting in this manner a quarter of an hour, without hearing Miss Bingley's voice, Elizabeth was roused by receiving from her a cold inquiry after the health of her family. She answered with equal indifference and brevity, and the other said no more.

The next variation which their visit afforded was produced by the entrance of servants with cold meat, cake, and a variety of all the finest fruits in season; but this did not take place till after many a significant look and smile from Mrs. Annesley to Miss Darcy had been given, to remind her of her post. There was now employment for the whole party; for though they could not all talk, they could all eat; and the beautiful pyramids of grapes, nectarines, and peaches soon collected them round the table.

While thus engaged, Elizabeth had a fair opportunity of deciding whether she most feared or wished for the appearance of Mr. Darcy by the feelings which prevailed on his entering the room; and then, though but a moment before she had believed her wishes to predominate, she began to regret that he came.

He had been some time with Mr. Gardiner, who, with two or three other gentlemen from the house, was engaged by the river, and had left him only on learning that the ladies of the family intended a visit to Georgiana that morning. No sooner did he appear than Elizabeth wisely resolved to be perfectly easy and unembarrassed— a resolution the more necessary to be made, but perhaps not the more easily kept, because she saw that the suspicions of the whole party were awakened against them, and that there was scarcely an eye which did not watch his behaviour when he first came into the room. In no countenance was attentive curiosity so strongly marked as in Miss Bingley's, in spite of the smiles which overspread her face whenever she spoke to one of its objects; for jealousy had not yet made her desperate,

224

and her attentions to Mr. Darcy were by no means over. Miss Darcy, on her brother's entrance, exerted herself much more to talk; and Elizabeth saw that he was anxious for his sister and herself to get acquainted, and forwarded, as much as possible, every attempt at conversation on either side. Miss Bingley saw all this likewise; and in the imprudence of anger, took the first opportunity of saying, with sneering civility,

"Pray, Miss Eliza, are not the ——shire militia removed from Meryton? They must be a great loss to *your* family."

In Darcy's presence she dared not mention Wickham's name; but Elizabeth instantly comprehended that he was uppermost in her thoughts; and the various recollections connected with him gave her a moment's distress; but exerting herself vigorously to repel the ill-natured attack, she presently answered the question in a tolerably disengaged tone. While she spoke, an involuntary glance showed her Darcy with an heightened complexion, earnestly looking at her, and his sister overcome with confusion, and unable to lift up her eyes. Had Miss Bingley known what pain she was then giving her beloved friend, she undoubtedly would have refrained from the hint; but she had merely intended to discompose Elizabeth by bringing forward the idea of a man to whom she believed her partial, to make her betray a sensibility which might injure her in Darcy's opinion, and perhaps to remind the latter of all the follies and absurdities by which some part of her family were connected with that corps. Not a syllable had ever reached her of Miss Darcy's meditated elopement. To no creature had it been revealed, where secrecy was possible, except to Elizabeth; and from all Bingley's connections her brother was particularly anxious to conceal it from that very wish which Elizabeth had long ago attributed to him, of their becoming hereafter her own. He had certainly formed such a plan, and without meaning that it should affect his endeavour to separate him from Miss Bennet, it is probable that it might add something to his lively concern for the welfare of his friend.

Elizabeth's collected behaviour, however, soon quieted his emotion; and as Miss Bingley, vexed and disappointed, dared not approach nearer to Wickham, Georgiana also recovered in time, though not enough to be able to speak any more. Her brother, whose eye she feared to meet, scarcely recollected her interest in the affair, and the very circumstance which had been designed to turn his thoughts from Elizabeth, seemed to have fixed them on her more and more cheerfully.

Their visit did not continue long after the question and answer above mentioned; and while Mr. Darcy was attending them to their carriage, Miss Bingley was venting her feelings in criticisms on Elizabeth's person, behaviour, and dress. But Georgiana would not join her. Her brother's recommendation was enough to ensure her favour: his judgment could not err, and he had spoken in such terms of Elizabeth as to leave Georgiana without the power of finding her otherwise than lovely and amiable. When Darcy returned to the saloon, Miss Bingley could not help repeating to him some part of what she had been saying to his sister.

"How very ill Eliza Bennet looks this morning, Mr. Darcy," she cried; "I never in my life saw any one so much altered as she is since the winter. She is grown so brown and coarse! Louisa and I were agreeing that we should not have known her again."

However little Mr. Darcy might have liked such an address, he contented himself with coolly replying that he perceived no other alteration than her being rather tanned—no miraculous consequence of travelling in the summer.

"For my own part," she rejoined, "I must confess that I never could see any beauty in her. Her face is too thin; her complexion has no brilliancy; and her features are not at all handsome. Her nose wants character; there is nothing marked in its lines. Her teeth are tolerable, but not out of the common way; and as for her eyes, which have sometimes been called so fine, I never could perceive anything extraordinary in them. They have a sharp, shrewish look, which I do not like at all; and in her air altogether, there is a self-sufficiency without fashion, which is intolerable."

Persuaded as Miss Bingley was that Darcy admired Elizabeth, this was not the best method of recommending herself; but angry people are not always wise; and in seeing him at last look somewhat nettled, she had all the success she expected. He was resolutely silent however; and, from a determination of making him speak, she continued,

"I remember when we first knew her in Hertfordshire how amazed we all were to find that she was a reputed beauty; and I particularly recollect your saying one night, after they had been dining at Netherfield, '*She* a beauty!—I should as soon call her mother a wit.' But afterwards she seemed to improve on you, and I believe you thought her rather pretty at one time."

"Yes," replied Darcy, who could contain himself no longer, "but *that* was only when I first knew her, for it is many months since I have considered her as one of the handsomest women of my acquaintance."

He then went away, and Miss Bingley was left to all the satisfaction of having forced him to say what gave no one any pain but herself.

Mrs. Gardiner and Elizabeth talked of all that had occurred during their visit, as they returned, except what had particularly interested them both. The looks and behaviour of everybody they had seen were discussed, except of the person who had mostly engaged their attention. They talked of his sister, his friends, his house, his fruit, of everything but himself; yet Elizabeth was longing to know what Mrs. Gardiner thought of him, and Mrs. Gardiner would have been highly gratified by her niece's beginning the subject.

CHAPTER FOUR

ELIZABETH had been a good deal disappointed in not finding a letter from Jane on their first arrival at Lambton; and this disappointment had been renewed on each of the mornings that had now been spent there; but on the third, her repining was over, and her sister justified by the receipt of two letters from her at once, on one of which was marked that it had been missent elsewhere. Elizabeth was not surprised at it, as Jane had written the direction remarkably ill.

They had just been preparing to walk as the letters came in; and her uncle and aunt, leaving her to enjoy them in quiet, set off by themselves. The one missent must be first attended to; it had been written five days ago. The beginning contained an account of all their little parties and engagements, with such news as the country afforded; but the latter half, which was dated a day later and written in evident agitation, gave more important intelligence. It was to this effect:

"Since writing the above, dearest Lizzy, something has occurred of a most unexpected and serious nature; but I am afraid of alarming you—be assured that we are all well. What I have to say relates to poor Lydia. An express came at twelve last night, just as we were all gone to bed, from Colonel Forster to inform us that she was gone off to Scotland with one of his officers; to own the truth, with Wickham!—Imagine our surprise. To Kitty, however, it does not seem so wholly unexpected. I am very, very sorry. So imprudent a match on both sides! But I am willing to hope the best, and that his character has been misunderstood. Thoughtless and indiscreet I can easily believe him, but this step (and let us rejoice over it) marks nothing bad at heart. His choice is disinterested at least, for he must know my father can give her nothing. Our poor mother is sadly grieved. My father bears it better. How thankful am I that we never let them know what has been said against him; we must forget it ourselves. They were off Saturday night about twelve, as is conjectured, but were not missed till yesterday morning at eight. The express was sent off directly. My dear Lizzy, they must have passed within ten miles of us. Colonel Forster gives us reason to expect him here soon. Lydia left a few lines for his wife, informing her of their intention. I must conclude, for I cannot be long from my poor mother. I am afraid you will not be able to make it out, but I hardly know what I have written."

Without allowing herself time for consideration, and scarcely knowing what she felt, Elizabeth on finishing this letter, instantly seized the other, and opening it with the utmost impatience, read as follows: it had been written a day later than the conclusion of the first.

"By this time, my dearest sister, you have received my hurried letter; I wish this may be more intelligible, but though not confined for time, my head is so bewildered that I cannot answer for being coherent. Dearest

Lizzy, I hardly know what I would write, but I have bad news for you, and it cannot be delayed. Imprudent as a marriage between Mr. Wickham and our poor Lydia would be, we are now anxious to be assured it has taken place, for there is but too much reason to fear they are not gone to Scotland. Colonel Forster came yesterday, having left Brighton the day before, not many hours after the express. Though Lydia's short letter to Mrs. F. gave them to understand that they were going to Gretna Green, something was dropped by Denny expressing his belief that W. never intended to go there, or to marry Lydia at all, which was repeated to Colonel F. who instantly taking the alarm, set off from B. intending to trace their route. He did trace them easily to Clapham, but no farther; for on entering that place they removed into a hackney-coach and dismissed the chaise that brought them from Epsom. All that is known after this is that they were seen to continue the London road. I know not what to think. After making every possible inquiry on that side London, Colonel F. came on into Hertfordshire, anxiously renewing them at all the turnpikes, and at the inns in Barnet and Hatfield, but without any success, no such people had been seen to pass through. With the kindest concern he came on to Longbourn, and broke his apprehensions to us in a manner most creditable to his heart. I am sincerely grieved for him and Mrs. F., but no one can throw any blame on them. Our distress, my dear Lizzy, is very great. My father and mother believe the worst, but I cannot think so ill of him. Many circumstances might make it more eligible for them to be married privately in town than to pursue their first plan; and even if *he* could form such a design against a young woman of Lydia's connections, which is not likely, can I suppose her so lost to everything?—Impossible. I grieve to find, however, that Colonel F. is not disposed to depend upon their marriage; he shook his head when I expressed my hopes, and said he feared W. was not a man to be trusted. My poor mother is really ill and keeps her room. Could she exert herself it would be better, but this is not to be expected; and as to my father, I never in my life saw him so affected. Poor Kitty has anger for having concealed their attachment; but as it was a matter of confidence one cannot wonder. I am truly glad, dearest Lizzy, that you have been spared something of these distressing scenes; but now as the first shock is over, shall I own that I long for your return? I am not so selfish, however, as to press for it, if inconvenient. Adieu. I take up my pen again to do what I have just told you I would not, but circumstances are such that I cannot help earnestly begging you all to come here as soon as possible. I know my dear uncle and aunt so well that I am not afraid of requesting it, though I have still something more to ask of the former. My father is going to London with Colonel Forster instantly to try to discover her. What he means to do I am sure I know not; but his excessive distress will not allow him to pursue any measure in the best and safest way, and Colonel Forster is obliged to be at Brighton again to-morrow evening. In such an exigence my uncle's advice and assistance would be everything in the world; he will immediately comprehend what I must feel, and I rely upon his goodness."

"Oh! where, where is my uncle?" cried Elizabeth, darting from her seat as she finished the letter, in eagerness to follow him, without losing a moment of the time so precious; but as she reached the door, it was opened by a servant, and Mr. Darcy appeared. Her pale face and impetuous manner made him start, and before he could recover himself enough to speak, she, in whose mind every idea was superseded by Lydia's situation, hastily exclaimed, "I beg your pardon, but I must leave you. I must find Mr. Gardiner this moment, on business that cannot be delayed; I have not an instant to lose."

"Good God! what is the matter?" cried he, with more feeling than politeness; then recollecting himself, "I will not detain you a minute, but let me, or let the servant, go after Mr. and Mrs. Gardiner. You are not well enough; you cannot go yourself."

Elizabeth hesitated, but her knees trembled under her, and she felt how little would be gained by her attempting to pursue them. Calling back the servant, therefore, she commissioned him, though in so breathless an accent as made her almost unintelligible, to fetch his master and mistress home instantly.

On his quitting the room, she sat down, unable to support herself, and looking so miserably ill that it was impossible for Darcy to leave her, or to refrain from saying, in a tone of gentleness and commiseration, "Let me call your maid. Is there nothing you could take to give you present relief?—A glass of wine; shall I get you one?—You are very ill."

"No, I thank you"; she replied, endeavouring to recover herself. "There is nothing the matter with me. I am quite well. I am only distressed by some dreadful news which I have just received from Longbourn."

She burst into tears as she alluded to it, and for a few minutes could not speak another word. Darcy, in wretched suspense, could only say something indistinctly of his concern, and observe her in compassionate silence. At length, she spoke again. "I have just had a letter from Jane, with such dreadful news. It cannot be concealed from anyone. My youngest sister has left all her friends—has eloped—has thrown herself into the power of—of Mr. Wickham. They are gone off together from Brighton. *You* know him too well to doubt the rest. She has no money, no connections, nothing that can tempt him to—she is lost forever."

Darcy was fixed in astonishment. "When I consider," she added, in a yet more agitated voice, "that *I* might have prevented it!—*I* who knew what he was. Had I but explained some part of it only—some part of what I learned to my own family! Had his character been known, this could not have happened. But it is all, all too late now."

"I am grieved, indeed," cried Darcy; "grieved—shocked. But is it certain, absolutely certain?"

"Oh yes!—They left Brighton together on Sunday night, and were traced almost to London, but not beyond; they are certainly not gone to Scotland."

"And what has been done, what has been attempted, to recover her?"

"My father is gone to London, and Jane has written to beg my uncle's immediate assistance, and we shall be off, I hope, in half an hour. But nothing can be done; I know very well that nothing can be done. How is such a man to be worked on? How are they even to be discovered? I have not the smallest hope. It is every way horrible!"

Darcy shook his head in silent acquiescence.

"When *my* eyes were opened to his real character. Oh! had I known what I ought, what I dared, to do! But I knew not—I was afraid of doing too much. Wretched, wretched mistake!"

Darcy made no answer. He seemed scarcely to hear her, and was walking up and down the room in earnest meditation, his brow contracted, his air gloomy. Elizabeth soon observed, and instantly understood it. Her power was sinking; everything *must* sink under such a proof of family weakness, such an assurance of the deepest disgrace. She could neither wonder nor condemn, but the belief of his self-conquest brought nothing consolatory to her bosom, afforded no palliation of her distress. It was, on the contrary, exactly calculated to make her understand her own wishes; and never had she so honestly felt that she could have loved him as now, when all love must be vain.

But self, though it would intrude, could not engross her. Lydia—the humiliation, the misery she was bringing on them all soon swallowed up every private care; and covering her face with her handkerchief, Elizabeth was soon lost to everything else; and after a pause of several minutes, was only recalled to a sense of her situation by the voice of her companion, who, in a manner which though it spoke compassion, spoke likewise restraint, said, "I am afraid you have been long desiring my absence, nor have I anything to plead in excuse of my stay, but real, though unavailing, concern. Would to heaven that anything could be either said or done on my part that might offer consolation to such distress.—But I will not torment you with vain wishes, which may seem purposely to ask for your thanks. This unfortunate affair will, I fear, prevent my sister's having the pleasure of seeing you at Pemberley to-day."

"Oh, yes. Be so kind as to apologize for us to Miss Darcy. Say that urgent business calls us home immediately. Conceal the unhappy truth as long as it is possible. —I know it cannot be long."

He readily assured her of his secrecy—again expressed his sorrow for her distress, wished it a happier conclusion than there was at present reason to hope, and leaving his compliments for her relations, with only one serious, parting look, went away.

As he quitted the room, Elizabeth felt how improbable it was that they should ever see each other again on such terms of cordiality as had marked their several meetings in Derbyshire; and as she threw a retrospective glance over the whole of their acquaintance, so full of contradictions and varieties, sighed at the perverseness of those feelings which would now have promoted its continuance, and would formerly have rejoiced in its termination.

If gratitude and esteem are good foundations of affection, Elizabeth's change of sentiment will be neither improbable nor faulty. But if otherwise, if the regard springing from such sources is unreasonable or unnatural, in comparison of what is so often described as arising on a first interview with its object, and even before two words have been exchanged, nothing can be said in her defense, except that she had given somewhat of a trial to the latter method, in her partiality for Wickham, and that its ill-success might perhaps authorize her to seek the other less interesting mode of attachment. Be that as it may, she saw him go with regret; and in this early example of what Lydia's infamy must produce, found additional anguish as she reflected on that wretched business. Never, since reading Jane's second letter, had she entertained a hope of Wickham's meaning to marry her. No one but Jane, she thought, could flatter herself with such an expectation. Surprise was the least of her feelings on this development. While the contents of the first letter remained on her mind, she was all surprise—all astonishment that Wickham should marry a girl whom it was impossible he could marry for money; and how Lydia could ever have attached him had appeared incomprehensible. But now it was all too natural. For such an attachment as this, she might have sufficient charms; and though she did not suppose Lydia to be deliberately engaging in an elopement, without the intention of marriage, she had no difficulty in believing that neither her virtue nor her understanding would preserve her from falling an easy prey.

She had never perceived, while the regiment was in Hertfordshire, that Lydia had any partiality for him, but she was convinced that Lydia had wanted only encouragement to attach herself to anybody. Sometimes one officer, sometimes another had been her favourite, as their attentions raised them in her opinion. Her affections had been continually fluctuating, but never without an object. The mischief of neglect and mistaken indulgence towards such a girl.—Oh! how acutely did she now feel it.

She was wild to be at home—to hear, to see, to be upon the spot, to share with Jane in the cares that must now fall wholly upon her in a family so deranged; a father absent, a mother incapable of exertion, and requiring constant attendance; and though almost persuaded that nothing could be done for Lydia, her uncle's interference seemed of the utmost importance, and till he entered the room, the misery of her impatience was severe. Mr. and Mrs. Gardiner had hurried back in alarm, supposing by the servant's account that their niece was taken suddenly ill; but satisfying them instantly on that head, she eagerly communicated the cause of their summons, reading the two letters aloud, and dwelling on the postscript of the last with trembling energy. Though Lydia had never been a favourite with them, Mr. and Mrs. Gardiner could not but be deeply affected. Not Lydia only, but all were concerned in it; and after the first exclamations of surprise and horror, Mr. Gardiner readily promised every assistance in his power. Elizabeth, though expecting no less, thanked him with tears of gratitude; and all three being actuated by one spirit, everything relating to their journey was speedily settled. They were to be off as soon as possible. "But what is to be done about Pemberley?" cried Mrs. Gardiner. "John told us Mr. Darcy was here when you sent for us; was it so?"

"Yes; and I told him we should not be able to keep our engagement. *That* is all settled."

"That is all settled," repeated the other, as she ran into her room to prepare. "And are they upon such terms as for her to disclose the real truth! Oh, that I knew how it was!"

But wishes were vain; or at best could serve only to amuse her in the hurry and confusion of the following hour. Had Elizabeth been at leisure to be idle, she would have remained certain that all employment was impossible to one so wretched as herself; but she had her share of business as well as her aunt, and amongst the rest there were notes to be written to all their friends in Lambton, with false excuses for their sudden departure. An hour, however, saw the whole completed; and Mr. Gardiner meanwhile having settled his account at the inn, nothing remained to be done but to go; and Elizabeth, after all the misery of the morning, found herself, in a shorter space of time than she could have supposed, seated in the carriage, and on the road to Longbourn.

CHAPTER FIVE

"I HAVE been thinking it over again, Elizabeth," said her uncle, as they drove from the town; "and really, upon serious consideration, I am much more inclined than I was to judge as your eldest sister does of the matter. It appears to me so very unlikely that any young man should form such a design against a girl who is by no means unprotected or friendless, and who was actually staying in his colonel's family, that I am strongly inclined to hope the best. Could he expect that her friends would not step forward? Could he expect to be noticed again by the regiment, after such an affront to Colonel Forster? His temptation is not adequate to the risk."

"Do you really think so?" cried Elizabeth, brightening up for a moment.

"Upon my word," said Mrs. Gardiner, "I begin to be of your uncle's opinion. It is really too great a violation of decency, honour, and interest for him to be guilty of it. I cannot think so very ill of Wickham. Can you, yourself, Lizzy, so wholly give him up as to believe him capable of it?"

"Not perhaps of neglecting his own interest. But of every other neglect I can believe him capable. If, indeed, it should be so! But I dare not hope it. Why should they not go on to Scotland, if that had been the case?"

"In the first place," replied Mr. Gardiner, "there is no absolute proof that they are not gone to Scotland."

"Oh! but their removing from the chaise into an hackney-coach is such a presumption! And, besides, no traces of them were to be found on the Barnet road."

"Well, then—supposing them to be in London. They may be there, though for the purpose of concealment, for no more exceptionable purpose. It is not likely that money should be very abundant on either side; and it might strike them that they could be more economically, though less expeditiously, married in London than in Scotland."

"But why all this secrecy? Why any fear of detection? Why must their marriage be private? Oh! no, no, this is not likely. His most particular friend, you see by Jane's account, was persuaded of his never intending to marry her. Wickham will never marry a woman without some money. He cannot afford it. And what claims has Lydia, what attractions has she beyond youth, health, and good humour that could make him for her sake forego every chance of benefiting himself by marrying well? As to what restraint the apprehension of disgrace in the corps might throw on a dishonourable elopement with her, I am not able to judge; for I know nothing of the effects that such a step might produce. But as to your other objection, I am afraid it will hardly hold good. Lydia has no brothers to step forward; and he might imagine, from my father's behaviour, from his indolence and the little attention he has ever seemed to give to what was going forward in his family, that *he* would do as little, and think as little about it, as any father could do in such a matter."

"But can you think that Lydia is so lost to everything but love of him as to consent to live with him on any other terms than marriage?"

"It does seem, and it is most shocking indeed," replied Elizabeth, with tears in her eyes, "that a sister's sense of decency and virtue in such a point should admit of doubt. But, really, I know not what to say. Perhaps I am not doing her justice. But she is very young; she has never been taught to think on serious subjects; and for the last half year, nay, for a twelvemonth, she has been given up to nothing but amusement and vanity. She has been allowed to dispose of her time in the most idle and frivolous manner, and to adopt any opinions that came in her sway. Since the ——shire were first quartered in Meryton, nothing but love, flirtation, and officers have been in her head. She has been doing everything in her power by thinking and talking on the subject to give greater—what shall I call it?—susceptibility to her feelings, which are naturally lively enough. And we all know that Wickham has every charm of person and address that can captivate a woman."

"But you see that Jane," said her aunt, "does not think so ill of Wickham as to believe him capable of the attempt."

"Of whom does Jane ever think ill? And who is there, whatever might be their former conduct, that she would believe capable of such an attempt, till it were proved against them? But Jane knows, as well as I do, what Wickham really is. We both know that he has been profligate in every sense of the word. That he has neither integrity nor honour. That he is as false and deceitful as he is insinuating."

"And do you really know all this?" cried Mrs. Gardiner, whose curiosity as to the mode of her intelligence was all alive.

"I do, indeed," replied Elizabeth colouring. "I told you the other day of his infamous behaviour to Mr. Darcy; and you, yourself, when last at Longbourn heard in what manner he spoke of the man who had behaved with such forbearance and liberality towards him. And there are other circumstances which I am not at liberty —which it is not worth-while to relate; but his lies about the whole Pemberley family are endless. From what he said of Miss Darcy, I was thoroughly prepared to see a proud, reserved, disagreeable girl. Yet he knew to the contrary himself. He must know that she was as amiable and unpretending as we have found her."

"But does Lydia know nothing of this? Can she be ignorant of what you and Jane seem so well to understand?"

"Oh, yes!—that, that is the worst of all. Till I was in Kent, and saw so much both of Mr. Darcy and his relation, Colonel Fitzwilliam, I was ignorant of the truth myself. And when I returned home, the ——shire was to leave Meryton in a week or fortnight's time. As that was the case, neither Jane, to whom I related the whole, nor I thought it necessary to make our knowledge public; for of what use could it apparently be to any one that the good opinion which all the neighbourhood had of him should then be overthrown? And even when it was settled that Lydia should go with Mrs. Forster, the necessity of opening her eyes to his character never occurred to me. That *she* could be in any danger from the deception never entered my head. That such a consequence as *this* should ensue you may easily believe was far enough from my thoughts."

"When they all removed to Brighton, therefore, you had no reason, I suppose, to believe them fond of each other."

"Not the slightest. I can remember no symptom of affection on either side; and had anything of the kind been perceptible, you must be aware that ours is not a family on which it could be thrown away. When first he entered the corps, she was ready enough to admire him; but so we all were. Every girl in, or near, Meryton was out of her senses about him for the first two months; but he never distinguished *her* by any particular attention, and consequently, after a moderate period of extravagant and wild admiration, her fancy for him gave way, and others of the regiment, who treated her with more distinction, again became her favourites."

It may be easily believed that however little of novelty could be added to their fears, hopes, and conjectures on this interesting subject by its repeated discussion, no other could detain them from it long during the whole of the journey. From Elizabeth's thoughts it was never absent. Fixed there by the keenest of all anguish, self-reproach, she could find no interval of ease or forgetfulness.

They travelled as expeditiously as possible; and sleeping one night on the road, reached Longbourn by dinner-time the next day. It was a comfort to Elizabeth to consider that Jane could not have been wearied by long expectations.

The little Gardiners, attracted by the sight of a chaise, were standing on the steps of the house as they entered the paddock; and when the carriage drove up to the door, the joyful surprise that lighted up their faces, and displayed itself over their whole bodies in a variety of capers and frisks, was the first pleasing earnest of their welcome.

Elizabeth jumped out; and after giving each of them an hasty kiss, hurried into the vestibule, where Jane, who came running downstairs from her mother's apartment, immediately met her.

Elizabeth, as she affectionately embraced her, whilst tears filled the eyes of both, lost not a moment in asking whether anything had been heard of the fugitives.

"Not yet," replied Jane. "But now that my dear uncle is come, I hope everything will be well."

"Is my father in town?"

"Yes, he went on Tuesday as I wrote you word."

"And have you heard from him often?"

"We have heard only once. He wrote me a few lines on Wednesday to say that he had arrived in safety, and to give me his directions, which I particularly begged him to do. He merely added that he should not write again till he had something of importance to mention."

"And my mother—How is she? How are you all?"

"My mother is tolerably well, I trust; though her spirits are greatly shaken. She is upstairs, and will have great satisfaction in seeing you all. She does not yet leave her dressing-room. Mary and Kitty, thank Heaven! are quite well."

"But you—How are you?" cried Elizabeth. "You look pale. How much you must have gone through!"

Her sister, however, assured her of her being perfectly well; and their conversation, which had been passing while Mr. and Mrs. Gardiner were engaged with their children, was now put an end to by the approach of the whole party. Jane ran to her uncle and aunt, and welcomed and thanked them both, with alternate smiles and tears.

When they were all in the drawing-room, the questions which Elizabeth had already asked were of course repeated by the others, and they soon found that Jane had no intelligence to give. The sanguine hope of good, however, which the benevolence of her heart suggested, had not yet deserted her; she still expected that it would all end well, and that every morning would bring some letter, either from Lydia or her father, to explain their proceedings, and perhaps announce the marriage.

Mrs. Bennet, to whose apartment they all repaired after a few minutes conversation together, received them exactly as might be expected; with tears and lamentations of regret, invectives against the villainous conduct of Wickham, and complaints of her own sufferings and ill-usage; blaming everybody but the person to whose ill-judging indulgence the errors of her daughter must be principally owing.

"If I had been able," said she, "to carry my point of going to Brighton with all my family, *this* would not have happened; but poor dear Lydia had nobody to take care of her. Why did the Forsters ever let her go out of their sight? I am sure there was some great neglect or other on their side, for she is not the kind of girl to do such a thing, if she had been well looked after. I always thought they were very unfit to have the charge of her; but I was overruled, as I always am. Poor dear child! And now here's Mr. Bennet gone away, and I know he will fight Wickham wherever he meets him, and then he will be killed, and what is to become of us all? The Collinses will turn us out before he is cold in his grave; and if you are not kind to us, brother, I do not know what we shall do."

They all exclaimed against such terrific ideas; and Mr. Gardiner, after general assurances of his affection for her and all her family, told her that he meant to be in London the very next day, and would assist Mr. Bennet in every endeavour for recovering Lydia.

"Do not give way to useless alarm," added he, "though it is right to be prepared for the worst, there is no occasion to look on it as certain. It is not quite a week since they left Brighton. In a few days more, we may gain some news of them, and till we know that they are not married and have no design of marrying, do not let us give the matter over as lost. As soon as I get to town, I shall go to my brother and make him come home with me to Gracechurch Street, and then we may consult together as to what is to be done."

"Oh! my dear brother," replied Mrs. Bennet, "that is exactly what I could most wish for. And now do, when you get to town, find them out, wherever they may be; and if they are not married already, *make* them marry. And as for wedding clothes, do not let them wait for that, but tell Lydia she shall have as much money as she chooses to buy them after they are married. And, above all things, keep Mr. Bennet from fighting. Tell him what a dreadful state I am in—that I am frightened out of my wits; and have such tremblings, such flutterings, all over me, such spasms in my side, and pains in my head, and such beatings at heart, that I can get no rest by night nor by day. And tell my dear Lydia not to give any directions about her clothes till she has seen me, for she does not know which are the best warehouses. Oh, brother, how kind you are! I know you will contrive it all."

But Mr. Gardiner, though he assured her again of his earnest endeavours in the cause, could not avoid recommending moderation to her, as well in her hopes as her fears; and after talking with her in this manner till dinner was on table, they left her to vent all her feelings on the housekeeper, who attended in the absence of her daughters.

Though her brother and sister were persuaded that there was no real occasion for such a seclusion from the family, they did not attempt to oppose it, for they knew that she had not prudence enough to hold her tongue before the servants while they waited at table, and judged it better that *one* only of the household, and the one whom they could most trust, should comprehend all her fears and solicitude on the subject.

In the dining-room they were soon joined by Mary and Kitty, who had been too busily engaged in their separate apartments to make their appearance before. One came from her books, and the other from her toilette. The faces of both, however, were tolerably calm; and no change was visible in either, except that the loss of her favourite sister, or the anger which she had herself incurred in the business, had given something more of fretfulness than usual to the accents of Kitty. As for Mary, she was mistress enough of herself to whisper to Elizabeth with a countenance of grave reflection soon after they were seated at table.

"This is a most unfortunate affair; and will probably be much talked of. But we must stem the tide of malice, and pour into the wounded bosoms of each other the balm of sisterly consolation."

Then, perceiving in Elizabeth no inclination of replying, she added, "Unhappy as the event must be for Lydia, we may draw from it this useful lesson: that loss of virtue in a female is irretrievable—that one false step involves her in endless ruin—that her reputation is no less brittle than it is beautiful—and that she cannot be too much guarded in her behaviour towards the undeserving of the other sex."

Elizabeth lifted up her eyes in amazement, but was too much oppressed to make any reply. Mary, however, continued to console herself with such kind of moral extractions from the evil before them.

In the afternoon, the two elder Miss Bennets were able to be for half an hour by themselves; and Elizabeth instantly availed herself of the opportunity of making many inquiries, which Jane was equally eager to satisfy. After joining in general lamentations over the dreadful sequel of this event, which Elizabeth considered as all but certain, and Miss Bennet could not assert to be wholly impossible, the former continued the subject by saying, "But tell me all and everything about it, which I have not already heard. Give me farther particulars. What did Colonel Forster say? Had they no apprehension of anything before the elopement took place? They must have seen them together forever."

"Colonel Forster did own that he had often suspected some partiality, especially on Lydia's side, but nothing to give him any alarm. I am so grieved for him. His behaviour was attentive and kind to the utmost. He *was* coming to us in order to assure us of his concern, before he had any idea of their not being gone to Scotland: when that apprehension first got abroad, it hastened his journey."

"And was Denny convinced that Wickham would not marry? Did he know of their intending to go off? Had Colonel Forster seen Denny himself?"

"Yes; but when questioned by *him* Denny denied knowing anything of their plan, and would not give his real opinion about it. He did not repeat his persuasion of their not marrying—and from *that,* I am inclined to hope he might have been misunderstood before."

"And till Colonel Forster came himself, not one of

you entertained a doubt, I suppose, of their being really married?"

"How was it possible that such an idea should enter our brains! I felt a little uneasy—a little fearful of my sister's happiness with him in marriage, because I knew that his conduct had not been always quite right. My father and mother knew nothing of that, they only felt how imprudent a match it must be. Kitty then owned, with a very natural triumph on knowing more than the rest of us, that in Lydia's last letter she had prepared her for such a step. She had known, it seems, of their being in love with each other many weeks."

"But not before they went to Brighton?"

"No, I believe not."

"And did Colonel Forster appear to think ill of Wickham himself? Does he know his real character?"

"I must confess that he did not speak so well of Wickham as he formerly did. He believed him to be imprudent and extravagant. And since this sad affair has taken place, it is said that he left Meryton greatly in debt; but I hope this may be false."

"Oh, Jane, had we been less secret, had we told what we knew of him, this could not have happened!"

"Perhaps it would have been better," replied her sister. "But to expose the former faults of any person, without knowing what their present feelings were, seemed unjustifiable. We acted with the best intentions."

"Could Colonel Forster repeat the particulars of Lydia's note to his wife?"

"He brought it with him for us to see."

Jane then took it from her pocket-book, and gave it to Elizabeth. These were the contents:

MY DEAR HARRIET,

You will laugh when you know where I am gone, and I cannot help laughing myself at your surprise to-morrow morning as soon as I am missed. I am going to Gretna Green, and if you cannot guess with who, I shall think you a simpleton, for there is but one man in the world I love, and he is an angel. I should never be happy without him, so think it no harm to be off. You need not send them word at Longbourn of my going, if you do not like it, for it will make the surprise the greater when I write to them, and sign my name Lydia Wickham. What a good joke it will be! I can hardly write for laughing. Pray make my excuses to Pratt, for not keeping my engagement and dancing with him tonight. Tell him I hope he will excuse me when he knows all, and tell him I will dance with him at the next ball we meet, with great pleasure. I shall send for my clothes when I get to Longbourn; but I wish you would tell Sally to mend a great slit in my worked muslin gown before they are packed up. Good-bye. Give my love to Colonel Forster, I hope you will drink to our good journey.

Your affectionate friend,

LYDIA BENNET

"Oh! thoughtless, thoughtless Lydia!" cried Elizabeth when she had finished it. "What a letter is this to be written at such a moment. But at least it shows that *she* was serious in the object of her journey. Whatever he might afterwards persuade her to, it was not on her side a *scheme* of infamy. My poor father! how he must have felt it!"

"I never saw anyone so shocked. He could not speak a word for full ten minutes. My mother was taken ill immediately, and the whole house in such confusion!"

"Oh! Jane," cried Elizabeth, "was there a servant belonging to it who did not know the whole story before the end of the day?"

"I do not know.—I hope there was.—But to be guarded at such a time is very difficult. My mother was in hysterics, and though I endeavoured to give her every assistance in my power, I am afraid I did not do so much as I might have done! But the horror of what might possibly happen almost took from me my faculties."

"Your attendance upon her has been too much for you. You do not look well. Oh! that I had been with you, you have had every care and anxiety upon yourself alone."

"Mary and Kitty have been very kind, and would have shared in every fatigue, I am sure, but I did not think it right for either of them. Kitty is slight and delicate, and Mary studies so much that her hours of repose

244

should not be broken in on. My aunt Philips came to Longbourn on Tuesday, after my father went away; and was so good as to stay till Thursday with me. She was of great use and comfort to us all, and Lady Lucas has been very kind; she walked here on Wednesday morning to condole with us, and offered her services, or any of her daughters, if they could be of use to us."

"She had better have stayed at home," cried Elizabeth; "perhaps she *meant* well, but under such a misfortune as this, one cannot see too little of one's neighbours. Assistance is impossible; condolence, insufferable. Let them triumph over us at a distance, and be satisfied."

She then proceeded to inquire into the measures which her father had intended to pursue while in town for the recovery of his daughter.

"He meant, I believe," replied Jane, "to go to Epsom, the place where they last changed horses, see the postilions, and try if anything could be made out from them. His principal object must be to discover the number of the hackney-coach which took them from Clapham. It had come with a fare from London; and as he thought the circumstance of a gentleman and lady's removing from one carriage into another might be remarked, he meant to make inquiries at Clapham. If he could anyhow discover at what house the coachman had before set down his fare, he determined to make inquiries there, and hoped it might not be impossible to find out the stand and number of the coach. I do not know of any other designs that he had formed: but he was in such a hurry to be gone, and his spirits so greatly discomposed, that I had difficulty in finding out even so much as this."

CHAPTER SIX

THE whole party were in hopes of a letter from Mr. Bennet the next morning, but the post came in without bringing a single line from him. His family knew him to be on all common occasions a most negligent and dilatory correspondent, but at such a time, they had hoped for exertion. They were forced to conclude that he had no pleasing intelligence to send, but even of *that* they would have been glad to be certain. Mr. Gardiner had waited only for the letters before he set off.

When he was gone, they were certain at least of receiving constant information of what was going on, and their uncle promised at parting to prevail on Mr. Bennet to return to Longbourn as soon as he could, to the great consolation of his sister, who considered it as the only security for her husband's not being killed in a duel.

Mrs. Gardiner and the children were to remain in Hertfordshire a few days longer, as the former thought her presence might be serviceable to her nieces. She shared in their attendance on Mrs. Bennet, and was a great comfort to them in their hours of freedom. Their other aunt also visited them frequently, and always, as she said, with the design of cheering and heartening them up, though as she never came without reporting some fresh instance of Wickham's extravagance or irregularity, she seldom went away without leaving them more dispirited than she found them.

All Meryton seemed striving to blacken the man, who but three months before, had been almost an angel of light. He was declared to be in debt to every tradesman in the place, and his intrigues, all honoured with the title of seduction, had been extended into every tradesman's family. Everybody declared that he was the wickedest young man in the world; and everybody began to find out that they had always distrusted the appearance of his goodness. Elizabeth, though she did not credit above half of what was said, believed enough to make her former assurance of her sister's ruin still more certain; and even Jane, who believed still less of it, became almost hopeless, more especially as the time was now come when if they had gone to Scotland, which she had never before entirely despaired of, they must in all probability have gained some news of them.

Mr. Gardiner left Longbourn on Sunday; on Tuesday his wife received a letter from him; it told them that on his arrival, he had immediately found out his brother, and persuaded him to come to Gracechurch Street. That Mr. Bennet had been to Epsom and Clapham before his arrival, but without gaining any satisfactory information; and that he was now determined to inquire at all the principal hotels in town, as Mr. Bennet thought it possible they might have gone to one of them on their first coming to London, before they procured lodgings. Mr. Gardiner himself did not expect any success from this measure, but as his brother was eager in it, he meant to assist him in pursuing it. He added that Mr. Bennet seemed wholly disinclined at present to leave London, and promised to write again very soon. There was also a postscript to this effect.

"I have written to Colonel Forster to desire him to find out, if possible, from some of the young man's intimates in the regiment whether Wickham has any relations or connections who would be likely to know in what part of the town he has now concealed himself. If there were any one that one could apply to with a probability of gaining such a clue as that, it might be of essential consequence. At present we have nothing to guide us. Colonel Forster will, I dare say, do everything in his power to satisfy us on this head. But, on second thoughts, perhaps Lizzy could tell us what relations he has now living better than any other person."

Elizabeth was at no loss to understand from whence this deference for her authority proceeded; but it was not in her power to give any information of so satisfactory a nature as the compliment deserved.

She had never heard of his having had any relations, except a father and mother, both of whom had been dead many years. It was possible, however, that some of his companions in the ——shire might be able to give more information; and though she was not very sanguine in expecting it, the application was a something to look forward to.

Everyday at Longbourn was now a day of anxiety; but the most anxious part of each was when the post was expected. The arrival of letters was the first grand object of every morning's impatience. Through letters, whatever of good or bad was to be told would be communicated, and every succeeding day was expected to bring some news of importance.

But before they heard again from Mr. Gardiner, a letter arrived for their father from a different quarter, from Mr. Collins; which, as Jane had received directions to open all that came for him in his absence, she accordingly read; and Elizabeth, who knew what curiosities his letters always were, looked over her, and read it likewise. It was as follows:

My dear Sir,

I feel myself called upon by our relationship, and my situation in life, to condole with you on the grievous affliction you are now suffering under, of which we were yesterday informed by a letter from Hertfordshire. Be assured, my dear sir, that Mrs. Collins and myself sincerely sympathize with you, and all your respectable family, in your present distress, which must be of the bitterest kind, because proceeding from a cause which no time can remove. No arguments shall be wanting on my part that can alleviate so severe a misfortune, or that may comfort you under a circumstance that must be of all others most afflicting to a parent's mind. The death of your daughter would have been a blessing in comparison of this. And it is the more to be lamented because there is reason to suppose, as my dear Charlotte informs me, that this licentiousness of behaviour in your daughter has proceeded from a faulty degree of indulgence, though at the same time, for the consolation of yourself and Mrs. Bennet, I am inclined to think that her own disposition must be naturally bad, or she could not be guilty of such an enormity at so early an age. Howsoever that may be, you are grievously to be pitied, in which opinion I am not only joined by Mrs. Collins, but likewise by Lady Catherine and her daughter, to whom I have related the affair. They agree with me in apprehending that this false step in one daughter will be injurious to the fortunes of all the others, for who, as Lady Catherine herself condescendingly says, will connect themselves with such a family. And this consideration leads me moreover to reflect with augmented satisfaction on a certain event of last November, for had it been otherwise, I must have been involved in all your sorrow and disgrace. Let me advise you then, my dear sir, to console yourself as much as possible, to throw off your unworthy child from your affection forever, and leave her to reap the fruits of her own heinous offence.

I AM, DEAR SIR, ETC. ETC.

Mr. Gardiner did not write again till he had received an answer from Colonel Forster; and then he had nothing of a pleasant nature to send. It was not known that Wickham had a single relation with whom he kept up any connection, and it was certain that he had no near one living. His former acquaintance had been numerous; but since he had been in the militia, it did not appear that he was on terms of particular friendship with any of them. There was no one therefore who could be pointed out as likely to give any news of him. And in the wretched state of his own finances, there was a very powerful motive for secrecy, in addition to his fear of discovery by Lydia's relations, for it had just transpired that he had left gaming debts behind him to a very considerable amount. Colonel Forster believed that more than a thousand pounds would be necessary to clear his expenses at Brighton. He owed a good deal in the town, but his debts of honour were still more formidable. Mr. Gardiner did not attempt to conceal these particulars from the Longbourn family; Jane heard them with horror. "A gamester!" she cried. "This is wholly unexpected. I had not an idea of it."

Mr. Gardiner added in his letter that they might expect to see their father at home on the following day, which was Saturday. Rendered spiritless by the ill-success of all their endeavours, he had yielded to his brother-in-law's entreaty that he would return to his family, and leave it to him to do whatever occasion might suggest to be advisable for continuing their pursuit. When Mrs. Bennet was told of this, she did not express so much satisfaction as her children expected, considering what her anxiety for his life had been before.

"What, is he coming home, and without poor Lydia!" she cried. "Sure he will not leave London before he has found them. Who is to fight Wickham, and make him marry her, if he comes away?"

As Mrs. Gardiner began to wish to be at home, it was settled that she and her children should go to London at the same time that Mr. Bennet came from it. The coach, therefore, took them the first stage of their journey, and brought its master back to Longbourn.

Mrs. Gardiner went away in all the perplexity about Elizabeth and her Derbyshire friend that had attended her from that part of the world. His name had never been voluntarily mentioned before them by her niece; and the kind of half-expectation which Mrs. Gardiner had formed of their being followed by a letter from him had ended in nothing. Elizabeth had received none since her return that could come from Pemberley.

The present unhappy state of the family rendered any other excuse for the lowness of her spirits unnecessary; nothing, therefore, could be fairly conjectured from *that,* though Elizabeth, who was by this time tolerably well acquainted with her own feelings, was perfectly aware that, had she known nothing of Darcy, she could have borne the dread of Lydia's infamy somewhat better. It would have spared her, she thought, one sleepless night out of two.

When Mr. Bennet arrived, he had all the appearance of his usual philosophic composure. He said as little as he had ever been in the habit of saying, made no mention of the business that had taken him away, and it was some time before his daughters had courage to speak of it.

It was not till the afternoon, when he joined them at tea, that Elizabeth ventured to introduce the subject; and then, on her briefly expressing her sorrow for what he must have endured, he replied, "Say nothing of that. Who should suffer but myself? It has been my own doing, and I ought to feel it."

"You must not be too severe upon yourself," replied Elizabeth.

"You may well warn me against such an evil. Human nature is so prone to fall into it! No, Lizzy, let me once in my life feel how much I have been to blame. I am not afraid of being overpowered by the impression. It will pass away soon enough."

"Do you suppose them to be in London?"

"Yes; where else can they be so well concealed?"

"And Lydia used to want to go to London," added Kitty.

"She is happy, then," said her father, dryly; "and her residence there will probably be of some duration."

Then, after a short silence, he continued, "Lizzy, I bear you no ill-will for being justified in your advice to me last May, which, considering the event, shows some greatness of mind."

They were interrupted by Miss Bennet, who came to fetch her mother's tea.

"This is a parade," cried he, "which does one good; it gives such an elegance to misfortune! Another day I will do the same; I will sit in my library, in my night-cap and powdering gown, and give as much trouble as I can —or, perhaps, I may defer it till Kitty runs away."

"I am not going to run away, Papa," said Kitty fretfully; "if *I* should ever go to Brighton, I would behave better than Lydia."

"*You* go to Brighton!—I would not trust you so near it as East Bourne for fifty pounds! No, Kitty, I have at last learned to be cautious, and you will feel the effects of it. No officer is ever to enter my house again, nor even to pass through the village. Balls will be absolutely prohibited, unless you stand up with one of your sisters. And you are never to stir out-of-doors, till you can prove that you have spent ten minutes of every day in a rational manner."

Kitty, who took all these threats in a serious light, began to cry.

"Well, well," said he, "do not make yourself unhappy. If you are a good girl for the next ten years, I will take you to a review at the end of them."

CHAPTER SEVEN

Two days after Mr. Bennet's return, as Jane and Elizabeth were walking together in the shrubbery behind the house, they saw the housekeeper coming towards them, and concluding that she came to call them to their mother, went forward to meet her; but instead of the expected summons, when they approached her, she said to Miss Bennet, "I beg your pardon, madam, for interrupting you, but I was in hopes you might have got some good news from town, so I took the liberty of coming to ask."

"What do you mean, Hill? We have heard nothing from town."

"Dear madam," cried Mrs. Hill, in great astonishment,

"don't you know there is an express come for master from Mr. Gardiner? He has been here this half hour, and master has had a letter."

Away ran the girls, too eager to get in to have time for speech. They ran through the vestibule into the breakfast-room, from thence to the library—their father was in neither; and they were on the point of seeking him upstairs with their mother, when they were met by the butler, who said,

"If you are looking for my master, ma'am, he is walking towards the little copse."

Upon this information, they instantly passed through the hall once more, and ran across the lawn after their father, who was deliberately pursuing his way towards a small wood on one side of the paddock.

Jane, who was not so light, nor so much in the habit of running as Elizabeth, soon lagged behind, while her sister, panting for breath, came up with him, and eagerly cried out,

"Oh, Papa, what news? what news? have you heard from my uncle?"

"Yes, I have had a letter from him by express."

"Well, and what news does it bring? good or bad?"

"What is there of good to be expected?" said he, taking the letter from his pocket; "but perhaps you would like to read it."

Elizabeth impatiently caught it from his hand. Jane now came up.

"Read it aloud," said their father, "for I hardly know myself what it is about."

Gracechurch Street, Monday,
August 2.

My dear Brother,

At last I am able to send you some tidings of my niece, and such as, upon the whole, I hope will give you satisfaction. Soon after you left me on Saturday, I was fortunate enough to find out in what part of London they were. The particulars I reserve till we meet. It is enough to know they are discovered, I have seen them both——

"Then it is as I always hoped," cried Jane; "they are married!"

Elizabeth read on; "I have seen them both. They are not married, nor can I find there was any intention of being so; but if you are willing to perform the engagements which I have ventured to make on your side, I hope it will not be long before they are. All that is required of you is to assure your daughter, by settlement, her equal share of the five thousand pounds, secured among your children after the decease of yourself and my sister; and, moreover, to enter into an engagement of allowing her during your life one hundred pounds per annum. These are conditions which, considering everything, I had no hesitation in complying with, as far as I thought myself privileged, for you. I shall send this by express that no time may be lost in bringing me your answer. You will easily comprehend from these particulars that Mr. Wickham's circumstances are not so hopeless as they are generally believed to be. The world has been deceived in that respect; and I am happy to say there will be some little money, even when all his debts are discharged, to settle on my niece, in addition to her own fortune. If, as I conclude will be the case, you send me full powers to act in your name throughout the whole of this business, I will immediately give directions to Haggerston for preparing a proper settlement. There will not be the smallest occasion for your coming to town again; therefore, stay quietly at Longbourn, and depend on my diligence and care. Send back your answer as soon as you can, and be careful to write explicitly. We have judged it best that my niece should be married from this house, of which I hope you will approve. She comes to us to-day. I shall write again as soon as anything more is determined on. Your's, etc.

"EDW. GARDINER."

"Is it possible!" cried Elizabeth, when she had finished. "Can it be possible that he will marry her?"

"Wickham is not so undeserving, then, as we have thought him," said her sister. "My dear father, I congratulate you."

"And have you answered the letter?" said Elizabeth.

"No; but it must be done soon."

Most earnestly did she then entreat him to lose no more time before he wrote.

"Oh! my dear father," she cried, "come back, and write immediately. Consider how important every moment is in such a case."

"Let me write for you," said Jane, "if you dislike the trouble yourself."

"I dislike it very much," he replied; "but it must be done."

And so saying, he turned back with them, and walked towards the house.

"And may I ask?" said Elizabeth, "but the terms, I suppose, must be complied with."

"Complied with! I am only ashamed of his asking so little."

"And they *must* marry! Yet he is *such* a man!"

"Yes, yes, they must marry. There is nothing else to be done. But there are two things that I want very much to know—one is, how much money your uncle has laid down to bring it about; and the other, how I am ever to pay him."

"Money! my uncle!" cried Jane, "what do you mean, sir?"

"I mean that no man in his senses would marry Lydia on so slight a temptation as one hundred a year during my life, and fifty after I am gone."

"That is very true," said Elizabeth; "though it had not occurred to me before. His debts to be discharged, and something still to remain! Oh! it must be my uncle's doings! Generous, good man, I am afraid he has distressed himself. A small sum could not do all this."

"No," said her father, "Wickham's a fool if he takes her with a farthing less than ten thousand pounds. I should be sorry to think so ill of him in the very beginning of our relationship."

"Ten thousand pounds! Heaven forbid! How is half such a sum to be repaid?"

Mr. Bennet made no answer, and each of them, deep in thought, continued silent till they reached the house. Their father then went to the library to write, and the girls walked into the breakfast-room.

"And they are really to be married!" cried Elizabeth, as soon as they were by themselves. "How strange this is! And for *this* we are to be thankful. That they should marry, small as is their chance of happiness, and wretched as is his character, we are forced to rejoice! Oh, Lydia!"

"I comfort myself with thinking," replied Jane, "that he certainly would not marry Lydia, if he had not a real regard for her. Though our kind uncle has done something towards clearing him, I cannot believe that ten thousand pounds, or anything like it, has been advanced. He has children of his own, and may have more. How could he spare half ten thousand pounds?"

"If we are ever able to learn what Wickham's debts have been," said Elizabeth, "and how much is settled on his side on our sister, we shall exactly know what Mr. Gardiner has done for them, because Wickham has not sixpence of his own. The kindness of my uncle and aunt can never be requited. Their taking her home, and affording her their personal protection and countenace, is such a sacrifice to her advantage as years of gratitude cannot enough acknowledge. By this time she is actually with them! If such goodness does not make her miserable now, she will never deserve to be happy! What a meeting for her when she first sees my aunt!"

"We must endeavour to forget all that has passed on either side," said Jane: "I hope and trust they will yet be happy. His consenting to marry her is a proof, I will believe, that he is come to a right way of thinking. Their mutual affection will steady them; and I flatter myself they will settle so quietly and live in so rational a manner as may in time make their past imprudence forgotten."

"Their conduct has been such," replied Elizabeth, "as neither you, nor I, nor anybody, can ever forget. It is useless to talk of it."

It now occurred to the girls that their mother was in all likelihood perfectly ignorant of what had happened. They went to the library, therefore, and asked their father, whether he would not wish them to make it known to her. He was writing, and, without raising his head, coolly replied,

"Just as you please."

"May we take my uncle's letter to read to her?"

"Take whatever you like, and get away."

Elizabeth took the letter from his writing table, and they went upstairs together. Mary and Kitty were both with Mrs. Bennet: one communication would, therefore, do for all. After a slight preparation for good news, the letter was read aloud. Mrs. Bennet could hardly contain herself. As soon as Jane had read Mr. Gardiner's hope of Lydia's being soon married, her joy burst forth, and every following sentence added to its exuberance. She was now in an irritation as violent from delight as she had ever been fidgety from alarm and vexation. To know that her daughter would be married was enough. She was disturbed by no fear for her felicity, nor humbled by any remembrance of her misconduct.

"My dear, dear Lydia!" she cried: "This is delightful indeed!—She will be married!—I shall see her again!—She will be married at sixteen!—My good, kind brother!—I knew how it would be—I knew he would manage everything. How I long to see her! and to see dear Wickham too! But the clothes, the wedding clothes! I will write to my sister Gardiner about them directly. Lizzy, my dear, run down to your father, and ask him how much he will give her. Stay, stay, I will go myself. Ring the bell, Kitty, for Hill. I will put on my things in a moment. My dear, dear Lydia!—How merry we shall be together when we meet!"

Her eldest daughter endeavoured to give some relief to the violence of these transports by leading her thoughts to the obligations which Mr. Gardiner's behaviour laid them all under.

"For we must attribute this happy conclusion," she added, "in a great measure to his kindness. We are persuaded that he has pledged himself to assist Mr. Wickham with money."

"Well," cried her mother, "it is all very right; who should do it but her own uncle? If he had not had a family of his own, I and my children must have had all his money you know, and it is the first time we have ever had anything from him, except a few presents. Well! I am so happy. In a short time, I shall have a daughter married. Mrs. Wickham! How well it sounds. And she was only sixteen last June. My dear Jane, I am in such a flutter that I am sure I can't write; so I will dictate, and you write for me. We will settle with your

256

father about the money afterwards; but the things should be ordered immediately."

She was then proceeding to all the particulars of calico, muslin, and cambric, and would shortly have dictated some very plentiful orders, had not Jane, though with some difficulty, persuaded her to wait till her father was at leisure to be consulted. One day's delay, she observed, would be of small importance; and her mother was too happy to be quite so obstinate as usual. Other schemes too came into her head.

"I will go to Meryton," said she, "as soon as I am dressed, and tell the good, good news to my sister Philips. And as I come back, I can call on Lady Lucas and Mrs. Long. Kitty, run down and order the carriage. An airing would do me a great deal of good, I am sure. Girls, can I do anything for you in Meryton? Oh! here comes Hill. My dear Hill, have you heard the good news? Miss Lydia is going to be married; and you shall all have a bowl of punch to make merry at her wedding."

Mrs. Hill began instantly to express her joy. Elizabeth received her congratulations amongst the rest, and then, sick of this folly, took refuge in her own room that she might think with freedom.

Poor Lydia's situation must, at best, be bad enough; but that it was no worse, she had need to be thankful. She felt it so; and though in looking forward neither rational happiness nor worldly prosperity could be justly expected for her sister, in looking back to what they had feared only two hours ago, she felt all the advantages of what they had gained.

CHAPTER EIGHT

MR. BENNET had very often wished, before this period of his life, that instead of spending his whole income, he had laid by an annual sum for the better provision of his children, and of his wife, if she survived him. He now wished it more than ever. Had he done his duty in that respect, Lydia need not have been indebted to her uncle, for whatever of honour or credit could now be purchased for her. The satisfaction of prevailing on one of the most

257

worthless young men in Great Britain to be her husband might then have rested in its proper place.

He was seriously concerned that a cause of so little advantage to any one should be forwarded at the sole expense of his brother-in-law, and he was determined, if possible, to find out the extent of his assistance, and to discharge the obligation as soon as he could.

When first Mr. Bennet had married, economy was held to be perfectly useless; for, of course, they were to have a son. This son was to join in cutting off the entail, as soon as he should be of age, and the widow and younger children would by that means be provided for. Five daughters successively entered the world, but yet the son was to come; and Mrs. Bennet, for many years after Lydia's birth, had been certain that he would. This event had at last been despaired of, but it was then too late to be saving. Mrs. Bennet had no turn of economy, and her husband's love of independence had alone prevented their exceeding their income.

Five thousand pounds was settled by marriage articles on Mrs. Bennet and the children. But in what proportions it should be divided amongst the latter depended on the will of the parents. This was one point, with regard to Lydia at least, which was now to be settled, and Mr. Bennet could have no hesitation in acceding to the proposal before him. In terms of grateful acknowledgment for the kindness of his brother, though expressed most concisely, he then delivered on paper his perfect approbation of all that was done, and his willingness to fulfil the engagements that had been made for him. He had never before supposed that could Wickham be prevailed on to marry his daughter it would be done with so little inconvenience to himself as by the present arrangement. He would scarcely be ten pounds a year the loser by the hundred that was to be paid them; for, what with her board and pocket allowance, and the continual presents in money which passed to her through her mother's hands, Lydia's expenses had been very little within that sum.

That it would be done with such trifling exertion on his side, too, was another very welcome surprise; for his chief wish at present was to have as little trouble in the business as possible. When the first transports of rage which had produced his activity in seeking her were over, he naturally returned to all his former indolence. His letter was soon dispatched; for though dilatory in undertaking business, he was quick in its execution. He begged to know farther particulars of what he was indebted to his brother; but was too angry with Lydia to send any message to her.

The good news quickly spread through the house; and with proportionate speed through the neighbourhood. It was borne in the latter with decent philosophy. To be sure it would have been more for the advantage of conversation had Miss Lydia Bennet come upon the town; or, as the happiest alternative, been secluded from the world in some distant farm-house. But there was much to be talked of in marrying her; and the good-natured wishes for her well-doing, which had proceeded before from all the spiteful old ladies in Meryton, lost but little of their spirit in this change of circumstances, because with such an husband, her misery was considered certain.

It was a fortnight since Mrs. Bennet had been downstairs, but on this happy day she again took her seat at the head of her table, and in spirits oppressively high. No sentiment of shame gave a damp to her triumph. The marriage of a daughter, which had been the first object of her wishes since Jane was sixteen, was now on the point of accomplishment, and her thoughts and her words ran wholly on those attendants of elegant nuptials, fine muslins, new carriages, and servants. She was busily searching through the neighbourhood for a proper situation for her daughter, and without knowing or considering what their income might be, rejected many as deficient in size and importance.

"Haye-Park might do," said she, "if the Gouldings would quit it, or the great house at Stoke, if the drawing-room were larger; but Ashworth is too far off! I could not bear to have her ten miles from me; and as for Purvis Lodge, the attics are dreadful."

Her husband allowed her to talk on without interruption, while the servants remained. But when they had withdrawn, he said to her, "Mrs. Bennet, before you take any, or all of these houses, for your son and daughter, let us come to a right understanding. Into *one* house in this neighbourhood they shall never have admittance. I will not encourage the impudence of either by receiving them at Longbourn."

A long dispute followed this declaration; but Mr. Bennet was firm: it soon led to another; and Mrs. Bennet found, with amazement and horror, that her husband would not advance a guinea to buy clothes for his daughter. He protested that she should receive from him no mark of affection whatever on the occasion. Mrs. Bennet could hardly comprehend it. That his anger could be carried to such a point of inconceivable resentment as to refuse his daughter a privilege, without which her marriage would scarcely seem valid, exceeded all that she could believe possible. She was more alive to the disgrace which the want of new clothes must reflect on her daughter's nuptials, than to any sense of shame at her eloping and living with Wickham a fortnight before they took place.

Elizabeth was now most heartily sorry that she had, from the distress of the moment, been led to make Mr. Darcy acquainted with their fears for her sister; for since her marriage would so shortly give the proper termination to the elopement, they might hope to conceal its unfavourable beginning from all those who were not immediately on the spot.

She had no fear of its spreading farther through his means. There were few people on whose secrecy she would have more confidently depended; but at the same time, there was no one whose knowledge of a sister's frailty would have mortified her so much. Not, however, from any fear of disadvantage from it individually to herself; for at any rate, there seemed a gulf impossible between them. Had Lydia's marriage been concluded on the most honourable terms, it was not to be supposed that Mr. Darcy would connect himself with a family, where to every other objection would now be added an alliance and relationship of the nearest kind with the man whom he so justly scorned.

From such a connection she could not wonder that he should shrink. The wish of procuring her regard, which she had assured herself of his feeling in Derbyshire, could not in rational expectation survive such a blow as this. She was humbled, she was grieved; she repented, though she hardly knew of what. She became jealous of his esteem, when she could no longer hope to be benefited by it. She wanted to hear of him, when there seemed the least chance of gaining intelligence. She was convinced that she could have been happy with him, when it was no longer likely they should meet.

What a triumph for him, as she often thought, could he know that the proposals which she had proudly spurned only four months ago would now have been gladly and gratefully received! He was as generous, she doubted not, as the most generous of his sex. But while he was mortal, there must be a triumph.

She began now to comprehend that he was exactly the man who, in disposition and talents, would most suit her. His understanding and temper, though unlike her own, would have answered all her wishes. It was an union that must have been to the advantage of both—by her ease and liveliness, his mind might have been softened, his manners improved; and from his judgment, information, and knowledge of the world, she must have received benefit of greater importance.

But no such happy marriage could now teach the admiring multitude what connubial felicity really was. An union of a different tendency, and precluding the possibility of the other, was soon to be formed in their family.

How Wickham and Lydia were to be supported in tolerable independence, she could not imagine. But how little of permanent happiness could belong to a couple who were only brought together because their passions were stronger than their virtue, she could easily conjecture.

Mr. Gardiner soon wrote again to his brother. To Mr. Bennet's acknowledgments he briefly replied, with assurances of his eagerness to promote the welfare of any of his family; and concluded with entreaties that the subject might never be mentioned to him again. The principal purport of his letter was to inform them that Mr. Wickham had resolved on quitting the militia.

"It was greatly my wish that he should do so," he added, "as soon as his marriage was fixed on. And I think you will agree with me in considering a removal from that corps as highly advisable, both on his account and my niece's. It is Mr. Wickham's intention to go into the regulars; and among his former friends, there are still some who are able and willing to assist him in the army. He has the promise of an ensigncy in General ————'s regiment, now quartered in the North. It is an advantage to have it so far from this part of the kingdom. He promises fairly, and I hope among different people, where they may each have a character to preserve, they will both be more prudent. I have written to Colonel Forster to inform him of our present arrangements, and to request that he will satisfy the various creditors of Mr. Wickham in and near Brighton, with assurances of speedy payment, for which I have pledged myself. And will you give yourself the trouble of carrying similar assurances to his creditors in Meryton, of whom I shall subjoin a list, according to his information. He has given in all his debts; I hope at least he has not deceived us. Haggerston has our directions, and all will be completed in a week. They will then join his regiment, unless they are first invited to Longbourn; and I understand from Mrs. Gardiner that my niece is very desirous of seeing you all before she leaves the South. She is well, and begs to be dutifully remembered to you and her mother.—Your's, etc.

E. Gardiner

Mr. Bennet and his daughters saw all the advantages of Wickham's removal from the ————shire, as clearly as Mr. Gardiner could do. But Mrs. Bennet was not so well pleased with it. Lydia's being settled in the North, just when she had expected most pleasure and pride in her company, for she had by no means given up her plan of their residing in Hertfordshire, was a severe disappointment; and besides, it was such a pity that Lydia should be taken from a regiment where she was acquainted with everybody, and had so many favourites.

"She is so fond of Mrs. Forster," said she, "it will be quite shocking to send her away! And there are several of the young men, too, that she likes very much. The officers may not be so pleasant in General ————'s regiment."

His daughter's request, for such it might be considered, of being admitted into her family again before she set off for the North received at first an absolute negative. But Jane and Elizabeth, who agreed in wishing, for the sake of their sister's feelings and consequence, that she should be noticed on her marriage by her parents, urged him so earnestly, yet so rationally and so mildly, to receive her and her husband at Longbourn, as soon as they were married, that he was prevailed on to think as they thought, and act as they wished. And their mother had the satisfaction of knowing that she should be able to show her married daughter in the neighbourhood before she was banished to the North. When Mr. Bennet wrote again to his brother, therefore, he sent his permission for them to come; and it was settled that as soon as the ceremony was over, they should proceed to Longbourn. Elizabeth was surprised, however, that Wickham should consent to such a scheme, and had she consulted only her own inclination, any meeting with him would have been the last object of her wishes.

CHAPTER NINE

THEIR sister's wedding day arrived; and Jane and Elizabeth felt for her probably more than she felt for herself. The carriage was sent to meet them at———, and they were to return in it by dinner-time. Their arrival was dreaded by the elder Miss Bennets; and Jane more especially, who gave Lydia the feelings which would have attended herself, had *she* been the culprit, was wretched in the thought of what her sister must endure.

They came. The family were assembled in the breakfast-room to receive them. Smiles decked the face of Mrs. Bennet as the carriage drove up to the door; her husband looked impenetrably grave; her daughters alarmed, anxious, uneasy.

Lydia's voice was heard in the vestibule; the door was thrown open, and she ran into the room. Her mother stepped forwards, embraced her, and welcomed her with rapture; gave her hand with an affectionate smile to Wickham, who followed his lady, and wished them both joy, with an alacrity which showed no doubt of their happiness.

Their reception from Mr. Bennet, to whom they then turned, was not quite so cordial. His countenance rather gained in austerity; and he scarcely opened his lips. The easy assurance of the young couple, indeed, was enough to provoke him. Elizabeth was disgusted, and even Miss Bennet was shocked. Lydia was Lydia still; untamed, unabashed, wild, noisy, and fearless. She turned from sister to sister, demanding their congratulations, and when at length they all sat down, looked eagerly round the room, took notice of some little alteration in it, and observed, with a laugh, that it was a great while since she had been there.

Wickham was not at all more distressed than herself, but his manners were always so pleasing that had his character and his marriage been exactly what they ought, his smiles and his easy address, while he claimed their relationship, would have delighted them all. Elizabeth had not before believed him quite equal to such assurance; but she sat down, resolving within herself to draw no limits in future to the impudence of an impudent man. *She* blushed, and Jane blushed; but the cheeks of the two who caused their confusion suffered no variation of colour.

There was no want of discourse. The bride and her mother could neither of them talk fast enough; and Wickham, who happened to sit near Elizabeth, began inquiring after his acquaintance in that neighbourhood with a good-humoured ease, which she felt very unable to equal in her replies. They seemed each of them to have the happiest memories in the world. Nothing of the past was recollected with pain; and Lydia led voluntarily to subjects which her sisters would not have alluded to for the world.

"Only think of its being three months," she cried, "since I went away; it seems but a fortnight I declare; and yet there have been things enough happened in the time. Good gracious! when I went away, I am sure I had no more idea of being married till I came back again! though I thought it would be very good fun if I was."

Her father lifted up his eyes. Jane was distressed,

Elizabeth looked expressively at Lydia; but she, who never heard nor saw anything of which she chose to be insensible, gaily continued, "Oh! Mamma, do the people here abouts know I am married to-day? I was afraid they might not; and we overtook William Goulding in his curricle, so I was determined he should know it, and so I let down the side glass next to him, and took off my glove, and let my hand just rest upon the window frame, so that he might see the ring, and then I bowed and smiled like anything."

Elizabeth could bear it no longer. She got up, and ran out of the room; and returned no more, till she heard them passing through the hall to the dining-parlour. She then joined them soon enough to see Lydia, with anxious parade, walk up to her mother's right hand, and hear her say to her eldest sister, "Ah! Jane, I take your place now, and you must go lower, because I am a married woman."

It was not to be supposed that time would give Lydia that embarrassment from which she had been so wholly free at first. Her ease and good spirits increased. She longed to see Mrs. Philips, the Lucases, and all their other neighbours, and to hear herself called "Mrs. Wickham" by each of them; and in the meantime, she went after dinner to show her ring and boast of being married to Mrs. Hill and the two housemaids.

"Well, Mamma," said she, when they were all returned to the breakfast-room, "and what do you think of my husband? Is not he a charming man? I am sure my sisters must all envy me. I only hope they may have half my good luck. They must all go to Brighton. That is the place to get husbands. What a pity it is, Mamma, we did not all go."

"Very true; and if I had my will, we should. But my dear Lydia, I don't at all like your going such a way off. Must it be so?"

"Oh, lord! yes; there is nothing in that. I shall like it of all things. You and Papa, and my sisters, must come down and see us. We shall be at Newcastle all the winter, and I dare say there will be some balls, and I will take care to get good partners for them all."

"I should like it beyond anything!" said her mother.

"And then when you go away, you may leave one

or two of my sisters behind you; and I dare say I shall get husbands for them before the winter is over."

"I thank you for my share of the favour," said Elizabeth; "but I do not particularly like your way of getting husbands."

Their visitors were not to remain above ten days with them. Mr. Wickham had received his commission before he left London, and he was to join his regiment at the end of a fortnight.

No one but Mrs. Bennet regretted that their stay would be so short; and she made the most of the time by visiting about with her daughter, and having very frequent parties at home. These parties were acceptable to all; to avoid a family circle was even more desirable to such as did think, than such as did not.

Wickham's affection for Lydia was just what Elizabeth had expected to find it, not equal to Lydia's for him. She had scarcely needed her present observation to be satisfied, from the reason of things, that their elopement had been brought on by the strength of her love, rather than by his; and she would have wondered why, without violently caring for her, he chose to elope with her at all, had she not felt certain that his flight was rendered necessary by distress of circumstances; and if that were the case, he was not the young man to resist an opportunity of having a companion.

Lydia was exceedingly fond of him. He was her dear Wickham on every occasion; no one was to be put in competition with him. He did everything best in the world; and she was sure he would kill more birds on the first of September than anybody else in the country.

One morning, soon after their arrival, as she was sitting with her two elder sisters, she said to Elizabeth,

"Lizzy, I never gave *you* an account of my wedding, I believe. You were not by when I told Mamma and the others all about it. Are not you curious to hear how it was managed?"

"No really," replied Elizabeth; "I think there cannot be too little said on the subject."

"La! You are so strange! But I must tell you how it went off. We were married, you know, at St. Clement's, because Wickham's lodgings were in that parish. And it was settled that we should all be there by eleven o'clock.

My uncle and aunt and I were to go together; and the others were to meet us at the church. Well, Monday morning came, and I was in such a fuss! I was so afraid you know that something would happen to put it off, and then I should have gone quite distracted. And there was my aunt all the time I was dressing, preaching and talking away just as if she was reading a sermon. However, I did not hear above one word in ten, for I was thinking, you may suppose, of my dear Wickham. I longed to know whether he would be married in his blue coat.

"Well, and so we breakfasted at ten as usual; I thought it would never be over; for, by the by, you are to understand, that my uncle and aunt were horrid unpleasant all the time I was with them. If you'll believe me, I did not once put my foot out-of-doors, though I was there a fortnight. Not one party, or scheme, or anything. To be sure London was rather thin, but however the Little Theatre was open. Well, and so just as the carriage came to the door, my uncle was called away upon business to that horrid man, Mr. Stone. And then, you know, when once they get together, there is no end of it. Well, I was so frightened I did not know what to do, for my uncle was to give me away; and if we were beyond the hour, we could not be married all day. But, luckily, he came back again in ten minutes time, and then we all set out. However, I recollected afterwards that if he *had* been prevented going, the wedding need not be put off, for Mr. Darcy might have done as well."

"Mr. Darcy!" repeated Elizabeth, in utter amazement.

"Oh, yes!—he was to come there with Wickham, you know. But gracious me! I quite forgot! I ought not to have said a word about it. I promised them so faithfully! What will Wickham say? It was to be such a secret!"

"If it was to be secret," said Jane, "say not another word on the subject. You may depend upon my seeking no further."

"Oh! certainly, said Elizabeth, though burning with curiosity; "we will ask you no questions."

"Thank you," said Lydia, "for if you did, I should certainly tell you all, and then Wickham would be angry."

On such encouragement to ask, Elizabeth was forced to put it out of her power by running away.

But to live in ignorance on such a point was impossible; or at least it was impossible not to try for information. Mr. Darcy had been at her sister's wedding. It was exactly a scene, and exactly among people, where he had apparently least to do and least temptation to go. Conjectures as to the meaning of it, rapid and wild, hurried into her brain; but she was satisfied with none. Those that best pleased her, as placing his conduct in the noblest light, seemed most improbable. She could not bear such suspense; and hastily seizing a sheet of paper, wrote a short letter to her aunt to request an explanation of what Lydia had dropped, if it were compatible with the secrecy which had been intended.

"You may readily comprehend," she added, "what my curiosity must be to know how a person unconnected with any of us, and (comparatively speaking) a stranger to our family, should have been amongst you at such a time. Pray write instantly and let me understand it—unless it is, for very cogent reasons, to remain in the secrecy which Lydia seems to think necessary; and then I must endeavour to be satisfied with ignorance."

"Not that I *shall* though," she added to herself, as she finished the letter; "and my dear aunt, if you do not tell me in an honourable manner, I shall certainly be reduced to tricks and stratagems to find it out."

Jane's delicate sense of honour would not allow her to speak to Elizabeth privately of what Lydia had let fall; Elizabeth was glad of it; till it appeared whether her inquiries would receive any satisfaction, she had rather be without a confidante.

CHAPTER TEN

ELIZABETH had the satisfaction of receiving an answer to her letter as soon as she possibly could. She was no sooner in possession of it, than hurrying into the little copse, where she was least likely to be interrupted, she sat down on one of the benches, and prepared to be happy; for the length of the letter convinced her that it did not contain a denial.

"MY DEAR NIECE,

"I have just received your letter, and shall devote this whole morning to answering it, as I foresee that a *little* writing will not comprise what I have to tell you. I must confess myself surprised by your application; I did not expect it from *you*. Don't think me angry, however, for I only mean to let you know that I had not imagined such inquiries to be necessary on *your* side. If you do not choose to understand me, forgive my impertinence. Your uncle is as much surprised as I am—and nothing but the belief of your being a party concerned would have allowed him to act as he has done. But if you are really innocent and ignorant, I must be more explicit. On the very day of my coming home from Longbourn, your uncle had a most unexpected visitor. Mr. Darcy called, and was shut up with him several hours. It was all over before I arrived; so my curiosity was not so dreadfully racked as *yours* seems to have been. He came to tell Mr. Gardiner that he had found out where your sister and Mr. Wickham were, and that he had seen and talked with them both, Wickham repeatedly, Lydia once. From what I can collect, he left Derbyshire only one day after ourselves, and came to town with the resolution of hunting for them. The motive professed was his conviction of its being owing to himself that Wickham's worthlessness had not been so well known, as to make it impossible for any young woman of character to love or confide in him. He generously imputed the whole to his mistaken pride, and confessed that he had before thought it beneath him to lay his private actions open to the world. His character was to speak for itself. He called it, therefore, his duty to step forward, and endeavour to remedy an evil which had been brought on by himself. If he *had another* motive, I am sure it would never disgrace him. He had been some days in town before he was able to discover them; but he had something to direct his search, which was more than *we* had; and the consciousness of this was another reason for his resolving to follow us. There is a lady, it seems, a Mrs. Younge, who was some time ago governess to Miss Darcy, and was dismissed from her charge on some cause of disapprobation, though he did not say what. She then took a large house in Edward Street and has since maintained herself by letting lodgings. This Mrs. Younge was, he knew, intimately acquainted with Wickham; and he went to her for intelligence of him as soon as he got to town. But it was two or three days before he could get from her what he wanted. She would not betray her trust, I suppose, without bribery and corruption, for she really did know where her friend was to be found. Wickham indeed had gone to her on their first arrival in London, and had she been able to receive them into her house, they would have taken up their abode with her. At length, however, our kind friend procured the wished-for direction. They were in————street. He saw Wickham, and afterwards insisted on seeing Lydia. His first object with her, he acknowledged, had been to persuade her to quit her present disgraceful situation, and return to her friends as soon as they could be prevailed on to receive her, offering his assistance, as far as it would go. But he found Lydia absolutely resolved on remaining where she was. She cared for none of her friends, she wanted no help of his, she would not hear of leaving Wickham. She was sure they should be married sometime or other, and it did not much signify when. Since such were her feelings, it only remained, he thought, to secure and expedite a marriage, which, in his very first conversation with Wickham, he easily learned had never been *his* design. He confessed himself obliged to leave the regiment on account of some debts of honour, which were very pressing; and scrupled not to lay all the ill-consequences of Lydia's flight on her own folly alone. He meant to resign his commission immediately; and as to his future situation, he could conjecture very little about it. He must go somewhere, but he did not know where, and he knew he should have nothing to live on. Mr. Darcy asked him why he had not married your sister at once. Though Mr. Bennet was not imagined to be very rich, he would have been able to do something for him, and his situation must have been benefited by marriage. But he found, in reply to this question, that Wickham still cherished the hope of more effectually making his fortune by marriage, in some other country. Under such circumstances, however, he was not likely to be proof against the temptation of immediate relief. They met several times, for there was much to be discussed. Wickham of course wanted more than he could get; but at length was reduced to be reasonable. Everything being settled between *them,* Mr. Darcy's next step was to make your uncle acquainted with it, and he first called in Gracechurch Street the evening before I came home. But Mr. Gardiner could not be seen, and Mr. Darcy found, on further inquiry, that your father was still with him, but would quit town the next morning. He did not judge your father to be a person whom he could so properly consult as your uncle, and therefore readily postponed seeing him, till after the departure of the former. He did not leave his name, and till the next day, it was only known that a gentleman had called on business. On Saturday he came again. Your father was gone, your uncle at home, and as I said before, they had a great deal of talk together. They met again on Sunday, and then *I* saw him too. It was not all settled before Monday: as soon as it was, the express was sent off to Longbourn. But our visitor was very obstinate. I fancy, Lizzy, that obstinacy is the real defect of his character after all. He has been accused of many faults at different times; but *this* is the true one. Nothing was to be done that he did not do himself; though I am sure (and I do not speak it to be thanked, therefore say nothing about it) your uncle would most readily have settled the whole. They battled it together for a long time, which was more than either the gentleman or lady concerned in it deserved. But at last your uncle was forced to yield, and instead of being allowed to be of use to his niece, was forced to put up with only having the probable credit of it, which went sorely against the grain; and I really believe your letter this morning gave him great pleasure, because it required an explanation that would rob him of his borrowed feathers, and give the praise where it was due. But, Lizzy, this must go no farther than yourself, or Jane at most. You know pretty well, I suppose, what has been done for the young people. His debts are to be paid, amounting, I believe, to considerably more than a thousand pounds, another thousand in addition to her own settled upon *her,* and his commission purchased. The reason why all this was to be done by him

alone was such as I have given above. It was owing
to him, to his reserve and want of proper consideration,
that Wickham's character had been so misunderstood,
and consequently that he had been received and noticed
as he was. Perhaps there was some truth in *this;* though
I doubt whether *his* reserve, or *anybody's* reserve, can
be answerable for the event. But in spite of all this fine
talking, my dear Lizzy, you may rest perfectly assured
that your uncle would never have yielded, if we had not
given him credit for *another interest* in the affair. When
all this was resolved on, he returned again to his friends,
who were still staying at Pemberley; but it was agreed
that he should be in London once more when the wedding took place, and all money matters were then to
receive the last finish. I believe I have now told you
everything. It is a relation which you tell me is to give
you great surprise; I hope at least it will not afford you
any displeasure. Lydia came to us; and Wickham had
constant admission to the house. *He* was exactly what
he had been when I knew him in Hertfordshire; but
I would not tell you how little I was satisfied with *her*
behaviour while she stayed with us, if I had not perceived, by Jane's letter last Wednesday, that her conduct
on coming home was exactly of a piece with it, and
therefore what I now tell you can give you no fresh
pain. I talked to her repeatedly in the most serious
manner, representing to her all the wickedness of what
she had done, and all the unhappiness she had brought
on her family. If she heard me, it was by good luck, for
I am sure she did not listen. I was sometimes quite provoked, but then I recollected my dear Elizabeth and
Jane, and for their sakes had patience with her. Mr.
Darcy was punctual in his return, and as Lydia informed
you, attended the wedding. He dined with us the next
day, and was to leave town again on Wednesday or
Thursday. Will you be very angry with me, my dear
Lizzy, if I take this opportunity of saying (what I was
never bold enough to say before) how much I like
him. His behaviour to us has in every respect been as
pleasing as when we were in Derbyshire. His understanding and opinions all please me; he wants nothing
but a little more liveliness, and *that,* if he marry *prudently,* his wife may teach him. I thought him very sly;

he hardly ever mentioned your name. But slyness seems the fashion. Pray forgive me if I have been very presuming, or at least do not punish me so far as to exclude me from P. I shall never be quite happy till I have been all round the park. A low phaeton, with a nice little pair of ponies, would be the very thing. But I must write no more. The children have been wanting me this half hour. Yours, very sincerely,

"M. GARDINER."

The contents of this letter threw Elizabeth into a flutter of spirits, in which it was difficult to determine whether pleasure or pain bore the greatest share. The vague and unsettled suspicions which uncertainty had produced of what Mr. Darcy might have been doing to forward her sister's match, which she had feared to encourage as an exertion of goodness too great to be probable, and at the same time dreaded to be just from the pain of obligation, were proved beyond their greatest extent to be true! He had followed them purposely to town, he had taken on himself all the trouble and mortification attendant on such a research; in which supplication had been necessary to a woman whom he must abominate and despise, and where he was reduced to meet, frequently meet, reason with, persuade, and finally bribe, the man whom he always most wished to avoid, and whose very name it was punishment to him to pronounce. He had done all this for a girl whom he could neither regard nor esteem. Her heart did whisper that he had done it for her. But it was a hope shortly checked by other considerations, and she soon felt that even her vanity was insufficient when required to depend on his affection for her, for a woman who had already refused him, as able to overcome a sentiment so natural as abhorrence against relationship with Wickham. Brother-in-law of Wickham! Every kind of pride must revolt from the connection. He had to be sure done much. She was ashamed to think how much. But he had given a reason for his interference, which asked no extraordinary stretch of belief. It was reasonable that he should feel he had been wrong; he had liberality, and he had the means of exercising it; and though she would not place herself as his principal inducement, she could, perhaps, believe that remaining partiality for her might assist his endeavours in a cause where her peace of mind must be materially concerned. It was painful, exceedingly painful, to know that they were under obligations to a person who could never receive a return. They owed the restoration of Lydia, her character, everything to him. Oh! how heartily did she grieve over every ungracious sensation she had ever encouraged, every saucy speech she had ever directed towards him. For herself she was humbled; but she was proud of him. Proud that in a cause of compassion and honour, he had been able to get the better of himself. She read over her aunt's commendation of him again and again. It was hardly enough; but it pleased her. She was even sensible of some pleasure, though mixed with regret, on finding how steadfastly both she and her uncle had been persuaded that affection and confidence subsisted between Mr. Darcy and herself.

She was roused from her seat, and her reflections, by someone's approach; and before she could strike into another path, she was overtaken by Wickham.

"I am afraid I interrupt your solitary ramble, my dear sister?" said he, as he joined her.

"You certainly do," she replied with a smile; "but it does not follow that the interruption must be unwelcome."

"I should be sorry indeed, if it were. *We* were always good friends; and now we are better."

"True. Are the others coming out?"

"I do not know. Mrs. Bennet and Lydia are going in the carriage to Meryton. And so, my dear sister, I find from our uncle and aunt that you have actually seen Pemberley."

She replied in the affirmative.

"I almost envy you the pleasure, and yet I believe it would be too much for me, or else I could take it in my way to Newcastle. And you saw the old housekeeper, I suppose? Poor Reynolds, she was always very fond of me. But of course she did not mention my name to you."

"Yes, she did."

"And what did she say?"

"That you were gone into the army, and she was

afraid had—not turned out well. At such a distance as *that,* you know, things are strangely misrepresented."

"Certainly," he replied, biting his lips. Elizabeth hoped she had silenced him; but he soon afterwards said,

"I was surprised to see Darcy in town last month. We passed each other several times. I wonder what he can be doing there."

"Perhaps preparing for his marriage with Miss de Bourgh," said Elizabeth. "It must be something particular to take him there at this time of year."

"Undoubtedly. Did you see him while you were at Lambton? I thought I understood from the Gardiners that you had."

"Yes; he introduced us to his sister."

"And do you like her?"

"Very much."

"I have heard, indeed, that she is uncommonly improved within this year or two. When I last saw her, she was not very promising. I am very glad you liked her. I hope she will turn out well."

"I dare say she will; she has got over the most trying age."

"Did you go by the village of Kympton?"

"I do not recollect that we did."

"I mention it because it is the living which I ought to have had. A most delightful place!—Excellent parsonage house! It would have suited me in every respect."

"How should you have liked making sermons?"

"Exceedingly well. I should have considered it as part of my duty, and the exertion would soon have been nothing. One ought not to repine; but to be sure, it would have been such a thing for me! The quiet, the retirement of such a life, would have answered all my ideas of happiness! But it was not to be. Did you ever hear Darcy mention the circumstances when you were in Kent?"

"I *have* heard from authority, which I thought *as good,* that it was left you conditionally only, and at the will of the present patron."

"You have. Yes, there was something in *that;* I told you so from the first, you may remember."

"I *did* hear, too, that there was a time when sermon-making was not so palatable to you as it seems to be at present; that you actually declared your resolution of never taking orders, and that the business had been compromised accordingly."

"You did! and it was not wholly without foundation. You may remember what I told you on that point when first we talked of it."

They were now almost at the door of the house, for she had walked fast to get rid of him; and unwilling, for her sister's sake, to provoke him, she only said in reply, with a good-humoured smile,

"Come, Mr. Wickham, we are brother and sister, you know. Do not let us quarrel about the past. In future, I hope we shall be always of one mind."

She held out her hand; he kissed it with affectionate gallantry, though he hardly knew how to look, and they entered the house.

CHAPTER ELEVEN

MR. WICKHAM was so perfectly satisfied with this conversation that he never again distressed himself, or provoked his dear sister Elizabeth, by introducing the subject of it; and she was pleased to find that she had said enough to keep him quiet.

The day of his and Lydia's departure soon came, and Mrs. Bennet was forced to submit to a separation, which, as her husband by no means entered into her scheme of their all going to Newcastle, was likely to continue at least a twelvemonth.

"Oh! my dear Lydia," she cried, "when shall we meet again?"

"Oh, lord! I don't know. Not these two or three years perhaps."

"Write to me very often, my dear."

"As often as I can. But you know married women have never much time for writing. My sisters may write to *me*. They will have nothing else to do."

Mr. Wickham's adieus were much more affectionate than his wife's. He smiled, looked handsome, and said many pretty things.

"He is as fine a fellow," said Mr. Bennet, as soon as they were out of the house, "as ever I saw. He simpers, and smirks, and makes love to us all. I am prodigiously proud of him. I defy even Sir William Lucas himself to produce a more valuable son-in-law."

The loss of her daughter made Mrs. Bennet very dull for several days.

"I often think," said she, "that there is nothing so bad as parting with one's friends. One seems so forlorn without them."

"This is the consequence you see, madam, of marrying a daughter," said Elizabeth. "It must make you better satisfied that your other four are single."

"It is no such thing. Lydia does not leave me because she is married; but only because her husband's regiment happens to be so far off. If that had been nearer, she would not have gone so soon."

But the spiritless condition which this event threw her into was shortly relieved, and her mind opened again to the agitation of hope by an article of news which then began to be in circulation. The housekeeper at Netherfield had received orders to prepare for the arrival of her master, who was coming down in a day or two to shoot there for several weeks. Mrs. Bennet was quite in the fidgets. She looked at Jane, and smiled, and shook her head by turns.

"Well, well, and so Mr. Bingley is coming down, sister" (for Mrs. Philips first brought her the news.) "Well, so much the better. Not that I care about it, though. He is nothing to us, you know, and I am sure *I* never want to see him again. But, however, he is very welcome to come to Netherfield, if he likes it. And who knows what *may* happen? But that is nothing to us. You know, sister, we agreed long ago never to mention a word about it. And so, is it quite certain he is coming?"

"You may depend on it," replied the other, "for Mrs. Nicholls was in Meryton last night; I saw her passing by and went out myself on purpose to know the truth of it; and she told me that it was certain true. He comes down on Thursday at the latest, very likely on Wednesday. She was going to the butcher's, she told me, on purpose to order in some meat on Wednesday, and she has got three couple of ducks, just fit to be killed."

Miss Bennet had not been able to hear of his coming without changing colour. It was many months since she had mentioned his name to Elizabeth; but now, as soon as they were alone together, she said,

"I saw you look at me to-day, Lizzy, when my aunt told us of the present report; and I know I appeared distressed. But don't imagine it was from any silly cause. I was only confused for the moment, because I felt that I *should* be looked at. I do assure you that the news does not affect me either with pleasure or pain. I am glad of one thing, that he comes alone; because we shall see the less of him. Not that I am afraid of *myself,* but I dread other people's remarks."

Elizabeth did not know what to make of it. Had she not seen him in Derbyshire, she might have supposed him capable of coming there with no other view than what was acknowledged; but she still thought him partial to Jane, and she wavered as to the greater probability of his coming there *with* his friend's permission, or being bold enough to come without it.

"Yet it is hard," she sometimes thought, "that this poor man cannot come to a house, which he has legally hired, without raising all this speculation! I *will* leave him to himself."

In spite of what her sister declared, and really believed to be her feelings, in the expectation of his arrival, Elizabeth could easily perceive that her spirits were affected by it. They were more disturbed, more unequal, than she had often seen them.

The subject which had been so warmly canvassed between their parents, about a twelvemonth ago, was now brought forward again.

"As soon as ever Mr. Bingley comes, my dear," said Mrs. Bennet, "you will wait on him of course."

"No, no. You forced me into visiting him last year, and promised if I went to see him, he should marry one of my daughters. But it ended in nothing, and I will not be sent on a fool's errand again."

His wife represented to him how absolutely necessary such an attention would be from all the neighbouring gentlemen on his returning to Netherfield.

" 'Tis an etiquette I despise," said he. "If he wants our society, let him seek it. He knows where we live. I will not spend *my* hours in running after my neighbours every time they go away and come back again."

"Well, all I know is, that it will be abominably rude if you do not wait on him. But, however, that shan't prevent my asking him to dine here, I am determined. We must have Mrs. Long and the Gouldings soon. That will make thirteen with ourselves, so there will be just room at table for him."

Consoled by this resolution, she was the better able to bear her husband's incivility; though it was very mortifying to know that her neighbours might well see Mr. Bingley, in consequence of it, before *they* did. As the day of his arrival drew near,

"I begin to be sorry that he comes at all," said Jane to her sister. "It would be nothing; I could see him with perfect indifference, but I can hardly bear to hear it thus perpetually talked of. My mother means well; but she does not know, no one can know, how much I suffer from what she says. Happy shall I be when his stay at Netherfield is over!"

"I wish I could say anything to comfort you," replied Elizabeth; "but it is wholly out of my power. You must feel it; and the usual satisfaction of preaching patience to a sufferer is denied me, because you have always so much."

Mr. Bingley arrived. Mrs. Bennet, through the assistance of servants, contrived to have the earliest tidings of it, that the period of anxiety and fretfulness on her side might be as long as it could. She counted the days that must intervene before their invitation could be sent, hopeless of seeing him before. But on the third morning after his arrival in Hertfordshire, she saw him from her dressing-room window enter the paddock, and ride towards the house.

Her daughters were eagerly called to partake of her joy. Jane resolutely kept her place at the table; but Elizabeth, to satisfy her mother, went to the window— she looked—she saw Mr. Darcy with him, and sat down again by her sister.

"There is a gentleman with him, Mamma," said Kitty; "who can it be?"

"Some acquaintance or other, my dear, I suppose; I am sure I do not know."

"La!" replied Kitty, "it looks just like that man that

used to be with him before. Mr. what's his name. That tall, proud man."

"Good gracious! Mr. Darcy!—and so it does I vow. Well, any friend of Mr. Bingley's will always be welcome here to be sure; but else I must say that I hate the very sight of him."

Jane looked at Elizabeth with surprise and concern. She knew but little of their meeting in Derbyshire, and therefore felt for the awkwardness which must attend her sister in seeing him almost for the first time after receiving his explanatory letter. Both sisters were uncomfortable enough. Each felt for the other, and of course for themselves; and their mother talked on, of her dislike of Mr. Darcy and her resolution to be civil to him only as Mr. Bingley's friend, without being heard by either of them. But Elizabeth had sources of uneasiness which could not be suspected by Jane, to whom she had never yet had courage to show Mrs. Gardiner's letter, or to relate her own change of sentiment towards him. To Jane, he could be only a man whose proposals she had refused, and whose merit she had undervalued; but to her own more extensive information, he was the person to whom the whole family were indebted for the first of benefits, and whom she regarded herself with an interest, if not quite so tender, at least as reasonable and just as what Jane felt for Bingley. Her astonishment at his coming—at his coming to Netherfield, to Longbourn, and voluntarily seeking her again, was almost equal to what she had known on first witnessing his altered behaviour in Derbyshire.

The colour which had been driven from her face returned for half a minute with an additional glow, and a smile of delight added lustre to her eyes, as she thought for that space of time that his affection and wishes must still be unshaken. But she would not be secure.

"Let me first see how he behaves," said she; "it will then be early enough for expectation."

She sat intently at work, striving to be composed, and without daring to lift up her eyes, till anxious curiosity carried them to the face of her sister, as the servant was approaching the door. Jane looked a little paler than usual, but more sedate than Elizabeth had expected. On the gentlemen's appearing, her colour increased; yet she received them with tolerable ease, and with a propriety of behaviour equally free from any symptom of resentment, or any unnecessary complaisance.

Elizabeth said as little to either as civility would allow, and sat down again to her work, with an eagerness which it did not often command. She had ventured only one glance at Darcy. He looked serious as usual; and she thought, more as he had been used to look in Hertfordshire, than as she had seen him at Pemberley. But, perhaps he could not in her mother's presence be what he was before her uncle and aunt. It was a painful, but not an improbable, conjecture.

Bingley, she had likewise seen for an instant, and in that short period saw him looking both pleased and embarrassed. He was received by Mrs. Bennet with a degree of civility which made her two daughters ashamed, especially when contrasted with the cold and ceremonious politeness of her curtsy and address to his friend.

Elizabeth particularly, who knew that her mother owed to the latter the preservation of her favourite daughter from irremediable infamy, was hurt and distressed to a most painful degree by a distinction so ill applied.

Darcy, after inquiring of her how Mr. and Mrs. Gardiner did, a question which she could not answer without confusion, said scarcely anything. He was not seated by her; perhaps that was the reason of his silence; but it had not been so in Derbyshire. There he had talked to her friends, when he could not to herself. But now several minutes elapsed without bringing the sound of his voice; and when occasionally, unable to resist the impulse of curiosity, she raised her eyes to his face, she as often found him looking at Jane as at herself, and frequently on no object but the ground. More thoughtfulness, and less anxiety to please than when they last met, were plainly expressed. She was disappointed, and angry with herself for being so.

"Could I expect it to be otherwise!" said she. "Yet why did he come?"

She was in no humour for conversation with anyone but himself; and to him she had hardly courage to speak.

She inquired after his sister, but could do no more.

"It is a long time, Mr. Bingley, since you went away," said Mrs. Bennet.

He readily agreed to it.

"I began to be afraid you would never come back again. People *did* say you meant to quit the place entirely at Michaelmas; but, however, I hope it is not true. A great many changes have happened in the neighbourhood since you went away. Miss Lucas is married and settled. And one of my own daughters. I suppose you have heard of it; indeed, you must have seen it in the papers. It was in the *Times* and the *Courier,* I know; though it was not put in as it ought to be. It was only said, 'Lately, George Wickham, Esq. to Miss Lydia Bennet,' without there being a syllable said of her father, or the place where she lived, or anything. It was my brother Gardiner's drawing up too, and I wonder how he came to make such an awkward business of it. Did you see it?"

Bingley replied that he did, and made his congratulations. Elizabeth dared not lift up her eyes. How Mr. Darcy looked, therefore, she could not tell.

"It is a delightful thing, to be sure, to have a daughter well married," continued her mother, "but at the same time, Mr. Bingley, it is very hard to have her taken such a way from me. They are gone down to Newcastle, a place quite northward, it seems, and there they are to stay, I do not know how long. His regiment is there; for I suppose you have heard of his leaving the——shire, and of his being gone into the regulars. Thank Heaven! he has *some* friends, though perhaps not so many as he deserves."

Elizabeth who knew this to be levelled at Mr. Darcy, was in such misery of shame that she could hardly keep her seat. It drew from her, however, the exertion of speaking, which nothing else had so effectually done before; and she asked Bingley whether he meant to make any stay in the country at present. A few weeks, he believed.

"When you have killed all your own birds, Mr. Bingley," said her mother, "I beg you will come here and shoot as many as you please on Mr. Bennet's manor. I am sure he will be vastly happy to oblige you, and will save all the best of the covies for you."

Elizabeth's misery increased at such unnecessary, such officious attention! Were the same fair prospect to arise at present as had flattered them a year ago, everything, she was persuaded, would be hastening to the same vexatious conclusion. At that instant she felt that years of happiness could not make Jane or herself amends for moments of such painful confusion.

"The first wish of my heart," said she to herself, "is never more to be in company with either of them. Their society can afford no pleasure that will atone for such wretchedness as this! Let me never see either one or the other again!

Yet the misery, for which years of happiness were to offer no compensation, received soon afterwards material relief from observing how much the beauty of her sister rekindled the admiration of her former lover. When first he came in, he had spoken to her but little; but every five minutes seemed to be giving her more of his attention. He found her as handsome as she had been last year; as good-natured, and as unaffected, though not quite so chatty. Jane was anxious that no difference should be perceived in her at all, and was really persuaded that she talked as much as ever. But her mind was so busily engaged that she did not always know when she was silent.

When the gentlemen rose to go away, Mrs. Bennet was mindful of her intended civility, and they were invited and engaged to dine at Longbourn in a few days time.

"You are quite a visit in my debt, Mr. Bingley," she added, "for when you went to town last winter, you promised to take a family dinner with us as soon as you returned. I have not forgot, you see; and I assure you, I was very much disappointed that you did not come back and keep your engagement."

Bingley looked a little silly at this reflection, and said something of his concern at having been prevented by business. They then went away.

Mrs. Bennet had been strongly inclined to ask them to stay and dine there that day; but, though she always kept a very good table, she did not think anything less than two courses could be good enough for a man on whom she had such anxious designs, or satisfy the appetite and pride of one who had ten thousand a year.

CHAPTER TWELVE

As soon as they were gone, Elizabeth walked out to recover her spirits; or in other words, to dwell without interruption on those subjects that must deaden them more. Mr. Darcy's behaviour astonished and vexed her.

"Why, if he came only to be silent, grave, and indifferent," said she, "did he come at all?"

She could settle it in no way that gave her pleasure.

"He could be still amiable, still pleasing to my uncle and aunt when he was in town; and why not to me? If he fears me, why come hither? If he no longer cares for me, why silent? Teasing, teasing man! I will think no more about him."

Her resolution was for a short time involuntarily kept by the approach of her sister, who joined her with a cheerful look, which showed her better satisfied with their visitors than Elizabeth.

"Now," said she, "that this first meeting is over I feel perfectly easy. I know my own strength, and I shall never be embarrassed again by his coming. I am glad he dines here on Tuesday. It will then be publicly seen that, on both sides, we meet only as common and indifferent acquaintance."

"Yes, very indifferent indeed," said Elizabeth laughingly. "Oh, Jane, take care."

"My dear Lizzy, you cannot think me so weak as to be in danger now."

"I think you are in very great danger of making him as much in love with you as ever."

They did not see the gentlemen again till Tuesday; and Mrs. Bennet, in the mean while, was giving way to all the happy schemes which the good humour and common politeness of Bingley, in half an hour's visit, had revived.

On Tuesday there was a large party assembled at Longbourn; and the two, who were most anxiously expected to the credit of their punctuality as sportsmen, were in very good time. When they repaired to the dining-room, Elizabeth eagerly watched to see whether Bingley would take the place which, in all their former parties, had belonged to him, by her sister. Her prudent mother, occupied by the same ideas, forbore to invite him to sit by herself. On entering the room, he seemed to hesitate; but Jane happened to look round, and happened to smile: it was decided. He placed himself by her.

Elizabeth, with a triumphant sensation, looked towards his friend. He bore it with noble indifference, and she would have imagined that Bingley had received his sanction to be happy, had she not seen his eyes likewise turned towards Mr. Darcy, with an expression of half-laughing alarm.

His behaviour to her sister was such during dinner-time, as showed an admiration of her, which, though more guarded than formerly, persuaded Elizabeth that if left wholly to himself, Jane's happiness, and his own, would be speedily secured. Though she dared not depend upon the consequence, she yet received pleasure from observing his behaviour. It gave her all the animation that her spirits could boast; for she was in no cheerful humour. Mr. Darcy was almost as far from her as the table could divide them. He was on one side of her mother. She knew how little such a situation would give pleasure to either, or make either appear to advantage. She was not near enough to hear any of their discourse, but she could see how seldom they spoke to each other, and how formal and cold was their manner whenever they did. Her mother's ungraciousness made the sense of what they owed him more painful to Elizabeth's mind; and she would, at times, have given anything to be privileged to tell him that his kindness was neither unknown nor unfelt by the whole of the family.

She was in hopes that the evening would afford some opportunity of bringing them together; that the whole of the visit would not pass away without enabling them to enter into something more of conversation than the mere ceremonious salutation attending his entrance. Anxious and uneasy, the period which passed in the drawing-room before the gentlemen came was wearisome and dull to a degree that almost made her uncivil. She looked forward to their entrance, as the point on which all her chance of pleasure for the evening must depend.

"If he does not come to me, *then*," said she, "I shall give him up forever."

The gentlemen came; and she thought he looked as if he would have answered her hopes; but, alas! the ladies had crowded round the table, where Miss Bennet was making tea and Elizabeth pouring out the coffee, in so close a confederacy that there was not a single vacancy near her which would admit of a chair. And on the gentlemen's approaching, one of the girls moved closer to her than ever, and said, in a whisper,

"The men shan't come and part us, I am determined. We want none of them; do we?"

Darcy had walked away to another part of the room. She followed him with her eyes, envied every one to whom he spoke, had scarcely patience enough to help anybody to coffee; and then was enraged against herself for being so silly!

"A man who has once been refused! How could I ever be foolish enough to expect a renewal of his love? Is there one among the sex who would not protest against such a weakness as a second proposal to the same woman? There is no indignity so abhorrent to their feelings!"

She was a little revived, however, by his bringing back his coffee cup himself; and she seized the opportunity of saying,

"Is your sister at Pemberley still?"

"Yes, she will remain there till Christmas."

"And quite alone? Have all her friends left her?"

"Mrs. Annesley is with her. The others have been gone on to Scarborough these three weeks."

She could think of nothing more to say; but if he wanted to converse with her, he might have better success. He stood by her, however, for some minutes, in silence; and, at last, on the young lady's whispering to Elizabeth again, he walked away.

When the tea-things were removed, and the card-tables placed, the ladies all rose, and Elizabeth was then hoping to be soon joined by him, when all her views were overthrown by seeing him fall a victim to her mother's rapacity for whist players, and in a few moments after seated with the rest of the party. She now lost every expectation of pleasure. They were confined for the evening at different tables, and she had nothing to hope, but that his eyes were so often turned towards her side of the room as to make him play as unsuccessfully as herself.

Mrs. Bennet had designed to keep the two Netherfield gentlemen to supper; but their carriage was unluckily ordered before any of the others, and she had no opportunity of detaining them.

"Well, girls," said she, as soon as they were left to themselves, "what say you to the day? I think every thing has passed off uncommonly well, I assure you. The dinner was as well-dressed as any I ever saw. The venison was roasted to a turn—and everybody said they never saw so fat a haunch. The soup was fifty times better than what we had at the Lucas's last week; and even Mr. Darcy acknowledged that the partridges were remarkably well done; and I suppose he has two or three French cooks at least. And, my dear Jane, I never saw you look in greater beauty. Mrs. Long said so too, for I asked her whether you did not. And what do you think she said besides? 'Ah! Mrs. Bennet, we shall have her at Netherfield at last.' She did indeed. I do think Mrs. Long is as good a creature as ever lived—and her nieces are very pretty behaved girls, and not at all handsome: I like them prodigiously."

Mrs. Bennet, in short, was in very great spirits; she had seen enough of Bingley's behaviour to Jane to be convinced that she would get him at last; and her expectations of advantage to her family, when in a happy humour, were so far beyond reason that she was quite disappointed at not seeing him there again the next day to make his proposals.

"It has been a very agreeable day," said Miss Bennet to Elizabeth. "The party seemed so well selected, so suitable one with the other. I hope we may often meet again."

Elizabeth smiled.

"Lizzy, you must not do so. You must not suspect me. It mortifies me. I assure you that I have now learned to enjoy his conversation as an agreeable and sensible young man, without having a wish beyond it. I am perfectly satisfied from what his manners now are that he never had any design of engaging my affection. It is only that he is blessed with greater sweetness of address, and a stronger desire of generally pleasing, than any other man."

"You are very cruel," said her sister, "you will not let me smile, and are provoking me to it every moment."

"How hard it is in some cases to be believed!"

"And how impossible in others!"

"But why should you wish to persuade me that I feel more than I acknowledge?"

"That is a question which I hardly know how to answer. We all love to instruct, though we can teach only what is not worth knowing. Forgive me; and if you persist in indifference, do not make *me* your confidante."

CHAPTER THIRTEEN

A FEW days after this visit, Mr. Bingley called again, and alone. His friend had left him that morning for London, but was to return home in ten days time. He sat with them above an hour, and was in remarkably good spirits. Mrs. Bennet invited him to dine with them; but, with many expressions of concern, he confessed himself engaged elsewhere.

"Next time you call," said she, "I hope we shall be more lucky."

He should be particularly happy at any time, etc. etc.; and if she would give him leave, would take an early opportunity of waiting on them.

"Can you come to-morrow?"

Yes, he had no engagement at all for to-morrow; and her invitation was accepted with alacrity.

He came, and in such very good time that the ladies were none of them dressed. In ran Mrs. Bennet to her daughter's room, in her dressing gown, and with her hair half-finished, crying out,

"My dear Jane, make haste and hurry down. He is come—Mr. Bingley is come.—He is, indeed. Make haste, make haste. Here, Sarah, come to Miss Bennet this moment, and help her on with her gown. Never mind Miss Lizzy's hair."

"We will be down as soon as we can," said Jane; "but I dare say Kitty is forwarder than either of us, for she went upstairs half an hour ago."

"Oh! hang Kitty! what has she to do with it? Come be quick, be quick! where is your sash my dear?"

But when her mother was gone, Jane would not be prevailed on to go down without one of her sisters.

The same anxiety to get them by themselves was visible again in the evening. After tea, Mr. Bennet retired to the library, as was his custom, and Mary went upstairs to her instrument. Two obstacles of the five being thus removed, Mrs. Bennet sat looking and winking at Elizabeth and Catherine for a considerable time, without making any impression on them. Elizabeth would not observe her; and when at last Kitty did, she very innocently said, "What is the matter Mamma? What do you keep winking at me for? What am I to do?"

"Nothing child, nothing. I did not wink at you." She then sat still five minutes longer; but unable to waste such a precious occasion, she suddenly got up, and saying to Kitty,

"Come here, my love, I want to speak to you," took her out of the room. Jane instantly gave a look at Elizabeth, which spoke her distress at such premeditation and her entreaty that *she* would not give into it. In a few minutes, Mrs. Bennet half opened the door and called out,

"Lizzy, my dear, I want to speak with you."

Elizabeth was forced to go.

"We may as well leave them by themselves, you know," said her mother as soon as she was in the hall. "Kitty and I are going upstairs to sit in my dressing-room."

Elizabeth made no attempt to reason with her mother, but remained quietly in the hall till she and Kitty were out of sight, then returned into the drawing-room.

Mrs. Bennet's schemes for this day were ineffectual. Bingley was everything that was charming, except the professed lover of her daughter. His ease and cheerfulness rendered him a most agreeable addition to their evening party; and he bore with the ill-judged officiousness of the mother, and heard all her silly remarks with a forbearance and command of countenance particularly grateful to the daughter.

He scarcely needed an invitation to stay supper; and before he went away, an engagement was formed, chiefly through his own and Mrs. Bennet's means, for his coming next morning to shoot with her husband.

After this day, Jane said no more of her indifference. Not a word passed between the sisters concerning Bingley; but Elizabeth went to bed in the happy belief that all must speedily be concluded, unless Mr. Darcy returned within the stated time. Seriously, however, she felt tolerably persuaded that all this must have taken place with that gentleman's concurrence.

Bingley was punctual to his appointment; and he and Mr. Bennet spent the morning together, as had been agreed on. The latter was much more agreeable than his companion expected. There was nothing of presumption or folly in Bingley that could provoke his ridicule, or disgust him into silence; and he was more communicative, and less eccentric than the other had ever seen him. Bingley of course returned with him to dinner; and in the evening Mrs. Bennet's invention was again at work to get everybody away from him and her daughter. Elizabeth, who had a letter to write, went into the breakfast-room for that purpose soon after tea; for as the others were all going to sit down to cards, she could not be wanted to counteract her mother's schemes.

But on returning to the drawing-room when her letter was finished, she saw, to her infinite surprise, there was reason to fear that her mother had been too ingenious for her. On opening the door, she perceived her sister and Bingley standing together over the hearth, as if engaged in earnest conversation; and had this led to no suspicion, the faces of both as they hastily turned round, and moved away from each other, would have told it all. *Their* situation was awkward enough; but *her's* she thought was still worse. Not a syllable was uttered by either; and Elizabeth was on the point of going away again, when Bingley, who as well as the other had sat down, suddenly rose, and whispering a few words to her sister, ran out of the room.

Jane could have no reserves from Elizabeth, where

confidence would give pleasure; and instantly embracing her, acknowledged, with the liveliest emotion, that she was the happiest creature in the world.

" 'Tis too much!" she added, "by far too much. I do not deserve it. Oh! why is not everybody as happy?"

Elizabeth's congratulations were given with a sincerity, a warmth, a delight, which words could but poorly express. Every sentence of kindness was a fresh source of happiness to Jane. But she would not allow herself to stay with her sister, or say half that remained to be said, for the present.

"I must go instantly to my mother," she cried. "I would not on any account trifle with her affectionate solicitude; or allow her to hear it from any one but myself. He is gone to my father already. Oh! Lizzy, to know that what I have to relate will give such pleasure to all my dear family! how shall I bear so much happiness!"

She then hastened away to her mother, who had purposely broken up the card party, and was sitting upstairs with Kitty.

Elizabeth, who was left by herself, now smiled at the rapidity and ease with which an affair was finally settled that had given them so many previous months of suspense and vexation.

"And this," said she, "is the end of all his friend's anxious circumspection! of all his sister's falsehood and contrivance! the happiest, wisest, most reasonable end!"

In a few minutes she was joined by Bingley, whose conference with her father had been short and to the purpose.

"Where is your sister?" said he hastily, as he opened the door.

"With my mother upstairs. She will be down in a moment, I dare say."

He then shut the door, and coming up to her, claimed the good wishes and affection of a sister. Elizabeth honestly and heartily expressed her delight in the prospect of their relationship. They shook hands with great cordiality; and then till her sister came down, she had to listen to all he had to say of his own happiness and of Jane's perfections; and in spite of his being a lover, Elizabeth really believed all his expectations of felicity to be rationally founded, because they had for basis the excellent understanding and super-excellent disposition of Jane, and a general similarity of feeling and taste between her and himself.

It was an evening of no common delight to them all; the satisfaction of Miss Bennet's mind gave a glow of such sweet animation to her face as made her look handsomer than ever. Kitty simpered and smiled, and hoped her turn was coming soon. Mrs. Bennet could not give her consent, or speak her approbation in terms warm enough to satisfy her feelings, though she talked to Bingley of nothing else for half an hour; and when Mr. Bennet joined them at supper, his voice and manner plainly showed how really happy he was.

Not a word, however, passed his lips in allusion to it, till their visitor took his leave for the night; but as soon as he was gone, he turned to his daughter and said,

"Jane, I congratulate you. You will be a very happy woman."

Jane went to him instantly, kissed him, and thanked him for his goodness.

"You are a good girl;" he replied, "and I have great pleasure in thinking you will be so happily settled. I have not a doubt of your doing very well together. Your tempers are by no means unlike. You are each of you so complying that nothing will ever be resolved on; so easy that every servant will cheat you; and so generous that you will always exceed your income."

"I hope not so. Imprudence or thoughtlessness in money matters would be unpardonable in *me*."

"Exceed their income! My dear Mr. Bennet," cried his wife, "what are you talking of? Why, he has four or five thousand a-year, and very likely more." Then addressing her daughter, "Oh! my dear, dear Jane, I am so happy! I am sure I sha'nt get a wink of sleep all night. I knew how it would be. I always said it must be so, at last. I was sure you could not be so beautiful for nothing! I remember, as soon as ever I saw him, when he first came into Hertfordshire last year, I thought how likely it was that you should come together. Oh! he is the handsomest young man that ever was seen!"

Wickham, Lydia, were all forgotten. Jane was beyond competition her favourite child. At that moment, she cared for no other. Her younger sisters soon began to make interest with her for objects of happiness which she might in future be able to dispense.

Mary petitioned for the use of the library at Netherfield; and Kitty begged very hard for a few balls there every winter.

Bingley, from this time, was of course a daily visitor at Longbourn; coming frequently before breakfast, and always remaining till after supper; unless when some barbarous neighbour, who could not be enough detested, had given him an invitation to dinner, which he thought himself obliged to accept.

Elizabeth had now but little time for conversation with her sister; for while he was present, Jane had no attention to bestow on any one else; but she found herself considerably useful to both of them in those hours of separation that must sometimes occur. In the absence of Jane, he always attached himself to Elizabeth, for the pleasure of talking of her; and when Bingley was gone, Jane constantly sought the same means of relief.

"He has made me so happy," said she, one evening, "by telling me that he was totally ignorant of my being in town last spring! I had not believed it possible."

"I suspected as much," replied Elizabeth. "But how did he account for it?"

"It must have been his sister's doing. They were certainly no friends to his acquaintance with me, which I cannot wonder at, since he might have chosen so much more advantageously in many respects. But when they see, as I trust they will, that their brother is happy with me, they will learn to be contented, and we shall be on good terms again; though we can never be what we once were to each other."

"That is the most unforgiving speech," said Elizabeth, "that I ever heard you utter. Good girl! It would vex me, indeed, to see you again the dupe of Miss Bingley's pretended regard."

"Would you believe it, Lizzy, that when he went to town last November, he really loved me, and nothing but a persuasion of *my* being indifferent would have prevented his coming down again!"

"He made a little mistake to be sure; but it is to the credit of his modesty."

This naturally introduced a panegyric from Jane on his diffidence, and the little value he put on his own good qualities.

Elizabeth was pleased to find that he had not betrayed the interference of his friend, for though Jane had the most generous and forgiving heart in the world, she knew it was a circumstance which must prejudice her against him.

"I am certainly the most fortunate creature that ever existed!" cried Jane. "Oh! Lizzy, why am I thus singled from my family, and blessed above them all! If I could but see *you* as happy! If there *were* but such another man for you!"

"If you were to give me forty such men, I never could be so happy as you. Till I have your disposition, your goodness, I never can have your happiness. No, no, let me shift for myself; and, perhaps, if I have very good luck, I may meet another Mr. Collins in time."

The situation of affairs in the Longbourn family could not be long a secret. Mrs. Bennet was privileged to whisper it to Mrs. Philips, and *she* ventured, without any permission, to do the same by all her neighbours in Meryton.

The Bennets were speedily pronounced to be the luckiest family in the world, though only a few weeks before, when Lydia had first run away, they had been generally proved to be marked out for misfortune.

CHAPTER FOURTEEN

ONE morning, about a week after Bingley's engagement with Jane had been formed, as he and the females of the family were sitting together in the dining-room, their attention was suddenly drawn to the window by the sound of a carriage; and they perceived a chaise and four driving up the lawn. It was too early in the morning for visitors, and besides, the equipage did not answer to that of any of their neighbours. The horses were post; and neither the carriage, nor the livery of the servant who preceded it, were familiar to them. As it was certain, however, that somebody was coming, Bingley instantly prevailed on Miss Bennet to avoid the confinement of such an intrusion, and walk away with him into the shrubbery. They both set off, and the conjectures of the remaining three continued, though with little satisfaction, till the door was thrown open, and their visitor entered. It was Lady Catherine de Bourgh.

They were of course all intending to be surprised; but their astonishment was beyond their expectation; and on the part of Mrs. Bennet and Kitty, though she was perfectly unknown to them, even inferior to what Elizabeth felt.

She entered the room with an air more than usually ungracious, made no other reply to Elizabeth's salutation than a slight inclination of the head, and sat down without saying a word. Elizabeth had mentioned her name to her mother on her ladyship's entrance, though no request of introduction had been made.

Mrs. Bennet all amazement, though flattered by having a guest of such high importance, received her with the utmost politeness. After sitting for a moment in silence, she said very stiffly to Elizabeth,

"I hope you are well, Miss Bennet. That lady I suppose is your mother."

Elizabeth replied very concisely that she was.

"And *that* I suppose is one of your sisters."

"Yes, madam," said Mrs. Bennet, delighted to speak to a Lady Catherine. "She is my youngest girl but one. My youngest of all is lately married, and my eldest is somewhere about the grounds, walking with a young man, who I believe will soon become a part of the family."

"You have a very small park here," returned Lady Catherine after a short silence.

"It is nothing in comparison of Rosings, my lady, I dare say; but I assure you it is much larger than Sir William Lucas's."

"This must be a most inconvenient sitting-room for the evening in summer; the windows are full west."

Mrs. Bennet assured her that they never sat there after dinner; and then added,

"May I take the liberty of asking your ladyship whether you left Mr. and Mrs. Collins well."

"Yes, very well. I saw them the night before last."

Elizabeth now expected that she would produce a letter for her from Charlotte, as it seemed the only probable motive for her calling. But no letter appeared, and she was completely puzzled.

Mrs. Bennet, with great civility, begged her ladyship to take some refreshment; but Lady Catherine very resolutely, and not very politely, declined eating anything; and then rising up, said to Elizabeth,

"Miss Bennet, there seemed to be a prettyish kind of a little wilderness on one side of your lawn. I should be glad to take a turn in it, if you will favour me with your company."

"Go, my dear," cried her mother, "and show her ladyship about the different walks. I think she will be pleased with the hermitage."

Elizabeth obeyed, and running into her own room for her parasol, attended her noble guest downstairs. As they passed through the hall, Lady Catherine opened the doors into the dining-parlour and drawing-room, and pronouncing them, after a short survey, to be decent looking rooms, walked on.

Her carriage remained at the door, and Elizabeth saw that her waiting-woman was in it. They proceeded in silence along the gravel walk that led to the copse; Elizabeth was determined to make no effort for conversation with a woman who was now more than usually insolent and disagreeable.

"How could I ever think her like her nephew?" said she, as she looked in her face.

As soon as they entered the copse, Lady Catherine began in the following manner:

"You can be at no loss, Miss Bennet, to understand the reason of my journey hither. Your own heart, your own conscience, must tell you why I come."

Elizabeth looked with unaffected astonishment.

"Indeed, you are mistaken, madam. I have not been at all able to account for the honour of seeing you here."

"Miss Bennet," replied her ladyship, in an angry tone, "you ought to know that I am not to be trifled with. But however insincere *you* may choose to be, you shall not find *me* so. My character has ever been celebrated for its sincerity and frankness, and in a cause of such moment as this, I shall certainly not depart from it. A report of a most alarming nature reached me two days ago. I was told that not only your sister was on the point of being most advantageously married, but that *you,* that Miss Elizabeth Bennet, would, in all likelihood, be soon afterwards united to my nephew, my own nephew, Mr. Darcy. Though I *know* it must be a scandalous falsehood, though I would not injure him so much as to suppose the truth of it possible, I instantly resolved on setting off for this place that I might make my sentiments known to you."

"If you believed it impossible to be true," said Elizabeth colouring with astonishment and disdain, "I wonder you took the trouble of coming so far. What could your ladyship propose by it?"

"At once to insist upon having such a report universally contradicted."

"Your coming to Longbourn to see me and my family," said Elizabeth coolly, "will be rather a confirmation of it, if, indeed, such a report is in existence."

"If! do you then pretend to be ignorant of it? Has it not been industriously circulated by yourselves? Do you not know that such a report is spread abroad?"

"I never heard that it was."

"And can you likewise declare that there is no *foundation* for it?"

"I do not pretend to possess equal frankness with your ladyship. *You* may ask questions, which *I* shall not choose to answer."

"This is not to be borne. Miss Bennet, I insist on being satisfied. Has he, has my nephew made you an offer of marriage?"

"Your ladyship has declared it to be impossible."

"It ought to be so; it must be so, while he retains the use of his reason. But *your* arts and allurements may, in a moment of infatuation, have made him forget what he owes to himself and to all his family. You may have drawn him in."

"If I have, I shall be the last person to confess it."

"Miss Bennet, do you know who I am? I have not been accustomed to such language as this. I am almost the nearest relation he has in the world, and am entitled to know all his dearest concerns."

"But you are not entitled to know *mine*; nor will such behaviour as this ever induce me to be explicit."

"Let me be rightly understood. This match, to which you have the presumption to aspire, can never take place. No, never. Mr. Darcy is engaged to *my daughter*. Now what have you to say?"

"Only this; that if he is so, you can have no reason to suppose he will make an offer to me."

Lady Catherine hesitated for a moment, and then replied,

"The engagement between them is of a peculiar kind. From their infancy, they have been intended for each other. It was the favourite wish of *his* mother, as well as of hers. While in their cradles, we planned the union: and now, at the moment when the wishes of both sisters would be accomplished in their marriage, to be prevented by a young woman of inferior birth, of no importance in the world, and wholly unallied to the family? Do you pay no regard to the wishes of his friends? To his tacit engagement with Miss De Bourgh? Are you lost to every feeling of propriety and delicacy? Have you not heard me say that from his earliest hours he was destined for his cousin?"

"Yes, and I had heard it before. But what is that to me? If there is no other objection to my marrying your nephew, I shall certainly not be kept from it by knowing that his mother and aunt wished him to marry Miss De Bourgh. You both did as much as you could in planning the marriage. Its completion depended on others. If Mr. Darcy is neither by honour nor inclination confined to his cousin, why is not he to make another choice? And if I am that choice, why may not I accept him."

"Because honour, decorum, prudence, nay, interest, forbid it. Yes, Miss Bennet, interest; for do not expect to be noticed by his family and friends, if you wilfully act against the inclinations of all. You will be censured, slighted, and despised, by everyone connected with him. Your alliance will be a disgrace; your name will never even be mentioned by any of us."

"These are heavy misfortunes," replied Elizabeth. "But the wife of Mr. Darcy must have such extraordinary sources of happiness necessarily attached to her situation that she could, upon the whole, have no cause to repine."

"Obstinate, headstrong girl! I am ashamed of you! Is this your gratitude for my attentions to you last spring? Is nothing due to me on that score?

"Let us sit down. You are to understand, Miss Bennet, that I came here with the determined resolution of carrying my purpose; nor will I be dissuaded from it. I have not been used to submit to any person's whims. I have not been in the habit of brooking disappointment."

"*That* will make your ladyship's situation at present more pitiable; but it will have no effect on *me*."

"I will not be interrupted. Hear me in silence. My daughter and my nephew are formed for each other. They are descended on the maternal side from the same noble line; and on the father's, from respectable, honourable, and ancient, though untitled families. Their fortune on both sides is splendid. They are destined for each other by the voice of every member of their respective houses; and what is to divide them? The upstart pretensions of a young woman without family, connections, or fortune. Is this to be endured! But it must not, shall not be. If you were sensible of your own good, you would not wish to quit the sphere in which you have been brought up."

"In marrying your nephew, I should not consider myself as quitting that sphere. He is a gentleman; I am a gentleman's daughter; so far we are equal."

"True. You *are* a gentleman's daughter. But who was your mother? Who are your uncles and aunts? Do not imagine me ignorant of their condition."

"Whatever my connections may be," said Elizabeth, "if your nephew does not object to them, they can be nothing to *you*."

"Tell me once for all, are you engaged to him?"

Though Elizabeth would not, for the mere purpose of obliging Lady Catherine, have answered this question; she could not but say, after a moment's deliberation,

"I am not."

Lady Catherine seemed pleased.

"And will you promise me never to enter into such an engagement?"

"I will make no promise of the kind."

"Miss Bennet I am shocked and astonished. I expected to find a more reasonable young woman. But do not deceive yourself into a belief that I will ever recede. I shall not go away till you have given me the assurance I require."

"And I certainly *never* shall give it. I am not to be intimidated into anything so wholly unreasonable. Your ladyship wants Mr. Darcy to marry your daughter; but would my giving you the wished-for promise make *their* marriage at all more probable? Supposing him to be attached to me, would *my* refusing to accept his hand make him wish to bestow it on his cousin? Allow me to say, Lady Catherine, that the arguments with which you have supported this extraordinary application have been as frivolous as the application was ill-judged. You have widely mistaken my character, if you think I can be worked on by such persuasions as these. How far your nephew might approve of your interference in *his* affairs, I cannot tell; but you have certainly no right to concern yourself in mine. I must beg, therefore, to be importuned no farther on the subject."

"Not so hasty, if you please. I have by no means done. To all the objections I have already urged, I have still another to add. I am no stranger to the particulars of your youngest sister's infamous elopement. I know it all; that the young man's marrying her was a patched-up business, at the expense of your father and uncles. And is *such* a girl to be my nephew's sister? Is *her* husband, is the son of his late father's steward, to be his brother? Heaven and earth!—of what are you thinking? Are the shades of Pemberley to be thus polluted?"

"You can *now* have nothing farther to say," she resentfully answered. "You have insulted me in every possible method. I must beg to return to the house."

And she rose as she spoke. Lady Catherine rose also, and they turned back. Her ladyship was highly incensed.

"You have no regard, then, for the honour and credit of my nephew! Unfeeling, selfish girl! Do you not consider that a connection with you must disgrace him in the eyes of everybody?"

"Lady Catherine, I have nothing farther to say. You know my sentiments."

"You are then resolved to have him?"

"I have said no such thing. I am only resolved to act in that manner which will, in my own opinion, constitute my happiness, without reference to *you,* or to any person so wholly unconnected with me."

"It is well. You refuse, then, to oblige me. You refuse to obey the claims of duty, honour, and gratitude. You are determined to ruin him in the opinion of all his friends, and make him the contempt of the world."

"Neither duty, nor honour, nor gratitude," replied Elizabeth, "have any possible claim on me in the present instance. No principle of either would be violated by my marriage with Mr. Darcy. And with regard to the resentment of his family, or the indignation of the world, if the former *were* excited by his marrying me, it would not give me one moment's concern—and the world in general would have too much sense to join in the scorn."

"And this is your real opinion! This is your final resolve! Very well. I shall now know how to act. Do not imagine, Miss Bennet, that your ambition will ever be gratified. I came to try you. I hoped to find you reasonable; but depend upon it I will carry my point."

In this manner Lady Catherine talked on, till they were at the door of the carriage, when turning hastily round, she added,

"I take no leave of you, Miss Bennet. I send no compliments to your mother. You deserve no such attention. I am most seriously displeased."

Elizabeth made no answer; and without attempting to persuade her ladyship to return into the house, walked quietly into it herself. She heard the carriage drive away as she proceeded upstairs. Her mother impatiently met her at the door of the dressing-room to ask why Lady Catherine would not come in again and rest herself.

"She did not choose it," said her daughter, "she would go."

"She is a very fine-looking woman! and her calling here was prodigiously civil! for she only came, I suppose, to tell us the Collinses were well. She is on her road somewhere, I dare say, and so passing through Meryton, thought she might as well call on you. I suppose she had nothing particular to say to you, Lizzy?"

Elizabeth was forced to give into a little falsehood here; for to acknowledge the substance of their conversation was impossible.

CHAPTER FIFTEEN

THE discomposure of spirits which this extraordinary visit threw Elizabeth into could not be easily overcome; nor could she for many hours learn to think of it less than incessantly. Lady Catherine, it appeared, had actually taken the trouble of this journey from Rosings for the sole purpose of breaking off her supposed engagement with Mr. Darcy. It was a rational scheme to be sure! but from what the report of their engagement could originate, Elizabeth was at a loss to imagine; till she recollected that *his* being the intimate friend of Bingley, and *her* being the sister of Jane, was enough, at a time when the expectation of one wedding made everybody eager for another, to supply the idea. She had not herself forgotten to feel that the marriage of her sister must bring them more frequently together. And her neighbours at Lucas lodge, therefore (for through their communication with the Collinses, the report she concluded had reached Lady Catherine), had only set *that* down as almost certain and immediate, which *she* had looked forward to as possible at some future time.

In revolving Lady Catherine's expressions, however, she could not help feeling some uneasiness as to the possible consequence of her persisting in this interference. From what she had said of her resolution to prevent their marriage, it occurred to Elizabeth that she must meditate an application to her nephew; and how *he* might take a similar representation of the evils attached to a connection with her, she dared not pronounce. She knew not the exact degree of his affection for his aunt, or his dependence on her judgment, but it was natural to suppose that he thought much higher of her ladyship than *she* could do; and it was certain that in enumerating the miseries of a marriage with *one,* whose immediate connections were so unequal to his own, his aunt would address him on his weakest side. With his notions of dignity, he would probably feel that the arguments, which to Elizabeth had appeared weak and ridiculous, contained much good sense and solid reasoning.

If he had been wavering before as to what he should

do, which had often seemed likely, the advice and entreaty of so near a relation might settle every doubt, and determine him at once to be as happy, as dignity unblemished could make him. In that case he would return no more. Lady Catherine might see him in her way through town; and his engagement to Bingley of coming again to Netherfield must give way.

"If, therefore, an excuse for not keeping his promise should come to his friend within a few days," she added, "I shall know how to understand it. I shall then give over every expectation, every wish of his constancy. If he is satisfied with only regretting me, when he might have obtained my affections and hand, I shall soon cease to regret him at all."

The surprise of the rest of the family on hearing who their visitor had been was very great; but they obligingly satisfied it with the same kind of supposition which had appeased Mrs. Bennet's curiosity; and Elizabeth was spared from much teasing on the subject.

The next morning, as she was going downstairs, she was met by her father, who came out of his library with a letter in his hand.

"Lizzy," said he, "I was going to look for you; come into my room."

She followed him thither; and her curiosity to know what he had to tell her was heightened by the supposition of its being in some manner connected with the letter he held. It suddenly struck her that it might be from Lady Catherine; and she anticipated with dismay all the consequent explanations.

She followed her father to the fire-place, and they both sat down. He then said,

"I have received a letter this morning that has astonished me exceedingly. As it principally concerns yourself, you ought to know its contents. I did not know before that I had *two* daughters on the brink of matrimony. Let me congratulate you on a very important conquest."

The colour now rushed into Elizabeth's cheeks in the instantaneous conviction of its being a letter from the nephew, instead of the aunt; and she was undetermined whether most to be pleased that he explained himself at all, or offended that his letter was not rather addressed to herself; when her father continued,

"You look conscious. Young ladies have great penetration in such matters as these; but I think I may defy even *your* sagacity to discover the name of your admirer. This letter is from Mr. Collins."

"From Mr. Collins! and what can *he* have to say?"

"Something very much to the purpose of course. He begins with congratulations on the approaching nuptials of my eldest daughter, of which it seems he has been told by some of the good-natured, gossiping Lucases. I shall not sport with your impatience by reading what he says on that point. What relates to yourself is as follows. 'Having thus offered you the sincere congratulations of Mrs. Collins and myself on this happy event, let me now add a short hint on the subject of another; of which we have been advertised by the same authority. Your daughter Elizabeth, it is presumed, will not long bear the name of Bennet, after her elder sister has resigned it, and the chosen partner of her fate may be reasonably looked up to as one of the most illustrious personages in this land.'

"Can you possibly guess, Lizzy, who is meant by this? 'This young gentleman is blessed in a peculiar way, with everything the heart of mortal can most desire—splendid property, noble kindred, and extensive patronage. Yet in spite of all these temptations, let me warn my cousin Elizabeth, and yourself, of what evils you may incur by a precipitate closure with this gentleman's proposals, which, of course, you will be inclined to take immediate advantage of.'

"Have you any idea, Lizzy, who this gentleman is? But now it comes out.

" 'My motive for cautioning you is as follows. We have reason to imagine that his aunt, Lady Catherine de Bourgh, does not look on the match with a friendly eye.'

"*Mr. Darcy,* you see, is the man! Now, Lizzy, I think I *have* surprised you. Could he, or the Lucases, have pitched on any man within the circle of our acquaintance whose name would have given the lie more effectually to what they related? Mr. Darcy, who never looks at any woman but to see a blemish, and who probably never looked at *you* in his life! It is admirable!"

Elizabeth tried to join in her father's pleasantry, but could only force one most reluctant smile. Never had his wit been directed in a manner so little agreeable to her.

"Are you not diverted?"

"Oh! yes. Pray read on."

" 'After mentioning the likelihood of this marriage to her ladyship last night, she immediately, with her usual condescension, expressed what she felt on the occasion; when it became apparent that on the score of some family objections on the part of my cousin, she would never give her consent to what she termed so disgraceful a match. I thought it my duty to give the speediest intelligence of this to my cousin, that she and her noble admirer may be aware of what they are about, and not run hastily into a marriage which has not been properly sanctioned.' Mr. Collins moreover adds, 'I am truly rejoiced that my cousin Lydia's sad business has been so well hushed up, and am only concerned that their living together before the marriage took place should be so generally known. I must not, however, neglect the duties of my station, or refrain from declaring my amazement, at hearing that you received the young couple into your house as soon as they were married. It was an encouragement of vice; and had I been the rector of Longbourn, I should very strenuously have opposed it. You ought certainly to forgive them as a Christian, but never to admit them in your sight, or allow their names to be mentioned in your hearing.' *That* is his notion of Christian forgiveness! The rest of his letter is only about his dear Charlotte's situation, and his expectation of a young olive-branch. But, Lizzy, you look as if you did not enjoy it. You are not going to be *missish,* I hope, and pretend to be affronted at an idle report. For what do we live, but to make sport of our neighbours, and laugh at them in our turn?"

"Oh!" cried Elizabeth, "I am excessively diverted. But it is so strange!"

"Yes—*that* is what makes it amusing. Had they fixed on any other man it would have been nothing; but *his* perfect indifference, and *your* pointed dislike, make it so delightfully absurd! Much as I abominate writing, I would not give up Mr. Collins's correspondence for any consideration. Nay, when I read a letter of his, I cannot

305

help giving him the preference even over Wickham, much as I value the impudence and hypocrisy of my son-in-law. And pray, Lizzy, what said Lady Catherine about this report? Did she call to refuse her consent?"

To this question his daughter replied only with a laugh; and as it had been asked without the least suspicion, she was not distressed by his repeating it. Elizabeth had never been more at a loss to make her feelings appear what they were not. It was necessary to laugh, when she would rather have cried. Her father had most cruelly mortified her by what he said of Mr. Darcy's indifference, and she could do nothing but wonder at such a want of penetration, or fear that perhaps instead of his seeing too *little,* she might have fancied too *much.*

CHAPTER SIXTEEN

INSTEAD of receiving any such letter of excuse from his friend, as Elizabeth half expected Mr. Bingley to do, he was able to bring Darcy with him to Longbourn before many days had passed after Lady Catherine's visit. The gentlemen arrived early; and before Mrs. Bennet had time to tell him of their having seen his aunt, of which her daughter sat in momentary dread, Bingley, who wanted to be alone with Jane, proposed their all walking out. It was agreed to. Mrs. Bennet was not in the habit of walking, Mary could never spare time, but the remaining five set off together. Bingley and Jane, however, soon allowed the others to outstrip them. They lagged behind, while Elizabeth, Kitty, and Darcy, were to entertain each other. Very little was said by either; Kitty was too much afraid of him to talk; Elizabeth was secretly forming a desperate resolution; and perhaps he might be doing the same.

They walked towards the Lucases, because Kitty wished to call upon Maria; and as Elizabeth saw no occasion for making it a general concern when Kitty left them, she went boldly on with him alone. Now was the moment for her resolution to be executed, and while her courage was high, she immediately said,

"Mr. Darcy, I am a very selfish creature; and, for the sake of giving relief to my own feelings, care not how much I may be wounding yours. I can no longer help thanking you for your unexampled kindness to my poor sister. Ever since I have known it, I have been most anxious to acknowledge to you how gratefully I feel it. Were it known to the rest of the family, I should not have merely my own gratitude to express."

"I am sorry, exceedingly sorry," replied Darcy, in a tone of surprise and emotion, "that you have ever been informed of what may, in a mistaken light, have given you uneasiness. I did not think Mrs. Gardiner was so little to be trusted."

"You must not blame my aunt. Lydia's thoughtlessness first betrayed to me that you had been concerned in the matter; and, of course, I could not rest till I knew the particulars. Let me thank you again and again, in the name of all my family, for that generous compassion which induced you to take so much trouble, and bear so many mortifications, for the sake of discovering them."

"If you *will* thank me," he replied, "let it be yourself alone. That the wish of giving happiness to you might add force to the other inducements which led me on, I shall not attempt to deny. But your *family* owe me nothing. Much as I respect them, I believe, I thought only of *you.*"

Elizabeth was too much embarrassed to say a word. After a short pause, her companion added, "You are too generous to trifle with me. If your feelings are still what they were last April, tell me so at once. *My* affections and wishes are unchanged, but one word from you will silence me on this subject forever."

Elizabeth feeling all the more than common awkwardness and anxiety of his situation now forced herself to speak; and immediately, though not very fluently, gave him to understand that her sentiments had undergone so material a change, since the period to which he alluded, as to make her receive with gratitude and pleasure his present assurances. The happiness which this reply produced was such as he had probably never felt before; and he expressed himself on the occasion as sensibly and as warmly as a man violently in love can be supposed to do. Had Elizabeth been able to encounter his eye, she might have seen how well the expression of heart-felt delight, diffused over his face, became him; but though she could not look, she could listen, and he told her of feelings, which, in proving of what importance she was to him, made his affection every moment more valuable.

They walked on, without knowing in what direction. There was too much to be thought, and felt, and said, for attention to any other objects. She soon learned that they were indebted for their present good understanding to the efforts of his aunt, who *did* call on him in her return through London, and there relate her journey to Longbourn, its motive, and the substance of her conversation with Elizabeth; dwelling emphatically on every expression of the latter, which, in her ladyship's apprehension, peculiarly denoted her perverseness and assurance in the belief that such a relation must assist her endeavours to obtain that promise from her nephew which *she* had refused to give. But, unluckily for her ladyship, its effect had been exactly contrariwise.

"It taught me to hope," said he, "as I had scarcely ever allowed myself to hope before. I knew enough of your disposition to be certain that, had you been absolutely, irrevocably decided against me, you would have acknowledged it to Lady Catherine, frankly and openly."

Elizabeth coloured and laughed as she replied, "Yes, you know enough of my *frankness* to believe me capable of *that*. After abusing you so abominably to your face, I could have no scruple in abusing you to all your relations."

"What did you say of me that I did not deserve? For, though your accusations were ill-founded, formed on mistaken premises, my behaviour to you at the time had merited the severest reproof. It was unpardonable. I cannot think of it without abhorrence."

"We will not quarrel for the greater share of blame annexed to that evening," said Elizabeth. "The conduct of neither, if strictly examined, will be irreproachable; but since then, we have both, I hope, improved in civility."

"I cannot be so easily reconciled to myself. The recollection of what I then said, of my conduct, my manners, my expressions during the whole of it, is now, and has been many months, inexpressibly painful to me.

Your reproof, so well applied, I shall never forget: 'had you behaved in a more gentlemanlike manner.' Those were your words. You know not, you can scarcely conceive, how they have tortured me; though it was some time, I confess, before I was reasonable enough to allow their justice."

"I was certainly very far from expecting them to make so strong an impression. I had not the smallest idea of their being ever felt in such a way."

"I can easily believe it. You thought me then devoid of every proper feeling, I am sure you did. The turn of your countenance I shall never forget, as you said that I could not have addressed you in any possible way that would induce you to accept me."

"Oh! do not repeat what I then said. These recollections will not do at all. I assure you that I have long been most heartily ashamed of it."

Darcy mentioned his letter. "Did it," said he, "did it *soon* make you think better of me? Did you, on reading it, give any credit to its contents?"

She explained what its effect on her had been, and how gradually all her former prejudices had been removed.

"I knew," said he, "that what I wrote must give you pain, but it was necessary. I hope you have destroyed the letter. There was one part especially, the opening of it, which I should dread your having the power of reading again. I can remember some expressions which might justly make you hate me."

"The letter shall certainly be burned, if you believe it essential to the preservation of my regard; but though we have both reason to think my opinions not entirely unalterable, they are not, I hope, quite so easily changed as that implies."

"When I wrote that letter," replied Darcy, "I believed myself perfectly calm and cool, but I am since convinced that it was written in a dreadful bitterness of spirit."

"The letter, perhaps, began in bitterness, but it did not end so. The adieu is charity itself. But think no more of the letter. The feelings of the person who wrote and the person who received it, are now so widely different from what they were then that every unpleasant circumstance attending it ought to be forgotten. You must learn some of my philosophy. Think only of the past as its remembrance gives your pleasure."

"I cannot give you credit for any philosophy of the kind. *Your* retrospections must be so totally void of reproach that the contentment arising from them is not of philosophy, but what is much better, of ignorance. But with *me,* it is not so. Painful recollections will intrude which cannot, which ought not to be repelled. I have been a selfish being all my life in practice, though not in principle. As a child I was taught what was *right,* but I was not taught to correct my temper. I was given good principles, but left to follow them in pride and conceit. Unfortunately an only son (for many years an only *child*) I was spoiled by my parents, who though good themselves (my father, particularly, all that was benevolent and amiable), allowed, encouraged, almost taught me to be selfish and overbearing, to care for none beyond my own family circle, to think meanly of all the rest of the world, to *wish* at least to think meanly of their sense and worth compared with my own. Such I was from eight to eight and twenty; and such I might still have been but for you, dearest, loveliest Elizabeth! What do I not owe you! You taught me a lesson, hard indeed at first, but most advantageous. By you I was properly humbled. I came to you without a doubt of my reception. You showed me how insufficient were all my pretensions to please a woman worthy of being pleased."

"Had you then persuaded yourself that I should?"

"Indeed I had. What will you think of my vanity? I believed you to be wishing, expecting my addresses."

"My manners must have been in fault, but not intentionally I asure you. I never meant to deceive you, but my spirits might often lead me wrong. How you must have hated me after *that* evening?"

"Hate you! I was angry perhaps at first, but my anger soon began to take a proper direction."

"I am almost afraid of asking what you thought of me when we met at Pemberley. You blamed me for coming?"

"No, indeed; I felt nothing but surprise."

"Your surprise could not be greater than *mine* in being noticed by you. My conscience told me that I deserved no extraordinary politeness, and I confess that I did not expect to receive *more* than my due."

"My object *then*," replied Darcy, "was to show you by every civility in my power that I was not so mean as to resent the past; and I hoped to obtain your forgiveness, to lessen your ill opinion, by letting you see that your reproofs had been attended to. How soon any other wishes introduced themselves I can hardly tell, but I believe in about half an hour after I had seen you."

He then told her of Georgiana's delight in her acquaintance, and of her disappointment at its sudden interruption; which naturally leading to the cause of that interruption, she soon learned that his resolution of following her from Derbyshire in quest of her sister had been formed before he quitted the inn, and that his gravity and thoughtfulness there had arisen from no other struggles than what such a purpose must comprehend.

She expressed her gratitude again, but it was too painful a subject to each to be dwelt on farther.

After walking several miles in a leisurely manner, and too busy to know anything about it, they found at last, on examining their watches, that it was time to be at home.

"What could become of Mr. Bingley and Jane!" was a wonder which introduced the discussion of *their* affairs. Darcy was delighted with their engagement; his friend had given him the earliest information of it.

"I must ask whether you were surprised?" said Elizabeth.

"Not at all. When I went away, I felt that it would soon happen."

"That is to say, you had given your permission. I guessed as much." And though he exclaimed at the term, she found that it had been pretty much the case.

"On the evening before my going to London," said he, "I made a confession to him, which I believe I ought to have made long ago. I told him of all that had occurred to make my former interference in his affairs absurd and impertinent. His surprise was great. He had never had the slightest suspicion. I told him, moreover, that I believed myself mistaken in supposing, as I had done, that your sister was indifferent to him; and as I could easily perceive that his attachment to her was unabated, I felt no doubt of their happiness together."

Elizabeth could not help smiling at his easy manner of directing his friend.

"Did you speak from your own observation," said she, "when you told him that my sister loved him, or merely from my information last spring?"

"From the former. I had narrowly observed her during the two visits which I had lately made her here; and I was convinced of her affection."

"And your assurance of it, I suppose, carried immediate conviction to him."

"It did. Bingley is most unaffectedly modest. His diffidence had prevented his depending on his own judgment in so anxious a case, but his reliance on mine made everything easy. I was obliged to confess one thing, which for a time, and not unjustly, offended him. I could not allow myself to conceal that your sister had been in town three months last winter, that I had known it, and purposely kept it from him. He was angry. But his anger, I am persuaded, lasted no longer than he remained in any doubt of your sister's sentiments. He has heartily forgiven me now."

Elizabeth longed to observe that Mr. Bingley had been a most delightful friend; so easily guided that his worth was invaluable; but she checked herself. She remembered that he had yet to learn to be laughed at, and it was rather too early to begin. In anticipating the happiness of Bingley, which of course was to be inferior only to his own, he continued the conversation till they reached the house. In the hall they parted.

CHAPTER SEVENTEEN

"My dear Lizzy, where can you have been walking to?" was a question which Elizabeth received from Jane as soon as she entered the room, and from all the others when they sat down to table. She had only to say in reply that they had wandered about till she was beyond her own knowledge. She coloured as she spoke; but neither that, nor anything else, awakened a suspicion of the truth.

The evening passed quietly, unmarked by anything extraordinary. The acknowledged lovers talked and laughed, the unacknowledged were silent. Darcy was not of a disposition in which happiness overflows in mirth; and Elizabeth, agitated and confused, rather *knew* that she was happy, than *felt* herself to be so; for, besides the immediate embarrassment, there were other evils before her. She anticipated what would be felt in the family when her situation became known; she was aware that no one liked him but Jane; and even feared that with the others it was a *dislike* which not all his fortune and consequence might do away with.

At night she opened her heart to Jane. Though suspicion was very far from Miss Bennet's general habits, she was absolutely incredulous here.

"You are joking, Lizzy. This cannot be!—engaged to Mr. Darcy! No, no, you shall not deceive me. I know it to be impossible."

"This is a wretched beginning indeed! My sole dependence was on you; and I am sure nobody else will believe me, if you do not. Yet, indeed, I am in earnest. I speak nothing but the truth. He still loves me, and we are engaged."

Jane looked at her doubtingly. "Oh, Lizzy! it cannot be. I know how much you dislike him."

"You know nothing of the matter. *That* is all to be forgot. Perhaps I did not always love him so well as I do now. But in such cases as these, a good memory is unpardonable. This is the last time I shall ever remember it myself."

Miss Bennet still looked all amazement. Elizabeth again, and more seriously, assured her of its truth.

"Good Heaven! can it be really so! Yet now I must believe you," cried Jane. "My dear, dear Lizzy, I would—I do congratulate you—but are you certain? forgive the question—are you quite certain that you can be happy with him?"

"There can be no doubt of that. It is settled between us already that we are to be the happiest couple in the world. But are you pleased, Jane? Shall you like to have such a brother?"

"Very, very much. Nothing could give either Bingley or myself more delight. But we considered it, we talked

313

of it as impossible. And do you really love him quite well enough? Oh, Lizzy! do anything rather than marry without affection. Are you quite sure that you feel what you ought to do?"

"Oh, yes! You will only think I feel *more* than I ought to do, when I tell you all."

"What do you mean?"

"Why, I must confess, that I love him better than I do Bingley. I am afraid you will be angry."

"My dearest sister, now *be* serious. I want to talk very seriously. Let me know everything that I am to know without delay. Will you tell me how long you have loved him?"

"It has been coming on so gradually that I hardly know when it began. But I believe I must date it from my first seeing his beautiful grounds at Pemberley."

Another entreaty that she would be serious, however, produced the desired effect; and she soon satisfied Jane by her solemn assurances of attachment. When convinced on that article, Miss Bennet had nothing farther to wish.

"Now I am quite happy," said she, "for you will be as happy as myself. I always had a value for him. Were it for nothing but his love of you, I must always have esteemed him; but now, as Bingley's friend and your husband, there can be only Bingley and yourself more dear to me. But Lizzy, you have been very sly, very reserved with me. How little did you tell me of what passed at Pemberley and Lambton! I owe all that I know of it to another, not to you."

Elizabeth told her the motives of her secrecy. She had been unwilling to mention Bingley; and the unsettled state of her own feelings had made her equally avoid the name of his friend. But now she would no longer conceal from her his share in Lydia's marriage. All was acknowledged, and half the night spent in conversation.

"Good gracious!" cried Mrs. Bennet, as she stood at a window the next morning, "if that disagreeable Mr. Darcy is not coming here again with our dear Bingley! What can he mean by being so tiresome as to be always coming here? I had no notion but he would go a shooting, or something or other, and not disturb us with his

314

company. What shall we do with him? Lizzy, you must walk out with him again, that he may not be in Bingley's way."

Elizabeth could hardly help laughing at so convenient a proposal; yet was really vexed that her mother should be always giving him such an epithet.

As soon as they entered, Bingley looked at her so expressively, and shook hands with such warmth, as left no doubt of his good information; and he soon afterwards said aloud, "Mr. Bennet, have you no more lanes hereabouts in which Lizzy may lose her way again to-day?"

"I advise Mr. Darcy and Lizzy and Kitty," said Mrs. Bennet, "to walk to Oakham Mount this morning. It is a nice long walk, and Mr. Darcy has never seen the view."

"It may do very well for the others," replied Mr. Bingley; "but I am sure it will be too much for Kitty. Won't it, Kitty?"

Kitty owned that she had rather stay at home. Darcy professed a great curiosity to see the view from the Mount, and Elizabeth silently consented. As she went upstairs to get ready, Mrs. Bennet followed her, saying,

"I am quite sorry, Lizzy, that you should be forced to have that disagreeable man all to yourself. But I hope you will not mind it: it is all for Jane's sake, you know; and there is no occasion for talking to him, except just now and then. So, do not put yourself to inconvenience."

During their walk, it was resolved that Mr. Bennet's consent should be asked in the course of the evening. Elizabeth reserved to herself the application for her mother's. She could not determine how her mother would take it; sometimes doubting whether all his wealth and grandeur would be enough to overcome her abhorrence of the man. But whether she were violently set against the match, or violently delighted with it, it was certain that her manner would be equally ill-adapted to do credit to her sense; and she could no more bear that Mr. Darcy should hear the first raptures of her joy, than the first vehemence of her disapprobation.

———

In the evening, soon after Mr. Bennet withdrew to

the library, she saw Mr. Darcy rise also and follow him, and her agitation on seeing it was extreme. She did not fear her father's opposition, but he was going to be made unhappy, and that it should be through her means, that *she,* his favourite child, should be distressing him by her choice, should be filling him with fears and regrets in disposing of her, was a wretched reflection, and she sat in misery till Mr. Darcy appeared again, when, looking at him, she was a little relieved by his smile. In a few minutes he approached the table where she was sitting with Kitty; and while pretending to admire her work, said in a whisper, "Go to your father, he wants you in the library." She was gone directly.

Her father was walking about the room, looking grave and anxious. "Lizzy," said he, "what are you doing? Are you out of your senses, to be accepting this man? Have not you always hated him?"

How earnestly did she then wish that her former opinions had been more reasonable, her expressions more moderate! It would have spared her from explanations and professions which it was exceedingly awkward to give; but they were now necessary, and she assured him, with some confusion, of her attachment to Mr. Darcy.

"Or in other words, you are determined to have him. He is rich, to be sure, and you may have more fine clothes and fine carriages than Jane. But will they make you happy?"

"Have you any other objection," said Elizabeth, "than your belief of my indifference?"

"None at all. We all know him to be a proud, unpleasant sort of man; but this would be nothing if you really liked him."

"I do, I do like him," she replied, with tears in her eyes, "I love him. Indeed he has no improper pride. He is perfectly amiable. You do not know what he really is; then pray do not pain me by speaking of him in such terms."

"Lizzy," said her father, "I have given him my consent. He is the kind of man, indeed, to whom I should never dare refuse anything which he condescended to ask. I now give it to *you,* if you are resolved on having him. But let me advise you to think better of it. I know your disposition, Lizzy. I know that you could be neither happy nor respectable, unless you truly esteemed your husband, unless you looked up to him as a superior. Your lively talents would place you in the greatest danger in an unequal marriage. You could scarcely escape discredit and misery. My child, let me not have the grief of seeing *you* unable to respect your partner in life. You know not what you are about."

Elizabeth, still more affected, was earnest and solemn in her reply; and at length, by repeated assurances that Mr. Darcy was really the object of her choice, by explaining the gradual change which her estimation of him had undergone, relating her absolute certainty that his affection was not the work of a day, but had stood the test of many months suspense, and enumerating with energy all his good qualities, she did conquer her father's incredulity, and reconcile him to the match.

"Well, my dear," said he, when she ceased speaking, "I have no more to say. If this be the case, he deserves you. I could not have parted with you, my Lizzy, to any one less worthy."

To complete the favourable impression, she then told him what Mr. Darcy had voluntarily done for Lydia. He heard her with astonishment.

"This is an evening of wonders, indeed! And so, Darcy did everything; made up the match, gave the money, paid the fellow's debts, and got him his commission! So much the better. It will save me a world of trouble and economy. Had it been your uncle's doing, I must and *would* have paid him; but these violent young lovers carry everything their own way. I shall offer to pay him to-morrow; he will rant and storm about his love for you, and there will be an end of the matter."

He then recollected her embarrassment a few days before on his reading Mr. Collins's letter; and after laughing at her some time, allowed her at last to go—saying, as she quitted the room, "If any young men come for Mary or Kitty, send them in, for I am quite at leisure."

Elizabeth's mind was now relieved from a very heavy weight; and after half an hour's quiet reflection in her own room, she was able to join the others with tolerable composure. Everything was too recent for gaiety, but the evening passed tranquilly away; there was no longer anything material to be dreaded, and the comfort of ease and familiarity would come in time.

When her mother went up to her dressing-room at night, she followed her, and made the important communication. Its effect was most extraordinary; for on first hearing it, Mrs. Bennet sat quite still and unable to utter a syllable. Nor was it under many, many minutes that she could comprehend what she heard, though not in general backward to credit what was for the advantage of her family, or that came in the shape of a lover to any of them. She began at length to recover, to fidget about in her chair, get up, sit down again, wonder, and bless herself.

"Good gracious! Lord bless me! only think! dear me! Mr. Darcy! Who would have thought it! And is it really true? Oh my sweetest Lizzy! how rich and how great you will be! What pin-money, what jewels, what carriages you will have! Jane's is nothing to it—nothing at all. I am so pleased—so happy. Such a charming man! —so handsome! so tall!—Oh, my dear Lizzy! pray apologize for my having disliked him so much before. I hope he will overlook it. Dear, dear Lizzy. A house in town! Everything that is charming! Three daughters married! Ten thousand a year! Oh, Lord! What will become of me. I shall go distracted."

This was enough to prove that her approbation need not be doubted: and Elizabeth, rejoicing that such an effusion was heard only by herself, soon went away. But before she had been three minutes in her own room, her mother followed her.

"My dearest child," she cried, "I can think of nothing else! Ten thousand a year, and very likely more! 'Tis as good as a lord! And a special license. You must and shall be married by a special license. But my dearest love, tell me what dish Mr. Darcy is particularly fond of, that I may have it to-morrow."

This was a sad omen of what her mother' behaviour to the gentleman himself might be; and Elizabeth found that though in the certain possession of his warmest affection, and secure of her relations' consent, there was still something to be wished for. But the morrow passed off much better than she expected; for Mrs. Bennet luckily stood in such awe of her intended son-in-law that she ventured not to speak to him, unless it was in her power to offer him any attentions, or mark her deference for his opinion.

Elizabeth had the satisfaction of seeing her father taking pains to get acquainted with him; and Mr. Bennet soon assured her that he was rising every hour in his esteem.

"I admire all my three sons-in-law highly," said he. "Wickham, perhaps, is my favourite; but I think I shall like *your* husband quite as well as Jane's."

CHAPTER EIGHTEEN

ELIZABETH'S spirits soon rising to playfulness again, she wanted Mr. Darcy to account for his having ever fallen in love with her. "How could you begin?" said she. "I can comprehend your going on charmingly when you had once made a beginning; but what could set you off in the first place?"

"I cannot fix on the hour, or the spot, or the look, or the words, which laid the foundation. It is too long ago. I was in the middle before I knew that I *had* begun."

"My beauty you had early withstood, and as for my manners—my behaviour to *you* was at least always bordering on the uncivil, and I never spoke to you without rather wishing to give you pain than not. Now be sincere; did you admire me for my impertinence?"

"For the liveliness of your mind, I did."

"You may as well call it impertinence at once. It was very little less. The fact is that you were sick of civility, of deference, of officious attention. You were disgusted with the women who were always speaking and looking and thinking for *your* approbation alone. I roused, and interested you, because I was so unlike *them*. Had you not been really amiable you would have hated me for it; but in spite of the pains you took to disguise yourself, your feelings were always noble and just; and in your heart, you thoroughly despised the persons who so assiduously courted you. There—I have saved you the trouble of accounting for it; and really, all things considered, I begin to think it perfectly reasonable. To be sure, you knew no actual good of me—but nobody thinks of *that* when they fall in love."

"Was there no good in your affectionate behaviour to Jane while she was ill at Netherfield?"

"Dearest Jane! who could have done less for her? But make a virtue of it by all means. My good qualities are under your protection, and you are to exaggerate them as much as possible; and, in return, it belongs to me to find occasions for teasing and quarrelling with you as often as may be; and I shall begin directly by asking you what made you so unwilling to come to the point at last. What made you so shy of me when you first called, and afterwards dined here? Why, especially, when you called did you look as if you did not care about me?"

"Because you were grave and silent, and gave me no encouragement."

"But I was embarrassed."

"And so was I."

"You might have talked to me more when you came to dinner."

"A man who had felt less might."

"How unlucky that you should have a reasonable answer to give, and that I should be so reasonable as to admit it! But I wonder how long you *would* have gone on, if you had been left to yourself. I wonder when you *would* have spoken, if I had not asked you! My resolution of thanking you for your kindness to Lydia had certainly great effect. *Too much,* I am afraid; for what becomes of the moral, if our comfort springs from a breach of promise, for I ought not to have mentioned the subject? This will never do."

"You need not distress yourself. The moral will be perfectly fair. Lady Catherine's unjustifiable endeavours to separate us were the means of removing all my doubts. I am not indebted for my present happiness to your eager desire of expressing your gratitude. I was not in a humour to wait for any opening of yours. My aunt's intelligence had given me hope, and I was determined at once to know everything."

"Lady Catherine has been of infinite use, which ought to make her happy, for she loves to be of use. But tell me, what did you come down to Netherfield for? Was it merely to ride to Longbourn and be embarrassed? or had you intended any more serious consequence?"

"My real purpose was to see *you*, and to judge, if I could, whether I might ever hope to make you love me. My avowed one, or what I avowed to myself, was to see whether your sister were still partial to Bingley, and if she were, to make the confession to him which I have since made."

"Shall you ever have courage to announce to Lady Catherine what is to befall her?"

"I am more likely to want time than courage, Elizabeth. But it ought to be done, and if you will give me a sheet of paper, it shall be done directly."

"And if I had not a letter to write myself, I might sit by you and admire the evenness of your writing, as another young lady once did. But I have an aunt, too, who must not be longer neglected."

From an unwillingness to confess how much her intimacy with Mr. Darcy had been overrated, Elizabeth had never yet answered Mrs. Gardiner's long letter, but now, having *that* to communicate which she knew would be most welcome, she was almost ashamed to find that her uncle and aunt had already lost three days of happiness, and immediately wrote as follows:

"I would have thanked you before, my dear aunt, as I ought to have done, for your long, kind, satisfactory detail of particulars; but to say the truth, I was too cross to write. You supposed more than really existed. But *now* suppose as much as you choose; give a loose to your fancy, indulge your imagination in every possible flight which the subject will afford, and unless you believe me actually married, you cannot greatly err. You must write again very soon, and praise him a great deal more than you did in your last. I thank you, again and again, for not going to the lakes. How could I be so silly as to wish it! Your idea of the ponies is delightful. We will go round the park everyday. I am the happiest creature in the world. Perhaps other people have said so before, but not one with such justice. I am happier even than Jane; she only smiles, I laugh. Mr. Darcy sends you all the love in the world that he can spare from me. You are all to come to Pemberley at Christmas. Your's, etc."

Mr. Darcy's letter to Lady Catherine was in a different style; and still different from either was what Mr. Bennet sent to Mr. Collins in reply to his last.

DEAR SIR,

I must trouble you once more for congratulations. Elizabeth will soon be the wife of Mr. Darcy. Console Lady Catherine as well as you can. But, if I were you, I would stand by the nephew. He has more to give.

YOURS SINCERELY, ETC.

Miss Bingley's congratulations to her brother on his approaching marriage were all that was affectionate and insincere. She wrote even to Jane on the occasion, to express her delight, and repeat all her former professions of regard. Jane was not deceived, but she was affected; and though feeling no reliance on her, could not help writing her a much kinder answer than she knew was deserved.

The joy which Miss Darcy expressed on receiving similar information was as sincere as her brother's in sending it. Four sides of paper were insufficient to contain all her delight and all her earnest desire of being loved by her sister.

Before any answer could arrive from Mr. Collins, or any congratulations to Elizabeth from his wife, the Longbourn family heard that the Collinses were come themselves to Lucas lodge. The reason of this sudden removal was soon evident. Lady Catherine had been rendered so exceedingly angry by the contents of her nephew's letter that Charlotte, really rejoicing in the match, was anxious to get away till the storm was blown over. At such a moment, the arrival of her friend was a sincere pleasure to Elizabeth, though in the course of their meetings she must sometimes think the pleasure dearly bought, when she saw Mr. Darcy exposed to all the parading and obsequious civility of her husband. He bore it however with admirable calmness. He could even listen to Sir William Lucas when he complimented him on carrying away the brightest jewel of the country, and expressed his hopes of their all meeting frequently at St James's, with very decent composure. If he did shrug his shoulders, it was not till Sir William was out of sight.

Mrs. Philip's vulgarity was another, and perhaps a greater tax on his forbearance; and though Mrs. Philips, as well as her sister, stood in too much awe of him to speak with the familiarity which Bingley's good humour encouraged, yet, whenever she *did* speak, she must be vulgar. Nor was her respect for him, though it made her more quiet, at all likely to make her more elegant. Elizabeth did all she could to shield him from the frequent notice of either, and was ever anxious to keep him to herself and to those of her family with whom he might converse without mortification; and though the uncomfortable feelings arising from all this took from the season of courtship much of its pleasure, it added to the hope of the future; and she looked forward with delight to the time when they should be removed from society so little pleasing to either, to all the comfort and elegance of their family party at Pemberley.

CHAPTER NINETEEN

HAPPY for all her maternal feelings was the day on which Mrs. Bennet got rid of her two most deserving daughters. With what delighted pride she afterwards visited Mrs. Bingley and talked of Mrs. Darcy may be guessed. I wish I could say, for the sake of her family, that the accomplishment of her earnest desire in the establishment of so many of her children produced so happy an effect as to make her a sensible, amiable, well-informed woman for the rest of her life; though perhaps it was lucky for her husband, who might not have relished domestic felicity in so unusual a form, that she still was occasionally nervous and invariably silly.

Mr. Bennet missed his second daughter exceedingly; his affection for her drew him oftener from home than anything else could do. He delighted in going to Pemberley, especially when he was least expected.

Mr. Bingley and Jane remained at Netherfield only a twelvemonth. So near a vicinity to her mother and Meryton relations was not desirable even to *his* easy temper, or *her* affectionate heart. The darling wish of his sisters was then gratified; he bought an estate in a neighbouring county to Derbyshire, and Jane and Elizabeth, in addition to every other source of happiness, were within thirty miles of each other.

Kitty, to her very material advantage, spent the chief of her time with her two elder sisters. In society so superior to what she had generally known, her improvement was great. She was not of so ungovernable a temper as Lydia, and removed from the influence of Lydia's example, she became, by proper attention and management, less irritable, less ignorant, and less insipid. From the farther disadvantage of Lydia's society she was of course carefully kept, and though Mrs. Wickham frequently invited her to come and stay with her, with the promise of balls and young men, her father would never consent to her going.

Mary was the only daughter who remained at home; and she was necessarily drawn from the pursuit of accomplishments by Mrs. Bennet's being quite unable to sit alone. Mary was obliged to mix more with the world, but she could still moralize over every morning visit; and as she was no longer mortified by comparisons between her sisters' beauty and her own, it was suspected by her father that she submitted to the change without much reluctance.

As for Wickham and Lydia, their characters suffered no revolution from the marriage of her sisters. He bore with philosophy the conviction that Elizabeth must now become acquainted with whatever of his ingratitude and falsehood had before been unknown to her; and in spite of everything, was not wholly without hope that Darcy might yet be prevailed on to make his fortune. The congratulatory letter which Elizabeth received from Lydia on her marriage explained to her that by his wife at least, if not by himself, such a hope was cherished. The letter was to this effect:

MY DEAR LIZZY,

I wish you joy. If you love Mr. Darcy half as well as I do my dear Wickham, you must be very happy. It is a great comfort to have you so rich; and when you have nothing else to do, I hope you will think of us. I am sure Wickam would like a place at court very much, and I do not think we shall have quite money enough to live upon without some help. Any place would do, of about three or four hundred a year; but, however, do not speak to Mr. Darcy about it, if you had rather not.

YOURS, ETC.

As it happened that Elizabeth had *much* rather not, she endeavoured in her answer to put an end to every entreaty and expectation of the kind. Such relief, however, as it was in her power to afford, by the practice of what might be called economy in her own private expenses, she frequently sent them. It had always been evident to her that such an income as theirs, under the direction of two persons so extravagant in their wants, and heedless of the future, must be very insufficient to their support; and whenever they changed their quarters, either Jane or herself were sure of being applied to for some little assistance towards discharging their bills. Their manner of living, even when the restoration of peace dismissed them to a home, was unsettled in the extreme. They were always moving from place to place in quest of a cheap situation, and always spending more than they ought. His affection for her soon sunk into indifference; hers lasted a little longer; and in spite of her youth and her manners, she retained all the claims to reputation which her marriage had given her.

Though Darcy could never receive *him* at Pemberley, yet, for Elizabeth's sake, he assisted him farther in his profession. Lydia was occasionally a visitor there, when her husband was gone to enjoy himself in London or Bath; and with the Bingleys they both of them frequently stayed so long that even Bingley's good humour was overcome, and he proceeded so far as to *talk* of giving them a hint to be gone.

Miss Bingley was very deeply mortified by Darcy's marriage; but as she thought it advisable to retain the right of visiting at Pemberley, she dropped all her resentment; was fonder than ever of Georgiana, almost as attentive to Darcy as heretofore, and paid off every arrear of civility to Elizabeth.

Pemberley was now Georgiana's home; and the attachment of the sisters was exactly what Darcy had hoped to see. They were able to love each other, even as well as they intended. Georgiana had the highest opinion in the world of Elizabeth; though at first she often listened with an astonishment bordering on alarm at her lively, sportive manner of talking to her brother. He, who had always inspired in herself a respect which almost overcame her affection, she now saw the object of open pleasantry. Her mind received knowledge which had never before fallen in her way. By Elizabeth's instructions she began to comprehend that a woman may take liberties with her husband, which a brother will not always allow in a sister more than ten years younger than himself.

Lady Catherine was extremely indignant on the marriage of her nephew; and as she gave way to all the genuine frankness of her character, in her reply to the letter which announced its arrangement, she sent him language so very abusive, especially of Elizabeth, that for some time all intercourse was at an end. But at length, by Elizabeth's persuasion, he was prevailed on to overlook the offence and seek a reconciliation; and after a little farther resistance on the part of his aunt, her resentment gave way, either to her affection for him, or her curiosity to see how his wife conducted herself; and she condescended to wait on them at Pemberley, in spite of that pollution which its woods had received, not merely from the presence of such a mistress, but the visits of her uncle and aunt from the city.

With the Gardiners they were always on the most intimate terms. Darcy, as well as Elizabeth, really loved them; and they were both ever sensible of the warmest gratitude towards the persons who, by bringing her into Derbyshire, had been the means of uniting them.

FINIS

326

WUTHERING HEIGHTS

by *Emily Brontë*

CHAPTER 1

1801—I have just returned from a visit to my landlord
—the solitary neighbour that I shall be troubled with.
This is certainly a beautiful country! In all England, I
do not believe that I could have fixed on a situation so
completely removed from the stir of society. A perfect
misanthropist's Heaven: and Mr. Heathcliff and I are
such a suitable pair to divide the desolation between us.
A capital fellow! He little imagined how my heart
warmed towards him when I beheld his black eyes with-
draw so suspiciously under their brows, as I rode up, and
when his fingers sheltered themselves, with a jealous
resolution, still further in his waistcoat, as I announced
my name.

"Mr. Heathcliff?" I said.

A nod was the answer.

"Mr. Lockwood, your new tenant, sir. I do myself the
honour of calling as soon as possible after my arrival, to
express the hope that I have not inconvenienced you
by my perseverance in soliciting the occupation of
Thrushcross Grange; I heard yesterday you had had
some thoughts——"

"Thrushcross Grange is my own, sir," he interrupted,
wincing. "I should not allow anyone to inconvenience
me, if I could hinder it—walk in!"

The "walk in" was uttered with closed teeth, and expressed the sentiment, "Go to the Deuce"; even the gate
over which he leant manifested no sympathizing movement to the words; and I think that circumstance determined me to accept the invitation; I felt interested in
a man who seemed more exaggeratedly reserved than
myself.

When he saw my horse's breast fairly pushing the barrier, he did pull out his hand to unchain it, and then
sullenly preceded me up the causeway, calling, as we
entered the court.

"Joseph, take Mr. Lockwood's horse; and bring up some wine."

"Here we have the whole establishment of domestics, I suppose," was the reflection, suggested by this compound order. "No wonder the grass grows up between the flags, and cattle are the only hedge-cutters."

Joseph was an elderly, nay, an old man; very old, perhaps, though hale and sinewy.

"The Lord help us!" he soliloquised in an undertone of peevish displeasure, while relieving me of my horse; looking, meantime, in my face so sourly that I charitably conjectured he must have need of divine aid to digest his dinner, and his pious ejaculation had no reference to my unexpected advent.

Wuthering Heights is the name of Mr. Heathcliff's dwelling. "Wuthering" being a significant provincial adjective, descriptive of the atmospheric tumult to which its station is exposed in stormy weather. Pure, bracing ventilation they must have up there at all times, indeed; one may guess the power of the north wind blowing over the edge, by the excessive slant of a few stunted firs at the end of the house; and by a range of gaunt thorns all stretching their limbs one way, as if craving alms of the sun. Happily, the architect had foresight to build it strong; the narrow windows are deeply set in the wall, and the corners defended with large jutting stones.

Before passing the threshold, I paused to admire a quantity of grotesque carving lavished over the front, and especially about the principal door; above which, among a wilderness of crumbling griffins and shameless little boys, I detected the date "1500," and the name "Hareton Earnshaw." I would have made a few comments, and requested a short history of the place from the surly owner; but his attitude at the door appeared to demand my speedy entrance, or complete departure, and I had no desire to aggravate his impatience previous to inspecting the penetralium.

One step brought us into the family sitting-room, without any introductory lobby or passage; they call it here "the house" pre-eminently. It includes kitchen and parlour, generally; but I believe at Wuthering Heights the kitchen is forced to retreat altogether into another quarter; at least I distinguished a chatter of tongues, and a clatter of culinary utensils, deep within; and I observed no signs of roasting, boiling, or baking, about the huge fireplace; nor any glitter of copper saucepans and tin cullenders on the walls. One end, indeed, reflected splendidly both light and heat from ranks of immense pewter dishes, interspersed with silver jugs and tankards, towering row after row, on a vast oak dresser, to the very roof. The latter had never been underdrawn: its entire anatomy lay bare to an inquiring eye, except where a frame of wood laden with oatcakes and clusters of legs of beef, mutton, and ham, concealed it. Above the chimney were sundry villainous old guns, and a couple of horse-pistols: and, by way of ornament, three gaudily painted canisters disposed along its ledge. The floor was of smooth, white stone; the chairs, high-backed, primitive structures, painted green; one or two heavy black ones lurking in the shade. In an arch under the dresser, reposed a huge, liver-coloured bitch pointer, surrounded by a swarm of squealing puppies; and other dogs haunted other recesses.

The apartment and furniture would have been nothing extraordinary as belonging to a homely, northern farmer, with a stubborn countenance, and stalwart limbs set out to advantage in knee-breeches and gaiters. Such an individual seated in his armchair, his mug of ale frothing on the round table before him, is to be seen in any circuit of five or six miles among these hills, if you go at the right time after dinner. But Mr. Heathcliff forms a singular contrast to his abode and style of living. He is a dark-skinned gypsy in aspect, in dress and manners a gentleman: that is, as much a gentleman as many a country squire; rather slovenly, perhaps, yet not looking amiss with his negligence, because he has an erect and handsome figure; and rather morose. Possibly, some people might suspect him of a degree of underbred pride; I have a sympathetic chord within that tells me it is nothing of the sort; I know, by instinct, his reserve springs from an aversion to showy displays of feeling—to manifestations of mutual kindliness. He'll love and hate equally under cover, and esteem it a species of impertinence to be loved or hated again. No, I'm running on too fast: I bestow my own attributes over liberally on him. Mr. Heathcliff may have entirely dissimilar reasons for keeping his hand out of the way when he meets a would-be acquaintance, to those which actuate me. Let me hope my constitution is almost peculiar; my dear mother used to say I should never have a comfortable home; and only last summer I proved myself perfectly unworthy of one.

While enjoying a month of fine weather at the sea-coast, I was thrown into the company of a most fascinating creature: a real goddess in my eyes, as long as she took no notice of me. I "never told my love" vocally; still, if looks have language, the merest idiot might have guessed I was over head and ears; she understood me at last, and looked a return—the sweetest of all imaginable looks. And what did I do? I confess it with shame—shrunk icily into myself, like a snail; at every glance retired colder and farther; till finally the poor innocent was led to doubt her own senses, and, overwhelmed with confusion at her supposed mistake, persuaded her mamma to decamp. By this curious turn of disposition I have gained the reputation of deliberate heartlessness; how undeserved, I alone can appreciate.

I took a seat at the end of the hearthstone opposite that towards which my landlord advanced, and filled up an interval of silence by attempting to caress the canine mother, who had left her nursery, and was sneaking wolfishly to the back of my legs, her lip curled up, and her white teeth watering for a snatch.

My caress provoked a long, guttural snarl.

"You'd better let the dog alone," growled Mr. Heath-cliff in unison, checking fiercer demonstrations with a punch of his foot. "She's not accustomed to be spoiled —not kept for a pet."

Then, striding to a side door, he shouted again.

"Joseph!"

Joseph mumbled indistinctly in the depths of the cellar, but gave no intimation of ascending; so his master dived down to him, leaving me vis-à-vis the ruffianly bitch and a pair of grim shaggy sheep dogs, who shared with her a jealous guardianship over all my movements.

Not anxious to come in contact with their fangs, I sat still; but, imagining they would scarcely understand tacit insults, I unfortunately indulged in winking and making faces at the trio, and some turn of my physiognomy so irritated madam, that she suddenly broke into a fury, and leapt on my knees. I flung her back, and hastened to interpose the table between us. This proceeding roused the whole hive. Half-a-dozen four-footed fiends, of various sizes and ages, issued from hidden dens to the common centre. I felt my heels and coat-laps peculiar subjects of assault; and, parrying off the larger combatants as effectually as I could with the poker, I was constrained to demand, aloud, assistance from some of the household in re-establishing peace.

Mr. Heathcliff and his man climbed the cellar steps with vexatious phlegm; I don't think they moved one second faster than usual, though the hearth was an absolute tempest of worrying and yelping.

Happily, an inhabitant of the kitchen made more dispatch: a lusty dame, with tucked-up gown, bare arms, and fire-flushed cheeks, rushed into the midst of us flourishing a frying-pan; and used that weapon, and her tongue, to such purpose, that the storm subsided magically, and she only remained, heaving like a sea after a high wind, when her master entered on the scene.

"What the devil is the matter?" he asked, eyeing me in a manner I could ill endure after this inhospitable treatment.

"What the devil, indeed!" I muttered. "The herd of possessed swine could have had no worse spirits in them than those animals of yours, sir. You might as well leave a stranger with a brood of tigers!"

"They won't meddle with persons who touch nothing," he remarked, putting the bottle before me, and restoring the displaced table. "The dogs do right to be vigilant. Take a glass of wine?"

"No thank you."

"Not bitten, are you?"

"If I had been, I would have set my signet on the biter."

Heathcliff's countenance relaxed into a grin.

"Come, come," he said, "you are flurried, Mr. Lockwood. Here, take a little wine. Guests are so exceedingly rare in this house that I and my dogs, I am willing to own, hardly know how to receive them. Your health, sir!"

I bowed and returned the pledge, beginning to perceive that it would be foolish to sit sulking for the misbehaviour of a pack of curs; besides, I felt loath to yield the fellow further amusement at my expense, since his humour took that turn.

He—probably swayed by prudential considerations of the folly of offending a good tenant—relaxed a little in the laconic style of chipping off his pronouns and auxiliary verbs, and introduced what he supposed would be a subject of interest to me—a discourse on the advantages and disadvantages of my present place of retirement.

I found him very intelligent on the topics we touched, and before I went home, I was encouraged so far as to volunteer another visit tomorrow.

He evidently wished no repetition of my intrusion. I shall go, notwithstanding. It is astonishing how sociable I feel myself compared with him.

CHAPTER 2

YESTERDAY afternoon set in misty and cold. I had half a mind to spend it by my study fire, instead of wading through heath and mud to Wuthering Heights.

On coming up from dinner, however (N.B.—I dine between twelve and one o'clock; the housekeeper, a matronly lady, taken as a fixture along with the house, could not, or would not, comprehend my request that I might be served at five)—on mounting the stairs with this lazy intention, and stepping into the room, I saw a servant girl on her knees, surrounded by brushes, and coal scuttles, and raising an infernal dust as she extinguished the flames with heaps of cinders. This spectacle drove me back immediately; I took my hat, and, after a four miles' walk, arrived at Heathcliff's garden gate just in time to escape the first feathery flakes of a snow shower.

On that bleak hilltop the earth was hard with a black frost, and the air made me shiver through every limb.

Being unable to remove the chain, I jumped over, and, running up the flagged causeway bordered with straggling gooseberry bushes, knocked vainly for admittance, till my knuckles tingled, and the dogs howled.

"Wretched inmates!" I ejaculated mentally, "you deserve perpetual isolation from your species for your churlish inhospitality. At least, I would not keep my doors barred in the daytime. I don't care—I will get in!"

So resolved, I grasped the latch and shook it vehemently. Vinegar-faced Joseph projected his head from a round window of the barn.

"Whet are ye for?" he shouted. "T' maister's dahn i' t' fowld. Goa rahned by th' end ut' laith, if yah went tuh spake tull him."

"Is there nobody inside to open the door?" I hallooed responsively.

"They's nobbut t' missis; and shoo'll nut open 't an ye mak yer flaysome dins till neeght."

"Why? Cannot you tell her who I am, eh, Joseph?"

"Nor-ne me! Aw'll hae noa hend wi't," muttered the head, vanishing.

The snow began to drive thickly. I seized the handle to essay another trial, when a young man without coat, and shouldering a pitchfork, appeared in the yard behind. He hailed me to follow him, and, after marching through a wash-house, and a paved area containing a coal-shed, pump, and pigeon-cote, we at length arrived in the huge, warm, cheerful apartment where I was formerly received.

It glowed delightfully in the radiance of an immense fire, compounded of coal, peat, and wood; and near the table, laid for a plentiful evening meal, I was pleased to observe the "missis," an individual whose existence I had never previously suspected. I bowed and waited, thinking she would bid me take a seat. She looked at me, leaning back in her chair, and remained motionless and mute.

"Rough weather!" I remarked. "I'm afraid, Mrs. Heathcliff, the door must bear the consequence of your servants' leisure attendance; I had hard work to make them hear me!"

She never opened her mouth. I stared—she stared also. At any rate, she kept her eyes on me in a cool, regardless manner, exceedingly embarrassing and disagreeable.

"Sit down," said the young man gruffly. "He'll be in soon."

I obeyed; and hemmed, and called the villain Juno, who deigned, at this second interview, to move the extreme tip of her tail, in token of owning my acquaintance.

"A beautiful animal!" I commenced again. "Do you intend parting with the little ones, madam?"

"They are not mine," said the amiable hostess, more repellingly than Heathcliff himself could have replied.

"Ah, your favourites are among these!" I continued, turning to an obscure cushion full of something like cats.

"A strange choice of favourites!" she observed scornfully.

Unluckily, it was a heap of dead rabbits. I hemmed once more, and drew closer to the hearth, repeating my comment on the wildness of the evening.

"You should not have come out," she said, rising and reaching from the chimney-piece two of the painted canisters.

Her position before was sheltered from the light; now, I had a distinct view of her whole figure and countenance. She was slender, and apparently scarcely past girlhood: an admirable form, and the most exquisite little face that I have ever had the pleasure of beholding: small features, very fair; flaxen ringlets, or rather golden, hanging loose on her delicate neck; and eyes—had they been agreeable in expression, they would have been irresistible; fortunately for my susceptible heart, the only sentiment they evinced hovered between scorn and a kind of desperation, singularly unnatural to be detected there.

The canisters were almost out of her reach; I made a motion to aid her; she turned upon me as a miser might turn if anyone attempted to assist him in counting his gold.

"I don't want your help," she snapped; "I can get them for myself."

"I beg your pardon," I hastened to reply.

"Were you asked to tea?" she demanded, tying an

apron over her neat black frock, and standing with a spoonful of the leaf poised over the pot.

"I shall be glad to have a cup," I answered.

"Were you asked?" she repeated.

"No," I said, half smiling. "You are the proper person to ask me."

She flung the tea back, spoon and all; and resumed her chair in a pet, her forehead corrugated, and her red underlip pushed out, like a child's, ready to cry.

Meanwhile, the young man had slung onto his person a decidedly shabby upper garment, and, erecting himself before the blaze, looked down on me, from the corner of his eyes, for all the world as if there were some mortal feud unavenged between us. I began to doubt whether he were a servant or not: his dress and speech were both rude, entirely devoid of the superiority observable in Mr. and Mrs. Heathcliff; his thick, brown curls were rough and uncultivated, his whiskers encroached bearishly over his cheeks, and his hands were embrowned like those of the common labourer; still his bearing was free, almost haughty, and he showed none of a domestic's assiduity in attending on the lady of the house.

In the absence of clear proofs of his condition, I deemed it best to abstain from noticing his curious conduct, and, five minutes afterwards, the entrance of Heathcliff relieved me, in some measure, from my uncomfortable state.

"You see, sir, I am come, according to promise!" I exclaimed, assuming the cheerful; "and I fear I shall be weatherbound for half an hour, if you can afford me shelter during that space."

"Half an hour?" he said, shaking the white flakes from his clothes; "I wonder you should select the thick of a snowstorm to ramble about in. Do you know that you run a risk of being lost in the marshes? People familiar with these moors often miss their road on such evenings; and, I can tell you, there is no chance of a change at present."

"Perhaps I can get a guide among your lads, and he might stay at the Grange till morning—could you spare me one?"

"No, I could not."

"Oh, indeed! Well, then, I must trust to my own sagacity."

"Umph!"

"Are you going to mak' th' tea?" demanded he of the shabby coat, shifting his ferocious gaze from me to the young lady.

"Is he to have any?" she asked, appealing to Heathcliff.

"Get it ready, will you?" was the answer, uttered so savagely that I started. The tone in which the words were said revealed a genuine bad nature. I no longer felt inclined to call Heathcliff a capital fellow.

When the preparations were finished, he invited me with—

"Now, sir, bring forward your chair." And we all, including the rustic youth, drew round the table, an austere silence prevailing while we discussed our meal.

I thought, if I had caused the cloud, it was my duty to make an effort to dispel it. They could not every day sit so grim and taciturn; and it was impossible, however ill-tempered they might be, that the universal scowl they wore was their everyday countenance.

"It is strange," I began, in the interval of swallowing one cup of tea and receiving another—"it is strange how custom can mould our tastes and ideas—many could not imagine the existence of happiness in a life of such complete exile from the world as you spend, Mr. Heathcliff; yet, I'll venture to say, that, surrounded by your family, and with your amiable lady as the presiding genius over your home and heart——"

"My amiable lady!" he interrupted, with an almost diabolical sneer on his face. "Where is she—my amiable lady?"

"Mrs. Heathcliff, your wife, I mean."

"Well, yes—Oh! you would intimate that her spirit has taken the post of ministering angel, and guards the fortunes of Wuthering Heights, even when her body is gone. Is that it?"

Perceiving myself in a blunder, I attempted to correct it. I might have seen that there was too great a disparity between the ages of the parties to make it likely that they were man and wife. One was about forty; a period of mental vigour at which men seldom cherish the delusion of being married for love, by girls; that

(18)

dream is reserved for the solace of our declining years. The other did not look seventeen.

Then it flashed upon me—"The clown at my elbow, who is drinking his tea out of a basin and eating his bread with unwashed hands, may be her husband. Heathcliff, junior, of course. Here is the consequence of being buried alive: she has thrown herself away upon that boor, from sheer ignorance that better individuals existed! A sad pity—I must beware how I cause her to regret her choice."

The last reflection may seem conceited; it was not. My neighbour struck me as bordering on repulsive; I knew, through experience, that I was tolerably attractive.

"Mrs. Heathcliff is my daughter-in-law," said Heathcliff, corroborating my surmise. He turned, as he spoke, a peculiar look in her direction, a look of hatred unless he has a most perverse set of facial muscles that will not, like those of other people, interpret the language of his soul.

"Ah, certainly—I see now; you are the favoured possessor of the beneficent fairy," I remarked, turning to my neighbour.

This was worse than before: the youth grew crimson, and clenched his fist, with every appearance of a meditated assault. But he seemed to recollect himself presently, and smothered the storm in a brutal curse, muttered on my behalf, which, however, I took care not to notice.

"Unhappy in your conjectures, sir!" observed my host; "we neither of us have the privilege of owning your good fairy; her mate is dead. I said she was my daughter-in-law, therefore, she must have married my son."

"And this young man is——"

"Not my son, assuredly!"

Heathcliff smiled again, as if it were rather too bold a jest to attribute the paternity of that bear to him.

"My name is Hareton Earnshaw," growled the other, "and I'd counsel you to respect it!"

"I've shown no disrespect," was my reply, laughing internally at the dignity with which he announced himself.

He fixed his eye on me longer than I cared to return

the stare, for fear I might be tempted either to box his ears, or render my hilarity audible. I began to feel unmistakably out of place in that pleasant family circle. The dismal spiritual atmosphere overcame, and more than neutralized, the glowing physical comforts round me; and I resolved to be cautious how I ventured under those rafters a third time.

The business of eating being concluded, and no one uttering a word of sociable conversation, I approached a window to examine the weather.

A sorrowful sight I saw: dark night coming down prematurely, and sky and hills mingled in one bitter swirl of wind and suffocating snow.

"I don't think it possible for me to get home now, without a guide," I could not help exclaiming. "The roads will be buried already; and, if they were bare, I could scarcely distinguish a foot in advance."

"Hareton, drive those dozen sheep into the barn porch. They 'll be covered if left in the fold all night: and put a plank before them," said Heathcliff.

"How must I do?" I continued, with rising irritation.

There was no reply to my question; and on looking round I saw only Joseph bringing in a pail of porridge for the dogs, and Mrs. Heathcliff leaning over the fire, diverting herself with burning a bundle of matches which had fallen from the chimney-piece as she restored the tea canister to its place.

The former, when he had deposited his burden, took a critical survey of the room; and, in cracked tones, grated out—

"Aw woonder hagh yah can faishion tuh stand theor i' idleness un war, when all on 'em 's goan aght! Bud yah 're a nowt, and it 's noa use talking—yah'll niver mend uh yer ill ways; bud, goa raight tuh t' divil, like yer mother afore ye!"

I imagined, for a moment, that this piece of eloquence was addressed to me; and, sufficiently enraged, stepped towards the aged rascal with an intention of kicking him out of the door. Mrs. Heathcliff, however, checked me by her answer.

"You scandalous old hypocrite!" she replied. "Are you not afraid of being carried away bodily, whenever you mention the devil's name? I warn you to refrain from provoking me, or I'll ask your abduction as a special favour. Stop, look here, Joseph," she continued, taking a long, dark book from a shelf. "I'll show you how far I've progressed in the Black Art: I shall soon be competent to make a clear house of it. The red cow didn't die by chance; and your rheumatism can hardly be reckoned among providential visitations!"

"Oh, wicked, wicked!" gasped the elder; "may the Lord deliver us from evil!"

"No, reprobate! you are a castaway—be off, or I'll hurt you seriously! I'll have you all modelled in wax and clay; and the first who passes the limits I fix, shall—I'll not say what he shall be done to—but, you 'll see! Go, I'm looking at you!"

The little witch put a mock malignity into her beautiful eyes, and Joseph, trembling with sincere horror, hurried out praying and ejaculating "wicked" as he went.

I thought her conduct must be prompted by a species of dreary fun; and, now that we were alone, I endeavoured to interest her in my distress.

"Mrs. Heathcliff," I said earnestly, "you must excuse me for troubling you—I presume, because, with that face, I'm sure you cannot help being good-hearted. Do point out some landmarks by which I may know my way home. I have no more idea how to get there than you would have how to get to London!"

"Take the road you came," she answered, ensconcing herself in a chair, with a candle and the long book open before her. "It is brief advice, but as sound as I can give."

"Then, if you hear of me being discovered dead in a bog or a pit full of snow, your conscience won't whisper that it is partly your fault?"

"How so? I cannot escort you. They wouldn't let me go to the end of the garden wall."

"You! I should be very sorry to ask you to cross the threshold, for my convenience, on such a night," I cried. "I want you to tell me my way, not to show it; or else to persuade Mr. Heathcliff to give me a guide."

"Who? There is himself, Earnshaw, Zillah, Joseph, and I. Which would you have?"

"Are there no boys at the farm?"

"No, those are all."

"Then, it follows that I am compelled to stay."

"That you may settle with your host. I have nothing to do with it."

"I hope it will be a lesson to you, to make no more rash journeys on these hills," cried Heathcliff's stern voice from the kitchen entrance. "As to staying here, I don't keep accommodations for visitors: you must share a bed with Hareton, or Joseph, if you do."

"I can sleep on a chair in this room," I replied.

"No, no! A stranger is a stranger, be he rich or poor: it will not suit me to permit anyone the range of the place while I am off guard!" said the unmannerly wretch.

With this insult, my patience was at an end. I uttered an expression of disgust, and pushed past him into the yard, running against Earnshaw in my haste. It was so dark that I could not see the means of exit; and, as I wandered round, I heard another specimen of their civil behaviour amongst each other.

At first, the young man appeared about to befriend me.

"I'll go with him as far as the park," he said.

"You'll go with him to hell!" exclaimed his master, or whatever relation he bore. "And who is to look after the horses, eh?"

"A man's life is of more consequence than one evening's neglect of the horses; somebody must go," murmured Mrs. Heathcliff, more kindly than I expected.

"Not at your command!" retorted Hareton. "If you set store on him, you'd better be quiet."

"Then I hope his ghost will haunt you; and I hope Mr. Heathcliff will never get another tenant, till the Grange is a ruin!" she answered sharply.

"Hearken, hearken, shoo's cursing on 'em!" muttered Joseph, towards whom I had been steering.

He sat within earshot, milking the cows by the light of a lantern, which I seized unceremoniously, and, calling out that I would send it back on the morrow, rushed to the nearest postern.

"Maister, maister, he 's staling t' lantern!" shouted the ancient, pursuing my retreat. "Hey, Gnasher! Hey, dog! Hey, Wolf, holld him, holld him!"

On opening the little door, two hairy monsters flew

at my throat, bearing me down and extinguishing the light; while a mingled guffaw, from Heathcliff and Hareton, put the copestone on my rage and humiliation.

Fortunately, the beasts seemed more bent on stretching their paws, and yawning, and flourishing their tails, than devouring me alive; but they would suffer no resurrection, and I was forced to lie till their malignant masters pleased to deliver me; then hatless, and trembling with wrath, I ordered the miscreants to let me out—on their peril to keep me one minute longer—with several incoherent threats of retaliation that, in their indefinite depth of virulency, smacked of King Lear.

The vehemence of my agitation brought on a copious bleeding at the nose, and still Heathcliff laughed, and still I scolded. I don't know what would have concluded the scene, had there not been one person at hand rather more rational than myself, and more benevolent than my entertainer. This was Zillah, the stout housewife; who at length issued forth to inquire into the nature of the uproar. She thought that some of them had been laying violent hands on me; and, not daring to attack her master, she turned her vocal artillery against the younger scoundrel.

"Well, Mr. Earnshaw," she cried, "I wonder what you'll have agait next! Are we going to murder folk on our very door-stones? I see this house will never do for me—look at t' poor lad, he's fair choking! Wisht, wisht! you mun'n't go on so. Come in, and I'll cure that. There now, hold ye still."

With these words she suddenly splashed a pint of icy water down my neck, and pulled me into the kitchen. Mr. Heathcliff followed, his accidental merriment expiring quickly in his habitual moroseness.

I was sick exceedingly, and dizzy and faint; and thus compelled, perforce, to accept lodgings under his roof. He told Zillah to give me a glass of brandy, and then passed on to the inner room, while she condoled with me on my sorry predicament; and having obeyed his orders, whereby I was somewhat revived, ushered me to bed.

CHAPTER 3

W HILE leading the way upstairs, she recommended that I should hide the candle, and not
make a noise, for her master had an odd notion about
the chamber she would put me in, and never let anybody lodge there willingly.

I asked the reason.

She did not know, she answered; she had only lived
there a year or two; and they had so many queer goings
on, she could not begin to be curious.

Too stupefied to be curious myself, I fastened my door
and glanced round for the bed. The whole furniture
consisted of a chair, a clothes press, and a large oak case,
with squares cut out near the top, resembling coach
windows.

Having approached this structure, I looked inside, and
perceived it to be a singular sort of old-fashioned couch,
very conveniently designed to obviate the necessity for
every member of the family having a room to himself.
In fact, it formed a little closet, and the ledge of a window, which it enclosed, served as a table.

I slid back the panelled sides, got in with my light,
pulled them together again, and felt secure against the
vigilance of Heathcliff, and everyone else.

The ledge, where I placed my candle, had a few mil-
dewed books piled up in one corner, and it was covered
with writing scratched on the paint. This writing, however, was nothing but a name repeated in all kinds of
characters, large and small—*Catherine Earnshaw*, here
and there varied to *Catherine Heathcliff*, and then again
to *Catherine Linton*.

In vapid listlessness I leant my head against the window, and continued spelling over Catherine Earnshaw
—Heathcliff—Linton, till my eyes closed; but they had
not rested five minutes when a glare of white letters
started from the dark, as vivid as spectres—the air

swarmed with Catherines; and rousing myself to dispel the obtrusive name, I discovered my candle wick reclining on one of the antique volumes, and perfuming the place with an odour of roasted calf-skin.

I snuffed it off, and, very ill at ease under the influence of cold and lingering nausea, sat up and spread open the injured tome on my knee. It was a Testament, in lean type, and smelling dreadfully musty: a flyleaf bore the inscription—"Catherine Earnshaw, her book," and a date some quarter of a century back.

I shut it, and took up another, and another, till I had examined all. Catherine's library was select, and its state of dilapidation proved it to have been well used, though not altogether for a legitimate purpose; scarcely one chapter had escaped a pen-and-ink commentary—at least, the appearance of one—covering every morsel of blank that the printer had left.

Some were detached sentences; other parts took the form of a regular diary, scrawled in an unformed, childish hand. At the top of an extra page (quite a treasure, probably, when first lighted on) I was greatly amused to behold an excellent caricature of my friend Joseph—rudely yet powerfully sketched.

An immediate interest kindled within me for the unknown Catherine, and I began, forthwith, to decipher her faded hieroglyphics.

"An awful Sunday!" commenced the paragraph beneath. "I wish my father were back again. Hindley is a detestable substitute—his conduct to Heathcliff is atrocious—H. and I are going to rebel—we took our initiatory step this evening.

"All day had been flooding with rain; we could not go to church, so Joseph must needs get up a congregation in the garret; and, while Hindley and his wife basked downstairs before a comfortable fire—doing anything but reading their Bibles, I'll answer for it—Heathcliff, myself, and the unhappy ploughboy were commanded to take our Prayer-books, and mount; we were ranged in a row on a sack of corn, groaning and shivering, and hoping that Joseph would shiver too, so that he might give us a short homily for his own sake. A vain idea! The service lasted precisely three hours; and yet my brother had the face to exclaim, when he saw us descending,

" 'What, done already?'

"On Sunday evenings we used to be permitted to play, if we did not make much noise; now a mere titter is sufficient to send us into corners!

" 'You forget you have a master here,' says the tyrant. 'I'll demolish the first who puts me out of temper! I insist on perfect sobriety and silence. Oh, boy! was that you? Frances, darling, pull his hair as you go by; I heard him snap his fingers.'

"Frances pulled his hair heartily, and then went and seated herself on her husband's knee; and there they were, like two babies, kissing and talking nonsense by the hour—foolish palaver that we should be ashamed of.

"We made ourselves as snug as our means allowed in the arch of the dresser. I had just fastened our pinafores together, and hung them up for a curtain, when in comes Joseph, on an errand from the stables. He tears down my handiwork, boxes my ears, and croaks—

" 'T' maister nobbut just buried, and Sabbath nut oe'red, und t' sahnd uht' gospel still i' yer lugs, and yah darr be laiking! shame on ye! sit ye dahn, ill childer! they 's good books eneugh if ye'll read 'em: sit ye dahn, and think uh yer sowls!'

"Saying this, he compelled us so to square our positions that we might receive from the far-off fire a dull ray to show us the text of the lumber he thrust upon us.

"I could not bear the employment. I took my dingy volume by the scroop, and hurled it into the dog kennel, vowing I hated a good book.

"Heathcliff kicked his to the same place.

"Then there was a hubbub!

" 'Maister Hindley!' shouted our chaplain. 'Maister, coom hither! Miss Cathy's riven th' back off "Th' Helmet uh Salvation," un' Heathcliff's pawsed his fit intuh t' first part uh "T' Brooad Way to Destruction!" It's fair flaysome ut yah let 'em goa on this gait. Ech! th' owd man ud uh laced 'em properly—bud he's goan!'

"Hindley hurried up from his paradise on the hearth, and seizing one of us by the collar and the other by the arm, hurled both into the back kitchen, where, Joseph asseverated, 'owd Nick' would fetch us as sure as we were living; and, so comforted, we each sought a separate nook to await his advent.

"I reached this book, and a pot of ink from the shelf, and pushed the house door ajar to give me light, and I have got the time on with writing for twenty minutes; but my companion is impatient, and proposes that we should appropriate the dairy woman's cloak, and have a scamper on the moors, under its shelter. A pleasant suggestion—and then, if the surly old man come in, he may believe his prophecy verified—we cannot be damper, or colder, in the rain than we are here."

I suppose Catherine fulfilled her project, for the next sentence took up another subject; she waxed lachrymose.

"How little did I dream that Hindley would ever make me cry so!" she wrote. "My head aches, till I cannot keep it on the pillow, and still I can't give over. Poor Heathcliff! Hindley calls him a vagabond, and won't let him sit with us, nor eat with us any more; and, he says, he and I must not play together, and threatens to turn him out of the house if we break his orders.

"He has been blaming our father (how dared he?) for treating H. too liberally; and swears he will reduce him to his right place——"

*   *   *   *   *   *

I began to nod drowsily over the dim page; my eye wandered from manuscript to print. I saw a red ornamented title—"Seventy Times Seven, and the First of the Seventy-First. A Pious Discourse delivered by the Reverend Jabes Branderham, in the Chapel of Gimmerden Sough." And while I was, half consciously, worrying my brain to guess what Jabes Branderham would make of his subject, I sank back in bed, and fell asleep.

Alas, for the effects of bad tea and bad temper! what else could it be that made me pass such a terrible night? I don't remember another that I can at all compare with it since I was capable of suffering.

I began to dream, almost before I ceased to be sensible of my locality. I thought it was morning, and I had set out on my way home, with Joseph for a guide. The snow lay yards deep in our road; and, as we floundered on, my companion wearied me with constant reproaches that I had not brought a pilgrim's staff, telling me that I could never get into the house without one, and boastfully flourishing a heavy-headed cudgel, which I understood to be so denominated.

For a moment I considered it absurd that I should need such a weapon to gain admittance into my own residence. Then a new idea flashed across me. I was not going there; we were journeying to hear the famous Jabes Branderham preach from the text—"Seventy Times Seven"; and either Joseph, the preacher, or I had committed the "First of the Seventy-First," and were to be publicly exposed and excommunicated.

We came to the chapel. I have passed it really in my walks, twice or thrice; it lies in a hollow, between two hills—an elevated hollow, near a swamp, whose peaty moisture is said to answer all the purposes of embalming on the few corpses deposited there. The roof has been kept whole hitherto; but as the clergyman's stipend is only twenty pounds per annum, and a house with two rooms, threatening speedily to determine into one, no clergyman will undertake the duties of pastor, especially as it is currently reported that his flock would rather let him starve than increase the living by one penny from their own pockets. However, in my dream, Jabes had a full and attentive congregation; and he preached—good God! what a sermon: divided into *four hundred and ninety* parts, each fully equal to an ordinary address from the pulpit, and each discussing a separate sin! Where he searched for them, I cannot tell. He had his private manner of interpreting the phrase, and it seemed necessary the brother should sin different sins on every occasion.

They were of the most curious character: odd transgressions that I never imagined previously.

Oh, how weary I grew. How I writhed, and yawned, and nodded, and revived! How I pinched and pricked myself, and rubbed my eyes, and stood up, and sat down again, and nudged Joseph to inform me if he would ever have done.

I was condemned to hear all out; finally, he reached the *"First of the Seventy-First."* At that crisis, a sudden inspiration descended on me; I was moved to rise and denounce Jabes Branderham as the sinner of the sin that no Christian need pardon.

"Sir," I exclaimed, "sitting here within these four walls, at one stretch, I have endured and forgiven the four hundred and ninety heads of your discourse. Seventy times seven times have I plucked up my hat and been about to depart—Seventy times seven times have you preposterously forced me to resume my seat. The four hundred and ninety-first is too much. Fellow-martyrs, have at him! Drag him down, and crush him to atoms, that the place which knows him may know him no more!"

"*Thou art the man!*" cried Jabes, after a solemn pause, leaning over his cushion. "Seventy times seven times didst thou gapingly contort thy visage—seventy times seven did I take counsel with my soul—Lo, this is human weakness; this also may be absolved! The First of the Seventy-First is come. Brethren, execute upon him the judgment written. Such honour have all His saints!"

With that concluding word the whole assembly, exalting their pilgrim's staves, rushed round me in a body; and I, having no weapon to raise in self-defence, commenced grappling with Joseph, my nearest and most ferocious assailant, for his. In the confluence of the multitude, several clubs crossed; blows, aimed at me, fell on other sconces. Presently the whole chapel resounded with rappings and counter-rappings; every man's hand was against his neighbour; and Branderham, unwilling to remain idle, poured forth his zeal in a shower of loud taps on the boards of the pulpit, which responded so smartly that, at last, to my unspeakable relief, they woke me.

And what was it that had suggested the tremendous tumult? What had played Jabes's part in the row? Merely the branch of a fir-tree that touched my lattice, as the blast wailed by, and rattled its dry cones against the panes!

I listened doubtingly an instant; detected the disturber, then turned and dosed, and dreamt again: if possible, still more disagreeably than before.

This time, I remembered I was lying in the oak closet, and I heard distinctly the gusty wind and the driving of the snow; I heard, also, the fir bough repeat its teasing sound, and ascribed it to the right cause; but it annoyed me so much, that I resolved to silence it, if possible; and I thought I rose and endeavoured to un-hasp the casement. The hook was soldered into the staple, a circumstance observed by me when awake, but forgotten.

"I must stop it, nevertheless!" I muttered, knocking my knuckles through the glass, and stretching an arm out to seize the importunate branch; instead of which, my fingers closed on the fingers of a little, ice-cold hand!

The intense horror of nightmare came over me; I tried to draw back my arm, but the hand clung to it, and a most melancholy voice sobbed,

"Let me in—let me in!"

"Who are you?" I asked, struggling, meanwhile, to dis-engage myself.

"Catherine Linton," it replied shiveringly (why did I think of *Linton*? I had read *Earnshaw* twenty times for Linton). "I'm come home: I'd lost my way on the moor!"

As it spoke, I discerned, obscurely, a child's face look-ing through the window. Terror made me cruel; and, finding it useless to attempt shaking the creature off, I pulled its wrist on to the broken pane, and rubbed it to and fro till the blood ran down and soaked the bed-clothes: still it wailed, "Let me in!" and maintained its tenacious gripe, almost maddening me with fear.

"How can I!" I said at length. "Let me go, if you want me to let you in!"

The fingers relaxed, I snatched mine through the hole, hurriedly piled the books up in a pyramid against it, and stopped my ears to exclude the lamentable prayer.

I seemed to keep them closed above a quarter of an hour; yet, the instant I listened again, there was the doleful cry moaning on!

"Begone!" I shouted, "I'll never let you in, not if you beg for twenty years."

"It is twenty years," mourned the voice, "twenty years. I've been a waif for twenty years!"

Thereat began a feeble scratching outside, and the pile of books moved as if thrust forward.

I tried to jump up, but could not stir a limb; and so yelled aloud, in a frenzy of fright.

To my confusion, I discovered the yell was not ideal: hasty footsteps approached my chamber door; somebody pushed it open, with a vigorous hand, and a light glimmered through the squares at the top of the bed. I sat shuddering yet, and wiping the perspiration from my forehead; the intruder appeared to hesitate, and muttered to himself.

At last, he said in a half-whisper, plainly not expecting an answer,

"Is anyone here?"

I considered it best to confess my presence, for I knew Heathcliff's accents, and feared he might search further, if I kept quiet.

With this intention, I turned and opened the panels. I shall not soon forget the effect my action produced.

Heathcliff stood near the entrance, in his shirt and trousers, with a candle dripping over his fingers, and his face as white as the wall behind him. The first creak of the oak startled him like an electric shock; the light leaped from his hold to a distance of some feet, and his agitation was so extreme, that he could hardly pick it up.

"It is only your guest, sir," I called out, desirous to spare him the humiliation of exposing his cowardice further. "I had the misfortune to scream in my sleep, owing to a frightful nightmare. I'm sorry I disturbed you."

"Oh, God confound you, Mr. Lockwood! I wish you were at the——" commenced my host, setting the candle on a chair, because he found it impossible to hold it steady.

"And who showed you up to this room?" he continued, crushing his nails into his palms, and grinding his teeth to subdue the maxillary convulsions. "Who was it? I've a good mind to turn them out of the house this moment!"

"It was your servant, Zillah," I replied, flinging myself on to the floor and rapidly resuming my garments. "I should not care if you did, Mr. Heathcliff; she richly deserves it. I suppose that she wanted to get another proof that the place was haunted, at my expense. Well, it is—swarming with ghosts and goblins! You have reason in shutting it up, I assure you. No one will thank you for a doze in such a den!"

"What do you mean?" asked Heathcliff, "and what are you doing? Lie down and finish out the night, since you are here; but, for Heaven's sake! don't repeat that horrid noise; nothing could excuse it, unless you were having your throat cut!"

"If the little fiend had got in at the window, she probably would have strangled me!" I returned. "I'm not going to endure the persecutions of your hospitable ancestors again. Was not the Reverend Jabes Branderham akin to you on the mother's side? And that minx, Catherine Linton, or Earnshaw, or however she was called —she must have been a changeling—wicked little soul! She told me she had been walking the earth these twenty years; a just punishment for her mortal transgressions, I've no doubt!"

Scarcely were these words uttered, when I recollected the association of Heathcliff's with Catherine's name in the book, which had completely slipped from my memory till thus awakened. I blushed at my inconsideration; but, without showing further consciousness of the offence, I hastened to add—

"The truth is, sir, I passed the first part of the night in—" here I stopped afresh—I was about to say "perusing those old volumes," then it would have revealed my knowledge of their written, as well as their printed, contents; so, correcting myself, I went on—"in spelling over the name scratched on that window ledge. A monotonous occupation, calculated to set me asleep, like counting, or——"

"What can you mean by talking in this way to me?" thundered Heathcliff with savage vehemence. "How—how dare you, under my roof?—God! he's mad to speak so!" And he struck his forehead with rage.

I did not know whether to resent this language or pursue my explanation; but he seemed so powerfully affected that I took pity and proceeded with my dreams; affirming I had never heard the appellation of "Catherine Linton" before, but reading it often over produced an impression which personified itself when I had no longer my imagination under control.

Heathcliff gradually fell back into the shelter of the bed, as I spoke, finally sitting down almost concealed behind it. I guessed, however, by his irregular and intercepted breathing, that he struggled to vanquish an excess of violent emotion.

Not liking to show him that I heard the conflict, I continued my toilette rather noisily, looked at my watch, and soliloquized on the length of the night:

"Not three o'clock yet! I could have taken oath it had been six. Time stagnates here—we must surely have retired to rest at eight!"

"Always at nine in winter, and always rise at four," said my host, suppressing a groan, and, as I fancied, by the motion of his shadow's arm, dashing a tear from his eyes.

"Mr. Lockwood," he added, "you may go into my room; you'll only be in the way, coming downstairs so early; and your childish outcry has sent sleep to the devil for me."

"And for me, too," I replied. "I'll walk in the yard till daylight, and then I'll be off; and you need not dread a repetition of my intrusion. I am now quite cured of seeking pleasure in society, be it country or town. A sensible man ought to find sufficient company in himself."

"Delightful company!" muttered Heathcliff. "Take the candle, and go where you please. I shall join you directly. Keep out of the yard, though, the dogs are unchained; and the house—Juno mounts sentinel there, and—nay, you can only ramble about the steps and passages. But, away with you! I'll come in two minutes!"

I obeyed, so far as to quit the chamber; when, ignorant where the narrow lobbies led, I stood still, and was witness, involuntarily, to a piece of superstition on the part of my landlord, which belied, oddly, his apparent sense.

He got on to the bed, and wrenched open the lattice, bursting, as he pulled at it, into an uncontrollable passion of tears.

"Come in! come in!" he sobbed. "Cathy, do come. Oh do—once more! Oh! my heart's darling! hear me this time, Catherine, at last!"

The spectre showed a spectre's ordinary caprice; it

gave no sign of being; but the snow and wind whirled wildly through, even reaching my station, and blowing out the light.

There was such anguish in the gush of grief that accompanied this raving, that my compassion made me overlook its folly, and I drew off, half angry to have listened at all, and vexed at having related my ridiculous nightmare, since it produced that agony; though why, was beyond my comprehension.

I descended cautiously to the lower regions, and landed in the back kitchen, where a gleam of fire, raked compactly together, enabled me to rekindle my candle.

Nothing was stirring except a brindled, grey cat, which crept from the ashes and saluted me with a querulous mew.

Two benches, shaped in sections of a circle, nearly enclosed the hearth; on one of these I stretched myself, and Grimalkin mounted the other. We were both of us nodding ere anyone invaded our retreat, and then it was Joseph, shuffling down a wooden ladder that vanished in the roof, through a trap: the ascent to his garret, I suppose.

He cast a sinister look at the little flame which I had enticed to play between the ribs, swept the cat from its elevation and bestowing himself in the vacancy, commenced the operation of stuffing a three-inch pipe with tobacco. My presence in his sanctum was evidently esteemed a piece of impudence too shameful for remark; he silently applied the tube to his lips, folded his arms, and puffed away.

I let him enjoy the luxury unannoyed; and after sucking out the last wreath and heaving a profound sigh, he got up, and departed as solemnly as he came.

A more elastic footstep entered next, and now I opened my mouth for a "good morning," but closed it again, the salutation unachieved; for Hareton Earnshaw was performing his orisons *sotto voce*, in a series of curses directed against every object he touched, while he rummaged a corner for a spade or shovel to dig through the drifts. He glanced over the back of the bench, dilating his nostrils, and thought as little of exchanging civilities with me as with my companion the cat.

I guessed, by his preparations, that egress was allowed, and, leaving my hard couch, made a movement to follow him. He noticed this, and thrust at an inner door with the end of his spade, intimating by an inarticulate sound that there was the place where I must go, if I changed my locality.

It opened into the house, where the females were already astir—Zillah urging flakes of flame up the chimney with a colossal bellows, and Mrs. Heathcliff, kneeling on the hearth, reading a book by the aid of the blaze.

She held her hand interposed between the furnace heat and her eyes, and seemed absorbed in her occupation, desisting from it only to chide the servant for covering her with sparks, or to push away a dog, now and then, that snoozled its nose over-forwardly into her face.

I was surprised to see Heathcliff there also. He stood by the fire, his back towards me, just finishing a stormy scene to poor Zillah, who ever and anon interrupted her labour to pluck up the corner of her apron, and heave an indignant groan.

"And you, you worthless ——" he broke out as I entered, turning to his daughter-in-law, and employing an epithet as harmless as duck, or sheep, but generally represented by a dash.

"There you are, at your idle tricks again? The rest of them do earn their bread—you live on my charity! Put your trash away, and find something to do. You shall pay me for the plague of having you eternally in my sight—do you hear, damnable jade?"

"I'll put my trash away, because you can make me, if I refuse," answered the young lady, closing her book, and throwing it on a chair. "But I'll not do anything, though you should swear your tongue out, except what I please!"

Heathcliff lifted his hand, and the speaker sprang to a safer distance, obviously acquainted with its weight.

Having no desire to be entertained by a cat-and-dog combat, I stepped forward briskly, as if eager to partake the warmth of the hearth, and innocent of any knowledge of the interrupted dispute. Each had enough decorum to suspend further hostilities. Heathcliff placed his fists, out of temptation, in his pockets; Mrs. Heathcliff curled her lip, and walked to a seat far off, where she kept her word by playing the part of a statue during the remainder of my stay.

That was not long. I declined joining their breakfast, and, at the first gleam of dawn, took an opportunity of escaping into the free air, now clear and still, and cold as impalpable ice.

My landlord hallooed for me to stop ere I reached the bottom of the garden, and offered to accompany me across the moor. It was well he did, for the whole hill-back was one billowy, white ocean, the swells and falls not indicating corresponding rises and depressions in the ground; many pits, at least, were filled to a level; and entire ranges of mounds, the refuse of the quarries, blotted out from the chart which my yesterday's walk left pictured in my mind.

I had remarked on one side of the road, at intervals of six or seven yards, a line of upright stones, continued through the whole length of the barren; these were erected, and daubed with lime on purpose to serve as guides in the dark, and also when a fall, like the present, confounded the deep swamps on either hand with the firmer path; but, excepting a dirty dot pointing up here and there, all traces of their existence had vanished, and my companion found it necessary to warn me frequently to steer to the right or left, when I imagined I was following correctly the windings of the road.

We exchanged little conversation, and he halted at the entrance of Thrushcross park, saying I could make no error there. Our adieux were limited to a hasty bow, and then I pushed forward, trusting to my own resources, for the porter's lodge is untenanted as yet.

The distance from the gate to the Grange is two miles. I believe I managed to make it four, what with losing myself among the trees, and sinking up to the neck in snow, a predicament which only those who have experienced it can appreciate. At any rate, whatever were my wanderings, the clock chimed twelve as I entered the house; and that gave exactly an hour for every mile of the usual way from Wuthering Heights.

My human fixture and her satellites rushed to welcome me, exclaiming, tumultuously, they had completely given me up; everybody conjectured that I perished last night, and they were wondering how they must set about the search for my remains.

I bid them be quiet, now that they saw me returned, and, benumbed to my very heart, I dragged upstairs; whence, after putting on dry clothes, and pacing to and fro thirty or forty minutes to restore the animal heat, I am adjourned to my study, feeble as a kitten—almost too much so to enjoy the cheerful fire and smoking coffee which the servant has prepared for my refreshment.

CHAPTER 4

WHAT vain weathercocks we are! I, who had determined to hold myself independent of all social intercourse, and thanked my stars that, at length, I had lighted on a spot where it was next to impracticable—I, weak wretch, after maintaining till dusk a struggle with low spirits and solitude, was finally compelled to strike my colours; and, under pretence of gaining information concerning the necessities of my establishment, I desired Mrs. Dean, when she brought in supper, to sit down while I ate it, hoping sincerely she would prove a regular gossip, and either rouse me to animation or lull me to sleep by her talk.

"You have lived here a considerable time," I commenced; "did you not say sixteen years?"

"Eighteen, sir; I came, when the mistress was married, to wait on her; after she died, the master retained me for his housekeeper."

"Indeed."

There ensued a pause. She was not a gossip, I feared, unless about her own affairs, and those could hardly interest me.

However, having studied for an interval, with a fist on either knee and a cloud of meditation over her ruddy countenance, she ejaculated—

"Ah, times are greatly changed since then!"

"Yes," I remarked, "you've seen a good many alterations, I suppose?"

"I have: and troubles too," she said.

"Oh, I'll turn the talk on my landlord's family!" I thought to myself. "A good subject to start—and that pretty girl-widow, I should like to know her history: whether she be a native of the country, or, as is more probable, an exotic that the surly indigenae will not recognize for kin."

With this intention I asked Mrs. Dean why Heathcliff let Thrushcross Grange and preferred living in a situation and residence so much inferior.

"Is he not rich enough to keep the estate in good order?" I enquired.

"Rich, sir!" she returned. "He has, nobody knows what money, and every year it increases. Yes, yes, he's rich enough to live in a finer house than this; but he's very near—close-handed; and, if he had meant to flit to Thrushcross Grange, as soon as he heard of a good tenant he could not have borne to miss the chance of getting a few hundreds more. It is strange people should be so greedy, when they are alone in the world!"

"He had a son, it seems?"

"Yes, he had one—he is dead."

"And that young lady, Mrs. Heathcliff, is his widow?"

"Yes."

"Where did she come from originally?"

"Why, sir, she is my late master's daughter; Catherine Linton was her maiden name. I nursed her, poor thing! I did wish Mr. Heathcliff would remove here, and then we might have been together again."

"What! Catherine Linton?" I exclaimed, astonished. But a minute's reflection convinced me it was not my ghostly Catherine. "Then," I continued, "my predecessor's name was Linton?"

"It was."

"And who is that Earnshaw, Hareton Earnshaw, who lives with Mr. Heathcliff? are they relations?"

"No; he is the late Mrs. Linton's nephew."

"The young lady's cousin, then?"

"Yes; and her husband was her cousin also, one on the mother's, the other on the father's side; Heathcliff married Mr. Linton's sister."

"I see the house at Wuthering Heights has 'Earnshaw' carved over the front door. Are they an old family?"

"Very old, sir; and Hareton is the last of them, as our Miss Cathy is of us—I mean, of the Lintons. Have you been to Wuthering Heights? I beg pardon for asking; but I should like to hear how she is."

"Mrs. Heathcliff? she looked very well, and very handsome; yet, I think, not very happy."

"Oh dear, I don't wonder! And how did you like the master?"

"A rough fellow, rather, Mrs. Dean. Is not that his character?"

"Rough as a saw-edge, and hard as whinstone! The less you meddle with him the better."

"He must have had some ups and downs in life to make him such a churl. Do you know anything of his history?"

"It's a cuckoo's, sir—I know all about it, except where he was born, and who were his parents, and how he got his money, at first. And Hareton has been cast out like an unfledged dunnock! The unfortunate lad is the only one in all this parish that does not guess how he has been cheated."

"Well, Mrs. Dean, it will be a charitable deed to tell me something of my neighbours. I feel I shall not rest, if I go to bed, so be good enough to sit and chat an hour."

"Oh, certainly, sir! I'll just fetch a little sewing, and then I'll sit as long as you please. But you've caught cold—I saw you shivering, and you must have some gruel to drive it out."

The worthy woman bustled off, and I crouched nearer the fire; my head felt hot, and the rest of me chill; moreover I was excited, almost to a pitch of foolishness, through my nerves and brain. This caused me to feel, not uncomfortable, but rather fearful (as I am still) of serious effects from the incidents of today and yesterday. She returned presently, bringing a smoking basin and a basket of work, and, having placed the former on the hob, drew in her seat, evidently pleased to find me so companionable.

Before I came to live here, she commenced—waiting

no further invitation to her story—I was almost always at Wuthering Heights; because my mother had nursed Mr. Hindley Earnshaw, that was Hareton's father, and I got used to playing with the children. I ran errands too, and helped to make hay, and hung about the farm ready for anything that anybody would set me to. One fine summer morning—it was the beginning of harvest, I remember—Mr. Earnshaw, the old master, came downstairs, dressed for a journey; and after he had told Joseph what was to be done during the day, he turned to Hindley and Cathy and me—for I sat eating my porridge with them—and he said, speaking to his son,

"Now, my bonny man, I'm going to Liverpool today. What shall I bring you? You may choose what you like, only let it be little, for I shall walk there and back—sixty miles each way, that is a long spell!"

Hindley named a fiddle, and then he asked Miss Cathy; she was hardly six years old, but she could ride any horse in the stable, and she chose a whip.

He did not forget me, for he had a kind heart, though he was rather severe sometimes. He promised to bring me a pocketful of apples and pears, and then he kissed his children, good-bye, and set off.

It seemed a long while to us all—the three days of his absence—and often did little Cathy ask when he would be home. Mrs. Earnshaw expected him by suppertime on the third evening, and she put the meal off hour after hour; there were no signs of his coming, however, and at last the children got tired of running down to the gate to look. Then it grew dark; she would have had them to bed, but they begged sadly to be allowed to stay up; and, just about eleven o'clock, the door latch was raised quietly, and in stepped the master. He threw himself into a chair, laughing and groaning, and bid them all stand off, for he was nearly killed—he would not have such another walk for the three kingdoms.

"And at the end of it, to be flighted to death!" he said, opening his greatcoat, which he held bundled up in his arms. "See here, wife! I was never so beaten with anything in my life; but you must e'en take it as a gift of God, though it's as dark almost as if it came from the devil."

We crowded round, and over Miss Cathy's head I had

a peep at a dirty, ragged, black-haired child, big enough both to walk and talk; indeed, its face looked older than Catherine's; yet, when it was set on its feet, it only stared round, and repeated over and over again some gibberish that nobody could understand. I was frightened, and Mrs. Earnshaw was ready to fling it out of doors; she did fly up, asking how he could fashion to bring that gipsy brat into the house, when they had their own bairns to feed and fend for? What he meant to do with it, and whether he were mad?

The master tried to explain the matter; but he was really half dead with fatigue, and all that I could make out, amongst her scolding, was a tale of his seeing it starving and houseless and as good as dumb in the streets of Liverpool, where he picked it up and inquired for its owner. Not a soul knew to whom it belonged, he said; and his money and time being both limited, he thought it better to take it home with him at once, than run into vain expenses there; because he was determined he would not leave it as he found it.

Well, the conclusion was that my mistress grumbled herself calm; and Mr. Earnshaw told me to wash it, and give it clean things, and let it sleep with the children.

Hindley and Cathy contented themselves with looking and listening till peace was restored; then, both began searching their father's pockets for the presents he had promised them. The former was a boy of fourteen, but when he drew out what had been a fiddle, crushed to morsels in the greatcoat, he blubbered aloud; and Cathy, when she learnt the master had lost her whip in attending on the stranger, showed her humour by grinning and spitting at the stupid little thing, earning for her pains a sound blow from her father to teach her cleaner manners.

They entirely refused to have it in bed with them, or even in their room, and I had no more sense, so I put it on the landing of the stairs, hoping it might be gone on the morrow. By chance, or else attracted by hearing his voice, it crept to Mr. Earnshaw's door, and there he found it on quitting his chamber. Inquiries were made as to how it got there; I was obliged to confess, and in recompense for my cowardice and inhumanity was sent out of the house.

This was Heathcliff's first introduction to the family. On coming back a few days afterwards (for I did not consider my banishment perpetual) I found they had christened him "Heathcliff"; it was the name of a son who died in childhood, and it has served him ever since, both for Christian and surname. Miss Cathy and he were now very thick, but Hindley hated him, and to say the truth I did the same; and we plagued and went on with him shamefully, for I wasn't reasonable enough to feel my injustice, and the mistress never put in a word on his behalf when she saw him wronged.

He seemed a sullen, patient child, hardened, perhaps, to ill-treatment; he would stand Hindley's blows without winking or shedding a tear, and my pinches moved him only to draw in a breath and open his eyes, as if he had hurt himself by accident and nobody was to blame.

This endurance made old Earnshaw furious, when he discovered his son persecuting the poor, fatherless child, as he called him. He took to Heathcliff strangely, believing all he said (for that matter, he said precious little, and generally the truth), and petting him up far above Cathy, who was too mischievous and wayward for a favourite.

So, from the very beginning, he bred bad feeling in the house; and at Mrs. Earnshaw's death, which happened in less than two years after, the young master had learnt to regard his father as an oppressor rather than a friend, and Heathcliff as a usurper of his father's affections and his privileges, and he grew bitter with brooding over these injuries.

I sympathized awhile; but when the children fell ill of the measles, and I had to tend them and take on me the cares of a woman at once, I changed my ideas. Heathcliff was dangerously sick, and while he lay at the worst he would have me constantly by his pillow; I suppose he felt I did a good deal for him, and he hadn't the wit to guess that I was compelled to do it. However, I will say this, he was the quietest child that ever nurse watched over. The difference between him and the others forced me to be less partial. Cathy and her brother harassed me terribly; he was as uncomplaining as a lamb; though hardness, not gentleness, made him give little trouble.

He got through, and the doctor affirmed it was in a great measure owing to me, and praised me for my care. I was vain of his commendations, and softened towards the being by whose means I earned them, and thus Hindley lost his last ally. Still I couldn't dote on Heathcliff, and I wondered often what my master saw to admire so much in the sullen boy, who never, to my recollection, repaid his indulgence by any sign of gratitude. He was not insolent to his benefactor, he was simply insensible, though knowing perfectly the hold he had on his heart, and conscious he had only to speak and all the house would be obliged to bend to his wishes.

As an instance, I remember Mr. Earnshaw once bought a couple of colts at the parish fair, and gave the lads each one. Heathcliff took the handsomest, but it soon fell lame, and when he discovered it, he said to Hindley—

"You must exchange horses with me. I don't like mine; and if you won't I shall tell your father of the three thrashings you've given me this week, and show him my arm, which is black to the shoulder."

Hindley put out his tongue, and cuffed him over the ears.

"You'd better do it at once," he persisted, escaping to the porch (they were in the stable). "You will have to; and if I speak of these blows, you'll get them again with interest."

"Off, dog!" cried Hindley, threatening him with an iron weight used for weighing potatoes and hay.

"Throw it," he replied, standing still, "and then I'll tell how you boasted that you would turn me out of doors as soon as he died, and see whether he will not turn you out directly."

Hindley threw it, hitting him on the breast, and down he fell, but staggered up immediately, breathless and white; and, had not I prevented it, he would have gone just so to the master, and got full revenge by letting his condition plead for him, intimating who had caused it.

"Take my colt, gipsy, then!" said young Earnshaw. "And I pray that he may break your neck; take him, and be damned, you beggarly interloper! and wheedle my father out of all he has; only afterwards show him what you are, imp of Satan! And take that—I hope he'll kick out your brains!"

Heathcliff had gone to loose the beast and shift it to his own stall; he was passing behind it, when Hindley finished his speech by knocking him under its feet, and without stopping to examine whether his hopes were fulfilled, ran away as fast as he could.

I was surprised to witness how coolly the child gathered himself up and went on with his intention, exchanging saddles and all, and then sitting down on a bundle of hay to overcome the qualm which the violent blow occasioned, before he entered the house. I persuaded him easily to let me lay the blame of his bruises on the horse; he minded little what tale was told since he had what he wanted. He complained so seldom, indeed, of such stirs as these, that I really thought him not vindictive. I was deceived completely, as you will hear.

CHAPTER 5

IN THE course of time, Mr. Earnshaw began to fail. He had been active and healthy, yet his strength left him suddenly; and when he was confined to the chimney-corner he grew grievously irritable. A nothing vexed him, and suspected slights of his authority nearly threw him into fits.

This was especially to be remarked if anyone attempted to impose upon, or domineer over, his favourite; he was painfully jealous lest a word should be spoken amiss to him, seeming to have got into his head the notion that, because he liked Heathcliff, all hated, and longed to do him an ill-turn.

It was a disadvantage to the lad, for the kinder among us did not wish to fret the master, so we humoured his partiality, and that humouring was rich nourishment to the child's pride and black tempers. Still it became in a manner necessary; twice, or thrice, Hindley's manifestations of scorn, while his father was near, roused the old man to a fury; he seized his stick to strike him, and shook with rage that he could not do it.

At last, our curate (we had a curate then who made the living answer by teaching the little Lintons and Earnshaws, and farming his bit of land himself) advised that the young man should be sent to college; and Mr. Earnshaw agreed, though with a heavy spirit, for he said—

"Hindley was naught, and would never thrive as where he wandered."

I hoped heartily we should have peace now. It hurt me to think the master should be made uncomfortable by his own good deed. I fancied the discontent of age and disease arose from his family disagreements, as he would have it that it did; really, you know, sir, it was in his sinking frame.

We might have got on tolerably, notwithstanding, but for two people, Miss Cathy and Joseph, the servant; you saw him, I dare say, up yonder. He was, and is yet, most likely, the wearisomest self-righteous pharisee that ever ransacked a Bible to rake the promises to himself and fling the curses on his neighbours. By his knack of sermonizing and pious discoursing, he contrived to make a great impression on Mr. Earnshaw, and the more feeble the master became, the more influence he gained.

He was relentless in worrying him about his soul's concerns, and about ruling his children rigidly. He encouraged him to regard Hindley as a reprobate, and, night after night, he regularly grumbled out a long string of tales against Heathcliff and Catherine, always minding to flatter Earnshaw's weakness by heaping the heaviest blame on the last.

Certainly, she had ways with her such as I never saw a child take up before, and she put all of us past our patience fifty times and oftener in a day; from the hour she came downstairs till the hour she went to bed, we had not a minute's security that she wouldn't be in mischief. Her spirits were always at high-water mark, her tongue always going—singing, laughing, and plaguing everybody who would not do the same. A wild, wicked slip she was—but she had the bonniest eye, and sweetest smile, and lightest foot in the parish; and, after all, I believe she meant no harm; for when once she made you cry in good earnest, it seldom happened that she would not keep you company, and oblige you to be quiet that you might comfort her.

She was much too fond of Heathcliff. The greatest punishment we could invent for her was to keep her separate from him; yet she got chided more than any of us on his account.

In play, she liked exceedingly to act the little mistress, using her hands freely, and commanding her companions. She did so to me, but I would not bear slapping and ordering, and so I let her know.

Now, Mr. Earnshaw did not understand jokes from his children; he had always been strict and grave with them, and Catherine, on her part, had no idea why her father should be crosser and less patient in his ailing condition than he was in his prime.

His peevish reproofs wakened in her a naughty delight to provoke him; she was never so happy as when we were all scolding her at once, and she defying us with her bold, saucy look, and her ready words; turning Joseph's religious curses into ridicule, baiting me, and doing just what her father hated most, showing how her pretended insolence, which he thought real, had more power over Heathcliff than his kindness; how the boy would do her bidding in anything, and his only when it suited his own inclination.

After behaving as badly as possible all day, she sometimes came fondling to make it up at night.

"Nay, Cathy," the old man would say, "I cannot love thee; thou 'rt worse than thy brother. Go, say thy prayers, child, and ask God's pardon. I doubt thy mother and I must rue that we ever reared thee!"

That made her cry, at first; and then, being repulsed continually hardened her, and she laughed if I told her to say she was sorry for her faults and beg to be forgiven.

But the hour came, at last, that ended Mr. Earnshaw's troubles on earth. He died quietly in his chair one October evening, seated by the fireside.

A high wind blustered round the house and roared in the chimney; it sounded wild and stormy, yet it was not cold, and we were all together—I, a little removed from the hearth, busy at my knitting, and Joseph reading his

Bible near the table (for the servants generally sat in the house then, after their work was done). Miss Cathy had been sick, and that made her still; she leant against her father's knee, and Heathcliff was lying on the floor with his head in her lap.

I remember the master, before he fell into a doze, stroking her bonny hair—it pleased him rarely to see her gentle—and saying—

"Why canst thou not always be a good lass, Cathy?"

And she turned her face up to his, and laughed, and answered,

"Why cannot you always be a good man, Father?"

But as soon as she saw him vexed again, she kissed his hand, and said she would sing him to sleep. She began singing very low, till his fingers dropped from hers, and his head sank on his breast. Then I told her to hush, and not stir, for fear she should wake him. We all kept as mute as mice a full half-hour, and should have done longer, only Joseph, having finished his chapter, got up and said that he must rouse the master for prayers and bed. He stepped forward, and called him by name, and touched his shoulder; but he would not move, so he took the candle and looked at him.

I thought there was something wrong as he set down the light, and seizing the children each by an arm, whispered them to "frame upstairs, and make little din —they might pray alone that evening—he had summut to do."

"I shall bid Father good night first," said Catherine, putting her arms round his neck before we could hinder her.

The poor thing discovered her loss directly—she screamed out—

"Oh, he's dead, Heathcliff! he's dead!"

And they both set up a heartbreaking cry.

I joined my wail to theirs, loud and bitter; but Joseph asked what we could be thinking of to roar in that way over a saint in heaven.

He told me to put on my cloak and run to Gimmerton for the doctor and the parson. I could not guess the use that either would be of, then. However, I went, through wind and rain, and brought one, the doctor, back with me; the other said he would come in the morning.

Leaving Joseph to explain matters, I ran to the children's room; their door was ajar, I saw they had never laid down, though it was past midnight; but they were calmer, and did not need me to console them. The little souls were comforting each other with better thoughts than I could have hit on; no parson in the world ever pictured heaven so beautifully as they did, in their innocent talk; and, while I sobbed, and listened, I could not help wishing we were all there safe together.

CHAPTER 6

Mr. HINDLEY came home to the funeral, and —a thing that amazed us, and set the neighbours gossiping right and left—he brought a wife with him.

What she was, and where she was born, he never informed us; probably, she had neither money nor name to recommend her, or he would scarcely have kept the union from his father.

She was not one that would have disturbed the house much on her own account. Every object she saw, the moment she crossed the threshold, appeared to delight her, and every circumstance that took place about her, except the preparing for the burial, and the presence of the mourners.

I thought she was half silly, from her behaviour while that went on; she ran into her chamber, and made me come with her, though I should have been dressing the children, and there she sat shivering and clasping her hands, and asking repeatedly—

"Are they gone yet?"

Then she began describing with hysterical emotion the effect it produced on her to see black; and started, and trembled, and, at last, fell a-weeping—and when I asked what was the matter, answered she didn't know, but she felt so afraid of dying!

I imagined her as little likely to die as myself. She was rather thin, but young and fresh complexioned, and her eyes sparkled as bright as diamonds. I did remark, to be sure, that mounting the stairs made her breathe very quick, that the least sudden noise set her all in a quiver, and that she coughed troublesomely sometimes; but I knew nothing of what these symptoms portended, and had no impulse to sympathize with her. We don't in general take to foreigners, here, Mr. Lockwood, unless they take to us first.

Young Earnshaw was altered considerably in the three years of his absence. He had grown sparer, and lost his colour, and spoke and dressed quite differently; and, on the very day of his return, he told Joseph and me we must thenceforth quarter ourselves in the back kitchen, and leave the house for him. Indeed, he would have carpeted and papered a small spare room for a parlour; but his wife expressed such pleasure at the white floor and huge glowing fireplace, at the pewter dishes and delftcase and dog kennel, and the wide space there was to move about in where they usually sat, that he thought it unnecessary to her comfort, and so dropped the intention.

She expressed pleasure, too, at finding a sister among her new acquaintance, and she prattled to Catherine, and kissed her, and ran about with her, and gave her quantities of presents, at the beginning. Her affection tired very soon, however, and when she grew peevish, Hindley became tyrannical. A few words from her, evincing a dislike to Heathcliff, were enough to rouse in him all his old hatred of the boy. He drove him from their company to the servants, deprived him of the instructions of the curate, and insisted that he should labour out of doors instead, compelling him to do so as hard as any other lad on the farm.

He bore his degradation pretty well at first, because Cathy taught him what she learnt, and worked or played with him in the fields. They both promised fair to grow up as rude as savages, the young master being entirely negligent how they behaved, and what they did, so they kept clear of him. He would not even have seen after their going to church on Sundays, only Joseph and the curate reprimanded his carelessness when they absented themselves, and that reminded him to order Heathcliff a flogging, and Catherine a fast from dinner or supper.

But it was one of their chief amusements to run away to the moors in the morning and remain there all day, and the after punishment grew a mere thing to laugh at. The curate might set as many chapters as he pleased for Catherine to get by heart, and Joseph might thrash Heathcliff till his arm ached; they forgot everything the minute they were together again—at least the minute they had contrived some naughty plan of revenge; and many a time I've cried to myself to watch them growing more reckless daily, and I not daring to speak a syllable, for fear of losing the small power I still retained over the unfriended creatures.

One Sunday evening, it chanced that they were banished from the sitting-room, for making a noise, or a light offence of the kind, and when I went to call them to supper, I could discover them nowhere.

We searched the house, above and below, and the yard and stables; they were invisible; and, at last, Hindley in a passion told us to bolt the doors, and swore nobody should let them in that night.

The household went to bed, and I, too anxious to lie down, opened my lattice and put my head out to harken, though it rained, determined to admit them in spite of the prohibition, should they return.

In a while, I distinguished steps coming up the road, and the light of a lantern glimmering through the gate.

I threw a shawl over my head and ran to prevent them from waking Mr. Earnshaw by knocking. There was Heathcliff, by himself; it gave me a start to see him alone.

"Where is Miss Catherine?" I cried hurriedly. "No accident, I hope?"

"At Thrushcross Grange," he answered, "and I would have been there too, but they had not the manners to ask me to stay."

"Well, you will catch it!" I said, "you'll never be content till you're sent about your business. What in the world led you wandering to Thrushcross Grange?"

"Let me get off my wet clothes, and I'll tell you all about it, Nelly," he replied.

I bid him beware of rousing the master, and while he

undressed and I waited to put out the candle, he continued—

"Cathy and I escaped from the wash-house to have a ramble at liberty, and getting a glimpse of the Grange lights, we thought we would just go and see whether the Lintons passed their Sunday evenings standing shivering in corners, while their father and mother sat eating and drinking, and singing and laughing, and burning their eyes out before the fire. Do you think they do? Or reading sermons, and being catechized by their man-servant, and set to learn a column of Scripture names if they don't answer properly?"

"Probably not," I responded. "They are good children, no doubt, and don't deserve the treatment you receive, for your bad conduct."

"Don't you cant, Nelly," he said; "nonsense! We ran from the top of the Heights to the park without stopping—Catherine completely beaten in the race, because she was barefoot. You'll have to seek for her shoes in the bog tomorrow. We crept through a broken hedge, groped our way up the path, and planted ourselves on a flower plot under the drawing-room window. The light came from thence; they had not put up the shutters, and the curtains were only half closed. Both of us were able to look in by standing on the basement and clinging to the ledge, and we saw—ah! it was beautiful—a splendid place carpeted with crimson, and crimson-covered chairs and tables, and a pure white ceiling bordered by gold, a shower of glass-drops hanging in silver chains from the centre, and shimmering with little soft tapers. Old Mr. and Mrs. Linton were not there; Edgar and his sister had it entirely to themselves. Shouldn't they have been happy? We should have thought ourselves in heaven! And now, guess what your good children were doing? Isabella—I believe she is eleven, a year younger than Cathy—lay screaming at the farther end of the room, shrieking as if witches were running red-hot needles into her. Edgar stood on the hearth weeping silently, and in the middle of the table sat a little dog, shaking its paw and yelping, which, from their mutual accusations, we understood they had nearly pulled in two between them. The idiots! That was their pleasure! to quarrel who should hold a heap of warm hair, and each begin to cry because both, after struggling to get it, refused to take it. We laughed outright at the petted things; we did despise them! When would you catch me wishing to have what Catherine wanted? or find us by ourselves, seeking entertainment in yelling, and sobbing, and rolling on the ground, divided by the whole room? I 'd not exchange, for a thousand lives, my condition here, for Edgar Linton's at Thrushcross Grange—not if I might have the privilege of flinging Joseph off the highest gable, and painting the house-front with Hindley's blood!"

"Hush, hush!" I interrupted. "Still you have not told me, Heathcliff, how Catherine is left behind?"

"I told you we laughed," he answered. "The Lintons heard us, and with one accord, they shot like arrows to the door; there was silence, and then a cry, 'Oh, Mamma, Mamma! Oh, Papa! Oh, Mamma, come here. Oh, Papa, oh!' They really did howl out something in that way. We made frightful noises to terrify them still more, and then we dropped off the ledge, because somebody was drawing the bars, and we felt we had better flee. I had Cathy by the hand, and was urging her on, when all at once she fell down.

" 'Run, Heathcliff, run!' she whispered. 'They have let the bulldog loose, and he holds me!'

"The devil had seized her ankle, Nelly; I heard his abominable snorting. She did not yell out—no! She would have scorned to do it, if she had been spitted on the horns of a mad cow. I did, though; I vociferated curses enough to annihilate any fiend in Christendom, and I got a stone and thrust it between his jaws, and tried with all my might to cram it down his throat. A beast of a servant came up with a lantern, at last, shouting—

" 'Keep fast, Skulker, keep fast!'

"He changed his note, however, when he saw Skulker's game. The dog was throttled off, his huge, purple tongue hanging half a foot out of his mouth, and his pendant lips streaming with bloody slaver.

"The man took Cathy up; she was sick, not from fear, I'm certain, but from pain. He carried her in; I followed, grumbling execrations and vengeance.

" 'What prey, Robert?' hallooed Linton from the entrance.

" 'Skulker has caught a little girl, sir,' he replied, 'and there's a lad here,' he added, making a clutch at me, 'who looks an out-and-outer! Very like, the robbers were for putting them though the window to open the doors to the gang after all were asleep, that they might murder us at their ease. Hold your tongue, you foulmouthed thief, you! you shall go to the gallows for this. Mr. Linton, sir, don't lay by your gun.'

" 'No, no, Robert,' said the old fool. 'The rascals knew that yesterday was my rent day; they thought to have me cleverly. Come in; I'll furnish them a reception. There, John, fasten the chain. Give Skulker some water, Jenny. To beard a magistrate in his stronghold, and on the Sabbath, too! Where will their insolence stop? Oh, my dear Mary, look here! Don't be afraid, it is but a boy —yet the villain scowls so plainly in his face; would it not be a kindness to the country to hang him at once, before he shows his nature in acts as well as features?'

"He pulled me under the chandelier, and Mrs. Linton placed her spectacles on her nose and raised her hands in horror. The cowardly children crept nearer, also, Isabella lisping—

" 'Frightful thing! Put him in the cellar, Papa. He's exactly like the son of the fortune-teller that stole my tame pheasant. Isn't he, Edgar?'

"While they examined me, Cathy came round; she heard the last speech, and laughed. Edgar Linton, after an inquisitive stare, collected sufficient wit to recognize her. They see us at church, you know, though we seldom meet them elsewhere.

" 'That's Miss Earnshaw!' he whispered to his mother, 'and look how Skulker has bitten her—how her foot bleeds!'

" 'Miss Earnshaw? Nonsense!' cried the dame. 'Miss Earnshaw scouring the county with a gipsy! And yet, my dear, the child is in mourning—surely it is—and she may be lamed for life!'

" 'What culpable carelessness in her brother!' exclaimed Mr. Linton, turning from me to Catherine. 'I've understood from Shielders' (that was the curate, sir) 'that he lets her grow up in absolute heathenism.

But who is this? Where did she pick up this companion? Oho! I declare he is that strange acquisition my late neighbour made, in his journey to Liverpool—a little Lascar, or an American or Spanish castaway.'

"'A wicked boy, at all events,' remarked the old lady, 'and quite unfit for a decent house! Did you notice his language, Linton? I'm shocked that my children should have heard it.'

."I recommended cursing—don't be angry, Nelly—and so Robert was ordered to take me off. I refused to go without Cathy; he dragged me into the garden, pushed the lantern into my hand, assured me that Mr. Earnshaw should be informed of my behaviour, and, bidding me march directly, secured the door again.

"The curtains were still looped up at one corner, and I resumed my station as spy, because, if Catherine had wished to return, I intended shattering their great glass panes to a million of fragments, unless they let her out.

"She sat on the sofa quietly. Mrs. Linton took off the grey cloak of the dairy maid which we had borrowed for our excursion, shaking her head and expostulating with her, I suppose; she was a young lady, and they made a distinction between her treatment and mine. Then the woman-servant brought a basin of warm water, and washed her feet; and Mr. Linton mixed a tumbler of negus, and Isabella emptied a plateful of cakes into her lap, and Edgar stood gaping at a distance. Afterwards, they dried and combed her beautiful hair, and gave her a pair of enormous slippers, and wheeled her to the fire; and I left her, as merry as she could be, dividing her food between the little dog and Skulker, whose nose she pinched as she ate, and kindling a spark of spirit in the vacant blue eyes of the Lintons—a dim reflection from her own enchanting face. I saw they were full of stupid admiration; she is so immeasurably superior to them—to everybody on earth, is she not, Nelly?"

"There will more come of this business than you reckon on," I answered, covering him up and extinguishing the light. "You are incurable, Heathcliff; and Mr. Hindley will have to proceed to extremities, see if he won't."

My words came truer than I desired. The luckless adventure made Earnshaw furious. And then Mr. Linton, to mend matters, paid us a visit himself on the morrow, and read the young master such a lecture on the road he guided his family, that he was stirred to look about him, in earnest.

Heathcliff received no flogging, but he was told that the first word he spoke to Miss Catherine should ensure a dismissal; and Mrs. Earnshaw undertook to keep her sister-in-law in due restraint when she returned home, employing art, not force: with force she would have found it impossible.

CHAPTER 7

CATHY stayed at Thrushcross Grange five weeks, till Christmas. By that time her ankle was thoroughly cured, and her manners much improved. The mistress visited her often in the interval, and commenced her plan of reform by trying to raise her self-respect with fine clothes and flattery, which she took readily; so that, instead of a wild, hatless little savage jumping into the house, rushing to squeeze us all breathless, there lighted from a handsome black pony a very dignified person, with brown ringlets falling from the cover of a feathered beaver, and a long cloth habit, which she was obliged to hold up with both hands that she might sail in.

Hindley lifted her from her horse, exclaiming delightedly,

"Why, Cathy, you are quite a beauty! I should scarcely have known you; you look like a lady now. Isabella Linton is not to be compared with her, is she, Frances?"

"Isabella has not her natural advantages," replied his wife; "but she must mind and not grow wild again here. Ellen, help Miss Catherine off with her things—Stay, dear, you will disarrange your curls—let me untie your hat."

I removed the habit, and there shone forth, beneath a

grand plaid silk frock, white trousers, and burnished shoes; and, while her eyes sparkled joyfully when the dogs came bounding up to welcome her, she dare hardly touch them lest they should fawn upon her splendid garments.

She kissed me gently—I was all flour making the Christmas cake, and it would not have done to give me a hug—and, then, she looked round for Heathcliff. Mr. and Mrs. Earnshaw watched anxiously their meeting, thinking it would enable them to judge, in some measure, what grounds they had for hoping to succeed in separating the two friends.

Heathcliff was hard to discover, at first. If he were careless and uncared for before Catherine's absence, he had been ten times more so since.

Nobody but I even did him the kindness to call him a dirty boy, and bid him wash himself, once a week; and children of his age seldom have a natural pleasure in soap and water. Therefore, not to mention his clothes, which had seen three months' service in mire and dust, and his thick uncombed hair, the surface of his face and hands was dismally beclouded. He might well skulk behind the settle on beholding such a bright, graceful damsel enter the house, instead of a rough-headed counterpart of himself, as he expected.

"Is Heathcliff not here?" she demanded, pulling off her gloves, and displaying fingers wonderfully whitened with doing nothing and staying in doors.

"Heathcliff, you may come forward," cried Mr. Hindley, enjoying his discomfiture and gratified to see what a forbidding young blackguard he would be compelled to present himself. "You may come and wish Miss Catherine welcome, like the other servants."

Cathy, catching a glimpse of her friend in his concealment, flew to embrace him; she bestowed seven or eight kisses on his cheek within the second, and then stopped, and drawing back, burst into a laugh, exclaiming,

"Why, how very black and cross you look! and how—how funny and grim! But that's because I'm used to Edgar and Isabella Linton. Well, Heathcliff, have you forgotten me?"

She had some reason to put the question, for shame

and pride threw double gloom over his countenance, and kept him immovable.

"Shake hands, Heathcliff," said Mr. Earnshaw condescendingly; "once in a way, that is permitted."

"I shall not," replied the boy, finding his tongue at last; "I shall not stand to be laughed at. I shall not bear it!"

And he would have broken from the circle, but Miss Cathy seized him again.

"I did not mean to laugh at you," she said. "I could not hinder myself. Heathcliff, shake hands, at least! What are you sulky for? It was only that you looked odd. If you wash your face, and brush your hair, it will be all right; but you are so dirty!"

She gazed concernedly at the dusky fingers she held in her own, and also at her dress, which she feared had gained no embellishment from its contact with his.

"You needn't have touched me!" he answered, following her eye and snatching away his hand. "I shall be as dirty as I please: and I like to be dirty, and I will be dirty."

With that he dashed head foremost out of the room, amid the merriment of the master and mistress, and to the serious disturbance of Catherine, who could not comprehend how her remarks should have produced such an exhibition of bad temper.

After playing lady's maid to the newcomer, and putting my cakes in the oven, and making the house and kitchen cheerful with great fires, befitting Christmas eve, I prepared to sit down and amuse myself by singing carols, all alone, regardless of Joseph's affirmations that he considered the merry tunes I chose as next door to songs.

He had retired to private prayer in his chamber, and Mr. and Mrs. Earnshaw were engaging Missy's attention by sundry gay trifles bought for her to present to the little Lintons, as an acknowledgment of their kindness.

They had invited them to spend the morrow at Wuthering Heights, and the invitation had been accepted, on one condition: Mrs. Linton begged that her darlings might be kept carefully apart from that "naughty swearing boy."

Under these circumstances I remained solitary. I smelt

the rich scent of the heating spices, and admired the shining kitchen utensils, the polished clock, decked in holly, the silver mugs ranged on a tray ready to be filled with mulled ale for supper, and, above all, the speckless purity of my particular care—the scoured and well-swept floor.

I gave due inward applause to every object, and then I remembered how old Earnshaw used to come in when all was tidied, and call me a cant lass, and slip a shilling into my hand as a Christmas box; and from that I went on to think of his fondness for Heathcliff, and his dread lest he should suffer neglect after death had removed him; and that naturally led me to consider the poor lad's situation now, and from singing I changed my mind to crying. It struck me soon, however, there would be more sense in endeavouring to repair some of his wrongs than shedding tears over them. I got up and walked into the court to seek him.

He was not far; I found him smoothing the glossy coat of the new pony in the stable, and feeding the other beasts, according to custom.

"Make haste, Heathcliff!" I said, "the kitchen is so comfortable; and Joseph is upstairs; make haste, and let me dress you smart before Miss Cathy comes out, and then you can sit together, with the whole hearth to yourselves, and have a long chatter till bedtime."

He proceeded with his task and never turned his head towards me.

"Come—are you coming?" I continued. "There's a little cake for each of you, nearly enough; and you'll need half-an-hour's donning."

I waited five minutes, but getting no answer left him. . . . Catherine supped with her brother and sister-in-law: Joseph and I joined at an unsociable meal, seasoned with reproofs on one side and sauciness on the other. His cake and cheese remained on the table all night for the fairies. He managed to continue work till nine o'clock, and then marched dumb and dour to his chamber.

Cathy sat up late, having a world of things to order for the reception of her new friends; she came into the kitchen once to speak to her old one, but he was gone, and she only stayed to ask what was the matter with him, and then went back.

In the morning he rose early; and as it was a holiday, carried his ill-humour onto the moors, not reappearing till the family were departed for church. Fasting and reflecting seemed to have brought him to a better spirit. He hung about me for a while, and having screwed up his courage, exclaimed abruptly—

"Nelly, make me decent, I'm going to be good."

"High time, Heathcliff," I said; "you *have* grieved Catherine: she's sorry she ever came home, I dare say! It looks as if you envied her, because she is more thought of than you."

The notion of *envying* Catherine was incomprehensible to him, but the notion of grieving her he understood clearly enough.

"Did she say she was grieved?" he inquired, looking very serious.

"She cried when I told her you were off again this morning."

"Well, *I* cried last night," he returned, "and I had more reason to cry than she."

"Yes, you had the reason of going to bed with a proud heart and an empty stomach," said I. "Proud people breed sad sorrows for themselves. But, if you be ashamed of your touchiness, you must ask pardon, mind, when she comes in. You must go up and offer to kiss her, and say—you know best what to say; only do it heartily, and not as if you thought her converted into a stranger by her grand dress. And now, though I have dinner to get ready, I'll steal time to arrange you so that Edgar Linton shall look quite a doll beside you—and that he does. You are younger, and yet, I'll be bound, you are taller and twice as broad across the shoulders; you could knock him down in a twinkling, don't you feel that you could?"

Heathcliff's face brightened a moment; then it was overcast afresh, and he sighed.

"But, Nelly, if I knocked him down twenty times, that wouldn't make him less handsome or me more so. I wish I had light hair and a fair skin, and was dressed and behaved as well, and had a chance of being as rich as he will be!"

"And cried for Mamma at every turn," I added, "and trembled if a country lad heaved his fist against you, and sat at home all day for a shower of rain. Oh, Heathcliff, you are showing a poor spirit! Come to the glass, and I'll let you see what you should wish. Do you mark those two lines between your eyes? And those thick brows, that instead of rising arched, sink in the middle? And that couple of black fiends, so deeply buried, who never open their windows boldly, but lurk glinting under them, like devil's spies? Wish and learn to smooth away the surly wrinkles, to raise your lids frankly, and change the fiends to confident, innocent angels, suspecting and doubting nothing, and always seeing friends where they are not sure of foes. Don't get the expression of a vicious cur that appears to know the kicks it gets are its desert, and yet hates all the world, as well as the kicker, for what it suffers."

"In other words, I must wish for Edgar Linton's great blue eyes and even forehead," he replied. "I do—and that won't help me to them."

"A good heart will help you to a bonny face, my lad," I continued, "if you were a regular black; and a bad one will turn the bonniest into something worse than ugly. And now that we've done washing, and combing, and sulking—tell me whether you don't think yourself rather handsome? I'll tell you, I do. You're fit for a prince in disguise. Who knows but your father was Emperor of China, and your mother an Indian queen, each of them able to buy up, with one week's income, Wuthering Heights and Thrushcross Grange together? And you were kidnapped by wicked sailors and brought to England. Were I in your place, I would frame high notions of my birth, and the thoughts of what I was should give me courage and dignity to support the oppressions of a little farmer!"

So I chattered on, and Heathcliff gradually lost his frown and began to look quite pleasant, when all at once our conversation was interrupted by a rumbling sound moving up the road and entering the court. He ran to the window and I to the door, just in time to behold the two Lintons descend from the family carriage, smothered in cloaks and furs, and the Earnshaws dismount from their horses: they often rode to church in winter.

Catherine took a hand of each of the children, and brought them into the house and set them before the fire, which quickly put colour into their white faces.

I urged my companion to hasten now and show his amiable humour, and he willingly obeyed; but ill-luck would have it that, as he opened the door leading from the kitchen on one side, Hindley opened it on the other. They met, and the master, irritated at seeing him clean and cheerful, or, perhaps, eager to keep his promise to Mrs. Linton, shoved him back with a sudden thrust, and angrily bade Joseph "keep the fellow out of the room—send him into the garret till dinner is over. He'll be cramming his fingers in the tarts and stealing the fruit, if left alone with them a minute."

"Nay, sir," I could not avoid answering, "he'll touch nothing, not he; and I suppose he must have his share of the dainties as well as we."

"He shall have his share of my hand, if I catch him downstairs again till dark," cried Hindley. "Begone, you vagabond! What! you are attempting the coxcomb, are you? Wait till I get hold of those elegant locks—see if I won't pull them a bit longer!"

"They are long enough already," observed Master Linton, peeping from the doorway. "I wonder they don't make his head ache. It's like a colt's mane over his eyes!"

He ventured this remark without any intention to insult, but Heathcliff's violent nature was not prepared to endure the appearance of impertinence from one whom he seemed to hate, even then, as a rival. He seized a tureen of hot applesauce, the first thing that came under his gripe, and dashed it full against the speaker's face and neck, who instantly commenced a lament that brought Isabella and Catherine hurrying to the place.

Mr. Earnshaw snatched up the culprit directly and conveyed him to his chamber, where, doubtless, he administered a rough remedy to cool the fit of passion, for he reappeared red and breathless. I got the dishcloth, and, rather spitefully, scrubbed Edgar's nose and mouth, affirming it served him right for meddling. His sister began weeping to go home, and Cathy stood by, confounded, blushing for all.

"You should not have spoken to him!" she expostulated with Master Linton. "He was in a bad temper, and now you've spoilt your visit; and he'll be flogged: I hate him to be flogged! I can't eat my dinner. Why did you speak to him, Edgar?"

"I didn't," sobbed the youth, escaping from my hands and finishing the remainder of the purification with his cambric pocket handkerchief. "I promised Mamma that I wouldn't say one word to him, and I didn't."

"Well, don't cry," replied Catherine, contemptuously; "you're not killed. Don't make more mischief, my brother is coming—be quiet! Give over, Isabella! Has anybody hurt you?"

"There, there, children—to your seats!" cried Hindley, bustling in. "That brute of a lad has warmed me nicely. Next time, Master Edgar, take the law into your own fists —it will give you an appetite!"

The little party recovered its equanimity at sight of the fragrant feast. They were hungry after their ride, and easily consoled, since no real harm had befallen them.

Mr. Earnshaw carved bountiful platefuls, and the mistress made them merry with lively talk. I waited behind her chair, and was pained to behold Catherine, with dry eyes and an indifferent air, commence cutting up the wing of a goose before her.

"An unfeeling child," I thought to myself; "how lightly she dismisses her old playmate's troubles. I could not have imagined her to be so selfish."

She lifted a mouthful to her lips; then set it down again; her cheeks flushed, and the tears gushed over them. She slipped her fork to the floor, and hastily dived under the cloth to conceal her emotion. I did not call her unfeeling long, for I perceived she was in purgatory throughout the day, and wearying to find an opportunity of getting by herself, or paying a visit to Heathcliff, who had been locked up by the master, as I discovered, on endeavouring to introduce to him a private mess of victuals.

In the evening we had a dance. Cathy begged that he might be liberated then, as Isabella Linton had no partner; her entreaties were vain, and I was appointed to supply the deficiency.

We got rid of all gloom in the excitement of the exercise, and our pleasure was increased by the arrival of the Gimmerton band, mustering fifteen strong: a trumpet, a trombone, clarionets, bassoons, French horns, and a bass viol, besides singers. They go the rounds of all the respectable houses, and receive contributions every Christmas, and we esteemed it a first-rate treat to hear them.

After the usual carols had been sung, we set them to songs and glees. Mrs. Earnshaw loved the music, and so they gave us plenty.

Catherine loved it too; but she said it sounded sweetest at the top of the steps, and she went up in the dark. I followed. They shut the house door below, never noting our absence, it was so full of people. She made no stay at the stairs' head, but mounted farther, to the garret where Heathcliff was confined, and called him. He stubbornly declined answering for a while; she persevered, and finally persuaded him to hold communion with her through the boards. I let the poor things converse unmolested, till I supposed the songs were going to cease, and the singers to get some refreshment; then I clambered up the ladder to warn her.

Instead of finding her outside, I heard her voice within. The little monkey had crept by the skylight of one garret along the roof, into the skylight of the other, and it was with the utmost difficulty I could coax her out again.

When she did come, Heathcliff came with her, and she insisted that I should take him into the kitchen, as my fellow-servant had gone to a neighbour's to be removed from the sound of our "devil's psalmody," as it pleased him to call it. I told them I intended by no means to encourage their tricks, but as the prisoner had never broken his fast since yesterday's dinner, I would wink at his cheating Mr. Hindley that once.

He went down; I set him a stool by the fire, and offered him a quantity of good things; but he was sick and could eat little, and my attempts to entertain him were thrown away. He leant his two elbows on his knees, and his chin on his hands, and remained wrapt in dumb meditation.

On my inquiring the subject of his thoughts, he answered gravely—

"I'm trying to settle how I shall pay Hindley back. I

don't care how long I wait, if I can only do it at last. I hope he will not die before I do!"

"For shame, Heathcliff!" said I. "It is for God to punish wicked people; we should learn to forgive."

"No, God won't have the satisfaction that I shall," he returned. "I only wish I knew the best way! Let me alone, and I 'll plan it out; while I 'm thinking of that I don't feel pain."

But, Mr. Lockwood, I forget these tales cannot divert you. I 'm annoyed how I should dream of chattering on at such a rate; and your gruel cold, and you nodding for bed! I could have told Heathcliff's history, all that you need hear, in half a dozen words.

Thus interrupting herself, the housekeeper rose, and proceeded to lay aside her sewing; but I felt incapable of moving from the hearth, and I was very far from nodding.

"Sit still, Mrs. Dean," I cried, "do sit still, another half hour! You 've done just right to tell the story leisurely. That is the method I like, and you must finish in the same style. I am interested in every character you have mentioned, more or less."

"The clock is on the stroke of eleven, sir."

"No matter—I 'm not accustomed to go to bed in the long hours. One or two is early enough for a person who lies till ten."

"You shouldn't lie till ten. There 's the very prime of the morning gone long before that time. A person who has not done one half his day's work by ten o'clock, runs a chance of leaving the other half undone."

"Nevertheless, Mrs. Dean, resume your chair; because tomorrow I intend lengthening the night till afternoon. I prognosticate for myself an obstinate cold, at least."

"I hope not, sir. Well, you must allow me to leap over some three years; during that space Mrs. Earnshaw——"

"No, no, I 'll allow nothing of the sort! Are you acquainted with the mood of mind in which, if you were seated alone, and the cat licking its kitten on the rug before you, you would watch the operation so intently that puss's neglect of one ear would put you seriously out of temper?"

"A terribly lazy mood, I should say."

"On the contrary, a tiresomely active one. It is mine, at present; and, therefore, continue minutely. I perceive that people in these regions acquire over people in towns the value that a spider in a dungeon does over a spider in a cottage, to their various occupants; and yet the deepened attraction is not entirely owing to the situation of the looker-on. They do live more in earnest, more in themselves, and less in surface change, and frivolous external things. I could fancy a love for life here almost possible; and I was a fixed unbeliever in any love of a year's standing. One state resembles setting a hungry man down to a single dish, on which he may concentrate his entire appetite and do it justice; the other, introducing him to a table laid out by French cooks: he can perhaps extract as much enjoyment from the whole, but each part is a mere atom in his regard and remembrance."

"Oh! here we are the same as anywhere else, when you get to know us," observed Mrs. Dean, somewhat puzzled at my speech.

"Excuse me," I responded; "you, my good friend, are a striking evidence against that assertion. Excepting a few provincialisms of slight consequence, you have no marks of the manners which I am habituated to consider peculiar to your class. I am sure you have thought a great deal more than the generality of servants think. You have been compelled to cultivate your reflective faculties for want of occasions for frittering your life away in silly trifles."

Mrs. Dean laughed.

"I certainly esteem myself a steady, reasonable kind of body," she said; "not exactly from living among the hills and seeing one set of faces and one series of actions, from year's end to year's end; but I have undergone sharp discipline, which has taught me wisdom; and then, I have read more than you would fancy, Mr. Lockwood. You could not open a book in this library that I have not looked into, and got something out of also: unless it be that range of Greek and Latin, and that of French, and those I know one from another; it is as much as you can expect of a poor man's daughter. However, if I am to follow my story in true gossip's fashion, I had better go on; and instead of leaping three years, I will be

content to pass to the next summer—the summer of
1778, that is nearly twenty-three years ago."

CHAPTER 8

ON THE morning of a fine June day, my first bonny
little nursling, and the last of the ancient Earnshaw
stock, was born.

We were busy with the hay in a faraway field, when
the girl that usually brought our breakfasts came running an hour too soon, across the meadow and up the
lane, calling me as she ran.

"Oh, such a grand bairn!" she panted out. "The finest
lad that ever breathed! But the doctor says missis must
go; he says she's been in a consumption these many
months. I heard him tell Mr. Hindley; and now she has
nothing to keep her, and she 'll be dead before winter.
You must come home directly. You 're to nurse it, Nelly,
to feed it with sugar and milk, and take care of it day
and night. I wish I were you, because it will be all yours
when there is no missis!"

"But is she very ill?" I asked, flinging down my rake,
and tying my bonnet.

"I guess she is, yet she looks bravely," replied the girl,
"and she talks as if she thought of living to see it grow
a man. She 's out of her head for joy, it 's such a beauty!
If I were her, I 'm certain I should not die. I should get
better at the bare sight of it, in spite of Kenneth. I was
fairly mad at him. Dame Archer brought the cherub
down to master, in the house, and his face just began
to light up, then the old croaker steps forward, and says
he—'Earnshaw, it 's a blessing your wife has been spared
to leave you this son. When she came, I felt convinced
we shouldn't keep her long; and now, I must tell you,
the winter will probably finish her. Don't take on, and
fret about it too much: it can't be helped. And besides,
you should have known better than to choose such a rush
of a lass!' "

"And what did the master answer?" I inquired.

"I think he swore; but I didn't mind him, I was straining to see the bairn," and she began again to describe it rapturously. I, as zealous as herself, hurried eagerly home to admire, on my part, though I was very sad for Hindley's sake. He had room in his heart only for two idols—his wife and himself; he doted on both, and adored one, and I couldn't conceive how he would bear the loss.

When we got to Wuthering Heights, there he stood at the front door; and, as I passed in, I asked, "how was the baby?"

"Nearly ready to run about, Nell!" he replied, putting on a cheerful smile.

"And the mistress?" I ventured to inquire; "the doctor says she's——"

"Damn the doctor!" he interrupted, reddening. "Frances is quite right: she'll be perfectly well by this time next week. Are you going upstairs? Will you tell her that I'll come, if she'll promise not to talk. I left her because she would not hold her tongue, and she must—tell her Mr. Kenneth says she must be quiet."

I delivered this message to Mrs. Earnshaw; she seemed in flighty spirits, and replied merrily—

"I hardly spoke a word, Ellen, and there he has gone out twice, crying. Well, say I promise I won't speak: but that does not bind me not to laugh at him!"

Poor soul! Till within a week of her death that gay heart never failed her, and her husband persisted doggedly, nay, furiously, in affirming her health improved every day. When Kenneth warned him that his medicines were useless at that stage of the malady, and he needn't put him to further expense by attending her, he retorted—

"I know you need not—she's well—she does not want any more attendance from you! She never was in a consumption. It was a fever, and it is gone; her pulse is as slow as mine now, and her cheek as cool."

He told his wife the same story, and she seemed to believe him. But one night, while leaning on his shoulder in the act of saying she thought she should be able to get up tomorrow, a fit of coughing took her—a very slight one—he raised her in his arms; she put her two hands about his neck, her face changed, and she was dead.

As the girl had anticipated, the child Hareton fell wholly into my hands. Mr. Earnshaw, provided he saw him healthy and never heard him cry, was contented, as far as regarded him. For himself, he grew desperate: his sorrow was of that kind that will not lament. He neither wept nor prayed; he cursed and defied, execrated God and man, and gave himself up to reckless dissipation.

The servants could not bear his tyrannical and evil conduct long; Joseph and I were the only two that would stay. I had not the heart to leave my charge; and besides, you know, I had been his foster-sister, and excused his behaviour more readily than a stranger would.

Joseph remained to hector over tenants and labourers, and because it was his vocation to be where he had plenty of wickedness to reprove.

The master's bad ways and bad companions formed a pretty example for Catherine and Heathcliff. His treatment of the latter was enough to make a fiend of a saint. And, truly, it appeared as if the lad were possessed of something diabolical at that period. He delighted to witness Hindley degrading himself past redemption, and became daily more notable for savage sullenness and ferocity.

I could not half tell what an infernal house we had. The curate dropped calling, and nobody decent came near us, at last, unless Edgar Linton's visits to Miss Cathy might be an exception. At fifteen she was the queen of the countryside; she had no peer; and she did turn out a haughty, headstrong creature! I own I did not like her, after her infancy was past; and I vexed her frequently by trying to bring down her arrogance: she never took an aversion to me, though. She had a wondrous constancy to old attachments; even Heathcliff kept his hold on her affections unalterably, and young Linton, with all his superiority, found it difficult to make an equally deep impression.

He was my late master; that is his portrait over the fireplace. It used to hang on one side, and his wife's on the other; but hers has been removed, or else you might see something of what she was. Can you make that out?

Mrs. Dean raised the candle, and I discerned a soft-featured face, exceedingly resembling the·young lady at the Heights, but more pensive and amiable in expression. It formed a sweet picture. The long light hair curled slightly on the temples; the eyes were large and serious; the figure almost too graceful. I did not marvel how Catherine Earnshaw could forget her first friend for such an individual. I marvelled much how he, with a mind to correspond with his person, could fancy my idea of Catherine Earnshaw.

"A very agreeable portrait," I observed to the housekeeper. "Is it like?"

"Yes," she answered; "but he looked better when he was animated; that is his everyday countenance; he wanted spirit in general."

Catherine had kept up her acquaintance with the Lintons since her five weeks' residence among them; and as she had no temptation to show her rough side in their company, and had the sense to be ashamed of being rude where she experienced such invariable courtesy, she imposed unwittingly on the old lady and gentleman, by her ingenious cordiality; gained the admiration of Isabella, and the heart and soul of her brother—acquisitions that flattered her from the first, for she was full of ambition, and led her to adopt a double character without exactly intending to deceive anyone.

In the place where she had heard Heathcliff termed a "vulgar young ruffian," and "worse than a brute," she took care not to act like him; but at home she had small inclination to practise politeness that would only be laughed at and restrain an unruly nature when it would bring her neither credit nor praise.

Mr. Edgar seldom mustered courage to visit Wuthering Heights openly. He had a terror of Earnshaw's reputation, and shrunk from encountering him; and yet he was always received with our best attempts at civility; the master himself avoided offending him, knowing why he came, and if he could not be gracious, kept out of the way. I rather think his appearance there was distasteful to Catherine: she was not artful, never played the coquette, and had evidently an objection to her two friends meeting at all, for when Heathcliff expressed contempt of Linton in his presence, she could not half coincide, as she did in his absence; and when Linton evinced disgust and antipathy to Heathcliff, she dare not treat his sentiments with indifference, as if depreciation of her playmate were of scarcely any consequence to her.

I 've had many a laugh at her perplexities and untold troubles, which she vainly strove to hide from my mockery. That sounds ill-natured: but she was so proud, it became really impossible to pity her distress, till she should be chastened into more humility.

She did bring herself, finally, to confess and confide in me; there was not a soul else that she might fashion into an adviser.

Mr. Hindley had gone from home, one afternoon, and Heathcliff presumed to give himself a holiday on the strength of it. He had reached the age of sixteen then, I think, and without having bad features or being deficient in intellect, he contrived to convey an impression of inward and outward repulsiveness that his present aspect retains no traces of.

In the first place, he had by that time lost the benefit of his early education; continual hard work, begun soon and concluded late, had extinguished any curiosity he once possessed in pursuit of knowledge, and any love for books or learning. His childhood's sense of superiority, instilled into him by the favours of old Mr. Earnshaw, was faded away. He struggled long to keep up an equality with Catherine in her studies, and yielded with poignant though silent regret; but he yielded completely, and there was no prevailing on him to take a step in the way of moving upward, when he found he must, necessarily, sink beneath his former level. Then personal appearance sympathized with mental deterioration; he acquired a slouching gait and ignoble look; his naturally reserved disposition was exaggerated into an almost idiotic excess of unsociable moroseness; and he took a grim pleasure, apparently, in exciting the aversion rather than the esteem of his few acquaintance.

Catherine and he were constant companions still at his seasons of respite from labour, but he had ceased to express his fondness for her in words, and recoiled with angry suspicion from her girlish caresses, as if conscious there could be no gratification in lavishing such marks of affection on him. On the before-named occasion he came into the house to announce his intention of doing nothing, while I was assisting Miss Cathy to arrange her dress; she had not reckoned on his taking it into his head to be idle, and imagining she would have the whole place to herself, she managed, by some means, to inform Mr. Edgar of her brother's absence, and was then preparing to receive him.

"Cathy, are you busy this afternoon?" asked Heathcliff. "Are you going anywhere?"

"No, it is raining," she answered.

"Why have you that silk frock on, then?" he said. "Nobody coming here, I hope?"

"Not that I know of," stammered Miss; "but you should be in the field now, Heathcliff. It is an hour past dinnertime. I thought you were gone."

"Hindley does not often free us from his accursed presence," observed the boy. "I 'll not work any more today; I 'll stay with you."

"Oh, but Joseph will tell," she suggested; "you'd better go!"

"Joseph is loading lime on the farther side of Penistone Crag; it will take him till dark, and he'll never know."

So saying, he lounged to the fire, and sat down. Catherine reflected an instant, with knitted brows—she found it needful to smooth the way for an intrusion.

"Isabella and Edgar Linton talked of calling this afternoon," she said, at the conclusion of a minute's silence. "As it rains, I hardly expect them; but they may come, and if they do, you run the risk of being scolded for no good."

"Order Ellen to say you are engaged, Cathy," he persisted. "Don't turn me out for those pitiful, silly friends of yours! I 'm on the point, sometimes, of complaining that they—but I 'll not——"

"That they what?" cried Catherine, gazing at him with a troubled countenance. "Oh, Nelly!" she added petulantly, jerking her head away from my hands, "you 've combed my hair quite out of curl! That 's enough; let me alone. What are you on the point of complaining about, Heathcliff?"

"Nothing—only look at the almanack on that wall." He pointed to a framed sheet hanging near the window, and continued—

"The crosses are for the evenings you have spent with the Lintons, the dots for those spent with me. Do you see? I've marked every day."

"Yes—very foolish; as if I took notice!" replied Catherine in a peevish tone. "And where is the sense of that?"

"To show that I do take notice," said Heathcliff.

"And should I always be sitting with you?" she demanded, growing more irritated. "What good do I get? What do you talk about? You might be dumb, or a baby, for anything you say to amuse me, or for anything you do, either!"

"You never told me before that I talked too little, or that you disliked my company, Cathy!" exclaimed Heathcliff in much agitation.

"It's no company at all, when people know nothing and say nothing," she muttered.

Her companion rose up, but he hadn't time to express his feelings further, for a horse's feet were heard on the flags, and having knocked gently, young Linton entered, his face brilliant with delight at the unexpected summons he had received.

Doubtless Catherine marked the difference between her friends, as one came in and the other went out. The contrast resembled what you see in exchanging a bleak, hilly, coal country for a beautiful fertile valley; and his voice and greeting were as opposite as his aspect. He had a sweet, low manner of speaking, and pronounced his words as you do; that's less gruff than we talk here, and softer.

"I'm not come too soon, am I?" he said, casting a look at me; I had begun to wipe the plate, and tidy some drawers at the far end in the dresser.

"No," answered Catherine. "What are you doing there, Nelly?"

"My work, Miss," I replied. (Mr. Hindley had given me directions to make a third party in any private visits Linton chose to pay.)

She stepped behind me and whispered crossly, "Take yourself and your dusters off; when company are in the house, servants don't commence scouring and cleaning in the room where they are!"

"It's a good opportunity, now that master is away," I answered aloud. "He hates me to be fidgeting over these things in his presence. I'm sure Mr. Edgar will excuse me."

"I hate you to be fidgeting in my presence," exclaimed the young lady imperiously, not allowing her guest time to speak; she had failed to recover her equanimity since the little dispute with Heathcliff.

"I'm sorry for it, Miss Catherine," was my response, and I proceeded assiduously with my occupation.

She, supposing Edgar could not see her, snatched the cloth from my hand, and pinched me, with a prolonged wrench, very spitefully on the arm.

I've said I did not love her, and rather relished mortifying her vanity now and then; besides, she hurt me extremely; so I started up from my knees, and screamed out,

"Oh, Miss, that's a nasty trick! You have no right to nip me, and I'm not going to bear it."

"I didn't touch you, you lying creature!" cried she, her fingers tingling to repeat the act, and her ears red with rage. She never had power to conceal her passion, it always set her whole complexion in a blaze.

"What's that, then?" I retorted, showing a decided purple witness to refute her.

She stamped her foot, wavered a moment, and then, irresistibly impelled by the naughty spirit within her, slapped me on the cheek a stinging blow that filled both eyes with water.

"Catherine, love! Catherine!" interposed Linton, greatly shocked at the double fault of falsehood and violence which his idol had committed.

"Leave the room, Ellen!" he repeated, trembling all over.

Little Hareton, who followed me everywhere, and was sitting near me on the floor, at seeing my tears commenced crying himself, and sobbed out complaints against "wicked Aunt Cathy," which drew her fury onto his unlucky head; she seized his shoulders, and shook him till the poor child waxed livid, and Edgar thoughtlessly laid hold of her hands to deliver him. In an instant one was wrung free, and the astonished young man felt it applied over his own ear in a way that could not be mistaken for jest.

He drew back in consternation. I lifted Hareton in my arms, and walked off to the kitchen with him, leaving the door of communication open, for I was curious to watch how they would settle their disagreement.

The insulted visitor moved to the spot where he had laid his hat, pale and with a quivering lip.

"That's right!" I said to myself. "Take warning and begone! It's a kindness to let you have a glimpse of her genuine disposition."

"Where are you going?" demanded Catherine, advancing to the door.

He swerved aside, and attempted to pass.

"You must not go!" she exclaimed energetically.

"I must and shall!" he replied in a subdued voice.

"No," she persisted, grasping the handle, "not yet, Edgar Linton. Sit down; you shall not leave me in that temper. I should be miserable all night, and I won't be miserable for you!"

"Can I stay after you have struck me?" asked Linton. Catherine was mute.

"You've made me afraid and ashamed of you," he continued; "I'll not come here again!"

Her eyes began to glisten, and her lids to twinkle.

"And you told a deliberate untruth!" he said.

"I didn't!" she cried, recovering her speech. "I did nothing deliberately. Well go, if you please—get away! And now I'll cry—I'll cry myself sick!"

She dropped down on her knees by a chair, and set to weeping in serious earnest.

Edgar persevered in his resolution as far as the court; there he lingered. I resolved to encourage him.

"Miss is dreadfully wayward, sir," I called out. "As bad as any marred child; you 'd better be riding home, or else she will be sick, only to grieve us."

The soft thing looked askance through the window; he possessed the power to depart, as much as a cat possesses the power to leave a mouse half killed, or a bird half eaten.

"Ah, I thought, there will be no saving him—he's doomed, and flies to his fate!

And so it was: he turned abruptly, hastened into the house again, shut the door behind him; and when I went in a while after to inform them that Earnshaw had come home rabid drunk, ready to pull the old place about our ears (his ordinary frame of mind in that condition), I saw the quarrel had merely effected a closer intimacy—had broken the outworks of youthful timidity, and enabled them to forsake the disguise of friendship, and confess themselves lovers.

Intelligence of Mr. Hindley's arrival drove Linton speedily to his horse, and Catherine to her chamber. I went to hide little Hareton, and to take the shot out of the master's fowling-piece, which he was fond of playing with in his insane excitement, to the hazard of the lives of any who provoked or even attracted his notice too much; and I had hit upon the plan of removing it, that he might do less mischief if he did go the length of firing the gun.

CHAPTER 9

HE ENTERED, vociferating oaths dreadful to hear, and caught me in the act of stowing his son away in the kitchen cupboard. Hareton was impressed with a wholesome terror of encountering either his wild-beast's fondness or his madman's rage; for in one he ran a chance of being squeezed and kissed to death, and in the other of being flung into the fire or dashed against the wall; and the poor thing remained perfectly quiet wherever I chose to put him.

"There, I 've found it out at last!" cried Hindley, pulling me back by the skin of my neck, like a dog. "By heaven and hell, you 've sworn between you to murder that child! I know how it is, now, that he is always out of my way. But, with the help of Satan, I shall make you swallow the carving-knife, Nelly! You needn't laugh; for I 've just crammed Kenneth, head-downmost, in the Blackhorse marsh; and two is the same as one—and I want to kill some of you; I shall have no rest till I do!"

"But I don't like the carving-knife, Mr. Hindley," I answered; "it has been cutting red herrings. I'd rather be shot, if you please."

"You'd rather be damned!" he said, "and so you shall. No law in England can hinder a man from keeping his house decent, and mine's abominable! open your mouth."

He held the knife in his hand, and pushed its point between my teeth; but, for my part, I was never much afraid of his vagaries. I spat out, and affirmed it tasted detestably—I would not take it on any account.

"Oh!" said he, releasing me, "I see that hideous little villain is not Hareton. I beg your pardon, Nell. If it be, he deserves flaying alive for not running to welcome me, and for screaming as if I were a goblin. Unnatural cub, come hither! I'll teach thee to impose on a good-hearted, deluded father. Now, don't you think the lad would be handsomer cropped? It makes a dog fiercer, and I love something fierce—get me a scissors—something fierce and trim! Besides, it's infernal affectation—devilish conceit it is, to cherish our ears—we're asses enough without them. Hush, child, hush! Well then, it is my darling! wisht, dry thy eyes—there's a joy; kiss me. What! it won't? Kiss me, Hareton! Damn thee, kiss me! By God, as if I would rear such a monster! As sure as I'm living, I'll break the brat's neck."

Poor Hareton was squalling and kicking in his father's arms with all his might, and redoubled his yells when he carried him upstairs and lifted him over the banister. I cried out that he would frighten the child into fits, and ran to rescue him.

As I reached them, Hindley leant forward on the rails to listen to a noise below, almost forgetting what he had in his hands.

"Who is that?" he asked, hearing someone approaching the stair's foot.

I leant forward, also, for the purpose of signing to Heathcliff, whose step I recognized, not to come further; and, at the instant when my eye quitted Hareton, he gave a sudden spring, delivered himself from the careless grasp that held him, and fell.

There was scarcely time to experience a thrill of horror

before we saw that the little wretch was safe. Heathcliff arrived underneath just at the critical moment; by a natural impulse, he arrested his descent, and setting him on his feet, looked up to discover the author of the accident.

A miser who has parted with a lucky lottery ticket for five shillings, and finds next day he has lost in the bargain five thousand pounds, could not show a blanker countenance than he did on beholding the figure of Mr. Earnshaw above. It expressed, plainer than words could do, the intensest anguish at having made himself the instrument of thwarting his own revenge. Had it been dark, I dare say, he would have tried to remedy the mistake by smashing Hareton's skull on the steps; but, we witnessed his salvation; and I was presently below with my precious charge pressed to my heart.

Hindley descended more leisurely, sobered and abashed.

"It is your fault, Ellen," he said, "you should have kept him out of sight: you should have taken him from me! Is he injured anywhere?"

"Injured!" I cried angrily. "If he's not killed, he'll be an idiot! Oh! I wonder his mother does not rise from her grave to see how you use him. You're worse than a heathen—treating your own flesh and blood in that manner!"

He attempted to touch the child, who, on finding himself with me, sobbed off his terror directly. At the first finger his father laid on him, however, he shrieked again louder than before, and struggled as if he would go into convulsions.

"You shall not meddle with him!" I continued. "He hates you—they all hate you—that's the truth! A happy family you have, and a pretty state you're come to!"

"I shall come to a prettier, yet, Nelly," laughed the misguided man, recovering his hardness. "At present, convey yourself and him away. And, hark you, Heathcliff! clear you too, quite from my reach and hearing. . . . I wouldn't murder you tonight, unless, perhaps, I set the house on fire; but that's as my fancy goes."

While saying this he took a pint bottle of brandy from the dresser and poured some into a tumbler.

"Nay, don't!" I entreated. "Mr. Hindley, do take warning. Have mercy on this unfortunate boy, if you care nothing for yourself!"

"Anyone will do better for him than I shall," he answered.

"Have mercy on your own soul!" I said, endeavouring to snatch the glass from his hand.

"Not I! On the contrary, I shall have great pleasure in sending it to perdition to punish its Maker," exclaimed the blasphemer. "Here's to its hearty damnation!"

He drank the spirits and impatiently bade us go, terminating his command with a sequel of horrid imprecations, too bad to repeat or remember.

"It's a pity he cannot kill himself with drink," observed Heathcliff, muttering an echo of curses back when the door was shut. "He's doing his very utmost; but his constitution defies him. Mr. Kenneth says he would wager his mare that he'll outlive any man on this side Gimmerton, and go to the grave a hoary sinner, unless some happy chance out of the common course befall him."

I went into the kitchen, and sat down to lull my little lamb to sleep. Heathcliff, as I thought, walked through to the barn. It turned out afterwards that he only got as far as the other side the settle, when he flung himself on a bench by the wall, removed from the fire, and remained silent.

I was rocking Hareton on my knee, and humming a song that began—

"It was far in the night, and the bairnies grat,
  The mither beneath the mools heard that,"

when Miss Cathy, who had listened to the hubbub from her room, put her head in and whispered—

"Are you alone, Nelly?"

"Yes, Miss," I replied.

She entered and approached the hearth. I, supposing she was going to say something, looked up. The expression of her face seemed disturbed and anxious. Her lips were half asunder, as if she meant to speak, and she drew a breath, but it escaped in a sigh instead of a sentence.

I resumed my song, not having forgotten her recent behaviour.

"Where's Heathcliff?" she said, interrupting me.

"About his work in the stable," was my answer.

He did not contradict me; perhaps he had fallen into a doze. There followed another long pause, during which I perceived a drop or two trickle from Catherine's cheek to the flags.

Is she sorry for her shameful conduct? I asked myself. That will be a novelty: but she may come to the point as she will—I shan't help her!

No, she felt small trouble regarding any subject, save her own concerns.

"Oh, dear!" she cried at last. "I'm very unhappy!"

"A pity," observed I. "You're hard to please: so many friends and so few cares, and can't make yourself content!"

"Nelly, will you keep a secret for me?" she pursued, kneeling down by me and lifting her winsome eyes to my face with that sort of look which turns off bad temper, even when one has all the right in the world to indulge it.

"Is it worth keeping?" I inquired, less sulkily.

"Yes, and it worries me, and I must let it out! I want to know what I should do. Today, Edgar Linton has asked me to marry him, and I've given him an answer. Now, before I tell you whether it was a consent or denial, you tell me which it ought to have been."

"Really, Miss Catherine, how can I know?" I replied. "To be sure, considering the exhibition you performed in his presence this afternoon, I might say it would be wise to refuse him; since he asked you after that, he must be either hopelessly stupid or a venturesome fool."

"If you talk so, I won't tell you any more," she returned peevishly, rising to her feet. "I accepted him, Nelly. Be quick, and say whether I was wrong!"

"You accepted him! Then what good is it discussing the matter? You have pledged your word, and cannot retract."

"But, say whether I should have done so—do!" she exclaimed in an irritated tone, chafing her hands together, and frowning.

"There are many things to be considered before that question can be answered properly," I said sententiously. "First and foremost, do you love Mr. Edgar?"

"Who can help it? Of course I do," she answered.

Then I put her through the following catechism—for a girl of twenty-two, it was not injudicious.

"Why do you love him, Miss Cathy?"

"Nonsense, I do—that's sufficient."

"By no means; you must say why."

"Well, because he is handsome, and pleasant to be with."

"Bad!" was my commentary.

"And because he is young and cheerful."

"Bad, still."

"And because he loves me."

"Indifferent, coming there."

"And he will be rich, and I shall like to be the greatest woman of the neighbourhood, and I shall be proud of having such a husband."

"Worst of all. And now say how you love him?"

"As everybody loves— You're silly, Nelly."

"Not at all— Answer."

"I love the ground under his feet, and the air over his head, and everything he touches, and every word he says. I love all his looks, and all his actions, and him entirely and altogether. There now!"

"And why?"

"Nay, you are making a jest of it; it is exceedingly ill-natured! It's no jest to me!" said the young lady, scowling, and turning her face to the fire.

"I'm very far from jesting, Miss Catherine," I replied. "You love Mr. Edgar, because he is handsome, and young, and cheerful, and rich, and loves you. The last, however, goes for nothing: you would love him without that, probably; and with it you wouldn't, unless he possessed the four former attractions."

"No, to be sure not; I should only pity him—hate him, perhaps, if he were ugly, and a clown."

"But there are several other handsome, rich young men in the world—handsomer, possibly, and richer than he is. What should hinder you from loving them?"

"If there be any, they are out of my way. I've seen none like Edgar."

"You may see some; and he won't always be handsome, and young, and may not always be rich."

"He is now; and I have only to do with the present. I wish you would speak rationally."

"Well, that settles it: if you have only to do with the present, marry Mr. Linton."

"I don't want your permission for that—I shall marry him; and yet you have not told whether I 'm right."

"Perfectly right, if people be right to marry only for the present. And now, let us hear what you are unhappy about. Your brother will be pleased. . . . The old lady and gentleman will not object, I think; you will escape from a disorderly comfortless home into a wealthy respectable one; and you love Edgar, and Edgar loves you. All seems smooth and easy: where is the obstacle?"

"*Here!* and *here!*" replied Catherine, striking one hand on her forehead and the other on her breast, "in whichever place the soul lives. In my soul and in my heart, I 'm convinced I 'm wrong!"

"That 's very strange! I cannot make it out."

"It 's my secret. But if you will not mock at me, I 'll explain it. I can't do it distinctly; but I 'll give you a feeling of how I feel."

She seated herself by me again; her countenance grew sadder and graver, and her clasped hands trembled.

"Nelly, do you never dream queer dreams?" she said suddenly, after some minutes' reflection.

"Yes, now and then," I answered.

"And so do I. I 've dreamt in my life dreams that have stayed with me ever after, and changed my ideas; they 've gone through and through me, like wine through water, and altered the colour of my mind. And this is one; I 'm going to tell it—but take care not to smile at any part of it."

"Oh! don't, Miss Catherine!" I cried. "We 're dismal enough without conjuring up ghosts and visions to perplex us. Come, come, be merry and like yourself! Look at little Hareton! *He's* dreaming nothing dreary. How sweetly he smiles in his sleep!"

"Yes, and how sweetly his father curses in his solitude! You remember him, I dare say, when he was just such another as that chubby thing, nearly as young and innocent. However, Nelly, I shall oblige you to listen; it 's not long, and I 've no power to be merry tonight."

"I won't hear it, I won't hear it!" I repeated hastily.

I was superstitious about dreams then, and am still, and Catherine had an unusual gloom in her aspect that made me dread something from which I might shape a prophecy, and foresee a fearful catastrophe.

She was vexed, but she did not proceed. Apparently taking up another subject, she recommenced in a short time.

"If I were in heaven, Nelly, I should be extremely miserable."

"Because you are not fit to go there," I answered. "All sinners would be miserable in heaven."

"But it is not for that. I dreamt once that I was there."

"I tell you I won't harken to your dreams, Miss Catherine! I'll go to bed," I interrupted again.

She laughed, and held me down, for I made a motion to leave my chair.

"This is nothing," cried she. "I was only going to say that heaven did not seem to be my home, and I broke my heart with weeping to come back to earth; and the angels were so angry that they flung me out into the middle of the heath on the top of Wuthering Heights, where I woke sobbing for joy. That will do to explain my secret, as well as the other. I've no more business to marry Edgar Linton than I have to be in heaven; and if the wicked man in there had not brought Heathcliff so low, I shouldn't have thought of it. It would degrade me to marry Heathcliff now; so he shall never know how I love him; and that, not because he's handsome, Nelly, but because he's more myself than I am. Whatever our souls are made of, his and mine are the same; and Linton's is as different as a moonbeam from lightning, or frost from fire."

Ere this speech ended, I became sensible of Heathcliff's presence. Having noticed a slight movement, I turned my head, and saw him rise from the bench, and steal out noiselessly. He had listened till he heard Catherine say it would degrade her to marry him, and then he stayed to hear no farther.

My companion, sitting on the ground, was prevented by the back of the settle from remarking his presence or departure; but I started, and bade her hush!

"Why?" she asked, gazing nervously round.

"Joseph is here," I answered, catching opportunely the

(82)

roll of his cartwheels up the road, "and Heathcliff will come in with him. I 'm not sure whether he were not at the door this moment."

"Oh, he couldn't overhear me at the door!" said she. "Give me Hareton, while you get the supper, and when it is ready ask me to sup with you. I want to cheat my uncomfortable conscience, and be convinced that Heathcliff has no notion of these things. He has not, has he? He does not know what being in love is?"

"I see no reason that he should not know, as well as you," I returned; "and if you are his choice, he 'll be the most unfortunate creature that ever was born! As soon as you become Mrs. Linton, he loses friend, and love, and all! Have you considered how you 'll bear the separation, and how he 'll bear to be quite deserted in the world? Because, Miss Catherine——"

"He quite deserted! We separated!" she exclaimed, with an accent of indignation. "Who is to separate us, pray? They 'll meet the fate of Milo! Not as long as I live, Ellen, for no mortal creature. Every Linton on the face of the earth might melt into nothing, before I could consent to forsake Heathcliff. Oh, that 's not what I intend—that 's not what I mean! I shouldn't be Mrs. Linton were such a price demanded! He'll be as much to me as he has been all his lifetime. Edgar must shake off his antipathy, and tolerate him, at least. He will, when he learns my true feelings towards him. Nelly, I see now, you think me a selfish wretch; but did it never strike you that if Heathcliff and I married, we should be beggars? whereas, if I marry Linton, I can aid Heathcliff to rise, and place him out of my brother's power."

"With your husband's money, Miss Catherine?" I asked. "You 'll find him not so pliable as you calculate upon; and though I 'm hardly a judge, I think that 's the worst motive you 've given yet for being the wife of young Linton."

"It is not," retorted she; "it is the best! The others were the satisfaction of my whims, and for Edgar's sake, too, to satisfy him. This is for the sake of one who comprehends in his person my feelings to Edgar and myself. I cannot express it; but surely you and everybody have a notion that there is or should be an existence of yours beyond you. What were the use of my creation, if

I were entirely contained here? My great miseries in this world have been Heathcliff's miseries, and I watched and felt each from the beginning; my great thought in living is himself. If all else perished, and he remained, I should still continue to be; and all else remained, and he were annihilated, the universe would turn to a mighty stranger; I should not seem a part of it. My love for Linton is like the foliage in the woods: time will change it, I'm well aware, as winter changes the trees. My love for Heathcliff resembles the eternal rocks beneath—a source of little visible delight, but necessary. Nelly, I am Heathcliff! He's always, always in my mind—not as a pleasure, any more than I am always a pleasure to myself, but as my own being. So don't talk of our separation again; it is impracticable, and——"

She paused, and hid her face in the folds of my gown, but I jerked it forcibly away. I was out of patience with her folly!

"If I can make any sense of your nonsense, Miss," I said, "it only goes to convince me that you are ignorant of the duties you undertake in marrying, or else that you are a wicked, unprincipled girl. But trouble me with no more secrets; I'll not promise to keep them."

"You'll keep that?" she asked eagerly.

"No, I'll not promise," I repeated.

She was about to insist, when the entrance of Joseph finished our conversation, and Catherine removed her seat to a corner and nursed Hareton, while I made the supper.

After it was cooked, my fellow-servant and I began to quarrel who should carry some to Mr. Hindley; and we didn't settle it till all was nearly cold. Then we came to the agreement that we would let him ask, if he wanted any, for we feared particularly to go into his presence when he had been some time alone.

"Und hah isn't that nowt comed in frough th' field, be this time? What is he abaht? girt eedle seeght!" demanded the old man, looking round for Heathcliff.

"I'll call him," I replied. "He's in the barn, I've no doubt."

I went and called, but got no answer. On returning, I whispered to Catherine that he had heard a good part of what she said, I was sure, and told how I saw him quit the kitchen just as she complained of her brother's conduct regarding him.

She jumped up in a fine fright, flung Hareton onto the settle, and ran to seek for her friend herself, not taking leisure to consider why she was so flurried, or how her talk would have affected him.

She was absent such a while that Joseph proposed we should wait no longer. He cunningly conjectured they were staying away in order to avoid hearing his protracted blessing. They were "ill eneugh for only fahl manners," he affirmed. And on their behalf he added that night a special prayer to the usual quarter of an hour's supplication before meat, and would have tacked another to the end of the grace, had not his young mistress broken in upon him with a hurried command that he must run down the road, and, wherever Heathcliff had rambled, find and make him re-enter directly!

"I want to speak to him, and I *must*, before I go upstairs," she said. "And the gate is open. He is somewhere out of hearing, for he would not reply, though I shouted at the top of the fold as loud as I could."

Joseph objected at first; she was too much in earnest, however, to suffer contradiction; and at last he placed his hat on his head, and walked grumbling forth.

Meantime, Catherine paced up and down the floor, exclaiming—

"I wonder where he *is*—I wonder where he can be! What did I say, Nelly? I've forgotten. Was he vexed at my bad humour this afternoon? Dear! tell me what I've said to grieve him? I do wish he'd come. I do wish he would!"

"What a noise for nothing!" I cried, though rather uneasy myself. "What a trifle scares you! It's surely no great cause of alarm that Heathcliff should take a moonlight saunter on the moors, or even lie too sulky to speak to us in the hayloft. I'll engage he's lurking there. See if I don't ferret him out!"

I departed to renew my search; its result was disappointment, and Joseph's quest ended in the same.

"Yon lad gets war un war!" observed he on re-entering. "He's left th' yate ut t' full swing, and miss's pony has trodden dahn two rigs uh corn, un plottered through, raight o'er intuh t' meadow! Hahsomdiver, t' maister 'ull

play t' devil to-morn, and he 'll do weel. He 's patience
itsseln wi' sich careless, offald craters—patience itsseln
he is! Bud he 'll nut be soa allus—yah 's see, all on ye!
Yah mum'n't drive him aht uf his heead fur nowt!"

"Have you found Heathcliff, you ass?" interrupted
Catherine. "Have you been looking for him, as I ordered?"

"Aw sud more likker look for th' horse," he replied.
"It 'ud be tuh more sense. Bud, aw can look for norther
horse, nur man uf a neeght loike this—as black as t'
chimbley! und Hathecliff's noan t' chap tuh coom ut
maw whistle—happen he 'll be less hard uh hearing wi'
ye!"

It was a very dark evening for summer; the clouds appeared inclined to thunder, and I said we had better all
sit down—the approaching rain would be certain to bring
him home without further trouble.

However, Catherine would not be persuaded into tranquillity. She kept wandering to and fro, from the gate
to the door, in a state of agitation which permitted no
repose; and at length took up a permanent position on
one side of the wall, near the road, where, heedless of
my expostulations and the growling thunder, and the
great drops that began to plash around her, she remained, calling at intervals, and then listening, and then
crying outright. She beat Hareton, or any child, at a good
passionate fit of crying.

About midnight, while we still sat up, the storm came
rattling over the Heights in full fury. There was a violent wind, as well as thunder, and either one or the other
split a tree off at the corner of the building; a huge
bough fell across the roof, and knocked down a portion
of the east chimney-stack, sending a clatter of stones and
soot into the kitchen fire.

We thought a bolt had fallen in the middle of us, and
Joseph swung onto his knees, beseeching the Lord to remember the patriarchs Noah and Lot, and, as in former
times, spare the righteous, though he smote the un-
godly. I felt some sentiment that it must be a judgment
on us also. The Jonah, in my mind, was Mr. Earnshaw;
and I shook the handle of his den that I might ascertain if he were yet living. He replied audibly enough, in
a fashion which made my companion vociferate, more

clamorously than before, that a wide distinction might be drawn between saints like himself and sinners like his master. But the uproar passed away in twenty minutes, leaving us all unharmed; excepting Cathy, who got thoroughly drenched for her obstinacy in refusing to take shelter, and standing bonnetless and shawlless to catch as much water as she could with her hair and clothes.

She came in and lay down on the settle, all soaked as she was, turning her face to the back, and putting her hands before it.

"Well, Miss!" I exclaimed, touching her shoulder, "you are not bent on getting your death, are you? Do you know what o'clock it is? Half-past twelve. Come, come to bed! There's no use waiting longer on that foolish boy; he'll be gone to Gimmerton, and he'll stay there now. He guesses we shouldn't wait for him till this late hour; at least, he guesses that only Mr. Hindley would be up; and he'd rather avoid having the door opened by the master."

"Nay, nay, he's noan at Gimmerton!" said Joseph. "Aw's niver wonder, bud he's at t' bothom uf a bug-hoile. This visitation worn't for nowt, und aw wod hev ye tuh look aht, Miss—yuh muh be t' next. Thank Hivin for all! All warks togither for gooid tuh them as is chozzen, and piked aht froo' th' rubbidge! Yah knaw what t' Scripture ses—"

And he began quoting several texts, referring us to the chapters and verses, where we might find them.

I, having vainly begged the wilful girl to rise and remove her wet things, left him preaching and her shivering, and betook myself to bed with little Hareton, who slept as fast as if everyone had been sleeping round him.

I heard Joseph read on a while afterwards; then I distinguished his slow step on the ladder, and then I dropped asleep.

Coming down somewhat later than usual, I saw, by the sunbeams piercing the chinks of the shutters, Miss Catherine still seated near the fireplace. The house door was ajar, too; light entered from its unclosed windows; Hindley had come out, and stood on the kitchen hearth, haggard and drowsy.

"What ails you, Cathy?" he was saying when I entered; "you look as dismal as a drowned whelp. Why are you so damp and pale, child?"

"I've been wet," she answered reluctantly, "and I'm cold, that's all."

"Oh, she is naughty!" I cried, perceiving the master to be tolerably sober. "She got steeped in the shower of yesterday evening, and there she has sat the night through, and I couldn't prevail on her to stir."

Mr. Earnshaw stared at us in surprise. "The night through," he repeated. "What kept her up? Not fear of the thunder, surely? That was over hours since."

Neither of us wished to mention Heathcliff's absence, as long as we could conceal it, so I replied, I didn't know how she took it into her head to sit up; and she said nothing.

The morning was fresh and cool; I threw back the lattice, and presently the room filled with sweet scents from the garden; but Catherine called peevishly to me,

"Ellen, shut the window. I'm starving!" And her teeth chattered as she shrunk closer to the almost extinguished embers.

"She's ill," said Hindley, taking her wrist; "I suppose that's the reason she would not go to bed. Damn it! I don't want to be troubled with more sickness here. What took you into the rain?"

"Running after t' lads, as usuald!" croaked Joseph, catching an opportunity, from our hesitation, to thrust in his evil tongue. "If Aw wur yah, maister, Aw'd just slam t' boards i' their faces all on 'em, gentle and simple! Never a day ut yah 're off, but yon cat uh Linton comes sneaking hither; and Miss Nelly shoo's a fine lass! shoo sits watching for ye i' t' kitchen; and as yah 're in at one door, he's aht at t' other; und, then, wer grand lady goes a coorting uf hor side! It's bonny behaviour, lurking amang t' fields, after twelve ut' night, wi' that fahl, flaysome divil uf a gipsy, Heathcliff! They think Aw 'm blind; but Aw 'm noan, nowt ut t' soart! Aw seed young Linton, boath coming and going, and Aw seed yah" (directing his discourse to me). "Yah gooid fur nowt, slattenly witch! nip up und bolt intuh th' hahs, t' minute yah heard t' maister's horse fit clatter up t' road."

"Silence, eavesdropper!" cried Catherine. "None of your insolence, before me! Edgar Linton came yesterday, by chance, Hindley; and it was I who told him to be off, because I knew you would not like to have met him as you were."

"You lie, Cathy, no doubt," answered her brother, "and you are a confounded simpleton! But never mind Linton at present; tell me, were you not with Heathcliff last night? Speak the truth, now. You need not be afraid of harming him; though I hate him as much as ever, he did me a good turn a short time since that will make my conscience tender of breaking his neck. To prevent it, I shall send him about his business, this very morning; and after he's gone, I'd advise you to look sharp: I shall only have the more humour for you."

"I never saw Heathcliff last night," answered Catherine, beginning to sob bitterly; "and if you do turn him out of doors, I'll go with him. But, perhaps, you'll never have an opportunity; perhaps he's gone." Here she burst into uncontrollable grief, and the remainder of her words were inarticulate.

Hindley lavished on her a torrent of scornful abuse, and bade her get to her room immediately, or she shouldn't cry for nothing! I obliged her to obey; and I shall never forget what a scene she acted when we reached her chamber; it terrified me. I thought she was going mad, and I begged Joseph to run for the doctor.

It proved the commencement of delirium; Mr. Kenneth, as soon as he saw her, pronounced her dangerously ill; she had a fever.

He bled her, and he told me to let her live on whey and water gruel, and take care she did not throw herself downstairs or out of the window; and then he left, for he had enough to do in the parish, where two or three miles was the ordinary distance between cottage and cottage.

Though I cannot say I made a gentle nurse, and Joseph and the master were no better, and though our patient was as wearisome and headstrong as a patient could be, she weathered it through.

Old Mrs. Linton paid us several visits, to be sure, and set things to rights, and scolded and ordered us all; and when Catherine was convalescent, she insisted on conveying her to Thrushcross Grange, for which deliverance we were very grateful. But the poor dame had reason to repent of her kindness; she and her husband both took the fever, and died within a few days of each other.

Our young lady returned to us, saucier and more passionate and haughtier than ever. Heathcliff had never been heard of since the evening of the thunderstorm; and, one day, I had the misfortune, when she provoked me exceedingly, to lay the blame of his disappearance on her, where indeed it belonged, as she well knew. From that period, for several months, she ceased to hold any communication with me, save in the relation of a mere servant. Joseph fell under a ban also; he would speak his mind, and lecture her all the same as if she were a little girl, and she esteemed herself a woman, and our mistress, and thought that her recent illness gave her a claim to be treated with consideration. Then the doctor had said that she would not bear crossing much, she ought to have her own way; and it was nothing less than murder in her eyes for anyone to presume to stand up and contradict her.

From Mr. Earnshaw and his companions she kept aloof; and tutored by Kenneth, and serious threats of a fit that often attended her rages, her brother allowed her whatever she pleased to demand, and generally avoided aggravating her fiery temper. He was rather too indulgent in humouring her caprices; not from affection, but from pride: he wished earnestly to see her bring honour to the family by an alliance with the Lintons, and as long as she let him alone she might trample us like slaves, for aught he cared!

Edgar Linton, as multitudes have been before and will be after him, was infatuated, and believed himself the happiest man alive on the day he led her to Gimmerton chapel, three years subsequent to his father's death.

Much against my inclination, I was persuaded to leave Wuthering Heights and accompany her here. Little Hareton was nearly five years old, and I had just begun to teach him his letters. We made a sad parting, but Catherine's tears were more powerful than ours. When I refused to go, and when she found her entreaties did not move me, she went lamenting to her husband and brother. The former offered me munificent wages; the latter ordered me to pack up—he wanted no women in the house, he said, now that there was no mistress, and as to Hareton, the curate should take him in hand, by and bye. And so I had but one choice left: to do as I was ordered. I told the master he got rid of all decent people only to run to ruin a little faster; I kissed Hareton good-bye; and since then he has been a stranger, and it's very queer to think it, but I've no doubt he has completely forgotten all about Ellen Dean, and that he was ever more than all the world to her, and she to him!

At this point of the housekeeper's story, she chanced to glance towards the time-piece over the chimney; and was in amazement on seeing the minute-hand measure half-past one. She would not hear of staying a second longer; in truth, I felt rather disposed to defer the sequel of her narrative myself. And now that she is vanished to her rest, and I have meditated for another hour or two, I shall summon courage to go, also, in spite of aching laziness of head and limbs.

CHAPTER 10

A CHARMING introduction to a hermit's life! Four weeks' torture, tossing and sickness! Oh, these bleak winds and bitter northern skies, and impassable roads, and dilatory country surgeons! And, oh, this dearth of the human physiognomy! And, worse than all, the terrible intimation of Kenneth that I need not expect to be out of doors till spring!

Mr. Heathcliff has just honoured me with a call. About seven days ago he sent me a brace of grouse—the last of the season. Scoundrel! He is not altogether guiltless in this illness of mine, and that I had a great mind to tell him. But, alas! how could I offend a man who was charitable enough to sit at my bedside a good hour, and talk on some other subject than pills, and draughts, blisters, and leeches?

This is quite an easy interval. I am too weak to read, yet I feel as if I could enjoy something interesting. Why not have up Mrs. Dean to finish her tale? I can recollect its chief incidents, as far as she had gone. Yes, I remember her hero had run off, and never been heard of for three years; and the heroine was married. I 'll ring; she 'll be delighted to find me capable of talking cheerfully.

Mrs. Dean came.

"It wants twenty minutes, sir, to taking the medicine," she commenced.

"Away, away with it!" I replied; "I desire to have——"

"The doctor says you must drop the powders."

"With all my heart! Don't interrupt me. Come and take your seat here. Keep your fingers from that bitter phalanx of vials. Draw your knitting out of your pocket —that will do—now continue the history of Mr. Heathcliff, from where you left off, to the present day. Did he finish his education on the Continent, and come back a gentleman? or did he get a sizar's place at college, or escape to America, and earn honours by drawing blood from his foster country? or make a fortune more promptly, on the English highways?"

"He may have done a little in all these vocations, Mr. Lockwood, but I couldn't give my word for any. I stated before that I didn't know how he gained his money; neither am I aware of the means he took to raise his mind from the savage ignorance into which it was sunk. But, with your leave, I 'll proceed in my own fashion, if you think it will amuse and not weary you. Are you feeling better this morning?"

"Much."

"That 's good news."

I got Miss Catherine and myself to Thrushcross Grange, and, to my agreeable disappointment, she behaved infinitely better than I dared to expect. She seemed almost overfond of Mr. Linton; and even to his sister, she showed plenty of affection. They were both very attentive to her comfort, certainly. It was not the thorn bending to the honeysuckles, but the honeysuckles embracing the thorn. There were no mutual concessions: one stood erect, and the other yielded; and who can be ill-natured and bad-tempered when they encounter neither opposition nor indifference?

I observed that Mr. Edgar had a deep-rooted fear of

ruffling her humour. He concealed it from her, but if ever he heard me answer sharply, or saw any other servant grow cloudy at some imperious order of hers, he would show his trouble by a frown of displeasure that never darkened on his own account. He many a time spoke sternly to me about my pertness, and averred that the stab of a knife could not inflict a worse pang than he suffered at seeing his lady vexed.

Not to grieve a kind master, I learned to be less touchy; and, for the space of half a year, the gunpowder lay as harmless as sand, because no fire came near to explode it. Catherine had seasons of gloom and silence, now and then: they were respected with sympathizing silence by her husband, who ascribed them to an alteration in her constitution, produced by her perilous illness, as she was never subject to depression of spirits before. The return of sunshine was welcomed by answering sunshine from him. I believe I may assert that they were really in possession of deep and growing happiness.

It ended. Well, we must be for ourselves in the long run; the mild and generous are only more justly selfish than the domineering; and it ended when circumstances caused each to feel that the one's interest was not the chief consideration in the other's thoughts.

On a mellow evening in September, I was coming from the garden with a heavy basket of apples which I had been gathering. It had got dusk, and the moon looked over the high wall of the court, causing undefined shadows to lurk in the corners of the numerous projecting portions of the building. I set my burden on the house steps by the kitchen door, and lingered to rest, and drew in a few more breaths of the soft, sweet air; my eyes were on the moon, and my back to the entrance, when I heard a voice behind me say—

"Nelly, is that you?"

It was a deep voice, and foreign in tone; yet there was something in the manner of pronouncing my name which made it sound familiar. I turned about to discover who spoke, fearfully, for the doors were shut, and I had seen nobody on approaching the steps.

Something stirred in the porch, and, moving nearer, I distinguished a tall man dressed in dark clothes, with dark face and hair. He leant against the side, and held his fingers on the latch as if intending to open for himself.

"Who can it be?" I thought. "Mr. Earnshaw? Oh, no! The voice has no resemblance to his."

"I have waited here an hour," he resumed, while I continued staring, "and the whole of that time all round has been as still as death. I dared not enter. You do not know me? Look, I'm not a stranger!"

A ray fell on his features; the cheeks were sallow, and half covered with black whiskers; the brows lowering, the eyes deep set and singular. I remembered the eyes.

"What!" I cried, uncertain whether to regard him as a worldly visitor, and I raised my hands in amazement. "What! you come back? Is it really you? Is it?"

"Yes, Heathcliff," he replied, glancing from me up to the windows, which reflected a score of glittering moons, but showed no lights from within. "Are they at home? where is she? Nelly, you are not glad! you needn't be so disturbed. Is she here? Speak! I want to have one word with her—your mistress. Go, and say some person from Gimmerton desires to see her."

"How will she take it?" I exclaimed. "What will she do? The surprise bewilders me—it will put her out of her head! And you are Heathcliff? But altered! Nay, there's no comprehending it. Have you been for a soldier?"

"Go and carry my message," he interrupted impatiently. "I'm in hell till you do!"

He lifted the latch, and I entered; but when I got to the parlour where Mr. and Mrs. Linton were, I could not persuade myself to proceed.

At length, I resolved on making an excuse to ask if they would have the candles lighted, and I opened the door.

They sat together in a window whose lattice lay back against the wall, and displayed, beyond the garden trees and the wild green park, the valley of Gimmerton, with a long line of mist winding nearly to its top (for very soon after you pass the chapel, as you may have noticed, the sough that runs from the marshes joins a beck which follows the bend of the glen). Wuthering Heights rose above this silvery vapour; but our old house was invisible; it rather dips down on the other side.

Both the room and its occupants, and the scene they gazed on, looked wondrously peaceful. I shrank reluctantly from performing my errand, and was actually going away leaving it unsaid, after having put my question about the candles, when a sense of my folly compelled me to return, and mutter,

"A person from Gimmerton wishes to see you, ma'am."

"What does he want?" asked Mrs. Linton.

"I did not question him," I answered.

"Well, close the curtains, Nelly," she said, "and bring up tea. I'll be back again directly."

She quitted the apartment; Mr. Edgar inquired, carelessly, who it was.

"Someone mistress does not expect," I replied. "That Heathcliff—you recollect him, sir—who used to live at Mr. Earnshaw's."

"What, the gipsy—the ploughboy?" he cried. "Why did you not say so to Catherine?"

"Hush! you must not call him by those names, master," I said. "She'd be sadly grieved to hear you. She was nearly heartbroken when he ran off. I guess his return will make a jubilee to her."

Mr. Linton walked to a window on the other side of the room that overlooked the court. He unfastened it, and leant out. I suppose they were below, for he exclaimed quickly,

"Don't stand there, love! Bring the person in, if it be anyone particular."

Ere long, I heard the click of the latch, and Catherine flew upstairs, breathless and wild, too excited to show gladness; indeed, by her face, you would rather have surmised an awful calamity.

"Oh, Edgar, Edgar!" she panted, flinging her arms round his neck. "Oh, Edgar, darling! Heathcliff's come back—he is!" And she tightened her embrace to a squeeze.

"Well, well," cried her husband crossly, "don't strangle me for that! He never struck me as such a marvellous treasure. There is no need to be frantic!"

"I know you didn't like him," she answered, repressing a little the intensity of her delight. "Yet, for my sake, you must be friends now. Shall I tell him to come up now?"

"Here?" he said. "Into the parlour?"

"Where else?" she asked.

He looked vexed, and suggested the kitchen as a more suitable place for him.

Mrs. Linton eyed him with a droll expression—half angry, half laughing at his fastidiousness.

"No," she added, after a while, "I cannot sit in the kitchen. Set two tables here, Ellen: one for your master and Miss Isabella, being gentry, the other for Heathcliff and myself, being of the lower orders. Will that please you, dear? Or must I have a fire lighted elsewhere? If so, give directions. I'll run down and secure my guest. I'm afraid the joy is too great to be real!"

She was about to dart off again; but Edgar arrested her.

"You bid him step up," he said, addressing me; "and, Catherine, try to be glad, without being absurd! The whole household need not witness the sight of your welcoming a runaway servant as a brother."

I descended, and found Heathcliff waiting under the porch, evidently anticipating an invitation to enter. He followed my guidance without waste of words, and I ushered him into the presence of the master and mistress, whose flushed cheeks betrayed signs of warm talking. But the lady's glowed with another feeling when her friend appeared at the door; she sprang forward, took both his hands, and led him to Linton, and then she seized Linton's reluctant fingers and crushed them into his.

Now fully revealed by the fire and candlelight, I was amazed, more than ever, to behold the transformation of Heathcliff. He had grown a tall, athletic, well-formed man, beside whom my master seemed quite slender and youthlike. His upright carriage suggested the idea of his having been in the army. His countenance was much older in expression and decision of feature than Mr. Linton's; it looked intelligent, and retained no marks of former degradation. A half-civilized ferocity lurked yet in the depressed brows and eyes full of black fire, but it was subdued; and his manner was even dignified, quite divested of roughness, though too stern for grace.

My master's surprise equalled or exceeded mine; he remained for a minute at a loss how to address the plough-boy, as he had called him. Heathcliff dropped his slight hand, and stood looking at him coolly till he chose to speak.

"Sit down, sir," he said, at length. "Mrs. Linton, recalling old times, would have me give you a cordial reception, and, of course, I am gratified when anything occurs to please her."

"And I also," answered Heathcliff, "especially if it be anything in which I have a part. I shall stay an hour or two willingly."

He took a seat opposite Catherine, who kept her gaze fixed on him as if she feared he would vanish were she to remove it. He did not raise his to her often; a quick glance now and then sufficed; but it flashed back, each time more confidently, the undisguised delight he drank from hers.

They were too much absorbed in their mutual joy to suffer embarrassment. Not so Mr. Edgar: he grew pale with pure annoyance, a feeling that reached its climax when his lady rose, and stepping across the rug, seized Heathcliff's hands again, and laughed like one beside herself.

"I shall think it a dream tomorrow!" she cried. "I shall not be able to believe that I have seen, and touched, and spoken to you once more. And yet, cruel Heathcliff! you don't deserve this welcome. To be absent and silent for three years, and never to think of me!"

"A little more than you have thought of me," he murmured. "I heard of your marriage, Cathy, not long since; and, while waiting in the yard below, I meditated this plan:—just to have one glimpse of your face, a stare of surprise, perhaps, and pretended pleasure; afterwards settle my score with Hindley; and then prevent the law by doing execution on myself. Your welcome has put these ideas out of my mind; but beware of meeting me with another aspect next time! Nay, you'll not drive me off again. You were really sorry for me, were you? Well, there was cause. I've fought through a bitter life since I last heard your voice, and you must forgive me, for I struggled only for you!"

"Catherine, unless we are to have cold tea, please to come to the table," interrupted Linton, striving to preserve his ordinary tone, and a due measure of politeness.

(97)

"Mr. Heathcliff will have a long walk, wherever he may lodge tonight; and I'm thirsty."

She took her post before the urn, and Miss Isabella came, summoned by the bell; then, having handed their chairs forward, I left the room.

The meal hardly endured ten minutes. Catherine's cup was never filled; she could neither eat nor drink. Edgar had made a slop in his saucer, and scarcely swallowed a mouthful.

Their guest did not protract his stay that evening above an hour longer. I asked, as he departed, if he went to Gimmerton.

"No, to Wuthering Heights," he answered. "Mr. Earnshaw invited me, when I called this morning."

Mr. Earnshaw invited *him!* and *he* called on Mr. Earnshaw! I pondered this sentence painfully after he was gone. Is he turning out a bit of a hypocrite and coming into the country to work mischief under a cloak? I mused. I had a presentiment, in the bottom of my heart, that he had better have remained away.

About the middle of the night, I was awakened from my first nap by Mrs. Linton gliding into my chamber, taking a seat on my bedside, and pulling me by the hair to rouse me.

"I cannot rest, Ellen," she said, by way of apology. "And I want some living creature to keep me company in my happiness! Edgar is sulky, because I'm glad of a thing that does not interest him; he refuses to open his mouth, except to utter pettish, silly speeches, and he affirmed I was cruel and selfish for wishing to talk when he was so sick and sleepy. He always contrives to be sick at the least cross! I gave a few sentences of commendation to Heathcliff, and he, either for a headache or a pang of envy, began to cry; so I got up and left him."

"What use is it praising Heathcliff to him?" I answered. "As lads they had an aversion to each other, and Heathcliff would hate just as much to hear him praised; it's human nature. Let Mr. Linton alone about him, unless you would like an open quarrel between them."

"But does it not show great weakness?" pursued she. "I'm not envious; I never feel hurt at the brightness of Isabella's yellow hair and the whiteness of her skin, at her dainty elegance, and the fondness all the family

(98)

exhibit for her. Even you, Nelly, if we have a dispute sometimes, you back Isabella at once, and I yield like a foolish mother; I call her a darling, and flatter her into a good temper. It pleases her brother to see us cordial, and that pleases me. But they are very much alike—they are spoiled children, and fancy the world was made for their accommodation; and though I humour both, I think a smart chastisement might improve them, all the same."

"You 're mistaken, Mrs. Linton," said I. "They humour you; I know what there would be to do if they did not. You can well afford to indulge their passing whims as long as their business is to anticipate all your desires. You may, however, fall out, at last, over something of equal consequence to both sides; and then those you term weak are very capable of being as obstinate as you."

"And then we shall fight to the death, shan't we, Nelly?" she returned, laughing. "No! I tell you, I have such faith in Linton's love, that I believe I might kill him, and he wouldn't wish to retaliate."

I advised her to value him the more for his affection.

"I do," she answered, "but he needn't resort to whining for trifles. It is childish; and, instead of melting into tears because I said that Heathcliff was now worthy of anyone's regard, and it would honour the first gentleman in the country to be his friend, he ought to have said it for me, and been delighted from sympathy. He must get accustomed to him, and he may as well like him; considering how Heathcliff has reason to object to him, I 'm sure he behaved excellently!"

"What do you think of his going to Wuthering Heights?" I inquired. "He is reformed in every respect, apparently—quite a Christian, offering the right hand of fellowship to his enemies all around!"

"He explained it," she replied. "I wondered as much as you. He said he called to gather information concerning me from you, supposing you resided there still, and Joseph told Hindley, who came out and fell to questioning him of what he had been doing, and how he had been living, and finally, desired him to walk in. There were some persons sitting at cards; Heathcliff joined them; my brother lost some money to him, and, finding him plentifully supplied, he requested that he would come again in the evening, to which he consented. Hindley is too reckless to select his acquaintance prudently; he doesn't trouble himself to reflect on the causes he might have for mistrusting one whom he has basely injured. But Heathcliff affirms his principal reason for resuming a connection with his ancient persecutor is a wish to install himself in quarters at walking distance from the Grange, and an attachment to the house where we lived together; and likewise a hope that I shall have more opportunities of seeing him there than I could have if he settled in Gimmerton. He means to offer liberal payment for permission to lodge at the Heights, and doubtless my brother's covetousness will prompt him to accept the terms—he was always greedy; though what he grasps with one hand he flings away with the other."

"It's a nice place for a young man to fix his dwelling in!" said I. "Have you no fear of the consequences, Mrs. Linton?"

"None for my friend," she replied; "his strong head will keep him from danger; a little for Hindley, but he can't be made morally worse than he is, and I stand between him and bodily harm. The event of this evening has reconciled me to God and humanity! I had risen in angry rebellion against Providence. Oh, I've endured very, very bitter misery, Nelly! If that creature knew how bitter, he'd be ashamed to cloud its removal with idle petulance. It was kindness for him which induced me to bear it alone; had I expressed the agony I frequently felt, he would have been taught to long for its alleviation as ardently as I. However, it's over, and I'll take no revenge on his folly; I can afford to suffer anything hereafter! Should the meanest thing alive slap me on the cheek, I'd not only turn the other, but I'd ask pardon for provoking it; and, as a proof, I'll go make my peace with Edgar instantly. Good night! I'm an angel!"

In this self-complacent conviction she departed; and the success of her fulfilled resolution was obvious on the morrow: Mr. Linton had not only abjured his peevishness (though his spirits seemed still subdued by Catherine's exuberance of vivacity), but he ventured no objection to her taking Isabella with her to Wuthering Heights in the afternoon; and she regarded him with such a summer of sweetness and affection in return, as made the house a paradise for several days, both master and servants profiting from the perpetual sunshine.

Heathcliff—Mr. Heathcliff, I should say in future—used the liberty of visiting at Thrushcross Grange cautiously, at first; he seemed estimating how far its owner would bear his intrusion. Catherine, also, deemed it judicious to moderate her expressions of pleasure in receiving him; and he gradually established his right to be expected.

He retained a great deal of the reserve for which his boyhood was remarkable, and that served to repress all startling demonstrations of feeling. My master's uneasiness experienced a lull, and further circumstances diverted it into another channel for a space.

His new source of trouble sprang from the not anticipated misfortune of Isabella Linton evincing a sudden and irresistible attraction towards the tolerated guest. She was at that time a charming young lady of eighteen; infantile in manners, though possessed of keen wit, keen feelings, and a keen temper, too, if irritated. Her brother, who loved her tenderly, was appalled at this fantastic preference. Leaving aside the degradation of an alliance with a nameless man, and the possible fact that his property, in default of heirs male, might pass into such a one's power, he had sense to comprehend Heathcliff's disposition—to know that, though his exterior was altered, his mind was unchangeable, and unchanged. And he dreaded that mind; it revolted him; he shrank forebodingly from the idea of committing Isabella to its keeping.

He would have recoiled still more had he been aware that her attachment rose unsolicited, and was bestowed where it awakened no reciprocation of sentiment; for the minute he discovered its existence, he laid the blame on Heathcliff's deliberate designing.

We had all remarked, during some time, that Miss Linton fretted and pined over something. She grew cross and wearisome, snapping at and teasing Catherine continually, at the imminent risk of exhausting her limited patience. We excused her to a certain extent, on the plea of ill-health: she was dwindling and fading before our eyes. But one day, when she had been particularly wayward, rejecting her breakfast, complaining that the servants did not do what she told them; that the mistress would allow her to be nothing in the house, and Edgar neglected her; that she had caught a cold with the doors being left open, and we let the parlour fire go out on purpose to vex her, with a hundred yet more frivolous accusations, Mrs. Linton peremptorily insisted that she should go to bed; and, having scolded her heartily, threatened to send for the doctor.

Mention of Kenneth caused her to exclaim, instantly, that her health was perfect, and it was only Catherine's harshness which made her unhappy.

"How can you say I am harsh, you naughty fondling?" cried the mistress, amazed at the unreasonable assertion. "You are surely losing your reason. When have I been harsh, tell me?"

"Yesterday," sobbed Isabella, "and now!"

"Yesterday!" said her sister-in-law. "On what occasion?"

"In our walk along the moor; you told me to ramble where I pleased, while you sauntered on with Mr. Heathcliff!"

"And that's your notion of harshness?" said Catherine, laughing. "It was no hint that your company was superfluous; we didn't care whether you kept with us or not. I merely thought Heathcliff's talk would have nothing entertaining for your ears."

"Oh no," wept the young lady, "you wished me away, because you know I liked to be there!"

"Is she sane?" asked Mrs. Linton, appealing to me. "I'll repeat our conversation, word for word, Isabella, and you point out any charm it could have had for you."

"I don't mind the conversation," she answered. "I wanted to be with——"

"Well!" said Catherine, perceiving her hesitate to complete the sentence.

"With him; and I won't be always sent off!" she continued, kindling up. "You are a dog in the manger, Cathy, and desire no one to be loved but yourself!"

"You are an impertinent little monkey!" exclaimed Mrs. Linton, in surprise. "But I'll not believe this idiocy! It is impossible that you can covet the admiration of Heathcliff—that you can consider him an agreeable person! I hope I have misunderstood you, Isabella?"

"No, you have not," said the infatuated girl. "I love him more than ever you loved Edgar; and he might love me, if you would let him!"

"I wouldn't be you for a kingdom, then!" Catherine declared, emphatically, and she seemed to speak sincerely. "Nelly, help me to convince her of her madness. Tell her what Heathcliff is—an unreclaimed creature, without refinement, without cultivation; an arid wilderness of furze and whinstone. I'd as soon put that little canary into the park on a winter's day, as recommend you to bestow your heart on him! It is deplorable ignorance of his character, child, and nothing else, which makes that dream enter your head. Pray, don't imagine that he conceals depths of benevolence and affection beneath a stern exterior! He's not a rough diamond—a pearl-containing oyster of a rustic: he's a fierce, pitiless, wolfish man. I never say to him, 'Let this or that enemy alone, because it would be ungenerous or cruel to harm them'; I say, 'Let them alone, because I should hate them to be wronged'; and he'd crush you like a sparrow's egg, Isabella, if he found you a troublesome charge. I know he couldn't love a Linton, and yet he'd be quite capable of marrying your fortune and expectations—avarice is growing with him a besetting sin. There's my picture; and I'm his friend—so much so, that had he thought seriously to catch you, I should, perhaps, have held my tongue, and let you fall into his trap."

Miss Linton regarded her sister-in-law with indignation.

"For shame! for shame!" she repeated angrily. "You are worse than twenty foes, you poisonous friend!"

"Ah! you won't believe me, then?" said Catherine. "You think I speak from wicked selfishness?"

"I'm certain you do," retorted Isabella, "and I shudder at you!"

"Good!" cried the other. "Try for yourself, if that be your spirit. I have done, and yield the argument to your saucy insolence."

"And I must suffer for her egotism!" she sobbed, as Mrs. Linton left the room. "All, all is against me; she has blighted my single consolation. But she uttered falsehoods, didn't she? Mr. Heathcliff is not a fiend; he has an honourable soul, and a true one, or how could he remember her?"

"Banish him from your thoughts, Miss," I said. "He's a bird of bad omen: no mate for you. Mrs. Linton spoke strongly, and yet I can't contradict her. She is better acquainted with his heart than I, or anyone besides, and she never would represent him as worse than he is. Honest people don't hide their deeds. How has he been living? how has he got rich? why is he staying at Wuthering Heights, the house of a man whom he abhors? They say Mr. Earnshaw is worse and worse since he came. They sit up all night together continually, and Hindley has been borrowing money on his land, and does nothing but play and drink, I heard only a week ago—it was Joseph who told me—I met him at Gimmerton:

"'Nelly,' he said, 'we's hae a Crahnr's 'quest enah, at ahr folks. One on 'em's a'most gotten his finger cut off wi' hauding t' other froo' sticking hisseln loike a cawlf. That's maister, yah knaw, ut's soa up uh going tuh t' grand 'sizes. He's noan feard uh t' Bench uh judges, norther Paul, nur Peter, nur John, nor Matthew, nor noan on 'em, nut he! He fair like's he langs tuh set his brazened face agean 'em! And yon bonny lad Heathcliff, yah mind, he's a rare un! He can girn a laugh, as well's onybody at a raight divil's jest. Does he niver say nowt of his fine living amang us, when he goas tuh t' Grange? This is t' way on 't—up at sun-dahn; dice, brandy, cloised shutters, und can'le lught till next day, at nooin; then, t' fooil gangs banning un raving tuh his cham'er, makking dacent fowks dig thur fingers i' thur lugs fur varry shaume; un' the knave, wah, he carn cahnt his brass, un' ate, un' sleep, un' off tuh his neighbour's tuh gossip wi' t' wife. I' course, he tells Dame Catherine hah hor father's goold runs intuh his pocket, and her fathur's son gallops dahn t' Broad road, while he flees afore tuh oppen t' pikes?' Now, Miss Linton, Joseph is an old rascal, but no liar; and, if his account of Heathcliff's conduct be true, you would never think of desiring such a husband, would you?"

"You are leagued with the rest, Ellen!" she replied. "I'll not listen to your slanders. What malevolence you must have to wish to convince me that there is no happiness in the world!"

Whether she would have got over this fancy if left to herself, or persevered in nursing it perpetually, I cannot say; she had little time to reflect. The day after, there was a justice meeting at the next town; my master was obliged to attend, and Mr. Heathcliff, aware of his absence, called rather earlier than usual.

Catherine and Isabella were sitting in the library, on hostile terms, but silent. The latter alarmed at her recent indiscretion, and the disclosure she had made of her secret feelings in a transcient fit of passion; the former, on mature consideration, really offended with her companion; and, if she laughed again at her pertness, inclined to make it no laughing matter to her.

She did laugh as she saw Heathcliff pass the window. I was sweeping the hearth, and I noticed a mischievous smile on her lips. Isabella, absorbed in her meditations, or a book, remained till the door opened; and it was too late to attempt an escape, which she would gladly have done had it been practicable.

"Come in, that's right!" exclaimed the mistress gaily, pulling a chair to the fire. "Here are two people sadly in need of a third to thaw the ice between them, and you are the very one we should both of us choose. Heathcliff, I'm proud to show you, at last, somebody that dotes on you more than myself. I expect you to feel flattered. Nay, it's not Nelly; don't look at her! My poor little sister-in-law is breaking her heart by mere contemplation of your physical and moral beauty. It lies in your own power to be Edgar's brother! No, no, Isabella, you sha'n't run off," she continued, arresting with feigned playfulness the confounded girl, who had risen indignantly. "We were quarreling like cats about you, Heathcliff, and I was fairly beaten in protestations of devotion and admiration; and, moreover, I was informed that if I would but have the manners to stand aside, my rival, as she will have herself to be, would shoot a shaft into your soul that would fix you forever, and send my image into eternal oblivion!"

"Catherine!" said Isabella, calling up her dignity, and disdaining to struggle from the tight grasp that held her. "I'd thank you to adhere to the truth and not slander me, even in joke! Mr. Heathcliff, be kind enough to bid this friend of yours release me; she forgets that you and I are not intimate acquaintances; and what amuses her is painful to me beyond expression."

As the guest answered nothing, but took his seat and looked thoroughly indifferent what sentiments she cherished concerning him, she turned and whispered an earnest appeal for liberty to her tormentor.

"By no means!" cried Mrs. Linton in answer. "I won't be named a dog in the manger again. You *shall* stay. Now then! Heathcliff, why don't you evince satisfaction at my pleasant news? Isabella swears that the love Edgar has for me is nothing to that she entertains for you. I'm sure she made some speech of the kind, did she not, Ellen? And she has fasted ever since the day before yesterday's walk, from sorrow and rage that I despatched her out of your society under the idea of its being unacceptable."

"I think you belie her," said Heathcliff, twisting his chair to face them. "She wishes to be out of my society now, at any rate!"

And he stared hard at the object of discourse, as one might do at a strange repulsive animal—a centipede from the Indies, for instance, which curiosity leads one to examine in spite of the aversion it raises.

The poor thing couldn't bear that; she grew white and red in rapid succession, and, while tears beaded her lashes, bent the strength of her small fingers to loosen the firm clutch of Catherine; and perceiving that as fast as she raised one finger off her arm another closed down, and she could not remove the whole together, she began to make use of her nails, and their sharpness presently ornamented the detainer's with crescents of red.

"There's a tigress!" exclaimed Mrs. Linton, setting her free, and shaking her hand with pain. "Begone, for God's sake, and hide your vixen face! How foolish to reveal those talons to him. Can't you fancy the conclusions he'll draw? Look, Heathcliff! they are instruments that will do execution—you must beware of your eyes."

"I'd wrench them off her fingers, if they ever menaced me," he answered brutally, when the door had closed after her. "But what did you mean by teasing the creature in that manner, Cathy? You were not speaking the truth, were you?"

"I assure you I was," she returned. "She has been pining for your sake several weeks, and raving about you this morning, and pouring forth a deluge of abuse, because I represented your failings in a plain light, for the purpose of mitigating her adoration. But don't notice it further; I wished to punish her sauciness, that's all. I like her too well, my dear Heathcliff, to let you absolutely seize and devour her up."

"And I like her too ill to attempt it," said he, "except in a very ghoulish fashion. You'd hear of odd things if I lived alone with that mawkish, waxen face; the most ordinary would be painting on its white the colours of the rainbow and turning the blue eyes black, every day or two; they detestably resemble Linton's."

"Delectably!" observed Catherine. "They are dove's eyes—angel's!"

"She's her brother's heir, is she not?" he asked, after a brief silence.

"I should be sorry to think so," returned his companion. "Half a dozen nephews shall erase her title, please Heaven. Abstract your mind from the subject at present—you are too prone to covet your neighbour's goods; remember *this* neighbour's goods are mine."

"If they were *mine*, they would be none the less that," said Heathcliff; "but though Isabella Linton may be silly, she is scarcely mad; and, in short, we'll dismiss the matter, as you advise."

From their tongues, they did dismiss it; and Catherine, probably, from her thoughts. The other, I felt certain, recalled it often in the course of the evening. I saw him smile to himself—grin rather—and lapse into ominous musing whenever Mrs. Linton had occasion to be absent from the apartment.

I determined to watch his movements. My heart invariably cleaved to the master's, in preference to Catherine's side—with reason I imagined, for he was kind, and trustful, and honourable; and she—she could not be called the *opposite*, yet she seemed to allow herself such wide latitude, that I had little faith in her principles, and still less sympathy for her feelings. I wanted something to happen which might have the effect of freeing both Wuthering Heights and the Grange of Mr. Heathcliff, quietly; leaving us as we had been prior to his advent. His visits were a continual nightmare to me, and, I suspected, to my master also. His abode at the Heights was an oppression past explaining. I felt that God had forsaken the stray sheep there to its own wicked wanderings, and an evil beast prowled between it and the fold, waiting his time to spring and destroy.

CHAPTER 11

SOMETIMES, while meditating on these things in solitude, I've got up in a sudden terror, and put on my bonnet to go and see how all was at the farm. I've persuaded my conscience that it was a duty to warn him how people talked regarding his ways; and then I've recollected his confirmed bad habits, and, hopeless of benefiting him, have flinched from re-entering the dismal house, doubting if I could bear to be taken at my word.

One time I passed the old gate, going out of my way, on a journey to Gimmerton. It was about the period that my narrative has reached—a bright frosty afternoon, the ground bare, and the road hard and dry.

I came to a stone where the highway branches off on to the moor at your left hand; a rough sand-pillar, with the letters W. H. cut on its north side, on the east, G., and on the southwest, T. G. It serves as guidepost to the Grange, and Heights, and village.

The sun shone yellow on its grey head, reminding me of summer; and I cannot say why, but all at once, a gush of child's sensations flowed into my heart. Hindley and I held it a favourite spot twenty years before.

I gazed long at the weather-worn block, and, stooping down, perceived a hole near the bottom still full of snail-shells and pebbles, which we were very fond of storing there with more perishable things; and, as fresh as reality, it appeared that I beheld my early playmate seated on the withered turf, his dark, square head bent forward, and his little hand scooping out the earth with a piece of slate.

"Poor Hindley!" I exclaimed involuntarily.

I started—my bodily eye was cheated into a momentary belief that the child lifted its face and stared straight into mine! It vanished in a twinkling, but immediately I felt an irresistible yearning to be at the Heights. Superstition urged me to comply with this impulse. Supposing he should be dead! I thought—or should die soon!—supposing it were a sign of death!

The nearer I got to the house the more agitated I grew, and on catching sight of it I trembled in every limb. The apparition had outstripped me: it stood looking through the gate. That was my first idea on observing an elf-locked, brown-eyed boy setting his ruddy countenance against the bars. Further reflection suggested this must be Hareton, my Hareton, not altered greatly since I left him, ten months since.

"God bless thee, darling!" I cried, forgetting instantaneously my foolish fears. "Hareton, it's Nelly! Nelly, thy nurse."

He retreated out of arm's length, and picked up a large flint.

"I am come to see thy father, Hareton," I added, guessing from the action that Nelly, if she lived in his memory at all, was not recognized as one with me.

He raised his missile to hurl it; I commenced a soothing speech, but could not stay the hand—the stone struck my bonnet; and then ensued, from the stammering lips of the little fellow, a string of curses, which, whether he comprehended them or not, were delivered with practised emphasis, and distorted his baby features into a shocking expression of malignity. You may be certain this grieved more than angered me. Fit to cry, I took an orange from my pocket, and offered it to propitiate him. He hesitated, and then snatched it from my hold, as if he fancied I only intended to tempt and disappoint him. I showed another, keeping it out of his reach.

"Who has taught you those fine words, my bairn?" I inquired. "The curate?"

"Damn the curate, and thee! Gie me that," he replied.

"Tell us where you got your lessons, and you shall have it," said I. "Who's your master?"

"Devil daddy," was his answer.

"And what do you learn from Daddy?" I continued.

He jumped at the fruit; I raised it higher. "What does he teach you?" I asked.

"Naught," said he, "but to keep out of his gait. Daddy cannot bide me, because I swear at him."

"Ah! and the devil teaches you to swear at Daddy?" I observed.

"Ay—nay," he drawled.

"Who, then?"

"Heathcliff."

I asked if he liked Mr. Heathcliff.

"Ay!" he answered again.

Desiring to have his reasons for liking him, I could only gather the sentences—"I known't—he pays Dad back what he gies to me—he curses Daddy for cursing me. He says I mun do as I will."

"And the curate does not teach you to read and write, then?" I pursued.

"No, I was told the curate should have his —— teeth dashed down his —— throat, if he stepped over the threshold—Heathcliff had promised that!"

I put the orange in his hand, and bade him tell his father that a woman called Nelly Dean was waiting to speak with him, by the garden gate.

He went up the walk, and entered the house; but, instead of Hindley, Heathcliff appeared on the door stones; and I turned directly and ran down the road as hard as ever I could race, making no halt till I gained the guidepost, and feeling as scared as if I had raised a goblin.

This is not much connected with Miss Isabella's affair; except that it urged me to resolve further on mounting vigilant guard, and doing my utmost to check the spread of such bad influence at the Grange, even though I should wake a domestic storm, by thwarting Mrs. Linton's pleasure.

The next time Heathcliff came, my young lady chanced to be feeding some pigeons in the court. She had never spoken a word to her sister-in-law for three days, but she had likewise dropped her fretful complaining, and we found it a great comfort.

Heathcliff had not the habit of bestowing a single unnecessary civility on Miss Linton, I knew. Now, as soon as he beheld her, his first precaution was to take a

sweeping survey of the house-front. I was standing by the
kitchen window, but I drew out of sight. He then
stepped across the pavement to her, and said something;
she seemed embarrassed, and desirous of getting away;
to prevent it, he laid his hand on her arm. She averted
her face—he apparently put some question which she
had no mind to answer. There was another rapid glance
at the house, and supposing himself unseen, the scoundrel had the impudence to embrace her.

"Judas! Traitor!" I ejaculated. "You are a hypocrite,
too, are you? A deliberate deceiver."

"Who is, Nelly?" said Catherine's voice at my elbow; I
had been over-intent on watching the pair outside to
mark her entrance.

"Your worthless friend!" I answered warmly; "the
sneaking rascal yonder. Ah, he has caught a glimpse of
us—he is coming in! I wonder will he have the art to
find a plausible excuse for making love to Miss, when he
told you he hated her?"

Mrs. Linton saw Isabella tear herself free, and run into
the garden; and a minute after, Heathcliff opened the
door.

I couldn't withhold giving some loose to my indignation; but Catherine angrily insisted on silence, and
threatened to order me out of the kitchen, if I dared
to be so presumptuous as to put in my insolent tongue.

"To hear you, people might think you were the mistress!" she cried. "You want setting down in your right
place! Heathcliff, what are you about, raising this stir? I
said you must let Isabella alone!—I beg you will, unless
you are tired of being received here, and wish Linton to
draw the bolts against you!"

"God forbid that he should try!" answered the black
villain. I detested him just then. "God keep him meek
and patient! Every day I grow madded after sending
him to heaven!"

"Hush!" said Catherine, shutting the inner door.
"Don't vex me. Why have you disregarded my request?
Did she come across you on purpose?"

"What is it to you?" he growled. "I have a right to
kiss her, if she chooses, and you have no right to object.
I'm not your husband; you needn't be jealous of me!"

"I'm not jealous of you," replied the mistress; "I'm

jealous for you. Clear your face; you shan't scowl at me! If you like Isabella, you shall marry her. But do you like her? Tell the truth, Heathcliff! There, you won't answer. I'm certain you don't!"

"And would Mr. Linton approve of his sister marrying that man?" I inquired.

"Mr. Linton should approve," returned my lady decisively.

"He might spare himself the trouble," said Heathcliff. "I could do as well without his approbation. And as to you, Catherine, I have a mind to speak a few words now, while we are at it. I want you to be aware that I know you have treated me infernally—infernally! Do you hear? And if you flatter yourself that I don't perceive it, you are a fool; and if you think I can be consoled by sweet words, you are an idiot; and if you fancy I'll suffer unrevenged, I'll convince you of the contrary, in a very little while! Meantime, thank you for telling me your sister-in-law's secret: I swear I'll make the most of it. And stand you aside!"

"What new phase of his character is this?" exclaimed Mrs. Linton, in amazement. "I've treated you infernally —and you'll take revenge! How will you take it, ungrateful brute? How have I treated you infernally?"

"I seek no revenge on you," replied Heathcliff less vehemently. "That's not the plan. The tyrant grinds down his slaves and they don't turn against him; they crush those beneath them. You are welcome to torture me to death for your amusement, only allow me to amuse myself a little in the same style, and refrain from insult as much as you are able. Having levelled my palace, don't erect a hovel and complacently admire your own charity in giving me that for a home. If I imagined you really wished me to marry Isabella, I'd cut my throat!"

"Oh, the evil is that I am not jealous, is it?" cried Catherine. "Well, I won't repeat my offer of a wife; it is as bad as offering Satan a lost soul. Your bliss lies, like his, in inflicting misery. You prove it. Edgar is restored from the ill-temper he gave way to at your coming; I begin to be secure and tranquil; and you, restless to know us at peace, appear resolved on exciting a quarrel. Quarrel with Edgar, if you please, Heathcliff, and deceive his sister; you'll hit on exactly the most efficient method of revenging yourself on me."

The conversation ceased. Mrs. Linton sat down by the fire, flushed and gloomy. The spirit which served her was growing intractable; she could neither lay nor control it. He stood on the hearth with folded arms, brooding on his evil thoughts; and in this position I left them to seek the master, who was wondering what kept Catherine below so long.

"Ellen," said he, when I entered, "have you seen your mistress?"

"Yes, she's in the kitchen, sir," I answered. "She's sadly put out by Mr. Heathcliff's behaviour, and, indeed, I do think it's time to arrange his visits on another footing. There's harm in being too soft, and now it's come to this——" And I related the scene in the court, and, as near as I dared, the whole subsequent dispute. I fancied it could not be very prejudicial to Mrs. Linton, unless she made it so afterwards, by assuming the defensive for her guest.

Edgar Linton had difficulty in hearing me to the close. His first words revealed that he did not clear his wife of blame.

"This is insufferable!" he exclaimed. "It is disgraceful that she should own him for a friend, and force his company on me! Call me two men out of the hall, Ellen. Catherine shall linger no longer to argue with the low ruffian—I have humoured her enough."

He descended, and bidding the servants wait in the passage, went, followed by me, to the kitchen. Its occupants had recommenced their angry discussion—Mrs. Linton, at least, was scolding with renewed vigour. Heathcliff had moved to the window, and hung his head, somewhat cowed by her violent rating apparently.

He saw the master first, and made a hasty motion that she should be silent, which she obeyed, abruptly, on discovering the reason of his intimation.

"How is this?" said Linton, addressing her; "what notion of propriety must you have to remain here, after the language which has been held to you by that blackguard? I suppose, because it is his ordinary talk, you think nothing of it; you are habituated to his baseness, and, perhaps, imagine I can get used to it too!"

"Have you been listening at the door, Edgar?" asked the mistress, in a tone particularly calculated to provoke her husband, implying both carelessness and contempt of his irritation.

Heathcliff, who had raised his eyes at the former speech, gave a sneering laugh at the latter, on purpose, it seemed, to draw Mr. Linton's attention to him.

He succeeded; but Edgar did not mean to entertain him with any high flights of passion.

"I have been so far forbearing with you, sir," he said quietly; "not that I was ignorant of your miserable, degraded character, but I felt you were only partly responsible for that; and Catherine wishing to keep up your acquaintance, I acquiesced—foolishly. Your presence is a moral poison that would contaminate the most virtuous. For that cause, and to prevent worse consequences, I shall deny you hereafter admission into this house, and give notice now that I require your instant departure. Three minutes' delay will render it involuntary and ignominious."

Heathcliff measured the height and breadth of the speaker with an eye full of derision.

"Cathy, this lamb of yours threatens like a bull!" he said. "It is in danger of splitting its skull against my knuckles. By God! Mr. Linton, I'm mortally sorry that you are not worth knocking down!"

My master glanced towards the passage, and signed me to fetch the men; he had no intention of hazarding a personal encounter.

I obeyed the hint, but Mrs. Linton, suspecting something, followed, and when I attempted to call them, she pulled me back, slammed the door to, and locked it.

"Fair means!" she said, in answer to her husband's look of angry surprise. "If you have not the courage to attack him, make an apology, or allow yourself to be beaten. It will correct you of feigning more valour than you possess. No, I'll swallow the key before you shall get it! I'm delightfully rewarded for my kindness to each! After constant indulgence of one's weak nature and the other's bad one, I earn, for thanks, two samples of blind ingratitude, stupid to absurdity! Edgar, I was defending you and yours; and I wish Heathcliff may flog you sick, for daring to think an evil thought of me!"

It did not need the medium of a flogging to produce that effect on the master. He tried to wrest the key from Catherine's grasp, and for safety she flung it into the hottest part of the fire; whereupon Mr. Edgar was taken with a nervous trembling, and his countenance grew deadly pale. For his life he could not avert that access of emotion; mingled anguish and humiliation overcame him completely. He leant on the back of a chair, and covered his face.

"Oh! Heavens! In old days this would win you knighthood!" exclaimed Mrs. Linton. "We are vanquished! we are vanquished! Heathcliff would as soon lift a finger at you as the king would march his army against a colony of mice. Cheer up! you sha'n't be hurt! Your type is not a lamb, it's a sucking leveret."

"I wish you joy of the milk-blooded coward, Cathy!" said her friend. "I compliment you on your taste. And that is the slavering, shivering thing you preferred to me! I would not strike him with my fist, but I'd kick him with my foot, and experience considerable satisfaction. Is he weeping, or is he going to faint for fear?"

The fellow approached and gave the chair on which Linton rested a push. He'd better have kept his distance: my master quickly sprang erect, and struck him full on the throat a blow that would have levelled a slighter man.

It took his breath for a minute; and, while he choked, Mr. Linton walked out by the back door into the yard, and from thence, to the front entrance.

"There! you've done with coming here," cried Catherine. "Get away, now; he'll return with a brace of pistols, and half a dozen assistants. If he did overhear us, of course, he'd never forgive you. You've played me an ill turn, Heathcliff! But, go—make haste! I'd rather see Edgar at bay than you."

"Do you suppose I'm going with that blow burning in my gullet?" he thundered. "By hell, no! I'll crush his ribs in like a rotten hazelnut, before I cross the threshold! If I don't floor him now, I shall murder him some time; so, as you value his existence, let me get at him!"

"He is not coming," I interposed, framing a bit of a lie. "There's the coachman, and the two gardeners; you'll surely not wait to be thrust into the road by them! Each has a bludgeon, and master will, very likely, be watching from the parlour windows to see that they fulfill his orders."

The gardeners and coachman were there; but Linton was with them. They had already entered the court. Heathcliff, on second thoughts, resolved to avoid a struggle against three underlings: he seized the poker, smashed the lock from the inner door, and made his escape as they tramped in.

Mrs. Linton, who was very much excited, bade me accompany her up stairs. She did not know my share in contributing to the disturbance, and I was anxious to keep her in ignorance.

"I'm nearly distracted, Nelly!" she exclaimed, throwing herself on the sofa. "A thousand smiths' hammers are beating in my head! Tell Isabella to shun me; this uproar is owing to her, and should she or any one else aggravate my anger at present, I shall get wild. And, Nelly, say to Edgar, if you see him again tonight, that I'm in danger of being seriously ill. I wish it may prove true. He has startled and distressed me shockingly! I want to frighten him. Besides, he might come and begin a string of abuse or complainings; I'm certain I should recriminate, and God knows where we should end! Will you do so, my good Nelly? You are aware that I am no way blameable in this matter. What possessed him to turn listener? Heathcliff's talk was outrageous, after you left us; but I could soon have diverted him from Isabella, and the rest meant nothing. Now, all is dashed wrong by the fool's craving to hear evil of self that haunts some people like a demon! Had Edgar never gathered our conversation, he would never have been the worse for it. Really, when he opened on me in that unreasonable tone of displeasure, after I had scolded Heathcliff till I was hoarse for *him*, I did not care, hardly, what they did to each other, especially as I felt that, however the scene closed, we should all be driven asunder for nobody knows how long! Well, if I cannot keep Heathcliff for my friend—if Edgar will be mean and jealous, I'll try to break their hearts by breaking my own. That will be a prompt way of finishing all, when I am pushed to extremity! But it's a deed to be reserved for a forlorn hope; I'd not take Linton by surprise with it. To this point he has been discreet in dreading to provoke me; you must represent the peril of quitting that policy, and remind him of my passionate temper, verging, when kindled, on frenzy. I wish you could dismiss that apathy out of your countenance, and look rather more anxious about me!"

The stolidity with which I received these instructions was, no doubt, rather exasperating; for they were delivered in perfect sincerity; but I believed a person who could plan the turning of her fits of passion to account, beforehand, might, by exerting her will, manage to control herself tolerably, even while under their influence, and I did not wish to "frighten" her husband, as she said, and multiply his annoyances for the purpose of serving her selfishness.

Therefore I said nothing when I met the master coming towards the parlour; but I took the liberty of turning back to listen whether they would resume their quarrel together.

He began to speak first.

"Remain where you are, Catherine," he said, without any anger in his voice, but with much sorrowful despondency. "I shall not stay. I am neither come to wrangle nor be reconciled; but I wish just to learn whether, after this evening's events, you intend to continue your intimacy with ——"

"Oh, for mercy's sake," interrupted the mistress, stamping her foot, "for mercy's sake, let us hear no more of it now! Your cold blood cannot be worked into a fever—your veins are full of ice-water; but mine are boiling, and the sight of such chillness makes them dance."

"To get rid of me, answer my question," persevered Mr. Linton. "You must answer it; and that violence does not alarm me. I have found that you can be as stoical as anyone, when you please. Will you give up Heathcliff hereafter, or will you give up me? It is impossible for you to be my friend and his at the same time, and I absolutely require to know which you choose."

"I require to be let alone!" exclaimed Catherine, furiously. "I demand it! Don't you see I can scarcely stand? Edgar, you—you leave me!"

She rung the bell till it broke with a twang; I entered leisurely. It was enough to try the temper of a saint, such senseless, wicked rages! There she lay dashing her head against the arm of the sofa, and grinding her teeth, so that you might fancy she would crash them to splinters!

Mr. Linton stood looking at her in sudden compunction and fear. He told me to fetch some water. She had no breath for speaking.

I brought a glass full, and, as she would not drink, I sprinkled it on her face. In a few seconds she stretched herself out stiff, and turned up her eyes, while her cheeks, at once blanched and livid, assumed the aspect of death.

Linton looked terrified.

"There is nothing in the world the matter," I whispered. I did not want him to yield, though I could not help being afraid in my heart.

"She has blood on her lips!" he said, shuddering.

"Never mind!" I answered tartly. And I told him how she had resolved, previous to his coming, on exhibiting a fit of frenzy.

I incautiously gave the account aloud, and she heard me, for she started up—her hair flying over her shoulders, her eyes flashing, the muscles of her neck and arms standing out preternaturally. I made up my mind for broken bones, at least; but she only glared about her for an instant, and then rushed from the room.

The master directed me to follow; I did, to her chamber door: she hindered me from going farther by securing it against me.

As she never offered to descend to breakfast next morning, I went to ask whether she would have some carried up.

"No!" she replied peremptorily.

The same question was repeated at dinner and tea; and again on the morrow after, and received the same answer.

Mr. Linton, on his part, spent his time in the library, and did not inquire concerning his wife's occupations. Isabella and he had had an hour's interview, during which he tried to elicit from her some sentiment of proper horror for Heathcliff's advances; but he could make nothing of her evasive replies, and was obliged to close the examination unsatisfactorily, adding, however, a solemn warning, that if she were so insane as to encourage that worthless suitor, it would dissolve all bonds of relationship between herself and him.

CHAPTER 12

WHILE Miss Linton moped about the park and garden, always silent, and almost always in tears; and her brother shut himself up among books that he never opened—wearying, I guessed, with a continual vague expectation that Catherine, repenting her conduct, would come of her own accord to ask pardon, and seek a reconciliation—and she fasted pertinaciously, under the idea, probably, that at every meal Edgar was ready to choke for her absence, and pride alone held him from running to cast himself at her feet; I went about my household duties, convinced that the Grange had but one sensible soul in its walls, and that lodged in my body.

I wasted no condolences on Miss, nor any expostulations on my mistress; nor did I pay attention to the sighs of my master, who yearned to hear his lady's name, since he might not hear her voice.

I determined they should come about as they pleased for me; and though it was a tiresomely slow process, I began to rejoice at length in a faint dawn of its progress —as I thought at first.

Mrs. Linton, on the third day, unbarred her door, and having finished the water in her pitcher and decanter, desired a renewed supply, and a basin of gruel, for she believed she was dying. That I set down as a speech meant for Edgar's ears; I believed no such thing, so I kept it to myself, and brought her some tea and dry toast.

She ate and drank eagerly; and sank back on her pillow again, clenching her hands and groaning.

"Oh, I will die," she exclaimed, "since no one cares anything about me. I wish I had not taken that."

Then a good while after I heard her murmur,

"No, I'll not die—he'd be glad—he does not love me at all—he would never miss me!"

"Did you want anything, ma'am?" I inquired, still preserving my external composure, in spite of her ghastly countenance and strange exaggerated manner.

"What is that pathetic being doing?" she demanded, pushing the thick entangled locks from her wasted face. "Has he fallen into a lethargy, or is he dead?"

"Neither," replied I, "if you mean Mr. Linton. He's tolerably well, I think, though his studies occupy him rather more than they ought; he is continually among his books, since he has no other society."

I should not have spoken so, if I had known her true condition, but I could not get rid of the notion that she acted a part of her disorder.

"Among his books!" she cried, confounded. "And I am dying! I on the brink of the grave! My God! does he know how I'm altered?" continued she, staring at her reflection in a mirror hanging against the opposite wall. "Is that Catherine Linton? He imagines me in a pet—in play, perhaps. Cannot you inform him that it is frightful earnest? Nelly, if it be not too late, as soon as I learn how he feels, I'll choose between these two; either to starve at once—that would be no punishment unless he had a heart—or to recover, and leave the country. Are you speaking the truth about him now? Take care. Is he actually so utterly indifferent for my life?"

"Why, ma'am," I answered, "the master has no idea of your being deranged; and of course he does not fear that you will let yourself die of hunger."

"You think not? Cannot you tell him I will?" she returned. "Persuade him! Speak of your own mind—say you are certain I will!"

"No, you forget, Mrs. Linton," I suggested, "that you have eaten some food with a relish this evening, and tomorrow you will perceive its good effects."

"If I were only sure it would kill him," she interrupted, "I'd kill myself directly! These three awful nights, I've never closed my lids—and oh, I've been tormented! I've been haunted, Nelly! But I begin to fancy you don't like me. How strange! I thought, though everybody hated and despised each other, they could not avoid loving me.

And they have all turned to enemies in a few hours; they have, I'm positive—the people here. How dreary to meet death, surrounded by their cold faces! Isabella, terrified and repelled, afraid to enter the room, it would be so terrible to watch Catherine go. And Edgar standing solemnly by to see it over; then offering prayers of thanks to God for restoring peace to his house, and going back to his books! What in the name of all that feels, has he to do with books, when I am dying?"

She could not bear the notion which I had put into her head of Mr. Linton's philosophical resignation. Tossing about, she increased her feverish bewilderment to madness, and tore the pillow with her teeth, then raising herself up all burning, desired that I would open the window. We were in the middle of winter, the wind blew strong from the northeast, and I objected.

Both the expressions flitting over her face, and the changes of her moods, began to alarm me terribly, and brought to my recollection her former illness, and the doctor's injunction that she should not be crossed.

A minute previously she was violent; now, supported on one arm, and not noticing my refusal to obey her, she seemed to find childish diversion in pulling the feathers from the rents she had just made, and ranging them on the sheet according to their different species: her mind had strayed to other associations.

"That's a turkey's," she murmured to herself, "and this is a wild duck's, and this is a pigeon's. Ah, they put pigeon's feathers in the pillows—no wonder I couldn't die! Let me take care to throw it on the floor when I lie down. And here is a moor cock's; and this—I should know it among a thousand—it's a lapwing's. Bonny bird, wheeling over our heads in the middle of the moor. It wanted to get to its nest, for the clouds had touched the swells, and it felt rain coming. This feather was picked up from the heath, the bird was not shot; we saw its nest in the winter, full of little skeletons. Heathcliff set a trap over it, and the old ones dare not come. I made him promise he'd never shoot a lapwing after that, and he didn't. Yes, here are more! Did he shoot my lapwings, Nelly? Are they red, any of them? Let me look."

"Give over with that baby-work!" I interrupted, dragging the pillow away, and turning the holes towards the mattress, for she was removing its contents by handfuls. "Lie down and shut your eyes: you're wandering. There's a mess! The down is flying about like snow."

I went here and there collecting it.

"I see in you, Nelly," she continued, dreamily, "an aged woman; you have grey hair and bent shoulders. This bed is the fairy cave under Penistone Crag, and you are gathering elf-bolts to hurt our heifers, pretending, while I am near, that they are only locks of wool. That's what you'll come to fifty years hence; I know you are not so now. I'm not wandering, you're mistaken—or else I should believe you really were that withered hag, and I should think I was under Penistone Crag; and I'm conscious it's night, and there are two candles on the table making the black press shine like jet."

"The black press? where is that?" I asked. "You are talking in your sleep!"

"It's against the wall, as it always is," she replied. "It does appear odd—I see a face in it!"

"There is no press in the room, and never was," said I, resuming my seat, and looping up the curtain that I might watch her.

"Don't you see that face?" she enquired, gazing earnestly at the mirror.

And say what I could, I was incapable of making her comprehend it to be her own; so I rose and covered it with a shawl.

"It's behind there still!" she pursued, anxiously. "And it stirred. Who is it? I hope it will not come out when you are gone! Oh! Nelly, the room is haunted! I'm afraid of being alone!"

I took her hand in mine, and bid her to be composed, for a succession of shudders convulsed her frame, and she would keep straining her gaze towards the glass.

"There's nobody here!" I insisted. "It was yourself, Mrs. Linton; you knew it a while since."

"Myself!" she gasped, "and the clock is striking twelve! It's true, then! That's dreadful!"

Her fingers clutched the clothes, and gathered them over her eyes. I attempted to steal to the door with an intention of calling her husband; but I was summoned back by a piercing shriek—the shawl had dropped from the frame.

"Why, what is the matter?" cried I. "Who is coward now? Wake up! That is the glass—the mirror, Mrs. Linton; and you see yourself in it, and there am I, too, by your side."

Trembling and bewildered, she held me fast, but the horror gradually passed from her countenance; its paleness gave place to a glow of shame.

"Oh, dear! I thought I was at home," she sighed. "I thought I was lying in my chamber at Wuthering Heights. Because I'm weak, my brain got confused, and I screamed unconsciously. Don't say anything, but stay with me. I dread sleeping; my dreams appal me."

"A sound sleep would do you good, ma'am," I answered; "and I hope this suffering will prevent your trying starving again."

"Oh, if I were but in my own bed in the old house!" she went on bitterly, wringing her hands. "And that wind sounding in the firs by the lattice. Do let me feel it—it comes straight down the moor—do let me have one breath!"

To pacify her, I held the casement ajar a few seconds. A cold blast rushed through; I closed it, and returned to my post.

She lay still now, her face bathed in tears. Exhaustion of body had entirely subdued her spirit; our fiery Catherine was no better than a wailing child.

"How long is it since I shut myself in here?" she asked, suddenly reviving.

"It was Monday evening," I replied, "and this is Thursday night, or rather Friday morning, at present."

"What! of the same week?" she exclaimed. "Only that brief time?"

"Long enough to live on nothing but cold water and ill-temper," observed I.

"Well, it seems a weary number of hours," she muttered doubtfully; "it must be more. I remember being in the parlour after they had quarrelled, and Edgar being cruelly provoking, and me running into this room desperate. As soon as ever I had barred the door, utter blackness overwhelmed me, and I fell on the floor. I couldn't explain to Edgar how certain I felt of having a fit, or going raging mad, if he persisted in teasing me! I had no command of tongue, or brain, and he did not guess my agony, perhaps; it barely left me sense to try to escape from him and his voice. Before I recovered sufficiently to see and hear, it began to be dawn, and, Nelly, I'll tell you what I thought, and what has kept recurring and recurring till I feared for my reason. I thought as I lay there, with my head against that table leg, and my eyes dimly discerning the grey square of the window, that I was enclosed in the oak-panelled bed at home; and my heart ached with some great grief which, just waking, I could not recollect. I pondered, and worried myself to discover what it could be, and, most strangely, the whole last seven years of my life grew a blank! I did not recall that they had been at all. I was a child; my father was just buried, and my misery arose from the separation that Hindley had ordered between me and Heathcliff. I was laid alone, for the first time, and, rousing from a dismal doze after a night of weeping, I lifted my hand to push the panels aside; it struck the tabletop! I swept it along the carpet, and then memory burst in; my late anguish was swallowed in a paroxysm of despair. I cannot say why I felt so wildly wretched; it must have been temporary derangement, for there is scarcely cause— But, supposing at twelve years old, I had been wrenched from the Heights, and every early association, and my all in all, as Heathcliff was at that time, and been converted at a stroke into Mrs. Linton, the lady of Thrushcross Grange, and the wife of a stranger: an exile, and outcast, thenceforth, from what had been my world— You may fancy a glimpse of the abyss where I grovelled! Shake your head as you will, Nelly, you have helped to unsettle me! You should have spoken to Edgar, indeed you should, and compelled him to leave me quiet! Oh, I'm burning! I wish I were out of doors! I wish I were a girl again, half savage and hardy, and free . . . and laughing at injuries, not maddening under them! Why am I so changed? why does my blood rush into a hell of tumult at a few words? I'm sure I should be myself were I once among the heather on those hills. Open the window again wide, fasten it open! Quick, why don't you move?"

"Because I won't give you your death of cold," I answered.

"You won't give me a chance of life, you mean," she said sullenly. "However, I'm not helpless yet; I'll open it myself."

And sliding from the bed before I could hinder her, she crossed the room, walking very uncertainly, threw it back, and bent out, careless of the frosty air that cut about her shoulders as keen as a knife.

I entreated, and finally attempted to force her to retire. But I soon found her delirious strength much surpassed mine (she was delirious, I became convinced by her subsequent actions and ravings).

There was no moon, and everything beneath lay in misty darkness: not a light gleamed from any house, far or near—all had been extinguished long ago; and those at Wuthering Heights were never visible—still she asserted she caught their shining.

"Look!" she cried eagerly, "that's my room with the candle in it, and the trees swaying before it . . . and the other candle is in Joseph's garret . . . Joseph sits up late, doesn't he? He's waiting till I come home that he may lock the gate. . . . Well, he'll wait a while yet. It's a rough journey, and a sad heart to travel it; and we must pass by Gimmerton Kirk, to go that journey! We've braved its ghosts often together, and dared each other to stand among the graves and ask them to come. . . . But Heathcliff, if I dare you now, will you venture? If you do, I'll keep you. I'll not lie there by myself; they may bury me twelve feet deep, and throw the church down over me, but I won't rest till you are with me. I never will!"

She paused, and resumed with a strange smile. "He's considering—he'd rather I'd come to him! Find a way, then! not through that Kirkyard. . . . You are slow! Be content, you always followed me!"

Perceiving it vain to argue against her insanity, I was planning how I could reach something to wrap about her, without quitting my hold of herself, for I could not trust her alone by the gaping lattice, when, to my consternation, I heard the rattle of the door-handle, and Mr. Linton entered. He had only then come from the library; and, in passing through the lobby, had noticed our talking and been attracted by curiosity, or fear, to examine what it signified, at that late hour.

"Oh, sir!" I cried, checking the exclamation risen to his lips at the sight which met him, and the bleak atmosphere of the chamber.

"My poor Mistress is ill, and she quite masters me, I cannot manage her at all; pray, come and persuade her to go to bed. Forget your anger, for she's hard to guide any way but her own."

"Catherine ill?" he said, hastening to us. "Shut the window, Ellen! Catherine! why . . ."

He was silent; the haggardness of Mrs. Linton's appearance smote him speechless, and he could only glance from her to me in horrified astonishment.

"She's been fretting here," I continued, "and eating scarcely anything, and never complaining. She would admit none of us till this evening, and so we couldn't inform you of her state, as we were not aware of it ourselves; but it is nothing."

I felt I uttered my explanations awkwardly; the master frowned. "It is nothing, is it, Ellen Dean?" he said sternly. "You shall account more clearly for keeping me ignorant of this!" And he took his wife in his arms, and looked at her with anguish.

At first she gave him no glance of recognition; he was invisible to her abstracted gaze. The delirium was not fixed, however; having weaned her eyes from contemplating the outer darkness, by degrees she centred her attention on him, and discovered who it was that held her.

"Ah! you are come, are you, Edgar Linton?" she said with angry animation. . . . "You are one of those things that are ever found when least wanted, and when you are wanted, never! I suppose we shall have plenty of lamentations now. . . . I see we shall . . . but they can't keep me from my narrow home out yonder: my resting place, where I'm bound before spring is over! There it is, not among the Lintons, mind, under the chapel roof, but in the open air, with a headstone; and you may please yourself, whether you go to them or come to me!"

"Catherine, what have you done?" commenced the

master. "Am I nothing to you any more? Do you love that wretch Heath——"

"Hush!" cried Mrs. Linton. "Hush, this moment! You mention that name and I end the matter instantly, by a spring from the window! What you touch at present you may have; but my soul will be on that hilltop before you lay hands on me again. I don't want you, Edgar, I'm past wanting you. Return to your books. I'm glad you possess a consolation, for all you had in me is gone."

"Her mind wanders, sir," I interposed. "She has been talking nonsense the whole evening; but, let her have quiet, and proper attendance, and she'll rally. . . . Hereafter, we must be cautious how we vex her."

"I desire no further advice from you," answered Mr. Linton. "You knew your mistress's nature, and you encouraged me to harass her. And not to give me one hint of how she has been these three days! It was heartless! Months of sickness could not cause such a change!"

I began to defend myself, thinking it too bad to be blamed for another's wicked waywardness.

"I knew Mrs. Linton's nature to be headstrong and domineering," cried I, "but I didn't know that you wished to foster her fierce temper! I didn't know that, to humour her, I should wink at Mr. Heathcliff. I performed the duty of a faithful servant in telling you, and I have got a faithful servant's wages! Well, it will teach me to be careful next time. Next time you may gather intelligence for yourself!"

"The next time you bring a tale to me, you shall quit my service, Ellen Dean," he replied.

"You'd rather hear nothing about it, I suppose, then, Mr. Linton?" said I. "Heathcliff has your permission to come a-courting to Miss, and to drop in at every opportunity your absence offers, on purpose to poison the mistress against you?"

Confused as Catherine was, her wits were alert at applying our conversation.

"Ah! Nelly has played traitor," she exclaimed, passionately. "Nelly is my hidden enemy. You witch! So you do seek elf-bolts to hurt us! Let me go, and I'll make her rue! I'll make her howl a recantation!"

A maniac's fury kindled under her brows; she struggled desperately to disengage herself from Linton's arms.

I felt no inclination to tarry the event, and, resolving to seek medical aid on my own responsibility, I quitted the chamber.

In passing the garden to reach the road, at a place where a bridle hook is driven into the wall, I saw something white moved irregularly, evidently by another agent than the wind. Notwithstanding my hurry, I stayed to examine it, lest ever after I should have the conviction impressed on my imagination that it was a creature of the other world.

My surprise and perplexity were great to discover, by touch more than vision, Miss Isabella's springer, Fanny, suspended to a handkerchief, and nearly at its last gasp.

I quickly released the animal, and lifted it into the garden. I had seen it follow its mistress upstairs, when she went to bed, and wondered much how it could have got out there, and what mischievous person had treated it so.

While untying the knot round the hook, it seemed to me that I repeatedly caught the beat of horses' feet galloping at some distance; but there were such a number of things to occupy my reflections that I hardly gave the circumstance a thought, though it was a strange sound, in that place, at two o'clock in the morning.

Mr. Kenneth was fortunately just issuing from his house to see a patient in the village as I came up the street, and my account of Catherine Linton's malady induced him to accompany me back immediately.

He was a plain rough man, and he made no scruple to speak his doubts of her surviving this second attack, unless she were more submissive to his directions than she had shown herself before.

"Nelly Dean," said he, "I can't help fancying there's an extra cause for this. What has there been to do at the Grange? We've odd reports up here. A stout, hearty lass like Catherine does not fall ill for a trifle; and that sort of people should not either. It's hard work bringing them through fevers, and such things. How did it begin?"

"The master will inform you," I answered; "but you are acquainted with the Earnshaws' violent dispositions, and Mrs. Linton caps them. I may say this: it commenced in a quarrel. She was struck during a tempest of passion with a kind of fit. That's her account, at least; for she flew off in the height of it, and locked herself up. Afterwards, she refused to eat, and now she alternately raves and remains in a half-dream, knowing those about her, but having her mind filled with all sorts of strange ideas and illusions."

"Mr. Linton will be sorry?" observed Kenneth, interrogatively.

"Sorry? He'll break his heart should anything happen!" I replied. "Don't alarm him more than necessary."

"Well, I told him to beware," said my companion, "and he must bide the consequences of neglecting my warning! Hasn't he been thick with Mr. Heathcliff lately?"

"Heathcliff frequently visits at the Grange," answered I, "though more on the strength of the mistress having known him when a boy, than because the master likes his company. At present, he's discharged from the trouble of calling, owing to some presumptuous aspirations after Miss Linton which he manifested. I hardly think he'll be taken in again."

"And does Miss Linton turn a cold shoulder on him?" was the doctor's next question.

"I'm not in her confidence," returned I, reluctant to continue the subject.

"No, she's a sly one," he remarked, shaking his head. "She keeps her own counsel! But she's a real little fool. I have it from good authority, that, last night (and a pretty night it was!) she and Heathcliff were walking in the plantation at the back of your house, above two hours; and he pressed her not to go in again, but just mount his horse and away with him! My informant said she could only put him off by pledging her word of honour to be prepared on their first meeting after that; when it was to be, he didn't hear, but you urge Mr. Linton to look sharp!"

This news filled me with fresh fears; I outstripped Kenneth, and ran most of the way back. The little dog was yelping in the garden yet. I spared a minute to open the gate for it, but instead of going to the house door, it coursed up and down snuffing the grass, and would have escaped to the road, had I not seized and conveyed it in with me.

On ascending to Isabella's room, my suspicions were

confirmed; it was empty. Had I been a few hours sooner, Mrs. Linton's illness might have arrested her rash step. But what could be done now? There was a bare possibility of overtaking them if I pursued instantly. I could not pursue them, however, and I dare not rouse the family, and fill the place with confusion, still less unfold the business to my master, absorbed as he was in his present calamity, and having no heart to spare for a second grief!

I saw nothing for it but to hold my tongue, and suffer matters to take their course; and Kenneth being arrived, I went with a badly composed countenance to announce him.

Catherine lay in a troubled sleep; her husband had succeeded in soothing the access of frenzy; he now hung over her pillow, watching every shade, and every change of her painfully expressive features.

The doctor, on examining the case for himself, spoke hopefully to him of its having a favourable termination, if we could only preserve around her perfect and constant tranquillity. To me, he signified the threatening danger was not so much death, as permanent alienation of intellect.

I did not close my eyes that night, nor did Mr. Linton; indeed, we never went to bed, and the servants were all up long before the usual hour, moving through the house with stealthy tread, and exchanging whispers as they encountered each other in their vocations. Everyone was active but Miss Isabella; and they began to remark how sound she slept; her brother, too, asked if she had risen, and seemed impatient for her presence, and hurt that she showed so little anxiety for her sister-in-law.

I trembled lest he should send me to call her; but I was spared the pain of being the first proclaimant of her flight. One of the maids, a thoughtless girl, who had been on an early errand to Gimmerton, came panting upstairs, open-mouthed, and dashed into the chamber, crying—

"Oh, dear, dear! What mun we have next? Master, master, our young lady——"

"Hold your noise!" cried I hastily, enraged at her clamourous manner.

"Speak lower, Mary—What is the matter?" said Mr. Linton. "What ails your young lady?"

"She's gone, she's gone! Yon' Heathcliff's run off wi' her!" gasped the girl.

"That is not true!" exclaimed Linton, rising in agitation. "It cannot be—how has the idea entered your head? Ellen Dean, go and seek her. It is incredible—it cannot be."

As he spoke he took the servant to the door, and then repeated his demand to know her reasons for such an assertion.

"Why, I met on the road a lad that fetches milk here," she stammered, "and he asked whether we weren't in trouble at the Grange. I thought he meant for missis's sickness, so I answered, yes. Then says he, 'They's somebody gone after 'em, I guess?' I stared. He saw I knew naught about it, and he told how a gentleman and lady had stopped to have a horse's shoe fastened at a blacksmith's shop, two miles out of Gimmerton, not very long after midnight! and how the blacksmith's lass had got up to spy who they were—she knew them both directly. And she noticed the man—Heathcliff it was, she felt certain, nob'dy could mistake him, besides— put a sovereign in her father's hand for payment. The lady had a cloak about her face; but having desired a sup of water, while she drank, it fell back, and she saw her very plain. Heathcliff held both bridles as they rode on, and they set their faces from the village, and went as fast as the rough roads would let them. The lass said nothing to her father, but she told it all over Gimmerton this morning."

I ran and peeped, for form's sake, into Isabella's room, confirming, when I returned, the servant's statement. Mr. Linton had resumed his seat by the bed; on my reentrance, he raised his eyes, read the meaning of my blank aspect, and dropped them without giving an order, or uttering a word.

"Are we to try any measures for overtaking and bringing her back?" I inquired. "How should we do,"

"She went of her own accord," answered the master; "she had a right to go if she pleased. Trouble me no more about her. Hereafter she is only my sister in name, not because I disown her, but because she has disowned me."

And that was all he said on the subject: he did not make a single inquiry further, nor mention her in any way, except directing me to send what property she had in the house to her fresh home, wherever it was, when I knew it.

CHAPTER 13

FOR TWO months the fugitives remained absent; in those two months, Mrs. Linton encountered and conquered the worst shock of what was denominated a brain fever. No mother could have nursed an only child more devotedly than Edgar tended her. Day and night he was watching, and patiently enduring all the annoyances that irritable nerves and a shaken reason could inflict; and, though Kenneth remarked that what he saved from the grave would only recompense his care by forming the source of constant future anxiety—in fact, that his health and strength were being sacrificed to preserve a mere ruin of humanity—he knew no limits in gratitude and joy when Catherine's life was declared out of danger; and hour after hour he would sit beside her, tracing the gradual return to bodily health, and flattering his too sanguine hopes with the illusion that her mind would settle back to its right balance also, and she would soon be entirely her former self.

The first time she left her chamber was at the commencement of the following March. Mr. Linton had put on her pillow, in the morning, a handful of golden crocuses; her eye, long stranger to any gleam of pleasure, caught them in waking, and shone delighted as she gathered them eagerly together.

"These are the earliest flowers at the Heights," she exclaimed. "They remind me of soft thaw winds, and warm sunshine, and nearly melted snow. Edgar, is there not a south wind, and is not the snow almost gone?"

"The snow is quite gone down here, darling," replied her husband, "and I only see two white spots on the whole range of moors; the sky is blue, and the larks are singing, and the becks and brooks are all brim full. Catherine, last spring at this time, I was longing to have you under this roof; now, I wish you were a mile or two up those hills—the air blows so sweetly, I feel that it would cure you."

"I shall never be there, but once more," said the invalid, "and then you'll leave me, and I shall remain forever. Next spring you'll long again to have me under this roof, and you'll look back and think you were happy today."

Linton lavished on her the kindest caresses, and tried to cheer her by the fondest words; but, vaguely regarding the flowers, she let the tears collect on her lashes and stream down her cheeks unheeding.

We knew she was really better, and, therefore, decided that long confinement to a single place produced much of this despondency, and it might be partially removed by a change of scene.

The master told me to light a fire in the many-weeks deserted parlour, and to set an easy chair in the sunshine by the window; and then he brought her down, and she sat a long while enjoying the genial heat, and, as we expected, revived by the objects round her, which, though familiar, were free from the dreary associations investing her hated sick-chamber. By evening, she seemed greatly exhausted; yet no arguments could persuade her to return to that apartment, and I had to arrange the parlour sofa for her bed, till another room could be prepared.

To obviate the fatigue of mounting and descending the stairs, we fitted up this, where you lie at present, on the same floor with the parlour, and she was soon strong enough to move from one to the other, leaning on Edgar's arm.

Ah, I thought myself, she might recover, so waited on as she was. And there was double cause to desire it, for on her existence depended that of another; we cherished the hope that in a little while, Mr. Linton's heart would be gladdened, and his lands secured from a stranger's gripe, by the birth of an heir.

I should mention that Isabella sent to her brother, some six weeks from her departure, a short note, announcing her marriage with Heathcliff. It appeared dry and cold; but at the bottom was dotted in with pencil an obscure apology, and an entreaty for kind remembrance and reconciliation, if her proceeding had offended him: asserting that she could not help it then, and being done, she had now no power to repeal it.

Linton did not reply to this, I believe; and, in a fortnight more, I got a long letter which I considered odd, coming from the pen of a bride just out of the honeymoon. I'll read it: for I keep it yet. Any relic of the dead is precious, if they were valued living.

DEAR ELLEN, it begins.

I came last night to Wuthering Heights, and heard, for the first time, that Catherine has been, and is yet, very ill. I must not write to her, I suppose, and my brother is either too angry or too distressed to answer what I send him. Still, I must write to somebody, and the only choice left me is you.

Inform Edgar that I'd give the world to see his face again—that my heart returned to Thrushcross Grange in twenty-four hours after I left it, and is there at this moment, full of warm feelings for him, and Catherine! *I can't follow it though*—(those words are underlined) they need not expect me, and they may draw what conclusions they please; taking care, however, to lay nothing at the door of my weak will or deficient affection.

The remainder of the letter is for yourself alone. I want to ask you two questions; the first is—

How did you contrive to preserve the common sympathies of human nature when you resided here? I cannot recognize any sentiment which those around share with me.

The second question, I have great interest in; it is this—

Is Mr. Heathcliff a man? If so, is he mad? And if not, is he a devil? I shan't tell my reasons for making this inquiry; but I beseech you to explain, if you can, what I have married: that is, when you call to see me; and you must call, Ellen, very soon. Don't write but come, and bring me something from Edgar.

Now, you shall hear how I have been received in my new home, as I am led to imagine the Heights will be. It is to amuse myself that I dwell on such subjects as the lack of external comforts; they never occupy my thoughts, except at the moment when I miss them. I should laugh and dance for joy, if I found their absence was the total of my miseries, and the rest was an unnatural dream!

The sun set behind the Grange, as we turned on to the moors; by that, I judged it to be six o'clock; and my companion halted half-an-hour, to inspect the park, and the gardens, and, probably, the place itself, as well as he could; so it was dark when we dismounted in the paved yard of the farmhouse, and your old fellow-servant, Joseph, issued out to receive us by the light of a dip candle. He did it with a courtesy that redounded to his credit. His first act was to elevate his torch to a level with my face, squint malignantly, project his under lip, and turn away.

Then he took the two horses, and led them into the stables, reappearing for the purpose of locking the outer gate, as if we lived in an ancient castle.

Heathcliff stayed to speak to him, and I entered the kitchen—a dingy, untidy hole; I dare say you would not know it, it is so changed since it was in your charge.

By the fire stood a ruffianly child, strong in limb and dirty in garb, with a look of Catherine in his eyes and about his mouth.

"This is Edgar's legal nephew," I reflected—"mine in a manner; I must shake hands, and,—yes—I must kiss him. It is right to establish a good understanding at the beginning."

I approached, and, attempting to take his chubby fist, said—

"How do you do, my dear?"

He replied in a jargon I did not comprehend.

"Shall you and I be friends, Hareton?" was my next essay at conversation.

An oath, and a threat to set Throttler on me if I did not "frame off" rewarded my perseverance.

"Hey, Throttler, lad!" whispered the little wretch, rousing a half-bred bulldog from its lair in a corner. "Now, wilt tuh be ganging?" he asked authoritatively.

Love for my life urged a compliance; I stepped over the threshold to wait till the others should enter. Mr. Heathcliff was nowhere visible; and Joseph, whom I followed to the stables, and requested to accompany me in, after staring and muttering to himself, screwed up his nose and replied—

"Mim! mim! mim! Did iver a Christian body hear owt like it? Minching un' munching! Hah can Aw tell whet ye say?"

"I say, I wish you to come with me into the house!" I cried, thinking him deaf, yet highly disgusted at his rudeness.

"Nor nuh me! Aw getten summet else to do," he answered, and continued his work, moving his lantern jaws meanwhile, and surveying my dress and countenance (the former a great deal too fine, but the latter, I'm sure, as sad as he could desire) with sovereign contempt.

I walked round the yard, and through a wicket, to another door, at which I took the liberty of knocking, in hopes some more civil servant might show himself.

After a short suspense, it was opened by a tall, gaunt man, without neckerchief, and otherwise extremely slovenly; his features were lost in masses of shaggy hair that hung on his shoulders; and his eyes, too, were like a ghostly Catherine's, with all their beauty annihilated.

"What's your business here?" he demanded, grimly. "Who are you?"

"My name was Isabella Linton," I replied. "You've seen me before, sir. I'm lately married to Mr. Heathcliff, and he has brought me here—I suppose by your permission."

"Is he come back, then?" asked the hermit, glaring like a hungry wolf.

"Yes—we came just now," I said; "but he left me by the kitchen door, and when I would have gone in, your little boy played sentinel over the place, and frightened me off by the help of a bulldog."

"It's well the hellish villain has kept his word!" growled my future host, searching the darkness beyond me in expectation of discovering Heathcliff; and then he indulged in a soliloquy of execrations, and threats of what he would have done had the "fiend" deceived him.

I repented having tried this second entrance, and was almost inclined to slip away before he finished cursing, but ere I could execute that intention, he ordered me in, and shut and re-fastened the door.

There was a great fire, and that was all the light in the huge apartment, whose floor had grown a uniform grey; and the once brilliant pewter dishes, which used to attract my gaze when I was a girl, partook of a similar obscurity, created by tarnish and dust.

I inquired whether I might call the maid, and be conducted to a bedroom? Mr. Earnshaw vouchsafed no answer. He walked up and down, with his hands in his pockets, apparently quite forgetting my presence; and his abstraction was evidently so deep, and his whole aspect so misanthropical, that I shrank from disturbing him again.

You'll not be surprised, Ellen, at my feeling particularly cheerless, seated in worse than solitude on that inhospitable hearth, and remembering that four miles distant lay my delightful home, containing the only people I loved on earth; and there might as well be the Atlantic to part us, instead of those four miles; I could not overpass them!

I questioned with myself—where must I turn for comfort? and—mind you don't tell Edgar, or Catherine—above every sorrow beside, this rose pre-eminent: despair at finding nobody who could or would be my ally against Heathcliff!

I had sought shelter at Wuthering Heights, almost gladly, because I was secured by that arrangement from living alone with him; but he knew the people we were coming amongst, and he did not fear their intermeddling.

I sat and thought a doleful time; the clock struck eight, and nine, and still my companion paced to and fro, his head bent on his breast, and perfectly silent, unless a groan or a bitter ejaculation forced itself out at intervals.

I listened to detect a woman's voice in the house, and filled the interim with wild regrets and dismal anticipations, which, at last, spoke audibly in irrepressible sighing and weeping.

I was not aware how openly I grieved, till Earnshaw

halted opposite, in his measured walk, and gave me a stare of newly awakened surprise. Taking advantage of his recovered attention, I exclaimed—

"I'm tired with my journey, and I want to go to bed! Where is the maid-servant? Direct me to her, as she won't come to me!"

"We have none," he answered; "you must wait on yourself!"

"Where must I sleep, then?" I sobbed; I was beyond regarding self-respect, weighed down by fatigue and wretchedness.

"Joseph will show you Heathcliff's chamber," said he; "open that door—he's in there."

I was going to obey, but he suddenly arrested me, and added in the strangest tone—

"Be so good as to turn your lock, and draw your bolt—don't omit it!"

"Well!" I said. "But why, Mr. Earnshaw?" I did not relish the notion of deliberately fastening myself in with Heathcliff.

"Look here!" he replied, pulling from his waistcoat a curiously constructed pistol, having a double-edged spring knife attached to the barrel. "That's a great tempter to a desperate man, is it not? I cannot resist going up with this every night, and trying his door. If once I find it open, he's done for! I do it invariably, even though the minute before I have been recalling a hundred reasons that should make me refrain; it is some devil that urges me to thwart my own schemes by killing him—you fight against that devil, for love, as long as you may; when the time comes, not all the angels in heaven shall save him!"

I surveyed the weapon inquisitively; a hideous notion struck me: how powerful I should be possessing such an instrument! I took it from his hand, and touched the blade. He looked astonished at the expression my face assumed during a brief second—it was not horror, it was covetousness. He snatched the pistol back, jealously, shut the knife, and returned it to its concealment.

"I don't care if you tell him," said he. "Put him on his guard, and watch for him. You know the terms we are on, I see—his danger does not shock you."

"What has Heathcliff done to you?" I asked. "In what

has he wronged you, to warrant this appalling hatred? Wouldn't it be wiser to bid him quit the house?"

"No!" thundered Earnshaw; "should he offer to leave me, he's a dead man; persuade him to attempt it, and you are a murderess! Am I to lose *all*, without a chance of retrieval? Is Hareton to be a beggar? Oh, damnation! I *will* have it back: and I'll have *his* gold too: and then his blood; and hell shall have his soul! It will be ten times blacker with that guest than ever it was before!"

You've acquainted me, Ellen, with your old master's habits. He is clearly on the verge of madness—he was so last night at least. I shuddered to be near him, and thought on the servant's ill-bred moroseness as comparatively agreeable.

He now recommenced his moody walk, and I raised the latch, and escaped into the kitchen.

Joseph was bending over the fire, peering into a large pan that swung above it; and a wooden bowl of oatmeal stood on the settle close by. The contents of the pan began to boil, and he turned to plunge his hand into the bowl; I conjectured that this preparation was probably for our supper, and, being hungry, I resolved it should be eatable; so, crying out sharply, "*I'll* make the porridge!" I removed the vessel out of his reach, and proceeded to take off my hat and riding habit. "Mr. Earnshaw," I continued, "directs me to wait on myself—I will. I'm not going to act the lady among you, for fear I should starve."

"Gooid Lord!" he muttered, sitting down, and stroking his ribbed stockings from the knee to the ankle. "If they's tuh be fresh ortherings—just when aw getten used tuh two maisters, if aw mun hev a *mistress* set o'er my heead, it's loike time tuh be flitting. Aw niver *did* think tuh say t' day ut aw mud lave th' owld place— but aw daht it's nigh at hend!"

This lamentation drew no notice from me; I went briskly to work, sighing to remember a period when it would have been all merry fun, but compelled speedily to drive off the remembrance. It racked me to recall past happiness, and the greater peril there was of conjuring up its apparition, the quicker the thible ran round, and the faster the handfuls of meal fell into the water.

Joseph beheld my style of cookery with growing indignation.

"Thear!" he ejaculated. "Hareton, thah willut sup thy porridge tuh neeght; they'll be nowt bud lumps as big as maw nave. Thear, agean! Aw'd fling in bowl un all, if aw wer yah! Thear, pale t' guilp off, un' then yah'll hae done wi't. Bang, bang. It's a marcy t' bothom isn't deaved aht!"

It was rather a rough mess, I own, when poured into the basins; four had been provided, and a gallon pitcher of new milk was brought from the dairy, which Hareton seized and commenced drinking and spilling from the expansive lip.

I expostulated, and desired that he should have his in a mug, affirming that I could not taste the liquid treated so dirtily. The old cynic chose to be vastly offended at this nicety; assuring me, repeatedly, that "the bairn was every bit as gooid" as I, "and every bit as wollsome," and wondering how I could fashion to be so conceited. Meanwhile, the infant ruffian continued sucking; and glowered up at me defyingly, as he slavered into the jug.

"I shall have my supper in another room," I said. "Have you no place you call a parlour?"

"Parlour!" he echoed, sneeringly, "parlour! Nay, we've noa parlours. If yah dunnut loike wer company, they's maister's; un' if yah dunnut loike maister, they's us."

"Then I shall go upstairs," I answered; "show me a chamber."

I put my basin on a tray, and went myself to fetch some more milk.

With great grumblings, the fellow rose, and preceded me in my ascent; we mounted to the garrets, he opening a door, now and then, to look into the apartments we passed.

"Here's a rahm," he said, at last, flinging back a cranky board on hinges. "It's weel eneugh tuh ate a few porridge in. They's a pack uh corn i' t' corner, thear, meeterly clane; if yah're feared uh muckying yer grand silk cloes, spread yer hankerchir ut t' top on 't."

The "rahm" was a kind of lumber-hole smelling strong of malt and grain, various sacks of which articles were piled around, leaving a wide, bare space in the middle.

"Why man!" I exclaimed, facing him angrily, "this is not a place to sleep in. I wish to see my bedroom."

"*Bed-rume!*" he repeated, in a tone of mockery. "Yah's see all t' *bed-rumes* thear is—yon's mine."

He pointed into the second garret, only differing from the first in being more naked about the walls, and having a large, low, curtainless bed, with an indigo-coloured quilt, at one end.

"What do I want with yours?" I retorted. "I suppose Mr. Heathcliff does not lodge at the top of the house, does he?"

"Oh, it's Maister *Hathecliff's* yah're wenting?" cried he, as if making a new discovery. "Couldn't ye uh said soa, at onst? un then, aw mud uh telled ye, baht all this wark, ut that's just one yah cannut sea—he allas keeps it locked, un' nob'dy iver mells on't but hisseln."

"You've a nice house, Joseph," I could not refrain from observing, "and pleasant inmates; and I think the concentrated essence of all the madness in the world took up its abode in my brain the day I linked my fate with theirs! However, that is not to the present purpose —there are other rooms. For Heaven's sake, be quick, and let me settle somewhere!"

He made no reply to this adjuration, only plodding doggedly down the wooden steps, and halting before an apartment which, from that halt and the superior quality of its furniture, I conjectured to be the best one. There was a carpet—a good one, but the pattern was obliterated by dust; a fireplace hung with cut paper, dropping to pieces; a handsome oak bedstead with ample crimson curtains of rather expensive material and modern make, but they had evidently experienced rough usage; the valances hung in festoons, wrenched from their rings, and the iron rod supporting them was bent in an arc, on one side, causing the drapery to trail upon the floor. The chairs were also damaged, many of them severely; and deep indentations deformed the panels of the walls.

I was endeavouring to gather resolution for entering, and taking possession, when my fool of a guide announced,

"This here is t' maister's."

My supper by this time was cold, my appetite gone,

and my patience exhausted. I insisted on being provided instantly with a place of refuge, and means of repose.

"Whear the divil," began the religious elder. "The Lord bless us! The Lord forgie us! Whear the *hell*, wold ye gang? ye marred, wearisome nowt! Yah seen all bud Hareton's bit uf a cham'er. They 's nut another hoile tuh lig dahn in i' th' hahse!"

I was so vexed, I flung my tray and its contents on the ground; and then seated myself at the stairs-head, hid my face in my hands, and cried.

"Ech! ech!" exclaimed Joseph. "Weel done, Miss Cathy! weel done, Miss Cathy! Hahsiver, t' maister sall just tum'le o'er them brocken pots; un' then we 's hear summut; we 's hear hah it 's tuh be. Gooid-for-nowt madling! yah desarve pining froo this tuh Churstmas, flingin t' precious gifts uh God under fooit i' yer flay-some rages! Bud, aw'm mista'en if yah shew yer sperrit lang. Will Hathecliff bide sich bonny ways, think ye? Aw nobbut wish he muh cotch ye i' that plisky. Aw nobbut wish he may."

And so he went scolding to his den beneath, taking the candle with him; and I remained in the dark.

The period of reflection succeeding this silly action compelled me to admit the necessity of smothering my pride and choking my wrath, and bestirring myself to remove its effects.

An unexpected aid presently appeared in the shape of Throttler, whom I now recognized as a son of our old Skulker; it had spent its whelphood at the Grange, and was given by my father to Mr. Hindley. I fancy it knew me; it pushed its nose against mine by way of salute, and then hastened to devour the porridge, while I groped from step to step, collecting the shattered earthenware, and drying the spatters of milk from the banister with my pocket-handkerchief.

Our labours were scarcely over when I heard Earnshaw's tread in the passage; my assistant tucked in his tail, and pressed to the wall; I stole into the nearest doorway. The dog's endeavour to avoid him was un-successful, as I guessed by a scutter downstairs, and a prolonged, piteous yelping. I had better luck: he passed on, entered his chamber, and shut the door.

Directly after Joseph came up with Hareton, to put

him to bed. I had found shelter in Hareton's room, and the old man, on seeing me, said—

"They's rahm fur boath yah, un yer pride, nah, aw sud think i' th' hahse. It's empty; yah muh hev it all tuh yerseln, un Him as allas maks a third, i' sich ill company!"

Gladly did I take advantage of this intimation; and the minute I flung myself into a chair, by the fire, I nodded, and slept.

My slumber was deep and sweet, though over far too soon. Mr. Heathcliff awoke me; he has just come in, and demanded, in his loving manner, what I was doing there?

I told him the cause of my staying up so late—that he had the key of our room in his pocket.

The adjective our gave mortal offence. He swore it was not, nor ever should be mine; and he'd—but I'll not repeat his language, nor describe his habitual conduct; he is ingenious and unresting in seeking to gain my abhorrence! I sometimes wonder at him with an intensity that deadens my fear, yet, I assure you, a tiger or a venomous serpent could not rouse terror in me equal to that which he wakens. He told me of Catherine's illness, and accused my brother of causing it, promising that I should be Edgar's proxy in suffering, till he could get hold of him.

I do hate him—I am wretched—I have been a fool! Beware of uttering one breath of this to anyone at the Grange. I shall expect you every day—don't disappoint me!

ISABELLA.

CHAPTER 14

A<small>S SOON</small> as I had perused this epistle, I went to the master and informed him that his sister had arrived at the Heights, and sent me a letter expressing her sorrow for Mrs. Linton's situation, and her ardent desire to see him, with a wish that he would transmit to her, as early as possible, some token of forgiveness by me.

"Forgiveness!" said Linton. "I have nothing to forgive her, Ellen. You may call at Wuthering Heights this afternoon, if you like, and say that I am not angry, but I'm sorry to have lost her, especially as I can never think she'll be happy. It is out of the question my going to see her, however; we are eternally divided; and should she really wish to oblige me, let her persuade the villain she has married to leave the country."

"And you won't write her a little note, sir?" I asked imploringly.

"No," he answered. "It is needless. My communication with Heathcliff's family shall be as sparing as his with mine. It shall not exist!"

Mr. Edgar's coldness depressed me exceedingly, and all the way from the Grange I puzzled my brains how to put more heart into what he said, when I repeated it; and how to soften his refusal of even a few lines to console Isabella.

I dare say she had been on the watch for me since morning: I saw her looking through the lattice, as I came up the garden causeway, and I nodded to her; but she drew back, as if afraid of being observed.

I entered without knocking. There never was such a dreary, dismal scene as the formerly cheerful house presented! I must confess, that if I had been in the young lady's place, I would, at least, have swept the hearth, and wiped the tables with a duster. But she already partook of the pervading spirit of neglect which encompassed her. Her pretty face was wan and listless, her hair uncurled, some locks hanging lankly down, and some carelessly twisted round her head. Probably she had not touched her dress since yester evening.

Hindley was not there. Mr. Heathcliff sat at a table, turning over some papers in his pocketbook; but he rose when I appeared, asked me how I did, quite friendly, and offered me a chair.

He was the only thing there that seemed decent, and I thought he never looked better. So much had circumstances altered their positions, that he would certainly have struck a stranger as a born and bred gentleman, and his wife as a thorough little slattern!

She came forward eagerly to greet me; and held out one hand to take the expected letter.

I shook my head. She wouldn't understand the hint, but followed me to a sideboard, where I went to lay my bonnet, and importuned me in a whisper to give her directly what I had brought.

Heathcliff guessed the meaning of her manœuvres, and said—

"If you have got anything for Isabella (as no doubt you have, Nelly), give it to her. You needn't make a secret of it: we have no secrets between us."

"Oh, I have nothing," I replied, thinking it best to speak the truth at once. "My master bid me tell his sister that she must not expect either a letter or a visit from him at present. He sends his love, ma'am, and his wishes for your happiness, and his pardon for the grief you have occasioned; but he thinks that after this time, his household and the household here should drop inter-communication, as nothing good could come of keeping it up."

Mrs. Heathcliff's lip quivered slightly, and she returned to her seat in the window. Her husband took his stand on the hearthstone, near me, and began to put questions concerning Catherine.

I told him as much as I thought proper of her illness, and he extorted from me, by cross-examination, most of the facts connected with its origin.

I blamed her, as she deserved, for bringing it all on herself, and ended by hoping that he would follow Mr. Linton's example, and avoid future interference with his family, for good or evil.

"Mrs. Linton is now just recovering," I said; "she 'll never be like she was, but her life is spared; and if you really have a regard for her, you 'll shun crossing her way again—nay, you 'll move out of this country entirely; and that you may not regret it, I 'll inform you Catherine Linton is as different now from your old friend Catherine Earnshaw, as that young lady is different from me. Her appearance is changed greatly, her character much more so; and the person who is compelled, of necessity, to be her companion, will only sustain his affection hereafter by the remembrance of what she once was, by common humanity, and a sense of duty!"

"That is quite possible," remarked Heathcliff, forcing himself to seem calm, "quite possible that your master should have nothing but common humanity and a sense of duty to fall back upon. But do you imagine that I shall leave Catherine to his *duty* and *humanity*? and can you compare my feelings respecting Catherine to his? Before you leave this house, I must exact a promise from you, that you'll get me an interview with her—consent, or refuse, I *will* see her! What do you say?"

"I say, Mr. Heathcliff," I replied, "you must not—you never shall, through my means. Another encounter between you and the master would kill her altogether."

"With your aid, that may be avoided," he continued; "and should there be danger of such an event—should he be the cause of adding a single trouble more to her existence—why, I think, I shall be justified in going to extremes! I wish you had sincerity enough to tell me whether Catherine would suffer greatly from his loss—the fear that she would restrains me. And there you see the distinction between our feelings—had he been in my place and I in his, though I hated him with a hatred that turned my life to gall, I never would have raised a hand against him. You may look incredulous, if you please! I never would have banished him from her society as long as she desired his. The moment her regard ceased, I would have torn his heart out, and drank his blood! But, till then—if you don't believe me, you don't know me—till then, I would have died by inches before I touched a single hair of his head!"

"And yet," I interrupted, "you have no scruples in completely ruining all hopes of her perfect restoration, by thrusting yourself into her remembrance now, when she has nearly forgotten you, and involving her in a new tumult of discord and distress."

"You suppose she has nearly forgotten me?" he said. "Oh, Nelly! you know she has not! You know as well as I do, that for every thought she spends on Linton, she spends a thousand on me! At a most miserable period of my life, I had a notion of the kind; it haunted me on my return to the neighbourhood last summer; but only her own assurance could make me admit the horrible idea again. And then, Linton would be nothing, nor Hindley, nor all the dreams that ever I dreamt. Two words would comprehend my future—*death* and *hell*; existence, after losing her, would be hell. Yet I was a fool to fancy for a moment that she valued Edgar Linton's attachment more than mine. If he loved with all the powers of his puny being, he couldn't love as much in eighty years as I could in a day. And Catherine has a heart as deep as I have; the sea could be as readily contained in that horse trough, as her whole affection be monopolized by him. Tush! He is scarcely a degree dearer to her than her dog, or her horse. It is not in him to be loved like me; how can she love in him what he has not?"

"Catherine and Edgar are as fond of each other as any two people can be," cried Isabella, with sudden vivacity. "No one has a right to talk in that manner, and I won't hear my brother depreciated in silence!"

"Your brother is wondrous fond of you too, isn't he?" observed Heathcliff scornfully. "He turns you adrift on the world with surprising alacrity."

"He is not aware of what I suffer," she replied. "I didn't tell him that."

"You have been telling him something, then; you have written, have you?"

"To say that I was married, I did write—you saw the note."

"And nothing since?"

"No."

"My young lady is looking sadly the worse for her change of condition," I remarked. "Somebody's love comes short in her case, obviously—whose, I may guess, but, perhaps, I shouldn't say."

"I should guess it was her own," said Heathcliff. "She degenerates into a mere slut! She is tired of trying to please me, uncommonly early. You'd hardly credit it, but the very morrow of our wedding, she was weeping to go home. However, she'll suit this house so much the better for not being over nice, and I'll take care she does not disgrace me by rambling abroad."

"Well, sir," returned I, "I hope you'll consider that Mrs. Heathcliff is accustomed to be looked after and waited on, and that she has been brought up like an only daughter, whom everyone was ready to serve. You must let her have a maid to keep things tidy about her, and you must treat her kindly. Whatever be your notion of Mr. Edgar, you cannot doubt that she has a capacity for strong attachments, or she wouldn't have abandoned the elegancies, and comforts, and friends of her former home, to fix contentedly, in such a wilderness as this, with you."

"She abandoned them under a delusion," he answered, "picturing in me a hero of romance, and expecting unlimited indulgences from my chivalrous devotion. I can hardly regard her in the light of a rational creature, so obstinately has she persisted in forming a fabulous notion of my character, and acting on the false impressions she cherished. But, at last, I think she begins to know me—I don't perceive the silly smiles and grimaces that provoked me at first, and the senseless incapability of discerning that I was in earnest, when I gave her my opinion of her infatuation and herself. It was a marvellous effort of perspicacity to discover that I did not love her. I believed, at one time, no lessons could teach her that! And yet it is poorly learnt, for this morning she announced, as a piece of appalling intelligence, that I had actually succeeded in making her hate me! A positive labour of Hercules, I assure you! If it be achieved, I have cause to return thanks. Can I trust your assertion, Isabella? Are you sure you hate me? If I let you alone for half a day, won't you come sighing and wheedling to me again? I dare say she would rather I had seemed all tenderness before you—it wounds her vanity to have the truth exposed. But I don't care who knows that the passion was wholly on one side, and I never told her a lie about it. She cannot accuse me of showing a bit of deceitful softness. The first thing she saw me do, on coming out of the Grange, was to hang up her little dog; and when she pleaded for it, the first words I uttered were a wish that I had the hanging of every being belonging to her, except one; possibly she took that exception for herself. But no brutality disgusted her—I suppose she has an innate admiration of it, if only her precious person were secure from injury! Now, was it not the depth of absurdity—of genuine idiocy, for that pitiful, slavish, mean-minded brach to dream that I could love her? Tell your master, Nelly, that I never, in all my life, met with such an abject thing as she is. She even disgraces the name of Linton; and I 've sometimes relented, from pure lack of invention, in my experiments on what she could endure, and still creep shamefully cringing back! But tell him, also, to set his fraternal and magisterial heart at ease, that I keep strictly within the limits of the law. I have avoided, up to this period, giving her the slightest right to claim a separation; and, what 's more, she 'd thank nobody for dividing us. If she desired to go, she might—the nuisance of her presence outweighs the gratification to be derived from tormenting her!"

"Mr. Heathcliff," said I, "this is the talk of a madman, and your wife, most likely, is convinced you are mad, and, for that reason, she has borne with you hitherto; but now that you say she may go, she 'll doubtless avail herself of the permission. You are not so bewitched, ma'am, are you, as to remain with him of your own accord?"

"Take care, Ellen!" answered Isabella, her eyes sparkling irefully; there was no misdoubting by their expression the full success of her partner's endeavours to make himself detested. "Don't put faith in a single word he speaks. He 's a lying fiend! a monster, and not a human being! I 've been told I might leave him before; and I 've made the attempt, but I dare not repeat it! Only, Ellen, promise you 'll not mention a syllable of his infamous conversation to my brother or Catherine. Whatever he may pretend, he wishes to provoke Edgar to desperation; he says he has married me on purpose to obtain power over him, and he shan't obtain it—I 'll die first! I just hope, I pray, that he may forget his diabolical prudence, and kill me! The single pleasure I can imagine, is to die, or to see him dead!"

"There—that will do for the present!" said Heathcliff. "If you are called upon in a court of law, you 'll remember her language, Nelly! And take a good look at that countenance—she 's near the point which would suit me. No; you 're not fit to be your own guardian, Isabella, now; and I, being your legal protector, must retain you in my custody, however distasteful the obligation may be. Go upstairs; I have something to say to

Ellen Dean in private. That's not the way—upstairs, I tell you! Why, this is the road upstairs, child!"

He seized, and thrust her from the room, and returned muttering—

"I have no pity! I have no pity! The more the worms writhe, the more I yearn to crush out their entrails! It's a moral teething; and I grind with greater energy, in proportion to the increase of pain."

"Do you understand what the word pity means?" I said, hastening to resume my bonnet. "Did you ever feel a touch of it in your life?"

"Put that down!" he interrupted, perceiving my intention to depart. "You are not going yet. Come here now, Nelly—I must either persuade or compel you to aid me in fulfilling my determination to see Catherine, and that without delay. I swear that I meditate no harm; I don't desire to cause any disturbance, or to exasperate or insult Mr. Linton; I only wish to hear from herself how she is, and why she has been ill, and to ask if anything that I could do would be of use to her. Last night, I was in the Grange garden six hours, and I'll return there tonight; and every night I'll haunt the place, and every day, till I find an opportunity of entering. If Edgar Linton meets me, I shall not hesitate to knock him down, and give him enough to insure his quiescence while I stay. If his servants oppose me, I shall threaten them off with these pistols. But wouldn't it be better to prevent my coming in contact with them, or their master? And you could do it so easily. I'd warn you when I came, and then you might let me in unobserved, as soon as she was alone, and watch till I departed, your conscience quite calm: you would be hindering mischief."

I protested against playing that treacherous part in my employer's house; and besides, I urged the cruelty and selfishness of his destroying Mrs. Linton's tranquillity for his satisfaction.

"The commonest occurrence startles her painfully," I said. "She's all nerves, and she couldn't bear the surprise, I'm positive. Don't persist, sir! or else, I shall be obliged to inform my master of your designs, and he'll take measures to secure his house and its inmates from any such unwarrantable intrusions!"

"In that case, I'll take measures to secure you, woman!" exclaimed Heathcliff; "you shall not leave Wuthering Heights till tomorrow morning. It is a foolish story to assert that Catherine could not bear to see me; and as to surprising her, I don't desire it; you must prepare her—ask her if I may come. You say she never mentions my name, and that I am never mentioned to her. To whom should she mention me if I am a forbidden topic in the house? She thinks you are all spies for her husband. Oh, I've no doubt she's in hell among you! I guess by her silence, as much as anything, what she feels. You say she is often restless, and anxious looking—is that a proof of tranquillity? You talk of her mind being unsettled. How the devil could it be otherwise in her frightful isolation? And that insipid, paltry creature attending her from *duty* and *humanity*! From *pity* and *charity*! He might as well plant an oak in a flower-pot, and expect it to thrive, as imagine he can restore her to vigour in the soil of his shallow cares! Let us settle it at once; will you stay here, and am I to fight my way to Catherine over Linton and his footmen? Or will you be my friend, as you have been hitherto, and do what I request? Decide! because there is no reason for my lingering another minute, if you persist in your stubborn ill-nature."

Well, Mr. Lockwood, I argued and complained, and flatly refused him fifty times; but in the long run he forced me to an agreement. I engaged to carry a letter from him to my mistress; and should she consent, I promised to let him have intelligence of Linton's next absence from home, when he might come, and get in as he was able—I wouldn't be there, and my fellow servants should be equally out of the way.

Was it right or wrong? I fear it was wrong, though expedient. I thought I prevented another explosion by my compliance; and I thought, too, it might create a favourable crisis in Catherine's mental illness; and then I remembered Mr. Edgar's stern rebuke of my carrying tales, and I tried to smooth away all disquietude on the subject, by affirming, with frequent iteration, that that betrayal of trust, if it merited so harsh an appellation, should be the last.

Notwithstanding, my journey homeward was sadder

than my journey thither; and many misgivings I had, ere I could prevail on myself to put the missive into Mrs. Linton's hand.

But here is Kenneth; I 'll go down, and tell him how much better you are. My history is dree, as we say, and will serve to wile away another morning.

Dree, and dreay! I reflected as the good woman descended to receive the doctor; and not exactly a kind which I should have chosen to amuse me. But never mind! I 'll extract wholesome medicines from Mrs. Dean's bitter herbs; and firstly, let me beware of the fascination that lurks in Catherine Heathcliff's brilliant eyes. I should be in a curious taking if I surrendered my heart to that young person and the daughter turned out a second edition of the mother!

CHAPTER 15

ANOTHER week over—and I am so many days nearer health, and spring! I have now heard all my neighbour's history, at different sittings, as the housekeeper could spare time from more important occupations. I 'll continue it in her own words, only a little condensed. She is, on the whole, a very fair narrator, and I don't think I could improve her style.

In the evening, she said, the evening of my visit to the Heights, I knew, as well as if I saw him, that Mr. Heathcliff was about the place; and I shunned going out, because I still carried his letter in my pocket, and didn't want to be threatened, or teased any more.

I had made up my mind not to give it till my master went somewhere, as I could not guess how its receipt would affect Catherine. The consequence was, that it did not reach her before the lapse of three days. The fourth was Sunday, and I brought it into her room after the family were gone to church.

There was a man-servant left to keep the house with me, and we generally made a practice of locking the doors during the hours of service; but on that occasion the weather was so warm and pleasant that I set them wide open, and, to fulfil my engagement, as I knew who would be coming, I told my companion that the mistress wished very much for some oranges, and he must run over to the village and get a few, to be paid for on the morrow. He departed, and I went upstairs.

Mrs. Linton sat in a loose, white dress, with a light shawl over her shoulders, in the recess of the open window, as usual. Her thick, long hair had been partly removed at the beginning of her illness, and now she wore it simply combed in its natural tresses over her temples and neck. Her appearance was altered, as I had told Heathcliff; but when she was calm, there seemed unearthly beauty in the change.

The flash of her eyes had been succeeded by a dreamy and melancholy softness; they no longer gave the impression of looking at the objects around her; they appeared always to gaze beyond, and far beyond—you would have said out of this world. Then, the paleness of her face—its haggard aspect having vanished as she recovered flesh—and the peculiar expression arising from her mental state, though painfully suggestive of their causes, added to the touching interest which she awakened; and—invariably to me, I know, and to any person who saw her, I should think—refuted more tangible proofs of convalescence, and stamped her as one doomed to decay.

A book lay spread on the sill before her, and the scarcely perceptible wind fluttered its leaves at intervals. I believe Linton had laid it there, for she never endeavoured to divert herself with reading, or occupation of any kind, and he would spend many an hour in trying to entice her attention to some subject which had formerly been her amusement.

She was conscious of his aim, and in her better moods endured his efforts placidly, only showing their uselessness by now and then suppressing a wearied sigh, and checking him at last with the saddest of smiles and kisses. At other times, she would turn petulantly away, and hide her face in her hands, or even push him off angrily;

and then he took care to let her alone, for he was certain of doing no good.

Gimmerton chapel bells were still ringing, and the full, mellow flow of the beck in the valley came soothingly on the ear. It was a sweet substitute for the yet absent murmur of the summer foliage, which drowned that music about the Grange when the trees were in leaf. At Wuthering Heights it always sounded on quiet days following a great thaw or a season of steady rain. And of Wuthering Heights Catherine was thinking as she listened—that is, if she thought or listened at all; but she had the vague, distant look I mentioned before, which expressed no recognition of material things either by ear or eye.

"There's a letter for you, Mrs. Linton," I said, gently inserting it in one hand that rested on her knee. "You must read it immediately, because it wants an answer. Shall I break the seal?"

"Yes," she answered, without altering the direction of her eyes.

I opened it—it was very short.

"Now," I continued, "read it."

She drew away her hand, and let it fall. I replaced it in her lap, and stood waiting till it should please her to glance down; but that movement was so long delayed that at last I resumed—

"Must I read it, ma'am? It is from Mr. Heathcliff."

There was a start and a troubled gleam of recollection, and a struggle to arrange her ideas. She lifted the letter, and seemed to peruse it; and when she came to the signature she sighed; yet still I found she had not gathered its import, for, upon my desiring to hear her reply, she merely pointed to the name, and gazed at me with mournful and questioning eagerness.

"Well, he wishes to see you," said I, guessing her need of an interpreter. "He's in the garden by this time, and impatient to know what answer I shall bring."

As I spoke, I observed a large dog lying on the sunny grass beneath raise its ears as if about to bark, and then smoothing them back, announce, by a wag of the tail, that someone approached whom it did not consider a stranger.

Mrs. Linton bent forward, and listened breathlessly.

The minute after a step traversed the hall; the open house was too tempting for Heathcliff to resist walking in—most likely he supposed that I was inclined to shirk my promise, and so resolved to trust to his own audacity.

With straining eagerness Catherine gazed towards the entrance of her chamber. He did not hit the right room directly; she motioned me to admit him; but he found it out, ere I could reach the door, and in a stride or two was at her side, and had her grasped in his arms.

He neither spoke nor loosed his hold for some five minutes, during which period he bestowed more kisses than ever he gave in his life before, I dare say: but then my mistress had kissed him first, and I plainly saw that he could hardly bear, for downright agony, to look into her face! The same conviction had stricken him as me, from the instant he beheld her, that there was no prospect of ultimate recovery there—she was fated, sure to die.

"Oh, Cathy! Oh, my life! how can I bear it?" was the first sentence he uttered, in a tone that did not seek to disguise his despair.

And now he stared at her so earnestly that I thought the very intensity of his gaze would bring tears into his eyes; but they burned with anguish, they did not melt.

"What now?" said Catherine, leaning back, and returning his look with a suddenly clouded brow—her humour was a mere vane for constantly varying caprices. "You and Edgar have broken my heart, Heathcliff! And you both come to bewail the deed to me, as if you were the people to be pitied! I shall not pity you, not I. You have killed me—and thriven on it, I think. How strong you are! How many years do you mean to live after I am gone?"

Heathcliff had knelt on one knee to embrace her; he attempted to rise, but she seized his hair, and kept him down.

"I wish I could hold you," she continued, bitterly, "till we were both dead! I shouldn't care what you suffered. I care nothing for your sufferings. Why shouldn't you suffer? I do! Will you forget me? Will you be happy when I am in the earth? Will you say twenty years hence, 'That's the grave of Catherine Earnshaw. I loved her long ago, and was wretched to lose her; but it is past.

I've loved many others since; my children are dearer to me than she was, and, at death, I shall not rejoice that I am going to her, I shall be sorry that I must leave them!' Will you say so, Heathcliff?"

"Don't torture me till I'm as mad as yourself," cried he, wrenching his head free, and grinding his teeth.

The two, to a cool spectator, made a strange and fearful picture. Well might Catherine deem that heaven would be a land of exile to her, unless with her mortal body she cast away her mortal character also. Her present countenance had a wild vindictiveness in its white cheek, and a bloodless lip and scintillating eye; and she retained in her closed fingers a portion of the locks she had been grasping. As to her companion, while raising himself with one hand, he had taken her arm with the other; and so inadequate was his stock of gentleness to the requirements of her condition, that on his letting go I saw four distinct impressions left blue in the colourless skin.

"Are you possessed with a devil," he pursued, savagely, "to talk in that manner to me when you are dying? Do you reflect that all those words will be branded in my memory, and eating deeper eternally after you have left me? You know you lie to say I have killed you, and, Catherine, you know that I could as soon forget you as my existence! Is it not sufficient for your infernal selfishness, that while you are at peace I shall writhe in the torments of hell?"

"I shall not be at peace," moaned Catherine, recalled to a sense of physical weakness by the violent, unequal throbbing of her heart, which beat visibly and audibly under this excess of agitation.

She said nothing further till the paroxysm was over; then she continued, more kindly—

"I'm not wishing you greater torment than I have, Heathcliff. I only wish us never to be parted: and should a word of mine distress you hereafter, think I feel the same distress underground, and for my own sake, forgive me! Come here and kneel down again! You never harmed me in your life. Nay, if you nurse anger, that will be worse to remember than my harsh words! Won't you come here again? Do!"

Heathcliff went to the back of her chair, and leant

(156)

over, but not so far as to let her see his face, which was livid with emotion. She bent round to look at him; he would not permit it; turning abruptly, he walked to the fireplace, where he stood, silent, with his back towards us.

Mrs. Linton's glance followed him suspiciously: every movement woke a new sentiment in her. After a pause, and a prolonged gaze, she resumed, addressing me in accents of indignant disappointment—

"Oh, you see, Nelly, he would not relent a moment to keep me out of the grave. *That* is how I'm loved! Well, never mind. That is not my Heathcliff. I shall love mine yet; and take him with me—he's in my soul. And," added she musingly, "the thing that irks me most is this shattered prison, after all. I'm tired, tired of being enclosed here. I'm wearying to escape into that glorious world, and to be always there: not seeing it dimly through tears, and yearning for it through the walls of an aching heart, but really with it, and in it. Nelly, you think you are better and more fortunate than I, in full health and strength; you are sorry for me—very soon that will be altered. I shall be sorry for you. I shall be incomparably beyond and above you all. I wonder he won't be near me!" She went on to herself. "I thought he wished it. Heathcliff, dear! you should not be sullen now. Do come to me, Heathcliff."

In her eagerness she rose and supported herself on the arm of the chair. At that earnest appeal he turned to her, looking absolutely desperate. His eyes wide, and wet at last, flashed fiercely on her; his breast heaved convulsively. An instant they held asunder, and then how they met I hardly saw, but Catherine made a spring, and he caught her, and they were locked in an embrace from which I thought my mistress would never be released alive—in fact, to my eyes, she seemed directly insensible. He flung himself into the nearest seat, and on my approaching hurriedly to ascertain if she had fainted, he gnashed at me, and foamed like a mad dog, and gathered her to him with greedy jealousy. I did not feel as if I were in the company of a creature of my own species; it appeared that he would not understand, though I spoke to him; so I stood off, and held my tongue, in great perplexity.

A movement of Catherine's relieved me a little

presently—she put up her hand to clasp his neck, and bring her cheek to his as he held her; while he, in return, covered her with frantic caresses, said wildly—

"You teach me how cruel you've been—cruel and false. Why did you despise me? Why did you betray your own heart, Cathy? I have not one word of comfort. You deserve this. You have killed yourself. Yes, you may kiss me, and cry, and wring out my kisses and tears; they'll blight you—they'll damn you. You loved me—then what *right* had you to leave me? What right—answer me—for the poor fancy you felt for Linton? Because misery, and degradation, and death, and nothing that God or Satan could inflict would have parted us, you, of your own will, did it. I have not broken your heart—you have broken it; and in breaking it, you have broken mine. So much the worse for me, that I am strong. Do I want to live? What kind of living will it be when you—oh, God! would you like to live with your soul in the grave?"

"Let me alone. Let me alone," sobbed Catherine. "If I've done wrong, I'm dying for it. It is enough! You left me too—but I won't upbraid you! I forgive you. Forgive me!"

"It is hard to forgive, and to look at those eyes, and feel those wasted hands," he answered. "Kiss me again; and don't let me see your eyes! I forgive what you have done to me. I love my murderer—but yours! How can I?"

They were silent—their faces hid against each other, and washed by each other's tears. At least, I suppose the weeping was on both sides; as it seemed Heathcliff *could* weep on a great occasion like this.

I grew very uncomfortable, meanwhile; for the afternoon wore fast away, the man whom I had sent off returned from his errand, and I could distinguish, by the shine of the westering sun up the valley, a concourse thickening outside Gimmerton chapel porch.

"Service is over," I announced. "My master will be here in half an hour."

Heathcliff groaned a curse, and strained Catherine closer; she never moved.

Ere long I perceived a group of the servants passing up the road towards the kitchen wing. Mr. Linton was not far behind; he opened the gate himself and sauntered slowly up, probably enjoying the lovely afternoon that breathed as soft as summer.

"Now he is here," I exclaimed. "For Heaven's sake, hurry down! You 'll not meet anyone on the front stairs. Do be quick; and stay among the trees till he is fairly in."

"I must go, Cathy," said Heathcliff, seeking to extricate himself from his companion's arms. "But, if I live, I 'll see you again before you are asleep. I won't stray five yards from your window."

"You must not go!" she answered, holding him as firmly as her strength allowed. "You shall not, I tell you."

"For one hour," he pleaded, earnestly.

"Not for one minute," she replied.

"I must—Linton will be up immediately," persisted the alarmed intruder.

He would have risen, and unfixed her fingers by the act—she clung fast, gasping; there was mad resolution in her face.

"No!" she shrieked. "Oh, don't, don't go. It is the last time! Edgar will not hurt us. Heathcliff, I shall die! I shall die!"

"Damn the fool! There he is," cried Heathcliff, sinking back into his seat. "Hush, my darling! Hush, hush, Catherine! I 'll stay. If he shot me so, I 'd expire with a blessing on my lips."

And there they were fast again. I heard my master mounting the stairs—the cold sweat ran from my forehead; I was horrified.

"Are you going to listen to her ravings?" I said, passionately. "She does not know what she says. Will you ruin her, because she has not wit to help herself? Get up! You could be free instantly. That is the most diabolical deed that ever you did. We are all done for—master, mistress, and servant."

I wrung my hands, and cried out, and Mr. Linton hastened his step at the noise. In the midst of my agitation, I was sincerely glad to observe that Catherine's arms had fallen relaxed, and her head hung down.

"She 's fainted, or dead," I thought; "so much the better. Far better that she should be dead, than lingering a burden and a misery-maker to all about her."

Edgar sprang to his unbidden guest, blanched with astonishment and rage. What he meant to do, I cannot tell; however, the other stopped all demonstrations, at once, by placing the lifeless-looking form in his arms.

"Look there!" he said. "Unless you be a fiend, help her first—then you shall speak to me!"

He walked into the parlour, and sat down. Mr. Linton summoned me, and with great difficulty, and after resorting to many means, we managed to restore her to sensation; but she was all bewildered; she sighed, and moaned, and knew nobody. Edgar, in his anxiety for her, forgot her hated friend. I did not. I went, at the earliest opportunity, and besought him to depart, affirming that Catherine was better, and he should hear from me in the morning, how she passed the night.

"I shall not refuse to go out of doors," he answered, "but I shall stay in the garden—and, Nelly, mind you keep your word tomorrow. I shall be under those larch trees. Mind! or I pay another visit, whether Linton be in or not."

He sent a rapid glance through the half-open door of the chamber, and, ascertaining that what I stated was apparently true, delivered the house of his luckless presence.

CHAPTER 16

ABOUT twelve o'clock, that night, was born the Catherine you saw at Wuthering Heights: a puny, seven months' child; and two hours after the mother died, having never recovered sufficient consciousness to miss Heathcliff, or know Edgar.

The latter's distraction at his bereavement is a subject too painful to be dwelt on; its after effects showed how deep the sorrow sunk.

A great addition, in my eyes, was his being left without an heir. I bemoaned that, as I gazed on the feeble orphan; and I mentally abused old Linton for (what was only natural partiality) the securing his estate to his own daughter, instead of his son's.

An unwelcomed infant it was, poor thing! It might have wailed out of life, and nobody cared a morsel, during those first hours of existence. We redeemed the neglect afterwards; but its beginning was as friendless as its end is likely to be.

Next morning—bright and cheerful out of doors—stole softened in through the blinds of the silent room, and suffused the couch and its occupant with a mellow, tender glow.

Edgar Linton had his head laid on the pillow, and his eyes shut. His young and fair features were almost as deathlike as those of the form beside him, and almost as fixed—but *his* was the hush of exhausted anguish, and *hers* of perfect peace. Her brow smooth, her lids closed, her lips wearing the expression of a smile—no angel in heaven could be more beautiful than she appeared. And I partook of the infinite calm in which she lay; my mind was never in a holier frame than while I gazed on that untroubled image of Divine rest. I instinctively echoed the words she had uttered a few hours before: "Incomparably beyond and above us all! Whether still on earth or now in heaven, her spirit is at home with God!"

I don't know if it be a peculiarity in me, but I am seldom otherwise than happy while watching in the chamber of death, should no frenzied or despairing mourner share the duty with me. I see a repose that neither earth nor hell can break, and I feel an assurance of the endless and shadowless hereafter—the Eternity they have entered—where life is boundless in its duration, and love in its sympathy, and joy in its fulness. I noticed on that occasion how much selfishness there is even in a love like Mr. Linton's, when he so regretted Catherine's blessed release!

To be sure, one might have doubted, after the wayward and impatient existence she had led, whether she merited a haven of peace at last. One might doubt in seasons of cold reflection; but not then, in the presence of her corpse. It asserted its own tranquillity, which seemed a pledge of equal quiet to its former inhabitant.

Do you believe such people are happy in the other world, sir? I'd give a great deal to know.

I declined answering Mrs. Dean's question, which struck me as something heterodox. She proceeded:

Retracing the course of Catherine Linton, I fear we have no right to think she is; but we'll leave her with her Maker.

The master looked asleep, and I ventured soon after sunrise to quit the room and steal out to the pure refreshing air. The servants thought me gone to shake off the drowsiness of my protracted watch; in reality, my chief motive was seeing Mr. Heathcliff. If he had remained among the larches all night, he would have heard nothing of the stir at the Grange, unless, perhaps, he might catch the gallop of the messenger going to Gimmerton. If he had come nearer, he would probably be aware, from the lights flitting to and fro, and the opening and shutting of the outer doors, that all was not right within.

I wished, yet feared, to find him. I felt the terrible news must be told, and I longed to get it over; but *how* to do it, I did not know.

He was there—at least a few yards further in the park, leant against an old ash tree, his hat off, and his hair soaked with the dew that had gathered on the budded branches, and fell pattering round him. He had been standing a long time in that position, for I saw a pair of ousels passing and repassing scarcely three feet from him, busy in building their nest, and regarding his proximity no more than that of a piece of timber. They flew off at my approach, and he raised his eyes and spoke:

"She's dead!" he said; "I've not waited for you to learn that. Put your handkerchief away—don't snivel before me. Damn you all! she wants none of your tears!"

I was weeping as much for him as her—we do sometimes pity creatures that have none of the feeling either for themselves or others; and when I first looked into his face, I perceived that he had got intelligence of the catastrophe, and a foolish notion struck me that his heart was quelled and he prayed, because his lips moved and his gaze was bent on the ground.

"Yes, she's dead!" I answered, checking my sobs and drying my cheeks. "Gone to heaven, I hope, where we may, every one, join her, if we take due warning and leave our evil ways to follow good!"

"Did she take due warning, then?" asked Heathcliff, attempting a sneer. "Did she die like a saint? Come, give me a true history of the event. How did——"

He endeavoured to pronounce the name, but could not manage it; and compressing his mouth he held a silent combat with his inward agony, defying, meanwhile, my sympathy with an unflinching, ferocious stare.

"How did she die?" he resumed, at last—fain, notwithstanding his hardihood, to have a support behind him; for, after the struggle, he trembled, in spite of himself, to his very finger-ends.

"Poor wretch!" I thought; "you have a heart and nerves the same as your brother men! Why should you be anxious to conceal them? Your pride cannot blind God! You tempt him to wring them, till he forces a cry of humiliation."

"Quietly as a lamb!" I answered aloud. "She drew a sigh, and stretched herself, like a child reviving, and sinking again to sleep; and five minutes after I felt one little pulse at her heart, and nothing more!"

"And—did she ever mention me?" he asked, hesitating, as if he dreaded the answer to his question would introduce details that he could not bear to hear.

"Her senses never returned; she recognized nobody from the time you left her," I said. "She lies with a sweet smile on her face; and her latest ideas wandered back to pleasant early days. Her life closed in a gentle dream—may she wake as kindly in the other world!"

"May she wake in torment!" he cried, with frightful vehemence, stamping his foot, and groaning in a sudden paroxysm of ungovernable passion. "Why, she's a liar to the end! Where is she? Not there—not in heaven—not perished—where? Oh! you said you cared nothing for my sufferings! And I pray one prayer—I repeat it till my tongue stiffens—Catherine Earnshaw, may you not rest as long as I am living! You said I killed you—haunt me, then! The murdered do haunt their murderers. I believe —I know that ghosts have wandered on earth. Be with me always—take any form—drive me mad! only do not leave me in this abyss, where I cannot find you! Oh

God! it is unutterable! I cannot live without my life! I cannot live without my soul!"

He dashed his head against the knotted trunk, and, lifting up his eyes, howled, not like a man, but like a savage beast getting goaded to death with knives and spears.

I observed several splashes of blood about the bark of the tree, and his hands and forehead were both stained; probably the scene I witnessed was a repetition of others acted during the night. It hardly moved my compassion —it appalled me; still I felt reluctant to quit him so. But the moment he recollected himself enough to notice me watching, he thundered a command for me to go, and I obeyed. He was beyond my skill to quiet or console!

Mrs. Linton's funeral was appointed to take place on the Friday following her decease; and till then her coffin remained uncovered, and strewn with flowers and scented leaves, in the great drawing-room. Linton spent his days and nights there, a sleepless guardian; and—a circumstance concealed from all but me—Heathcliff spent his nights, at least, outside, equally a stranger to repose.

I held no communication with him; still I was conscious of his design to enter, if he could; and on the Tuesday, a little after dark, when my master, from sheer fatigue, had been compelled to retire a couple of hours, I went and opened one of the windows, moved by his perseverance to give him a chance of bestowing on the fading image of his idol one final adieu.

He did not omit to avail himself of the opportunity, cautiously and briefly—too cautiously to betray his presence by the slightest noise. Indeed, I shouldn't have discovered that he had been there, except for the disarrangement of the drapery about the corpse's face, and for observing on the floor a curl of light hair, fastened with a silver thread, which, on examination, I ascertained to have been taken from a locket hung round Catherine's neck. Heathcliff had opened the trinket and cast out its contents, replacing them by a black lock of his own. I twisted the two, and enclosed them together.

Mr. Earnshaw was, of course, invited to attend the remains of his sister to the grave; and he sent no excuse, but he never came; so that, besides her husband, the mourners were wholly composed of tenants and servants. Isabella was not asked.

The place of Catherine's interment, to the surprise of the villagers, was neither in the chapel, under the carved monument of the Lintons, nor yet by the tombs of her own relations, outside. It was dug on a green slope in a corner of the kirkyard, where the wall is so low that heath and bilberry plants have climbed over it from the moor; and peat mould almost buries it. Her husband lies in the same spot now; and they have each a simple headstone above, and a plain grey block at their feet, to mark the graves.

CHAPTER 17

THAT Friday made the last of our fine days, for a month. In the evening, the weather broke; the wind shifted from south to northeast, and brought rain first, and then sleet and snow.

On the morrow one could hardly imagine that there had been three weeks of summer; the primroses and crocuses were hidden under wintry drifts, the larks were silent, the young leaves of the early trees smitten and blackened. And dreary, and chill, and dismal that morrow did creep over! My master kept his room; I took possession of the lonely parlour, converting it into a nursery, and there I was sitting, with the moaning doll of a child laid on my knee, rocking it to and fro, and watching, meanwhile, the still driving flakes build up the uncurtained window, when the door opened, and some person entered, out of breath and laughing!

My anger was greater than my astonishment for a minute. I supposed it one of the maids, and I cried—

"Have done! How dare you show your giddiness here? What would Mr. Linton say if he heard you?"

"Excuse me!" answered a familiar voice, "but I know Edgar is in bed, and I cannot stop myself."

With that the speaker came forward to the fire, panting and holding her hand to her side.

"I have run the whole way from Wuthering Heights!" she continued, after a pause; "except where I 've flown. I couldn't count the number of falls I 've had. Oh, I 'm aching all over! Don't be alarmed! There shall be an explanation as soon as I can give it; only just have the goodness to step out and order the carriage to take me on to Gimmerton, and tell a servant to seek up a few clothes in my wardrobe."

The intruder was Mrs. Heathcliff. She certainly seemed in no laughing predicament, her hair streaming on her shoulders, dripping with snow and water; she was dressed in the girlish dress she commonly wore, befitting her age more than her position—a low frock with short sleeves, and nothing on either head or neck. The frock was of light silk, and clung to her with wet, and her feet were protected merely by thin slippers; add to this a deep cut under one ear, which only the cold prevented from bleeding profusely, a white face scratched and bruised, and a frame hardly able to support itself, through fatigue, and you may fancy my first fright was not much allayed when I had leisure to examine her.

"My dear young lady," I exclaimed, "I 'll stir nowhere, and hear nothing, till you have removed every article of your clothes, and put on dry things; and certainly you shall not go to Gimmerton tonight, so it is needless to order the carriage."

"Certainly, I shall," she said, "walking or riding; yet I 've no objection to dress myself decently. And—ah, see how it flows down my neck now! The fire does make it smart."

She insisted on my fulfilling her directions, before she would let me touch her; and not till after the coachman had been instructed to get ready, and a maid set to pack up some necessary attire, did I obtain her consent for binding the wound and helping to change her garments.

"Now, Ellen," she said, when my task was finished, and she was seated in an easy chair on the hearth, with a cup of tea before her, "you sit down opposite me, and put poor Catherine's baby away—I don't like to see it! You mustn't think I care little for Catherine, because I behaved so foolishly on entering. I 've cried too, bitterly —yes, more than anyone else has reason to cry. We parted unreconciled, you remember, and I shan't forgive myself. But, for all that, I was not going to sympathize with him—the brute beast! O, give me the poker! This is the last thing of his I have about me." She slipped the gold ring from her third finger, and threw it on the floor. "I 'll smash it!" she continued, striking it with childish spite, "and then I 'll burn it!" and she took and dropped the misused article among the coals. "There! he shall buy another, if he gets me back again. He 'd be capable of coming to seek me, to tease Edgar—I dare not stay, lest that notion should possess his wicked head! And besides, Edgar has not been kind, has he? And I won't come suing for his assistance; nor will I bring him into more trouble. Necessity compelled me to seek shelter here; though, if I had not learnt he was out of the way, I 'd have halted at the kitchen, washed my face, warmed myself, got you to bring what I wanted, and departed again to anywhere out of reach of my accursed—of that incarnate goblin! Ah, he was in such a fury! If he had caught me! It 's a pity Earnshaw is not his match in strength; I wouldn't have run till I 'd seen him all but demolished, had Hindley been able to do it!"

"Well, don't talk so fast, Miss!" I interrupted, "you 'll disorder the handkerchief I have tied round your face, and make the cut bleed again. Drink your tea, and take breath, and give over laughing—laughter is sadly out of place under this roof, and in your condition!"

"An undeniable truth," she replied. "Listen to that child! It maintains a constant wail—send it out of my hearing for an hour; I shan't stay any longer."

I rang the bell, and committed it to a servant's care; and then I inquired what had urged her to escape from Wuthering Heights in such an unlikely plight, and where she meant to go, as she refused remaining with us.

"I ought, and I wish to remain," answered she, "to cheer Edgar and take care of the baby, for two things, and because the Grange is my right home. But I tell you he wouldn't let me! Do you think he could bear to see me grow fat and merry; and could bear to think that we were tranquil, and not resolve on poisoning our comfort?

Now, I have the satisfaction of being sure that he detests me to the point of its annoying him seriously to have me within earshot, or eyesight; I notice, when I enter his presence, the muscles of his countenance are involuntarily distorted into an expression of hatred, partly arising from his knowledge of the good causes I have to feel that sentiment for him, and partly from original aversion. It is strong enough to make me feel pretty certain that he would not chase me over England, supposing I contrived a clear escape; and therefore I must get quite away. I've recovered from my first desire to be killed by him—I'd rather he'd kill himself! He has extinguished my love effectually, and so I'm at my ease. I can recollect yet how I loved him; and can dimly imagine that I could still be loving him, if—no, no! Even if he had doted on me, the devilish nature would have revealed its existence somehow. Catherine had an awfully perverted taste to esteem him so dearly, knowing him so well. Monster! would that he could be blotted out of creation, and out of my memory!"

"Hush, hush! He's a human being," I said. "Be more charitable; there are worse men than he is yet!"

"He's not a human being," she retorted, "and he has no claim on my charity. I gave him my heart, and he took and pinched it to death, and flung it back to me. People feel with their hearts, Ellen, and since he has destroyed mine, I have not power to feel for him; and I would not, though he groaned from this to his dying day, and wept tears of blood for Catherine! No, indeed, indeed, I wouldn't!" And here Isabella began to cry; but, immediately dashing the water from her lashes, she recommenced.

"You asked, what has driven me to flight at last? I was compelled to attempt it, because I had succeeded in rousing his rage a pitch above his malignity. Pulling out the nerves with red-hot pincers requires more coolness than knocking on the head. He was worked up to forget the fiendish prudence he boasted of, and proceeded to murderous violence. I experienced pleasure in being able to exasperate him; the sense of pleasure woke my instinct of self-preservation, so I fairly broke free; and if ever I come into his hands again he is welcome to a signal revenge.

"Yesterday, you know, Mr. Earnshaw should have been at the funeral. He kept himself sober for the purpose—tolerably sober, not going to bed mad at six o'clock and getting up drunk at twelve. Consequently, he rose, in suicidal low spirits, as fit for the church as for a dance; and instead, he sat down by the fire and swallowed gin or brandy by tumblerfuls.

"Heathcliff—I shudder to name him!—has been a stranger in the house from last Sunday till today. Whether the angels have fed him, or his kin beneath, I cannot tell, but he has not eaten a meal with us for nearly a week. He has just come home at dawn, and gone upstairs to his chamber, locking himself in—as if anybody dreamt of coveting his company! There he has continued, praying like a Methodist—only the deity he implored is senseless dust and ashes, and God, when addressed, was curiously confounded with his own black father! After concluding these precious orisons—and they lasted generally till he grew hoarse and his voice was strangled in his throat—he would be off again, always straight down to the Grange! I wonder Edgar did not send for a constable, and give him into custody! For me, grieved as I was about Catherine, it was impossible to avoid regarding this season of deliverance from degrading oppression as a holiday.

"I recovered spirits sufficient to hear Joseph's eternal lectures without weeping, and to move up and down the house less with the foot of a frightened thief than formerly. You wouldn't think that I should cry at anything Joseph could say; but he and Hareton are detestable companions. I 'd rather sit with Hindley, and hear his awful talk, than with 't' little maister' and his staunch supporter, that odious old man!

"When Heathcliff is in, I 'm often obliged to seek the kitchen and their society, or starve among the damp uninhabited chambers; when he is not, as was the case this week, I establish a table and chair at one corner of the house fire, and never mind how Mr. Earnshaw may occupy himself; and he does not interfere with my arrangements. He is quieter now than he used to be, if no one provokes him—more sullen and depressed, and less furious. Joseph affirms he 's sure he 's an altered man, that the Lord has touched his heart, and he is saved 'so as by fire.' I'm puzzled to detect signs of the favourable change—but it is not my business.

"Yester-evening I sat in my nook reading some old books till late on towards twelve. It seemed so dismal to go upstairs, with the wild snow blowing outside, and my thoughts continually reverting to the kirkyard and the new-made grave! I dared hardly lift my eyes from the page before me, that melancholy scene so instantly usurped its place.

"Hindley sat opposite, his head leant on his hand, perhaps meditating on the same subject. He had ceased drinking at a point below irrationality, and had neither stirred nor spoken during two or three hours. There was no sound through the house but the moaning wind which shook the windows every now and then, the faint crackling of the coals, and the click of my snuffers as I removed at intervals the long wick of the candle. Hareton and Joseph were probably fast asleep in bed. It was very, very sad, and while I read I sighed, for it seemed as if all joy had vanished from the world, never to be restored.

"The doleful silence was broken at length by the sound of the kitchen latch—Heathcliff had returned from his watch earlier than usual, owing, I suppose, to the sudden storm.

"That entrance was fastened, and we heard him coming round to get in by the other. I rose with an irrepressible expression of what I felt on my lips, which induced my companion, who had been staring towards the door, to turn and look at me.

" 'I'll keep him out five minutes,' he exclaimed. 'You won't object?'

" 'No, you may keep him out the whole night for me,' I answered. 'Do! put the key in the lock, and draw the bolts.'

"Earnshaw accomplished this ere his guest reached the front; he then came and brought his chair to the other side of my table, leaning over it, and searching in my eyes for a sympathy with the burning hate that gleamed from his; as he both looked and felt like an assassin, he couldn't exactly find that; but he discovered enough to encourage him to speak.

" 'You and I,' he said, 'have each a great debt to settle with the man out yonder! If we were neither of us cowards, we might combine to discharge it. Are you as soft as your brother? Are you willing to endure to the last, and not once attempt a repayment?'

" 'I 'm weary of enduring now,' I replied; 'and I 'd be glad of a retaliation that wouldn't recoil on myself; but treachery and violence are spears pointed at both ends —they wound those who resort to them, worse than their enemies.'

" 'Treachery and violence are a just return for treachery and violence!' cried Hindley. 'Mrs. Heathcliff, I 'll ask you to do nothing, but sit still and be dumb. Tell me now, can you? I 'm sure you would have as much pleasure as I in witnessing the conclusion of the fiend's existence; he 'll be your death unless you overreach him; and he 'll be my ruin. Damn the hellish villain! He knocks at the door as if he were master here already! Promise to hold your tongue, and before that clock strikes—it wants three minutes of one—you 're a free woman!'

"He took the implements which I described to you in my letter from his breast, and would have turned down the candle. I snatched it away, however, and seized his arm.

" 'I 'll not hold my tongue!' I said; 'you mustn't touch him. Let the door remain shut, and be quiet!'

" 'No! I 've formed my resolution, and by God, I 'll execute it!' cried the desperate being. 'I 'll do you a kindness in spite of yourself, and Hareton justice! And you needn't trouble your head to screen me; Catherine is gone. Nobody alive would regret me, or be ashamed, though I cut my throat this minute—and it 's time to make an end!'

"I might as well have struggled with a bear, or reasoned with a lunatic. The only resource left me was to run to a lattice and warn his intended victim of the fate which awaited him.

" 'You 'd better seek shelter somewhere else tonight!' I exclaimed in a rather triumphant tone. 'Mr. Earnshaw has a mind to shoot you, if you persist in endeavouring to enter.'

" 'You 'd better open the door, you ——,' he answered, addressing me by some elegant term that I don't care to repeat.

" 'I shall not meddle in the matter,' I retorted again.

'Come in and get shot, if you please! I 've done my duty.'

"With that I shut the window and returned to my place by the fire, having too small a stock of hypocrisy at my command to pretend any anxiety for the danger that menaced him.

Earnshaw swore passionately at me, affirming that I loved the villain yet, and calling me all sorts of names for the base spirit I evinced. And I, in my secret heart (and conscience never reproached me), thought what a blessing it would be for *him*, should Heathcliff put him out of misery; and what a blessing for *me*, should he send Heathcliff to his right abode! As I sat nursing these reflections, the casement behind me was banged on to the floor by a blow from the latter individual, and his black countenance looked blightingly through. The stanchions stood too close to suffer his shoulders to follow, and I smiled, exulting in my fancied security. His hair and clothes were whitened with snow, and his sharp cannibal teeth, revealed by cold and wrath, gleamed through the dark.

" 'Isabella, let me in, or I 'll make you repent!' he 'girned,' as Joseph calls it.

" 'I cannot commit murder,' I replied. 'Mr. Hindley stands sentinel with a knife and loaded pistol.'

" 'Let me in by the kitchen door,' he said.

" 'Hindley will be there before me,' I answered; 'and that 's a poor love of yours that cannot bear a shower of snow! We were left at peace in our beds as long as the summer moon shone, but the moment a blast of winter returns, you must run for shelter! Heathcliff, if I were you, I 'd go stretch myself over her grave and die like a faithful dog. The world is surely not worth living in now, is it? You had distinctly impressed on me the idea that Catherine was the whole joy of your life; I can't imagine how you think of surviving her loss.'

" 'He 's there, is he?' exclaimed my companion, rushing to the gap. 'If I can get my arm out I can hit him!'

"I 'm afraid, Ellen, you 'll set me down as really wickèd; but you don't know all, so don't judge. I wouldn't have aided or abetted an attempt on even *his* life for anything. Wish that he were dead, I must; and therefore I was fearfully disappointed, and unnerved by terror for the consequences of my taunting speech, when he flung himself on Earnshaw's weapon and wrenched it from his grasp.

"The charge exploded, and the knife, in springing back, closed into its owner's wrist. Heathcliff pulled it away by main force, slitting up the flesh as it passed on, and thrust it dripping into his pocket. He then took a stone, struck down the division between two windows, and sprung in. His adversary had fallen senseless with excessive pain, and the flow of blood that gushed from an artery or a large vein.

"The ruffian kicked and trampled on him, and dashed his head repeatedly against the flags, holding me with one hand, meantime, to prevent me summoning Joseph.

"He exerted preter-human self-denial in abstaining from finishing him completely; but getting out of breath he finally desisted, and dragged the apparently inanimate body onto the settle.

"There he tore off the sleeve of Earnshaw's coat, and bound up the wound with brutal roughness, spitting and cursing during the operation as energetically as he had kicked before.

"Being at liberty, I lost no time in seeking the old servant, who, having gathered by degrees the purport of my hasty tale, hurried below, gasping, as he descended the steps two at once.

" 'Whet is thur tuh do, nah? whet is thur tuh do, nah?'

" 'There's this to do,' thundered Heathcliff, 'that your master's mad, and should he last another month, I'll have him to an asylum. And how the devil did you come to fasten me out, you toothless hound? Don't stand muttering and mumbling there. Come, I'm not going to nurse him. Wash that stuff away; and mind the sparks of your candle—it is more than half brandy!'

" 'Und, soa, yah been murthering on him?' exclaimed Joseph, lifting his hands and eyes in horror. 'If iver Aw seed a seeght loike this! May the Lord——'

"Heathcliff gave him a push onto his knees in the middle of the blood, and flung a towel to him; but instead of proceeding to dry it up, he joined his hands, and began a prayer which excited my laughter from its odd phraseology. I was in the condition of mind to be shocked at nothing—in fact, I was as reckless as some malefactors show themselves at the foot of the gallows.

" 'Oh, I forgot you,' said the tyrant. 'You shall do that. Down with you. And you conspire with him against me, do you, viper? There, that is work fit for you!'

"He shook me till my teeth rattled, and pitched me beside Joseph, who steadily concluded his supplications and then rose, vowing he would set off for the Grange directly. Mr. Linton was a magistrate, and though he had fifty wives dead, he should inquire into this.

"He was so obstinate in his resolution, that Heathcliff deemed it expedient to compel from my lips a recapitulation of what had taken place, standing over me, heaving with malevolence, as I reluctantly delivered the account in answer to his questions.

"It required a great deal of labour to satisfy the old man that he was not the aggressor; especially with my hardly wrung replies. However, Mr. Earnshaw soon convinced him that he was alive still; he hastened to administer a dose of spirits, and by their succour his master presently regained motion and consciousness.

"Heathcliff, aware that he was ignorant of the treatment received while insensible, called him deliriously intoxicated, and said he should not notice his atrocious conduct further, but advised him to get to bed. To my joy, he left us, after giving this judicious counsel, and Hindley stretched himself on the hearthstone. I departed to my own room, marvelling that I had escaped so easily.

"This morning, when I came down, about half-an-hour before noon, Mr. Earnshaw was sitting by the fire, deadly sick; his evil genius, almost as gaunt and ghastly, leant against the chimney. Neither appeared inclined to dine, and, having waited till all was cold on the table, I commenced alone.

"Nothing hindered me from eating heartily, and I experienced a certain sense of satisfaction and superiority, as, at intervals, I cast a look towards my silent companions, and felt the comfort of a quiet conscience within me.

"After I had done, I ventured on the unusual liberty of

drawing near the fire, going round Earnshaw's seat, and kneeling in the corner beside him.

"Heathcliff did not glance my way, and I gazed up, and contemplated his features almost as confidently as if they had been turned to stone. His forehead, that I once thought so manly, and that I now think so diabolical, was shaded with a heavy cloud; his basilisk eyes were nearly quenched by sleeplessness—and weeping, perhaps, for the lashes were wet then; his lips devoid of their ferocious sneer, and sealed in an expression of unspeakable sadness. Had it been another, I would have covered my face, in the presence of such grief. In *his* case, I was gratified, and, ignoble as it seems to insult a fallen enemy, I couldn't miss this chance of sticking in a dart—his weakness was the only time when I could taste the delight of paying wrong for wrong."

"Fie, fie, Miss!" I interrupted. "One might suppose you had never opened a Bible in your life. If God afflict your enemies, surely that ought to suffice you. It is both mean and presumptuous to add your torture to his!"

"In general, I'll allow that it would be, Ellen," she continued; "but what misery laid on Heathcliff could content me, unless I have a hand in it? I'd rather he suffered *less*, if I might cause his sufferings and he might *know* that I was the cause. Oh, I owe him so much. On only one condition can I hope to forgive him. It is, if I may take an eye for an eye, a tooth for a tooth; for every wrench of agony return a wrench—reduce him to my level. As he was the first to injure, make him the first to implore pardon; and then—why then, Ellen, I might show you some generosity. But it is utterly impossible I can ever be revenged, and therefore I cannot forgive him. Hindley wanted some water, and I handed him a glass, and asked him how he was.

"'Not as ill as I wish,' he replied. 'But leaving out my arm, every inch of me is as sore as if I had been fighting with a legion of imps!'

"'Yes, no wonder,' was my next remark. 'Catherine used to boast that she stood between you and bodily harm; she meant that certain persons would not hurt you for fear of offending her. It's well people don't *really* rise from their grave, or, last night, she might have witnessed a repulsive scene! Are not you bruised, and cut over your chest and shoulders?'

" 'I can't say,' he answered—'but what do you mean? Did he dare to strike me when I was down?'

" 'He trampled on, and kicked you, and dashed you on the ground,' I whispered. 'And his mouth watered to tear you with his teeth; because, he's only half a man—not so much.'

"Mr. Earnshaw looked up, like me, to the countenance of our mutual foe, who, absorbed in his anguish, seemed insensible to anything around him; the longer he stood, the plainer his reflections revealed their blackness through his features.

" 'Oh, if God would but give me strength to strangle him in my last agony, I'd go to hell with joy,' groaned the impatient man, writhing to rise, and sinking back in despair, convinced of his inadequacy for the struggle.

" 'Nay, it's enough that he has murdered one of you,' I observed aloud. 'At the Grange, everyone knows your sister would have been living now, had it not been for Mr. Heathcliff. After all, it is preferable to be hated than loved by him. When I recollect how happy we were—how happy Catherine was before he came—I'm fit to curse the day.'

"Most likely, Heathcliff noticed more the truth of what was said than the spirit of the person who said it. His attention was roused, I saw, for his eyes rained down tears among the ashes, and he drew his breath in suffocating sighs. I stared full at him, and laughed scornfully. The clouded windows of hell flashed a moment towards me; the fiend which usually looked out, however, was so dimmed and drowned that I did not fear to hazard another sound of derision.

" 'Get up, and begone out of my sight,' said the mourner.

"I guessed he uttered those words, at least, though his voice was hardly intelligible.

" 'I beg your pardon,' I replied. 'But I loved Catherine too; and her brother requires attendance which, for her sake, I shall supply. Now that she's dead, I see her in Hindley; Hindley has exactly her eyes, if you had not tried to gouge them out, and made them black and red, and her——'

" 'Get up, wretched idiot, before I stamp you to death!'
he cried, making a movement that caused me to make
one also.

" 'But then,' I continued, holding myself ready to flee,
'if poor Catherine had trusted you, and assumed the
ridiculous, contemptible, degrading title of Mrs. Heathcliff, she would soon have presented a similar picture!
She wouldn't have borne your abominable behaviour
quietly—her detestation and disgust must have found
voice.'

"The back of the settle and Earnshaw's person interposed between me and him, so instead of endeavouring
to reach me, he snatched a dinner knife from the table
and flung it at my head. It struck beneath my ear, and
stopped the sentence I was uttering; but, pulling it out,
I sprang to the door and delivered another which I hope
went a little deeper than his missile.

"The last glimpse I caught of him was a furious rush
on his part, checked by the embrace of his host, and
both fell locked together on the hearth.

"In my flight through the kitchen I bid Joseph speed
to his master; I knocked over Hareton, who was hanging
a litter of puppies from a chairback in the doorway, and,
blest as a soul escaped from purgatory, I bounded, leaped,
and flew down the steep road; then, quitting its windings,
shot direct across the moor, rolling over banks, and wading through marshes, precipitating myself, in fact, towards the beacon light of the Grange. And far rather
would I be condemned to a perpetual dwelling in the
infernal regions, than, even for one night, abide beneath
the roof of Wuthering Heights again."

Isabella ceased speaking, and took a drink of tea; then
she rose, and bidding me put on her bonnet, and a great
shawl I had brought, and turning a deaf ear to my entreaties for her to remain another hour, she stepped onto
a chair, kissed Edgar's and Catherine's portraits, bestowed a similar salute on me, and descended to the
carriage, accompanied by Fanny, who yelped wild with
joy at recovering her mistress. She was driven away,
never to revisit this neighbourhood; but a regular correspondence was established between her and my master when things were more settled.

I believe her new abode was in the south, near London;

there she had a son born, a few months subsequent to her escape. He was christened Linton, and, from the first, she reported him to be an ailing, peevish creature.

Mr. Heathcliff, meeting me one day in the village, inquired where she lived. I refused to tell. He remarked that it was not of any moment, only she must beware of coming to her brother—she should not be with him, if he had to keep her himself.

Though I would give no information, he discovered, through some of the other servants, both her place of residence and the existence of the child. Still he didn't molest her, for which forbearance she might thank his aversion, I suppose.

He often asked about the infant, when he saw me; and on hearing its name, smiled grimly, and observed—

"They wish me to hate it too, do they?"

"I don't think they wish you to know anything about it," I answered.

"But I'll have it," he said, "when I want it. They may reckon on that!"

Fortunately, its mother died before the time arrived, some thirteen years after the decease of Catherine, when Linton was twelve, or a little more.

On the day succeeding Isabella's unexpected visit, I had no opportunity of speaking to my master; he shunned conversation, and was fit for discussing nothing. When I could get him to listen, I saw it pleased him that his sister had left her husband, whom he abhorred with an intensity which the mildness of his nature would scarcely seem to allow. So deep and sensitive was his aversion, that he refrained from going anywhere where he was likely to see or hear of Heathcliff. Grief, and that together, transformed him into a complete hermit; he threw up his office of magistrate, ceased even to attend church, avoided the village on all occasions, and spent a life of entire seclusion within the limits of his park and grounds, only varied by solitary rambles on the moors, and visits to the grave of his wife, mostly at evening, or early morning before other wanderers were abroad.

But he was too good to be thoroughly unhappy long. He didn't pray for Catherine's soul to haunt him. Time brought resignation, and a melancholy sweeter than common joy. He recalled her memory with ardent, tender love, and hopeful aspiring to the better world, where, he doubted not, she was gone.

And he had earthly consolation and affections, also. For a few days, I said, he seemed regardless of the puny successor to the departed; that coldness melted as fast as snow in April, and ere the tiny thing could stammer a word or totter a step, it wielded a despot's sceptre in his heart.

It was named Catherine, but he never called it the name in full, as he had never called the first Catherine short—probably because Heathcliff had a habit of doing so. The little one was always Cathy; it formed to him a distinction from the mother, and yet, a connection with her; and his attachment sprang from its relation to her, far more than from its being his own.

I used to draw a comparison between him and Hindley Earnshaw, and perplex myself to explain satisfactorily why their conduct was so opposite in similar circumstances. They had both been fond husbands, and were both attached to their children; and I could not see how they shouldn't both have taken the same road, for good or evil. But, I thought in my mind, Hindley, with apparently the stronger head, has shown himself sadly the worse and the weaker man. When his ship struck, the captain abandoned his post; and the crew, instead of trying to save her, rushed into riot and confusion, leaving no hope for their luckless vessel. Linton, on the contrary, displayed the true courage of a loyal and faithful soul; he trusted God; and God comforted him. One hoped, and the other despaired: they chose their own lots, and were righteously doomed to endure them.

But you 'll not want to hear my moralizing, Mr. Lockwood; you 'll judge as well as I can, all these things—at least, you 'll think you will, and that's the same.

The end of Earnshaw was what might have been expected; it followed fast on his sister's; there were scarcely six months between them. We, at the Grange, never got a very succinct account of his state preceding it; all that I did learn was on occasion of going to aid in the preparations for the funeral. Mr. Kenneth came to announce the event to my master.

"Well, Nelly," said he, riding into the yard one morning, too early not to alarm me with an instant presentiment of bad news. "It's yours and my turn to go into mourning at present. Who's given us the slip now, do you think?"

"Who?" I asked in a flurry.

"Why, guess!" he returned, dismounting, and slinging his bridle on a hook by the door. "And nip up the corner of your apron—I'm certain you'll need it."

"Not Mr. Heathcliff, surely?" I exclaimed.

"What! would you have tears for him?" said the doctor. "No, Heathcliff's a tough young fellow; he looks blooming today. I've just seen him. He's rapidly regaining flesh since he lost his better half."

"Who is it, then, Mr. Kenneth?" I repeated impatiently.

"Hindley Earnshaw! Your old friend Hindley," he replied, "and my wicked gossip—though he's been too wild for me this long while. There! I said we should draw water. But cheer up! He died true to his character—drunk as a lord. Poor lad; I'm sorry, too. One can't help missing an old companion, though he had the worst tricks with him that ever man imagined, and has done me many a rascally turn. He's barely twenty-seven, it seems; that's your own age—who would have thought you were born in one year?"

I confess this blow was greater to me than the shock of Mrs. Linton's death: ancient associations lingered round my heart; I sat down in the porch and wept as for a blood relation, desiring Kenneth to get another servant to introduce him to the master.

I could not hinder myself from pondering on the question—"Had he had fair play?" Whatever I did, that idea would bother me; it was so tiresomely pertinacious that I resolved on requesting leave to go to Wuthering Heights, and assist in the last duties to the dead. Mr. Linton was extremely reluctant to consent, but I pleaded eloquently for the friendless condition in which he lay; and I said my old master and foster-brother had a claim on my services as strong as his own. Besides, I reminded him that the child Hareton was his wife's nephew, and, in the absence of nearer kin, he ought to act as its guardian; and he ought to and must inquire how the property was left, and look over the concerns of his brother-in-law.

He was unfit for attending to such matters then, but he bid me speak to his lawyer; and at length permitted me to go. His lawyer had been Earnshaw's also; I called at the village, and asked him to accompany me. He shook his head, and advised that Heathcliff should be let alone, affirming, if the truth were known, Hareton would be found little else than a beggar.

"His father died in debt," he said; "the whole property is mortgaged, and the sole chance for the natural heir is to allow him an opportunity of creating some interest in the creditor's heart, that he may be inclined to deal leniently towards him."

When I reached the Heights, I explained that I had come to see everything carried on decently, and Joseph, who appeared in sufficient distress, expressed satisfaction at my presence. Mr. Heathcliff said he did not perceive that I was wanted; but I might stay and order the arrangements for the funeral, if I chose.

"Correctly," he remarked, "that fool's body should be buried at the crossroads, without ceremony of any kind. I happened to leave him ten minutes yesterday afternoon, and in that interval he fastened the two doors of the house against me, and he has spent the night in drinking himself to death deliberately! We broke in this morning, for we heard him snorting like a horse; and there he was, laid over the settle; flaying and scalping would not have wakened him. I sent for Kenneth, and he came—but not till the beast had changed into carrion; he was both dead and cold, and stark; and so you'll allow, it was useless making more stir about him!"

The old servant confirmed his statement, but muttered—

"Aw'd rayther he'd goan hisseln fur t' doctor! Aw sud uh taen tent uh t' maister better nur him—un he warn't deead when Aw left, nowt uh t' soart!"

I insisted on the funeral being respectable. Mr. Heathcliff said I might have my own way there too; only, he desired me to remember that the money for the whole affair came out of his pocket.

He maintained a hard, careless deportment, indicative of neither joy nor sorrow: if anything, it expressed a flinty gratification at a piece of difficult work successfully executed. I observed once, indeed, something like exultation in his aspect—it was just when the people were bearing the coffin from the house. He had the hypocrisy to represent a mourner; and previous to following with Hareton, he lifted the unfortunate child on to the table and muttered, with peculiar gusto,

"Now, my bonny lad, you are mine! And we'll see if one tree won't grow as crooked as another, with the same wind to twist it!"

The unsuspecting thing was pleased at this speech—he played with Heathcliff's whiskers, and stroked his cheek—but I divined its meaning, and observed tartly,

"That boy must go back with me to Thrushcross Grange, sir. There is nothing in the world less yours than he is!"

"Does Linton say so?" he demanded.

"Of course—he has ordered me to take him," I replied.

"Well," said the scoundrel, "we'll not argue the subject now; but I have a fancy to try my hand at rearing a young one, so intimate to your master that I must supply the place of this with my own, if he attempt to remove it. I don't engage to let Hareton go, undisputed; but I'll be pretty sure to make the other come! Remember to tell him."

This hint was enough to bind our hands. I repeated its substance on my return, and Edgar Linton, little interested at the commencement, spoke no more of interfering. I'm not aware that he could have done it to any purpose, had he been ever so willing.

The guest was now the master of Wuthering Heights; he held firm possession, and proved to the attorney—who, in his turn, proved it to Mr. Linton—that Earnshaw had mortgaged every yard of land he owned, for cash to supply his mania for gaming; and he, Heathcliff, was the mortgagee.

In that manner Hareton, who should now be the first gentleman in the neighbourhood, was reduced to a state of complete dependence on his father's inveterate enemy, and lives in his own house as a servant, deprived of the advantage of wages, and quite unable to right himself, because of his friendlessness, and his ignorance that he has been wronged.

CHAPTER 18

THE twelve years, continued Mrs. Dean, following that dismal period, were the happiest of my life; my greatest troubles in their passage rose from our little lady's trifling illnesses, which she had to experience in common with all children, rich and poor.

For the rest, after the first six months, she grew like a larch, and could walk and talk too, in her own way, before the heath blossomed a second time over Mrs. Linton's dust.

She was the most winning thing that ever brought sunshine into a desolate house—a real beauty in face, with the Earnshaws' handsome dark eyes, but the Lintons' fair skin, and small features, and yellow curling hair. Her spirit was high, though not rough, and qualified by a heart sensitive and lively to excess in its affections. That capacity for intense attachments reminded me of her mother; still she did not resemble her; for she could be soft and mild as a dove, and she had a gentle voice and pensive expression; her anger was never furious, her love never fierce—it was deep and tender.

However, it must be acknowledged, she had faults to foil her gifts. A propensity to be saucy was one; and a perverse will, that indulged children invariably acquire, whether they be good tempered or cross. If a servant chanced to vex her, it was always—"I shall tell Papa!" And if he reproved her, even by a look, you would have thought it a heartbreaking business: I don't believe he ever did speak a harsh word to her.

He took her education entirely on himself, and made it an amusement. Fortunately, curiosity and a quick intellect urged her into an apt scholar; she learnt rapidly and eagerly, and did honour to his teaching.

Till she reached the age of thirteen, she had not once been beyond the range of the park by herself. Mr. Linton would take her with him a mile or so outside, on

rare occasions; but he trusted her to no one else. Gimmerton was an unsubstantial name in her ears, the chapel, the only building she had approached or entered, except her own home. Wuthering Heights and Mr. Heathcliff did not exist for her; she was a perfect recluse, and, apparently, perfectly contented. Sometimes, indeed, while surveying the country from her nursery window, she would observe—

"Ellen, how long will it be before I can walk to the top of those hills? I wonder what lies on the other side —is it the sea?"

"No, Miss Cathy," I would answer, "it is hills again, just like these."

"And what are those golden rocks like, when you stand under them?" she once asked.

The abrupt descent of Penistone Crags particularly attracted her notice, especially when the setting sun shone on it and the topmost heights, and the whole extent of landscape besides lay in shadow.

I explained that they were bare masses of stone, with hardly enough earth in their clefts to nourish a stunted tree.

"And why are they bright so long after it is evening here?" she pursued.

"Because they are a great deal higher up than we are," replied I; "you could not climb them, they are too high and steep. In winter the frost is always there before it comes to us; and deep into summer I have found snow under that black hollow on the northeast side!"

"Oh, you have been on them!" she cried, gleefully. "Then I can go, too, when I am a woman. Has Papa been, Ellen?"

"Papa would tell you, Miss," I answered, hastily, "that they are not worth the trouble of visiting. The moors, where you ramble with him, are much nicer; and Thrushcross park is the finest place in the world."

"But I know the park, and I don't know those," she murmured to herself. "And I should delight to look round me from the brow of that tallest point; my little pony Minny shall take me sometime."

One of the maids mentioning the Fairy cave quite turned her head with a desire to fulfil this project; she teased Mr. Linton about it, and he promised she should have the journey when she got older. But Miss Catherine measured her age by months, and,

"Now, am I old enough to go to Penistone Crags?" was the constant question in her mouth.

The road thither wound close by Wuthering Heights. Edgar had not the heart to pass it, so she received as constantly the answer,

"Not yet, love: not yet."

I said Mrs. Heathcliff lived above a dozen years after quitting her husband. Her family were of a delicate constitution; she and Edgar both lacked the ruddy health that you will generally meet in these parts. What her last illness was, I am not certain; I conjecture, they died of the same thing, a kind of fever, slow at its commencement, but incurable, and rapidly consuming life towards the close.

She wrote to inform her brother of the probable conclusion of a four months' indisposition under which she had suffered, and entreated him to come to her, if possible, for she had much to settle, and she wished to bid him adieu, and deliver Linton safely into his hands. Her hope was that Linton might be left with him, as he had been with her—his father, she would fain convince herself, had no desire to assume the burden of his maintenance or education.

My master hesitated not a moment in complying with her request: reluctant as he was to leave home at ordinary calls, he flew to answer this, commending Catherine to my peculiar vigilance, in his absence, with reiterated orders that she must not wander out of the park, even under my escort; he did not calculate on her going unaccompanied.

He was away three weeks; the first day or two, my charge sat in a corner of the library, too sad for either reading or playing—in that quiet state she caused me little trouble; but it was succeeded by an interval of impatient, fretful weariness; and being too busy, and too old then, to run up and down amusing her, I hit on a method by which she might entertain herself.

I used to send her on travels round the grounds—now on foot, and now on a pony, indulging her with a patient audience of all her real and imaginary adventures, when she returned.

The summer shone in full prime, and she took such a taste for this solitary rambling that she often contrived to remain out from breakfast till tea; and then the evenings were spent in recounting her fanciful tales. I did not fear her breaking bounds, because the gates were generally locked, and I thought she would scarcely venture forth alone, if they had stood wide open.

Unluckily, my confidence proved misplaced. Catherine came to me, one morning, at eight o'clock, and said she was that day an Arabian merchant, going to cross the Desert with his caravan; and I must give her plenty of provision for herself and beasts: a horse, and three camels, personated by a large hound and a couple of pointers.

I got together a good store of dainties, and slung them in a basket on one side of the saddle; and she sprang up as gay as a fairy, sheltered by her wide-brimmed hat and gauze veil from the July sun, and trotted off with a merry laugh, mocking my cautious counsel to avoid galloping, and come back early.

The naughty thing never made her appearance at tea. One traveller, the hound, being an old dog and fond of its ease, returned; but neither Cathy, nor the pony, nor the two pointers were visible in any direction; and I dispatched emissaries down this path, and that path, and at last went wandering in search of her myself.

There was a labourer working at a fence round a plantation, on the borders of the grounds. I enquired of him if he had seen our young lady.

"I saw her at morn," he replied; "she would have me to cut her a hazel switch, and then she leapt her Galloway over the hedge yonder, where it is lowest, and galloped out of sight."

You may guess how I felt at hearing this news. It struck me directly she must have started for Penistone Crags.

"What will become of her?" I ejaculated, pushing through a gap which the man was repairing, and making straight to the highroad.

I walked as if for a wager, mile after mile, till a turn brought me in view of the Heights; but no Catherine could I detect, far or near.

The Crags lie about a mile and a half beyond Mr.

Heathcliff's place, and that is four from the Grange, so I began to fear night would fall ere I could reach them.

"And what if she should have slipped in clambering among them," I reflected, "and been killed, or broken some of her bones?"

My suspense was truly painful; and, at first, it gave me delightful relief to observe, in hurrying by the farm-house, Charlie, the fiercest of the pointers, lying under a window, with swelled head and bleeding ear. I opened the wicket and ran to the door, knocking vehemently for admittance. A woman whom I knew, and who formerly lived at Gimmerton, answered—she had been servant there since the death of Mr. Earnshaw.

"Ah," said she, "you are come a seeking your little mistress! Don't be frightened. She's here safe: but I'm glad it isn't the master."

"He is not at home then, is he?" I panted, quite breathless with quick walking and alarm.

"No, no," she replied, "both he and Joseph are off, and I think they won't return this hour or more. Step in and rest you a bit."

I entered, and beheld my stray lamb seated on the hearth, rocking herself in a little chair that had been her mother's when a child. Her hat was hung against the wall, and she seemed perfectly at home, laughing and chattering, in the best spirits imaginable, to Hareton—now a great, strong lad of eighteen—who stared at her with considerable curiosity and astonishment, comprehending precious little of the fluent succession of remarks and questions which her tongue never ceased pouring forth.

"Very well, Miss!" I exclaimed, concealing my joy under an angry countenance. "This is your last ride, till Papa comes back. I'll not trust you over the threshold again, you naughty, naughty girl!"

"Aha, Ellen!" she cried, gaily, jumping up, and running to my side. "I shall have a pretty story to tell tonight—and so you've found me out. Have you ever been here in your life before?"

"Put that hat on, and home at once," said I. "I'm dreadfully grieved at you, Miss Cathy; you've done extremely wrong! It's no use pouting and crying—that won't repay the trouble I've had, scouring the country after you. To think how Mr. Linton charged me to keep you in, and you stealing off so! It shows you are a cunning little fox, and nobody will put faith in you any more."

"What have I done?" sobbed she, instantly checked. "Papa charged me nothing; he'll not scold me, Ellen—he's never cross, like you!"

"Come, come!" I repeated. "I'll tie the riband. Now, let us have no petulance. Oh, for shame. You thirteen years old, and such a baby!"

This exclamation was caused by her pushing the hat from her head, and retreating to the chimney out of my reach.

"Nay," said the servant, "don't be hard on the bonny lass, Mrs. Dean. We made her stop—she'd fain have ridden forwards, afeared you should be uneasy. But Hareton offered to go with her, and I thought he should; it's a wild road over the hills."

Hareton, during the discussion, stood with his hands in his pockets, too awkward to speak, though he looked as if he did not relish my intrusion.

"How long am I to wait?" I continued, disregarding the woman's interference. "It will be dark in ten minutes. Where is the pony, Miss Cathy? And where is Phœnix? I shall leave you unless you be quick; so please yourself."

"The pony is in the yard," she replied, "and Phœnix is shut in there. He's bitten—and so is Charlie. I was going to tell you all about it; but you are in a bad temper, and don't deserve to hear."

I picked up her hat, and approached to reinstate it; but perceiving that the people of the house took her part, she commenced capering round the room, and on my giving chase, ran like a mouse over and under and behind the furniture, rendering it ridiculous for me to pursue.

Hareton and the woman laughed, and she joined them, and waxed more impertinent still; till I cried, in great irritation—

"Well, Miss Cathy, if you were aware whose house this is, you'd be glad enough to get out."

"It's your father's, isn't it?" she said, turning to Hareton.

"Nay," he replied, looking down, and blushing bashfully.

He could not stand a steady gaze from her eyes, though they were just his own.

"Whose, then—your master's?" she asked.

He coloured deeper, with a different feeling, muttered an oath, and turned away.

"Who is his master?" continued the tiresome girl, appealing to me. "He talked about 'our house,' and 'our folk.' I thought he had been the owner's son. And he never said, Miss; he should have done, shouldn't he, if he's a servant?"

Hareton grew black as a thundercloud at this childish speech. I silently shook my questioner, and at last succeeded in equipping her for departure.

"Now, get my horse," she said, addressing her unknown kinsman as she would one of the stableboys at the Grange. "And you may come with me. I want to see where the goblin-hunter rises in the marsh, and to hear about the *fairishes*, as you call them: but make haste! What's the matter? Get my horse, I say."

"I'll see thee damned before I be *thy* servant!" growled the lad.

"You'll see me *what?*" asked Catherine in surprise.

"Damned—thou saucy witch!" he replied.

"There, Miss Cathy! you see you have got into pretty company," I interposed. "Nice words to be used to a young lady! Pray don't begin to dispute with him. Come, let us seek for Minny ourselves, and begone."

"But Ellen," cried she, staring, fixed in astonishment. "How dare he speak so to me? Mustn't he be made to do as I ask him? You wicked creature, I shall tell Papa what you said. Now then!"

Hareton did not appear to feel this threat; so the tears sprung into her eyes with indignation. "You bring the pony," she exclaimed, turning to the woman, "and let my dog free this moment!"

"Softly, Miss," answered the addressed; "you'll lose nothing by being civil. Though Mr. Hareton, there, be not the master's son, he's your cousin; and I was never hired to serve you."

"*He* my cousin!" cried Cathy, with a scornful laugh.

"Yes, indeed," responded her reprover.

"Oh, Ellen! don't let them say such things," she pursued in great trouble. "Papa is gone to fetch my cousin from London—my cousin is a gentleman's son. That my——" She stopped, and wept outright, upset at the bare notion of relationship with such a clown.

"Hush, hush!" I whispered, "people can have many cousins and of all sorts, Miss Cathy, without being any the worse for it; only they needn't keep their company, if they be disagreeable and bad."

"He's not—he's not my cousin, Ellen!" she went on, gathering fresh grief from reflection, and flinging herself into my arms for refuge from the idea.

I was much vexed at her and the servant for their mutual revelations; having no doubt of Linton's approaching arrival, communicated by the former, being reported to Mr. Heathcliff; and feeling as confident that Catherine's first thought on her father's return would be to seek an explanation of the latter's assertion concerning her rude-bred kindred.

Hareton, recovering from his disgust at being taken for a servant, seemed moved by her distress; and, having fetched the pony round to the door, he took, to propitiate her, a fine crooked-legged terrier whelp from the kennel, and putting it into her hand bid her wisht! for he meant naught.

Pausing in her lamentations, she surveyed him with a glance of awe and horror, then burst forth anew.

I could scarcely refrain from smiling at this antipathy to the poor fellow, who was a well-made, athletic youth, good looking in features, and stout and healthy, but attired in garments befitting his daily occupations of working on the farm, and lounging among the moors after rabbits and game. Still, I thought I could detect in his physiognomy a mind owning better qualities than his father ever possessed. Good things lost amid a wilderness of weeds, to be sure, whose rankness far overtopped their neglected growth, yet, notwithstanding, evidence of a wealthy soil, that might yield luxuriant crops under other and favourable circumstances. Mr. Heathcliff, I believe, had not treated him physically ill, thanks to his fearless nature, which offered no temptation to that course of oppression; it had none of the timid susceptibility that would have given zest to ill-treatment, in Heathcliff's judgment. He appeared to have bent his malevolence on making him a brute; he was never taught to read or write, never rebuked for any bad habit which did not annoy his keeper, never led a single step towards virtue, or guarded by a single precept against vice. And from what I heard, Joseph contributed much to his deterioration, by a narrow-minded partiality which prompted him to flatter and pet him, as a boy, because he was the head of the old family. And as he had been in the habit of accusing Catherine Earnshaw and Heathcliff, when children, of putting the master past his patience, and compelling him to seek solace in drink by what he termed their "offalld ways," so at present he laid the whole burden of Hareton's faults on the shoulders of the usurper of his property.

If the lad swore, he wouldn't correct him; nor however culpably he behaved. It gave Joseph satisfaction, apparently, to watch him go the worst lengths—he allowed that he was ruined, that his soul was abandoned to perdition, but then, he reflected that Heathcliff must answer for it. Hareton's blood would be required at his hands; and there lay immense consolation in that thought.

Joseph had instilled into him a pride of name, and of his lineage; he would, had he dared, have fostered hate between him and the present owner of the Heights; but his dread of that owner amounted to superstition, and he confined his feelings regarding him to muttered innuendoes and private comminations.

I don't pretend to be intimately acquainted with the mode of living customary in those days at Wuthering Heights; I only speak from hearsay; for I saw little. The villagers affirmed Mr. Heathcliff was near, and a cruel hard landlord to his tenants; but the house, inside, had regained its ancient aspect of comfort under female management, and the scenes of riot common in Hindley's time were not now enacted within its walls. The master was too gloomy to seek companionship with any people, good or bad; and he is yet.

This, however, is not making progress with my story. Miss Cathy rejected the peace-offering of the terrier, and demanded her own dogs, Charlie and Phœnix. They came limping, and hanging their heads, and we set out for home, sadly out of sorts, every one of us.

I could not wring from my little lady how she had

spent the day, except that, as I supposed, the goal of her pilgrimage was Penistone Crags, and she arrived without adventure to the gate of the farmhouse, when Hareton happened to issue forth, attended by some canine followers, who attacked her train.

They had a smart battle, before their owners could separate them; that formed an introduction. Catherine told Hareton who she was, and where she was going, and asked him to show her the way, finally, beguiling him to accompany her.

He opened the mysteries of the Fairy cave, and twenty other queer places. But, being in disgrace, I was not favoured with a description of the interesting objects she saw.

I could gather, however, that her guide had been a favourite till she hurt his feelings by addressing him as a servant, and Heathcliff's housekeeper hurt hers by calling him her cousin.

Then the language he had held to her rankled in her heart—she who was always "love," and "darling," and "queen," and "angel," with everybody at the Grange, to be insulted so shockingly by a stranger! She did not comprehend it, and hard work I had to obtain a promise that she would not lay the grievance before her father.

I explained how he objected to the whole household at the Heights, and how sorry he would be to find she had been there; but I insisted most on the fact, that if she revealed my negligence of his orders, he would perhaps be so angry, that I should have to leave; and Cathy couldn't bear that prospect—she pledged her word, and kept it, for my sake. After all, she was a sweet little girl.

CHAPTER 19

A LETTER, edged with black, announced the day of my master's return. Isabella was dead; and he wrote to bid me to get mourning for his daughter, and arrange a room, and other accommodations, for his youthful nephew.

Catherine ran wild with joy at the idea of welcoming her father back, and indulged most sanguine anticipations of the innumerable excellences of her "real" cousin.

The evening of their expected arrival came. Since early morning, she had been busy ordering her own small affairs, and now, attired in her new black frock—poor thing! her aunt's death impressed her with no definite sorrow—she obliged me, by constant worrying, to walk with her down through the grounds to meet them.

"Linton is just six months younger than I am," she chattered, as we strolled leisurely over the swells and hollows of mossy turf, under shadow of the trees. "How delightful it will be to have him for a playfellow! Aunt Isabella sent Papa a beautiful lock of his hair; it was lighter than mine—more flaxen, and quite as fine. I have it carefully preserved in a little glass box, and I've often thought what pleasure it would be to see its owner. Oh! I am happy—and Papa, dear, Dear Papa! Come, Ellen, let us run! come run!"

She ran, and returned and ran again, many times before my sober footsteps reached the gate, and then she seated herself on the grassy bank beside the path, and tried to wait patiently, but that was impossible—she couldn't be still a minute.

"How long they are!" she exclaimed. "Ah, I see some dust on the road—they are coming! No! When will they be here? May we not go a little way—half a mile, Ellen, only just half a mile? Do say yes, to that clump of birches at the turn!"

I refused staunchly: and, at length, her suspense was ended; the travelling carriage rolled in sight.

Miss Cathy shrieked, and stretched out her arms, as soon as she caught her father's face looking from the window. He descended, nearly as eager as herself; and a considerable interval elapsed ere they had a thought to spare for any but themselves.

While they exchanged caresses, I took a peep in to see after Linton. He was asleep in a corner, wrapped in a warm, fur-lined cloak, as if it had been winter. A pale, delicate, effeminate boy, who might have been taken for my master's younger brother, so strong was the resemblance: but there was a sickly peevishness in his aspect that Edgar Linton never had.

The latter saw me looking, and having shaken hands, advised me to close the door, and leave him undisturbed, for the journey had fatigued him.

Cathy would fain have taken one glance, but her father told her to come on, and they walked together up the park, while I hastened before to prepare the servants.

"Now, darling," said Mr. Linton, addressing his daughter, as they halted at the bottom of the front steps, "your cousin is not so strong or so merry as you are, and he has lost his mother, remember, a very short time since; therefore, don't expect him to play and run about with you directly. And don't harass him much by talking; let him be quiet this evening, at least, will you?"

"Yes, yes, Papa," answered Catherine, "but I do want to see him, and he hasn't once looked out."

The carriage stopped; and the sleeper, being roused, was lifted to the ground by his uncle.

"This is your cousin Cathy, Linton," he said, putting their little hands together. "She's fond of you already; and mind you don't grieve her by crying tonight. Try to be cheerful now; the travelling is at an end, and you have nothing to do but rest and amuse yourself as you please."

"Let me go to bed, then," answered the boy, shrinking from Catherine's salute; and he put his fingers to his eyes to remove incipient tears.

"Come, come, there's a good child," I whispered, leading him in. "You'll make her weep too—see how sorry she is for you!"

I do not know whether it were sorrow for him, but his cousin put on as sad a countenance as himself, and returned to her father. All three entered, and mounted to the library, where tea was laid ready.

I proceeded to remove Linton's cap and mantle, and placed him on a chair by the table, but he was no sooner seated than he began to cry afresh. My master inquired what was the matter.

"I can't sit on a chair," sobbed the boy.

"Go to the sofa, then, and Ellen shall bring you some tea," answered his uncle, patiently.

He had been greatly tried during the journey, I felt convinced, by his fretful ailing charge.

Linton slowly trailed himself off, and lay down. Cathy carried a footstool and her cup to his side.

At first she sat silent; but that could not last; she had resolved to make a pet of her little cousin, as she would have him to be; and she commenced stroking his curls, and kissing his cheek, and offering him tea in her saucer, like a baby. This pleased him, for he was not much better; he dried his eyes, and lightened into a faint smile.

"Oh, he 'll do very well," said the master to me, after watching them a minute. "Very well, if we can keep him, Ellen. The company of a child of his own age will instil new spirit into him soon, and by wishing for strength he 'll gain it."

"Ay, if we can keep him!" I mused to myself, and sore misgivings came over me that there was slight hope of that. And then, I thought, however will that weakling live at Wuthering Heights, between his father and Hareton? what playmates and instructors they 'll be.

Our doubts were presently decided—even earlier than I expected. I had just taken the children upstairs, after tea was finished, and seen Linton asleep—he would not suffer me to leave him till that was the case—I had come down, and was standing by the table in the hall, lighting a bedroom candle for Mr. Edgar, when a maid stepped out of the kitchen and informed me that Mr. Heathcliff's servant Joseph was at the door, and wished to speak with the master.

"I shall ask him what he wants first," I said, in considerable trepidation. "A very unlikely hour to be troubling people, and the instant they have returned from a long journey. I don't think the master can see him."

Joseph had advanced through the kitchen as I uttered these words, and now presented himself in the hall. He was donned in his Sunday garments, with his most sanctimonious and sourest face, and, holding his hat in one hand and his stick in the other, he proceeded to clean his shoes on the mat.

"Good evening, Joseph," I said, coldly. "What business brings you here tonight?"

"It 's Maister Linton Aw mun spake tull," he answered, waving me disdainfully aside.

"Mr. Linton is going to bed; unless you have something particular to say, I 'm sure he won't hear it now," I continued. "You had better sit down in there, and entrust your message to me."

"Which is his rahm?" pursued the fellow, surveying the range of closed doors.

I perceived he was bent on refusing my mediation, so very reluctantly I went up to the library, and announced the unseasonable visitor, advising that he should be dismissed till next day.

Mr. Linton had no time to empower me to do so, for he mounted close at my heels, and, pushing into the apartment, planted himself at the far side of the table, with his two fists clapped on the head of his stick, and began in an elevated tone, as if anticipating opposition—

"Hathecliff has send me for his lad, un Aw munn't goa back 'baht him."

Edgar Linton was silent a minute; an expression of exceeding sorrow overcast his features; he would have pitied the child on his own account, but, recalling Isabella's hopes and fears, and anxious wishes for her son, and her commendations of him to his care, he grieved bitterly at the prospect of yielding him up, and searched in his heart how it might be avoided. No plan offered itself—the very exhibition of any desire to keep him would have rendered the claimant more peremptory—there was nothing left but to resign him. However, he was not going to rouse him from his sleep.

"Tell Mr. Heathcliff," he answered, calmly, "that his son shall come to Wuthering Heights tomorrow. You may also tell him that the mother of Linton desired him to remain under my guardianship; and, at present, his health is very precarious."

"Noa!" said Joseph, giving a thud with his prop on the floor, and assuming an authoritative air. "Noa! that manes nowt—Hathecliff maks noa 'cahnt uh t' mother, nur yah norther; but he 'll hev his lad; und Aw mun tak him—soa nah yah knaw!"

"You shall not tonight!" answered Linton, decisively. "Walk downstairs at once, and repeat to your master what I have said. Ellen, show him down. Go——"

And, aiding the indignant elder with a lift by the arm, he rid the room of him, and closed the door.

"Varrah weel!" shouted Joseph, as he slowly drew off. "Tuh morn, he's come hisseln, un' thrust *him* aht, if yah darr!"

CHAPTER 20

To obviate the danger of this threat being fulfilled, Mr. Linton commissioned me to take the boy home early, on Catherine's pony; and, said he—

"As we shall now have no influence over his destiny, good or bad, you must say nothing of where he is gone to my daughter; she cannot associate with him hereafter, and it's better for her to remain in ignorance of his proximity, lest she should be restless, and anxious to visit the Heights—merely tell her, his father sent for him suddenly, and he has been obliged to leave us."

Linton was very reluctant to be roused from his bed at five o'clock, and astonished to be informed that he must prepare for further travelling; but I softened off the matter by stating that he was going to spend some time with his father, Mr. Heathcliff, who wished to see him so much, he did not like to defer the pleasure till he should recover from his late journey.

"My father!" he cried, in strange perplexity. "Mamma never told me I had a father. Where does he live? I'd rather stay with Uncle."

"He lives a little distance from the Grange," I replied, "just beyond those hills—not so far, but you may walk over here when you get hearty. And you should be glad to go home, and to see him. You must try to love him, as you did your mother, and then he will love you."

"But why have I not heard of him before?" asked Linton. "Why didn't Mamma and he live together, as other people do?"

"He had business to keep him in the north," I answered, "and your mother's health required her to reside in the south."

"And why didn't Mamma speak to me about him?" persevered the child. "She often talked of Uncle, and I learnt to love him long ago. How am I to love Papa? I don't know him."

"Oh, all children love their parents," I said. "Your mother, perhaps, thought you would want to be with him if she mentioned him often to you. Let us make haste. An early ride on such a beautiful morning is much preferable to an hour's more sleep."

"Is she to go with us," he demanded, "the little girl I saw yesterday?"

"Not now," replied I.

"Is Uncle?" he continued.

"No, I shall be your companion there," I said.

Linton sank back on his pillow, and fell into a brown study.

"I won't go without Uncle," he cried at length; "I can't tell where you mean to take me."

I attempted to persuade him of the naughtiness of showing reluctance to meet his father; still he obstinately resisted any progress towards dressing, and I had to call for my master's assistance in coaxing him out of bed.

The poor thing was finally got off with several delusive assurances that his absence should be short, that Mr. Edgar and Cathy would visit him, and other promises, equally ill-founded, which I invented and reiterated at intervals throughout the way.

The pure heather-scented air, and the bright sunshine, and the gentle canter of Minny, relieved his despondency, after a while. He began to put questions concerning his new home, and its inhabitants, with greater interest and liveliness.

"Is Wuthering Heights as pleasant a place as Thrushcross Grange?" he inquired, turning to take a last glance into the valley, whence a light mist mounted and formed a fleecy cloud on the skirts of the blue.

"It is not so buried in trees," I replied, "and it is not quite so large, but you can see the country beautifully, all round; and the air is healthier for you—fresher and dryer. You will, perhaps, think the building old and dark at first—though it is a respectable house, the next best in the neighbourhood. And you will have such nice rambles on the moors. Hareton Earnshaw—that is Miss Cathy's other cousin, and so yours in a manner—will show you all the sweetest spots; and you can bring a book in fine weather, and make a green hollow your study; and, now and then, your uncle may join you in a walk; he does, frequently, walk out on the hills.'

"And what is my father like?" he asked. "Is he as young and handsome as Uncle?"

"He's as young," said I, "but he has black hair and eyes; and looks sterner; and he is taller and bigger altogether. He 'll not seem to you so gentle and kind at first, perhaps, because it is not his way—still, mind you be frank and cordial with him, and naturally he 'll be fonder of you than any uncle, for you are his own."

"Black hair and eyes!" mused Linton. "I can't fancy him. Then I am not like him, am I?"

"Not much," I answered . . . not a morsel, I thought, surveying with regret the white complexion and slim frame of my companion, and his large languid eyes . . . his mother's eyes, save that, unless a morbid touchiness kindled them a moment, they had not a vestige of her sparkling spirit.

"How strange that he should never come to see Mama, and me!" he murmured. "Has he ever seen me? If he have, I must have been a baby—I remember not a single thing about him!"

"Why, Master Linton," said I, "three hundred miles is a great distance, and ten years seem very different in length to a grown-up person compared with what they do to you. It is probable Mr. Heathcliff proposed going, from summer to summer, but never found a convenient opportunity; and now it is too late. Don't trouble him with questions on the subject; it will disturb him for no good."

The boy was fully occupied with his own cogitations for the remainder of the ride, till we halted before the farmhouse garden gate. I watched to catch his impressions in his countenance. He surveyed the carved front and low-browed lattices, the straggling gooseberry bushes and crooked firs, with solemn intentness, and then shook his head—his private feelings entirely disapproved of the exterior of his new abode. But he had sense to postpone complaining; there might be compensation within.

Before he dismounted, I went and opened the door. It was half-past six; the family had just finished breakfast; the servant was clearing and wiping down the table: Joseph stood by his master's chair telling some tale concerning a lame horse; and Hareton was preparing for the hay-field.

"Hallo, Nelly!" cried Mr. Heathcliff, when he saw me. "I feared I should have to come down and fetch my property myself. You 've brought it, have you? Let us see what we can make of it."

He got up and strode to the door; Hareton and Joseph followed in gaping curiosity. Poor Linton ran a frightened eye over the faces of the three.

"Sure-ly," said Joseph after a grave inspection, "he 's swopped wi' ye, maister, an' yon 's his lass!"

Heathcliff, having stared his son into an ague of confusion, uttered a scornful laugh.

"God! what a beauty! what a lovely, charming thing!" he exclaimed. "Haven't they reared it on snails and sour milk, Nelly? Oh, damn my soul! but that 's worse than I expected—and the devil knows I was not sanguine!"

I bid the trembling and bewildered child get down, and enter. He did not thoroughly comprehend the meaning of his father's speech, or whether it were intended for him—indeed, he was not yet certain that the grim, sneering stranger was his father; but he clung to me with growing trepidation, and on Mr. Heathcliff's taking a seat, and bidding him "come hither," he hid his face on my shoulder, and wept.

"Tut, tut!" said Heathcliff, stretching out a hand and dragging him roughly between his knees, and then holding up his head by the chin. "None of that nonsense! We 're not going to hurt thee, Linton—isn't that thy name? Thou art thy mother's child, entirely! Where is my share in thee, puling chicken?"

He took off the boy's cap and pushed back his thick flaxen curls, felt his slender arms and his small fingers, during which examination Linton ceased crying, and lifted his great blue eyes to inspect the inspector.

"Do you know me?" asked Heathcliff, having satisfied himself that the limbs were all equally frail and feeble.

"No," said Linton, with a gaze of vacant fear.

"You 've heard of me, I dare say?"

"No," he replied again.

"No? What a shame of your mother, never to waken your filial regard for me! You are my son, then, I 'll tell you; and your mother was a wicked slut to leave you in ignorance of the sort of father you possessed. Now, don't wince, and colour up! Though it is something to see you have not white blood. Be a good lad; and I 'll do for you. Nelly, if you be tired you may sit down; if not, get home again. I guess you 'll report what you hear, and see, to the cipher at the Grange; and this thing won't be settled while you linger about it."

"Well," replied I, "I hope you 'll be kind to the boy, Mr. Heathcliff, or you 'll not keep him long; and he 's all you have akin in the wide world, that you will ever know—remember."

"I 'll be very kind to him, you needn't fear," he said, laughing. "Only nobody else must be kind to him—I 'm jealous of monopolizing his affection. And, to begin my kindness, Joseph! bring the lad some breakfast. Hareton, you infernal calf, begone to your work. Yes, Nell," he added when they had departed, "my son is prospective owner of your place, and I should not wish him to die till I was certain of being his successor. Besides he 's mine, and I want the triumph of seeing my descendant fairly lord of their estates, my child hiring their children to till their fathers' lands for wages. That is the sole consideration which can make me endure the whelp— I despise him for himself, and hate him for the memories he revives! But that consideration is sufficient; he 's as safe with me, and shall be tended as carefully as your master tends his own. I have a room upstairs, furnished for him in handsome style; I 've engaged a tutor, also, to come three times a week, from twenty miles distance, to teach him what he pleases to learn. I 've ordered Hareton to obey him; and in fact I 've arranged every thing with a view to preserve the superior and the gentleman in him, above his associates. I do regret, however, that he so little deserves the trouble; if I wished any blessing in the world, it was to find him a worthy object of pride, and I 'm bitterly disappointed with the whey-faced whining wretch!"

While he was speaking, Joseph returned, bearing a basin of milk-porridge, and placed it before Linton. He stirred round the homely mess with a look of aversion, and affirmed he could not eat it.

I saw the old man-servant shared largely in his master's scorn of the child, though he was compelled to retain the sentiment in his heart, because Heathcliff plainly meant his underlings to hold him in honour.

"Cannot ate it?" repeated he, peering in Linton's face, and subduing his voice to a whisper, for fear of being overheard. "But Maister Hareton nivir ate nowt else, when he wer a little un—und what wer gooid eneugh fur him 's gooid eneugh fur yah, Aw 's rayther think!"

"I shan't eat it!" answered Linton, snappishly. "Take it away."

Joseph snatched up the food indignantly, and brought it to us.

"Is there owt ails th' victuals?" he asked, thrusting the tray under Heathcliff's nose.

"What should ail them?" he said.

"Wah!" answered Joseph, "yon dainty chap says he cannut ate 'em. Bud Aw guess it 's raight! His mother wer just soa—we wer a'most too mucky tuh sow t' corn fur makking her breead."

"Don't mention his mother to me," said the master, angrily. "Get him something that he can eat, that 's all. What is his usual food, Nelly?"

I suggested boiled milk or tea, and the housekeeper received instructions to prepare some.

Come, I reflected, his father's selfishness may contribute to his comfort. He perceives his delicate constitution, and the necessity of treating him tolerably. I 'll console Mr. Edgar by acquainting him with the turn Heathcliff's humour has taken.

Having no excuse for lingering longer, I slipped out, while Linton was engaged in timidly rebuffing the advances of a friendly sheep dog. But he was too much on the alert to be cheated—as I closed the door, I heard a cry, and a frantic repetition of the words—

"Don't leave me! I 'll not stay here! I 'll not stay here!"

Then the latch was raised and fell; they did not suffer

him to come forth. I mounted Minny, and urged her to a trot; and so my brief guardianship ended.

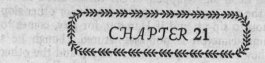

CHAPTER 21

WE HAD sad work with little Cathy that day; she rose in high glee, eager to join her cousin, and such passionate tears and lamentations followed the news of his departure, that Edgar himself was obliged to sooth her, by affirming he should come back soon—he added, however, "if I can get him," and there were no hopes of that.

This promise poorly pacified her; but time was more potent, and though still at intervals she inquired of her father when Linton would return, before she did see him again his features had waxed so dim in her memory that she did not recognize him.

When I chanced to encounter the housekeeper of Wuthering Heights, in paying business visits to Gimmerton, I used to ask how the young master got on; for he lived almost as secluded as Catherine herself, and was never to be seen. I could gather from her that he continued in weak health, and was a tiresome inmate. She said Mr. Heathcliff seemed to dislike him ever longer and worse, though he took some trouble to conceal it. He had an antipathy to the sound of his voice, and could not do at all with his sitting in the same room with him many minutes together.

There seldom passed much talk between them: Linton learnt his lessons and spent his evenings in a small apartment they called the parlour; or else lay in bed all day, for he was constantly getting coughs, and colds, and aches, and pains of some sort.

"And I never knew such a faint-hearted creature," added the woman, "nor one so careful of hisseln. He will go on, if I leave the window open a bit late in the evening. Oh! it's killing, a breath of night air! And he must have a fire in the middle of summer; and

Joseph's bacca pipe is poison; and he must always have sweets and dainties, and always milk, milk forever—heeding naught how the rest of us are pinched in winter; and there he'll sit, wrapped in his furred cloak in his chair by the fire, and some toast and water or other slop on the hob to sip at; and if Hareton, for pity, comes to amuse him—Hareton is not bad-natured, though he's rough—they're sure to part, one swearing and the other crying. I believe the master would relish Earnshaw's thrashing him to a mummy, if he were not his son; and I'm certain he would be fit to turn him out of doors, if he knew half the nursing he gives hisseln. But then, he won't go into danger of temptation; he never enters the parlour, and should Linton show those ways in the house where he is, he sends him upstairs directly."

I divined, from this account, that utter lack of sympathy had rendered young Heathcliff selfish and disagreeable, if he were not so originally, and my interest in him, consequently, decayed—though still I was moved with a sense of grief at his lot, and a wish that he had been left with us.

Mr. Edgar encouraged me to gain information; he thought a great deal about him, I fancy, and would have run some risk to see him; and he told me once to ask the housekeeper whether he ever came into the village.

She said he had only been twice, on horseback, accompanying his father, and both times he pretended to be quite knocked up for three or four days afterwards.

That housekeeper left, if I recollect rightly, two years after he came, and another, whom I did not know, was her successor; she lives there still.

Time wore on at the Grange in its former pleasant way, till Miss Cathy reached sixteen. On the anniversary of her birth we never manifested any signs of rejoicing, because it was also the anniversary of my late mistress's death. Her father invariably spent that day alone in the library, and walked, at dusk, as far as Gimmerton kirkyard, where he would frequently prolong his stay beyond midnight. Therefore Catherine was thrown on her own resources for amusement.

This twentieth of March was a beautiful spring day, and when her father had retired, my young lady came down dressed for going out, and said she had asked to have a ramble on the edge of the moors with me, and Mr. Linton had given her leave, if we went only a short distance and were back within the hour.

"So make haste, Ellen!" she cried. "I know where I wish to go; where a colony of moor-game are settled: I want to see whether they have made their nests yet."

"That must be a good distance up," I answered; "they don't breed on the edge of the moor."

"No, it's not," she said. "I've gone very near with Papa."

I put on my bonnet and sallied out, thinking nothing more of the matter. She bounded before me, and returned to my side, and was off again like a young greyhound; and, at first, I found plenty of entertainment in listening to the larks singing far and near, and enjoying the sweet, warm sunshine; and watching her, my pet, and my delight, with her golden ringlets flying loose behind, and her bright cheek, as soft and pure in its bloom as a wild rose, and her eyes radiant with cloudless pleasure. She was a happy creature, and an angel, in those days. It's a pity she could not be content.

"Well," said I, "where are your moor-game, Miss Cathy? We should be at them; the Grange park fence is a great way off now."

"Oh, a little further—only a little further, Ellen," was her answer, continually. "Climb to that hillock, pass that bank, and by the time you reach the other side I shall have raised the birds."

But there were so many hillocks and banks to climb and pass, that, at length, I began to be weary, and told her we must halt, and retrace our steps.

I shouted to her, as she had outstripped me, a long way; she either did not hear or did not regard, for she still sprang on, and I was compelled to follow. Finally, she dived into a hollow; and before I came in sight of her again, she was two miles nearer Wuthering Heights than her own home; and I beheld a couple of persons arrest her, one of whom I felt convinced was Mr. Heathcliff himself.

Cathy had been caught in the fact of plundering, or, at least, hunting out the nests of the grouse.

The Heights were Heathcliff's land, and he was reproving the poacher.

"I 've neither taken any nor found any," she said, as I toiled to them, expanding her hands in corroboration of the statement. "I didn't mean to take them; but Papa told me there were quantities up here, and I wished to see the eggs."

Heathcliff glanced at me with an ill-meaning smile, expressing his acquaintance with the party, and, consequently, his malevolence towards it, and demanded who "Papa" was?

"Mr. Linton of Thrushcross Grange," she replied. "I thought you did not know me, or you wouldn't have spoken in that way."

"You suppose Papa is highly esteemed and respected, then?" he said, sarcastically.

"And what are you?" inquired Catherine, gazing curiously on the speaker. "That man I 've seen before. Is he your son?"

She pointed to Hareton, the other individual, who had gained nothing but increased bulk and strength by the addition of two years to his age; he seemed as awkward and rough as ever.

"Miss Cathy," I interrupted, "it will be three hours instead of one that we are out, presently. We really must go back."

"No, that man is not my son," answered Heathcliff, pushing me aside. "But I have one, and you have seen him before, too; and, though your nurse is in a hurry, I think both you and she would be the better for a little rest. Will you just turn this nab of heath, and walk into my house? You 'll get home earlier for the ease; and you shall receive a kind welcome."

I whispered Catherine that she mustn't, on any account, accede to the proposal; it was entirely out of the question.

"Why?" she asked, aloud. "I 'm tired of running, and the ground is dewy—I can't sit here. Let us go, Ellen. Besides, he says I have seen his son. He 's mistaken, I think; but I guess where he lives—at the farmhouse I visited in coming from Penistone Crags. Don't you?"

"I do. Come, Nelly, hold your tongue—it will be a treat for her to look in on us. Hareton, get forwards with the lass. You shall walk with me, Nelly."

"No, she 's not going to any such place," I cried, struggling to release my arm, which he had seized; but she was almost at the door-stones already, scampering round the brow at full speed. Her appointed companion did not pretend to escort her; he shied off by the roadside, and vanished.

"Mr. Heathcliff, it's very wrong," I continued; "you know you mean no good. And there she'll see Linton, and all will be told, as soon as ever we return; and I shall have the blame."

"I want her to see Linton," he answered; "he's looking better these few days—it's not often he's fit to be seen. And we'll soon persuade her to keep the visit secret; where is the harm of it?"

"The harm of it is, that her father would hate me if he found I suffered her to enter your house; and I am convinced you have a bad design in encouraging her to do so," I replied.

"My design is as honest as possible. I'll inform you of its whole scope," he said. "That the two cousins may fall in love, and get married. I'm acting generously to your master; his young chit has no expectations, and should she second my wishes, she'll be provided for at once as joint successor with Linton."

"If Linton died," I answered, "and his life is quite uncertain, Catherine would be the heir."

"No, she would not," he said. "There is no clause in the will to secure it so—his property would go to me; but, to prevent disputes, I desire their union, and am resolved to bring it about."

"And I'm resolved she shall never approach your house with me again," I returned, as we reached the gate, where Miss Cathy waited our coming.

Heathcliff bid me be quiet; and, preceding us up the path, hastened to open the door. My young lady gave him several looks, as if she could not exactly make up her mind what to think of him; but now he smiled when he met her eye, and softened his voice in addressing her; and I was foolish enough to imagine the memory of her mother might disarm him from desiring her injury.

Linton stood on the hearth. He had been out, walking in the fields, for his cap was on, and he was calling to Joseph to bring him dry shoes.

He had grown tall of his age, still wanting some months of sixteen. His features were pretty yet, and his eye and complexion brighter than I remembered them, though with merely temporary lustre borrowed from the salubrious air and genial sun.

"Now, who is that?" asked Mr. Heathcliff, turning to Cathy. "Can you tell?"

"Your son?" she said, having doubtfully surveyed first one and then the other.

"Yes, yes," answered he; "but is this the only time you have beheld him? Think! Ah! you have a short memory. Linton, don't you recall your cousin, that you used to tease us so with wishing to see?"

"What, Linton!" cried Cathy, kindling into joyful surprise at the name. "Is that little Linton? He's taller than I am! Are you, Linton?"

The youth stepped forward, and acknowledged himself; she kissed him fervently, and they gazed with wonder at the change time had wrought in the appearance of each.

Catherine had reached her full height; her figure was both plump and slender, elastic as steel, and her whole aspect sparkling with health and spirits. Linton's looks and movements were very languid, and his form extremely slight; but there was a grace in his manner that mitigated these defects, and rendered him not unpleasing.

After exchanging numerous marks of fondness with him, his cousin went to Mr. Heathcliff, who lingered by the door, dividing his attention between the objects inside and those that lay without—pretending, that is, to observe the latter, and really noting the former alone.

"And you are my uncle, then?" she cried, reaching up to salute him. "I thought I liked you, though you were cross, at first. Why don't you visit at the Grange with Linton? To live all these years such close neighbours, and never see us, is odd—what have you done so for?"

"I visited it once or twice too often before you were born," he answered. "There—damn it! If you have any kisses to spare, give them to Linton: they are thrown away on me."

"Naughty Ellen!" exclaimed Catherine, flying to attack me next with her lavish caresses. "Wicked Ellen! to try to hinder me from entering. But I 'll take this walk every morning in future—may I, Uncle?—and sometimes bring Papa. Won't you be glad to see us?"

"Of course!" replied the uncle, with a hardly suppressed grimace, resulting from his deep aversion to both the proposed visitors. "But stay," he continued, turning towards the young lady. "Now I think of it, I 'd better tell you. Mr. Linton has a prejudice against me; we quarrelled at one time of our lives, with unchristian ferocity, and, if you mention coming here to him, he 'll put a veto on your visits altogether. Therefore, you must not mention it, unless you be careless of seeing your cousin hereafter; you may come, if you will, but you must not mention it."

"Why did you quarrel?" asked Catherine, considerably crestfallen.

"He thought me too poor to wed his sister," answered Heathcliff, "and was grieved that I got her; his pride was hurt, and he 'll never forget it."

"That 's wrong!" said the young lady; "sometime, I 'll tell him so. But Linton and I have no share in your quarrel. I 'll not come here, then; he shall come to the Grange."

"It will be too far for me," murmured her cousin; "to walk four miles would kill me. No, come here, Miss Catherine, now and then—not every morning, but once or twice a week."

The father launched towards his son a glance of bitter contempt.

"I am afraid, Nelly, I shall lose my labour," he muttered to me. "Miss Catherine, as the ninny calls her, will discover his value, and send him to the devil. Now, if it had been Hareton!—Do you know that, twenty times a day, I covet Hareton, with all his degradation? I 'd have loved the lad had he been someone else. But I think he 's safe from her love. I 'll pit him against that paltry creature, unless it bestir itself briskly. We calculate it will scarcely last till it is eighteen. Oh, confound the vapid thing! He 's absorbed in drying his feet, and never looks at her—Linton!"

"Yes, Father," answered the boy.

"Have you nothing to show your cousin, anywhere about—not even a rabbit, or a weasel's nest? Take her into the garden, before you change your shoes, and into the stable to see your horse."

"Wouldn't you rather sit here?" asked Linton, addressing Cathy in a tone which expressed reluctance to move again.

"I don't know," she replied, casting a longing look at the door, and evidently eager to be active.

He kept his seat, and shrank closer to the fire.

Heathcliff rose, and went into the kitchen, and from thence to the yard, calling out for Hareton. Hareton responded, and presently the two re-entered. The young man had been washing himself, as was visible by the glow on his cheeks, and his wetted hair.

"Oh, I 'll ask you, Uncle," cried Miss Cathy, recollecting the housekeeper's assertion. "That is not my cousin, is he?"

"Yes," he replied, "your mother's nephew. Don't you like him?"

Catherine looked queer.

"Is he not a handsome lad?" he continued.

The uncivil little thing stood on tiptoe, and whispered a sentence in Heathcliff's ear.

He laughed; Hareton darkened; I perceived he was very sensitive to suspected slights, and had obviously a dim notion of his inferiority. But his master or guardian chased the frown by exclaiming—

"You 'll be the favourite among us, Hareton! She says you are a—what was it? Well, something very flattering. Here! you go with her round the farm. And behave like a gentleman, mind! Don't use any bad words; and don't stare, when the young lady is not looking at you, and be ready to hide your face when she is; and, when you speak, say your words slowly, and keep your hands out of your pockets. Be off, and entertain her as nicely as you can."

He watched the couple walking past the window. Earnshaw had his countenance completely averted from his companion. He seemed studying the familiar landscape with a stranger's and an artist's interest.

Catherine took a sly look at him, expressing small admiration. She then turned her attention to seeking out objects of amusement for herself, and tripped merrily on, lilting a tune to supply the lack of conversation.

"I've tied his tongue," observed Heathcliff. "He'll not venture a single syllable, all the time! Nelly, you recollect me at his age—nay, some years younger. Did I ever look so stupid—so 'gaumless,' as Joseph calls it?"

"Worse," I replied, "because more sullen with it."

"I've a pleasure in him," he continued reflecting aloud. "He has satisfied my expectations. If he were a born fool I should not enjoy it half so much. But he's no fool; and I can sympathize with all his feelings, having felt them myself. I know what he suffers now, for instance, exactly; it is merely a beginning of what he shall suffer, though. And he'll never be able to emerge from his bathos of coarseness and ignorance. I've got him faster than his scoundrel of a father secured me, and lower; for he takes a pride in his brutishness. I've taught him to scorn everything extra-animal as silly and weak. Don't you think Hindley would be proud of his son, if he could see him? almost as proud as I am of mine. But there's this difference; one is gold put to the use of paving-stones, and the other is tin polished to ape a service of silver. *Mine* has nothing valuable about it; yet I shall have the merit of making it go as far as such poor stuff can go. *His* had first-rate qualities, and they are lost, rendered worse than unavailing. I have nothing to regret; he would have more than any, but I, are aware of. And the best of it is, Hareton is damnably fond of me! You'll own that I've outmatched Hindley there. If the dead villain could rise from his grave to abuse me for his offspring's wrongs, I should have the fun of seeing the said offspring fight him back again, indignant that he should dare to rail at the one friend he has in the world!"

Heathcliff chuckled a fiendish laugh at the idea. I made no reply, because I saw that he expected none.

Meantime, our young companion, who sat too removed from us to hear what was said, began to evince symptoms of uneasiness, probably repenting that he had denied himself the treat of Catherine's society for fear of a little fatigue.

His father remarked the restless glances wandering to the window, and the hand irresolutely extended towards his cap.

"Get up, you idle boy!" he exclaimed with assumed

heartiness. "Away after them! they are just at the corner, by the stand of hives."

Linton gathered his energies, and left the hearth. The lattice was open, and, as he stepped out, I heard Cathy inquiring of her unsociable attendant, what was that inscription over the door? Hareton stared up, and scratched his head like a true clown.

"It 's some damnable writing," he answered. "I cannot read it."

"Can't read it?" cried Catherine. "I can read it, it 's English. But I want to know why it is there."

Linton giggled—the first appearance of mirth he had exhibited.

"He does not know his letters," he said to his cousin. "Could you believe in the existence of such a colossal dunce?"

"Is he all as he should be?" asked Miss Cathy seriously; "or is he simple—not right? I 've questioned him twice now, and each time he looked so stupid I think he does not understand me. I can hardly understand him, I 'm sure!"

Linton repeated his laugh, and glanced at Hareton tauntingly, who certainly did not seem quite clear of comprehension at that moment.

"There 's nothing the matter, but laziness, is there, Earnshaw?" he said. "My cousin fancies you are an idiot. There you experience the consequence of scorning 'book-larning,' as you would say. Have you noticed, Catherine, his frightful Yorkshire pronunciation?"

"Why, where the devil is the use on 't?" growled Hareton, more ready in answering his daily companion. He was about to enlarge further, but the two youngsters broke into a noisy fit of merriment; my giddy Miss being delighted to discover that she might turn his strange talk to matter of amusement.

"Where is the use of the devil in that sentence?" tittered Linton. "Papa told you not to say any bad words, and you can't open your mouth without one. Do try to behave like a gentleman, now do!"

"If thou weren't more a lass than a lad, I 'd fell thee this minute, I would; pitiful lath of a crater!" retorted the angry boor, retreating, while his face burnt with mingled rage and mortification; for he was conscious of being insulted, and embarrassed how to resent it.

Mr. Heathcliff, having overheard the conversation as well as I, smiled when he saw him go; but immediately afterwards cast a look of singular aversion on the flippant pair, who remained chattering in the doorway—the boy finding animation enough while discussing Hareton's faults and deficiencies, and relating anecdotes of his goings on, and the girl relishing his pert and spiteful sayings, without considering the ill-nature they evinced; but I began to dislike, more than to compassionate, Linton, and to excuse his father, in some measure, for holding him cheap.

We stayed till afternoon; I could not tear Miss Cathy away, before; but happily my master had not quitted his apartment, and remained ignorant of our prolonged absence.

As we walked home, I would fain have enlightened my charge on the characters of the people we had quitted; but she got it into her head that I was prejudiced against them.

"Aha!" she cried, "you take Papa's side, Ellen; you are partial, I know—or else you wouldn't have cheated me so many years into the notion that Linton lived a long way from here. I 'm really extremely angry, only, I 'm so pleased, I can't show it! But you must hold your tongue about my uncle; he 's my uncle, remember, and I 'll scold papa for quarrelling with him."

And so she ran on, till I dropped endeavouring to convince her of her mistake.

She did not mention the visit that night, because she did not see Mr. Linton. Next day it all came out, sadly to my chagrin; and still I was not altogether sorry: I thought the burden of directing and warning would be more efficiently borne by him than me, but he was too timid in giving satisfactory reasons for his wish that she would shun connection with the household of the Heights, and Catherine liked good reasons for every restraint that harassed her petted will.

"Papa!" she exclaimed, after the morning's salutations, "guess whom I saw yesterday, in my walk on the moors. Ah, Papa, you started! you 've not done right, have you, now? I saw—But listen, and you shall hear how I found you out, and Ellen, who is in league with you, and yet pretended to pity me so, when I kept hoping, and was always disappointed about Linton's coming back!"

She gave a faithful account of her excursion and its consequences, and my master, though he cast more than one reproachful look at me, said nothing till she had concluded. Then he drew her to him, and asked if she knew why he had concealed Linton's near neighbourhood from her? Could she think it was to deny her a pleasure that she might harmlessly enjoy?

"It was because you disliked Mr. Heathcliff," she answered.

"Then you believe I care more for my own feelings than yours, Cathy?" he said. "No, it was not because I disliked Mr. Heathcliff, but because Mr. Heathcliff dislikes me; and is a most diabolical man, delighting to wrong and ruin those he hates, if they give him the slightest opportunity. I knew that you could not keep up an acquaintance with your cousin, without being brought into contact with him; and I knew he would detest you, on my account; so for your own good, and nothing else, I took precautions that you should not see Linton again. I meant to explain this some time as you grew older, and I'm sorry I delayed it."

"But Mr. Heathcliff was quite cordial, Papa," observed Catherine, not at all convinced, "and he didn't object to our seeing each other; he said I might come to his house when I pleased, only I must not tell you, because you had quarrelled with him, and would not forgive him for marrying Aunt Isabella. And you won't. You are the one to be blamed: he is willing to let us be friends, at least—Linton and I—and you are not."

My master, perceiving that she would not take his word for her uncle-in-law's evil disposition, gave a hasty sketch of his conduct to Isabella, and the manner in which Wuthering Heights became his property. He could not bear to discourse long upon the topic; for though he spoke little of it, he still felt the same horror and detestation of his ancient enemy that had occupied his heart ever since Mrs. Linton's death. "She might have been living yet, if it had not been for him!" was his constant bitter reflection, and, in his eyes, Heathcliff seemed a murderer.

Miss Cathy—conversant with no bad deeds except her own slight acts of disobedience, injustice, and passion, rising from hot temper and thoughtlessness, and repented of on the day they were committed—was amazed at the blackness of spirit that could brood on and cover revenge for years, and deliberately prosecute its plans without a visitation of remorse. She appeared so deeply impressed and shocked at this new view of human nature—excluded from all her studies and all her ideas till now—that Mr. Edgar deemed it unnecessary to pursue the subject. He merely added—

"You will know hereafter, darling, why I wish you to avoid his house and family; now, return to your old employments and amusements, and think no more about them!"

Catherine kissed her father, and sat down quietly to her lessons for a couple of hours, according to custom; then she accompanied him into the grounds, and the whole day passed as usual; but in the evening, when she had retired to her room, and I went to help her to undress, I found her crying, on her knees by the bedside.

"Oh, fie, silly child!" I exclaimed. "If you had any real griefs, you'd be ashamed to waste a tear on this little contrariety. You never had one shadow of substantial sorrow, Miss Catherine. Suppose, for a minute, that master and I were dead, and you were by yourself in the world—how would you feel then? Compare the present occasion with such an affliction as that, and be thankful for the friends you have, instead of coveting more."

"I'm not crying for myself, Ellen," she answered, "it's for him. He expected to see me again tomorrow, and there, he'll be so disappointed—and he'll wait for me, and I shan't come!"

"Nonsense!" said I, "do you imagine he has thought as much of you as you have of him? Hasn't he Hareton for a companion? Not one in a hundred would weep at losing a relation they had just seen twice, for two afternoons. Linton will conjecture how it is, and trouble himself no further about you."

"But may I not write a note to tell him why I cannot come?" she asked, rising to her feet. "And just send those books I promised to lend him? His books are not as nice as mine, and he wanted to have them extremely, when I told him how interesting they were. May I not, Ellen?"

"No, indeed! no, indeed!" replied I with decision. "Then he would write to you, and there'd never be an end to it. No, Miss Catherine, the acquaintance must be dropped entirely; so Papa expects, and I shall see that it is done."

"But how can one little note——" she recommenced, putting on an imploring countenance.

"Silence!" I interrupted. "We'll not begin with your little notes. Get into bed."

She threw at me a very naughty look, so naughty that I would not kiss her good night at first; I covered her up, and shut her door, in great displeasure; but, repenting halfway, I returned softly, and lo! there was Miss, standing at the table with a bit of blank paper before her and a pencil in her hand, which she guiltily slipped out of sight, on my re-entrance.

"You'll get nobody to take that, Catherine," I said, "if you write it; and at present I shall put out your candle."

I set the extinguisher on the flame, receiving as I did so a slap on my hand, and a petulant "cross thing!" I then quitted her again, and she drew the bolt in one of her worst, most peevish humours.

The letter was finished and forwarded to its destination by a milk-fetcher who came from the village—but that I didn't learn till some time afterwards. Weeks passed on, and Cathy recovered her temper, though she grew wondrous fond of stealing off to corners by herself, and often, if I came near her suddenly while reading, she would start and bend over the book, evidently desirous to hide it, and I detected edges of loose paper sticking out beyond the leaves.

She also got a trick of coming down early in the morning, and lingering about the kitchen, as if she were expecting the arrival of something; and she had a small drawer in a cabinet in the library, which she would trifle over for hours, and whose key she took special care to remove when she left it.

One day, as she inspected this drawer, I observed that

the playthings and trinkets, which recently formed its contents, were transmuted into bits of folded paper.

My curiosity and suspicions were roused; I determined to take a peep at her mysterious treasures; so, at night, as soon as she and my master were safe upstairs, I searched and readily found among my house keys one that would fit the lock. Having opened, I emptied the whole contents into my apron, and took them with me to examine at leisure in my own chamber.

Though I could not but suspect, I was still surprised to discover that they were a mass of correspondence— daily, almost, it must have been—from Linton Heath- cliff, answers to documents forwarded by her. The earlier dated were embarrassed and short; gradually, however, they expanded into copious love letters, foolish as the age of the writer rendered natural, yet with touches, here and there, which I thought were borrowed from a more experienced source.

Some of them struck me as singularly odd compounds of ardour and flatness, commencing in strong feeling, and concluding in the affected, wordy way that a school- boy might use to a fancied, incorporeal sweetheart.

Whether they satisfied Cathy, I don't know; but they appeared very worthless trash to me.

After turning over as many as I thought proper, I tied them in a handkerchief and set them aside, re- locking the vacant drawer.

Following her habit, my young lady descended early, and visited the kitchen; I watched her go to the door, on the arrival of a certain little boy, and, while the dairy maid filled his can, she tucked something into his jacket pocket, and plucked something out.

I went round by the garden, and laid wait for the messenger, who fought valorously to defend his trust, and we spilt the milk between us; but I succeeded in ab- stracting the epistle; and, threatening serious conse- quences if he did not look sharp home, I remained under the wall and perused Miss Cathy's affectionate composition. It was more simple and more eloquent than her cousin's—very pretty and very silly.

I shook my head, and went meditating into the house. The day being wet, she could not divert herself with rambling about the park, so, at the conclusion of her morning studies, she resorted to the solace of the drawer. Her father sat reading at the table, and I, on purpose, had sought a bit of work in some unripped fringes of the window curtain, keeping my eye steadily fixed on her proceedings.

Never did any bird flying back to a plundered nest which it had left brim-full of chirping young ones, express more complete despair in its anguished cries and flutterings, than she by her single "Oh!" and the change that transfigured her late happy countenance. Mr. Linton looked up.

"What is the matter, love? Have you hurt yourself?" he said.

His tone and look assured her he had not been the discoverer of the hoard.

"No, Papa—" she gasped. "Ellen! Ellen! come upstairs— I'm sick!"

I obeyed her summons, and accompanied her out.

"Oh, Ellen! you have got them," she commenced immediately, dropping on her knees, when we were enclosed alone. "O, give them to me, and I'll never do so again! Don't tell Papa. You have not told Papa, Ellen say you have not! I've been exceedingly naughty, but I won't do it any more!"

With a grave severity in my manner, I bid her stand up.

"So," I exclaimed, "Miss Catherine, you are tolerably far on, it seems; you may well be ashamed of them! A fine bundle of trash you study in your leisure hours, to be sure—why it's good enough to be printed! And what do you suppose the master will think, when I display it before him? I haven't shown it yet, but you needn't imagine I shall keep your ridiculous secrets. For shame! and you must have led the way in writing such absurdities—he would not have thought of beginning, I'm certain."

"I didn't! I didn't!" sobbed Cathy, fit to break her heart. "I didn't once think of loving him till——"

"Loving!" cried I, as scornfully as I could utter the word. "Loving! Did anybody ever hear the like! I might just as well talk of loving the miller who comes once a year to buy our corn. Pretty loving, indeed! and both times together you have seen Linton hardly four hours in your life! Now here is the babyish trash. I'm going with it to the library; and we'll see what your father says to such *loving*."

She sprang at her precious epistles, but I held them above my head; and then she poured out further frantic entreaties that I would burn them—do anything rather than show them. And being really fully as inclined to laugh as scold—for I esteemed it all girlish vanity—I at length relented in a measure, and asked—

"If I consent to burn them, will you promise faithfully, neither to send nor receive a letter again, nor a book (for I perceive you have sent him books), nor locks of hair, nor rings, nor playthings?"

"We don't send playthings!" cried Catherine, her pride overcoming her shame.

"Nor anything at all, then, my lady!" I said. "Unless you will, here I go."

"I promise, Ellen!" she cried, catching my dress. "Oh, put them in the fire, do, do!"

But when I proceeded to open a place with the poker, the sacrifice was too painful to be borne. She earnestly supplicated that I would spare her one or two.

"One or two, Ellen, to keep for Linton's sake!"

I unknotted the handkerchief, and commenced dropping them in from an angle, and the flame curled up the chimney.

"I will have one, you cruel wretch!" she screamed, darting her hand into the fire, and drawing forth some half-consumed fragments, at the expense of her fingers.

"Very well—and I will have some to exhibit to Papa!" I answered, shaking back the rest into the bundle, and turning anew to the door.

She emptied her blackened pieces into the flames, and motioned me to finish the immolation. It was done; I stirred up the ashes, and interred them under a shovel full of coals; and she mutely, and with a sense of intense injury, retired to her private apartment. I descended to tell my master that the young lady's qualm of sickness was almost gone, but I judged it best for her to lie down a while.

She wouldn't dine; but she reappeared at tea, pale, and red about the eyes, and marvellously subdued in outward aspect.

Next morning, I answered the letter by a slip of paper, inscribed, "Master Heathcliff is requested to send no more notes to Miss Linton, as she will not receive them." And, thenceforth, the little boy came with vacant pockets.

CHAPTER 22

SUMMER drew to an end, and early Autumn—it was past Michaelmas, but the harvest was late that year, and a few of our fields were still uncleared.

Mr. Linton and his daughter would frequently walk out among the reapers; at the carrying of the last sheaves, they stayed till dusk, and the evening happening to be chill and damp, my master caught a bad cold, that settling obstinately on his lungs, confined him indoors throughout the whole of the winter, nearly without intermission.

Poor Cathy, frightened from her little romance, had been considerably sadder and duller since its abandonment; and her father insisted on her reading less, and taking more exercise. She had his companionship no longer; I esteemed it a duty to supply its lack, as much as possible, with mine—an inefficient substitute, for I could only spare two or three hours, from my numerous diurnal occupations, to follow her footsteps, and then my society was obviously less desirable than his.

On an afternoon in October, or the beginning of November—a fresh watery afternoon, when the turf and paths were rustling with moist, withered leaves, and the cold, blue sky was half hidden by clouds—dark grey streamers, rapidly mounting from the west, and boding abundant rain—I requested my young lady to forego her ramble because I was certain of showers. She refused, and I unwillingly donned a cloak, and took my umbrella to accompany her on a stroll to the bottom of the park, a formal walk which she generally affected if low-spirited —and that she invariably was when Mr. Edgar had been worse than ordinary, a thing never known from his confession, but guessed both by her and me from his increased silence, and the melancholy of his countenance.

She went sadly on: there was no running or bounding now, though the chill wind might well have tempted her to a race. And often, from the side of my eye, I could detect her raising a hand, and brushing something off her cheek.

I gazed round for a means of diverting her thoughts. On one side of the road rose a high, rough bank, where hazels and stunted oaks, with their roots half exposed, held uncertain tenure—the soil was too loose for the latter, and strong winds had blown some nearly horizontal. In summer, Miss Catherine delighted to climb along these trunks, and sit in the branches, swinging twenty feet above the ground; and I, pleased with her agility and her light, childish heart, still considered it proper to scold every time I caught her at such an elevation, but so that she knew there was no necessity for descending. From dinner to tea she would lie in her breeze-rocked cradle, doing nothing except singing old songs—my nursery lore—to herself, or watching the birds, joint tenants, feed and entice their young ones to fly; or nestling with closed lids, half thinking, half dreaming, happier than words can express.

"Look, Miss!" I exclaimed, pointing to a nook under the roots of one twisted tree. "Winter is not here yet. There's a little flower, up yonder, the last bud from the multitude of bluebells that clouded those turf steps in July with a lilac mist. Will you clamber up, and pluck it to show to Papa?"

Cathy stared a long time at the lonely blossom trembling in its earthly shelter, and replied, at length—

"No, I'll not touch it; but it looks melancholy, does it not, Ellen?"

"Yes," I observed, "about as starved and sackless as you—your cheeks are bloodless; let us take hold of hands and run. You're so low, I dare say I shall keep up with you."

"No," she repeated, and continued sauntering on, pausing at intervals, to muse over a bit of moss, or a tuft of blanched grass, or a fungus spreading its bright orange among the heaps of brown foliage; and, ever and anon, her hand was lifted to her averted face.

"Catherine, why are you crying, love?" I asked, approaching and putting my arm over her shoulder. "You mustn't cry because Papa has a cold; be thankful it is nothing worse."

She now put no further restraint on her tears; her breath was stifled by sobs.

"Oh, it will be something worse," she said. "And what shall I do when Papa and you leave me, and I am by myself? I can't forget your words, Ellen; they are always in my ear. How life will be changed, how dreary the world will be, when Papa and you are dead."

"None can tell, whether you won't die before us," I replied. "It's wrong to anticipate evil. We'll hope there are years and years to come before any of us go; master is young, and I am strong, and hardly forty-five. My mother lived till eighty, a canty dame to the last. And suppose Mr. Linton were spared till he saw sixty, that would be more years than you have counted, Miss. And would it not be foolish to mourn a calamity above twenty years beforehand?"

"But Aunt Isabella was younger than Papa," she remarked, gazing up with timid hope to seek further consolation.

"Aunt Isabella had not you and me to nurse her," I replied. "She wasn't as happy as master; she hadn't as much to live for. All you need do is to wait well on your father, and cheer him by letting him see you cheerful, and avoid giving him anxiety on any subject—mind that, Cathy! I'll not disguise but you might kill him, if you were wild and reckless, and cherished a foolish, fanciful affection for the son of a person who would be glad to have him in his grave, and allowed him to discover that you fretted over the separation he has judged it expedient to make."

"I fret about nothing on earth except Papa's illness," answered my companion. "I care for nothing in comparison with Papa. And I'll never—never—oh, never, while I have my senses, do an act or say a word to vex him. I love him better than myself, Ellen, and I know it by this: I pray every night that I may live after him, because I would rather be miserable than that he should be—that proves I love him better than myself."

"Good words," I replied. "But deeds must prove it also; and after he is well, remember you don't forget resolutions formed in the hour of fear."

As we talked, we neared a door that opened on the road; and my young lady, lightening into sunshine again, climbed up, and seated herself on the top of the wall, reaching over to gather some hips that bloomed scarlet on the summit branches of the wild rose trees, shadowing the highway side—the lower fruit had disappeared, but only birds could touch the upper, except from Cathy's present station.

In stretching to pull them, her hat fell off, and as the door was locked, she proposed scrambling down to recover it. I bid her to be cautious lest she got a fall, and she nimbly disappeared.

But the return was no such easy matter; the stones were smooth and neatly cemented, and the rosebushes and blackberry stragglers could yield no assistance in reascending. I, like a fool, didn't recollect that, till I heard her laughing and exclaiming—

"Ellen, you'll have to fetch the key, or else I must run round to the porter's lodge. I can't scale the ramparts on this side!"

"Stay where you are," I answered. "I have my bundle of keys in my pocket; perhaps I may manage to open it; if not, I'll go."

Catherine amused herself with dancing to and fro before the door, while I tried all the large keys in succession. I had applied the last, and found that none would do; so, repeating my desire that she would remain there, I was about to hurry home as fast as I could, when an approaching sound arrested me. It was the trot of a horse; Cathy's dance stopped; and in a minute the horse stopped also.

"Who is that?" I whispered.

"Ellen, I wish you could open the door," whispered back my companion, anxiously.

"Ho, Miss Linton!" cried a deep voice (the rider's), "I'm glad to meet you. Don't be in haste to enter, for I have an explanation to ask and obtain."

"I shan't speak to you, Mr. Heathcliff," answered

Catherine. "Papa says you are a wicked man, and you hate both him and me; and Ellen says the same."

"That is nothing to the purpose," said Heathcliff. (He it was.) "I don't hate my son, I suppose; and it is concerning him that I demand your attention. Yes! you have cause to blush. Two or three months since, were you not in the habit of writing to Linton? making love in play, eh? You deserved, both of you, flogging for that! You especially, the elder, and less sensitive, as it turns out. I've got your letters, and if you give me any pertness I'll send them to your father. I presume you grew weary of the amusement and dropped it, didn't you? Well, you dropped Linton with it, into a Slough of Despond. He was in earnest—in love, really. As true as I live, he's dying for you; breaking his heart at your fickleness—not figuratively, but actually. Though Hareton has made him a standing jest for six weeks, and I have used more serious measures, and attempted to frighten him out of his idiocy, he gets worse daily, and he'll be under the sod before summer, unless you restore him!"

"How can you lie so glaringly to the poor child!" I called from the inside. "Pray ride on! How can you deliberately get up such paltry falsehoods? Miss Cathy, I'll knock the lock off with a stone; you won't believe that vile nonsense. You can feel in yourself, it is impossible that a person should die for the love of a stranger."

"I was not aware there were eavesdroppers," muttered the detected villain. "Worthy Mrs. Dean, I like you, but I don't like your double dealing," he added, aloud. "How could you lie so glaringly, as to affirm I hated the 'poor child?' and invent bugbear stories to terrify her from my door-stones? Catherine Linton (the very name warms me), my bonny lass, I shall be from home all this week; go and see if I have not spoken truth: do, there's a darling! Just imagine your father in my place, and Linton in yours; then think how you would value your careless lover if he refused to stir a step to comfort you, when your father, himself, entreated him; and don't, from pure stupidity, fall into the same error. I swear, on my salvation, he's going to his grave, and none but you can save him!"

The lock gave way, and I issued out.

"I swear Linton is dying," repeated Heathcliff, looking hard at me. "And grief and disappointment are hastening his death. Nelly, if you won't let her go, you can walk over yourself. But I shall not return till this time next week; and I think your master himself would scarcely object to her visiting her cousin!"

"Come in," said I, taking Cathy by the arm and half forcing her to re-enter; for she lingered, viewing with troubled eyes the features of the speaker, too stern to express his inward deceit.

He pushed his horse close, and, bending down, observed—

"Miss Catherine, I'll own to you that I have little patience with Linton; and Hareton and Joseph have less. I'll own that he's with a harsh set. He pines for kindness, as well as love; and a kind word from you would be his best medicine. Don't mind Mrs. Dean's cruel cautions; but be generous, and contrive to see him. He dreams of you day and night, and cannot be persuaded that you don't hate him, since you neither write nor call."

I closed the door, and rolled a stone to assist the loosened lock in holding it; and spreading my umbrella, I drew my charge underneath, for the rain began to drive through the moaning branches of the trees, and warned us to avoid delay.

Our hurry prevented any comment on the encounter with Heathcliff, as we stretched towards home; but I divined instinctively that Catherine's heart was clouded now in double darkness. Her features were so sad, they did not seem hers; she evidently regarded what she had heard as every syllable true.

The master had retired to rest before we came in. Cathy stole to his room to inquire how he was; he had fallen asleep. She returned, and asked me to sit with her in the library. We took our tea together; and afterwards she lay down on the rug, and told me not to talk for she was weary.

I got a book, and pretended to read. As soon as she supposed me absorbed in my occupation, she recommenced her silent weeping—it appeared, at present, her favourite diversion. I suffered her to enjoy it a while; then I expostulated, deriding and ridiculing all Mr. Heathcliff's assertions about his son, as if I were certain she would coincide. Alas! I hadn't the skill to counter-act the effect his account had produced; it was just what he intended.

"You may be right, Ellen," she answered, "but I shall never feel at ease till I know. And I must tell Linton it is not my fault that I don't write, and convince him that I shall not change."

What use were anger and protestations against her silly credulity? We parted that night—hostile; but next day beheld me on the road to Wuthering Heights, by the side of my wilful young mistress's pony. I couldn't bear to witness her sorrow, to see her pale, dejected countenance, and heavy eyes, and I yielded, in the faint hope that Linton himself might prove, by his reception of us, how little of the tale was founded on fact.

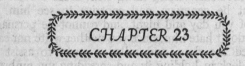

CHAPTER 23

THE rainy night had ushered in a misty morn-ing—half frost, half drizzle—and temporary brooks crossed our path, gurgling from the uplands. My feet were thoroughly wetted; I was cross and low—exactly the humour suited for making the most of these dis-agreeable things.

We entered the farmhouse by the kitchen way, to as-certain whether Mr. Heathcliff were really absent, be-cause I put slight faith in his own affirmation.

Joseph seemed sitting in a sort of elysium alone, be-side a roaring fire, a quart of ale on the table near him, bristling with large pieces of toasted oat cake, and his black, short pipe in his mouth.

Catherine ran to the hearth to warm herself. I asked if the master was in?

My question remained so long unanswered, that I thought the old man had grown deaf, and repeated it louder.

"Na—ay!" he snarled, or rather screamed through his

nose. "Na—ay! yah muh goa back whear yah coom frough."

"Joseph!" cried a peevish voice, simultaneously with me, from the inner room. "How often am I to call you? There are only a few red ashes now. Joseph! come this moment."

Vigorous puffs, and a resolute stare into the grate, declared he had no ear for this appeal. The housekeeper and Hareton were invisible, one gone on an errand, and the other at his work, probably. We knew Linton's tones and entered.

"Oh, I hope you'll die in a garret! starved to death," said the boy, mistaking our approach for that of his negligent attendant.

He stopped, on observing his error; his cousin flew to him.

"Is that you, Miss Linton?" he said, raising his head from the arm of the great chair, in which he reclined. "No—don't kiss me. It takes my breath—dear me! Papa said you would call," continued he, after recovering a little from Catherine's embrace, while she stood by looking very contrite. "Will you shut the door, if you please? you left it open; and those—those *detestable* creatures won't bring coals to the fire. It's so cold!"

I stirred up the cinders, and fetched a scuttle full myself. The invalid complained of being covered with ashes; but he had a tiresome cough, and looked feverish and ill, so I did not rebuke his temper.

"Well, Linton," murmured Catherine, when his corrugated brow relaxed. "Are you glad to see me? Can I do you any good?"

"Why didn't you come before?" he said. "You should have come, instead of writing. It tired me dreadfully, writing those long letters. I'd far rather have talked to you. Now, I can neither bear to talk, nor anything else. I wonder where Zillah is! Will you" (looking at me) "step into the kitchen and see?"

I had received no thanks for my other service; and being unwilling to run to and fro at his behest, I replied—

"Nobody is out there but Joseph."

"I want to drink," he exclaimed, fretfully, turning away. "Zillah is constantly gadding off to Gimmerton since Papa went. It's miserable! And I 'm obliged to come down here—they resolved never to hear me upstairs."

"Is your father attentive to you, Master Heathcliff?" I asked, perceiving Catherine to be checked in her friendly advances.

"Attentive? He makes *them* a little more attentive, at least," he cried. "The wretches! Do you know, Miss Linton, that brute Hareton laughs at me! I hate him! indeed, I hate them all—they are odious beings."

Cathy began searching for some water; she lighted on a pitcher in the dresser, filled a tumbler, and brought it. He bid her add a spoonful of wine from a bottle on the table; and having swallowed a small portion, appeared more tranquil, and said she was very kind.

"And are you glad to see me?" asked she, reiterating her former question, and pleased to detect the faint dawn of a smile.

"Yes, I am. It 's something new to hear a voice like yours!" he replied. "But I *have* been vexed, because you wouldn't come. And Papa swore it was owing to me; he called me a pitiful, shuffling, worthless thing; and said you despised me; and if he had been in my place, he would be more the master of the Grange than your father, by this time. But you don't despise me, do you, Miss——"

"I wish you would say Catherine, or Cathy," interrupted my young lady. "Despise you? No! Next to Papa, and Ellen, I love you better than anybody living. I don't love Mr. Heathcliff, though; and I dare not come when he returns; will he stay away many days?"

"Not many," answered Linton; "but he goes onto the moors frequently, since the shooting season commenced, and you might spend an hour or two with me, in his absence. Do! say you will! I think I should not be peevish with you—you 'd not provoke me, and you 'd be always ready to help me, wouldn't you?"

"Yes," said Catherine, stroking his long soft hair, "if I could only get Papa's consent, I 'd spend half my time with you. Pretty Linton! I wish you were my brother."

"And then you would like me as well as your father?" observed he, more cheerfully. "But Papa says you would love me better than him and all the world, if you were my wife; so I 'd rather you were that."

"No! I should never love anybody better than Papa," she returned gravely. "And people hate their wives, sometimes, but not their sisters and brothers; and if you were the latter, you would live with us, and Papa would be as fond of you as he is of me."

Linton denied that people ever hated their wives; but Cathy affirmed they did, and, in her wisdom, instanced his own father's aversion to her aunt.

I endeavoured to stop her thoughtless tongue. I couldn't succeed till everything she knew was out. Master Heathcliff, much irritated, asserted her relation was false.

"Papa told me; and Papa does not tell falsehoods!" she answered pertly.

"My papa scorns yours!" cried Linton. "He calls him a sneaking fool!"

"Yours is a wicked man," retorted Catherine, "and you are very naughty to dare to repeat what he says. He must be wicked, to have made Aunt Isabella leave him as she did!"

"She didn't leave him," said the boy; "you shan't contradict me!"

"She did!" cried my young lady.

"Well, I'll tell you something!" said Linton. "Your mother hated your father: now then."

"Oh!" exclaimed Catherine, too enraged to continue.

"And she loved mine!" added he.

"You little liar! I hate you now," she panted, and her face grew red with passion.

"She did! she did!" sang Linton, sinking into the recess of his chair, and leaning back his head to enjoy the agitation of the other disputant, who stood behind.

"Hush, Master Heathcliff!" I said; "that's your father's tale too, I suppose."

"It isn't: you hold your tongue!" he answered. "She did, she did, Catherine! she did, she did!"

Cathy, beside herself, gave the chair a violent push, and caused him to fall against one arm. He was immediately seized by a suffocating cough that soon ended his triumph.

It lasted so long that it frightened even me. As to his

cousin, she wept with all her might, aghast at the mischief she had done, though she said nothing.

I held him till the fit exhausted itself. Then he thrust me away, and leant his head down silently. Catherine quelled her lamentations also, took a seat opposite, and looked solemnly into the fire.

"How do you feel now, Master Heathcliff?" I inquired after waiting ten minutes.

"I wish *she* felt as I do," he replied, "spiteful, cruel thing! Hareton never touches me—he never struck me in his life. And I was better today, and there——" His voice died in a whimper.

"*I* didn't strike you!" muttered Cathy, chewing her lip to prevent another burst of emotion.

He sighed and moaned like one under great suffering, and kept it up for a quarter of an hour—on purpose to distress his cousin, apparently, for whenever he caught a stifled sob from her he put renewed pain and pathos into the inflexions of his voice.

"I'm sorry I hurt you, Linton," she said at length, racked beyond endurance. "But *I* couldn't have been hurt by that little push, and I had no idea that you could, either—you're not much, are you, Linton? Don't let me go home thinking I've done you harm. Answer! speak to me."

"I can't speak to you," he murmured; "you've hurt me so, that I shall lie awake all night, choking with this cough! If you had it you'd know what it was; but you'll be comfortably asleep, while I'm in agony—and nobody near me! I wonder how you would like to pass those fearful nights!" And he began to wail aloud, for very pity of himself.

"Since you are in the habit of passing dreadful nights," I said, "it won't be Miss who spoils your ease—you'd be the same had she never come. However, she shall not disturb you again; and perhaps you'll get quieter when we leave you."

"Must I go?" asked Catherine dolefully, bending over him. "Do you want me to go, Linton?"

"You can't alter what you've done," he replied pettishly, shrinking from her, "unless you alter it for the worse, by teasing me into a fever."

"Well, then I must go?" she repeated.

"Let me alone, at least," said he; "I can't bear your talking!"

She lingered, and resisted my persuasions to departure, a tiresome while; but as he neither looked up nor spoke, she finally made a movement to the door and I followed.

We were recalled by a scream. Linton had slid from his seat on to the hearthstone, and lay writhing in the mere perverseness of an indulged plague of a child, determined to be as grievous and harassing as it can.

I thoroughly gauged his disposition from his behaviour, and saw at once it would be folly to attempt humouring him. Not so my companion; she ran back in terror, knelt down, and cried, and soothed, and entreated, till he grew quiet from lack of breath, by no means from compunction at distressing her.

"I shall lift him on the settle," I said, "and he may roll about as he pleases; we can't stop to watch him. I hope you are satisfied, Miss Cathy, that you are not the person to benefit him, and that his condition of health is not occasioned by attachment to you. Now then, there he is! Come away; as soon as he knows there is nobody by to care for his nonsense, he'll be glad to lie still!"

She placed a cushion under his head, and offered him some water; he rejected the latter, and tossed uneasily on the former, as if it were a stone or a block of wood. She tried to put it more comfortably.

"I can't do with that," he said; "it's not high enough!"

Catherine brought another to lay above it.

"That's too high!" murmured the provoking thing.

"How must I arrange it, then?" she asked despairingly.

He twined himself up to her, as she half knelt by the settle, and converted her shoulder into a support.

"No, that won't do," I said. "You'll be content with the cushion, Master Heathcliff. Miss has wasted too much time on you already—we cannot remain five minutes longer."

"Yes, yes, we can!" replied Cathy. "He's good and patient now. He's beginning to think I shall have far greater misery than he will tonight, if I believe he is the worse for my visit; and then, I dare not come again. Tell the truth about it, Linton, for I mustn't come, if I have hurt you."

"You must come, to cure me," he answered. "You ought to come because you have hurt me—you know you have, extremely! I was not as ill when you entered as I am at present—was I?"

"But you 've made yourself ill by crying, and being in a passion."

"I didn't do it all," said his cousin. "However, we 'll be friends now. And you want me—you would wish to see me sometimes, really?"

"I told you I did," he replied impatiently. "Sit on the settle and let me lean on your knee. That's as Mamma used to do, whole afternoons together. Sit quite still, and don't talk; but you may sing a song if you can sing; or you may say a nice long interesting ballad—one of those you promised to teach me; or a story. I 'd rather have a ballad, though—begin."

Catherine repeated the longest she could remember. The employment pleased both mightily. Linton would have another, and after that another, notwithstanding my strenuous objections; and so they went on until the clock struck twelve, and we heard Hareton in the court, returning for his dinner.

"And tomorrow, Catherine, will you be here to-morrow?" asked young Heathcliff, holding her frock as she rose reluctantly.

"No!" I answered, "nor next day neither." She, however, gave a different response, evidently, for his forehead cleared as she stooped and whispered in his ear.

"You won't go tomorrow, recollect, Miss!" I commenced, when we were out of the house. "You are not dreaming of it, are you?"

She smiled.

"Oh, I 'll take good care," I continued; "I 'll have that lock mended, and you can escape by no way else."

"I can get over the wall," she said, laughing. "The Grange is not a prison, Ellen, and you are not my jailer. And besides, I 'm almost seventeen—I 'm a woman. And I 'm certain Linton would recover quickly if he had me to look after him. I 'm older than he is, you know, and wiser, less childish, am I not? And he 'll soon do as I direct him, with some slight coaxing. He 's a pretty little darling when he 's good. I 'd make such a pet of him, if he were mine. We should never quarrel, should we, after we were used to each other? Don't you like him, Ellen?"

"Like him?" I exclaimed. "The worst-tempered bit of a sickly slip that ever struggled into its teens! Happily, as Mr. Heathcliff conjectured, he'll not win twenty! I doubt whether he'll see spring, indeed. And small loss to his family whenever he drops off. And lucky it is for us that his father took him—the kinder he was treated, the more tedious and selfish he'd be! I'm glad you have no chance of having him for a husband, Miss Catherine!"

My companion waxed serious at hearing this speech. To speak of his death so regardlessly wounded her feelings.

"He's younger than I," she answered, after a protracted pause of meditation, "and he ought to live the longest; he will—he must live as long as I do. He's as strong now as when he first came into the North, I'm positive of that! It's only a cold that ails him, the same as Papa has. You say Papa will get better, and why shouldn't he?"

"Well, well," I cried, "after all, we needn't trouble ourselves; for listen, Miss—and mind, I'll keep my word —if you attempt going to Wuthering Heights again, with or without me, I shall inform Mr. Linton, and, unless he allow it, the intimacy with your cousin must not be revived."

"It has been revived!" muttered Cathy sulkily.

"Must not be continued, then!" I said.

"We'll see!" was her reply, and she set off at a gallop, leaving me to toil in the rear.

We both reached home before our dinner-time; my master supposed we had been wandering through the park, and therefore he demanded no explanation of our absence. As soon as I entered, I hastened to change my soaked shoes and stockings; but sitting such a while at the Heights had done the mischief. On the succeeding morning I was laid up, and during three weeks I remained incapacitated for attending to my duties—a calamity never experienced prior to that period, and never, I am thankful to say, since.

My little mistress behaved like an angel in coming to wait on me, and cheer my solitude—the confinement brought me exceedingly low. It is wearisome, to a stirring active body; but few have slighter reasons for complaint than I had. The moment Catherine left Mr. Linton's room, she appeared at my bedside. Her day was divided between us; no amusement usurped a minute; she neglected her meals, her studies, and her play, and she was the fondest nurse that ever watched. She must have had a warm heart, when she loved her father so, to give so much to me!

I said her days were divided between us; but the master retired early, and I generally needed nothing after six o'clock, thus the evening was her own.

Poor thing! I never considered what she did with herself after tea. And though frequently, when she looked in to bid me good night, I remarked a fresh colour in her cheeks and a pinkness over her slender fingers, instead of fancying the hue borrowed from a cold ride across the moors, I laid it to the charge of a hot fire in the library.

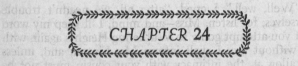

CHAPTER 24

AT THE close of three weeks, I was able to quit my chamber, and move about the house. And on the first occasion of my sitting up in the evening, I asked Catherine to read to me, because my eyes were weak. We were in the library, the master having gone to bed; she consented, rather unwillingly, I fancied, and imagining my sort of books did not suit her, I bid her please herself in the choice of what she perused.

She selected one of her own favourites, and got forward steadily about an hour; then came frequent questions.

"Ellen, are not you tired? Hadn't you better lie down now? You'll be sick, keeping up so long, Ellen."

"No, no, dear, I'm not tired," I returned, continually.

Perceiving me immovable, she essayed another method

of showing her dis-relish for her occupation. It changed to yawning, and stretching, and—

"Ellen, I'm tired."

"Give over then and talk," I answered.

That was worse; she fretted and sighed, and looked at her watch till eight, and finally went to her room, completely overdone with sleep, judging by her peevish, heavy look, and the constant rubbing she inflicted on her eyes.

The following night she seemed more impatient still; and on the third from recovering my company, she complained of a headache, and left me.

I thought her conduct odd; and having remained alone a long while, I resolved on going, and inquiring whether she were better, and asking her to come and lie on the sofa, instead of upstairs in the dark.

No Catherine could I discover upstairs, and none below. The servants affirmed they had not seen her. I listened at Mr. Edgar's door; all was silence. I returned to her apartment, extinguished my candle, and seated myself in the window.

The moon shone bright; a sprinkling of snow covered the ground, and I reflected that she might, possibly, have taken it into her head to walk about the garden, for refreshment. I did detect a figure creeping along the inner fence of the park; but it was not my young mistress; on its emerging into the light, I recognized one of the grooms.

He stood a considerable period, viewing the carriage road through the grounds; then started off at a brisk pace, as if he had detected something, and reappeared presently, leading Miss's pony; and there she was, just dismounted, and walking by its side.

The man took his charge stealthily across the grass towards the stable. Cathy entered by the casement window of the drawing-room, and glided noiselessly up to where I awaited her.

She put the door gently to, slipped off her snowy shoes, untied her hat, and was proceeding, unconscious of my espionage, to lay aside her mantle, when I suddenly rose and revealed myself. The surprise petrified her an instant; she uttered an inarticulate exclamation, and stood fixed.

"My dear Miss Catherine," I began, too vividly impressed by her recent kindness to break into a scold, "where have you been riding out at this hour? And why should you try to deceive me by telling a tale? Where have you been? Speak!"

"To the bottom of the park," she stammered. "I didn't tell a tale."

"And nowhere else?" I demanded.

"No," was the muttered reply.

"Oh, Catherine!" I cried, sorrowfully. "You know you have been doing wrong, or you wouldn't be driven to uttering an untruth to me. That does grieve me. I'd rather be three months ill, than hear you frame a deliberate lie."

She sprang forward and, bursting into tears, threw her arms round my neck.

"Well, Ellen, I'm so afraid of you being angry," she said. "Promise not to be angry, and you shall know the very truth. I hate to hide it."

We sat down in the window-seat; I assured her I would not scold, whatever her secret might be, and I guessed it, of course; so she commenced—

"I've been to Wuthering Heights, Ellen, and I've never missed going a day since you fell ill, except thrice before and twice after you left your room. I gave Michael books and pictures to prepare Minny every evening, and to put her back in the stable—you mustn't scold *him* either, mind. I was at the Heights by half-past six, and generally stayed till half-past eight, and then galloped home. It was not to amuse myself that I went—I was often wretched all the time. Now and then, I was happy; once in a week perhaps. At first, I expected there would be sad work persuading you to let me keep my word to Linton, for I had engaged to call again next day, when we quitted him; but, as you stayed upstairs on the morrow, I escaped that trouble; and while Michael was refastening the lock of the park door in the afternoon, I got possession of the key, and told him how my cousin wished me to visit him, because he was sick, and couldn't come to the Grange; and how Papa would object to my going; and then I negotiated with him about the pony. He is fond of reading, and he thinks of leaving soon to get married; so he offered, if I would lend him books out of the library, to do what I wished; but I preferred giving him my own, and that satisfied him better.

"On my second visit, Linton seemed in lively spirits; and Zillah (that is their housekeeper) made us a clean room and a good fire, and told us that, as Joseph was out at a prayer meeting and Hareton Earnshaw was off with his dogs—robbing our woods of pheasants, as I heard afterwards—we might do what we liked.

"She brought me some warm wine and gingerbread, and appeared exceedingly good-natured; and Linton sat in the armchair, and I in the little rocking chair on the hearthstone, and we laughed and talked so merrily, and found so much to say; we planned where we would go, and what we would do in summer. I needn't repeat that, because you would call it silly.

"One time, however, we were near quarrelling. He said the pleasantest manner of spending a hot July day was lying from morning till evening on a bank of heath in the middle of the moors, with the bees humming dreamily about among the bloom, and the larks singing high up overhead, and the blue sky and bright sun shining steadily and cloudlessly. That was his most perfect idea of heaven's happiness; mine was rocking in a rustling green tree, with a west wind blowing, and bright white clouds flitting rapidly above; and not only larks, but throstles, and blackbirds, and linnets, and cuckoos pouring out music on every side, and the moors seen at a distance, broken into cool dusky dells; but close by great swells of long grass undulating in waves to the breeze; and woods and sounding water, and the whole world awake and wild with joy. He wanted all to lie in an ecstasy of peace; I wanted all to sparkle, and dance in a glorious jubilee.

"I said his heaven would be only half alive, and he said mine would be drunk; I said I should fall asleep in his, and he said he could not breathe in mine, and began to grow very snappish. At last, we agreed to try both, as soon as the right weather came; and then we kissed each other and were friends. After sitting still an hour, I looked at the great room with its smooth uncarpeted floor, and thought how nice it would be to play in, if we removed the table; and I asked Linton to call Zillah in to help us, and we'd have a game at blind-man's buff;

she should try to catch us—you used to, you know, Ellen.
He wouldn't; there was no pleasure in it, he said; but he
consented to play at ball with me. We found two in a
cupboard, among a heap of old toys: tops, and hoops,
battledoors, and shuttlecocks. One was marked C., and
the other H.; I wished to have the C., because that stood
for Catherine, and the H. might be for Heathcliff, his
name; but the bran came out of H., and Linton didn't
like it.

"I beat him constantly, and he got cross again, and
coughed, and returned to his chair. That night, though,
he easily recovered his good humour; he was charmed
with two or three pretty songs—your songs, Ellen; and
when I was obliged to go, he begged and entreated me
to come the following evening; and I promised.

"Minny and I went flying home as light as air; and I
dreamt of Wuthering Heights and my sweet, darling
cousin, till morning.

"On the morrow, I was sad; partly because you were
poorly, and partly that I wished my father knew, and
approved of my excursions. But it was beautiful moonlight after tea; and, as I rode on, the gloom cleared.

"I shall have another happy evening, I thought to myself, and what delights me more, my pretty Linton will.

"I trotted up their garden, and was turning round to
the back, when that fellow Earnshaw met me, took my
bridle, and bid me go in by the front entrance. He pat-
ted Minny's neck, and said she was a bonny beast, and
appeared as if he wanted me to speak to him. I only told
him to leave my horse alone, or else it would kick him.

"He answered in his vulgar accent,

"'It wouldn't do mitch hurt if it did'; and surveyed
its legs with a smile.

"I was half inclined to make it try; however, he moved
off to open the door, and, as he raised the latch, he
looked up to the inscription above, and said, with a
stupid mixture of awkwardness and elation—

"'Miss Catherine! I can read yon, nah.'

"'Wonderful,' I exclaimed. 'Pray let us hear you—you
are grown clever!'

"He spelt, and drawled over by syllables, the name
—'Hareton Earnshaw.'

" 'And the figures?' I cried, encouragingly, perceiving that he came to a dead halt.

" 'I cannot tell them yet,' he answered.

" 'Oh, you dunce!' I said, laughing heartily at his failure.

"The fool stared, with a grin hovering about his lips, and a scowl gathering over his eyes, as if uncertain whether he might not join in my mirth—whether it were not pleasant familiarity, or what it really was, contempt.

"I settled his doubts, by suddenly retrieving my gravity and desiring him to walk away, for I came to see Linton not him.

"He reddened—I saw that by the moonlight—dropped his hand from the latch, and skulked off, a picture of mortified vanity. He imagined himself to be as accomplished as Linton, I suppose, because he could spell his own name, and was marvellously discomfited that I didn't think the same."

"Stop, Miss Catherine, dear!" I interrupted. "I shall not scold, but I don't like your conduct there. If you had remembered that Hareton was your cousin as much as Master Heathcliff, you would have felt how improper it was to behave in that way. At least, it was praiseworthy ambition for him to desire to be as accomplished as Linton; and probably he did not learn merely to show off; you had made him ashamed of his ignorance before, I have no doubt, and he wished to remedy it and please you. To sneer at his imperfect attempt was very bad breeding. Had you been brought up in his circumstances, would you be less rude? He was as quick and as intelligent a child as ever you were; and I'm hurt that he should be despised now, because that base Heathcliff has treated him so unjustly."

"Well, Ellen, you won't cry about it, will you?" she exclaimed, surprised at my earnestness. "But wait, and you shall hear if he conned his A B C to please me, and if it were worth while being civil to the brute. I entered; Linton was lying on the settle, and half got up to welcome me.

" 'I'm ill tonight, Catherine, love,' he said; 'and you must have all the talk, and let me listen. Come, and sit by me. I was sure you wouldn't break your word, and I'll make you promise again, before you go.'

"I knew now that I mustn't tease him, as he was ill; and I spoke softly and put no questions, and avoided irritating him in any way. I had brought some of my nicest books for him; he asked me to read a little of one, and I was about to comply, when Earnshaw burst the door open, having gathered venom with reflection. He advanced direct to us, seized Linton by the arm, and swung him off the seat.

" 'Get to thy own room!' he said in a voice almost inarticulate with passion, and his face looked swelled and furious. 'Take her there if she comes to see thee—thou shalln't keep me out of this. Begone, wi' ye both!'

"He swore at us, and left Linton no time to answer, nearly throwing him into the kitchen; and he clenched his fist as I followed, seemingly longing to knock me down. I was afraid for a moment, and I let one volume fall; he kicked it after me, and shut us out.

"I heard a malignant, crackly laugh by the fire, and turning, beheld that odious Joseph standing rubbing his bony hands, and quivering.

" 'Aw wer sure he 'd sarve ye eht! He 's a grand lad! He 's getten t' raight sperrit in him! He knaws—Aye, he knaws, as weel as Aw do, who sud be t' maister yonder—Ech, ech, ech! He mad ye skift properly! Ech, ech, ech!'

" 'Where must we go?' I said to my cousin, disregarding the old wretch's mockery.

"Linton was white and trembling. He was not pretty then, Ellen. Oh no! he looked frightful! for his thin face and large eyes were wrought into an expression of frantic, powerless fury. He grasped the handle of the door, and shook it; it was fastened inside.

" 'If you don't let me in I 'll kill you!—If you don't let me in I 'll kill you!' he rather shrieked than said. 'Devil! devil!—I 'll kill you—I 'll kill you!'

"Joseph uttered his croaking laugh again.

" 'Thear that's t' father!' he cried. 'That 's father! We've allas summut uh orther side in us. Niver heed Hareton, lad—dunnut be 'feared—he cannot get at thee!'

"I took hold of Linton's hands, and tried to pull him away, but he shrieked so shockingly that I dared not proceed. At last, his cries were choked by a dreadful fit of coughing; blood gushed from his mouth, and he fell on the ground.

"I ran into the yard, sick with terror, and called for Zillah, as loud as I could. She soon heard me—she was milking the cows in a shed behind the barn, and hurrying from her work—she inquired what there was to do?

"I hadn't breath to explain; dragging her in, I looked about for Linton. Earnshaw had come out to examine the mischief he had caused, and he was then conveying the poor thing upstairs. Zillah and I ascended after him, but he stopped me at the top of the steps, and said I shouldn't go in, I must go home.

"I exclaimed that he had killed Linton, and I *would* enter.

"Joseph locked the door, and declared I should do 'no sich stuff,' and asked me whether I were 'bahn to be as mad as him.'

"I stood crying, till the housekeeper re-appeared. She affirmed that he would be better in a bit, but he couldn't do with that shrieking and din; and she took me, and nearly carried me into the house.

"Ellen, I was ready to tear my hair off my head! I sobbed and wept so that my eyes were almost blind; and the ruffian you have such sympathy with stood opposite, presuming every now and then to bid me 'wisht,' and denying that it was his fault; and finally, frightened by my assertions that I would tell Papa, and that he should be put in prison and hanged, he commenced blubbering himself, and hurried out to hide his cowardly agitation.

"Still, I was not rid of him; when at length they compelled me to depart, and I had got some hundred yards off the premises, he suddenly issued from the shadow of the roadside, and checked Minny and took hold of me.

"'Miss Catherine, I 'm ill grieved,' he began, 'but it 's rayther too bad——'

"I gave him a cut with my whip, thinking perhaps he would murder me. He let go, thundering one of his horrid curses, and I galloped home more than half out of my senses.

"I didn't bid you good night, that evening, and I didn't go to Wuthering Heights, the next; I wished to, exceedingly, but I was strangely excited, and dreaded to hear that Linton was dead, sometimes; and sometimes shuddered at the thought of encountering Hareton.

"On the third day I took courage—at least, I couldn't

bear longer suspense, and stole off once more. I went at five o'clock, and walked, fancying I might manage to creep into the house, and up to Linton's room, unobserved. However, the dogs gave notice of my approach. Zillah received me, and saying 'the lad was mending nicely,' showed me into a small, tidy, carpeted apartment, where, to my inexpressible joy, I beheld Linton laid on a little sofa, reading one of my books. But he would neither speak to me nor look at me, through a whole hour, Ellen—he has such an unhappy temper. And what quite confounded me, when he did open his mouth it was to utter the falsehood that I had occasioned the uproar, and Hareton was not to blame!

"Unable to reply, except passionately, I got up and walked from the room. He sent after me a faint 'Catherine!' He did not reckon on being answered so; but I wouldn't turn back; and the morrow was the second day on which I stayed at home, nearly determined to visit him no more.

"But it was so miserable going to bed, and getting up, and never hearing anything about him, that my resolution melted into air before it was properly formed. It had appeared wrong to take the journey once; now it seemed wrong to refrain. Michael came to ask if he must saddle Minny; I said 'Yes,' and considered myself doing a duty as she bore me over the hills.

"I was forced to pass the front windows to get to the court; it was no use trying to conceal my presence.

"'Young master is in the house,' said Zillah, as she saw me making for the parlour.

"I went in; Earnshaw was there also, but he quitted the room directly. Linton sat in the great armchair half asleep; walking up to the fire, I began in a serious tone, partly meaning it to be true—

"'As you don't like me, Linton, and as you think I come on purpose to hurt you, and pretend that I do so every time, this is our last meeting: let us say good-bye; and tell Mr. Heathcliff that you have no wish to see me, and that he mustn't invent any more falsehoods on the subject.'

"'Sit down and take your hat off, Catherine,' he answered. 'You are so much happier than I am, you ought to be better. Papa talks enough of my defects, and shows enough scorn of me, to make it natural I should doubt myself. I doubt whether I am not altogether as worthless as he calls me, frequently; and then I feel so cross and bitter, I hate everybody! I am worthless, and bad in temper, and bad in spirit, almost always; and if you choose, you may say good-bye: you'll get rid of an annoyance. Only, Catherine, do me this justice: believe that if I might be as sweet, and as kind, and as good as you are, I would be, as willingly, and more so, than as happy and as healthy. And believe that your kindness has made me love you deeper than if I deserved your love; and though I couldn't, and cannot help showing my nature to you, I regret it and repent it, and shall regret and repent it till I die!'

"I felt he spoke the truth; and I felt I must forgive him—and, though he should quarrel the next moment, I must forgive him again. We were reconciled; but we cried, both of us, the whole time I stayed—not entirely for sorrow, yet I was sorry Linton had that distorted nature. He 'll never let his friends be at ease, and he 'll never be at ease himself!

"I have always gone to his little parlour, since that night; because his father returned the day after. About three times, I think, we have been merry and hopeful, as we were the first evening; the rest of my visits were dreary and troubled, now with his selfishness and spite, and now with his sufferings; but I 've learnt to endure the former with nearly as little resentment as the latter.

"Mr. Heathcliff purposely avoids me; I have hardly seen him at all. Last Sunday, indeed, coming earlier than usual, I heard him abusing poor Linton, cruelly, for his conduct of the night before. I can't tell how he knew of it, unless he listened. Linton had certainly behaved provokingly—however, it was the business of nobody but me, and I interrupted Mr. Heathcliff's lecture by entering and telling him so. He burst into a laugh, and went away, saying he was glad I took that view of the matter. Since then, I 've told Linton he must whisper his bitter things.

"Now, Ellen, you have heard all; and I can't be prevented from going to Wuthering Heights, except by inflicting misery on two people; whereas, if you 'll only not tell Papa, my going need disturb the tranquillity of none.

You 'll not tell, will you? It will be very heartless if you do."

"I 'll make up my mind on that point by tomorrow, Miss Catherine," I replied. "It requires some study; and so I 'll leave you to your rest, and go think it over."

I thought it over aloud, in my master's presence; walking straight from her room to his, and relating the whole story: with the exception of her conversations with her cousin, and any mention of Hareton.

Mr. Linton was alarmed and distressed more than he would acknowledge to me. In the morning, Catherine learnt my betrayal of her confidence, and she learnt also that her secret visits were to end.

In vain she wept and writhed against the interdict, and implored her father to have pity on Linton. All she got to comfort her was a promise that he would write, and give him leave to come to the Grange when he pleased, but explaining that he must no longer expect to see Catherine at Wuthering Heights. Perhaps, had he been aware of his nephew's disposition and state of health, he would have seen fit to withhold even that slight consolation.

CHAPTER 25

THESE things happened last winter, sir," said Mrs. Dean, "hardly more than a year ago. Last winter, I did not think, at another twelve months' end, I should be amusing a stranger to the family with relating them! Yet, who knows how long you 'll be a stranger? You 're too young to rest always contented, living by yourself; and I some way fancy, no one could see Catherine Linton, and not love her. You smile—but why do you look so lively and interested, when I talk about her? and why have you asked me to hang her picture over your fireplace? and why——"

"Stop, my good friend!" I cried. "It may be very possible that I should love her; but would she love me? I doubt it too much to venture my tranquillity by running into temptation—and then my home is not here. I'm of the busy world, and to its arms I must return. Go on. Was Catherine obedient to her father's commands?"

"She was," continued the housekeeper. "Her affection for him was still the chief sentiment in her heart; and he spoke without anger; he spoke in the deep tenderness of one about to leave his treasure amid perils and foes, where his remembered words would be the only aid that he could bequeath to guide her. He said to me, a few days afterwards,

"'I wish my nephew would write, Ellen, or call. Tell me, sincerely, what you think of him: is he changed for the better, or is there a prospect of improvement, as he grows a man?'

"'He's very delicate, sir,' I replied, 'and scarcely likely to reach manhood; but this I can say, he does not resemble his father; and if Miss Catherine had the misfortune to marry him, he would not be beyond her control, unless she were extremely and foolishly indulgent. However, master, you'll have plenty of time to get acquainted with him, and see whether he would suit her—it wants four years and more to his being of age.'"

Edgar sighed; and, walking to the window, looked out towards Gimmerton Kirk. It was a misty afternoon, but the February sun shone dimly, and we could just distinguish the two fir trees in the yard, and the sparely scattered gravestones.

"I've prayed often," he half soliloquized, "for the approach of what is coming; and now I begin to shrink, and fear it. I thought the memory of the hour I came down that glen a bridegroom would be less sweet than the anticipation that I was soon, in a few months, or, possibly, weeks, to be carried up, and laid in its lonely hollow! Ellen, I've been very happy with my little Cathy. Through winter nights and summer days she was a living hope at my side. But I've been as happy musing by myself among those stones, under that old church: lying, through the long June evenings, on the green mound of her mother's grave, and wishing, yearning for the time when I might lie beneath it. What can I do for Cathy? How must I quit her? I'd not care one moment for Linton being Heathcliff's son, nor for his taking her from me, if he could console her for my loss. I'd not care that Heathcliff gained his ends, and triumphed in robbing me of my last blessing! But should Linton be unworthy—only a feeble tool to his father—I cannot abandon her to him! And, hard though it be to crush her buoyant spirit, I must persevere in making her sad while I live, and leaving her solitary when I die. Darling! I'd rather resign her to God, and lay her in the earth before me."

"Resign her to God, as it is, sir," I answered, "and if we should lose you—which may He forbid—under His providence, I'll stand her friend and counsellor to the last. Miss Catherine is a good girl; I don't fear that she will go wilfully wrong; and people who do their duty are always finally rewarded."

Spring advanced; yet my master gathered no real strength, though he resumed his walks in the grounds with his daughter. To her inexperienced notions, this itself was a sign of convalescence; and then his cheek was often flushed, and his eyes were bright—she felt sure of his recovering.

On her seventeenth birthday, he did not visit the churchyard; it was raining, and I observed—

"You'll surely not go out tonight, sir?"

He answered—

"No, I'll defer it, this year, a little longer."

He wrote again to Linton, expressing his great desire to see him; and, had the invalid been presentable, I've no doubt his father would have permitted him to come. As it was, being instructed, he returned an answer, intimating that Mr. Heathcliff objected to his calling at the Grange; but his uncle's kind remembrance delighted him, and he hoped to meet him, sometimes, in his rambles, and personally to petition that his cousin and he might not remain long so utterly divided.

That part of his letter was simple, and probably his own. Heathcliff knew he could plead eloquently enough for Catherine's company, then—

"I do not ask," he said, "that she may visit here; but, am I never to see her, because my father forbids me to go to her home, and you forbid her to come to mine? Do, now and then, ride with her towards the Heights, and let us exchange a few words, in your presence! We have done nothing to deserve this separation; and you are not angry with me—you have no reason to dislike me, you allow, yourself. Dear uncle! send me a kind note tomorrow, and leave to join you anywhere you please, except at Thrushcross Grange. I believe an interview would convince you that my father's character is not mine; he affirms I am more your nephew than his son; and though I have faults which render me unworthy of Catherine, she has excused them, and, for her sake, you should also. You inquire after my health—it is better; but while I remain cut off from all hope, and doomed to solitude, or the society of those who never did and never will like me, how can I be cheerful and well?"

Edgar, though he felt for the boy, could not consent to grant his request, because he could not accompany Catherine.

He said, in summer, perhaps, they might meet; meantime, he wished him to continue writing at intervals, and engaged to give him what advice and comfort he was able by letter, being well aware of his hard position in his family.

Linton complied; and had he been unrestrained, would probably have spoiled all by filling his epistles with complaints and lamentations, but his father kept a sharp watch over him, and, of course, insisted on every line that my master sent being shown; so, instead of penning his peculiar personal sufferings and distresses, the themes constantly uppermost in his thoughts, he harped on the cruel obligation of being held asunder from his friend and love, and gently intimated that Mr. Linton must allow an interview soon, or he should fear he was purposely deceiving him with empty promises.

Cathy was a powerful ally at home; and, between them, they at length persuaded my master to acquiesce in their having a ride or a walk together, about once a week, under my guardianship, and on the moors nearest the Grange; for June found him still declining; and though he had set aside, yearly, a portion of his income for my young lady's fortune, he had a natural desire that she might retain—or at least return in a short time to—the house of her ancestors, and he considered her only prospect of doing that was by a union with his heir; he had no idea that the latter was failing almost as fast as himself, nor had anyone, I believe—no doctor visited the Heights, and no one saw Master Heathcliff to make report of his condition, among us.

I, for my part, began to fancy my forebodings were false, and that he must be actually rallying, when he mentioned riding and walking on the moors, and seemed so earnest in pursuing his object.

I could not picture a father treating a dying child as tyrannically and wickedly as I afterwards learnt Heathcliff had treated him, to compel this apparent eagerness, his efforts redoubling the more imminently his avaricious and unfeeling plans were threatened with defeat by death.

CHAPTER 26

Summer was already past its prime, when Edgar reluctantly yielded his assent to their entreaties, and Catherine and I set out on our first ride to join her cousin.

It was a close, sultry day, devoid of sunshine, but with a sky too dappled and hazy to threaten rain; and our place of meeting had been fixed at the guide-stone, by the crossroads. On arriving there, however, a little herd-boy, despatched as a messenger, told us that—

"Maister Linton wer just ut this side th' Heights, and he'd be mitch obleeged to us to gang on a bit further."

"Then Master Linton has forgot the first injunction of his uncle," I observed; "he bid us keep on the Grange land, and here we are, off at once."

"Well, we'll turn our horses' heads round, when we reach him," answered my companion, "our excursion shall lie towards home."

But when we reached him, and that was scarcely a quarter of a mile from his own door, we found he had no horse; and we were forced to dismount, and leave ours to graze.

He lay on the heath, awaiting our approach, and did

not rise till we came within a few yards. Then he walked so feebly, and looked so pale, that I immediately exclaimed—

"Why, Master Heathcliff, you are not fit for enjoying a ramble, this morning. How ill you do look!"

Catherine surveyed him with grief and astonishment, and changed the ejaculation of joy on her lips, to one of alarm, and the congratulation on their long postponed meeting to an anxious inquiry, whether he were worse than usual.

"No—better—better!" he panted, trembling, and retaining her hand as if he needed its support, while his large blue eyes wandered timidly over her, the hollowness round them transforming to haggard wildness the languid expression they once possessed.

"But you have been worse," persisted his cousin, "worse than when I saw you last—you are thinner, and——"

"I'm tired," he interrupted, hurriedly. "It is too hot for walking, let us rest here. And, in the morning, I often feel sick—Papa says I grow so fast."

Badly satisfied, Cathy sat down, and he reclined beside her.

"This is something like your paradise," said she, making an effort at cheerfulness. "You recollect the two days we agreed to spend in the place and the way each thought pleasantest? This is nearly yours, only there are clouds; but then they are so soft and mellow, it is nicer than sunshine. Next week, if you can, we'll ride down to the Grange Park, and try mine."

Linton did not appear to remember what she talked of; and he had evidently great difficulty in sustaining any kind of conversation. His lack of interest in the subjects she started, and his equal incapacity to contribute to her entertainment, were so obvious, that she could not conceal her disappointment. An indefinite alteration had come over his whole person and manner. The pettishness that might be caressed into fondness, had yielded to a listless apathy; there was less of the peevish temper of a child which frets and teases on purpose to be soothed, and more of the self-absorbed moroseness of a confirmed invalid, repelling consolation, and ready to regard the good-humoured mirth of others, as an insult.

Catherine perceived, as well as I did, that he held it

rather a punishment, than a gratification, to endure our company, and she made no scruple of proposing, presently, to depart.

That proposal, unexpectedly, roused Linton from his lethargy, and threw him into a strange state of agitation. He glanced fearfully towards the Heights, begging she would remain another half-hour, at least.

"But, I think," said Cathy, "you'd be more comfortable at home than sitting here; and I cannot amuse you today, I see, by my tales, and songs, and chatter; you have grown wiser than I, in these six months; you have little taste for my diversions now; or else, if I could amuse you, I'd willingly stay."

"Stay to rest yourself," he replied. "And, Catherine, don't think, or say that I'm very unwell; it is the heavy weather and heat that make me dull; and I walked about, before you came, a great deal, for me. Tell Uncle, I'm in tolerable health, will you?"

"I'll tell him that you say so, Linton. I couldn't affirm that you are," observed my young lady, wondering at his pertinacious assertion of what was evidently an untruth.

"And be here again next Thursday," continued he, shunning her puzzled gaze. "And give him my thanks for permitting you to come—my best thanks, Catherine. And—and, if you did meet my father, and he asked you about me, don't lead him to suppose that I've been extremely silent and stupid—don't look sad and downcast, as you are doing—he'll be angry."

"I care nothing for his anger," exclaimed Cathy, imagining she would be its object.

"But I do," said her cousin, shuddering. "Don't provoke him against me, Catherine, for he is very hard."

"Is he severe to you, Master Heathcliff?" I inquired. "Has he grown weary of indulgence, and passed from passive to active hatred?"

Linton looked at me, but did not answer; and, after keeping her seat by his side another ten minutes, during which his head fell drowsily on his breast, and he uttered nothing except suppressed moans of exhaustion or pain, Cathy began to seek solace in looking for bilberries, and sharing the produce of her researches with me—she did not offer them to him, for she saw further notice would only weary and annoy.

"Is it half an hour now, Ellen!" she whispered in my ear, at last. "I can't tell why we should stay. He's asleep, and Papa will be wanting us back."

"Well, we must not leave him asleep," I answered; "wait till he wakes, and be patient. You were mighty eager to set off, but your longing to see poor Linton has soon evaporated!"

"Why did *he* wish to see me?" returned Catherine. "In his crossest humours, formerly, I liked him better than I do in his present curious mood. It's just as if it were a task he was compelled to perform—this interview—for fear his father should scold him. But I'm hardly going to come to give Mr. Heathcliff pleasure, whatever reason he may have for ordering Linton to undergo this penance. And, though I'm glad he's better in health, I'm sorry he's so much less pleasant, and so much less affectionate to me."

"You think *he is* better in health, then?" I said.

"Yes," she answered, "because he always made such a great deal of his sufferings, you know. He is not tolerably well, as he told me to tell Papa; but he's better, very likely."

"There you differ with me, Miss Cathy," I remarked; "I should conjecture him to be far worse."

Linton here started from his slumber in bewildered terror, and asked if anyone had called his name.

"No," said Catherine, "unless in dreams. I cannot conceive how you manage to doze out of doors, in the morning."

"I thought I heard my father," he gasped, glancing up to the frowning nab above us. "You are sure nobody spoke?"

"Quite sure," replied his cousin. "Only Ellen and I were disputing concerning your health. Are you truly stronger, Linton, than when we separated in winter? If you be, I'm certain one thing is not stronger—your regard for me—speak, are you?"

The tears gushed from Linton's eyes as he answered, "Yes, yes, I am!"

And, still under the spell of the imaginary voice, his gaze wandered up and down to detect its owner.

Cathy rose.

"For today we must part," she said. "And I won't conceal that I have been sadly disappointed with our meeting, though I'll mention it to nobody but you—not that I stand in awe of Mr. Heathcliff!"

"Hush," murmured Linton; "for God's sake, hush! He's coming." And he clung to Catherine's arm, striving to detain her; but at that announcement she hastily disengaged herself, and whistled to Minny, who obeyed like a dog.

"I'll be here next Thursday," she cried, springing to the saddle. "Good-bye. Quick, Ellen!"

And so we left him, scarcely conscious of our departure, so absorbed was he in anticipating his father's approach.

Before we reached home, Catherine's displeasure softened into a perplexed sensation of pity and regret, largely blended with vague, uneasy doubts about Linton's actual circumstances, physical and social, in which I partook, though I counselled her not to say much; for a second journey would make us better judges.

My master requested an account of our on-goings. His nephew's offering of thanks was duly delivered, Miss Cathy gently touching on the rest; I also threw little light on his inquiries, for I hardly knew what to hide, and what to reveal.

CHAPTER 27

SEVEN days glided away, every one marking its course by the henceforth rapid alteration of Edgar Linton's state. The havoc that months had previously wrought was now emulated by the inroads of hours.

Catherine, we would fain have deluded yet, but her own quick spirit refused to delude her—it divined in secret, and brooded on the dreadful probability, gradually ripening into certainty.

She had not the heart to mention her ride, when Thursday came round; I mentioned it for her, and obtained permission to order her out of doors; for the library, where her father stopped a short time daily—the brief period he could bear to sit up—and his chamber, had become her whole world. She grudged each moment that did not find her bending over his pillow, or seated by his side. Her countenance grew wan with watching and sorrow, and my master gladly dismissed her to what he flattered himself would be a happy change of scene and society, drawing comfort from the hope that she would not now be left entirely alone after his death.

He had a fixed idea, I guessed by several observations he let fall, that as his nephew resembled him in person, he would resemble him in mind; for Linton's letters bore few or no indications of his defective character. And I, through pardonable weakness, refrained from correcting the error, asking myself what good there would be in disturbing his last moments with information that he had neither power nor opportunity to turn to account.

We deferred our excursion till the afternoon; a golden afternoon of August—every breath from the hills so full of life, that it seemed whoever respired it, though dying, might revive.

Catherine's face was just like the landscape—shadows and sunshine flitting over it in rapid succession; but the shadows rested longer, and the sunshine was more transient; and her poor little heart reproached itself for even that passing forgetfulness of its cares.

We discerned Linton watching at the same spot he had selected before. My young mistress alighted, and told me that as she was resolved to stay a very little while, I had better hold the pony and remain on horseback; but I dissented—I wouldn't risk losing sight of the charge committed to me a minute; so we climbed the slope of heath together.

Master Heathcliff received us with greater animation on this occasion—not the animation of high spirits though, nor yet of joy; it looked more like fear.

"It is late!" he said, speaking short and with difficulty. "Is not your father very ill? I thought you wouldn't come."

"Why won't you be candid?" cried Catherine, swallowing her greeting. "Why cannot you say at once, you don't want me? It is strange, Linton, that for the second time you have brought me here on purpose, apparently, to distress us both, and for no reason besides!"

Linton shivered, and glanced at her, half supplicating, half ashamed; but his cousin's patience was not sufficient to endure this enigmatical behaviour.

"My father is very ill," she said, "and why am I called from his bedside—why didn't you send to absolve me from my promise, when you wished I wouldn't keep it? Come! I desire an explanation; playing and trifling are completely banished out of my mind, and I can't dance attendance on your affectations, now!"

"My affectations!" he murmured; "what are they? For Heaven's sake, Catherine, don't look so angry! Despise me as much as you please; I am a worthless, cowardly wretch—I can't be scorned enough! But I'm too mean for your anger—hate my father, and spare me, for contempt."

"Nonsense!" cried Catherine, in a passion. "Foolish, silly boy! And there! he trembles, as if I were really going to touch him! You needn't bespeak contempt, Linton; anybody will have it spontaneously, at your service. Get off! I shall return home; it is folly dragging you from the hearthstone, and pretending—what do we pretend? Let go my frock! If I pitied you for crying and looking so very frightened, you should spurn such pity. Ellen, tell him how disgraceful this conduct is. Rise, and don't degrade yourself into an abject reptile—don't."

With streaming face and an expression of agony, Linton had thrown his nerveless frame along the ground; he seemed convulsed with exquisite terror.

"Oh!" he sobbed, "I cannot bear it! Catherine, Catherine, I'm a traitor too, and I dare not tell you! But leave me and I shall be killed! Dear Catherine, my life is in your hands: and you have said you loved me—and if you did, it wouldn't harm you. You'll not go, then? kind, sweet, good Catherine! And perhaps you will consent—and he'll let me die with you!"

My young lady, on witnessing his intense anguish, stooped to raise him. The old feeling of indulgent tenderness overcame her vexation, and she grew thoroughly moved and alarmed.

"Consent to what?" she asked. "To stay? Tell me the meaning of this strange talk, and I will. You contradict your own words, and distract me! Be calm and frank, and confess at once all that weighs on your heart. You wouldn't injure me, Linton, would you? You wouldn't let any enemy hurt me, if you could prevent it? I'll believe you are a coward, for yourself, but not a cowardly betrayer of your best friend."

"But my father threatened me," gasped the boy, clasping his attenuated fingers, "and I dread him—I dread him! I dare not tell!"

"Oh well!" said Catherine, with scornful compassion, "keep your secret, I'm no coward—save yourself; I'm not afraid!"

Her magnanimity provoked his tears; he wept wildly, kissing her supporting hands, and yet could not summon courage to speak out.

I was cogitating what the mystery might be, and determined Catherine should never suffer to benefit him or anyone else, by my good will, when hearing a rustle among the ling, I looked up, and saw Mr. Heathcliff almost close upon us, descending the Heights. He didn't cast a glance towards my companions, though they were sufficiently near for Linton's sobs to be audible; but hailing me in the almost hearty tone he assumed to none besides, and the sincerity of which, I couldn't avoid doubting, he said—

"It is something to see you so near to my house, Nelly! How are you at the Grange? Let us hear! The rumour goes," he added in a lower tone, "that Edgar Linton is on his deathbed—perhaps they exaggerated his illness?"

"No; my master is dying," I replied, "it is true enough. A sad thing it will be for us all, but a blessing for him!"

"How long will he last, do you think?" he asked.

"I don't know," I said.

"Because," he continued, looking at the two young people, who were fixed under his eye—Linton appeared as if he could not venture to stir, or raise his head, and Catherine could not move, on his account—"Because that lad yonder seems determined to beat me, and I'd thank his uncle to be quick, and go before him—Hallo! Has the whelp been playing that game long? I *did* give him some lessons about snivelling. Is he pretty lively with Miss Linton generally?"

"Lively? No—he has shown the greatest distress," I

answered. "To see him, I should say, that instead of rambling with his sweetheart on the hills, he ought to be in bed, under the hands of a doctor."

"He shall be, in a day or two," muttered Heathcliff. "But first—get up, Linton! Get up!" he shouted. "Don't grovel on the ground, there—up this moment!"

Linton had sunk prostrate again in another paroxysm of helpless fear, caused by his father's glance towards him, I suppose—there was nothing else to produce such humiliation. He made several efforts to obey, but his little strength was annihilated for the time, and he fell back again with a moan.

Mr. Heathcliff advanced, and lifted him to lean against a ridge of turf.

"Now," said he, with curbed ferocity, "I'm getting angry; and if you don't command that paltry spirit of yours—Damn you! Get up, directly!"

"I will, Father!" he panted. "Only, let me alone, or I shall faint! I've done as you wished, I'm sure. Catherine will tell you that I—that I—have been cheerful. Ah! keep by me, Catherine; give me your hand."

"Take mine," said his father; "stand on your feet. There now—she'll lend you her arm—that's right, look at her. You would imagine I was the devil himself, Miss Linton, to excite such horror. Be so kind as to walk home with him, will you? He shudders, if I touch him."

"Linton, dear!" whispered Catherine, "I can't go to Wuthering Heights . . . Papa has forbidden me . . . He'll not harm you—why are you so afraid?"

"I can never re-enter that house," he answered. "I'm not to re-enter it without you!"

"Stop . . ." cried his father. "We'll respect Catherine's filial scruples. Nelly, take him in, and I'll follow your advice concerning the doctor, without delay."

"You'll do well," replied I, "but I must remain with my mistress. To mind your son is not my business."

"You are very stiff," said Heathcliff, "I know that—but you'll force me to pinch the baby, and make it scream, before it moves your charity. Come then, my hero. Are you willing to return, escorted by me?"

He approached once more, and made as if he would seize the fragile being; but shrinking back, Linton clung to his cousin, and implored her to accompany him, with a frantic importunity that admitted no denial.

However I disapproved, I couldn't hinder her—indeed how could she have refused him herself? What was filling him with dread we had no means of discerning, but there he was, powerless under its gripe, and any addition seemed capable of shocking him into idiocy.

We reached the threshold; Catherine walked in; and I stood waiting till she had conducted the invalid to a chair, expecting her out immediately, when Mr. Heathcliff, pushing me forward, exclaimed—

"My house is not stricken with the plague, Nelly; and I have a mind to be hospitable today; sit down, and allow me to shut the door."

He shut and locked it also. I started.

"You shall have tea, before you go home," he added. "I am by myself. Hareton is gone with some cattle to the Lees—and Zillah and Joseph are off on a journey of pleasure. And, though I 'm used to being alone, I 'd rather have some interesting company, if I can get it. Miss Linton, take your seat by *him*. I give you what I have—the present is hardly worth accepting, but, I have nothing else to offer. It is Linton, I mean. How she does stare! It 's odd what a savage feeling I have to anything that seems afraid of me! Had I been born where laws are less strict, and tastes less dainty, I should treat myself to a slow vivisection of those two, as an evening's amusement."

He drew in his breath, struck the table, and swore to himself, "By hell! I hate them."

"I 'm not afraid of you!" exclaimed Catherine, who could not hear the latter part of his speech.

She stepped close up, her black eyes flashing with passion and resolution. "Give me that key—I will have it!" she said. "I wouldn't eat or drink here, if I were starving."

Heathcliff had the key in his hand that remained on the table. He looked up, seized with a sort of surprise at her boldness; or, possibly, reminded by her voice and glance of the person from whom she inherited it.

She snatched at the instrument, and half succeeded in getting it out of his loosened fingers—but her action recalled him to the present; he recovered it speedily.

"Now, Catherine Linton," he said, "stand off, or I shall knock you down; and that will make Mrs. Dean mad."

Regardless of this warning, she captured his closed hand and its contents again.

"We will go!" she repeated, exerting her utmost efforts to cause the iron muscles to relax; and finding that her nails made no impression, she applied her teeth pretty sharply.

Heathcliff glanced at me a glance that kept me from interfering a moment. Catherine was too intent on his fingers to notice his face. He opened them suddenly, and resigned the object of dispute; but, ere she had well secured it, he seized her with the liberated hand, and, pulling her on his knee, administered with the other a shower of terrific slaps on both sides of the head, each sufficient to have fulfilled his threat, had she been able to fall.

At this diabolical violence, I rushed on him furiously. "You villain!" I began to cry, "you villain!"

A touch on the chest silenced me; I am stout, and soon put out of breath, and, what with that and the rage, I staggered dizzily back, and felt ready to suffocate, or to burst a blood-vessel.

The scene was over in two minutes; Catherine, released, put her two hands to her temples, and looked just as if she were not sure whether her ears were off or on. She trembled like a reed, poor thing, and leant against the table perfectly bewildered.

"I know how to chastise children, you see," said the scoundrel, grimly, as he stooped to repossess himself of the key, which had dropped to the floor. "Go to Linton now, as I told you, and cry at your ease! I shall be your father, tomorrow—all the father you 'll have in a few days—and you shall have plenty of that—you can bear plenty—you 're no weakling—you shall have a daily taste, if I catch such a devil of a temper in your eyes again!"

Cathy ran to me instead of Linton, and knelt down, and put her burning cheek on my lap, weeping aloud. Her cousin had shrunk into a corner of the settle, as quiet as a mouse, congratulating himself, I dare say, that the correction had lighted on another than him.

Mr. Heathcliff, perceiving us all confounded, rose, and expeditiously made the tea himself. The cups and saucers were laid ready. He poured it out, and handed me a cup.

"Wash away your spleen," he said. "And help your own naughty pet and mine. It is not poisoned, though I prepared it. I'm going out to seek your horses."

Our first thought, on his departure, was to force an exit somewhere. We tried the kitchen door, but that was fastened outside; we looked at the windows—they were too narrow for even Cathy's little figure.

"Master Linton," I cried, seeing we were regularly imprisoned, "you know what your diabolical father is after, and you shall tell us, or I'll box your ears, as he has done your cousin's."

"Yes, Linton; you must tell," said Catherine. "It was for your sake I came, and it will be wickedly ungrateful if you refuse."

"Give me some tea, I'm thirsty, and then I'll tell you," he answered. "Mrs. Dean, go away. I don't like you standing over me. Now, Catherine, you are letting your tears fall into my cup! I won't drink that. Give me another."

Catherine pushed another to him, and wiped her face. I felt disgusted at the little wretch's composure, since he was no longer in terror for himself. The anguish he had exhibited on the moor subsided as soon as ever he entered Wuthering Heights; so I guessed he had been menaced with an awful visitation of wrath if he failed in decoying us there; and, that accomplished, he had no further immediate fears.

"Papa wants us to be married," he continued, after sipping some of the liquid. "And he knows your papa wouldn't let us marry now; and he's afraid of my dying, if we wait; so we are to be married in the morning, and you are to stay here all night; and, if you do as he wishes, you shall return home next day, and take me with you."

"Take you with her, pitiful changeling?" I exclaimed. "You marry? Why, the man is mad! or he thinks us fools, every one. And do you imagine that beautiful young lady, that healthy, hearty girl, will tie herself to a little perishing monkey like you? Are you cherishing the notion that anybody, let alone Miss Catherine Linton, would have you for a husband? You want whipping for bringing us in here at all, with your dastardly, puling tricks; and—don't look so silly now! I've a very good mind to shake you severely, for your contemptible treachery, and your imbecile conceit."

I did give him a slight shaking; but it brought on the cough, and he took to his ordinary resource of moaning and weeping, and Catherine rebuked me.

"Stay all night? No!" she said, looking slowly round. "Ellen, I'll burn that door down, but I'll get out."

And she would have commenced the execution of her threat directly, but Linton was up in alarm, for his dear self, again. He clasped her in his two feeble arms, sobbing—

"Won't you have me, and save me—not let me come to the Grange? Oh! darling Catherine! you mustn't go, and leave me, after all. You must obey my father, you must!"

"I must obey my own," she replied, "and relieve him from this cruel suspense. The whole night! What would he think? He'll be distressed already. I'll either break or burn a way out of the house. Be quiet! You're in no danger—but, if you hinder me—Linton, I love Papa better than you!"

The mortal terror he felt of Mr. Heathcliff's anger restored to the boy his coward's eloquence. Catherine was near distraught; still, she persisted that she must go home, and tried entreaty, in her turn, persuading him to subdue his selfish agony.

While they were thus occupied, our jailer re-entered.

"Your beasts have trotted off," he said, "and— Now, Linton! snivelling again? What has she been doing to you? Come, come—have done, and get to bed. In a month or two, my lad, you'll be able to pay her back her present tyrannies, with a vigorous hand. You're pining for pure love, are you not? nothing else in the world— and she shall have you! There, to bed! Zillah won't be here tonight; you must undress yourself. Hush! hold your noise! Once in your own room, I'll not come near you, you needn't fear. By chance, you've managed tolerably. I'll look to the rest."

He spoke these words, holding the door open for his son to pass, and the latter achieved his exit exactly as a spaniel might, which suspected the person who attended on it of designing a spiteful squeeze.

The lock was re-secured. Heathcliff approached the

fire, where my mistress and I stood silent. Catherine looked up, and instinctively raised her hand to her cheek—his neighbourhood revived a painful sensation. Anybody else would have been incapable of regarding the childish act with sternness, but he scowled on her, and muttered—

"Oh, you are not afraid of me? Your courage is well disguised—you seem damnably afraid!"

"I am afraid now," she replied, "because if I stay, Papa will be miserable; and how can I endure making him miserable—when he—when he—Mr. Heathcliff, let me go home! I promise to marry Linton: Papa would like me to, and I love him—and why should you wish to force me to do what I'll willingly do of myself?"

"Let him dare to force you!" I cried. "There's law in the land, thank God, there is! though we be in an out-of-the-way place. I'd inform, if he were my own son, and it's felony without benefit of clergy!"

"Silence!" said the ruffian. "To the devil with your clamour! I don't want you to speak. Miss Linton, I shall enjoy myself remarkably in thinking your father will be miserable—I shall not sleep for satisfaction. You could have hit on no surer way of fixing your residence under my roof, for the next twenty-four hours, than informing me that such an event would follow. As to your promise to marry Linton, I'll take care you shall keep it; for you shall not quit this place till it is fulfilled."

"Send Ellen then, to let Papa know I'm safe!" exclaimed Catherine, weeping bitterly. "Or marry me now. Poor Papa! Ellen, he'll think we're lost. What shall we do?"

"Not he! He'll think you are tired of waiting on him, and run off, for a little amusement," answered Heathcliff. "You cannot deny that you entered my house of your own accord, in contempt of his injunctions to the contrary. And it is quite natural that you should desire amusement at your age, and that you should weary of nursing a sick man, and that man only your father. Catherine, his happiest days were over when your days began. He cursed you, I dare say, for coming into the world (I did, at least). And it would just do if he cursed you as he went out of it. I'd join him. I don't love you! How should I? Weep away. As far as I can see, it will be your chief diversion hereafter, unless Linton make amends for other losses—and your provident parent appears to fancy he may. His letters of advice and consolation entertained me vastly. In his last, he recommended my jewel to be careful of his, and kind to her when he got her. Careful and kind—that's paternal. But Linton requires his whole stock of care and kindness for himself. Linton can play the little tyrant well. He'll undertake to torture any number of cats if their teeth be drawn, and their claws pared. You'll be able to tell his uncle fine tales of his kindness, when you get home again, I assure you."

"You're right there!" I said; "explain your son's character. Show his resemblance to yourself; and then, I hope, Miss Cathy will think twice before she takes the cockatrice!"

"I don't much mind speaking of his amiable qualities now," he answered, "because she must either accept him or remain a prisoner, and you along with her, till your master dies. I can detain you both, quite concealed, here. If you doubt, encourage her to retract her word, and you'll have an opportunity of judging!"

"I'll not retract my word," said Catherine. "I'll marry him, within this hour, if I may go to Thrushcross Grange afterwards. Mr. Heathcliff, you're a cruel man, but you're not a fiend; and you won't, from mere malice, destroy, irrevocably, all my happiness. If Papa thought I had left him, on purpose, and if he died before I returned, could I bear to live? I've given over crying, but I'm going to kneel here, at your knee; and I'll not get up, and I'll not take my eyes from your face, till you look back at me! No, don't turn away! do look! You'll see nothing to provoke you. I don't hate you. I'm not angry that you struck me. Have you never loved anybody, in all your life, Uncle? Never? Ah! you must look once—I'm so wretched—you can't help being sorry and pitying me."

"Keep your eft's fingers off; and move, or I'll kick you!" cried Heathcliff, brutally repulsing her. "I'd rather be hugged by a snake. How the devil can you dream of fawning on me? I detest you!"

He shrugged his shoulders, shook himself, indeed, as if his flesh crept with aversion, and thrust back his chair, while I got up, and opened my mouth, to commence a downright torrent of abuse; but I was rendered dumb in the middle of the first sentence, by a threat that I should be shown into a room by myself, the very next syllable I uttered.

It was growing dark—we heard a sound of voices at the garden gate. Our host hurried out instantly; he had his wits about him; we had not. There was a talk of two or three minutes, and he returned alone.

"I thought it had been your cousin, Hareton," I observed to Catherine. "I wish he would arrive! Who knows but he might take our part?"

"It was three servants sent to seek you from the Grange," said Heathcliff, overhearing me. "You should have opened a lattice and called out—but I could swear that chit is glad you didn't. She's glad to be obliged to stay, I'm certain."

At learning the chance we had missed, we both gave vent to our grief without control, and he allowed us to wail on till nine o'clock. Then he bade us go upstairs, through the kitchen, to Zillah's chamber, and I whispered my companion to obey—perhaps we might contrive to get through the window there, or into a garret, and out by its skylight.

The window, however, was narrow, like those below, and the garret trap was safe from our attempts, for we were fastened in as before.

We neither of us lay down; Catherine took her station by the lattice, and watched anxiously for morning, a deep sigh being the only answer I could obtain to my frequent entreaties that she would try to rest.

I seated myself in a chair, and rocked, to and fro, passing harsh judgment on my many derelictions of duty, from which, it struck me then, all the misfortunes of all my employers sprang. It was not the case, in reality, I am aware; but it was, in my imagination, that dismal night; and I thought Heathcliff himself less guilty than I.

At seven o'clock he came, and inquired if Miss Linton had risen.

She ran to the door immediately, and answered, "Yes."

"Here, then," he said, opening it, and pulling her out. I rose to follow, but he turned the lock again. I demanded my release.

"Be patient," he replied; "I'll send up your breakfast in a while."

I thumped on the panels, and rattled the latch angrily; and Catherine asked why I was still shut up? He answered, I must try to endure it another hour, and they went away.

I endured it two or three hours; at length, I heard a footstep, not Heathcliff's.

"I've brought you something to eat," said a voice; "oppen t' door!"

Complying eagerly, I beheld Hareton, laden with food enough to last me all day.

"Tak' it," he added, thrusting the tray into my hand.

"Stay one minute," I began.

"Nay!" cried he, and retired, regardless of any prayers I could pour forth to detain him.

And there I remained enclosed, the whole day, and the whole of the next night; and another, and another. Five nights and four days I remained, altogether, seeing nobody but Hareton, once every morning; and he was a model of a jailer—surly, and dumb, and deaf to every attempt at moving his sense of justice or compassion.

CHAPTER 28

ON THE fifth morning, or rather afternoon, a different step approached—lighter and shorter—and, this time, the person entered the room. It was Zillah; donned in her scarlet shawl, with a black silk bonnet on her head, and a willow basket swung to her arm.

"Eh, dear! Mrs. Dean," she exclaimed. "Well! there is a talk about you at Gimmerton. I never thought you were sunk in the Blackhorse marsh, and Missy with you, till master told me you'd been found, and he'd lodged you here! What, and you must have got on an island, sure? And how long were you in the hole? Did master save you, Mrs. Dean? But you're not so thin—you've not been so poorly, have you?"

"Your master is a true scoundrel!" I replied. "But he shall answer for it. He needn't have raised that tale; it shall all be laid bare!"

"What do you mean?" asked Zillah. "It's not his tale; they tell that in the village—about your being lost in the marsh; and I calls to Earnshaw, when I came in—'Eh, they's queer things, Mr. Hareton, happened since I went off. It's a sad pity of that likely young lass, and cant Nelly Dean.'

"He stared. I thought he had not heard aught, so I told him the rumour.

"The master listened, and he just smiled to himself, and said,

"'If they have been in the marsh, they are out now, Zillah. Nelly Dean is lodged, at this minute, in your room. You can tell her to flit, when you go up; here is the key. The bog-water got into her head, and she would have run home, quite flighty, but I fixed her, till she came round to her senses. You can bid her go to the Grange, at once, if she be able, and carry a message from me, that her young lady will follow in time to attend the squire's funeral.'"

"Mr. Edgar is not dead?" I gasped. "Oh! Zillah, Zillah!"

"No, no; sit you down, my good mistress," she replied, "your right sickly yet. He's not dead; Doctor Kenneth thinks he may last another day. I met him on the road and asked."

Instead of sitting down, I snatched my outdoor things, and hastened below, for the way was free.

On entering the house, I looked about for someone to give information of Catherine.

The place was filled with sunshine, and the door stood wide open; but nobody seemed at hand.

As I hesitated whether to go off at once, or return and seek my mistress, a slight cough drew my attention to the hearth.

Linton lay on the settle, sole tenant, sucking a stick of sugar-candy, and pursuing my movements with apathetic eyes.

"Where is Miss Catherine?" I demanded, sternly, supposing I could frighten him into giving intelligence, by catching him thus, alone.

He sucked on like an innocent.

"Is she gone?" I said.

"No," he replied; "she's upstairs: she's not to go; we won't let her."

"You won't let her, little idiot!" I exclaimed. "Direct me to her room immediately, or I'll make you sing out sharply."

"Papa would make you sing out, if you attempted to get there," he answered. "He says I'm not to be soft with Catherine—she's my wife, and it's shameful that she should wish to leave me! He says, she hates me, and wants me to die, that she may have my money; but she shan't have it—and she shan't go home! She never will! —she may cry, and be sick as much as she pleases!"

He resumed his former occupation, closing his lids, as if he meant to drop asleep.

"Master Heathcliff," I resumed, "have you forgotten all Catherine's kindness to you, last winter, when you affirmed you loved her, and when she brought you books, and sung you songs, and came many a time through wind and snow to see you? She wept to miss one evening, because you would be disappointed; and you felt then that she was a hundred times too good to you: and now you believe the lies your father tells, though you know he detests you both! And you join him against her. That's fine gratitude, is it not?"

The corner of Linton's mouth fell, and he took the sugar-candy from his lips.

"Did she come to Wuthering Heights because she hated you?" I continued. "Think for yourself! As to your money, she does not even know that you will have any. And you say she's sick; and yet, you leave her alone, up there in a strange house! You, who have felt what it is to be so neglected! You could pity your own sufferings, and she pitied them, too, but you won't pity hers! I shed tears, Master Heathcliff, you see—an elderly woman, and a servant merely—and you, after pretending such affection, and having reason to worship her, almost, store up every tear you have for yourself, and lie there quite at ease. Ah! you're a heartless, selfish boy!"

"I can't stay with her," he answered crossly. "I'll not stay, by myself. She cries so I can't bear it. And she won't give over, though I say I'll call my father. I did call him once, and he threatened to strangle her, if she was not quiet; but she began again, the instant he left the room, moaning and grieving all night long, though I screamed for vexation that I couldn't sleep."

"Is Mr. Heathcliff out?" I inquired, perceiving that the wretched creature had no power to sympathize with his cousin's mental tortures.

"He's in the court," he replied, "talking to Doctor Kenneth who says Uncle is dying, truly, at last. I'm glad, for I shall be master of the Grange after him—and Catherine always spoke of it as her house. It isn't hers! It's mine—Papa says everything she has is mine. All her nice books are mine—she offered to give me them, and her pretty birds, and her pony Minny, if I would get the key of our room, and let her out; but I told her she had nothing to give, they were all, all mine. And then she cried, and took a little picture from her neck, and said I should have that; two pictures in a gold case—on one side her mother, and on the other, Uncle, when they were young. That was yesterday—I said they were mine, too, and tried to get them from her. The spiteful thing wouldn't let me—she pushed me off, and hurt me. I shrieked out —that frightens her—she heard Papa coming, and she broke the hinges, and divided the case and gave me her mother's portrait; the other she attempted to hide; but Papa asked what was the matter and I explained it. He took the one I had away; and ordered her to resign hers to me; she refused, and he—he struck her down, and wrenched it off the chain, and crushed it with his foot."

"And were you pleased to see her struck?" I asked, having my designs in encouraging his talk.

"I winked," he answered. "I wink to see my father strike a dog, or a horse, he does it so hard. Yet I was glad at first—she deserved punishing for pushing me; but when Papa was gone, she made me come to the window and showed me her cheek cut on the inside, against her teeth, and her mouth filling with blood; and then she gathered up the bits of the picture, and went and sat down with her face to the wall, and she has never spoken to me since—and I sometimes think she can't speak for pain. I don't like to think so! but she's a naughty thing for crying continually; and she looks so pale and wild, I'm afraid of her!"

"And you can get the key if you choose?" I said.

"Yes, when I am upstairs," he answered; "but I can't walk upstairs now."

"In what apartment is it?" I asked.

"Oh," he cried, "I shan't tell you where it is! It is our secret. Nobody, neither Hareton, nor Zillah are to know. There! you 've tired me—go away, go away!" And he turned his face onto his arm, and shut his eyes again.

I considered it best to depart without seeing Mr. Heathcliff, and bring a rescue for my young lady, from the Grange.

On reaching it, the astonishment of my fellow servants to see me, and their joy also, was intense; and when they heard that their little mistress was safe, two or three were about to hurry up, and shout the news at Mr. Edgar's door, but I bespoke the announcement of it, myself.

How changed I found him, even in those few days! He lay an image of sadness, and resignation, waiting his death. Very young he looked—though his actual age was thirty-nine, one would have called him ten years younger, at least. He thought of Catherine for he murmured her name. I touched his hand, and spoke.

"Catherine is coming, dear master!" I whispered; "she is alive, and well, and will be here I hope tonight."

I trembled at the first effects of this intelligence; he half rose up, looked eagerly round the apartment, and then sunk back in a swoon.

As soon as he recovered, I related our compulsory visit, and detention at the Heights. I said Heathcliff forced me to go in, which was not quite true. I uttered as little as possible against Linton; nor did I describe all his father's brutal conduct—my intentions being to add no bitterness, if I could help it, to his already overflowing cup.

He divined that one of his enemy's purposes was to secure the personal property, as well as the estate, to his son, or rather himself; yet why he did not wait till his decease was a puzzle to my master, because ignorant how nearly he and his nephew would quit the world together.

However, he felt that his will had better be altered: instead of leaving Catherine's fortune at her own disposal, he determined to put it in the hands of trustees, for her use during life, and for her children, if she had any, after her. By that means, it could not fall to Mr. Heathcliff should Linton die.

Having received his orders, I despatched a man to fetch the attorney, and four more, provided with serviceable weapons, to demand my young lady of her jailer. Both parties were delayed very late. The single servant returned first.

He said Mr. Green, the lawyer, was out when he arrived at his house, and he had to wait two hours for his re-entrance; and then Mr. Green told him he had a little business in the village that must be done, but he would be at Thrushcross Grange before morning.

The four men came back unaccompanied, also. They brought word that Catherine was ill—too ill to quit her room—and Heathcliff would not suffer them to see her.

I scolded the stupid fellows well, for listening to that tale, which I would not carry to my master, resolving to take a whole bevy up to the Heights, at daylight, and storm it, literally, unless the prisoner were quietly surrendered to us.

Her father *shall* see her, I vowed, and vowed again, if that devil be killed on his own door-stones in trying to prevent it!

Happily, I was spared the journey, and the trouble.

I had gone downstairs at three o'clock to fetch a jug of water, and was passing through the hall with it in my hand, when a sharp knock at the front door made me jump.

"Oh! it is Green," I said, recollecting myself—"only Green," and I went on, intending to send somebody else to open it; but the knock was repeated, not loud, and still importunately.

I put the jug on the banister, and hastened to admit him myself.

The harvest moon shone clear outside. It was not the attorney. My own sweet little mistress sprung on my neck, sobbing—

"Ellen! Ellen! Is Papa alive?"

"Yes!" I cried, "yes, my angel, he is. God be thanked, you are safe with us again!"

She wanted to run, breathless as she was, upstairs to

Mr. Linton's room; but I compelled her to it down on a chair, and made her drink, and washed her pale face, chafing it into a faint colour with my apron. Then I said I must go first, and tell of her arrival, imploring her to say, she should be happy with young Heathcliff. She stared, but soon comprehending why I counselled her to utter the falsehood, she assured me she would not complain.

I couldn't abide to be present at their meeting. I stood outside the chamber door a quarter of an hour, and hardly ventured near the bed, then.

All was composed, however; Catherine's despair was as silent as her father's joy. She supported him calmly, in appearance; and he fixed on her features his raised eyes that seemed dilating with ecstasy.

He died blissfully, Mr. Lockwood; he died so. Kissing her cheek, he murmured,

"I am going to her; and you darling child shall come to us"; and never stirred or spoke again, but continued that rapt, radiant gaze, till his pulse imperceptibly stopped, and his soul departed. None could have noticed the exact minute of his death, it was so entirely without a struggle.

Whether Catherine had spent her tears, or whether the grief were too weighty to let them flow, she sat there dry-eyed till the sun rose; she sat till noon, and would still have remained, brooding over that deathbed, but I insisted on her coming away, and taking some repose.

It was well I succeeded in removing her, for at dinnertime appeared the lawyer, having called at Wuthering Heights to get his instructions how to behave. He had sold himself to Mr. Heathcliff, and that was the cause of his delay in obeying my master's summons. Fortunately, no thought of worldly affairs crossed the latter's mind, to disturb him, after his daughter's arrival.

Mr. Green took upon himself to order everything and everybody about the place. He gave all the servants but me notice to quit. He would have carried his delegated authority to the point of insisting that Edgar Linton should not be buried beside his wife, but in the chapel, with his family. There was the will, however, to hinder that, and my loud protestations against any infringement of its directions.

The funeral was hurried over; Catherine, Mrs. Linton Heathcliff now, was suffered to stay at the Grange till her father's corpse had quitted it.

She told me that her anguish had at last spurred Linton to incur the risk of liberating her. She heard the men I sent, disputing at the door, and she gathered the sense of Heathcliff's answer. It drove her desperate. Linton, who had been conveyed up to the little parlour soon after I left, was terrified into fetching the key before his father re-ascended.

He had the cunning to unlock and re-lock the door, without shutting it; and when he should have gone to bed, he begged to sleep with Hareton, and his petition was granted, for once.

Catherine stole out before break of day. She dare not try the doors, lest the dogs should raise an alarm; she visited the empty chambers, and examined their windows; and, luckily, lighting on her mother's, she got easily out of its lattice, and onto the ground, by means of the fir tree, close by. Her accomplice suffered for his share in the escape, notwithstanding his timid contrivances.

CHAPTER 29

THE evening after the funeral, my young lady and I were seated in the library, now musing mournfully—one of us despairingly—on our loss, now venturing conjectures as to the gloomy future.

We had just agreed the best destiny which could await Catherine would be a permission to continue resident at the Grange, at least during Linton's life—he being allowed to join her there, and I to remain as housekeeper. That seemed rather too favourable an arrangement to be hoped for; and yet I did hope, and began to cheer up under the prospect of retaining my home, and my employment, and, above all, my beloved young mistress, when a servant—one of the discarded ones, not yet departed—rushed hastily in, and said, "that devil Heathcliff" was coming through the court—should he fasten the door in his face?

If we had been mad enough to order that proceeding, we had not time. He made no ceremony of knocking, or announcing his name—he was master, and availed himself of the master's privilege to walk straight in, without saying a word.

The sound of our informant's voice directed him to the library; he entered, and motioning him out, shut the door.

It was the same room into which he had been ushered, as a guest, eighteen years before; the same moon shone through the window, and the same autumn landscape lay outside. We had not yet lighted a candle, but all the apartment was visible, even to the portraits on the wall—the splendid head of Mrs. Linton, and the graceful one of her husband.

Heathcliff advanced to the hearth. Time had little altered his person either. There was the same man, his dark face rather sallower, and more composed, his frame a stone or two heavier, perhaps, with no other difference.

Catherine had risen, with an impulse to dash out, when she saw him.

"Stop!" he said, arresting her by the arm. "No more runnings away! Where would you go? I'm come to fetch you home; and I hope you'll be a dutiful daughter, and not encourage my son to further disobedience. I was embarrassed how to punish him, when I discovered his part in the business—he's such a cobweb, a pinch would annihilate him—but you'll see by his look that he has received his due! I brought him down one evening, the day before yesterday, and just set him in a chair, and never touched him afterwards. I sent Hareton out, and we had the room to ourselves. In two hours, I called Joseph to carry him up again; and, since then, my presence is as potent on his nerves as a ghost—and I fancy he sees me often, though I am not near. Hareton says he wakes and shrieks in the night by the hour together, and calls you to protect him from me; and, whether you like your precious mate or not, you must come—he's your concern now; I yield all my interest in him to you."

"Why not let Catherine continue here?" I pleaded, "and send Master Linton to her. As you hate them both, you'd not miss them; they can only be a daily plague to your unnatural heart."

"I'm seeking a tenant for the Grange," he answered, "and I want my children about me, to be sure—besides, that lass owes me her services for her bread; I'm not going to nurture her in luxury and idleness after Linton is gone. Make haste and get ready now. And don't oblige me to compel you."

"I shall," said Catherine. "Linton is all I have to love in the world, and, though you have done what you could to make him hateful to me, and me to him, you cannot make us hate each other! and I defy you to hurt him when I am by, and I defy you to frighten me."

"You are a boastful champion," replied Heathcliff; "but I don't like you well enough to hurt him—you shall get the full benefit of the torment, as long as it lasts. It is not I who will make him hateful to you—it is his own sweet spirit. He's as bitter as gall at your desertion, and its consequences; don't expect thanks for this noble devotion. I heard him draw a pleasant picture to Zillah of what he would do, if he were as strong as I; the inclination is there, and his very weakness will sharpen his wits to find a substitute for strength."

"I know he has a bad nature," said Catherine; "he's your son. But I'm glad I've a better, to forgive it; and I know he loves me, and for that reason I love him. Mr. Heathcliff, you have nobody to love you, and, however miserable you make us, we shall still have the revenge of thinking that your cruelty arises from your greater misery! You are miserable, are you not? Lonely, like the devil, and envious like him? Nobody loves you—nobody will cry for you when you die! I wouldn't be you!"

Catherine spoke with a kind of dreary triumph; she seemed to have made up her mind to enter into the spirit of her future family, and draw pleasure from the griefs of her enemies.

"You shall be sorry to be yourself presently," said her father-in-law, "if you stand there another minute. Begone, witch, and get your things."

She scornfully withdrew.

In her absence, I began to beg for Zillah's place at the

Heights, offering to resign mine to her; but he would suffer it on no account. He bid me be silent; and then, for the first time, allowed himself a glance round the room, and a look at the pictures. Having studied Mrs. Linton, he said—

"I shall have that home. Not because I need it, but——"

He turned abruptly to the fire, and continued, with what, for lack of a better word, I must call a smile—

"I'll tell you what I did yesterday! I got the sexton, who was digging Linton's grave, to remove the earth off her coffin-lid, and I opened it. I thought, once, I would have stayed there, when I saw her face again—it is hers yet—he had hard work to stir me; but he said it would change, if the air blew on it, and so I struck one side of the coffin loose, and covered it up—not Linton's side, damn him! I wish he'd been soldered in lead—and I bribed the sexton to pull it away, when I'm laid there, and slide mine out too. I'll have it made so, and then, by the time Linton gets to us, he'll not know which is which!"

"You were very wicked, Mr. Heathcliff!" I exclaimed; "were you not ashamed to disturb the dead?"

"I disturbed nobody, Nelly," he replied, "and I gave some ease to myself. I shall be a great deal more comfortable now; and you'll have a better chance of keeping me underground, when I get there. Disturbed her? No! she has disturbed me, night and day, through eighteen years—incessantly—remorselessly—till yesternight; and yesternight I was tranquil. I dreamt I was sleeping the last sleep by that sleeper, with my heart stopped and my cheek frozen against hers."

"And if she had been dissolved into earth, or worse, what would you have dreamt of then?" I said.

"Of dissolving with her, and being more happy still!" he answered. "Do you suppose I dread any change of that sort? I expected such a transformation on raising the lid, but I'm better pleased that it should not commence till I share it. Besides, unless I had received a distinct impression of her passionless features, that strange feeling would hardly have been removed. It began oddly. You know, I was wild after she died, and eternally, from dawn to dawn, praying her to return to me—her spirit—I have a strong faith in ghosts; I have a conviction that they can, and do exist, among us!

"The day she was buried, there came a fall of snow. In the evening I went to the churchyard. It blew bleak as winter—all round was solitary; I didn't fear that her fool of a husband would wander up the den so late, and no one else had business to bring them there.

"Being alone, and conscious two yards of loose earth was the sole barrier between us, I said to myself—

"'I'll have her in my arms again! If she be cold, I'll think it is this north wind that chills me; and if she be motionless, it is sleep.'

"I got a spade from the toolhouse, and began to delve with all my might—it scraped the coffin; I fell to work with my hands; the wood commenced cracking about the screws, I was on the point of attaining my object, when it seemed that I heard a sigh from someone above, close at the edge of the grave, and bending down. 'If I can only get this off,' I muttered, 'I wish they may shovel in the earth over us both!' and I wrenched more desperately still. There was another sigh, close at my ear. I appeared to feel the warm breath of it displacing the sleet-laden wind. I knew no living thing in flesh and blood was by; but as certainly as you perceive the approach to some substantial body in the dark, though it cannot be discerned, so certainly I felt that Cathy was there: not under me, but on the earth.

"A sudden sense of relief flowed, from my heart, through every limb. I relinquished my labour of agony, and turned consoled at once, unspeakably consoled. Her presence was with me; it remained while I re-filled the grave, and led me home. You may laugh, if you will, but I was sure I should see her there. I was sure she was with me, and I could not help talking to her.

"Having reached the Heights, I rushed eagerly to the door. It was fastened; and, I remember, that accursed Earnshaw and my wife opposed my entrance. I remember stopping to kick the breath out of him, and then hurrying upstairs, to my room, and hers. I looked round impatiently—I felt her by me—I could *almost* see her, and yet I *could not!* I ought to have sweat blood then, from the anguish of my yearning—from the fervour of my supplications to have but one glimpse! I had not one.

She showed herself, as she often was in life, a devil to me! And, since then, sometimes more and sometimes less, I've been the sport of that intolerable torture! Infernal—keeping my nerves at such a stretch, that, if they had not resembled catgut, they would, long ago, have relaxed to the feebleness of Linton's.

"When I sat in the house with Hareton, it seemed that on going out, I should meet her; when I walked on the moors I should meet her coming in. When I went from home, I hastened to return—she *must* be somewhere at the Heights, I was certain! And when I slept in her chamber—I was beaten out of that—I couldn't lie there; for the moment I closed my eyes, she was either outside the window, or sliding back the panels, or entering the room, or even resting her darling head on the same pillow as she did when a child. And I must open my lids to see. And so I opened and closed them a hundred times a night—to be always disappointed! It racked me! I've often groaned aloud, till that old rascal Joseph no doubt believed that my conscience was playing the fiend inside of me.

"Now, since I've seen her, I'm pacified—a little. It was a strange way of killing, not by inches, but by fractions of hairbreadths, to beguile me with the spectre of a hope, through eighteen years!"

Mr. Heathcliff paused and wiped his forehead; his hair clung to it, wet with perspiration; his eyes were fixed on the red embers of the fire; the brows not contracted, but raised next the temples, diminishing the grim aspect of his countenance, but imparting a peculiar look of trouble, and a painful appearance of mental tension towards one absorbing subject. He only half addressed me, and I maintained silence—I didn't like to hear him talk!

After a short period, he resumed his meditation on the picture, took it down and leant it against the sofa to contemplate it at better advantage; and while so occupied Catherine entered, announcing that she was ready, when her pony should be saddled.

"Send that over tomorrow," said Heathcliff to me, then turning to her he added, "you may do without your pony; it is a fine evening, and you'll need no ponies at Wuthering Heights; for what journeys you take, your own feet will serve you. Come along."

"Good-bye, Ellen!" whispered my dear little mistress. As she kissed me, her lips felt like ice. "Come and see me, Ellen, don't forget."

"Take care you do no such thing, Mrs. Dean!" said her new father. "When I wish to speak to you I'll come here. I want none of your prying at my house!"

He signed her to precede him; and casting back a look that cut my heart, she obeyed.

I watched them from the window walk down the garden, Heathcliff fixed Catherine's arm under his, though she disputed the act, at first, evidently, and with rapid strides, he hurried her into the alley, whose trees concealed them.

CHAPTER 30

I HAVE paid a visit to the Heights, but I have not seen her since she left; Joseph held the door in his hand, when I called to ask after her, and wouldn't let me pass. He said Mrs. Linton was "thrang," and the master was not in. Zillah has told me something of the way they go on, otherwise I should hardly know who was dead and who living.

She thinks Catherine haughty, and does not like her, I can guess by her talk. My young lady asked some aid of her when she first came; but Mr. Heathcliff told her to follow her own business, and let his daughter-in-law look after herself, and Zillah willingly acquiesced, being a narrow-minded selfish woman. Catherine evinced a child's annoyance at this neglect; repaid it with contempt, and thus enlisted my informant among her enemies, as securely as if she had done her some great wrong.

I had a long talk with Zillah, about six weeks ago, a little before you came, one day, when we foregathered on the moor; and this is what she told me.

"The first thing Mrs. Linton did," she said, "on her arrival at the Heights, was to run upstairs without even wishing good evening to me and Joseph; she shut herself into Linton's room, and remained till morning. Then, while the master and Earnshaw were at breakfast, she entered the house, and asked all in a quiver if the doctor might be sent for? her cousin was very ill.

" 'We know that!' answered Heathcliff; 'but his life is not worth a farthing, and I won't spend a farthing on him.'

" 'But I cannot tell how to do,' she said; 'and if nobody will help me, he 'll die!'

" 'Walk out of the room,' cried the master, 'and let me never hear a word more about him! None here care what becomes of him; if you do, act the nurse; if you do not, lock him up and leave him.'

"Then she began to bother me, and I said I 'd had enough plague with the tiresome thing; we each had our tasks, and hers was to wait on Linton, Mr. Heathcliff bid me leave that labour to her.

"How they managed together, I can't tell. I fancy he fretted a great deal, and moaned hisseln, night and day; and she had precious little rest, one could guess by her white face, and heavy eyes—she sometimes came into the kitchen all wildered like, and looked as if she would fain beg assistance; but I was not going to disobey the master: I never dare disobey him, Mrs. Dean; and though I thought it wrong that Kenneth should not be sent for, it was no concern of mine, either to advise or complain; and I always refused to meddle.

"Once or twice, after we had gone to bed, I 've happened to open my door again, and seen her sitting crying, on the stairs' top; and then I 've shut myself in, quick, for fear of being moved to interfere. I did pity her then, I 'm sure; still I didn't want to lose my place, you know!

"At last, one night she came boldly into my chamber, and frightened me out of my wits, by saying—

" 'Tell Mr. Heathcliff that his son is dying—I 'm sure he is, this time. Get up, instantly, and tell him!'

"Having uttered this speech, she vanished again. I lay a quarter of an hour listening and trembling. Nothing stirred—the house was quiet.

" 'She 's mistaken,' I said to myself. 'He 's got over it. I needn't disturb them.' And I began to doze. But my sleep was marred a second time, by a sharp ringing of the bell—the only bell we have, put up on purpose for Linton; and the master called to me to see what was the matter, and inform them that he wouldn't have that noise repeated.

"I delivered Catherine's message. He cursed to himself, and in a few minutes came out with a lighted candle, and proceeded to their room. I followed. Mrs. Heathcliff was seated by the bedside, with her hands folded on her knees. Her father-in-law went up, held the light to Linton's face, looked at him, and touched him; afterwards he turned to her.

" 'Now—Catherine,' he said, 'how do you feel?'

"She was dumb.

" 'How do you feel, Catherine?' he repeated.

" 'He 's safe, and I 'm free,' she answered. 'I should feel well—but,' she continued with a bitterness she couldn't conceal, 'you have left me so long to struggle against death, alone, that I feel and see only death! I feel like death!'

"And she looked like it, too! I gave her a little wine. Hareton and Joseph, who had been wakened by the ringing, and the sound of feet, and heard our talk from outside, now entered. Joseph was fain, I believe, of the lad's removal; Hareton seemed a thought bothered—though he was more taken up with staring at Catherine than thinking of Linton. But the master bid him get off to bed again; we didn't want his help. He afterwards made Joseph remove the body to his chamber, and told me to return to mine, and Mrs. Heathcliff remained by herself.

"In the morning, he sent me to tell her she must come down to breakfast; she had undressed, and appeared going to sleep; and said she was ill, at which I hardly wondered. I informed Mr. Heathcliff, and he replied—

" 'Well, let her be till after the funeral; and go up now and then to get her what is needful; and as soon as she seems better, tell me.' "

Cathy stayed upstairs a fortnight, according to Zillah, who visited her twice a day, and would have been rather more friendly, but her attempts at increasing kindness were proudly and promptly repelled.

Heathcliff went up at once, to show her Linton's will. He had bequeathed the whole of his and what had been her movable property to his father. The poor creature was threatened, or coaxed, into that act during her week's absence, when his uncle died. The lands, being a minor, he could not meddle with. However, Mr. Heathcliff has claimed and kept them in his wife's right, and his also; I suppose legally, at any rate, Catherine, destitute of cash and friends, cannot disturb his possession.

"Nobody," said Zillah, "ever approached her door, except that once, but I . . . and nobody asked anything about her. The first occasion of her coming down into the house was on a Sunday afternoon. She had cried out, when I carried up her dinner, that she couldn't bear any longer being in the cold; and I told her the master was going to Thrushcross Grange, and Earnshaw and I needn't hinder her from descending; so, as soon as she heard Heathcliff's horse trot off, she made her appearance, donned in black, and her yellow curls combed back behind her ears, as plain as a Quaker—she couldn't comb them out.

"Joseph and I generally go to chapel on Sundays," (the Kirk, you know, has no minister now, explained Mrs. Dean; and they call the Methodists' or Baptists' place, I can't say which it is, at Gimmerton, a chapel). "Joseph had gone," she continued, "but I thought proper to bide at home. Young folks are always the better for an elder's over-looking; and Hareton, with all his bashfulness, isn't a model of nice behaviour. I let him know that his cousin would very likely sit with us, and she had been always used to see the Sabbath respected; so he had as good leave his guns and bits of indoor work alone, while she stayed.

"He coloured up at the news, and cast his eyes over his hands and clothes. The train-oil and gunpowder were shoved out of sight in a minute. I saw he meant to give her his company, and I guessed, by his way, he wanted to be presentable; so, laughing, as I durst not laugh when the master is by, I offered to help him, if he would, and joked at his confusion. He grew sullen, and began to swear.

"Now, Mrs. Dean," she went on, seeing me not pleased by her manner, "you happen think your young lady too fine for Mr. Hareton; and happen you're right: but, I own, I should love well to bring her pride a peg lower. And what will all her learning and her daintiness do for her, now? She's as poor as you or I—poorer, I'll be bound; you're saving, and I'm doing my little all, that road."

Hareton allowed Zillah to give him her aid; and she flattered him into a good humour; so, when Catherine came, half forgetting her former insults, he tried to make himself agreeable, by the housekeeper's account.

"Missis walked in," she said, "as chill as an icicle, and as high as a princess. I got up and offered her my seat in the armchair. No, she turned up her nose at my civility. Earnshaw rose too, and bid her come to the settle, and sit close by the fire; he was sure she was starved.

"'I've been starved a month and more,' she answered, resting on the word, as scornful as she could.

"And she got a chair for herself, and placed it at a distance from both of us. Having sat till she was warm, she began to look round, and discovered a number of books in the dresser; she was instantly upon her feet again, stretching to reach them; but they were too high up.

"Her cousin, after watching her endeavours a while, at last summoned courage to help her; she held her frock, and he filled it with the first that came to hand.

"That was a great advance for the lad. She didn't thank him; still, he felt gratified that she had accepted his assistance, and ventured to stand behind as she examined them, and even to stoop and point out what struck his fancy in certain old pictures which they contained; nor was he daunted by the saucy style in which she jerked the page from his finger—he contented himself with going a bit farther back, and looking at her instead of the book.

"She continued reading, or seeking for something to read. His attention became, by degrees, quite centred in the study of her thick, silky curls—her face he couldn't see, and she couldn't see him. And, perhaps, not quite awake to what he did, but attracted like a child to a candle, at last he proceeded from staring to touching; he put out his hand and stroked one curl, as gently as if it were a bird. He might have stuck a knife into her neck, she started round in such a taking.

"'Get away, this moment! How dare you touch me? Why are you stopping there?' she cried, in a tone of disgust. 'I can't endure you! I'll go upstairs again, if you come near me.'

"Mr. Hareton recoiled, looking as foolish as he could do; he sat down in the settle, very quiet, and she continued turning over her volumes another half-hour; finally, Earnshaw crossed over, and whispered to me.

"'Will you ask her to read to us, Zillah? I'm stalled of doing naught; and I do like—I could like to hear her! Dunnot say I wanted it, but ask of yourseln.'

"'Mr. Hareton wishes you would read to us, ma'am,' I said, immediately. 'He'd take it very kind—he'd be much obliged.'

"She frowned; and, looking up, answered—

"'Mr. Hareton, and the whole set of you, will be good enough to understand that I reject any pretence at kindness you have the hypocrisy to offer! I despise you, and will have nothing to say to any of you! When I would have given my life for one kind word, even to see one of your faces, you all kept off. But I won't complain to you! I'm driven down here by the cold, not either to amuse you, or enjoy your society.'

"'What could I ha' done?' began Earnshaw. 'How was I to blame?'

"'Oh! you are an exception,' answered Mrs. Heathcliff. 'I never missed such a concern as you.'

"'But I offered more than once, and asked,' he said, kindling up at her pertness, 'I asked Mr. Heathcliff to let me wake for you——'

"'Be silent! I'll go out of doors, or anywhere, rather than have your disagreeable voice in my ear!' said my lady.

"Hareton muttered, she might go to hell, for him! and unslinging his gun, restrained himself from his Sunday occupations no longer.

"He talked now, freely enough; and she presently saw fit to retreat to her solitude; but the frost had set in, and, in spite of her pride, she was forced to condescend to our company, more and more. However, I took care there should be no further scorning at my good nature; ever since, I've been as stiff as herself; and she has no lover or liker among us—and she does not deserve one, for, let them say the least word to her, and she'll curl back without respect of anyone! She'll snap at the master himself, and as good as dares him to thrash her; and the more hurt she gets, the more venomous she grows."

At first, on hearing this account from Zillah, I determined to leave my situation, take a cottage, and get Catherine to come and live with me; but Mr. Heathcliff would as soon permit that, as he would set up Hareton in an independent house; and I can see no remedy, at present, unless she could marry again: and that scheme it does not come within my province to arrange.

Thus ended Mrs. Dean's story. Notwithstanding the doctor's prophecy, I am rapidly recovering strength; and, though it be only the second week in January, I propose getting out on horseback in a day or two, and riding over to Wuthering Heights, to inform my landlord that I shall spend the next six months in London; and, if he likes, he may look out for another tenant to take the place, after October—I would not pass another winter here for much.

CHAPTER 31

YESTERDAY was bright, calm, and frosty. I went to the Heights as I proposed; my housekeeper entreated me to bear a little note from her to her young lady, and I did not refuse, for the worthy woman was not conscious of anything odd in her request.

The front door stood open, but the jealous gate was fastened, as at my last visit; I knocked, and invoked Earnshaw from among the garden beds; he unchained it, and I entered. The fellow is as handsome a rustic as need be seen. I took particular notice of him this time; but then he does his best, apparently, to make the least of his advantages.

I asked if Mr. Heathcliff were at home. He answered, no, but he would be in at dinner-time. It was eleven o'clock, and I announced my intention of going in, and waiting for him, at which he immediately flung down his tools and accompanied me, in the office of watchdog, not as a substitute for the host.

We entered together; Catherine was there, making herself useful in preparing some vegetables for the approaching meal; she looked more sulky and less spirited than when I had seen her first. She hardly raised her eyes to notice me, and continued her employment with the same disregard to common forms of politeness, as before, never returning my bow and good-morning by the slightest acknowledgment.

"She does not seem so amiable," I thought, "as Mrs. Dean would persuade me to believe. She's a beauty, it is true; but not an angel."

Earnshaw surlily bid her remove her things to the kitchen.

"Remove them yourself," she said, pushing them from her as soon as she had done, and retiring to a stool by the window, where she began to carve figures of birds and beasts out of the turnip parings in her lap.

I approached her, pretending to desire a view of the garden; and, as I fancied, adroitly dropped Mrs. Dean's note onto her knee, unnoticed by Hareton—but she asked aloud,

"What is that?" And chucked it off.

"A letter from your old acquaintance, the housekeeper at the Grange," I answered, annoyed at her exposing my kind deed, and fearful lest it should be imagined a missive of my own.

She would gladly have gathered it up at this information, but Hareton beat her; he seized, and put it in his waistcoat, saying Mr. Heathcliff should look at it first. Thereat, Catherine silently turned her face from us, and, very stealthily, drew out her pocket-handkerchief and applied it to her eyes; and her cousin, after struggling a while to keep down his softer feelings, pulled out the letter and flung it on the floor beside her, as ungraciously as he could.

Catherine caught and perused it eagerly; then she put a few questions to me concerning the inmates, rational and irrational, of her former home; and gazing towards the hills, murmured in soliloquy—

"I should like to be riding Minny down there! I should

like to be climbing up there—Oh! I'm tired—I'm stalled, Hareton!"

And she leant her pretty head back against the sill, with half a yawn and half a sigh, and lapsed into an aspect of abstracted sadness: neither caring nor knowing whether we remarked her.

"Mrs. Heathcliff," I said, after sitting some time mute, "are you not aware that I am an acquaintance of yours? so intimate, that I think it strange you won't come and speak to me. My housekeeper never wearies of talking about and praising you, and she'll be greatly disappointed if I return with no news of or from you, except that you received her letter and said nothing!"

She appeared to wonder at this speech and asked—

"Does Ellen like you?"

"Yes, very well," I replied unhesitatingly.

"You must tell her," she continued, "that I would answer her letter, but I have no materials for writing—not even a book from which I might tear a leaf."

"No books!" I exclaimed. "How do you contrive to live here without them? if I may take the liberty to inquire. Though provided with a large library, I'm frequently very dull at the Grange; take my books away, and I should be desperate!"

"I was always reading, when I had them," said Catherine, "and Mr. Heathcliff never reads; so he took it into his head to destroy my books. I have not had a glimpse of one, for weeks. Only once, I searched through Joseph's store of theology, to his great irritation; and once, Hareton, I came upon a secret stock in your room . . . some Latin and Greek, and some tales and poetry, all old friends—I brought the last here—and you gathered them, as a magpie gathers silver spoons, for the mere love of stealing! They are of no use to you; or else you concealed them in the bad spirit, that as you cannot enjoy them, nobody else shall. Perhaps your envy counselled Mr. Heathcliff to rob me of my treasures? But I've most of them written on my brain and printed in my heart, and you cannot deprive me of those!"

Earnshaw blushed crimson when his cousin made this revelation of his private literary accumulations, and stammered an indignant denial of her accusations.

"Mr. Hareton is desirous of increasing his amount of

knowledge," I said, coming to his rescue. "He is not envious but emulous of your attainments. He'll be a clever scholar in a few years!"

"And he wants me to sink into a dunce, meantime," answered Catherine. "Yes, I hear him trying to spell and read to himself, and pretty blunders he makes! I wish you would repeat Chevy Chase as you did yesterday: it was extremely funny! I heard you . . . and I heard you turning over the dictionary, to seek out the hard words, and then cursing, because you couldn't read their explanations!"

The young man evidently thought it too bad that he should be laughed at for his ignorance, and then laughed at for trying to remove it. I had a similar notion, and, remembering Mrs. Dean's anecdote of his first attempt at enlightening the darkness in which he had been reared, I observed—

"But, Mrs. Heathcliff, we have each had a commencement, and each stumbled and tottered on the threshold, and had our teachers scorned, instead of aiding us, we should stumble and totter yet."

"Oh!" she replied, "I don't wish to limit his acquirements . . . still, he has no right to appropriate what is mine, and make it ridiculous to me with his vile mistakes and mispronunciations! Those books, both prose and verse, were consecrated to me by other associations, and I hate to have them debased and profaned in his mouth! Besides, of all, he has selected my favourite pieces that I love the most to repeat, as if out of deliberate malice!"

Hareton's chest heaved in silence a minute; he laboured under a severe sense of mortification and wrath, which it was no easy task to suppress.

I rose and, from a gentlemanly idea of relieving his embarrassment, took up my station in the doorway, surveying the external prospect as I stood.

He followed my example, and left the room; but presently re-appeared, bearing half a dozen volumes in his hands, which he threw into Catherine's lap, exclaiming—

"Take them! I never want to hear, or read, or think of them again!"

"I won't have them, now," she answered. "I shall connect them with you, and hate them."

She opened one that had obviously been often turned over, and read a portion in the drawling tone of a beginner; then laughed, and threw it from her.

"And listen," she continued provokingly, commencing a verse of an old ballad in the same fashion.

But his self-love would endure no further torment; I heard, and not altogether disapprovingly, a manual check given to her saucy tongue. The little wretch had done her utmost to hurt her cousin's sensitive though uncultivated feelings, and a physical argument was the only mode he had of balancing the account and repaying its effects on the inflicter.

He afterwards gathered the books and hurled them on the fire. I read in his countenance what anguish it was to offer that sacrifice to spleen—I fancied that as they were consumed, he recalled the pleasure they had already imparted, and the triumph and ever-increasing pleasure he had anticipated from them; and I fancied, I guessed the incitement to his secret studies, also. He had been content with daily labour and rough animal enjoyments, till Catherine crossed his path. Shame at her scorn and hope of her approval were his first prompters to higher pursuits; and instead of guarding him from one, and winning him the other, his endeavours to raise himself had produced just the contrary result.

"Yes, that's all the good that such a brute as you can get from them!" cried Catherine, sucking her damaged lip, and watching the conflagration with indignant eyes.

"You'd better hold your tongue, now!" he answered fiercely.

And his agitation precluding further speech, he advanced hastily to the entrance, where I made way for him to pass. But, ere he had crossed the door-stones, Mr. Heathcliff, coming up the causeway, encountered him, and laying hold of his shoulder, asked—

"What's to do now, my lad?"

"Naught, naught!" he said, and broke away, to enjoy his grief and anger in solitude.

Heathcliff gazed after him, and sighed.

"It will be odd, if I thwart myself!" he muttered, unconscious that I was behind him. "But, when I look for his father in his face, I find her every day more! How the devil is he so like? I can hardly bear to see him."

He bent his eyes to the ground, and walked moodily in. There was a restless, anxious expression in his countenance I had never remarked there before, and he looked sparer in person.

His daughter-in-law, on perceiving him through the window, immediately escaped to the kitchen, so that I remained alone.

"I'm glad to see you out of doors again, Mr. Lockwood," he said in reply to my greeting, "from selfish motives partly; I don't think I could readily supply your loss in this desolation. I've wondered, more than once, what brought you here."

"An idle whim, I fear, sir," was my answer; "or else an idle whim is going to spirit me away. I shall set out for London next week; and I must give you warning, that I feel no disposition to retain Thrushcross Grange beyond the twelve months I agreed to rent it. I believe I shall not live there any more."

"Oh, indeed! you're tired of being banished from the world, are you?" he said. "But, if you be coming to plead off paying for a place you won't occupy, your journey is useless; I never relent in exacting my due from anyone."

"I'm coming to plead off nothing about it!" I exclaimed, considerably irritated. "Should you wish it, I'll settle with you now," and I drew my note-book from my pocket.

"No, no," he replied coolly; "you'll leave sufficient behind to cover your debts, if you fail to return; I'm not in such a hurry—sit down and take your dinner with us; a guest that is safe from repeating his visit can generally be made welcome. Catherine! bring the things in—where are you?"

Catherine re-appeared, bearing a tray of knives and forks.

"You may get your dinner with Joseph," muttered Heathcliff aside, "and remain in the kitchen till he is gone."

She obeyed his directions very punctually—perhaps she had no temptation to transgress. Living among clowns and misanthropists, she probably cannot appreciate a better class of people, when she meets them.

With Mr. Heathcliff, grim and saturnine, on one hand,

and Hareton, absolutely dumb, on the other, I made a somewhat cheerless meal, and bid adieu early. I would have departed by the back way, to get a last glimpse of Catherine, and annoy old Joseph; but Hareton received orders to lead up my horse, and my host himself escorted me to the door, so I could not fulfill my wish.

"How dreary life gets over in that house!" I reflected, while riding down the road. "What a realization of something more romantic than a fairy tale it would have been for Mrs. Linton Heathcliff, had she and I struck up an attachment, as her good nurse desired, and migrated together into the stirring atmosphere of the town!"

CHAPTER 32

1802—This September, I was invited to devastate the moors of a friend, in the North; and, on my journey to his abode, I unexpectedly came within fifteen miles of Gimmerton. The hostler at a roadside public-house was holding a pail of water to refresh my horses, when a cart of very green oats, newly reaped, passed by, and he remarked—

"Yon 's frough Gimmerton, nah! They 're allas three wick' after other folk wi' ther harvest."

"Gimmerton?" I repeated—my residence in that locality had already grown dim and dreamy. "Ah! I know! How far is it from this?"

"Happen fourteen mile' o'er th' hills, and a rough road," he answered.

A sudden impulse seized me to visit Thrushcross Grange. It was scarcely noon, and I conceived that I might as well pass the night under my own roof, as in an inn. Besides, I could spare a day easily, to arrange matters with my landlord, and thus save myself the trouble of invading the neighbourhood again.

Having rested a while, I directed my servant to inquire the way to the village; and, with great fatigue to our beasts, we managed the distance in some three hours.

I left him there, and proceeded down the valley alone. The grey church looked greyer, and the lonely churchyard lonelier. I distinguished a moor sheep cropping the short turf on the graves. It was sweet, warm weather—too warm for travelling; but the heat did not hinder me from enjoying the delightful scenery above and below; had I seen it nearer August, I 'm sure it would have tempted me to waste a month among its solitudes. In winter nothing more dreary, in summer nothing more divine, than those glens shut in by hills, and those bluff, bold swells of heath.

I reached the Grange before sunset, and knocked for admittance; but the family had retreated into the back premises, I judged by one thin, blue wreath curling from the kitchen chimney, and they did not hear.

I rode into the court. Under the porch, a girl of nine or ten sat knitting, and an old woman reclined on the house-steps, smoking a meditative pipe.

"Is Mrs. Dean within?" I demanded of the dame.

"Mistress Dean? Nay!" she answered, "shoo doesn't bide here; shoo 's up at th' Heights."

"Are you the housekeeper, then?" I continued.

"Eea, Aw keep th' hause," she replied.

"Well, I 'm Mr. Lockwood, the master. Are there any rooms to lodge me in, I wonder? I wish to stay here all night."

"T' maister!" she cried in astonishment. "Whet, whoiver knew yah wur coming? Yah sud ha' send word! They 's nowt norther dry—nor mensful abaht t' place; nowt there is n't!"

She threw down her pipe and bustled in, the girl followed, and I entered too; soon perceiving that her report was true, and, moreover, that I had almost upset her wits by my unwelcome apparition.

I bid her be composed—I would go out for a walk; and, meantime, she must try to prepare a corner of a sitting-room for me to sup in, and a bedroom to sleep in. No sweeping and dusting, only good fires and dry sheets were necessary.

She seemed willing to do her best; though she thrust the hearth-brush into the grates in mistake for the poker, and malappropriated several other articles of her craft: but I retired, confiding in her energy for a resting-place against my return. Wuthering Heights was the goal of my proposed excursion. An afterthought brought me back, when I had quitted the court.

"All well at the Heights?" I enquired of the woman.

"Eea f'r owt Ee knaw!" she answered, scurrying away with a pan of hot cinders.

I would have asked why Mrs. Dean had deserted the Grange, but it was impossible to delay her at such a crisis, so I turned away and made my exit, rambling leisurely along, with the glow of a sinking sun behind and the mild glory of a rising moon in front—one fading, and the other brightening, as I quitted the park, and climbed the stony by-road branching off to Mr. Heathcliff's dwelling.

Before I arrived in sight of it, all that remained of day was a beamless, amber light along the west; but I could see every pebble on the path, and every blade of grass, by that splendid moon.

I had neither to climb the gate, nor to knock—it yielded to my hand.

That is an improvement! I thought. And I noticed another, by the aid of my nostrils—a fragrance of stocks and wallflowers, wafted on the air, from amongst the homely fruit trees.

Both doors and lattices were open; and yet, as is usually the case in a coal district, a fine, red fire illumined the chimney; the comfort which the eye derives from it renders the extra heat endurable. But the house of Wuthering Heights is so large, that the inmates have plenty of space for withdrawing out of its influence; and, accordingly, what inmates there were had stationed themselves not far from one of the windows. I could both see them and hear them talk before I entered, and looked and listened in consequence, being moved thereto by a mingled sense of curiosity, and envy that grew as I lingered.

"Con-trary!" said a voice, as sweet as a silver bell—"That for the third time, you dunce! I'm not going to tell you, again. Recollect, or I pull your hair!"

"Contrary, then," answered another, in deep but softened tones. "And now, kiss me, for minding so well."

"No, read it over first correctly, without a single mistake."

The male speaker began to read; he was a young man, respectably dressed, and seated at a table, having a book before him. His handsome features glowed with pleasure, and his eyes kept impatiently wandering from the page to a small white hand over his shoulder, which recalled him by a smart slap on the cheek whenever its owner detected such signs of inattention.

Its owner stood behind, her light shining ringlets blending, at intervals, with his brown locks, as she bent to superintend his studies; and her face—it was lucky he could not see her face, or he would never have been so steady—I could, and I bit my lip, in spite, at having thrown away the chance I might have had, of doing something besides staring at its smiting beauty.

The task was done, not free from further blunders, but the pupil claimed a reward, and received at least five kisses, which, however, he generously returned. Then, they came to the door, and from their conversation, I judged they were about to issue out and have a walk on the moors. I supposed I should be condemned in Hareton Earnshaw's heart, if not by his mouth, to the lowest pit in the infernal regions, if I showed my unfortunate person in his neighbourhood then; and feeling very mean and malignant, I skulked round to seek refuge in the kitchen.

There was unobstructed admittance on that side also, and, at the door, sat my old friend, Nelly Dean, sewing and singing a song, which was often interrupted from within, by harsh words of scorn and intolerance, uttered in far from musical accents.

"Aw'd rayther, by th' haulf, hev 'em swearing i' my lugs frough morn tuh neeght, nur hearken yah, hah-siver!" said the tenant of the kitchen, in answer to an unheard speech of Nelly's. "It's a blazing shaime, ut Aw cannut oppen t' Blessed Book, bud yah set up them glories tuh sattan, un' all t' flaysome wickednesses ut iver wer born intuh t' warld! Oh! yah 're a raight nowt; un' shoo 's another; un' that poor lad 'ull be lost, atween ye. Poor lad!" he added, with a groan; "he 's witched, Aw 'm sartin on 't! O, Lord, judge 'em, fur they 's norther law nur justice amang wer rullers!"

"No! or we should be sitting in flaming fagots, I suppose," retorted the singer. "But wisht, old man, and read your Bible, like a christian, and never mind me. This is 'Fairy Annie's Wedding'—a bonny tune—it goes to a dance."

Mrs. Dean was about to recommence, when I advanced; and recognizing me directly, she jumped to her feet, crying—

"Why, bless you, Mr. Lockwood! How could you think of returning in this way? All's shut up at Thrushcross Grange. You should have given us notice!"

"I 've arranged to be accommodated there, for as long as I shall stay," I answered. "I depart again tomorrow. And how are you transplanted here, Mrs. Dean? tell me that."

"Zillah left, and Mr. Heathcliff wished me to come, soon after you went to London, and stay till you returned. But, step in, pray! Have you walked from Gimmerton this evening?"

"From the Grange," I replied; "and, while they make me lodging room there, I want to finish my business with your master, because I don't think of having another opportunity in a hurry."

"What business, sir?" said Nelly, conducting me into the house. "He's gone out at present, and won't return soon."

"About the rent," I answered.

"Oh! then it is with Mrs. Heathcliff you must settle," she observed, "or rather with me. She has not learnt to manage her affairs yet, and I act for her—there's nobody else."

I looked surprised.

"Ah! you have not heard of Heathcliff's death, I see!" she continued.

"Heathcliff dead?" I exclaimed, astonished. "How long ago?"

"Three months since; but, sit down, and let me take your hat, and I'll tell you all about it. Stop, you have had nothing to eat, have you?"

"I want nothing. I have ordered supper at home. You sit down too. I never dreamt of his dying! Let me hear how it came to pass. You say you don't expect them back for some time—the young people?"

"No—I have to scold them every evening, for their late rambles; but they don't care for me. At least, have

(293)

a drink of our old ale; it will do you good—you seem weary."

She hastened to fetch it, before I could refuse, and I heard Joseph asking whether "it warn't a crying scandal that she should have fellies at her time of life? And then, to get them jocks out uh' t' Maister's cellar! He fair shaamed to 'bide still and see it."

She did not stay to retaliate, but re-entered, in a minute, bearing a reaming silver pint whose contents I lauded with becoming earnestness. And afterwards she furnished me with the sequel of Heathcliff's history. He had a "queer" end, as she expressed it.

I was summoned to Wuthering Heights, within a fortnight of your leaving us, she said; and I obeyed joyfully, for Catherine's sake.

My first interview with her grieved and shocked me! she had altered so much since our separation. Mr. Heathcliff did not explain his reasons for taking a new mind about my coming here; he only told me he wanted me, and he was tired of seeing Catherine; I must make the little parlour my sitting room, and keep her with me. It was enough if he were obliged to see her once or twice a day.

She seemed pleased at this arrangement; and, by degrees, I smuggled over a great number of books, and other articles, that had formed her amusement at the Grange; and flattered myself we should get on in tolerable comfort.

The delusion did not last long. Catherine, contented at first, in a brief space grew irritable and restless. For one thing, she was forbidden to move out of the garden, and it fretted her sadly to be confined to its narrow bounds, as Spring drew on; for another, in following the house, I was forced to quit her frequently, and she complained of loneliness; she preferred quarrelling with Joseph in the kitchen to sitting at peace in her solitude.

I did not mind their skirmishes; but Hareton was often obliged to seek the kitchen also, when the master wanted to have the house to himself; and though, in the beginning, she either left it at his approach, or quietly joined in my occupations, and shunned remarking or addressing him—and though he was always as sullen and silent as possible—after a while, she changed her behaviour, and became incapable of letting him alone—talking at him, commenting on his stupidity and idleness, expressing her wonder how he could endure the life he lived—how he could sit a whole evening staring into the fire, and dozing.

"He's just like a dog, is he not, Ellen?" she once observed, "or a cart-horse? He does his work, eats his food, and sleeps, eternally! What a blank, dreary mind he must have! Do you ever dream, Hareton? And, if you do, what is it about? But you can't speak to me!"

Then she looked at him, but he would neither open his mouth nor look again.

"He's perhaps dreaming now," she continued. "He's twitched his shoulder as Juno twitches hers. Ask him, Ellen."

"Mr. Hareton will ask the master to send you upstairs, if you don't behave!" I said. He had not only twitched his shoulder but clenched his fist, as if tempted to use it.

"I know why Hareton never speaks, when I am in the kitchen," she exclaimed, on another occasion. "He is afraid I shall laugh at him. Ellen, what do you think? He began to teach himself to read once, and, because I laughed, he burned his books, and dropped it—was he not a fool?"

"Were not you naughty?" I said; "answer me that."

"Perhaps I was," she went on, "but I did not expect him to be so silly. Hareton, if I gave you a book, would you take it now? I'll try!"

She placed one she had been perusing on his hand; he flung it off, and muttered, if she did not give over, he would break her neck.

"Well, I shall put it here," she said, "in the table drawer; and I'm going to bed."

Then she whispered me to watch whether he touched it, and departed. But he would not come near it, and so I informed her in the morning, to her great disappointment. I saw she was sorry for his persevering sulkiness and indolence; her conscience reproved her for frightening him off improving himself—she had done it effectually.

But her ingenuity was at work to remedy the injury; while I ironed, or pursued other stationary employments

I could not well do in the parlour, she would bring some pleasant volume and read it aloud to me. When Hareton was there, she generally paused in an interesting part, and left the book lying about—that she did repeatedly; but he was as obstinate as a mule, and, instead of snatching at her bait, in wet weather he took to smoking with Joseph, and they sat like automatons, one on each side of the fire, the elder happily too deaf to understand her wicked nonsense, as he would have called it, the younger doing his best to seem to disregard it. On fine evenings the latter followed his shooting expeditions, and Catherine yawned and sighed, and teased me to talk to her, and ran off into the court or garden, the moment I began; and, as a last resource, cried and said, she was tired of living—her life was useless.

Mr. Heathcliff, who grew more and more disinclined to society, had almost banished Earnshaw out of his apartment. Owing to an accident, at the commencement of March, he became for some days a fixture in the kitchen. His gun burst while out on the hills by himself; a splinter cut his arm, and he lost a good deal of blood before he could reach home. The consequence was, that, perforce, he was condemned to the fireside and tranquillity till he made it up again.

It suited Catherine to have him there—at any rate, it made her hate her room upstairs more than ever, and she would compel me to find out business below, that she might accompany me.

On Easter Monday, Joseph went to Gimmerton fair with some cattle; and, in the afternoon, I was busy getting up linen in the kitchen. Earnshaw sat, morose as usual, at the chimney corner, and my little mistress was beguiling an idle hour with drawing pictures on the windowpanes, varying her amusement by smothered bursts of songs, and whispered ejaculations, and quick glances of annoyance and impatience in the direction of her cousin, who steadfastly smoked, and looked into the grate.

At a notice that I could do with her no longer, intercepting my light, she removed to the hearthstone. I bestowed little attention on her proceedings, but presently, I heard her begin—

"I've found out, Hareton, that I want—that I'm glad —that I should like you to be my cousin, now, if you had not grown so cross to me, and so rough."

Hareton returned no answer.

"Hareton, Hareton, Hareton! do you hear?" she continued.

"Get off wi' ye!" he growled, with uncompromising gruffness.

"Let me take that pipe," she said, cautiously advancing her hand, and abstracting it from his mouth.

Before he could attempt to recover it, it was broken, and behind the fire. He swore at her and seized another.

"Stop," she cried, "you must listen to me, first; and I can't speak while those clouds are floating in my face."

"Will you go to the devil!" he exclaimed, ferociously, "and let me be!"

"No," she persisted, "I won't—I can't tell what to do to make you talk to me, and you are determined not to understand. When I call you stupid, I don't mean anything, I don't mean that I despise you. Come, you shall take notice of me, Hareton—you are my cousin, and you shall own me."

"I shall have naught to do wi' you, and your mucky pride, and your damned, mocking tricks!" he answered. "I'll go to hell, body and soul, before I look sideways after you again! Side out of t' gait, now, this minute!"

Catherine frowned, and retreated to the window-seat, chewing her lip, and endeavouring, by humming an eccentric tune, to conceal a growing tendency to sob.

"You should be friends with your cousin, Mr. Hareton," I interrupted, "since she repents of her sauciness! It would do you a great deal of good; it would make you another man, to have her for a companion."

"A companion?" he cried; "when she hates me, and does not think me fit to wipe her shoon! Nay, if it made me a king, I'd not be scorned for seeking her good will any more."

"It is not I who hate you, it is you who hate me!" wept Cathy, no longer disguising her trouble. "You hate me as much as Mr. Heathcliff does, and more."

"You're a damned liar," began Earnshaw; "why have I made him angry, by taking your part then, a hundred times? and that, when you sneered at, and despised me, and— Go on plaguing me, and I'll step in yonder, and say you worried me out of the kitchen!"

"I didn't know you took my part," she answered, drying her eyes, "and I was miserable and bitter at everybody; but, now I thank you, and beg you to forgive me, what can I do besides?"

She returned to the hearth, and frankly extended her hand. He blackened, and scowled like a thundercloud, and kept his fists resolutely clenched, and his gaze fixed on the ground.

Catherine, by instinct, must have divined it was obdurate perversity, and not dislike, that prompted this dogged conduct; for, after remaining an instant undecided, she stooped, and impressed on his cheek a gentle kiss.

The little rogue thought I had not seen her, and, drawing back, she took her former station by the window, quite demurely.

I shook my head reprovingly; and then she blushed, and whispered—

"Well! what should I have done, Ellen? He wouldn't shake hands, and he wouldn't look; I must show him some way that I like him—that I want to be friends."

Whether the kiss convinced Hareton, I cannot tell— he was very careful, for some minutes, that his face should not be seen, and when he did raise it, he was sadly puzzled where to turn his eyes.

Catherine employed herself in wrapping a handsome book neatly in white paper; and having tied it with a bit of riband, and addressed it to "Mr. Hareton Earnshaw," she desired me to be her ambassadress, and convey the present to its destined recipient.

"And tell him, if he'll take it, I'll come and teach him to read it right," she said; "and, if he refuse it, I'll go upstairs and never tease him again."

I carried it, and repeated the message, anxiously watched by my employer. Hareton would not open his fingers, so I laid it on his knee. He did not strike it off, either. I returned to my work; Catherine leaned her head and arms on the table, till she heard the slight rustle of the covering being removed; then she stole away, and quietly seated herself beside her cousin. He trembled, and his face glowed; all his rudeness and all his surly harshness had deserted him; he could not summon courage, at first, to utter a syllable, in reply to her questioning look, and her murmured petition.

"Say you forgive me, Hareton, do! You can make me so happy, by speaking that little word."

He muttered something inaudible.

"And you'll be my friend?" added Catherine, interrogatively.

"Nay! you'll be ashamed of me every day of your life," he answered. "And the more, the more you know me, and I cannot bide it."

"So, you won't be my friend?" she said, smiling as sweet as honey, and creeping close up.

I overheard no further distinguishable talk, but on looking round again I perceived two such radiant countenances bent over the page of the accepted book, that I did not doubt the treaty had been ratified, on both sides, and the enemies were, thenceforth, sworn allies.

The work they studied was full of costly pictures, and those, and their position, had charm enough to keep them unmoved, till Joseph came home. He, poor man, was perfectly aghast at the spectacle of Catherine, seated on the same bench with Hareton Earnshaw, leaning her hand on his shoulder, and confounded at his favourite's endurance of her proximity. It affected him too deeply to allow an observation on the subject that night. His emotion was only revealed by the immense sighs he drew, as he solemnly spread his large Bible on the table, and overlaid it with dirty banknotes from his pocket-book, the produce of the day's transactions. At length, he summoned Hareton from his seat.

"Tak' these in tuh t' maister, lad," he said, "un' bide theare; Aw's gang up tuh my awn rahm. This hoile's norther mensful, nor seemly fur us—we mun side aht, and seearch another!"

"Come, Catherine," I said, "we must 'side out' too; I've done my ironing, are you ready to go?"

"It is not eight o'clock!" she answered, rising unwillingly. "Hareton, I'll leave this book upon the chimney-piece, and I'll bring some more tomorrow."

"Ony books ut yah leave, Aw suall tak' intuh th' hahse," said Joseph, "un' it'll be mitch if yah find 'em agean; soa, yah muh plase yourseln!"

Cathy threatened that his library should pay for hers; and, smiling as she passed Hareton, went singing upstairs, lighter of heart, I venture to say, than ever she had been under that roof before, except, perhaps, during her earliest visits to Linton.

The intimacy thus commenced grew rapidly—though it encountered temporary interruptions. Earnshaw was not to be civilized with a wish, and my young lady was no philosopher, and no paragon of patience; but both their minds tending to the same point—one loving and desiring to esteem, and the other loving and desiring to be esteemed—they contrived in the end to reach it.

You see, Mr. Lockwood, it was easy enough to win Mrs. Heathcliff's heart. But now, I'm glad you did not try. The crown of all my wishes will be the union of those two. I shall envy no one on their wedding-day—there won't be a happier woman than myself in England!

CHAPTER 33

O N THE morrow of that Monday, Earnshaw being still unable to follow his ordinary employments, and therefore remaining about the house, I speedily found it would be impracticable to retain my charge beside me, as heretofore.

She got downstairs before me, and out into the garden, where she had seen her cousin performing some easy work; and when I went to bid them come to breakfast, I saw she had persuaded him to clear a large space of ground from currant and gooseberry bushes, and they were busy planning together an importation of plants from the Grange.

I was terrified at the devastation which had been accomplished in a brief half hour; the black currant trees were the apple of Joseph's eye, and she had just fixed her choice of a flower bed in the midst of them!

"There! That will be all shown to the master," I exclaimed, "the minute it is discovered. And what excuse have you to offer for taking such liberties with the garden? We shall have a fine explosion on the head of it, see if we don't! Mr. Hareton, I wonder you should have no more wit than to go and make that mess at her bidding!"

"I'd forgotten they were Joseph's," answered Earnshaw, rather puzzled, "but I'll tell him I did it."

We always ate our meals with Mr. Heathcliff. I held the mistress's post in making tea and carving, so I was indispensable at table. Catherine usually sat by me; but today she stole nearer to Hareton, and I presently saw she would have no more discretion in her friendship, than she had in her hostility.

"Now, mind you don't talk with and notice your cousin too much," were my whispered instructions as we entered the room. "It will certainly annoy Mr. Heathcliff, and he'll be mad at you both."

"I'm not going to," she answered.

The minute after, she had sidled to him, and was sticking primroses in his plate of porridge.

He dared not speak to her, there—he dared hardly look—and yet she went on teasing, till he was twice on the point of being provoked to laugh; and I frowned, and then, she glanced towards the master, whose mind was occupied on other subjects than his company, as his countenance evinced, and she grew serious for an instant, scrutinizing him with deep gravity. Afterwards she turned, and re-commenced her nonsense; at last, Hareton uttered a smothered laugh.

Mr. Heathcliff started; his eye rapidly surveyed our faces. Catherine met it with her accustomed look of nervousness, and yet defiance, which he abhorred.

"It is well you are out of my reach," he exclaimed. "What fiend possesses you to stare back at me, continually, with those infernal eyes? Down with them! and don't remind me of your existence again. I thought I had cured you of laughing!"

"It was me," muttered Hareton.

"What do you say?" demanded the master.

Hareton looked at his plate, and did not repeat the confession.

Mr. Heathcliff looked at him a bit, and then silently resumed his breakfast, and his interrupted musing.

We had nearly finished, and the two young people prudently shifted wider asunder, so I anticipated no further disturbance during that sitting—when Joseph appeared at the door, revealing by his quivering lip and furious eyes that the outrage committed on his precious shrubs was detected.

He must have seen Cathy and her cousin about the spot before he examined it, for while his jaws worked like those of a cow chewing its cud, and rendered his speech difficult to understand, he began—

"Aw mun hev my wage, and Aw mun goa! Aw hed aimed tuh dee, wheare Aw'd sarved fur sixty year; un' Aw thowt Aw'd lug my books up intuh t' garret, 'un all my bits uh stuff, un' they sud hev t' kitchen tuh theirseln; fur t' sake uh quietness. It wur hard tuh gie up my awn hearthstun, bud Aw thowt Aw *could* do that! Bud, nah, shoo's taan my garden frough me, un' by th' heart! Maister, Aw cannot stand it! Yah muh bend tuh th' yoak, and ye will—Aw' noan used to 't and an ow'd man doesn't sooin get used tuh new barthens—Aw'd rayther arn my bite, an' my sup, wi' a hammer in th' road!"

"Now, now, idiot!" interrupted Heathcliff, "cut it short! What's your grievance? I'll interfere in no quarrels between you and Nelly—she may thrust you into the coal-hole for anything I care."

"It's noan Nelly!" answered Joseph. "Aw sudn't shift fur Nelly—Nasty, ill nowt as shoo is, Thank God! shoo cannot stale t' sowl uh nob'dy! Shoo wer niver soa handsome, bud whet a body mud look at her 'baht winking. It's yon flaysome, graceless quean, ut's witched ahr lad, wi' her bold een, un' her forrard ways—till—Nay! It fair bursts my heart! He's forgetten all E done for him, un made on him, un' goan un' riven up a whole row ut t' grandest currant trees, i' t' garden!" and here he lamented outright, unmanned by a sense of his bitter injuries, and Earnshaw's ingratitude and dangerous condition.

"Is the fool drunk?" asked Mr. Heathcliff. "Hareton, is it you he's finding fault with?"

"I've pulled up two or three bushes," replied the young man, "but I'm going to set 'em again."

"And why have you pulled them up?" said the master. Catherine wisely put in her tongue.

"We wanted to plant some flowers there," she cried. "I'm the only person to blame, for I wished him to do it."

"And who the devil gave you leave to touch a stick about the place?" demanded her father-in-law, much surprised. "And who ordered you to obey her?" he added, turning to Hareton.

The latter was speechless; his cousin replied—

"You shouldn't grudge a few yards of earth, for me to ornament, when you have taken all my land!"

"Your land, insolent slut? you never had any!" said Heathcliff.

"And my money," she continued, returning his angry glare, and meantime, biting a piece of crust, the remnant of her breakfast.

"Silence!" he exclaimed. "Get done, and begone!"

"And Hareton's land, and his money," pursued the reckless thing. "Hareton and I are friends now, and I shall tell him all about you!"

The master seemed confounded a moment; he grew pale, and rose up, eyeing her all the while, with an expression of mortal hate.

"If you strike me, Hareton will strike you!" she said; "so you may as well sit down."

"If Hareton does not turn you out of the room, I'll strike him to Hell," thundered Heathcliff. "Damnable witch! dare you pretend to rouse him against me? Off with her! Do you hear? Fling her into the kitchen! I'll kill her, Ellen Dean, if you let her come into my sight again!"

Hareton tried under his breath to persuade her to go.

"Drag her away!" he cried savagely. "Are you staying to talk?" And he approached to execute his own command.

"He'll not obey you, wicked man, any more!" said Catherine; "and he'll soon detest you as much as I do!"

"Wisht! wisht!" muttered the young man reproachfully. "I will not hear you speak so to him. Have done."

"But you won't let him strike me?" she cried.

"Come then!" he whispered earnestly.

It was too late—Heathcliff had caught hold of her.

"Now you go!" he said to Earnshaw. "Accursed witch! this time she has provoked me, when I could not bear it, and I'll make her repent it for ever!"

He had his hand in her hair; Hareton attempted to release the locks, entreating him not to hurt her that once. His black eyes flashed; he seemed ready to tear Catherine in pieces, and I was just worked up to risk coming to the rescue, when of a sudden, his fingers relaxed, he shifted his grasp from her head to her arm, and gazed intently in her face—Then, he drew his hand over his eyes, stood a moment to collect himself apparently, and turning anew to Catherine, said with assumed calmness,

"You must learn to avoid putting me in a passion, or I shall really murder you sometime! Go with Mrs. Dean, and keep with her, and confine your insolence to her ears. As to Hareton Earnshaw, if I see him listen to you, I'll send him seeking his bread where he can get it! Your love will make him an outcast, and a beggar. Nelly, take her, and leave me, all of you! Leave me!"

I led my young lady out; she was too glad of her escape to resist; the other followed, and Mr. Heathcliff had the room to himself, till dinner. I had counselled Catherine to get hers upstairs; but, as soon as he perceived her vacant seat, he sent me to call her. He spoke to none of us, ate very little, and went out directly afterwards, intimating that he should not return before evening.

The two new friends established themselves in the house, during his absence, when I heard Hareton sternly check his cousin, on her offering a revelation of her father-in-law's conduct to his father.

He said he wouldn't suffer a word to be uttered to him, in his disparagement; if he were the devil, it didn't signify; he would stand by him; and he'd rather she would abuse himself, as she used to, than begin on Mr. Heathcliff.

Catherine was waxing cross at this; but he found means to make her hold her tongue, by asking, how she would like *him* to speak ill of her father? and then she comprehended that Earnshaw took the master's reputation home to himself, and was attached by ties stronger than reason could break—chains, forged by habit, which it would be cruel to attempt to loosen.

She showed a good heart, thenceforth, in avoiding both complaints and expressions of antipathy concerning Heathcliff, and confessed to me her sorrow that she had endeavoured to raise a bad spirit between him and Hareton—indeed, I don't believe she has ever breathed a syllable, in the latter's hearing, against her oppressor, since.

When this slight disagreement was over, they were thick again, and as busy as possible, in their several occupations, of pupil, and teacher. I came in to sit with them, after I had done my work, and I felt so soothed and comforted to watch them, that I did not notice how time got on. You know, they both appeared in a measure my children; I had long been proud of one, and now, I was sure, the other would be a source of equal satisfaction. His honest, warm, and intelligent nature shook off rapidly the clouds of ignorance and degradation in which it had been bred; and Catherine's sincere commendations acted as a spur to his industry. His brightening mind brightened his features, and added spirit and nobility to their aspect—I could hardly fancy it the same individual I had beheld on the day I discovered my little lady at Wuthering Heights, after her expedition to the Crags.

While I admired, and they laboured, dusk grew on, and with it returned the master. He came upon us quite unexpectedly, entering by the front way, and had a full view of the whole three, ere we could raise our heads to glance at him.

Well, I reflected, there was never a pleasanter or more harmless sight; and it will be a burning shame to scold them. The red fire-light glowed on their two bonny heads, and revealed their faces, animated with the eager interest of children; for, though he was twenty-three, and she eighteen, each had so much of novelty to feel and learn, that neither experienced nor evinced the sentiments of sober disenchanted maturity.

They lifted their eyes together, to encounter Mr. Heathcliff—perhaps you have never remarked that their eyes are precisely similar, and they are those of Catherine Earnshaw. The present Catherine has no other likeness to her, except a breadth of forehead, and a certain arch of the nostril that makes her appear rather haughty, whether she will or not. With Hareton the resemblance is carried farther—it is singular, at all times —then it was particularly striking, because his senses were alert, and his mental faculties wakened to unwonted activity.

I suppose this resemblance disarmed Mr. Heathcliff: he walked to the hearth in evident agitation, but it quickly subsided, as he looked at the young man—or, I should say, altered its character, for it was there yet.

He took the book from his hand, and glanced at the open page, then returned it without any observation, merely signing Catherine away; her companion lingered very little behind her, and I was about to depart also, but he bid me sit still.

"It is a poor conclusion, is it not," he observed, having brooded a while on the scene he had just witnessed. "An absurd termination to my violent exertions? I get levers and mattocks to demolish the two houses, and train myself to be capable of working like Hercules, and when everything is ready, and in my power, I find the will to lift a slate off either roof has vanished! My old enemies have not beaten me; now would be the precise time to revenge myself on their representatives—I could do it, and none could hinder me. But where is the use? I don't care for striking, I can't take the trouble to raise my hand! That sounds as if I had been labouring the whole time, only to exhibit a fine trait of magnanimity. It is far from being the case—I have lost the faculty of enjoying their destruction, and I am too idle to destroy for nothing.

"Nelly, there is a strange change approaching—I'm in its shadow at present. I take so little interest in my daily life, that I hardly remember to eat and drink. Those two who have left the room are the only objects which retain a distinct material appearance to me; and, that appearance causes me pain, amounting to agony. About her I won't speak; and I don't desire to think; but I earnestly wish she were invisible—her presence invokes only maddening sensations. He moves me differently— and yet if I could do it without seeming insane, I'd never see him again! You'll perhaps think me rather inclined to become so," he added, making an effort to smile, "if I try to describe the thousand forms of past associations, and ideas he awakens, or embodies. But you 'll not talk of what I tell you, and my mind is so eternally secluded in itself, it is tempting, at last, to turn it out to another.

"Five minutes ago, Hareton seemed a personification of my youth, not a human being; I felt to him in such a variety of ways, that it would have been impossible to have accosted him rationally.

"In the first place, his startling likeness to Catherine connected him fearfully with her. That however which you may suppose the most potent to arrest my imagination, is actually the least—for what is not connected with her to me? and what does not recall her? I cannot look down to this floor, but her features are shaped on the flags! In every cloud, in every tree—filling the air at night, and caught by glimpses in every object, by day I am surrounded with her image! The most ordinary faces of men, and women—my own features mock me with a resemblance. The entire world is a dreadful collection of memoranda that she did exist, and that I have lost her!

"Well, Hareton's aspect was the ghost of my immortal love, of my wild endeavours to hold my right, my degradation, my pride, my happiness, and my anguish—

"But it is frenzy to repeat these thoughts to you; only it will let you know, why, with a reluctance to be always alone, his society is no benefit, rather an aggravation of the constant torment I suffer, and it partly contributes to render me regardless how he and his cousin go on together. I can give them no attention, any more."

"But what do you mean by a *change*, Mr. Heathcliff?" I said, alarmed at his manner, though he was neither in danger of losing his senses, nor dying; according to my judgment he was quite strong and healthy, and, as to his reason, from childhood he had a delight in dwelling on dark things, and entertaining odd fancies. He might have had a monomania on the subject of his departed idol; but on every other point his wits were as sound as mine.

"I shall not know that, till it comes," he said; "I 'm only half conscious of it now."

"You have no feeling of illness, have you?" I asked.

"No, Nelly, I have not," he answered.

"Then, you are not afraid of death?" I pursued.

"Afraid? No!" he replied. "I have neither a fear, nor a presentiment, nor a hope of death. Why should I? With my hard constitution and temperate mode of living, and unperilous occupations, I ought to, and probably *shall* remain above ground, till there is scarcely a black hair on my head. And yet I cannot continue in this condition! I have to remind myself to breathe—almost to remind my heart to beat! And it is like bending back a stiff spring—it is by compulsion that I do the slightest act not prompted by one thought, and by compulsion, that I notice anything alive or dead, which is not associated with one universal idea. I have a single wish, and my whole being and faculties are yearning to attain it. They have yearned towards it so long, and so unwaveringly, that I 'm convinced it *will* be reached —and soon—because it has devoured my existence; I am swallowed in the anticipation of its fulfillment. My confessions have not relieved me, but they may account for some otherwise unaccountable phases of humour which I show. O, God! It is a long fight. I wish it were over!"

He began to pace the room, muttering terrible things to himself, till I was inclined to believe, as he said Joseph did, that conscience had turned his heart to an earthly hell. I wondered greatly how it would end.

Though he seldom before had revealed this state of mind, even by looks, it was his habitual mood, I had no doubt—he asserted it himself; but not a soul, from his general bearing, would have conjectured the fact. You did not, when you saw him, Mr. Lockwood; and at the period of which I speak, he was just the same as then, only fonder of continued solitude, and perhaps still more laconic in company.

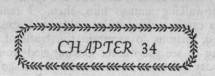

CHAPTER 34

FOR some days after that evening, Mr. Heathcliff shunned meeting us at meals; yet he would not consent, formally, to exclude Hareton and Cathy. He had an aversion to yielding so completely to his feelings, choosing rather to absent himself—and eating once in twenty-four hours seemed sufficient sustenance for him.

One night, after the family were in bed, I heard him go downstairs, and out at the front door. I did not hear him re-enter, and in the morning I found he was still away.

We were in April then; the weather was sweet and warm, the grass as green as showers and sun could make it, and the two dwarf apple trees, near the southern wall, in full bloom.

After breakfast, Catherine insisted on my bringing a chair, and sitting with my work under the fir trees at the end of the house; and she beguiled Hareton, who had perfectly recovered from his accident, to dig and arrange her little garden, which was shifted to that corner by the influence of Joseph's complaints.

I was comfortably reveling in the spring fragrance around, and the beautiful soft blue overhead, when my young lady, who had run down near the gate to procure some primrose roots for a border, returned only half laden, and informed us that Mr. Heathcliff was coming in.

"And he spoke to me," she added, with a perplexed countenance.

"What did he say?" asked Hareton.

"He told me to begone as fast as I could," she answered. "But he looked so different from his usual look that I stopped a moment to stare at him."

"How?" he enquired.

"Why, almost bright and cheerful. No, almost nothing—very much excited, and wild and glad!" she replied.

"Night-walking amuses him, then," I remarked, affecting a careless manner—in reality, as surprised as she was. And, anxious to ascertain the truth of her statement, for to see the master looking glad would not be an everyday spectacle, I framed an excuse to go in.

Heathcliff stood at the open door; he was pale, and he trembled; yet, certainly, he had a strange joyful glitter in his eyes that altered the aspect of his whole face.

"Will you have some breakfast?" I said. "You must be hungry, rambling about all night!"

I wanted to discover where he had been, but I did not like to ask directly.

"No, I'm not hungry," he answered, averting his head, and speaking rather contemptuously, as if he guessed I was trying to divine the occasion of his good humour.

I felt perplexed—I didn't know whether it were not a proper opportunity to offer a bit of admonition.

"I don't think it right to wander out of doors," I observed, "instead of being in bed—it is not wise, at any rate, this moist season. I dare say you'll catch a bad cold, or a fever—you have something the matter with you now!"

"Nothing but what I can bear," he replied, "and with the greatest pleasure, provided you'll leave me alone—get in, and don't annoy me."

I obeyed; and, in passing, I noticed he breathed as fast as a cat.

"Yes!" I reflected to myself, "we shall have a fit of illness. I cannot conceive what he has been doing!"

That noon, he sat down to dinner with us, and received a heaped-up plate from my hands, as if he intended to make amends for previous fasting.

"I've neither cold nor fever, Nelly," he remarked, in allusion to my morning's speech, "and I'm ready to do justice to the food you give me."

He took his knife and fork, and was going to commence eating, when the inclination appeared to become suddenly extinct. He laid them on the table, looked eagerly towards the window, then rose and went out.

We saw him walking to and fro in the garden while we concluded our meal, and Earnshaw said he'd go and ask why he would not dine; he thought we had grieved him some way.

"Well, is he coming?" cried Catherine, when her cousin returned.

"Nay," he answered, "but he 's not angry—he seemed rare and pleased indeed; only, I made him impatient by speaking to him twice, and then he bid me be off to you; he wondered how I could want the company of anybody else."

I set his plate to keep warm on the fender, and after an hour or two he re-entered, when the room was clear, in no degree calmer: the same unnatural—it was unnatural—appearance of joy under his black brows; the same bloodless hue, and his teeth visible, now and then, in a kind of smile; his frame shivering, not as one shivers with chill or weakness, but as a tight-stretched cord vibrates—a strong thrilling, rather than trembling.

I will ask what is the matter, I thought, or who should? And I exclaimed—

"Have you heard any good news, Mr. Heathcliff? You look uncommonly animated."

"Where should good news come from, to me?" he said. "I 'm animated with hunger; and, seemingly, I must not eat."

"Your dinner is here," I returned; "why won't you get it?"

"I don't want it now," he muttered, hastily; "I 'll wait till supper. And, Nelly, once for all, let me beg you to warn Hareton and the other away from me. I wish to be troubled by nobody—I wish to have this place to myself."

"Is there some new reason for this banishment?" I inquired. "Tell me why you are so queer, Mr. Heathcliff? Where were you last night? I 'm not putting the question through idle curiosity, but——"

"You are putting the question through very idle curiosity," he interrupted, with a laugh. "Yet, I 'll answer it. Last night, I was on the threshold of hell. Today, I am within sight of my heaven. I have my eyes on it, hardly three feet to sever me! And now you 'd better go. You 'll neither see nor hear anything to frighten you, if you refrain from prying."

Having swept the hearth and wiped the table, I departed more perplexed than ever.

He did not quit the house again that afternoon, and no one intruded on his solitude, till, at eight o'clock, I deemed it proper, though unsummoned, to carry a candle and his supper to him.

He was leaning against the ledge of an open lattice, but not looking out—his face was turned to the interior gloom. The fire had smouldered to ashes; the room was filled with the damp, mild air of the cloudy evening; and so still, that not only the murmur of the beck down Gimmerton was distinguishable, but its ripples and its gurgling over the pebbles, or through the large stones which it could not cover.

I uttered an ejaculation of discontent at seeing the dismal grate, and commenced shutting the casements, one after another, till I came to his.

"Must I close this?" I asked, in order to rouse him; for he would not stir.

The light flashed on his features as I spoke. Oh, Mr. Lockwood, I cannot express what a terrible start I got, by the momentary view! Those deep black eyes! That smile, and ghastly paleness! It appeared to me, not Mr. Heathcliff, but a goblin; and, in my terror, I let the candle bend towards the wall, and it left me in darkness.

"Yes, close it," he replied, in his familiar voice. "There, that is pure awkwardness! Why did you hold the candle horizontally? Be quick, and bring another."

I hurried out in a foolish state of dread, and said to Joseph—

"The master wishes you to take him a light and rekindle the fire." For I dared not go in myself again just then.

Joseph rattled some fire into the shovel, and went; but he brought it back immediately, with the supper-tray in his other hand, explaining that Mr. Heathcliff was going to bed, and he wanted nothing to eat till morning.

We heard him mount the stairs directly; he did not proceed to his ordinary chamber, but turned into that with the panelled bed; its window, as I mentioned before, is wide enough for anybody to get through, and it struck me that he plotted another midnight excursion, which he had rather we had no suspicion of.

"Is he a ghoul, or a vampire?" I mused. I had read of such hideous, incarnate demons. And then I set myself to reflect how I had tended him in infancy; and watched him grow to youth; and followed him almost through his whole course; and what absurd nonsense it was to yield to that sense of horror.

"But where did he come from, the little dark thing, harboured by a good man to his bane?" muttered superstition, as I dozed into unconsciousness. And I began, half dreaming, to weary myself with imagining some fit parentage for him; and repeating my waking meditations, I tracked his existence over again, with grim variations; at last, picturing his death and funeral, of which, all I can remember is, being exceedingly vexed at having the task of dictating an inscription for his monument, and consulting the sexton about it; and, as he had no surname, and we could not tell his age, we were obliged to content ourselves with the single word, "Heathcliff." That came true—we were. If you enter the kirkyard, you 'll read on his headstone, only that, and the date of his death.

Dawn restored me to common sense. I rose, and went into the garden, as soon as I could see, to ascertain if there were any footmarks under his window. There were none.

"He has stayed at home," I thought, "and he 'll be all right today."

I prepared breakfast for the household, as was my usual custom, but told Hareton and Catherine to get theirs ere the master came down, for he lay late. They preferred taking it out of doors, under the trees, and I set a little table to accommodate them.

On my re-entrance, I found Mr. Heathcliff below. He and Joseph were conversing about some farming business; he gave clear, minute directions concerning the matter discussed, but he spoke rapidly, and turned his head continually aside, and had the same excited expression, even more exaggerated.

When Joseph quitted the room, he took his seat in the place he generally chose, and I put a basin of coffee before him. He drew it nearer, and then rested his arms on the table, and looked at the opposite wall, as I supposed, surveying one particular portion, up and down, with glittering, restless eyes, and with such eager interest that he stopped breathing, during half a minute together.

"Come now," I exclaimed, pushing some bread against his hand. "Eat and drink that, while it is hot—it has been waiting near an hour."

He didn't notice me, and yet he smiled. I'd rather have seen him gnash his teeth than smile so.

"Mr. Heathcliff! master!" I cried. "Don't, for God's sake, stare as if you saw an unearthly vision."

"Don't, for God's sake, shout so loud," he replied. "Turn round, and tell me, are we by ourselves?"

"Of course," was my answer; "of course we are!"

Still, I involuntarily obeyed him, as if I were not quite sure.

With a sweep of his hand he cleared a vacant space in front among the breakfast things, and leant forward to gaze more at his ease.

Now, I perceived he was not looking at the wall; for when I regarded him alone, it seemed exactly that he gazed at something within two yards distance. And whatever it was, it communicated, apparently, both pleasure and pain, in exquisite extremes—at least, the anguished yet raptured expression of his countenance suggested that idea.

The fancied object was not fixed, either; his eyes pursued it with unwearied vigilance, and, even in speaking to me, were never weaned away.

I vainly reminded him of his protracted abstinence from food; if he stirred to touch anything in compliance with my entreaties, if he stretched his hand out to get a piece of bread, his fingers clenched before they reached it, and remained on the table, forgetful of their aim.

I sat, a model of patience, trying to attract his absorbed attention from its engrossing speculation, till he grew irritable, and got up, asking why I would not allow him to have his own time in taking his meals? and saying that, on the next occasion, I needn't wait, I might set the things down and go.

Having uttered these words he left the house, slowly

sauntered down the garden path, and disappeared through the gate.

The hours crept anxiously by; another evening came. I did not retire to rest till late, and when I did, I could not sleep. He returned after midnight, and, instead of going to bed, shut himself into the room beneath. I listened, and tossed about; and, finally, dressed, and descended. It was too irksome to lie up there, harassing my brain with a hundred idle misgivings.

I distinguished Mr. Heathcliff's step, restlessly measuring the floor, and he frequently broke the silence by a deep inspiration, resembling a groan. He muttered detached words, also; the only one I could catch was the name "Catherine," coupled with some wild term of endearment or suffering, and spoken as one would speak to a person present—low and earnest, and wrung from the depth of his soul.

I had not courage to walk straight into the apartment; but I desired to divert him from his reverie, and therefore fell foul of the kitchen fire, stirred it, and began to scrape the cinders. It drew him forth sooner than I expected. He opened the door immediately, and said—

"Nelly, come here—is it morning? Come in with your light."

"It is striking four," I answered. "You want a candle to take upstairs—you might have lit one at this fire."

"No, I don't wish to go upstairs," he said. "Come in, and kindle me a fire, and do anything there is to do about the room."

"I must blow the coals red first, before I can carry any," I replied, getting a chair and the bellows.

He roamed to and fro, meantime, in a state approaching distraction, his heavy sighs succeeding each other so thick as to leave no space for common breathing between.

"When day breaks I'll send for Green," he said; "I wish to make some legal inquiries of him while I can bestow a thought on those matters, and while I can act calmly. I have not written my will yet, and how to leave my property I cannot determine! I wish I could annihilate it from the face of the earth."

"I would not talk so, Mr. Heathcliff," I interposed. "Let your will be, a while—you'll be spared to repent of your many injustices, yet! I never expected that your nerves would be disordered; they are, at present, marvellously so, however, and almost entirely through your own fault. The way you've passed these three last days might knock up a Titan. Do take some food, and some repose. You need only look at yourself in a glass to see how you require both. Your cheeks are hollow, and your eyes bloodshot, like a person starving with hunger, and going blind with loss of sleep."

"It is not my fault that I cannot eat or rest," he replied. "I assure you it is through no settled designs. I'll do both, as soon as I possibly can. But you might as well bid a man struggling in the water rest within arm's length of the shore! I must reach it first, and then I'll rest. Well, never mind Mr. Green; as to repenting of my injustices, I've done no injustice, and I repent of nothing—I'm too happy, and yet I'm not happy enough. My soul's bliss kills my body, but does not satisfy itself."

"Happy, master?" I cried. "Strange happiness! If you would hear me without being angry, I might offer some advice that would make you happier."

"What is that?" he asked. "Give it."

"You are aware, Mr. Heathcliff," I said, "that from the time you were thirteen years old, you have lived a selfish, unchristian life; and probably hardly had a Bible in your hands during all that period. You must have forgotten the contents of the book, and you may not have space to search it now. Could it be hurtful to send for someone—some minister of any denomination, it does not matter which, to explain it, and show you how very far you have erred from its precepts, and how unfit you will be for its heaven, unless a change takes place before you die?"

"I'm rather obliged than angry, Nelly," he said, "for you remind me of the manner that I desire to be buried in—it is to be carried to the churchyard, in the evening. You and Hareton may, if you please, accompany me; and mind, particularly, to notice that the sexton obeys my directions concerning the two coffins! No minister need come, nor need anything be said over me—I tell you, I have nearly attained my heaven, and that of others is altogether unvalued and uncoveted by me!"

"And supposing you persevered in your obstinate fast,

and died by that means, and they refused to bury you in the precincts of the kirk?" I said, shocked at his godless indifference. "How would you like it?"

"They won't do that," he replied; "if they did, you must have me removed secretly; and if you neglect it, you shall prove, practically, that the dead are not annihilated!"

As soon as he heard the other members of the family stirring he retired to his den, and I breathed freer. But in the afternoon, while Joseph and Hareton were at their work, he came into the kitchen again, and with a wild look, bid me come, and sit in the house—he wanted somebody with him.

I declined, telling him plainly that his strange talk and manner frightened me, and I had neither the nerve nor the will to be his companion, alone.

"I believe you think me a fiend!" he said, with his dismal laugh, "something too horrible to live under a decent roof!"

Then turning to Catherine, who was there, and who drew behind me at his approach, he added, half sneeringly—

"Will you come, chuck? I'll not hurt you. No! to you, I've made myself worse than the devil. Well, there is one who won't shrink from my company! By God! she's relentless. Oh, damn it! It's unutterably too much for flesh and blood to bear—even mine."

He solicited the society of no one more. At dusk, he went into his chamber. Through the whole night, and far into the morning, we heard him groaning, and murmuring to himself. Hareton was anxious to enter, but I bid him fetch Mr. Kenneth, and he should go in and see him.

When he came, and I requested admittance and tried to open the door, I found it locked; and Heathcliff bid us be damned. He was better, and would be left alone; so the doctor went away.

The following evening was very wet—indeed it poured down, till day-dawn; and, as I took my morning walk round the house, I observed the master's window swinging open, and the rain driving straight in.

He cannot be in bed, I thought; those showers would

drench him through! He must either be up or out. But I'll make no more ado, I'll go boldly and look!

Having succeeded in obtaining entrance with another key, I ran to unclose the panels, for the chamber was vacant; quickly pushing them aside, I peeped in. Mr. Heathcliff was there—laid on his back. His eyes met mine so keen and fierce, I started; and then he seemed to smile.

I could not think him dead—but his face and throat were washed with rain; the bed-clothes dripped, and he was perfectly still. The lattice, flapping to and fro, had grazed one hand that rested on the sill; no blood trickled from the broken skin, and when I put my fingers to it, I could doubt no more—he was dead and stark!

I hasped the window; I combed his black long hair from his forehead; I tried to close his eyes, to extinguish, if possible, that frightful, lifelike gaze of exultation, before anyone else beheld it. They would not shut—they seemed to sneer at my attempts, and his parted lips and sharp white teeth sneered too! Taken with another fit of cowardice, I cried for Joseph. Joseph shuffled up and made a noise, but resolutely refused to meddle with him.

"Th' divil's harried off his soul," he cried, "and he muh hev his carcass intuh t' bargin, for ow't Aw care! Ech! what a wicked un he looks grinning at death!" and the old sinner grinned in mockery.

I thought he intended to cut a caper round the bed; but suddenly composing himself, he fell on his knees, and raised his hands, and returned thanks that the lawful master and the ancient stock were restored to their rights.

I felt stunned by the awful event; and my memory unavoidably recurred to former times with a sort of oppressive sadness. But poor Hareton, the most wronged, was the only one that really suffered much. He sat by the corpse all night, weeping in bitter earnest. He pressed its hand, and kissed the sarcastic, savage face that everyone else shrank from contemplating, and bemoaned him with that strong grief which springs naturally from a generous heart, though it be tough as tempered steel.

Kenneth was perplexed to pronounce of what disorder

the master died. I concealed the fact of his having swallowed nothing for four days, fearing it might lead to trouble, and then, I am persuaded he did not abstain on purpose—it was the consequence of his strange illness, not the cause.

We buried him, to the scandal of the whole neighbourhood, as he had wished. Earnshaw and I, the sexton and six men to carry the coffin, comprehended the whole attendance.

The six men departed when they had let it down into the grave; we stayed to see it covered. Hareton, with a streaming face, dug green sods, and laid them over the brown mould himself; at present it is as smooth and verdant as its companion mounds—and I hope its tenant sleeps as soundly. But the country folks, if you asked them, would swear on their Bible that he *walks*. There are those who speak to having met him near the church, and on the moor, and even within this house. Idle tales, you 'll say, and so say I. Yet that old man by the kitchen fire affirms he has seen two on 'em looking out of his chamber window, on every rainy night since his death—and an odd thing happened to me about a month ago.

I was going to the Grange one evening—a dark evening threatening thunder—and, just at the turn of the Heights, I encountered a little boy with a sheep and two lambs before him; he was crying terribly, and I supposed the lambs were skittish, and would not be guided.

"What is the matter, my little man?" I asked.

"They's Heathcliff, and a woman, yonder, under t' Nab," he blubbered, "un' Aw darnut pass 'em."

I saw nothing; but neither the sheep nor he would go on; so I bid him take the road lower down.

He probably raised the phantoms from thinking, as he traversed the moors alone, on the nonsense he had heard his parents and companions repeat—yet still, I don't like being out in the dark, now; and I don't like being left by myself in this grim house—I cannot help it; I shall be glad when they leave it, and shift to the Grange!

"They are going to the Grange then?" I said.

"Yes," answered Mrs. Dean, "as soon as they are married; and that will be on New Year's day."

"And who will live here then?"

"Why, Joseph will take care of the house, and, perhaps, a lad to keep him company. They will live in the kitchen, and the rest will be shut up."

"For the use of such ghosts as choose to inhabit it," I observed.

"No, Mr. Lockwood," said Nelly, shaking her head. "I believe the dead are at peace, but it is not right to speak of them with levity."

At that moment the garden gate swung to; the ramblers were returning.

"They are afraid of nothing," I grumbled, watching their approach through the window. "Together, they would brave satan and all his legions."

As they stepped onto the door-stones, and halted to take a last look at the moon—or, more correctly, at each other, by her light—I felt irresistibly impelled to escape them again; and, pressing a remembrance into the hand of Mrs. Dean, and disregarding her expostulations at my rudeness, I vanished through the kitchen as they opened the house-door: and so should have confirmed Joseph in his opinion of his fellow-servant's gay indiscretions, had he not fortunately recognized me for a respectable character by the sweet ring of a sovereign at his feet.

My walk home was lengthened by a diversion in the direction of the kirk. When beneath its walls, I perceived decay had made progress, even in seven months; many a window showed black gaps deprived of glass, and slates jutted off, here and there, beyond the right line of the roof, to be gradually worked off in coming autumn storms.

I sought, and soon discovered, the three head-stones on the slope next the moor—the middle one grey, and half buried in heath; Edgar Linton's only harmonized by the turf, and moss creeping up its foot; Heathcliff's still bare.

I lingered round them, under that benign sky; watched the moths fluttering among the heath and hare-bells; listened to the soft wind breathing through the grass; and wondered how anyone could ever imagine unquiet slumbers for the sleepers in that quiet earth.

SILAS MARNER

———————•◆•———————

by George Eliot

PART ONE

CHAPTER I

IN THE DAYS when the spinning wheels hummed busily in the farmhouses—and even great ladies, clothed in silk and thread lace, had their toy spinning wheels of polished oak—there might be seen, in districts far away among the lanes, or deep in the bosom of the hills, certain pallid undersized men who, by the side of the brawny countryfolk, looked like the remnants of a disinherited race. The shepherd's dog barked fiercely when one of these alien-looking men appeared on the upland, dark against the early winter sunset; for what dog likes a figure bent under a heavy bag?—and these pale men rarely stirred abroad without that mysterious burden. The shepherd himself, though he had good reason to believe that the bag held nothing but flaxen thread, or else the long rolls of strong linen spun from that thread, was not quite sure that this trade of weaving, indispensable though it was, could be carried on entirely without the help of the Evil One. In that far-off time superstition clung easily round every person or thing that was at all unwonted, or even intermittent and occasional merely, like the visits of the peddler or the knife grinder. No one knew where wandering men had their homes or their origin; and how was a man to be explained unless you at least knew somebody who knew his father and mother? To the peasants of old times, the world outside their own direct experience was a region of vagueness and mystery: to their untravelled thought a state of wandering was a conception as dim as the winter life of the swallows that came back with the spring; and even a settler, if he came from distant parts, hardly ever ceased to be viewed with a remnant of distrust, which would have prevented any surprise if a long course of inoffensive conduct on his part had ended in the commission of a crime; especially if he had any reputation for knowledge, or showed any skill in handicraft. All cleverness, whether in the rapid use of that difficult instrument the tongue, or in some other art unfamiliar to villagers, was in itself suspicious: honest folk, born and bred in a visible manner, were mostly not overwise or clever—at least, not beyond such a matter as knowing the signs of the weather; and the process by which rapidity and dexterity of any kind were acquired was so wholly hidden, that they partook of the nature of conjuring. In this way it came to pass that those scattered linen weavers—emigrants from the town into the country—were to the last regarded as aliens by their rustic neighbours, and usually contracted the eccentric habits which belong to a state of loneliness.

In the early years of this century, such a linen weaver, named Silas Marner, worked at his vocation in a stone cottage that stood among the nutty hedgerows near the village of Raveloe, and not far from the edge of a deserted stone pit. The questionable sound of Silas's loom, so unlike the natural cheerful trotting of the winnowing machine, or the simpler rhythm of the flail, had a half-fearful fascination for the Raveloe boys, who would often leave off their nutting or birds'-nesting to peep in at the window of the stone cottage, counterbalancing a certain awe at the mysterious action of the loom by a pleasant sense of scornful superiority, drawn from the mockery of its alternating noises, along with the bent, treadmill attitude of the weaver. But sometimes it happened that Marner, pausing to adjust an irregularity in his thread, became aware of the small scoundrels, and, though chary of his time, he liked their intrusion so ill that he would descend from his loom, and, opening the door, would fix on them a gaze that was always enough to make them take to their legs in terror. For how was it possible to believe that those large brown protuberant eyes in Silas Marner's pale face really saw nothing very distinctly that was not close to them, and not rather that their dreadful stare could dart cramp, or rickets, or a wry mouth at any boy who happened to be in the rear? They had, perhaps, heard their fathers and mothers hint that Silas Marner could cure folks' rheumatism if he had a mind, and add, still more darkly, that if you could only speak the devil fair enough, he might save you the cost of the doctor. Such strange lingering echoes of the old demon worship might perhaps even now be caught by the diligent listener among the grey-haired peasantry; for the rude mind with difficulty associates the ideas of power and benignity. A shadowy conception of power that by much persuasion can be induced to refrain from inflicting harm is the shape most easily taken by the sense of the Invisible in the minds of men who have always been pressed close by primitive wants, and to whom a life of hard toil has never been illuminated by any enthusiastic religious faith. To them pain and mishap present a far wider range of possibilities than gladness and enjoyment: their imagination is almost barren of the images that feed desire and hope, but is all overgrown by recollections that are a perpetual pasture to fear. "Is there anything you can fancy that you would like to eat?" I once said to an old labouring man, who was in his last illness, and who had refused all the food his wife had offered him. "No," he answered, "I've never been used to nothing but common victual, and I can't eat that." Experience had bred no fancies in him that could raise the phantasm of appetite.

And Raveloe was a village where many of the old echoes lingered, undrowned by new voices. Not that it was one of those barren parishes lying on the outskirts of civilization—inhabited by meagre sheep and thinly scattered shepherds: on the contrary, it lay in the rich central plain of what we are pleased to call Merry England, and held farms which, speaking from a spiritual point of view, paid highly desirable tithes. But it was nestled in a snug, well-wooded hollow, quite an hour's journey on horseback from any turnpike, where it was never reached by the vibrations of the coach horn, or of public opinion. It was an important-looking village, with a fine old church and large churchyard in the heart of it, and two or three large brick-and-stone homesteads, with well-walled orchards and ornamental weathercocks, standing close upon the road, and lifting more imposing fronts than the rectory, which peeped from among the

trees on the other side of the churchyard—a village which
showed at once the summits of its social life, and told the
practised eye that there was no great park and manor
house in the vicinity, but that there were several chiefs
in Raveloe who could farm badly quite at their ease,
drawing enough money from their bad farming, in those
wartimes, to live in a rollicking fashion, and keep a jolly
Christmas, Whitsun, and Easter tide.

It was fifteen years since Silas Marner had first come to
Raveloe; he was then simply a pallid young man, with
prominent, short-sighted brown eyes, whose appearance
would have had nothing strange for people of average
culture and experience, but for the villagers near whom
he had come to settle it had mysterious peculiarities which
corresponded with the exceptional nature of his occupation, and his advent from an unknown region called
"North'ard." So had his way of life—he invited no
comer to step across his doorsill, and he never strolled into
the village to drink a pint at the Rainbow, or to gossip at
the wheelwright's; he sought no man or woman, save for
the purposes of his calling, or in order to supply himself
with necessaries; and it was soon clear to the Raveloe
lasses that he would never urge one of them to accept him
against her will—quite as if he had heard them declare
that they would never marry a dead man come to life
again. This view of Marner's personality was not without
another ground than his pale face and unexampled eyes;
for Jem Rodney, the molecatcher, averred that, one evening as he was returning homeward, he saw Silas Marner
leaning against a stile with a heavy bag on his back, instead of resting the bag on the stile as a man in his senses
would have done; and that, on coming up to him, he saw
that Marner's eyes were set like a dead man's, and he
spoke to him, and shook him, and his limbs were stiff, and
his hands clutched the bag as if they'd been made of iron;
but just as he had made up his mind that the weaver was
dead, he came all right again, like, as you might say, in
the winking of an eye, and said "Good night," and walked
off. All this Jem swore he had seen, more by token, that it
was the very day he had been mole-catching on Squire
Cass's land, down by the old saw pit. Some said Marner
must have been in a "fit," a word which seemed to explain

things otherwise incredible; but the argumentative Mr.
Macey, clerk of the parish, shook his head, and asked if
anybody was ever known to go off in a fit and not fall
down. A fit was a stroke, wasn't it? and it was in the
nature of a stroke to partly take away the use of a man's
limbs and throw him on the parish, if he'd got no children to look to. No, no; it was no stroke that would let a
man stand on his legs, like a horse between the shafts, and
then walk off as soon as you can say "Gee!" But there
might be such a thing as a man's soul being loose from his
body, and going out and in, like a bird out of its nest and
back; and that was how folks got overwise, for they went
to school in this shell-less state to those who could teach
them more than their neighbours could learn with their
five senses and the parson. And where did Master Marner
get his knowledge of herbs from—and charms, too, if he
liked to give them away? Jem Rodney's story was no more
than what might have been expected by anybody who had
seen how Marner had cured Sally Oates, and made her
sleep like a baby, when her heart had been beating
enough to burst her body, for two months and more,
while she had been under the doctor's care. He might cure
more folks if he would; but he was worth speaking fair,
if it was only to keep him from doing you a mischief.

It was partly to this vague fear that Marner was indebted for protecting him from the persecution that his
singularities might have drawn upon him, but still more
to the fact that, the old linen weaver in the neighbouring
parish of Tarley being dead, his handicraft made him a
highly welcome settler to the richer housewives of the
district, and even to the more provident cottagers, who
had their little stock of yarn at the year's end; and their
sense of his usefulness would have counteracted any repugnance or suspicion which was not confirmed by a
deficiency in the quality or the tale of the cloth he wove
for them. And the years had rolled on without producing
any change in the impressions of the neighbours concerning Marner, except the change from novelty to habit. At
the end of fifteen years the Raveloe men said just the
same things about Silas Marner as at the beginning: they
did not say them quite so often, but they believed them
much more strongly when they did say them. There was

only one important addition which the years had brought:
it was that Master Marner had laid by a fine sight of
money somewhere, and that he could buy up "bigger
men" than himself.

But while opinion concerning him had remained nearly
stationary, and his daily habits had presented scarcely any
visible change, Marner's inward life had been a history
and a metamorphosis, as that of every fervid nature must
be when it has fled, or been condemned, to solitude. His
life, before he came to Raveloe, had been filled with the
movement, the mental activity, and the close fellowship
which, in that day as in this, marked the life of an artisan
early incorporated in a narrow religious sect, where the
poorest layman has the chance of distinguishing himself
by gifts of speech, and has, at the very least, the weight of
a silent voter in the government of his community.
Marner was highly thought of in that little hidden world,
known to itself as the church assembling in Lantern Yard;
he was believed to be a young man of exemplary life and
ardent faith; and a peculiar interest had been centered in
him ever since he had fallen, at a prayer meeting, into a
mysterious rigidity and suspension of consciousness which,
lasting for an hour or more, had been mistaken for death.
To have sought a medical explanation for this phenom-
enon would have been held by Silas himself, as well as by
his minister and fellow members, a wilful self-exclusion
from the spiritual significance that might lie therein.
Silas was evidently a brother selected for a peculiar
discipline, and though the effort to interpret this discipline was discouraged by the absence, on his part, of any
spiritual vision during his outward trance, yet it was believed by himself and others that its effect was seen in an
accession of light and fervour. A less truthful man than he
might have been tempted into the subsequent creation of
a vision in the form of resurgent memory; a less sane
man might have believed in such a creation; but Silas was
both sane and honest, though, as with many honest and
fervent men, culture had not defined any channels for his
sense of mystery, and so it spread itself over the proper
pathway of inquiry and knowledge. He had inherited
from his mother some acquaintance with medicinal herbs
and their preparation—a little store of wisdom which she

had imparted to him as a solemn bequest—but of late years he had had doubts about the lawfulness of applying this knowledge, believing that herbs could have no efficacy without prayer, and that prayer might suffice without herbs; so that the inherited delight he had in wandering in the fields in search of foxglove and dandelion and coltsfoot began to wear to him the character of a temptation.

Among the members of his church there was one young man, a little older than himself, with whom he had long lived in such close friendship that it was the custom of their Lantern Yard brethren to call them David and Jonathan. The real name of the friend was William Dane, and he, too, was regarded as a shining instance of youthful piety, though somewhat given to over severity towards weaker brethren, and to be so dazzled by his own light as to hold himself wiser than his teachers. But whatever blemishes others might discern in William, to his friend's mind he was faultless; for Marner had one of those impressible self-doubting natures which, at an inexperienced age, admire imperativeness and lean on contradiction. The expression of trusting simplicity in Marner's face, heightened by that absence of special observation, that defenceless, deer-like gaze which belongs to large prominent eyes, was strongly contrasted by the self-complacent suppression of inward triumph that lurked in the narrow slanting eyes and compressed lips of William Dane. One of the most frequent topics of conversation between the two friends was assurance of salvation: Silas confessed that he could never arrive at anything higher than hope mingled with fear, and listened with longing wonder when William declared that he had possessed unshaken assurance ever since, in the period of his conversion, he had dreamed that he saw the words "calling and election sure" standing by themselves on a white page in the open Bible. Such colloquies have occupied many a pair of pale-faced weavers, whose unnurtured souls have been like young winged things, fluttering forsaken in the twilight.

It had seemed to the unsuspecting Silas that the friendship had suffered no chill even from his formation of another attachment of a closer kind. For some months he had been engaged to young servant woman, waiting only

for a little increase to their mutual savings in order to
their marriage; and it was a great delight to him that
Sarah did not object to William's occasional presence in
their Sunday interviews. It was at this point in their
history that Silas's cataleptic fit occurred during the
prayer meeting; and amidst the various queries and expressions of interest addressed to him by his fellow members, William's suggestion alone jarred with the general
sympathy towards a brother thus singled out for special
dealings. He observed that, to him, this trance looked
more like a visitation of Satan than a proof of divine
favour, and exhorted his friend to see that he hid no accursed thing within his soul. Silas, feeling bound to accept
rebuke and admonition as a brotherly office, felt no resentment, but only pain, at his friend's doubts concerning
him; and to this was soon added some anxiety at the
perception that Sarah's manner towards him began to
exhibit a strange fluctuation between an effort at an increased manifestation of regard and involuntary signs of
shrinking and dislike. He asked her if she wished to break
off their engagement; but she denied this: their engagement was known to the church, and had been recognised
in the prayer meetings; it could not be broken off without
strict investigation, and Sarah could render no reason that
would be sanctioned by the feeling of the community. At
this time the senior deacon was taken dangerously ill, and,
being a childless widower, he was tended night and day
by some of the younger brethren or sisters. Silas frequently took his turn in the night-watching with William,
the one relieving the other at two in the morning. The
old man, contrary to expectation, seemed to be on the
way to recovery, when one night Silas, sitting up by his
bedside, observed that his usually audible breathing had
ceased. The candle was burning low, and he had to lift
it to see the patient's face distinctly. Examination convinced him that the deacon was dead—had been dead
some time, for the limbs were rigid. Silas asked himself if
he had been asleep, and looked at the clock: it was already
four in the morning. How was it that William had not
come? In much anxiety he went to seek for help, and soon
there were several friends assembled in the house, the
minister among them, while Silas went away to his work,

wishing he could have met William to know the reason
of his nonappearance. But at six o'clock, as he was thinking of going to seek his friend, William came, and with
him the minister. They came to summon him to Lantern
Yard, to meet the church members there; and to his inquiry concerning the cause of the summons the only
reply was, "You will hear." Nothing further was said
until Silas was seated in the vestry, in front of the minister, with the eyes of those who to him represented God's
people fixed solemnly upon him. Then the minister, taking out a pocket knife, showed it to Silas, and asked him
if he knew where he had left that knife? Silas said he did
not know that he had left it anywhere out of his own
pocket—but he was trembling at this strange interroga-
tion. He was then exhorted not to hide his sin, but to
confess and repent. The knife had been found in the
bureau by the departed deacon's bedside—found in the
place where the little bag of church money had lain,
which the minister himself had seen the day before. Some
hand had removed that bag; and whose hand could it be,
if not that of the man to whom the knife belonged? For
some time Silas was mute with astonishment; then he
said, "God will clear me: I know nothing about the knife
being there, or the money being gone. Search me and my
dwelling: you will find nothing but three pound five of
my own savings, which William Dane knows I have had
these six months." At this William groaned, but the
minister said, "The proof is heavy against you, brother
Marner. The money was taken in the night last past, and
no man was with our departed brother but you, for William Dane declares to us that he was hindered by sudden
sickness from going to take his place as usual, and you
yourself said that he had not come; and, moreover, you
neglected the dead body."

"I must have slept," said Silas. Then, after a pause, he
added, "Or I must have had another visitation like that
which you have all seen me under, so that the thief must
have come and gone while I was not in the body, but out
of the body. But, I say again, search me and my dwelling,
for I have been nowhere else."

The search was made, and it ended—in William Dane's
finding the well-known bag, empty, tucked behind the

chest of drawers in Silas's chamber! On this William exhorted his friend to confess, and not to hide his sin any
longer. Silas turned a look of keen reproach on him, and
said, "William, for nine years that we have gone in and
out together, have you ever known me tell a lie? But God
will clear me."

"Brother," said William, "how do I know what you
may have done in the secret chambers of your heart, to
give Satan an advantage over you?"

Silas was still looking at his friend. Suddenly a deep
flush came over his face, and he was about to speak
impetuously, when he seemed checked again by some
inward shock, that sent the flush back and made him
tremble. But at last he spoke feebly, looking at William.

"I remember now—the knife wasn't in my pocket."

William said, "I know nothing of what you mean."
The other persons present, however, began to inquire
where Silas meant to say that the knife was, but he would
give no further explanation; he only said, "I am sore
stricken; I can say nothing. God will clear me."

On their return to the vestry there was further deliberation. Any resort to legal measures for ascertaining the
culprit was contrary to the principles of the church:
prosecution was held by them to be forbidden to Chris-
tians, even if it had been a case in which there was no
scandal to the community. But they were bound to take
other measures for finding out the truth, and they resolved on praying and drawing lots. This resolution can
be a ground of surprise only to those who are unacquainted with that obscure religious life which has gone
on in the alleys of our towns. Silas knelt with his brethren,
relying on his own innocence being certified by immediate divine interference, but feeling that there was
sorrow and mourning behind for him even then—that his
trust in man had been cruelly bruised. *The lots declared
that Silas Marner was guilty*. He was solemnly suspended
from church membership, and called upon to render up
the stolen money; only on confession, as the sign of repentance, could he be received once more within the fold
of the church. Marner listened in silence. At last, when
everyone rose to depart, he went towards William Dane
and said, in a voice shaken by agitation:

"The last time I remember using my knife was when I took it out to cut a strap for you. I don't remember putting it in my pocket again. *You* stole the money, and you have woven a plot to lay the sin at my door. But you may prosper, for all that: there is no just God that governs the earth righteously, but a God of lies, that bears witness against the innocent."

There was a general shudder at this blasphemy.

William said meekly, "I leave our brethren to judge whether this is the voice of Satan or not. I can do nothing but pray for you, Silas."

Poor Marner went out with that despair in his soul— that shaken trust in God and man which is little short of madness to a loving nature. In the bitterness of his wounded spirit, he said to himself, "*She* will cast me off too." And he reflected that, if she did not believe the testimony against him, her whole faith must be upset, as his was. To people accustomed to reason about the forms in which their religious feeling has incorporated itself, it is difficult to enter into that simple, untaught state of mind in which the form and the feeling have never been severed by an act of reflection. We are apt to think it in- evitable that a man in Marner's position should have begun to question the validity of an appeal to the divine judgment by drawing lots; but to him this would have been an effort of independent thought such as he had never known; and he must have made the effort at a moment when all his energies were turned into the anguish of disappointed faith. If there is an angel who records the sorrows of men as well as their sins, he knows how many and deep are the sorrows that spring from false ideas for which no man is culpable.

Marner went home, and for a whole day sat alone, stunned by despair, without any impulse to go to Sarah and attempt to win her belief in his innocence. The sec- ond day he took refuge from benumbing unbelief by getting into his loom and working away as usual; and before many hours were past, the minister and one of the deacons came to him with the message from Sarah, that she held her engagement to him at an end. Silas received the message mutely, and then turned away from the messengers to work at his loom again. In little more than a month from that time, Sarah was married to William Dane; and not long afterwards it was known to the brethren in Lantern Yard that Silas Marner had departed from the town.

CHAPTER II

EVEN PEOPLE whose lives have been made various by learning sometimes find it hard to keep a fast hold on their habitual views of life, on their faith in the Invisible —nay, on the sense that their past joys and sorrows are a real experience, when they are suddenly transported to a new land, where the beings around them know nothing of their history, and share none of their ideas—where their mother earth shows another lap, and human life has other forms than those on which their souls have been nourished. Minds that have been unhinged from their old faith and love have perhaps sought this Lethean influence of exile in which the past becomes dreamy because its symbols have all vanished, and the present too is dreamy because it is linked with no memories. But even *their* experience may hardly enable them thoroughly to imagine what was the effect on a simple weaver like Silas Marner, when he left his own country and people and came to settle in Raveloe. Nothing could be more unlike his native town, set within sight of the widespread hill-sides, than this low, wooded region, where he felt hidden even from the heavens by the screening trees and hedgerows. There was nothing here, when he rose in the deep morning quiet and looked out on the dewy brambles and rank tufted grass, that seemed to have any relation with that life centering in Lantern Yard, which had once been to him the altar place of high dispensations. The white-washed walls; the little pews where well-known figures entered with a subdued rustling, and where first one well-known voice and then another, pitched in a peculiar key of petition, uttered phrases at once occult and famil-iar, like the amulet worn on the heart; the pulpit where the minister delivered unquestioned doctrine, and swayed to and fro, and handled the book in a long-accustomed manner; the very pauses between the couplets of the hymn, as it was given out, and the recurrent swell of voices in song: these things had been the channel of divine influences to Marner—they were the fostering home of his religious emotions—they were Christianity and God's kingdom upon earth. A weaver who finds hard words in his hymnbook knows nothing of abstractions; as the little child knows nothing of parental love, but only knows one face and one lap towards which it stretches its arms for refuge and nurture.

And what could be more unlike that Lantern Yard world than the world in Raveloe?—orchards looking lazy with neglected plenty; the large church in the wide churchyard, which men gazed at lounging at their own doors in service time; the purple-faced farmers jogging along the lanes or turning in at the Rainbow; homesteads, where men supped heavily and slept in the light of the evening hearth, and where women seemed to be laying up a stock of linen for the life to come. There were no lips in Raveloe from which a word could fall that would stir Silas Marner's benumbed faith to a sense of pain. In the early ages of the world, we know, it was believed that each territory was inhabited and ruled by its own divinities, so that a man could cross the bordering heights and be out of the reach of his native gods, whose presence was confined to the streams and the groves and the hills among which he had lived from his birth. And poor Silas was vaguely conscious of something not unlike the feeling of primitive men, when they fled thus, in fear or in sullenness, from the face of an unpropitious deity. It seemed to him that the Power in which he had vainly trusted among the streets and in the prayer meetings was very far away from this land in which he had taken refuge, where men lived in careless abundance, knowing and needing nothing of that trust which, for him, had been turned to bitterness. The little light he possessed spread its beams so narrowly that frustrated belief was a curtain broad enough to create for him the blackness of night.

His first movement after the shock had been to work in his loom; and he went on with this unremittingly, never asking himself why, now he was come to Raveloe, he

worked far on into the night to finish the tale of Mrs.
Osgood's table linen sooner than she expected—without
contemplating beforehand the money she would put into
his hand for the work. He seemed to weave, like the
spider, from pure impulse, without reflection. Every
man's work, pursued steadily, tends in this way to become
an end in itself, and so to bridge over the loveless chasms
of his life. Silas's hand satisfied itself with throwing the
shuttle, and his eye with seeing the little squares in the
cloth complete themselves under his effort. Then there
were the calls of hunger; and Silas, in his solitude, had to
provide his own breakfast, dinner, and supper, to fetch
his own water from the well, and put his own kettle on
the fire; and all these immediate promptings helped,
along with the weaving, to reduce his life to the unques-
tioning activity of a spinning insect. He hated the
thought of the past; there was nothing that called out
his love and fellowship toward the strangers he had come
amongst; and the future was all dark, for there was no
Unseen Love that cared for him. Thought was arrested
by utter bewilderment, now its old narrow pathway was
closed, and affection seemed to have died under the
bruise that had fallen on its keenest nerves.

But at last Mrs. Osgood's table linen was finished, and
Silas was paid in gold. His earnings in his native town,
where he worked for a wholesale dealer, had been after a
lower rate; he had been paid weekly, and of his weekly
earnings a large proportion had gone to objects of piety
and charity. Now, for the first time in his life, he had five
bright guineas put into his hand; no man expected a
share of them, and he loved no man that he should offer
him a share. But what were the guineas to him who saw
no vista beyond countless days of weaving? It was needless
for him to ask that, for it was pleasant to him to feel them
in his palm, and look at their bright faces, which were all
his own: it was another element of life, like the weaving
and the satisfaction of hunger, subsisting quite aloof from
the life of belief and love from which he had been cut off.
The weaver's hand had known the touch of hard-won
money even before the palm had grown to its full
breadth; for twenty years, mysterious money had stood
to him as the symbol of earthly good, and the immediate

object of toil. He had seemed to love it little in the years
when every penny had its purpose for him; for he loved
the *purpose* then. But now, when all purpose was gone,
that habit of looking towards the money and grasping
it with a sense of fulfilled effort made a loam that was
deep enough for the seeds of desire; and as Silas walked
homeward across the fields in the twilight, he drew out
the money and thought it was brighter in the gathering
gloom.

About this time an incident happened which seemed to
open a possibility of some fellowship with his neighbours.
One day, taking a pair of shoes to be mended, he saw the
cobbler's wife seated by the fire, suffering from the terrible symptoms of heart disease and dropsy, which he had
witnessed as the precursors of his mother's death. He felt
a rush of pity at the mingled sight and remembrance,
and, recalling the relief his mother had found from a
simple preparation of foxglove, he promised Sally Oates
to bring her something that would ease her, since the
doctor did her no good. In this office of charity, Silas felt,
for the first time since he had come to Raveloe, a sense of
unity between his past and present life, which might have
been the beginning of his rescue from the insectlike
existence into which his nature had shrunk. But Sally
Oates's disease had raised her into a personage of much
interest and importance among the neighbours, and the
fact of her having found relief from drinking Silas
Marner's "stuff" became a matter of general discourse.
When Doctor Kimble gave physic, it was natural that it
should have an effect; but when a weaver, who came from
nobody knew where, worked wonders with a bottle of
brown waters, the occult character of the process was
evident. Such a sort of thing had not been known since
the Wise Woman at Tarley died; and she had charms as
well as "stuff": everybody went to her when their children
had fits. Silas Marner must be a person of the same sort,
for how did he know what would bring back Sally Oates's
breath, if he didn't know a fine sight more than that?
The Wise Woman had words that she muttered to herself, so that you couldn't hear what they were, and if she
tied a bit of red thread round the child's toe the while, it
would keep off the water in the head. There were women

in Raveloe, at that present time, who had worn one of
the Wise Woman's little bags round their necks, and, in
consequence, had never had an idiot child, as Ann
Coulter had. Silas Marner could very likely do as much,
and more; and now it was all clear how he should have
come from unknown parts, and be so "comical looking."
But Sally Oates must mind and not tell the doctor, for
he would be sure to set his face against Marner: he was
always angry about the Wise Woman, and used to
threaten those who went to her that they should have
none of his help any more.

Silas now found himself and his cottage suddenly beset
by mothers who wanted him to charm away the whoop-
ing cough, or bring back the milk, and by men who
wanted stuff against the rheumatics or the knots in the
hands; and, to secure themselves against a refusal, the
applicants brought silver in their palms. Silas might have
driven a profitable trade in charms as well as in his small
list of drugs; but money on this condition was no temptation to him: he had never known an impulse towards
falsity, and he drove one after another away with growing
irritation, for the news of him as a wise man had spread
even to Tarley, and it was long before people ceased to
take long walks for the sake of asking his aid. But the
hope in his wisdom was at length changed into dread, for
no one believed him when he said he knew no charms
and could work no cures, and every man and woman who
had an accident or a new attack after applying to him set
the misfortune down to Master Marner's ill will and
irritated glances. Thus it came to pass that his movement
of pity towards Sally Oates, which had given him a
transient sense of brotherhood, heightened the repulsion
between him and his neighbours, and made his isolation
more complete.

Gradually the guineas, the crowns, and the half-
crowns grew to a heap, and Marner drew less and less
for his own wants, trying to solve the problem of keeping
himself strong enough to work sixteen hours a day on as
small an outlay as possible. Have not men, shut up in
solitary imprisonment, found an interest in marking the
moments by straight strokes of a certain length on the
wall, until the growth of the sum of straight strokes,

arranged in triangles, has become a mastering purpose? Do we not wile away moments of inanity or fatigued waiting by repeating some trivial movement or sound, until the repetition has bred a want, which is incipient habit? That will help us to understand how the love of accumulating money grows an absorbing passion in men whose imaginations, even in the very beginning of their hoard, showed them no purpose beyond it. Marner wanted the heaps of ten to grow into a square, and then into a larger square; and every added guinea, while it was itself a satisfaction, bred a new desire. In this strange world, made a hopeless riddle to him, he might, if he had had a less intense nature, have sat weaving, weaving—looking towards the end of his pattern, or towards the end of his web, till he forgot the riddle, and everything else but his immediate sensations; but the money had come to mark off his weaving into periods, and the money not only grew, but it remained with him. He began to think it was conscious of him, as his loom was, and he would on no account have exchanged those coins, which had become his familiars, for other coins with unknown faces. He handled them, he counted them, till their form and colour were like the satisfaction of a thirst to him; but it was only in the night, when his work was done, that he drew them out to enjoy their companionship. He had taken up some bricks in his floor underneath his loom, and here he had made a hole in which he set the iron pot that contained his guineas and silver coins, covering the bricks with sand whenever he replaced them. Not that the idea of being robbed presented itself often or strongly to his mind: hoarding was common in country districts in those days; there were old labourers in the parish of Raveloe who were known to have their savings by them, probably inside their flock beds; but their rustic neighbours, though not all of them as honest as their ancestors in the days of King Alfred, had not imaginations bold enough to lay a plan of burglary. How could they have spent the money in their own village without betraying themselves? They would be obliged to "run away"—a course as dark and dubious as a balloon journey.

So, year after year, Silas Marner had lived in this solitude, his guineas rising in the iron pot, and his life

narrowing and hardening itself more and more into a
mere pulsation of desire and satisfaction that had no
relation to any other being. His life had reduced itself
to the mere functions of weaving and hoarding, without
any contemplation of an end towards which the functions
tended. The same sort of process has perhaps been undergone by wiser men, when they have been cut off from
faith and love—only, instead of a loom and a heap of
guineas, they have had some erudite research, some
ingenious project, or some well-knit theory. Strangely
Marner's face and figure shrank and bent themselves into
a constant mechanical relation to the objects of his life,
so that he produced the same sort of impression as a
handle or a crooked tube, which has no meaning standing
apart. The prominent eyes that used to look trusting and
dreamy now looked as if they had been made to see only
one kind of thing that was very small, like tiny grain, for
which they hunted everywhere: and he was so withered
and yellow that, though he was not yet forty, the children
always called him "Old Master Marner."

Yet even in this stage of withering a little incident
happened, which showed that the sap of affection was
not all gone. It was one of his daily tasks to fetch his
water from a well a couple of fields off, and for this
purpose, ever since he came to Raveloe, he had had a
brown earthenware pot, which he held as his most
precious utensil, among the very few conveniences he had
granted himself. It had been his companion for twelve
years, always standing on the same spot, always lending
its handle to him in the early morning, so that its form
had an expression for him of willing helpfulness, and the
impress of its handle on his palm gave a satisfaction
mingled with that of having the fresh clear water. One
day as he was returning from the well, he stumbled
against the step of the stile, and his brown pot, falling
with force against the stones that overarched the ditch
below him, was broken in three pieces. Silas picked up
the pieces and carried them home with grief in his heart.
The brown pot could never be of use to him any more,
but he stuck the bits together and propped the ruin in
its old place for a memorial.

This is the history of Silas Marner until the fifteenth year after he came to Raveloe. The livelong day he sat in his loom, his ear filled with its monotony, his eyes bent close down on the slow growth of sameness in the brownish web, his muscles moving with such even repetition that their pause seemed almost as much a constraint as the holding of his breath. But at night came his revelry: at night he closed his shutters, and made fast his doors, and drew out his gold. Long ago the heap of coins had become too large for the iron pot to hold them, and he had made for them two thick leather bags, which wasted no room in their resting place, but lent themselves flexibly to every corner. How the guineas shone as they came pouring out of the dark leather mouths! The silver bore no large proportion in amount to the gold, because the long pieces of linen which formed his chief work were always partly paid for in gold, and out of the silver he supplied his own bodily wants, choosing always the shillings and sixpences to spend in this way. He loved the guineas best, but he would not change the silver—the crowns and half-crowns that were his own earnings, begotten by his labour; he loved them all. He spread them out in heaps and bathed his hands in them; then he counted them and set them up in regular piles, and felt their rounded outline between his thumb and fingers, and thought fondly of the guineas that were only half-earned by the work in his loom, as if they had been unborn children—thought of the guineas that were coming slowly through the coming years, through all his life, which spread far away before him, the end quite hidden by countless days of weaving. No wonder his thoughts were still with his loom and his money when he made his journeys through the fields and the lanes to fetch and carry home his work, so that his steps never wandered to the hedge banks and the lane side in search of the once familiar herbs: these too belonged to the past, from which his life had shrunk away, like a rivulet that has sunk far down from the grassy fringe of its old breadth into a little shivering thread, that cuts a groove for itself in the barren sand.

But about the Christmas of that fifteenth year, a second

great change came over Marner's life, and his history became blent in a singular manner with the life of his neighbours.

CHAPTER III

THE GREATEST MAN in Raveloe was Squire Cass, who lived in the large red house, with the handsome flight of stone steps in front and the high stables behind it, nearly opposite the church. He was only one among several landed parishioners, but he alone was honoured with the title of Squire; for though Mr. Osgood's family was also understood to be of timeless origin—the Raveloe imagination having never ventured back to that fearful blank when there were no Osgoods—still, he merely owned the farm he occupied; whereas Squire Cass had a tenant or two, who complained of the game to him quite as if he had been a lord.

It was still that glorious wartime which was felt to be a peculiar favour of Providence towards the landed interest, and the fall of prices had not yet come to carry the race of small squires and yeomen down that road to ruin for which extravagant habits and bad husbandry were plentifully anointing their wheels. I am speaking now in relation to Raveloe and the parishes that resembled it; for our old fashioned country life had many different aspects, as all life must have when it is spread over a various surface, and breathed on variously by multitudinous currents, from the winds of heaven to the thoughts of men, which are forever moving and crossing each other, with incalculable results. Raveloe lay low among the bushy trees and the rutted lanes, aloof from the currents of industrial energy and Puritan earnestness: the rich ate and drank freely, and accepted gout and apoplexy as things that ran mysteriously in respectable families, and the poor thought that the rich were entirely in the right of it to lead a jolly life; besides, their feasting caused a multiplication of orts, which were the heirlooms of the poor. Betty Jay scented the boiling of Squire Cass's hams, but her longing was arrested by the unctuous liquor in which they were boiled; and when the seasons brought round the great merrymakings, they were regarded on all hands as a fine thing for the poor. For the Raveloe feasts were like the rounds of beef and the barrels of ale—they were on a large scale, and lasted a good while, especially in the winter time. When ladies had packed up their best gowns and top knots in band boxes, and had incurred the risk of fording streams on pillions with the precious burden in rainy or snowy weather, when there was no knowing how high the water would rise, it was not to be supposed that they looked forward to a brief pleasure. On this ground it was always contrived in the dark seasons, when there was little work to be done, and the hours were long, that several neighbours should keep open house in succession. When Squire Cass's standing dishes diminished in plenty and freshness, his guests had nothing to do but to walk a little higher up the village to Mr. Osgood's, at the Orchards, and they found hams and chines uncut, pork pies with the scent of the fire in them, spun butter in all its freshness—everything, in fact, that appetites at leisure could desire, in perhaps greater perfection, though not in greater abundance, than at Squire Cass's.

For the Squire's wife had died long ago, and the Red House was without that presence of the wife and mother which is the fountain of wholesome love and fear in parlour and kitchen; and this helped to account not only for there being more profusion than finished excellence in the holiday provisions, but also for the frequency with which the proud Squire condescended to preside in the parlour of the Rainbow rather than under the shadow of his own dark wainscot; perhaps, also, for the fact that his sons had turned out rather ill. Raveloe was not a place where moral censure was severe, but it was thought a weakness in the Squire that he had kept all his sons at home in idleness; and though some licence was to be allowed to young men whose fathers could afford it, people shook their heads at the courses of the second son, Dunstan, commonly called Dunsey Cass, whose taste for swopping and betting might turn out to be a sowing of something worse than wild oats. To be sure, the neighbours said, it was no matter what became of Dunsey—a spiteful jeering fellow, who seemed to enjoy his drink

the more when other people went dry—always provided
that his doings did not bring trouble on a family like
Squire Cass's, with a monument in the church, and tankards older than King George. But it would be a thousand
pities if Mr. Godfrey, the eldest, a fine, open-faced, good-
natured young man, who was to come into the land some
day, should take to going along the same road as his
brother, as he had seemed to do of late. If he went on in
that way, he would lose Miss Nancy Lammeter, for it was
well known that she had looked very shyly on him ever
since last Whitsuntide twelvemonth, when there was so
much talk about his being away from home days and days
together. There was something wrong, more than common—that was quite clear; for Mr. Godfrey didn't look
half so fresh-coloured and open as he used to do. At one
time everybody was saying what a handsome couple he
and Miss Nancy Lammeter would make! and if she could
come to be mistress at the Red House, there would be a
fine change, for the Lammeters had been brought up in
that way, that they never suffered a pinch of salt to be
wasted, and yet everybody in their household had of the
best, according to his place. Such a daughter-in-law would
be a saving to the old Squire, if she never brought a penny
to her fortune, for it was to be feared that, notwithstanding his incomings, there were more holes in his pocket
than the one where he put his own hand in. But if Mr.
Godfrey didn't turn over a new leaf, he might say "Good-
bye" to Miss Nancy Lammeter.

It was the once hopeful Godfrey who was standing,
with his hands in his side pockets and his back to the fire,
in the dark wainscoted parlour, one late November afternoon, in that fifteenth year of Silas Marner's life at Raveloe. The fading grey light fell dimly on the walls decor-
ated with guns, whips, and foxes' brushes, on coats and
hats flung on the chairs, on tankards sending forth a
scent of flat ale, and on a half-choked fire, with pipes
propped up in the chimney corners: signs of a domestic
life destitute of any hallowing charm, with which the look
of gloomy vexation on Godfrey's blond face was in sad
accordance. He seemed to be waiting and listening for
someone's approach, and presently the sound of a heavy

step, with an accompanying whistle, was heard across the large, empty entrance hall.

The door opened, and a thickset, heavy-looking young man entered, with the flushed face and the gratuitously elated bearing, which mark the first stage of intoxication. It was Dunsey, and at the sight of him Godfrey's face parted with some of its gloom to take on the more active expression of hatred. The handsome brown spaniel that lay on the hearth retreated under the chair in the chimney corner.

"Well, Master Godfrey, what do you want with me?" said Dunsey, in a mocking tone. "You're my elders and betters, you know; I was obliged to come when you sent for me."

"Why, this is what I want—and just shake yourself sober and listen, will you?" said Godfrey, savagely. He had himself been drinking more than was good for him, trying to turn his gloom into uncalculating anger. "I want to tell you, I must hand over that rent of Fowler's to the Squire, or else tell him I gave it you; for he's threatening to distrain for it, and it'll all be out soon, whether I tell him or not. He said, just now, before he went out, he should send word to Cox to distrain, if Fowler didn't come and pay up his arrears this week. The Squire's short o' cash, and in no humour to stand any nonsense; and you know what he threatened, if ever he found you making away with his money again. So, see and get the money, and pretty quickly, will you?"

"Oh!" said Dunsey, sneeringly, coming nearer to his brother and looking in his face. "Suppose, now, you get the money yourself, and save me the trouble, eh? Since you was so kind as to hand it over to me, you'll not refuse me the kindness to pay it back for me: it was your brotherly love made you do it, you know."

Godfrey bit his lips and clenched his fist. "Don't come near me with that look, else I'll knock you down."

"Oh no, you won't," said Dunsey, turning away on his heel, however. "Because I'm such a good-natured brother, you know. I might get you turned out of house and home, and cut off with a shilling any day. I might tell the Squire how his handsome son was married to that nice young woman, Molly Farren, and was very unhappy because he

couldn't live with his drunken wife, and I should slip into
your place as comfortable as could be. But, you see, I
don't do it—I'm so easy and good-natured. You'll take any
trouble for me. You'll get the hundred pounds for me—
I know you will."

"How can I get the money?" said Godfrey, quivering.
"I haven't a shilling to bless myself with. And it's a lie
that you'd slip into my place: you'd get yourself turned
out too, that's all. For if you begin telling tales, I'll follow.
Bob's my father's favourite—you know that very well.
He'd only think himself well rid of you."

"Never mind," said Dunsey, nodding his head sideways
as he looked out of the window. "It 'ud be very pleasant
to me to go in your company—you're such a handsome
brother, and we've always been so fond of quarrelling
with one another, I shouldn't know what to do without
you. But you'd like better for us both to stay at home together; I know you would. So you'll manage to get that
little sum o' money, and I'll bid you good-bye, though I'm
sorry to part."

Dunstan was moving off, but Godfrey rushed after him
and seized him by the arm, saying, with an oath:

"I tell you, I have no money: I can get no money."

"Borrow of old Kimble."

"I tell you, he won't lend me any more, and I shan't
ask him."

"Well then, sell Wildfire."

"Yes, that's easy talking. I must have the money
directly."

"Well, you've only got to ride him to the hunt to-
morrow. There'll be Bryce and Keating there, for sure.
You'll get more bids than one."

"I daresay, and get back home at eight o'clock, splashed
up to the chin. I'm going to Mrs. Osgood's birthday
dance."

"Oho!" said Dunsey, turning his head on one side, and
trying to speak in a small mincing treble. "And there's
sweet Miss Nancy coming; and we shall dance with her,
and promise never to be naughty again, and be taken into
favour, and—"

"Hold your tongue about Miss Nancy, you fool," said
Godfrey, turning red, "else I'll throttle you."

"What for," said Dunsey, still in an artificial tone, but taking a whip from the table and beating the butt end of it on his palm. "You've a very good chance. I'd advise you to creep up her sleeve again: it 'ud be saving time if Molly should happen to take a drop too much laudanum someday, and make a widower of you. Miss Nancy wouldn't mind being a second, if she didn't know it. And you've got a good-natured brother, who'll keep your secret well, because you'll be so very obliging to him."

"I tell you what it is," said Godfrey, quivering, and pale again, "My patience is pretty near at an end. If you'd a little more sharpness in you, you might know that you may urge a man a bit too far, and make one leap as easy as another. I don't know but what it is so now: I may as well tell the Squire everything myself—I should get you off my back, if I got nothing else. And, after all, he'll know sometime. She's been threatening to come herself and tell him. So, don't flatter yourself that your secrecy's worth any price you choose to ask. You drain me of money till I've got nothing to pacify *her* with, and she'll do as she threatens some day. It's all one. I'll tell my father everything myself, and you may go to the devil."

Dunsey perceived that he had overshot his mark, and that there was a point at which even the hesitating Godfrey might be driven into decision. But he said, with an air of unconcern:

"As you please; but I'll have a draught of ale first." And ringing the bell, he threw himself across two chairs, and began to rap the window seat with the handle of his whip.

Godfrey stood, still with his back to the fire, uneasily moving his fingers among the contents of his side pockets, and looking at the floor. That big muscular frame of his held plenty of animal courage, but helped him to no decision when the dangers to be braved were such as could neither be knocked down nor throttled. His natural irresolution and moral cowardice were exaggerated by a position in which dreaded consequences seemed to press equally on all sides, and his irritation had no sooner provoked him to defy Dunstan and anticipate all possible betrayals, than the miseries he must bring on himself by such a step seemed more unendurable to him than the present evil. The results of confession were not contingent, they were certain; whereas betrayal was not certain. From the near vision of that certainty he fell back on suspense and vacillation with a sense of repose. The disinherited son of a small squire, equally disinclined to dig and to beg, was almost as helpless as an uprooted tree which, by the favour of earth and sky, has grown to a handsome bulk on the spot where it first shot upward. Perhaps it would have been possible to think of digging with some cheerfulness if Nancy Lammeter were to be won on those terms; but, since he must irrevocably lose *her* as well as the inheritance, and must break every tie but the one that degraded him and left him without motive for trying to recover his better self, he could imagine no future for himself on the other side of confession but that of "listing for a soldier"—the most desperate step, short of suicide, in the eyes of respectable families. No! he would rather trust to casualties than to his own resolve—rather go on sitting at the feast and sipping the wine he loved, though with the sword hanging over him and terror in his heart, than rush away into the cold darkness where there was no pleasure left. The utmost concession to Dunstan about the horse began to seem easy, compared with the fulfillment of his own threat. But his pride would not let him recommence the conversation otherwise than by continuing the quarrel. Dunstan was waiting for this, and took his ale in shorter draughts than usual.

"It's just like you," Godfrey burst out, in a bitter tone, "to talk about my selling Wildfire in that cool way—the last thing I've got to call my own, and the best bit of horseflesh I ever had in my life. And if you'd got a spark of pride in you, you'd be ashamed to see the stables emptied, and everybody sneering about it. But it's my belief you'd sell yourself, if it was only for the pleasure of making somebody feel he'd got a bad bargain."

"Ay, ay," said Dunstan, very placably, "you do me justice, I see. You know I'm a jewel for 'ticing people into bargains. For which reason I advise you to let *me* sell Wildfire. I'd ride him to the hunt tomorrow for you, with pleasure. I shouldn't look so handsome as you in the saddle, but it's the horse they'll bid for, and not the rider."

"Yes, I daresay—trust my horse to you!"

"As you please," said Dunstan, rapping the window seat again with an air of great unconcern. "It's *you* have got to pay Fowler's money; it's none of my business. You received the money from him when you went to Bramcote, and *you* told the Squire it wasn't paid. I'd nothing to do with that; you chose to be so obliging as give it me, that was all. If you don't want to pay the money, let it alone; it's all one to me. But I was willing to accommodate you by undertaking to sell the horse, seeing it's not convenient to you to go so far tomorrow."

Godfrey was silent for some moments. He would have liked to spring on Dunstan, wrench the whip from his hand, and flog him to within an inch of his life; and no bodily fear could have deterred him; but he was mastered by another sort of fear, which was fed by feelings stronger even than his resentment. When he spoke again it was in a half-conciliatory tone.

"Well, you mean no nonsense about the horse, eh? You'll sell him all fair, and hand over the money? If you don't, you know, everything'll go to smash, for I've got nothing else to trust to. And you'll have less pleasure in pulling the house over my head, when your own skull's to be broken too."

"Ay, ay," said Dunstan, rising, "all right. I thought you'd come round. I'm the fellow to bring old Bryce up to the scratch. I'll get you a hundred and twenty for him, if I get you a penny."

"But it'll perhaps rain cats and dogs tomorrow, as it did yesterday, and then you can't go," said Godfrey, hardly knowing whether he wished for that obstacle or not.

"Not *it*," said Dunstan. "I'm always lucky in my weather. It might rain if you wanted to go yourself. You never hold trumps, you know—I always do. You've got the beauty, you see, and I've got the luck, so you must keep me by you for your crooked sixpence; you'll *never* get along without me."

"Confound you, hold your tongue!" said Godfrey, impetuously. "And take care to keep sober tomorrow, else you'll get pitched on your head coming home, and Wildfire might be the worse for it."

"Make your tender heart easy," said Dunstan, opening the door. "You never knew me see double when I'd got

a bargain to make; it 'ud spoil the fun. Besides, whenever
I fall, I'm warranted to fall on my legs."

With that, Dunstan slammed the door behind him, and
left Godfrey to that bitter rumination on his personal
circumstances which was now unbroken from day to day
save by the excitement of sporting, drinking, card-play-
ing, or the rarer and less oblivious pleasure of seeing Miss
Nancy Lammeter. The subtle and varied pains springing
from the higher sensibility that accompanies higher culture are perhaps less pitiable than that dreary absence
of impersonal enjoyment and consolation which leaves
ruder minds to the perpetual urgent companionship of
their own griefs and discontents. The lives of those rural
forefathers, whom we are apt to think very prosaic
figures—men whose only work was to ride round their
land, getting heavier and heavier in their saddles, and
who passed the rest of their days in the half-listless gratification of senses dulled by monotony—had a certain
pathos in them nevertheless. Calamities came to *them*
too, and their early errors carried hard consequences:
perhaps the love of some sweet maiden, the image of
purity, order, and calm, had opened their eyes to the
vision of a life in which the days would not seem too long,
even without rioting; but the maiden was lost, and the
vision passed away, and then what was left to them, especially when they had become too heavy for the hunt, or
for carrying a gun over the furrows, but to drink and get
merry, or to drink and get angry, so that they might be
independent of variety, and say over again with eager
emphasis the things they had said already any time that
twelvemonth? Assuredly, among those flushed and dull-
eyed men there were some whom—thanks to their native
human kindness—even riot could never drive into brutality; men who, when their cheeks were fresh, had felt
the keen point of sorrow or remorse, had been pierced
by the reeds they leaned on, or had lightly put their limbs
in fetters from which no struggle could loose them, and
under these sad circumstances, common to us all, their
thoughts could find no resting place outside the ever-
trodden round of their own petty history.

That, at least, was the condition of Godfrey Cass in this
six-and-twentieth year of his life. A movement of com-

punction, helped by those small indefinable influences which every personal relation exerts on a pliant nature, had urged him into a secret marriage, which was a blight on his life. It was an ugly story of low passion, delusion, and waking from delusion, which needs not to be dragged from the privacy of Godfrey's bitter memory. He had long known that the delusion was partly due to a trap laid for him by Dunstan, who saw in his brother's degrading marriage the means of gratifying at once his jealous hate and his cupidity. And if Godfrey could have felt himself simply a victim, the iron bit that destiny had put into his mouth would have chafed him less intolerably. If the curses he muttered half aloud when he was alone had had no other object than Dunstan's diabolical cunning, he might have shrunk less from the consequences of avowal. But he had something else to curse—his own vicious folly, which now seemed as mad and unaccountable to him as almost all our follies and vices do when their promptings have long passed away. For four years he had thought of Nancy Lammeter, and wooed her with tacit patient worship, as the woman who made him think of the future with joy: she would be his wife, and would make home lovely to him, as his father's home had never been; and it would be easy, when she was always near, to shake off those foolish habits that were no pleasures, but only a feverish way of annulling vacancy. Godfrey's was an essentially domestic nature, bred up in a home where the hearth had no smiles, and where the daily habits were not chastised by the presence of household order; his easy disposition made him fall in unresistingly with the family courses, but the need of some tender permanent affection, the longing for some influence that would make the good he preferred easy to pursue, caused the neatness, purity, and liberal orderliness of the Lammeter household, sunned by the smile of Nancy, to seem like those fresh, bright hours of the morning, when temptations go to sleep, and leave the ear open to the voice of the good angel, inviting to industry, sobriety, and peace. And yet the hope of this paradise had not been enough to save him from a course which shut him out of it forever. Instead of keeping fast hold of the strong silken rope by which Nancy would have drawn him safe to the green banks, where it was easy to step firmly, he had let himself be dragged back into mud and slime, in which it was useless to struggle. He had made ties for himself which robbed him of all wholesome motive, and were a constant exasperation.

Still, there was one position worse than the present: it was the position he would be in when the ugly secret was disclosed; and the desire that continually triumphed over every other was that of warding off the evil day when he would have to bear the consequences of his father's violent resentment for the wound inflicted on his family pride—would have, perhaps, to turn his back on that hereditary ease and dignity which, after all, was a sort of reason for living, and would carry with him the certainty that he was banished forever from the sight and esteem of Nancy Lammeter. The longer the interval, the more chance there was of deliverance from some, at least, of the hateful consequences to which he had sold himself— the more opportunities remained for him to snatch the strange gratification of seeing Nancy, and gathering some faint indications of her lingering regard. Towards this gratification he was impelled, fitfully, every now and then, after having passsed weeks in which he had avoided her as the far-off, bright-winged prize, that only made him spring forward, and find his chain all the more galling. One of those fits of yearning was on him now, and it would have been strong enough to have persuaded him to trust Wildfire to Dunstan rather than disappoint the yearning, even if he had not had another reason for his disinclination towards the morrow's hunt. That other reason was the fact that the morning's meet was near Batherley, the market town where the unhappy woman lived whose image became more odious to him every day; and to his thought the whole vicinage was haunted by her. The yoke a man creates for himself by wrongdoing will breed hate in the kindliest nature; and the good-humoured, affectionate-hearted Godfrey Cass was fast becoming a bitter man, visited by cruel wishes, that seemed to enter, and depart, and enter again, like demons who had found in him a ready-garnished home.

What was he to do this evening to pass the time? He might as well go to the Rainbow, and hear the talk about the cockfighting: everybody was there, and what else was there to be done? Though, for his own part, he did not care a button for cockfighting. Snuff, the brown spaniel, who had placed herself in front of him, and had been watching him for some time, now jumped up in impatience for the expected caress. But Godfrey thrust her away without looking at her, and left the room, followed humbly by the unresenting Snuff—perhaps because she saw no other career open to her.

CHAPTER IV

DUNSTAN CASS, setting off in the raw morning, at the judiciously quiet pace of a man who is obliged to ride to cover on his hunter, had to take his way along the lane which, at its farther extremity, passed by the piece of unenclosed ground called the Stone Pit, where stood the cottage, once a stonecutter's shed, now for fifteen years inhabited by Silas Marner. The spot looked very dreary at this season, with the moist trodden clay about it, and the red, muddy water high up in the deserted quarry. That was Dunstan's first thought as he approached it; the second was that the old fool of a weaver, whose loom he heard rattling already, had a great deal of money hidden somewhere. How was it that he, Dunstan Cass, who had often heard talk of Marner's miserliness, had never thought of suggesting to Godfrey that he should frighten or persuade the old fellow into lending the money on the excellent security of the young Squire's prospects? The resource occurred to him now as so easy and agreeable, especially as Marner's hoard was likely to be large enough to leave Godfrey a handsome surplus beyond his immediate needs, and enable him to accommodate his faithful brother, that he had almost turned the horse's head towards home again. Godfrey would be ready enough to accept the suggestion: he would snatch eagerly at a plan that might save him from parting with Wildfire. But when Dunstan's meditation reached this point, the inclination to go on grew strong and prevailed. He didn't want to give Godfrey that pleasure: he preferred that Master Godfrey should be vexed. Moreover, Dunstan enjoyed the self-important consciousness of having a horse to sell, and the opportunity of driving a bargain, swaggering, and, possibly, taking somebody in. He might have all the satisfaction attendant on selling his brother's horse, and not the less have the further satisfaction of setting Godfrey to borrow Marner's money. So he rode on to cover.

Bryce and Keating were there, as Dunstan was quite sure they would be—he was such a lucky fellow.

"Heyday!" said Bryce, who had long had his eye on Wildfire, "you're on your brother's horse today: how's that?"

"Oh, I've swapped with him," said Dunstan, whose delight in lying, grandly independent of utility, was not to be diminished by the likelihood that his hearer would not believe him. "Wildfire's mine now."

"What! has he swapped with you for that big-boned hack of yours?" said Bryce, quite aware that he should get another lie in answer.

"Oh, there was a little account between us," said Dunsey, carelessly, "and Wildfire made it even. I accommodated him by taking the horse, though it was against my will, for I'd got an itch for a mare o' Jortin's—as rare a bit o'blood as ever you threw your leg across. But I shall keep Wildfire, now I've got him; though I'd a bid of a hundred and fifty for him the other day, from a man over at Flitton—he's buying for Lord Cromleck—a fellow with a cast in his eye, and a green waistcoat. But I mean to stick to Wildfire: I shan't get a better at a fence in a hurry. The mare's got more blood, but she's a bit too weak in the hind quarters."

Bryce of course divined that Dunstan wanted to sell the horse, and Dunstan knew that he divined it (horse-dealing is only one of many human transactions carried on in this ingenious manner) ; and they both considered that the bargain was in its first stage, when Bryce replied ironically:

"I wonder at that now; I wonder you mean to keep him; for I never heard of a man who didn't want to sell his horse getting a bid of half as much again as the horse was worth. You'll be lucky if you get a hundred."

Keating rode up now, and the transaction became

more complicated. It ended in the purchase of the horse
by Bryce for a hundred and twenty, to be paid on the
delivery of Wildfire, safe and sound, at the Batherley
stables. It did occur to Dunsey that it might be wise for
him to give up the day's hunting, proceed at once to
Batherley, and, having waited for Bryce's return, hire a
horse to carry him home with the money in his pocket.
But the inclination for a run, encouraged by confidence
in his luck, and by a draught of brandy from his pocket
pistol at the conclusion of the bargain, was not easy to
overcome, especially with a horse under him that would
take the fences to the admiration of the field. Dunstan,
however, took one fence too many, and "staked" his horse.
His own ill-favoured person, which was quite unmarket-
able, escaped without injury, but poor Wildfire, unconscious of his price, turned on his flank, and painfully
panted his last. It happened that Dunstan, a short time
before, having had to get down to arrange his stirrup, had
muttered a good many curses at this interruption, which
had thrown him in the rear of the hunt near the moment
of glory, and under this exasperation had taken the fences
more blindly. He would soon have been up with the
hounds again, when the fatal accident happened; and
hence he was between eager riders in advance, not
troubling themselves about what happened behind them,
and far-off stragglers, who were as likely as not to pass
quite aloof from the line of road in which Wildfire had
fallen. Dunstan, whose nature it was to care more for
immediate annoyances than for remote consequences, no
sooner recovered his legs, and saw that it was all over
with Wildfire, than he felt a satisfaction at the absence
of witnesses to a position which no swaggering could
make enviable. Reinforcing himself, after his shake, with
a little brandy and much swearing, he walked as fast as
he could to a coppice on his right hand, through which
it occurred to him that he could make his way to Batherley without danger of encountering any member of the
hunt. His first intention was to hire a horse there and
ride home forthwith, for to walk many miles without a
gun in his hand, and along an ordinary road, was as
much out of the question to him as to other spirited
young men of his kind. He did not much mind about

taking the bad news to Godfrey, for he had to offer him
at the same time the resource of Marner's money; and
if Godfrey kicked, as he always did, at the notion of
making a fresh debt, from which he himself got the smallest share of advantage, why, he wouldn't kick long:
Dunstan felt sure he could worry Godfrey into anything.
The idea of Marner's money kept growing in vividness,
now the want of it had become immediate; the prospect
of having to make his appearance with the muddy boots
of a pedestrian at Batherley, and encounter the grinning
queries of stablemen, stood unpleasantly in the way of
his impatience to be back at Raveloe and carry out his
felicitous plan; and a casual visitation of his waistcoat
pocket, as he was ruminating, awakened his memory to
the fact that the two or three small coins his forefinger encountered there were of too pale a colour to cover that
small debt, without payment of which Jennings had
declared he would never do any more business with
Dunsey Cass. After all, according to the direction in
which the run had brought him, he was not so very much
farther from home than he was from Batherley; but
Dunsey, not being remarkable for clearness of head, was
only led to this conclusion by the gradual perception that
there were other reasons for choosing the unprecedented
course of walking home. It was now nearly four o'clock,
and a mist was gathering: the sooner he got into the road
the better. He remembered having crossed the road and
seen the finger post only a little while before Wildfire
broke down; so, buttoning his coat, twisting the lash of
his hunting whip compactly round the handle, and rapping the tops of his boots with a self-possessed air, as if
to assure himself that he was not at all taken by surprise,
he set off with the sense that he was undertaking a remarkable feat of bodily exertion, which somehow, and at
some time, he should be able to dress up and magnify to
the admiration of a select circle at the Rainbow. When
a young gentleman like Dunsey is reduced to so exceptional a mode of locomotion as walking, a whip in his
hand is a desirable corrective to a too bewildering dreamy
sense of unwontedness in his position; and Dunstan, as
he went along through the gathering mist, was always
rapping his whip somewhere. It was Godfrey's whip,

which he had chosen to take without leave because it had a gold handle; of course no one could see, when Dunstan held it, that the name *Godfrey Cass* was cut in deep letters on that gold handle—they could only see that it was a very handsome whip. Dunsey was not without fear that he might meet some acquaintance in whose eyes he would cut a pitiable figure, for mist is no screen when people get close to each other; but when he at last found himself in the well-known Raveloe lanes without having met a soul, he silently remarked that that was part of his usual good luck. But now the mist, helped by the evening darkness, was more of a screen than he desired, for it hid the ruts into which his feet were liable to slip—hid everything, so that he had to guide his steps by dragging his whip along the low bushes in advance of the hedgerow. He must soon, he thought, be getting near the opening at the Stone Pits: he should find it out by the break in the hedgerow. He found it out, however, by another circumstance which he had not expected— namely, by certain gleams of light, which he presently guessed to proceed from Silas Marner's cottage. That cottage and the money hidden within it had been in his mind continually during his walk, and he had been imagining ways of cajoling and tempting the weaver to part with the immediate possession of his money for the sake of receiving interest. Dunstan felt as if there must be a little frightening added to the cajolery, for his own arithmetical convictions were not clear enough to afford him any forcible demonstration as to the advantages of interest; and as for security, he regarded it vaguely as the means of cheating a man, by making him believe that he would be paid. Altogether, the operation on the miser's mind was a task that Godfrey would be sure to hand over to his more daring and cunning brother: Dunstan had made up his mind to that; and by the time he saw the light gleaming through the chinks of Marner's shutters, the idea of a dialogue with the weaver had be- come so familiar to him that it occurred to him as quite a natural thing to make the acquaintance forthwith. There might be several conveniences attending this course: the weaver had possibly got a lantern, and Dunstan was tired of feeling his way. He was still nearly three-quarters of a mile from home, and the lane was becoming unpleasantly slippery, for the mist was passing into rain. He turned up the bank, not without some fear lest he might miss the right way, since he was not certain whether the light were in front or on the side of the cottage. But he felt the ground before him cautiously with his whip handle, and at last arrived safely at the door. He knocked loudly, rather enjoying the idea that the old fellow would be frightened at the sudden noise. He heard no movement in reply: all was silence in the cottage. Was the weaver gone to bed, then? If so, why had he left a light? That was a strange forgetfulness in a miser. Dunstan knocked still more loudly, and, without pausing for a reply, pushed his fingers through the latch hole, intending to shake the door and pull the latch-string up and down, not doubting that the door was fastened. But, to his surprise, at this double motion the door opened, and he found himself in front of a bright fire, which lit up every corner of the cottage—the bed, the loom, the three chairs, and the table—and showed him that Marner was not there.

Nothing at that moment could be much more inviting to Dunsey than the bright fire on the brick hearth: he walked in and seated himself by it at once. There was something in front of the fire, too, that would have been inviting to a hungry man, if it had been in a different stage of cooking. It was a small bit of pork suspended from the kettle hanger by a string passed through a large door key, in a way known to primitive housekeepers unpossessed of jacks. But the pork had been hung at the farthest extremity of the hanger, apparently to prevent the roasting from proceeding too rapidly during the owner's absence. The old staring simpleton had hot meat for his supper, then? thought Dunstan. People had always said he lived on mouldy bread, on purpose to check his appetite. But where could he be at this time, and on such an evening, leaving his supper in this stage of preparation, and his door unfastened? Dunstan's own recent difficulty in making his way suggested to him that the weaver had perhaps gone outside his cottage to fetch in fuel, or for some such brief purpose, and had slipped into the Stone Pit. That was an interesting idea to Dunstan, carrying consequences of entire novelty. If the weaver was dead, who had a right to his money? Who would know where his money was hidden? *Who would know that anybody had come to take it away?* He went no farther into the subtleties of evidence: the pressing question, "Where *is* the money?" now took such entire possession of him as to make him quite forget that the weaver's death was not a certainty. A dull mind, once arriving at an inference that flatters a desire, is rarely able to retain the impression that the notion from which the inference started was purely problematic. And Dunstan's mind was as dull as the mind of a possible felon usually is. There were only three hiding places where he had ever heard of cottagers' hoards being found: the thatch, the bed, and a hole in the floor. Marner's cottage had no thatch; and Dunstan's first act, after a train of thought made rapid by the stimulus of cupidity, was to go up to the bed; but while he did so, his eyes travelled eagerly over the floor, where the bricks, distinct in the firelight, were discernible under the sprinkling of sand. But not everywhere; for there was one spot, and one only, which was quite covered with sand, and sand showing the marks of fingers which had apparently been careful to spread it over a given space. It was near the treddles of the loom. In an instant Dunstan darted to that spot, swept away the sand with his whip, and, inserting the thin end of the hook between the bricks, found that they were loose. In haste he lifted up two bricks, and saw what he had no doubt was the object of his search; for what could there be but money in those two leathern bags? And, from their weight, they must be filled with guineas. Dunstan felt round the hole, to be certain that it held no more; then hastily replaced the bricks, and spread the sand over them. Hardly more than five minutes had passed since he entered the cottage, but it seemed to Dunstan like a long while; and though he was without any distinct recognition of the possibility that Marner might be alive, and might re-enter the cottage at any moment, he felt an undefinable dread laying hold on him, as he rose to his feet with the bags in his hand. He would hasten out into the darkness, and then consider what he should do with the bags. He closed the door behind him immediately, that he might shut in the

stream of light: a few steps would be enough to carry him
beyond betrayal by the gleams from the shutter chinks
and the latch hole. The rain and darkness had got thick-
er, and he was glad of it; though it was awkward walking
with both hands filled, so that it was as much as he could
do to grasp his whip along with one of the bags. But when
he had gone a yard or two, he might take his time. So he
stepped forward into the darkness.

CHAPTER V

WHEN DUNSTAN CASS turned his back on the cottage,
Silas Marner was not more than a hundred yards away
from it, plodding along from the village with a sack
thrown round his shoulders as an overcoat, and with a
horn lantern in his hand. His legs were weary, but his
mind was at ease, free from the presentiment of change.
The sense of security more frequently springs from habit
than from conviction, and for this reason it often subsists
after such a change in the conditions as might have been
expected to suggest alarm. The lapse of time during
which a given event has not happened is, in this logic
of habit, constantly alleged as a reason why the event
should never happen, even when the lapse of time is
precisely the added condition which makes the event imminent. A man will tell you that he has worked in a mine
for forty years unhurt by an accident, as a reason why he
should apprehend no danger, though the roof is beginning to sink; and it is often observable that the older a
man gets, the more difficult it is to him to retain a believing conception of his own death. This influence of habit
was necessarily strong in a man whose life was so monotonous as Marner's—who saw no new people and heard
of no new events to keep alive in him the idea of the unexpected and the changeful; and it explains, simply
enough, why his mind could be at ease, though he had
left his house and his treasure more defenceless than
usual. Silas was thinking with double complacency of his
supper: first, because it would be hot and savoury; and
secondly, because it would cost him nothing. For the little

bit of pork was a present from that excellent housewife, Miss Priscilla Lammeter, to whom he had this day carried home a handsome piece of linen; and it was only on occasion of a present like this, that Silas indulged himself with roast meat. Supper was his favourite meal, because it came at his time of revelry, when his heart warmed over his gold; whenever he had roast meat, he always chose to have it for supper. But this evening, he had no sooner ingeniously knotted his string fast round his bit of pork, twisted the string according to rule over his door key, passed it throught the handle, and made it fast on the hanger, than he remembered that a piece of very fine twine was indispensable to his "setting up" a new piece of work in his loom early in the morning. It had slipped his memory, because, in coming from Mr. Lammeter's, he had not to pass through the village; but to lose time by going on errands in the morning was out of the question. It was a nasty fog to turn out into, but there were things Silas loved better than his own comfort; so, drawing his pork to the extremity of the hanger, and arming himself with his lantern and his old sack, he set out on what, in ordinary weather, would have been a twenty minutes' errand. He could not have locked his door without undoing his well-knotted string and retarding his supper; it was not worth his while to make that sacrifice. What thief would find his way to the Stone Pits on such a night as this? and why should he come on this particular night, when he had never come through all the fifteen years before? These questions were not distinctly present in Silas's mind; they merely serve to represent the vaguely felt foundation of his freedom from anxiety.

He reached his door in much satisfaction that his errand was done: he opened it, and to his shortsighted eyes everything remained as he left it, except that the fire sent out a welcome increase of heat. He trod about the floor while putting by his lantern and throwing aside his hat and sack, so as to merge the marks of Dunstan's feet on the sand in the marks of his own nailed boots. Then he moved his pork nearer to the fire, and sat down to the agreeable business of tending the meat and warming himself at the same time.

Anyone who had looked at him as the red light shone

upon his pale face, strange straining eyes, and meagre
form would perhaps have understood the mixture of contemptuous pity, dread, and suspicion with which he was
regarded by his neighbours in Raveloe. Yet few men
could be more harmless than poor Marner. In his truthful, simple soul, not even the growing greed and worship
of gold could beget any vice directly injurious to others.
The light of his faith quite put out, and his affections
made desolate, he had clung with all the force of his
nature to his work and his money; and like all objects to
which a man devotes himself, they had fashioned him
into correspondence with themselves. His loom, as he
wrought in it without ceasing, had in its turn wrought on
him, and confirmed more and more the monotonous craving for its monotonous response. His gold, as he hung
over it and saw it grow, gathered his power of loving together into a hard isolation like its own.

As soon as he was warm he began to think it would be
a long while to wait till after supper before he drew out
his guineas, and it would be pleasant to see them on the
table before him as he ate his unwonted feast. For joy is
the best of wine, and Silas's guineas were golden wine of
that sort.

He rose and placed his candle unsuspectingly on the
floor near his loom, swept away the sand without noticing
any change, and removed the bricks. The sight of the
empty hole made his heart leap violently, but the belief
that his gold was gone could not come at once—only
terror, and the eager effort to put an end to the terror. He
passed his trembling hand all about the hole, trying to
think it possible that his eyes had deceived him; then he
held the candle in the hole and examined it curiously,
trembling more and more. At last he shook so violently
that he let fall the candle, and lifted his hands to his
head, trying to steady himself, that he might think. Had
he put his gold somewhere else, by a sudden resolution
last night, and then forgotten it? A man falling into dark
water seeks a momentary footing even on sliding stones;
and Silas, by acting as if he believed in false hopes,
warded off the moment of despair. He searched in every
corner, he turned his bed over, and shook it, and kneaded
it; he looked in his brick oven where he laid his sticks.

When there was no other place to be searched, he kneeled down again and felt once more all round the hole. There was no untried refuge left for a moment's shelter from the terrible truth.

Yes, there was a sort of refuge which always comes with the prostration of thought under an overpowering passion: it was that expectation of impossibilities, that belief in contradictory images, which is still distinct from madness, because it is capable of being dissipated by the external fact. Silas got up from his knees trembling, and looked round at the table: didn't the gold lie there after all? The table was bare. Then he turned and looked behind him—looked all round his dwelling, seeming to strain his brown eyes after some possible appearance of the bags where he had already sought them in vain. He could see every object in his cottage—and his gold was not there.

Again he put his trembling hands to his head, and gave a wild wringing scream, the cry of desolation. For a few moments after, he stood motionless; but the cry had relieved him from the first maddening pressure of the truth. He turned, and tottered towards his loom, and got into the seat where he worked, instinctively seeking this as the strongest assurance of reality.

And now that all the false hopes had vanished, and the first shock of certainty was past, the idea of a thief began to present itself, and he entertained it eagerly, because a thief might be caught and made to restore the gold. The thought brought some new strength with it, and he started from his loom to the door. As he opened it the rain beat in upon him, for it was falling more and more heavily. There were no footsteps to be tracked on such a night—footsteps? When had the thief come? During Silas' absence in the daytime the door had been locked, and there had been no marks of any inroad on his return by daylight. And in the evening, too, he said to himself, everything was the same as when he had left it. The sand and bricks looked as if they had not been moved. *Was* it a thief who had taken the bags? or was it a cruel power that no hands could reach, which had delighted in making him a second time desolate? He shrank from this vaguer dread, and fixed his mind with struggling effort on the robber with hands, who could be reached by hands. His thoughts glanced at all the neighbours who had made any remarks, or asked any questions which he might now regard as a ground of suspicion. There was Jem Rodney, a known poacher and otherwise disreputable: he had often met Marner in his journeys across the fields, and had said something jestingly about the weaver's money; nay, he had once irritated Marner, by lingering at the fire when he called to light his pipe, instead of going about his business. Jem Rodney was the man—there was ease in the thought. Jem could be found and made to restore the money: Marner did not want to punish him, but only to get back his gold which had gone from him, and left his soul like a forlorn traveller on an unknown desert. The robber must be laid hold of. Marner's ideas of legal authority were confused, but he felt that he must go and proclaim his loss; and the great people in the village—the clergyman, the constable, and Squire Cass—would make Jem Rodney, or somebody else, deliver up the stolen money. He rushed out in the rain, under the stimulus of this hope, forgetting to cover his head, not caring to fasten his door; for he felt as if he had nothing left to lose. He ran swiftly till want of breath compelled him to slacken his pace as he was entering the village at the turning close to the Rainbow.

The Rainbow, in Marner's view, was a place of luxurious resort for rich and stout husbands, whose wives had superfluous stores of linen; it was the place where he was likely to find the powers and dignities of Raveloe, and where he could most speedily make his loss public. He lifted the latch, and turned into the bright bar or kitchen on the right hand, where the less lofty customers of the house were in the habit of assembling, the parlour on the left being reserved for the more select society in which Squire Cass frequently enjoyed the double pleasure of conviviality and condescension. But the parlour was dark tonight, the chief personages who ornamented its circle being all at Mrs. Osgood's birthday dance, as Godfrey Cass was. And in consequence of this, the party on the high-screened seats in the kitchen was more numerous than usual; several personages, who would otherwise have been admitted into the parlour and enlarged the opportunity of hectoring and condescension for their betters, being content this evening to vary their enjoyment by taking their spirits-and-water where they could themselves hector and condescend in company that called for beer.

CHAPTER VI

THE CONVERSATION, which was at a high pitch of animation when Silas approached the door of the Rainbow, had, as usual, been slow and intermittent when the company first assembled. The pipes began to be puffed in a silence which had an air of severity; the more important customers, who drank spirits and sat nearest the fire, staring at each other as if a bet were depending on the first man who winked; while the beer drinkers, chiefly men in fustian jackets and smock frocks, kept their eyelids down and rubbed their hands across their mouths, as if their draughts of beer were a funereal duty attended with embarrassing sadness. At last, Mr. Snell, the landlord, a man of a neutral disposition, accustomed to stand aloof from human differences as those of beings who were all alike in need of liquor, broke silence, by saying in a doubtful tone to his cousin the butcher:

"Some folks 'ud say that was a fine beast you druv in yesterday, Bob."

The butcher, a jolly, smiling, red-haired man, was not disposed to answer rashly. He gave a few puffs before he spat and replied, "And they wouldn't be fur wrong, John."

After this feeble delusive thaw, the silence set in as severely as before.

"Was it a red Durham?" said the farrier, taking up the thread of discourse after the lapse of a few minutes.

The farrier looked at the landlord, and the landlord looked at the butcher, as the person who must take the responsibility of answering.

"Red it was," said the butcher, in his good-humoured husky treble, "and a Durham it was."

"Then you needn't tell *me* who you bought it of," said

the farrier, looking round with some triumph; "I know
who it is has got the red Durhams o' this countryside.
And she'd a white star on her brow, I'll bet a penny?"
The farrier leaned forward with his hands on his knees
as he put this question, and his eyes twinkled knowingly.

"Well; yes—she might," said the butcher slowly, considering that he was giving a decided affirmative. "I don't
say contrairy."

"I knew that very well," said the farrier, throwing himself backward again, and speaking defiantly; "if *I* don't
know Mr. Lammeter's cows, I should like to know who
does—that's all. And as for the cow you've bought, bargain or no bargain, I've been at the drenching of her—
contradick me who will."

The farrier looked fierce, and the mild butcher's con-
versational spirit was roused a little.

"I'm not for contradicking no man," he said; "I'm for
peace and quietness. Some are for cutting long ribs—I'm
for cutting 'em short, myself; but *I* don't quarrel with
'em. All I say is, it's a lovely carkiss—and anybody as was
reasonable, it 'ud bring tears into their eyes to look
at it."

"Well, it's the cow as I drenched, whatever it is," pursued the farrier angrily; "and it was Mr. Lammeter's cow,
else you told a lie when you said it was a red Durham."

"I tell no lies," said the butcher, with the same mild
huskiness as before, "and I contradick none—not if a man
was to swear himself black: he's no meat o' mine, nor
none o' my bargains. All I say is, it's a lovely carkiss. And
what I say, I'll stick to; but I'll quarrel wi' no man."

"No," said the farrier, with bitter sarcasm, looking at
the company generally; "and p'rhaps you aren't pig-
headed; and p'rhaps you didn't say the cow was a red
Durham; and p'rhaps you didn't say she'd got a star on
her brow—stick to that, now you're at it."

"Come, come," said the landlord; "let the cow alone.
The truth lies atween you: you're both right and both
wrong, as I allays say. And as for the cow's being Mr.
Lammeter's, I say nothing to that; but this I say, as the
Rainbow's the Rainbow. And for the matter o' that, if
the talk is to be o' the Lammeters, *you* know the most
upo' that head, eh, Mr. Macey? You remember when first

Mr. Lammeter's father come into these parts, and took the Warrens?"

Mr. Macey, tailor and parish clerk, the latter of which functions rheumatism had of late obliged him to share with a small-featured young man who sat opposite him, held his white head on one side, and twirled his thumbs with an air of complacency, slightly seasoned with criticism. He smiled pityingly, in answer to the landlord's appeal, and said:

"Ay, ay; I know, I know; but I let other folks talk. I've laid by now, and gev up to the young uns. Ask them as have been to school at Tarley: they've learnt pernouncing; that's come up since my day."

"If you're pointing at me, Mr. Macey," said the deputy clerk, with an air of anxious propriety, "I'm nowise a man to speak out of my place. As the psalm says:

'I know what's right, nor only so,
But also practise what I know.' "

"Well, then, I wish you'd keep hold o' the tune when it's set for you; if you're for prac*tis*ing, I wish you'd prac*tise* that," said a large, jocose-looking man, an excellent wheelwright in his weekday capacity, but on Sundays leader of the choir. He winked, as he spoke, at two of the company, who were known officially as the "bassoon" and the "key bugle," in the confidence that he was expressing the sense of the musical profession in Raveloe.

Mr. Tookey, the deputy clerk, who shared the unpopularity common to deputies, turned very red, but replied, with careful moderation, "Mr. Winthrop, if you'll bring me any proof as I'm in the wrong, I'm not the man to say I won't alter. But there's people set up their own ears for a standard, and expect the whole choir to follow 'em. There may be two opinions, I hope."

"Ay, ay," said Mr. Macey, who felt very well satisfied with this attack on youthful presumption; "you're right there, Tookey: there's allays two 'pinions; there's the 'pinion a man has of himsen, and there's the 'pinion other folks have on him. There'd be two 'pinions about a cracked bell, if the bell could hear itself."

"Well, Mr. Macey," said poor Tookey, serious amidst

the general laughter, "I undertook to partially fill up the office of parish clerk by Mr. Crackenthorp's desire, whenever your infirmities should make you unfitting; and it's one of the rights thereof to sing in the choir—else why have you done the same yourself?"

"Ah! but the old gentleman and you are two folks," said Ben Winthrop. "The old gentleman's got a gift. Why, the Squire used to invite him to take a glass, only to hear him sing the 'Red Rovier'; didn't he, Mr. Macey? It's a natural gift. There's my little lad Aaron, he's got a gift—he can sing a tune off straight, like a throstle. But as for you, Master Tookey, you'd better stick to your 'Amens': your voice is well enough when you keep it up in your nose. It's your inside as isn't right made for music: it's no better nor a hollow stalk."

This kind of unflinching frankness was the most piquant form of joke to the company at the Rainbow, and Ben Winthrop's insult was felt by everybody to have capped Mr. Macey's epigram.

"I see what it is plain enough," said Mr. Tookey, unable to keep cool any longer. "There's a consperacy to turn me out o' the choir, as I shouldn't share the Christmas money—that's where it is. But I shall speak to Mr. Crackenthorp; I'll not be put upon by no man."

"Nay, nay, Tookey," said Ben Winthrop. "We'll pay you your share to keep out of it—that's what we'll do. There's things folk 'ud pay to be rid on, besides varmin."

"Come, come," said the landlord, who felt that paying people for their absence was a principle dangerous to society; "a joke's a joke. We're all good friends here, I hope. We must give and take. You're both right and you're both wrong, as I say. I agree wi' Mr. Macey here, as there's two opinions; and if mine was asked, I should say they're both right. Tookey's right and Winthrop's right, and they've only got to split the difference and make themselves even."

The farrier was puffing his pipe rather fiercely, in some contempt at this trivial discussion. He had no ear for music himself, and never went to church, as being of the medical profession, and likely to be in requisition for delicate cows. But the butcher, having music in his soul, had listened with a divided desire for Tookey's defeat, and for the preservation of the peace.

"To be sure," he said, following up the landlord's conciliatory view, "we're fond of our old clerk; it's nat'ral, and him used to be such a singer, and got a brother as is known for the first fiddler in this countryside. Eh, it's a pity but what Solomon lived in our village, and could give us a tune when we liked; eh, Mr. Macey? I'd keep him in liver and lights for nothing—that I would."

"Ay, ay," said Mr. Macey, in the height of complacency; "our family's been known for musicianers as far back as anybody can tell. But them things are dying out, as I tell Solomon every time he comes round; there's no voices like what there used to be, and there's nobody remembers what we remember, if it isn't the old crows."

"Ay, you remember when first Mr. Lammeter's father came into these parts, don't you, Mr. Macey?" said the landlord.

"I should think I did," said the old man, who had now gone through that complimentary process necessary to bring him up to the point of narration; "and a fine old gentleman he was—as fine, and finer, nor the Mr. Lammeter as now is. He came from a bit north'ard, so far as I could ever make out. But there's nobody rightly knows about those parts: only it couldn't be far north'ard, nor much different from this country, for he brought a fine breed o' sheep with him, so there must be pastures there, and everything reasonable. We heard tell as he'd sold his own land to come and take the Warrens', and that seemed odd for a man as had land of his own, to come and rent a farm in a strange place. But they said it was along of his wife's dying; though there's reasons in things as nobody knows on—that's pretty much what I've made out; though some folks are so wise, they'll find you fifty reasons straight off, and all the while the real reason's winking at 'em in the corner, and they niver see't. Howsomever, it was soon seen as we'd got a new parish'ner as know'd the rights and customs o' things, and kep a good house, and was well looked on by everybody. And the young man—that's the Mr. Lammeter as now is, for he'd niver a sister—soon begun to court Miss Osgood, that's the sister o' the Mr. Osgood as now is, and a fine hand-

some lass she was—eh, you can't think—they pretend this
young lass is like her, but that's the way wi' people as
don't know what come before 'em. *I* should know, for I
helped the old rector, Mr. Drumlow as was, I helped him
marry 'em."

Here Mr. Macey paused; he always gave his narrative
in instalments, expecting to be questioned according to
precedent.

"Ay, and a partic'lar thing happened, didn't it, Mr.
Macey, so as you were likely to remember that marriage?"
said the landlord, in a congratulatory tone.

"I should think there did—a *very* partic'lar thing," said
Mr. Macey, nodding sideways. "For Mr. Drumlow—poor
old gentleman, I was fond on him, though he'd got a bit
confused in his head, what wi' age and wi' taking a drop
o' summat warm when the service come of a cold morning. And young Mr. Lammeter, he'd have no way but he
must be married in Janiwary, which, to be sure, 's a unreasonable time to be married in, for it isn't like a christening or a burying, as you can't help; and so Mr. Drumlow—poor old gentleman, I was fond on him—but when
he come to put the questions, he put 'em by the rule o'
contrairy like, and he says, 'Wilt thou have this man to
thy wedded wife?' says he, and then he says, 'Wilt thou
have this woman to thy wedded husband?' says he. But
the partic'larest thing of all is as nobody took any notice
on it but me, and they answered straight off 'yes,' like as
if it had been me saying 'Amen' i' the right place, without listening to what went before."

"But *you* knew what was going on well enough, didn't
you, Mr. Macey? You were live enough, eh?" said the
butcher.

"Lor' bless you!" said Mr. Macey, pausing, and smiling
in pity at the impotence of his hearer's imagination;
"why, I was all of a tremble: it was as if I'd been a coat
pulled by the two tails, like; for I couldn't stop the parson, I couldn't take upon me to do that; and yet I said
to myself, I says, 'Suppose they shouldn't be fast married,
'cause the words are contrairy?' and my head went working like a mill, for I was allays uncommon for turning
things over and seeing all round 'em; and I says to myself, 'Is't the meanin' or the words as makes folks fast i'

wedlock?' For the parson meant right, and the bride and bridegroom meant right. But then, when I come to think on it, meanin' goes but a little way i' most things, for you may mean to stick things together and your glue may be bad, and then where are you? And so I says to mysen, 'It isn't the meanin', it's the glue.' And I was worreted as if I'd got three bells to pull at once, when we got into the vestry, and they begun to sign their names. But where's the use o' talking?—you can't think what goes on in a 'cute man's inside."

"But you held in for all that, didn't you, Mr. Macey?" said the landlord.

"Ay, I held in tight till I was by mysen wi' Mr. Drumlow, and then I out wi' everything, but respectful, as I allays did. And he made light on it, and he says, 'Pooh, pooh, Macey, make yourself easy,' he says, 'it's neither the meaning nor the words—it's the re*ges*ter does it—that's the glue.' So you see he settled it easy; for parsons and doctors know everything by heart, like, so as they aren't worreted wi' thinking what's the rights and wrongs o' things, as I'n been many and many's the time. And sure enough the wedding turned out all right, on'y poor Mrs. Lammeter—that's Miss Osgood as was—died afore the lasses were growed up; but for prosperity and everything respectable, there's no family more looked on."

Everyone of Mr. Macey's audience had heard this story many times, but it was listened to as if it had been a favourite tune, and at certain points the puffing of the pipes was momentarily suspended, that the listeners might give their whole minds to the expected words. But there was more to come; and Mr. Snell, the landlord, duly put the leading question.

"Why, old Mr. Lammeter had a pretty fortin, didn't they say, when he come into these parts?"

"Well, yes," said Mr. Macey; "but I daresay it's as much as this Mr. Lammeter's done to keep it whole. For there was allays a talk as nobody could get rich on the Warrens: though he holds it cheap, for it's what they call Charity Land."

"Ay, and there's few folks know so well as you how it come to be Charity Land, eh, Mr. Macey?" said the butcher.

"How should they?" said the old clerk, with some contempt. "Why, my grandfather made the grooms' livery for that Mr. Cliff as came and built the big stables at the Warrens. Why, they're stables four times as big as Squire Cass's, for he thought o' nothing but hosses and hunting, Cliff didn't—a Lunnon tailor, some folks said, as had gone mad wi' cheating. For he couldn't ride; lor bless you! They said he'd got no more grip o' the hoss than if his legs had been cross sticks: my grandfather heared old Squire Cass say so many and many a time. But ride he would, as if Old Harry had been a-driving him; and he'd a son, a lad o' sixteen; and nothing would his father have him do, but he must ride and ride—though the lad was frighted, they said. And it was a common saying as the father wanted to ride the tailor out o' the lad, and make a gentleman on him—not but what I'm a tailor myself, but in respect as God made me such, I'm proud on it, for 'Macey, tailor,' 's been wrote up over our door since afore the Queen's heads went out on the shillings. But Cliff, he was ashamed o' being called a tailor, and he was sore vexed as his riding was laughed at, and nobody o' the gentlefolks hereabout could abide him. Howsomever, the poor lad got sickly and died, and the father didn't live long after him, for he got queerer nor ever, and they said he used to go out i' the dead o' the night, wi' a lantern in his hand, to the stables, and set a lot o' lights burning, for he got as he couldn't sleep; and there he'd stand, cracking his whip and looking at his hosses; and they said it was a mercy as the stables didn't get burnt down wi' the poor dumb creaturs in 'em. But at last he died raving, and they found as he'd left all his property, Warrens and all, to a Lunnon Charity, and that's how the Warrens come to be Charity Land; though, as for the stables, Mr. Lammeter never uses 'em—they're out o' all charicter—lor bless you! if you was to set the doors a-banging in 'em, it 'ud sound like thunder half o'er the parish."

"Ay, but there's more going on in the stables than what folks see by daylight, eh, Mr. Macey?" said the landlord.

"Ay, ay; go that way of a dark night, that's all," said Mr. Macey, winking mysteriously, "and then make believe, if you like, as you didn't see lights i' the stables, nor hear the stamping o' the hosses, nor the cracking o' the whips, and howling, too, if it's tow'rt daybreak. 'Cliff's Holiday' has been the name of it ever sin' I were a boy; that's to say, some said as it was the holiday old Harry gev him from roasting, like. That's what my father told me, and he was a reasonable man, though there's folks nowadays know what happened afore they were born better nor they know their own business."

"What do you say to that, eh, Dowlas?" said the landlord, turning to the farrier, who was swelling with impatience for his cue. "There's a nut for *you* to crack."

Mr. Dowlas was the negative spirit in the company, and was proud of his position.

"Say? I say what a man *should* say as doesn't shut his eyes to look at a finger post. I say as I'm ready to wager any man ten pound, if he'll stand out wi' me any dry night in the pasture before the Warren stables, as we shall neither see lights nor hear noises, if it isn't the blowing of our own noses. That's what I say, and I've said it many a time; but there's nobody 'ull ventur a ten-pun' note on their ghos'es as they make so sure of."

"Why, Dowlas, that's easy betting, that is," said Ben Winthrop. "You might as well bet a man as he wouldn't catch the rheumatise if he stood up to's neck in the pool of a frosty night. It 'ud be fine fun for a man to win his bet as he'd catch the rheumatise. Folks as believe in Cliff's Holiday aren't a-going to ventur near it for a matter o' ten pound."

"If Master Dowlas wants to know the truth on it," said Mr. Macey, with a sarcastic smile, tapping his thumbs together, "he's no call to lay any bet—let him go and stan' by himself—there's nobody 'ull hinder him; and then he can let the parish'ners know if they're wrong."

"Thank you! I'm obliged to you," said the farrier, with a snort of scorn. "If folks are fools, it's no business o' mine. *I* don't want to make out the truth about ghos'es: *I* know it a'ready. But I'm not against a bet—everything fair and open. Let any man bet me ten pound as I shall see Cliff's Holiday, and I'll go and stand by myself. I want no company. I'd as lief do it as I'd fill this pipe."

"Ah, but who's to watch you, Dowlas, and see you do it? That's no fair bet," said the butcher.

"No fair bet?" replied Mr. Dowlas angrily. "I should

like to hear any man stand up and say I want to bet un-
fair. Come now, Master Lundy, I should like to hear you
say it."

"Very like you would," said the butcher. "But it's no
business o' mine. You're none o' my bargains, and I
aren't a-going to try and 'bate your price. If anybody'll
bid for you at your own vallying, let him. I'm for peace
and quietness, I am."

"Yes, that's what every yapping cur is, when you hold
a stick up at him," said the farrier. "But I'm afraid o'
neither man nor ghost, and I'm ready to lay a fair bet—
I aren't a turn-tail cur."

"Ay, but there's this in it, Dowlas," said the landlord,
speaking in a tone of much candour and tolerance.
"There's folks, i' my opinion, they can't see ghos'es, not if
they stood as plain as a pikestaff before 'em. And there's
reason i' that. For there's my wife, now, can't smell, not
if she'd the strongest o' cheese under her nose. I never
see'd a ghost myself, but then I says to myself, 'Very like
I haven't got the smell for 'em.' I mean, putting a ghost
for a smell, or else contrairiways. And so, I'm for holding
with both sides; for, as I say, the truth lies between 'em.
And if Dowlas was to go and stand, and say he'd never
seen a wink o' Cliff's Holiday all the night through, I'd
back him; and if anybody said as Cliff's Holiday was certain sure, for all that, I'd back him too. For the smell's
what I go by."

The landlord's analogical argument was not well received by the farrier—a man intensely opposed to compro-
mise.

"Tut, tut," he said, setting down his glass with re-
freshed irritation; "what's the smell got to do with it?
Did ever a ghost give a man a black eye? That's what I
should like to know. If ghos'es want me to believe in 'em,
let 'em leave off skulking i' the dark and i' lone places—
let 'em come where there's company and candles."

"As if ghos'es 'ud want to be believed in by anybody so
ignirant!" said Mr. Macey, in deep disgust at the farrier's
crass incompetence to apprehend the conditions of ghostly phenomena.

CHAPTER VII

YET THE NEXT MOMENT there seemed to be some evidence that ghosts had a more condescending disposition than Mr. Macey attributed to them; for the pale, thin figure of Silas Marner was suddenly seen standing in the warm light, uttering no word, but looking round at the company with his strange, unearthly eyes. The long pipes gave a simultaneous movement, like the antennae of startled insects, and every man present, not excepting even the sceptical farrier, had an impression that he saw, not Silas Marner in the flesh, but an apparition; for the door by which Silas had entered was hidden by the high-screen seats, and no one had noticed his approach. Mr. Macey, sitting a long way off the ghost, might be supposed to have felt an argumentative triumph, which would tend to neutralise his share of the general alarm. Had he not always said that when Silas Marner was in that strange trance of his, his soul went loose from his body? Here was the demonstration: nevertheless, on the whole, he would have been as well contented without it. For a few moments there was a dead silence, Marner's want of breath and agitation not allowing him to speak. The landlord, under the habitual sense that he was bound to keep his house open to all company, and confident in the protection of his unbroken neutrality, at last took on himself the task of adjuring the ghost.

"Master Marner," he said, in a conciliatory tone, "what's lacking to you? What's your business here?"

"Robber!" said Silas, gaspingly. "I've been robbed! I want the constable—and the Justice—and Squire Cass—and Mr. Crackenthorp."

"Lay hold on him, Jem Rodney," said the landlord, the idea of a ghost subsiding; "he's off his head, I doubt. He's wet through."

Jem Rodney was the outermost man, and sat conveniently near Marner's standing place; but he declined to give his services.

"Come and lay hold of him yourself, Mr. Snell, if you've

57

a mind," said Jem, rather sullenly. "He's been robbed, and murdered too, for what I know," he added, in a muttering tone.

"Jem Rodney!" said Silas, turning and fixing his strange eyes on the suspected man.

"Ay, Master Marner, what do you want wi' me?" said Jem, trembling a little, and seizing his drinking can as a defensive weapon.

"If it was you stole my money," said Silas, clasping his hands entreatingly, and raising his voice to a cry, "give it me back, and I won't meddle with you. I won't set the constable on you. Give it me back, and I'll let you—I'll let you have a guinea."

"Me stole your money!" said Jem, angrily. "I'll pitch this can at your eye if you talk o' *my* stealing your money."

"Come, come, Master Marner," said the landlord, now rising resolutely, and seizing Marner by the shoulder, "if you've got any information to lay, speak it out sensible, and show as you're in your right mind, if you expect anybody to listen to you. You're as wet as a drowned rat. Sit down and dry yourself, and speak straight forrard."

"Ah, to be sure, man," said the farrier, who began to feel that he had not been quite on a par with himself and the occasion. "Let's have no more staring and screaming, else we'll have you strapped for a madman. That was why I didn't speak at the first—thinks I, the man's run mad."

"Ay, ay, make him sit down," said several voices at once, well pleased that the reality of ghosts remained still an open question.

The landlord forced Marner to take off his coat, and then to sit down on a chair aloof from everyone else, in the centre of the circle, and in the direct rays of the fire. The weaver, too feeble to have any distinct purpose beyond that of getting help to recover his money, submitted unresistingly. The transient fears of the company were now forgotten in their strong curiosity, and all faces were turned toward Silas, when the landlord, having seated himself again, said:

"Now then, Master Marner, what's this you've got to say, as you've been robbed? Speak out."

"He'd better not say again as it was me robbed him," cried Jem Rodney, hastily. "What could I ha' done with his money? I could as easy steal the parson's surplice, and wear it."

"Hold your tongue, Jem, and let's hear what's he's got to say," said the landlord. "Now then, Master Marner."

Silas now told his story under frequent questioning, as the mysterious character of the robbery became evident.

This strangely novel situation of opening his trouble to his Raveloe neighbours, of sitting in the warmth of a hearth not his own, and feeling the presence of faces and voices which were his nearest promise of help, had doubtless its influence on Marner, in spite of his passionate preoccupation with his loss. Our consciousness rarely registers the beginning of a growth within us any more than without us: there have been many circulations of the sap before we detect the smallest sign of the bud.

The slight suspicion with which his hearers at first listened to him gradually melted away before the convincing simplicity of his distress: it was impossible for the neighbours to doubt that Marner was telling the truth, not because they were capable of arguing at once from the nature of his statements to the absence of any motive for making them falsely, but because, as Mr. Macey observed, "Folks as had the devil to back 'em were not likely to be so mushed" as poor Silas was. Rather, from the strange fact that the robber had left no traces, and had happened to know the nick of time, utterly incalculable by mortal agents, when Silas would go away from home without locking his door, the more probable conclusion seemed to be, that his disreputable intimacy in that quarter, if it ever existed, had been broken up, and that, in consequence, this ill turn had been done to Marner by somebody it was quite in vain to set the constable after. Why this preternatural felon should be obliged to wait till the door was unlocked was a question which did not present itself.

"It isn't Jem Rodney as has done this work, Master Marner," said the landlord. "You mustn't be a-casting your eye at poor Jem. There may be a bit of a reckoning against Jem for the matter of a hare or so, if anybody was bound to keep their eyes staring open, and niver to wink—but Jem's been a-sitting here drinking his can, like the decentest man i' the parish, since before you left your house, Master Marner, by your own account."

"Ay, ay," said Mr. Macey; "let's have no accusing o' the innicent. That isn't the law. There must be folks to swear again' a man before he can be ta'en up. Let's have no accusing o' the innicent, Master Marner."

Memory was not so utterly torpid in Silas that it could not be wakened by these words. With a movement of compunction, as new and strange to him as everything else within the last hour, he started from his chair and went close up to Jem, looking at him as if he wanted to assure himself of the expression in his face.

"I was wrong," he said, "yes, yes—I ought to have thought. There's nothing to witness against you, Jem. Only you'd been into my house oftener than anybody else, and so you came into my head. I don't accuse you—I won't accuse anybody—only," he added, lifting up his hands to his head, and turning away with bewildered misery, "I try —I try to think where my money can be."

"Ay, ay, they're gone where it's hot enough to melt 'em, I doubt," said Mr. Macey.

"Tchuh!" said the farrier. And then he asked, with a cross-examining air, "How much money might there be in the bags, Master Marner?"

"Two hundred and seventy-two pounds, twelve and six-pence, last night when I counted it," said Silas, seating himself again, with a groan.

"Pooh! why, they'd be none so heavy to carry. Some tramp's been in, that's all; and as for the no footmarks, and the bricks and the sand being all right—why, your eyes are pretty much like a insect's, Master Marner; they're obliged to look so close, you can't see much at a time. It's my opinion as, if I'd been you, or you'd been me—for it comes to the same thing—you wouldn't have thought you'd found everything as you left it. But what I vote is, as two of the sensiblest o' the company should go with you to Master Kench, the constable's—he's ill i' bed, I know that much—and get him to appoint one of us his deppity; for that's the law, and I don't think anybody 'ull take upon him to contradick me there. It isn't much of a walk to Kench's; and then, if it's me as is deppity, I'll go back with you, Master Marner, and examine your primises;

and if anybody's got any fault to find with that, I'll thank him to stand up and say it out like a man."

By this pregnant speech the farrier had re-established his self-complacency, and waited with confidence to hear himself named as one of the superlatively sensible men.

"Let us see how the night is, though," said the landlord, who also considered himself personally concerned in this proposition. "Why, it rains heavy still," he said, returning from the door.

"Well, I'm not the man to be afraid o' the rain," said the farrier. "For it'll look bad when Justice Malam hears as respectable men like us had a information laid before 'em and took no steps."

The landlord agreed with this view, and after taking the sense of the company, and duly rehearsing a small ceremony known in high ecclesiastical life as the *nolo episcopari*, he consented to take on himself the chill dignity of going to Kench's. But to the farrier's strong disgust, Mr. Macey now started an objection to his proposing himself as a deputy constable; for that oracular old gentleman, claiming to know the law, stated, as a fact delivered to him by his father, that no doctor could be a constable.

"And you're a doctor, I reckon, though you're only a cow doctor—for a fly's a fly, though it may be a hoss fly," concluded Mr. Macey, wondering a little at his own "cuteness."

There was a hot debate upon this, the farrier being of course indisposed to renounce the quality of doctor, but contending that a doctor could be a constable if he liked—the law meant, he needn't be one if he didn't like. Mr. Macey thought this was nonsense, since the law was not likely to be fonder of doctors than of other folks. Moreover, if it was in the nature of doctors more than of other men not to like being constables, how came Mr. Dowlas to be so eager to act in that capacity?

"*I* don't want to act the constable," said the farrier, driven into a corner by this merciless reasoning; "and there's no man can say it of me, if he'd tell the truth. But if there's to be any jealousy and en*vy*ing about going to Kench's in the rain, let them go as like it—you won't get me to go, I can tell you."

By the landlord's intervention, however, the dispute

was accommodated. Mr. Dowlas consented to go as a second person disinclined to act officially; and so poor Silas, furnished with some old coverings, turned out with his two companions into the rain again, thinking of the long night hours before him, not as those do who long to rest, but as those who expect to "watch for the morning."

CHAPTER VIII

WHEN GODFREY CASS returned from Mrs. Osgood's party at midnight, he was not much surprised to learn that Dunsey had not come home. Perhaps he had not sold Wildfire, and was waiting for another chance—perhaps, on that foggy afternoon, he had preferred housing himself at the Red Lion at Batherley for the night, if the run had kept him in that neighbourhood; for he was not likely to feel much concern about leaving his brother in suspense. Godfrey's mind was too full of Nancy Lammeter's looks and behaviour, too full of the exasperation against himself and his lot, which the sight of her always produced in him, for him to give much thought to Wildfire or to the probabilities of Dunstan's conduct.

The next morning the whole village was excited by the story of the robbery, and Godfrey, like everyone else, was occupied in gathering and discussing news about it, and in visiting the Stone Pits. The rain had washed away all possibility of distinguishing footmarks, but a close investigation of the spot had disclosed, in the direction opposite to the village, a tinderbox, with a flint and steel, half sunk in the mud. It was not Silas's tinderbox, for the only one he had ever had was still standing on his shelf; and the inference generally accepted was that the tinderbox in the ditch was somehow connected with the robbery. A small minority shook their heads, and intimated their opinion that it was not a robbery to have much light thrown on it by tinderboxes, that Master Marner's tale had a queer look with it, and that such things had been known as a man's doing himself a mischief, and then setting the justice to look for the doer. But when questioned closely as to their grounds for this opinion, and what

Master Marner had to gain by such false pretences, they only shook their heads as before, and observed that there was no knowing what some folks counted gain; moreover, that everybody had a right to their own opinions, grounds or no grounds, and that the weaver, as everybody knew, was partly crazy. Mr. Macey, though he joined in the defence of Marner against all suspicions of deceit, also pooh-poohed the tinderbox; indeed, repudiated it as a rather impious suggestion, tending to imply that everything must be done by human hands, and that there was no power which could make away with the guineas without moving the bricks. Nevertheless, he turned round rather sharply on Mr. Tookey, when the zealous deputy, feeling that this was a view of the case peculiarly suited to a parish clerk, carried it still further, and doubted whether it was right to inquire into a robbery at all when the circumstances were so mysterious.

"As if," concluded Mr. Tookey, "as if there was nothing but what could be made out by justices and constables."

"Now, don't you be for overshooting the mark, Tookey," said Mr. Macey, nodding his head aside, admonishingly. "That's what you're allays at; if I throw a stone and hit, you think there's summat better than hitting, and you try to throw a stone beyond. What I said was against the tinderbox: I said nothing against justices and constables, for they're o' King George's making, and it 'ud be ill-becoming a man in a parish office to fly out again' King George."

While these discussions were going on amongst the group outside the Rainbow, a higher consultation was being carried on within, under the presidency of Mr. Crackenthorp, the rector, assisted by Squire Cass and other substantial parishioners. It had just occurred to Mr. Snell, the landlord—he being, as he observed, a man accustomed to put two and two together—to connect with the tinderbox, which, as deputy constable, he himself had had the honourable distinction of finding, certain recollections of a peddler who had called to drink at the house about a month before, and had actually stated that he carried a tinderbox about with him to light his pipe. Here, surely, was a clue to be followed out. And as memory, when duly impregnated with ascertained facts, is sometimes surprisingly fertile, Mr. Snell gradually recovered a vivid impression of the effect produced on him by the peddler's countenance and conversation. He had a "look with his eye" which fell unpleasantly on Mr. Snell's sensitive organism. To be sure, he didn't say anything particular—no, except that about the tinderbox—but it isn't what a man says, it's the way he says it. Moreover he had a swarthy foreignness of complexion which boded little honesty.

"Did he wear earrings?" Mr. Crackenthorp wished to know, having some acquaintance with foreign customs.

"Well—stay—let me see," said Mr. Snell, like a docile clairvoyant, who would really not make a mistake if she could help it. After stretching the corners of his mouth and contracting his eyes, as if he were trying to see the earrings, he appeared to give up the effort, and said, "Well, he'd got earrings in his box to sell, so it's nat'ral to suppose he might wear 'em. But he called at every house, a'most, in the village; there's somebody else, mayhap, saw 'em in his ears, though I can't take upon me rightly to say."

Mr. Snell was correct in his surmise, that somebody else would remember the peddler's earrings. For, on the spread of inquiry among the villagers, it was stated with gathering emphasis that the parson had wanted to know whether the peddler wore earrings in his ears, and an impression was created that a great deal depended on the eliciting of this fact. Of course everyone who heard the question, not having any distinct image of the peddler as *without* earrings, immediately had an image of him *with* earrings, larger or smaller, as the case might be; and the image was presently taken for a vivid recollection, so that the glazier's wife, a well-intentioned woman, not given to lying, and whose house was among the cleanest in the village, was ready to declare, as sure as ever she meant to take the sacrament, the very next Christmas that was ever coming, that she had seen big earrings, in the shape of the young moon, in the peddler's two ears; while Jinny Oates, the cobbler's daughter, being a more imaginative person, stated not only that she had seen them too, but that they made her blood creep, as it did at that very moment while there she stood.

Also, by way of throwing further light on this clue of the tinderbox, a collection was made of all the articles purchased from the peddler at various houses, and carried to the Rainbow to be exhibited there. In fact, there was a general feeling in the village, that for the clearing-up of this robbery there must be a great deal done at the Rainbow, and that no man need offer his wife an excuse for going there while it was the scene of severe public duties.

Some disappointment was felt, and perhaps a little indignation also, when it became known that Silas Marner, on being questioned by the Squire and the parson, had retained no other recollection of the peddler than that he had called at his door, but had not entered his house, having turned away at once when Silas, holding the door ajar, had said that he wanted nothing. This had been Silas's testimony, though he clutched strongly at the idea of the peddler's being the culprit, if only because it gave him a definite image of a whereabout for his gold, after it had been taken away from its hiding place: he could see it now in the peddler's box. But it was observed with some irritation in the village, that anybody but a "blind creatur" like Marner would have seen the man prowling about, for how came he to leave his tinderbox in the ditch close by, if he hadn't been lingering there? Doubtless, he had made his observations when he saw Marner at the door. Anybody might know—and only look at him—that the weaver was a half-crazy miser. It was a wonder the peddler hadn't murdered him; men of that sort, with rings in their ears, had been known for murderers often and often; there had been one tried at the 'sizes, not so long ago but what there were people living who remembered it.

Godfrey Cass, indeed, entering the Rainbow during one of Mr. Snell's frequently repeated recitals of his testimony, had treated it lightly, stating that he himself had bought a penknife of the peddler, and thought him a merry grinning fellow enough; it was all nonsense, he said, about the man's evil looks. But this was spoken of in the village as the random talk of youth, "as if it was only Mr. Snell who had seen something odd about the peddler!" On the contrary, there were at least half a dozen who were ready to go before Justice Malam, and give in much more striking testimony than any the landlord could furnish. It was to

be hoped Mr. Godfrey would not go to Tarley and throw
cold water on what Mr. Snell said there, and so prevent
the justice from drawing up a warrant. He was suspected
of intending this when, after midday, he was seen setting
off on horseback in the direction of Tarley.

But by this time Godfrey's interest in the robbery had
faded before his growing anxiety about Dunstan and
Wildfire, and he was going, not to Tarley, but to Batherley, unable to rest in uncertainty about them any longer.
The possibility that Dunstan had played him the ugly
trick of riding away with Wildfire, to return at the end of
a month, when he had gambled away or otherwise
squandered the price of the horse, was a fear that urged
itself upon him more, even, than the thought of an accidental injury; and now that the dance at Mrs. Osgood's
was past, he was irritated with himself that he had trusted
his horse to Dunstan. Instead of trying to still his fears, he
encouraged them, with that superstitious impression
which clings to us all, that if we expect evil very strongly
it is the less likely to come; and when he heard a horse
approaching at a trot, and saw a hat rising above a hedge
beyond an angle of the lane, he felt as if his conjuration
had succeeded. But no sooner did the horse come within
sight, than his heart sank again. It was not Wildfire; and
in a few moments more he discerned that the rider was not
Dunstan, but Bryce, who pulled up to speak, with a face
that implied something disagreeable.

"Well, Mr. Godfrey, that's a lucky brother of yours,
that Master Dunsey, isn't he?"

"What do you mean?" said Godfrey hastily.

"Why, hasn't he been home yet?" said Bryce.

"Home? No. What has happened? Be quick. What has
he done with my horse?"

"Ah, I thought it was yours, though he pretended you
had parted with it to him."

"Has he thrown him down and broken his knees?" said
Godfrey, flushed with exasperation.

"Worse than that," said Bryce. "You see, I'd made a
bargain with him to buy the horse for a hundred and
twenty—a swinging price, but I always liked the horse.
And what does he do but go and stake him—fly at a hedge
with stakes in it, atop of a bank with a ditch before it.

The horse had been dead a pretty good while when he was found. So he hasn't been home since, has he?"

"Home? No," said Godfrey, "and he'd better keep away. Confound me for a fool! I might have known this would be the end of it."

"Well, to tell you the truth," said Bryce, "after I'd bargained for the horse, it did come into my head that he might be riding and selling the horse without your knowledge, for I didn't believe it was his own. I knew Master Dunsey was up to his tricks sometimes. But where can he be gone? He's never been seen at Batherley. He couldn't have been hurt, for he must have walked off."

"Hurt," said Godfrey, bitterly. "He'll never be hurt—he's made to hurt other people."

"And so you *did* give him leave to sell the horse, eh?" said Bryce.

"Yes; I wanted to part with the horse—he was always a little too hard in the mouth for me," said Godfrey; his pride making him wince under the idea that Bryce guessed the sale to be a matter of necessity. "I was going to see after him—I thought some mischief had happened. I'll go back now," he added, turning the horse's head, and wishing he could get rid of Bryce; for he felt that the long-dreaded crisis in his life was close upon him. "You're coming on to Raveloe, aren't you?"

"Well, no, not now," said Bryce. "I *was* coming round there, for I had to go to Flitton, and I thought I might as well take you in my way, and just let you know all I knew myself about the horse. I suppose Master Dunsey didn't like to show himself till the ill news had blown over a bit. He's perhaps gone to pay a visit at the Three Crowns, by Whitbridge—I know he's fond of the house."

"Perhaps he is," said Godfrey, rather absently. Then rousing himself, he said, with an effort at carelessness, "We shall hear of him soon enough, I'll be bound."

"Well, here's my turning," said Bryce, not surprised to perceive that Godfrey was rather "down"; "so I'll bid you good day, and wish I may bring you better news another time."

Godfrey rode along slowly, representing to himself the scene of confession to his father from which he felt that there was now no longer any escape. The revelation about

the money must be made the very next morning; and if
he withheld the rest, Dunstan would be sure to come back
shortly, and finding that he must bear the brunt of his
father's anger, would tell the whole story out of spite,
even though he had nothing to gain by it. There was one
step, perhaps, by which he might still win Dunstan's
silence and put off the evil day: he might tell his father
that he had himself spent the money paid to him by
Fowler; and as he had never been guilty of such an
offence before, the affair would blow over after a little
storming. But Godfrey could not bend himself to this.
He felt that in letting Dunstan have the money, he had
already been guilty of a breach of trust hardly less culpable than that of spending the money directly for his own
behoof; and yet there was a distinction between the two
acts which made him feel that the one was so much more
blackening than the other as to be intolerable to him.

"I don't pretend to be a good fellow," he said to himself; "but I'm not a scoundrel—at least, I'll stop short
somewhere. I'll bear the consequences of what I *have*
done sooner than make believe I've done what I never
would have done. I'd never have spent the money for my
own pleasure—I was tortured into it."

Through the remainder of this day Godfrey, with only
occasional fluctuations, kept his will bent in the direction
of a complete avowal to his father, and he withheld the
story of Wildfire's loss till the next morning, that it might
serve him as an introduction to heavier matter. The old
Squire was accustomed to his son's frequent absence from
home, and thought neither Dunstan's nor Wildfire's nonappearance a matter calling for remark. Godfrey said to
himself again and again that if he let slip this one opportunity of confession, he might never have another; the
revelation might be made even in a more odious way
than by Dunstan's malignity: *she* might come, as she had
threatened to do. And then he tried to make the scene
easier to himself by rehearsal: he made up his mind how
he would pass from the admission of his weakness in letting Dunstan have the money to the fact that Dunstan
had a hold on him which he had been unable to shake
off, and how he would work up his father to expect something very bad before he told him the fact. The old

Squire was an implacable man: he made resolutions in violent anger, but he was not to be moved from them after his anger had subsided—as fiery volcanic matters cool and harden into rock. Like many violent and implacable men, he allowed evils to grow under favour of his own heedlessness, till they pressed upon him with exasperating force, and then he turned round with fierce severity and became unrelentingly hard. This was his system with his tenants: he allowed them to get into arrears, neglect their fences, reduce their stock, sell their straw, and otherwise go the wrong way—and then, when he became short of money in consequence of this indulgence, he took the hardest measures and would listen to no appeal. Godfrey knew all this, and felt it with the greater force because he had constantly suffered annoyance from witnessing his father's sudden fits of unrelentingness, for which his own habitual irresolution deprived him of all sympathy. (He was not critical on the faulty indulgence which preceded these fits; *that* seemed to him natural enough.) Still there was just the chance, Godfrey thought, that his father's pride might see this marriage in a light that would induce him to hush it up, rather than turn his son out and make the family the talk of the country for ten miles round.

This was the view of the case that Godfrey managed to keep before him pretty closely till midnight, and he went to sleep thinking that he had done with inward debating. But when he awoke in the still morning darkness he found it impossible to reawaken his evening thoughts; it was as if they had been tired out and were not to be roused to further work. Instead of arguments for confession, he could now feel the presence of nothing but its evil consequences: the old dread of disgrace came back— the old shrinking from the thought of raising a hopeless barrier between himself and Nancy—the old disposition to rely on chances which might be favourable to him, and save him from betrayal. Why, after all, should he cut off the hope of them by his own act? He had seen the matter in a wrong light yesterday. He had been in a rage with Dunstan, and had thought of nothing but a thorough breakup of their mutual understanding; but what it would be really wisest for him to do was to try and soften

his father's anger against Dunsey, and keep things as
nearly as possible in their old condition. If Dunsey did
not come back for a few days (and Godfrey did not know
but that the rascal had enough money in his pocket to
enable him to keep away still longer), everything might
blow over.

CHAPTER IX

GODFREY ROSE and took his own breakfast earlier than
usual, but lingered in the wainscoted parlour till his
younger brothers had finished their meal and gone out,
awaiting his father, who always went out and had a walk
with his managing man before breakfast. Everyone breakfasted at a different hour in the Red House, and the
Squire was always the latest, giving a long chance to a
rather feeble morning appetite before he tried it. The
table had been spread with substantial eatables nearly
two hours before he presented himself—a tall, stout man
of sixty, with a face in which the knit brow and rather
hard glance seemed contradicted by the slack and feeble
mouth. His person showed marks of habitual neglect, his
dress was slovenly; and yet there was something in the
presence of the old Squire distinguishable from that of
the ordinary farmers in the parish, who were perhaps
every whit as refined as he, but, having slouched their
way through life with a consciousness of being in the
vicinity of their "betters," wanted that self-possession and
authoritativeness of voice and carriage which belonged to
a man who thought of superiors as remote existences,
with whom he had personally little more to do than with
America or the stars. The Squire had been used to parish
homage all his life, used to the presupposition that his
family, his tankards, and everything that was his were the
oldest and best; and as he never associated with any gentry higher than himself, his opinion was not disturbed by
comparison.

He glanced at his son as he entered the room, and said,
"What, sir! haven't *you* had your breakfast yet?" but
there was no pleasant morning greeting between them;

not because of any unfriendliness, but because the sweet flower of courtesy is not a growth of such homes as the Red House.

"Yes sir," said Godfrey, "I've had my breakfast, but I was waiting to speak to you."

"Ah! well," said the Squire, throwing himself indifferently into his chair, and speaking in a ponderous coughing fashion, which was felt in Raveloe to be a sort of privilege of his rank, while he cut a piece of beef, and held it up before the deerhound that had come in with him. "Ring the bell for my ale, will you? You youngsters' business is your own pleasure, mostly. There's no hurry about it for anybody but yourselves."

The Squire's life was quite as idle as his sons', but it was a fiction kept up by himself and his contemporaries in Raveloe that youth was exclusively the period of folly, and that their aged wisdom was constantly in a state of endurance mitigated by sarcasm. Godfrey waited, before he spoke again, until the ale had been brought and the door closed—an interval during which Fleet, the deerhound, had consumed enough bits of beef to make a poor man's holiday dinner.

"There's been a cursed piece of ill luck with Wildfire," he began; "happened the day before yesterday."

"What! broke his knees?" said the Squire, after taking a draught of ale. "I thought you knew how to ride better than that, sir. I never threw a horse down in my life. If I had, I might ha' whistled for another, for *my* father wasn't quite so ready to unstring as some other fathers I know of. But they must turn over a new leaf—*they* must. What with mortgages and arrears, I'm as short o' cash as a roadside pauper. And that fool Kimble says the newspaper's talking about peace. Why, the country wouldn't have a leg to stand on. Prices 'ud run down like a jack, and I should never get my arrears, not if I sold all the fellows up. And there's that damned Fowler, I won't put up with him any longer; I've told Winthrop to go to Cox this very day. The lying scoundrel told me he'd be sure to pay me a hundred last month. He takes advantage because he's on that outlying farm, and thinks I shall forget him."

The Squire had delivered this speech in a coughing

and interrupted manner, but with no pause long enough
for Godfrey to make it a pretext for taking up the word
again. He felt that his father meant to ward off any
request for money on the ground of the misfortune with
Wildfire, and that the emphasis he had thus been led to
lay on his shortness of cash and his arrears was likely to
produce an attitude of mind the utmost unfavourable for
his own disclosure. But he must go on, now he had begun.

"It's worse than breaking the horse's knees—he's been
staked and killed," he said, as soon as his father was silent,
and had begun to cut his meat. "But I wasn't thinking of
asking you to buy me another horse; I was only thinking
I'd lost the means of paying you with the price of Wildfire, as I'd meant to do. Dunsey took him to the hunt to
sell him for me the other day, and after he'd made a bargain for a hundred and twenty with Bryce, he went after
the hounds, and took some fool's leap or other, that did
for the horse at once. If it hadn't been for that, I should
have paid you a hundred pounds this morning."

The Squire had laid down his knife and fork, and was
staring at his son in amazement, not being sufficiently
quick of brain to form a probable guess as to what could
have caused so strange an inversion of the paternal and
filial relations as this proposition of his son to pay him a
hundred pounds.

"The truth is, sir—I'm very sorry—I was quite to
blame," said Godfrey. "Fowler did pay that hundred
pounds. He paid it to me, when I was over there one day
last month. And Dunsey bothered me for the money, and
I let him have it, because I hoped I should be able to pay
it you before this."

The Squire was purple with anger before his son had
done speaking, and found utterance difficult. "You let
Dunsey have it, sir? And how long have you been so
thick with Dunsey that you must *collogue* with him to
embezzle my money? Are you turning out a scamp? I tell
you, I won't have it. I'll turn the whole pack of you out
of the house together, and marry again. I'd have you to
remember, sir, my property's got no entail on it; since
my grandfather's time the Casses can do as they like with
their land. Remember that, sir. Let Dunsey have the

money! Why should you let Dunsey have the money? There's some lie at the bottom of it."

"There's no lie, sir," said Godfrey. "I wouldn't have spent the money myself, but Dunsey bothered me, and I was a fool and let him have it. But I meant to pay it, whether he did or not. That's the whole story. I never meant to embezzle money, and I'm not the man to do it. You never knew me do a dishonest trick, sir."

"Where's Dunsey, then? What do you stand talking there for? Go and fetch Dunsey, as I tell you, and let him give account of what he wanted the money for, and what he's done with it. He shall repent it. I'll turn him out. I said I would, and I'll do it. He shan't brave me. Go and fetch him."

"Dunsey isn't come back, sir."

"What! did he break his own neck then?" said the Squire, with some disgust at the idea that, in that case, he could not fulfil his threat.

"No, he wasn't hurt, I believe, for the horse was found dead, and Dunsey must have walked off. I daresay we shall see him again by and by. I don't know where he is."

"And what must you be letting him have my money for? Answer me that," said the Squire, attacking Godfrey again, since Dunsey was not within reach.

"Well, sir, I don't know," said Godfrey, hesitatingly. That was a feeble evasion, but Godfrey was not fond of lying, and, not being sufficiently aware that no sort of duplicity can long flourish without the help of vocal falsehoods, he was quite unprepared with invented motives.

"You don't know? I tell you what it is, sir. You've been up to some trick, and you've been bribing him not to tell," said the Squire, with a sudden acuteness which startled Godfrey, who felt his heart beat violently at the nearness of his father's guess. The sudden alarm pushed him on to take the next step—a very slight impulse suffices for that on a downward road.

"Why, sir," he said, trying to speak with careless ease, "it was a little affair between me and Dunsey; it's no matter to anybody else. It's hardly worth while to pry into young men's fooleries: it wouldn't have made any difference to you, sir, if I'd not had the bad luck to lose Wildfire. I should have paid you the money."

"Fooleries! Pshaw! It's time you'd done with fooleries. And I'd have you know, sir, you *must* ha' done with 'em," said the Squire, frowning and casting an angry glance at his son. "Your goings-on are not what I shall find money for any longer. There's my grandfather had his stables full o' horses, and kept a good house too, and in worse times by what I can make out; and so might I, if I hadn't four good-for-nothing fellows to hang on me like horse leeches. I've been too good a father to you all—that's what it is. But I shall pull up, sir."

Godfrey was silent. He was not likely to be very penetrating in his judgments, but he had always had a sense that his father's indulgence had not been kindness, and had had a vague longing for some discipline that would have checked his own errant weakness, and helped his better will. The Squire ate his bread and meat hastily, took a deep draught of ale, then turned his chair from the table, and began to speak again.

"It'll be all the worse for you, you know—you'd need try and help me keep things together."

"Well, sir, I've often offered to take the management of things, but you know you've taken it ill always, and seemed to think I wanted to push you out of your place."

"I know nothing o' your offering or o' my taking it ill," said the Squire, whose memory consisted in certain strong impressions unmodified by detail; "but I know, one while you seemed to be thinking o' marrying, and I didn't offer to put any obstacles in your way, as some fathers would. I'd as lieve you married Lammeter's daughter as anybody. I suppose, if I'd said you nay, you'd ha' kept on with it; but, for want o' contradiction, you've changed your mind. You're a shilly-shallow fellow: you take after your poor mother. She never had a will of her own; a woman has no call for one, if she's got a proper man for her husband. But *your* wife had need have one, for you hardly know your own mind enough to make both your legs walk one way. The lass hasn't said downright she won't have you, has she?"

"No," said Godfrey, feeling very hot and uncomfortable; "but I don't think she will."

"Think! Why, haven't you the courage to ask her? Do you stick to it, you want to have *her*—that's the thing?"

"There's no other woman I want to marry," said Godfrey evasively.

"Well, then, let me make the offer for you, that's all, if you haven't the pluck to do it yourself. Lammeter isn't likely to be loath for his daughter to marry into *my* family, I should think. And as for the pretty lass, she wouldn't have her cousin—and there's nobody else, as I see, could ha' stood in your way."

"I'd rather let it be, please sir, at present," said Godfrey, in alarm. "I think she's a little offended with me just now, and I should like to speak for myself. A man must manage these things for himself."

"Well, speak then and manage it, and see if you can't turn over a new leaf. That's what a man must do when he thinks o' marrying."

"I don't see how I can think of it at present, sir. You wouldn't like to settle me on one of the farms, I suppose, and I don't think she'd come to live in this house with all my brothers. It's a different sort of life to what she's been used to."

"Not come to live in this house? Don't tell me. You ask her, that's all," said the Squire, with a short, scornful laugh.

"I'd rather let the thing be, at present, sir," said Godfrey. "I hope you won't try to hurry it on by saying anything."

"I shall do what I choose," said the Squire, "and I shall let you know I'm master; else you may turn out and find an estate to drop into somewhere else. Go out and tell Winthrop not to go to Cox's, but wait for me. And tell 'em to get my horse saddled. And stop: look out and get that hack o' Dunsey's sold, and hand me the money, will you? He'll keep no more hacks at my expense. And if you know where he's sneaking—I daresay you do—you may tell him to spare himself the journey o' coming back home. Let him turn ostler, and keep himself. He shan't hang on me any more."

"I don't know where he is, sir; and if I did, it isn't my place to tell him to keep away," said Godfrey, moving towards the door.

"Confound it, sir, don't stay arguing, but go and order my horse," said the Squire, taking up a pipe.

Godfrey left the room, hardly knowing whether he were more relieved by the sense that the interview was ended without having made any change in his position, or more uneasy that he had entangled himself still further in prevarication and deceit. What had passed about his proposing to Nancy had raised a new alarm, lest by some after-dinner words of his father's to Mr. Lammeter he should be thrown into the embarrassment of being obliged absolutely to decline her when she seemed to be within his reach. He fled to his usual refuge, that of hoping for some unforeseen turn of fortune, some favourable chance which would save him from unpleasant consequences—perhaps even justify his insincerity by manifesting its prudence. And in this point of trusting to some throw of fortune's dice, Godfrey can hardly be called specially old-fashioned. Favourable Chance, I fancy, is the god of all men who follow their own devices instead of obeying a law they believe in. Let even a polished man of these days get into a position he is ashamed to avow, and his mind will be bent on all the possible issues that may deliver him from the calculable results of that position. Let him live outside his income, or shirk the resolute honest work that brings wages, and he will presently find himself dreaming of a possible benefactor, a possible simpleton who may be cajoled into using his interest, a possible state of mind in some possible person not yet forthcoming. Let him neglect the responsibilities of his office, and he will inevitably anchor himself on the chance, that the thing left undone may turn out not to be of the supposed importance. Let him betray his friend's confidence, and he will adore that same cunning complexity called Chance, which gives him the hope that his friend will never know; let him forsake a decent craft that he may pursue the gentilities of a profession to which nature never called him, and his religion will infallibly be the worship of blessed Chance, which he will believe in as the mighty creator of success. The evil principle deprecated in that religion is the orderly sequence by which the seed brings forth a crop after its kind.

CHAPTER X

JUSTICE MALAM was naturally regarded in Tarley and Raveloe as a man of capacious mind, seeing that he could draw much wider conclusions without evidence than could be expected of his neighbours who were not on the Commission of the Peace. Such a man was not likely to neglect the clue of the tinderbox, and an inquiry was set on foot concerning a peddler, name unknown, with curly black hair and a foreign complexion, carrying a box of cutlery and jewellery, and wearing large rings in his ears. But either because inquiry was too slow-footed to overtake him, or because the description applied to so many peddlers that inquiry did not know how to choose among them, weeks passed away, and there was no other result concerning the robbery than a gradual cessation of the excitement it had caused in Raveloe. Dunstan Cass's absence was hardly a subject of remark: he had once before had a quarrel with his father, and had gone off, nobody knew whither, to return at the end of six weeks, take up his old quarters unforbidden, and swagger as usual. His own family, who equally expected this issue, with the sole difference that the Squire was determined this time to forbid him the old quarters, never mentioned his absence; and when his uncle Kimble or Mr. Osgood noticed it, the story of his having killed Wildfire, and committed some offence against his father, was enough to prevent surprise. To connect the fact of Dunsey's disappearance with that of the robbery occurring on the same day, lay quite away from the track of everyone's thought—even Godfrey's, who had better reason than anyone else to know what his brother was capable of. He remembered no mention of the weaver between them since the time, twelve years ago, when it was their boyish sport to deride him; and, besides, his imagination constantly created an alibi for Dunstan: he saw him continually in some congenial haunt, to which he had walked off on leaving Wildfire—saw him sponging on chance acquaintances, and meditating a return home to the old amusement of

tormenting his elder brother. Even if any brain in Raveloe had put the said two facts together, I doubt whether
a combination so injurious to the prescriptive respectability of a family with a mural monument and venerable
tankards would not have been suppressed as of unsound
tendency. But Christmas puddings, brawn, and abundance of spirituous liquors, throwing the mental origi-
nality into the channel of nightmare, are great preserva-
tives against a dangerous spontaneity of waking thought.

When the robbery was talked of at the Rainbow and
elsewhere, in good company, the balance continued to
waver between the rational explanation founded on the
tinderbox, and the theory of an impenetrable mystery
that mocked investigation. The advocates of the tinder-
box-and-peddler view considered the other side a muddle-
headed and credulous set who, because they themselves
were walleyed, supposed everybody else to have the same
blank outlook; and the adherents of the inexplicable
more than hinted that their antagonists were animals inclined to crow before they had found any corn—mere
skimming dishes in point of depth—whose clear-sighted-
ness consisted in supposing there was nothing behind a
barn door because they couldn't see through it; so that,
though their controversy did not serve to elicit the fact
concerning the robbery, it elicited some true opinions of
collateral importance.

But while poor Silas's loss served thus to brush the slow
current of Raveloe conversation, Silas himself was feeling
the withering desolation of that bereavement, about
which his neighbours were arguing at their ease. To anyone who had observed him before he lost his gold, it
might have seemed that so withered and shrunken a life
as his could hardly be susceptible of a bruise, could hardly endure any subtraction but such as would put an end
to it altogether. But in reality it had been an eager life,
filled with immediate purpose, which fenced him in from
the wide, cheerless unknown. It had been a clinging life;
and though the object round which its fibres had clung
was a dead, disrupted thing, it satisfied the need for clinging. But now the fence was broken down—the support
was snatched away. Marner's thoughts could no longer
move in their old round, and were baffled by a blank like

that which meets a plodding ant when the earth has broken away on its homeward path. The loom was there, and the weaving, and the growing pattern in the cloth; but the bright treasure in the hole under his feet was gone; the prospect of handling and counting it was gone: the evening had no phantasm of delight to still the poor soul's craving. The thought of the money he would get by his actual work could bring no joy, for its meagre image was only a fresh reminder of his loss; and hope was too heavily crushed by the sudden blow for his imagination to dwell on the growth of a new hoard from that small beginning.

He filled up the blank with grief. As he sat weaving, he every now and then moaned low, like one in pain: it was the sign that his thoughts had come round again to the sudden chasm—to the empty evening time. And all the evening, as he sat in his loneliness by his dull fire, he leaned his elbows on his knees, and clasped his head with his hands, and moaned very low—not as one who seeks to be heard.

And yet he was not utterly forsaken in his trouble. The repulsion Marner had always created in his neighbours was partly dissipated by the new light in which this misfortune had shown him. Instead of a man who had more cunning than honest folks could come by, and, what was worse, had not the inclination to use that cunning in a neighbourly way, it was now apparent that Silas had not cunning enough to keep his own. He was generally spoken of as a "poor mushed creatur"; and that avoidance of his neighbours which had before been referred to his ill will, and to a probable addiction to worse company, was now considered mere craziness.

This change to a kindlier feeling was shown in various ways. The odour of Christmas cooking being on the wind, it was the season when superfluous pork and black puddings are suggestive of charity in well-to-do families; and Silas's misfortune had brought him uppermost in the memory of housekeepers like Mrs. Osgood. Mr. Crackenthorp, too, while he admonished Silas that his money had probably been taken from him because he thought too much of it, and never came to church, enforced the doctrine by a present of pigs' pettitoes, well calculated to dissipate unfounded prejudices against the clerical character. Neighbours, who had nothing but verbal consolation to give, showed a disposition not only to greet Silas, and discuss his misfortune at some length when they encountered him in the village, but also to take the trouble of calling at his cottage, and getting him to repeat all the details on the very spot; and then they would try to cheer him by saying, "Well, Master Marner, you're no worse off nor other poor folks, after all; and if you was to be crippled, the parish 'ud give you a 'lowance."

I suppose one reason why we are seldom able to comfort our neighbours with our words is that our good will gets adulterated, in spite of ourselves, before it can pass our lips. We can send black puddings and pettitoes without giving them a flavour of our own egoism; but language is a stream that is almost sure to smack of a mingled soil. There was a fair proportion of kindness in Raveloe; but it was often of a beery and bungling sort, and took the shape least allied to the complimentary and hypocritical.

Mr. Macey, for example, coming one evening expressly to let Silas know that recent events had given him the advantage of standing more favourably in the opinion of a man whose judgment was not formed lightly, opened the conversation by saying, as soon as he had seated himself and adjusted his thumbs:

"Come, Master Marner, why, you've no call to sit a-moaning. You're a deal better off to ha' lost your money nor to ha' kep it by foul means. I used to think, when you first come into these parts, as you were no better nor you should be; you were younger a deal than what you are now; but you were allays a staring, white-faced creatur, partly like a bald-faced calf, as I may say. But there's no knowing: it isn't every queer-looksed thing as Old Harry's had the making of—I mean, speaking o' toads and such; for they're often harmless, like, and useful against varmin. And it's pretty much the same wi' you, as fur as I can see. Though as to the yarbs and stuff to cure the breathing, if you brought that sort o' knowledge from distant parts, you might ha' been a bit freer of it. And if the knowledge wasn't well come by, why, you might ha' made up for it by coming to church reg'lar; for, as for the children as the Wise Woman charmed, I've been at the christening of 'em again and again, and they took the water just as well. And that's reasonable; for if Old Harry's a mind to do a bit o' kindness for a holiday, like, who's got anything against it? That's my thinking; and I've been clerk o' this parish forty year, and I know, when the parson and me does the cussing of a Ash Wednesday, there's no cussing o' folks as have a mind to be cured without a doctor, let Kimble say what he will. And so, Master Marner, as I was saying—for there's windings i' things as they may carry you to the fur end o' the prayer book afore you get back to 'em—my advice is, as you keep up your sperrits; for as for thinking you're a deep 'un, and ha' got more inside you nor 'ull bear daylight, I'm not o' that opinion at all, and so I tell the neighbours. For, says I, you talk o' Master Marner making out a tale —why, it's nonsense, that is: it 'ud take a 'cute man to make a tale like that; and, says I, he looked as scared as a rabbit."

During this discursive address Silas had continued motionless in his previous attitude, leaning his elbows on his knees, and pressing his hands against his head. Mr. Macey, not doubting that he had been listened to, paused, in the expectation of some appreciatory reply, but Marner remained silent. He had a sense that the old man meant to be good-natured and neighbourly; but the kindness fell on him as sunshine falls on the wretched—he had no heart to taste it, and felt that it was very far off him.

"Come, Master Marner, have you got nothing to say to that?" said Mr. Macey at last, with a slight accent of impatience.

"Oh," said Marner slowly, shaking his head between his hands, "I thank you—thank you—kindly."

"Ay, ay, to be sure: I thought you would," said Mr. Macey; "and my advice is—have you got a Sunday suit?"

"No," said Marner.

"I doubted it was so," said Mr. Macey. "Now, let me advise you to get a Sunday suit: there's Tookey, he's a poor creatur, but he's got my tailoring business, and some o' my money in it, and he shall make a suit at a low price, and give you trust, and then you can come to church, and be a bit neighbourly. Why, you've never heard me say

'Amen' since you come into these parts, and I recommend you to lose no time for it'll be poor work when
Tookey has it all to himself, for I mayn't be equil to stand
i' the desk at all, come another winter." Here Mr. Macey
paused, perhaps expecting some sign of emotion in his
hearer; but not observing any, he went on. "And as for
the money for the suit o' clothes, why, you get a matter of
a pound a week at your weaving, Master Marner, and
you're a young man, eh, for all you look so mushed. Why,
you couldn't ha' been five-and-twenty when you come
into these parts, eh?"

Silas started a little at the change to a questioning tone,
and answered mildly, "I don't know; I can't rightly say
—it's a long while since."

After receiving such an answer as this, it is not surprising that Mr. Macey observed, later on in the evening at
the Rainbow, that Marner's head was "all of a muddle,"
and that it was to be doubted if he ever knew when Sunday came round, which showed him a worse heathen than
many a dog.

Another of Silas's comforters, besides Mr. Macey, came
to him with a mind highly charged on the same topic.
This was Mrs. Winthrop, the wheelwright's wife. The
inhabitants of Raveloe were not severely regular in their
churchgoing, and perhaps there was hardly a person in
the parish who would not have held that to go to church
every Sunday in the calendar would have shown a greedy
desire to stand well with Heaven, and get an undue advantage over their neighbours—a wish to be better than
the "common run," that would have implied a reflection
on those who had had godfathers and godmothers as well
as themselves, and had an equal right to the burying
service. At the same time, it was understood to be requisite for all who were not household servants, or young
men, to take the sacrament at one of the great festivals:
Squire Cass himself took it on Christmas day; while those
who were held to be "good livers" went to church with
greater, though still with moderate, frequency.

Mrs. Winthrop was one of these; she was in all respects
a woman of scrupulous conscience, so eager for duties that
life seemed to offer them too scantily unless she rose at
half-past four, though this threw a scarcity of work over

the more advanced hours of the morning, which it was a
constant problem with her to remove. Yet she had not the
vixenish temper which is sometimes supposed to be a necessary condition of such habits: she was a very mild, patient woman, whose nature it was to seek out all the
sadder and more serious elements of life, and pasture her
mind upon them. She was the person always first thought
of in Raveloe when there was illness or death in a
family, when leeches were to be applied, or there was
a sudden disappointment in a monthly nurse. She was
a "comfortable woman"—good-looking, fresh-complex-
ioned, having her lips always slightly screwed, as if she
felt herself in a sickroom with the doctor or the clergyman present. But she was never whimpering; no one
had seen her shed tears; she was simply grave and inclined to shake her head and sigh, almost imperceptibly,
like a funeral mourner who is not a relation. It seemed
surprising that Ben Winthrop, who loved his quart pot
and his joke, got along so well with Dolly; but she took
her husband's jokes and joviality as patiently as everything else, considering that "men *would* be so," and viewing the stronger sex in the light of animals whom it had
pleased Heaven to make naturally troublesome, like bulls
and turkey cocks.

This good, wholesome woman could hardly fail to
have her mind drawn strongly towards Silas Marner, now
that he appeared in the light of a sufferer; and one Sunday afternoon she took her little boy Aaron with her, and
went to call on Silas, carrying in her hand some small
lard cakes, flat, pastelike articles, much esteemed in Raveloe. Aaron, an apple-cheeked youngster of seven, with a
clean starched frill, which looked like a plate for the apples, needed all his adventurous curiosity to embolden
him against the possibility that the big-eyed weaver might
do him some bodily injury; and his dubiety was much
increased when, on arriving at the Stone Pits, they heard
the mysterious sound of the loom.

"Ah, it is as I thought," said Mrs. Winthrop, sadly.

They had to knock loudly before Silas heard them; but
when he did come to the door he showed no impatience,
as he would once have done, at a visit that had been unasked for and unexpected. Formerly, his heart had been

as a locked casket with its treasure inside; but now the casket was empty, and the lock was broken. Left groping in darkness, with his prop utterly gone, Silas had inevitably a sense, though a dull and half-despairing one, that if any help came to him it must come from without; and there was a slight stirring of expectation at the sight of his fellow men, a faint consciousness of dependence on their good will. He opened the door wide to admit Dolly, but without otherwise returning her greeting than by moving the armchair a few inches as a sign that she was to sit down in it. Dolly, as soon as she was seated, removed the white cloth that covered her lard cakes, and said in her gravest way:

"I'd a baking yisterday, Master Marner, and the lard cakes turned out better nor common, and I'd ha' asked you to accept some, if you'd thought well. I don't eat such things myself, for a bit o' bread's what I like from one year's end to the other; but men's stomichs are made so comical, they want a change—they do, I know, God help 'em."

Dolly sighed gently as she held out the cakes to Silas, who thanked her kindly, and looked very close at them, absently, being accustomed to look so at everything he took into his hand—eyed all the while by the wondering bright orbs of the small Aaron, who had made an outwork of his mother's chair, and was peering round from behind it.

"There's letters pricked on 'em," said Dolly. "I can't read 'em myself, and there's nobody, not Mr. Macey himself, rightly knows what they mean; but they've a good meaning, for they're the same as is on the pulpit cloth at church. What are they, Aaron, my dear?"

Aaron retreated completely behind his outwork.

"Oh, go, that's naughty," said his mother mildly.

"Well, whativer the letters are, they've a good meaning; and it's a stamp as has been in our house, Ben says, ever since he was a little un, and his mother used to put it on cakes, and I've allays put it on too; for if there's any good, we've need of it i' this world."

"It's I.H.S.," said Silas, at which proof of learning Aaron peeped round the chair again.

"Well, to be sure, you can read 'em off," said Dolly.

"Ben's read 'em to me many and many a time, but they slip out o' my mind again; the more's the pity, for they're good letters, else they wouldn't be in the church; and so I prick 'em on all the loaves and all the cakes; though sometimes they won't hold, because o' the rising—for, as I said, if there's any good to be got, we've need of it i' this world—that we have; and I hope they'll bring good to you, Master Marner, for it's wi' that will I brought you the cakes; and you see the letters have held better nor common."

Silas was as unable to interpret the letters as Dolly, but there was no possibility of misunderstanding the desire to give comfort that made itself heard in her quiet tones. He said, with more feeling than before, "Thank you—thank you kindly." But he laid down the cakes and seated himself absently—drearily unconscious of any distinct benefit towards which the cake and the letters, or even Dolly's kindness, could tend for him.

"Ah, if there's good anywhere, we've need of it," repeated Dolly, who did not lightly forsake a serviceable phrase. She looked at Silas pityingly as she went on. "But you didn't hear the church bells this morning, Master Marner? I doubt you didn't know it was Sunday. Living so lone here, you lose your count, I daresay; and then, when your loom makes a noise, you can't hear the bells, more partic'lar now the frost kills the sound."

"Yes, I did; I heard 'em," said Silas, to whom Sunday bells were a mere accident of the day, and not part of its sacredness. There had been no bells in Lantern Yard.

"Dear heart!" said Dolly, pausing before she spoke again. "But what a pity it is you should work of a Sunday, and not clean yourself—if you *didn't* go to church; for if you'd a roasting bit, it might be as you couldn't leave it, being a lone man. But there's the bakehus, if you could make up your mind to spend a twopence on the oven now and then,—not every week, in course—I shouldn't like to do that myself—you might carry your bit o' dinner there, for it's nothing but right to have a bit o' summat hot of a Sunday, and not to make it as you can't know your dinner from Saturday. But now, upo' Christmas day, this blessed Christmas as is ever coming, if you was to take your dinner to the bakehus, and go to church, and see the holly and the yew, and hear the an-thim, and then take the sacramen', you'd be a deal the better, and you'd know which end you stood on, and you could put your trust i' Them as knows better nor we do, seein' you'd ha' done what it lies on us all to do."

Dolly's exhortation, which was an unusually long effort of speech for her, was uttered in the soothing, persuasive tone with which she would have tried to prevail on a sick man to take his medicine, or a basin of gruel for which he had no appetite. Silas had never before been closely urged on the point of his absence from church, which had only been thought of as a part of his general queer-ness; and he was too direct and simple to evade Dolly's appeal.

"Nay, nay," he said. "I know nothing o' church. I've never been to church."

"No!" said Dolly, in a low tone of wonderment. Then bethinking herself of Silas's advent from an unknown country, she said, "Could it ha' been as they'd no church where you was born?"

"Oh, yes," said Silas, meditatively, sitting in his usual posture of leaning on his knees, and supporting his head. "There was churches—a many—it was a big town. But I knew nothing of 'em—I went to chapel."

Dolly was much puzzled at this new world, but she was rather afraid of inquiring further, lest "chapel" meant some haunt of wickedness. After a little thought, she said:

"Well, Master Marner, it's niver too late to turn over a new leaf, and if you've niver had no church, there's no telling the good it'll do you. For I feel so set up and com-fortable as niver was, when I've been and heard the prayers, and the singing to the praise and glory o' God, as Mr. Macey gives out—and Mr. Crackenthorp saying good words, and more partic'lar on Sacramen' Day; and if a bit o' trouble comes, I feel as I can put up wi' it, for I've looked for help i' the right quarter, and gev myself up to Them as we must all give ourselves up to at the last; and if we'n done our part, it isn't to be believed as Them as are above us 'ull be worse nor we are, and come short o' Theirn."

Poor Dolly's exposition of her simple Raveloe theology

fell rather unmeaningly on Silas's ears, for there was no word in it that could rouse a memory of what he had known as religion, and his comprehension was quite baffled by the plural pronoun, which was no heresy of Dolly's, but only her way of avoiding a presumptuous familiarity. He remained silent, not feeling inclined to assent to the part of Dolly's speech which he fully understood —her recommendation that he should go to church. Indeed, Silas was so unaccustomed to talk beyond the brief questions and answers necessary for the transaction of his simple business, that words did not easily come to him without the urgency of a distinct purpose.

But now, little Aaron, having become used to the weaver's awful presence, had advanced to his mother's side, and Silas, seeming to notice him for the first time, tried to return Dolly's signs of good will by offering the lad a bit of lard cake. Aaron shrank back a little, and rubbed his head against his mother's shoulder, but still thought the piece of cake worth the risk of putting his hand out for it.

"Oh, for shame, Aaron," said his mother, taking him on her lap, however; "why, you don't want cake again yet awhile. He's wonderful hearty," she went on, with a little sigh, "that he is, God knows. He's my youngest, and we spoil him sadly, for either me or the father must allays hev him in our sight—that we must."

She stroked Aaron's brown head, and thought it must do Master Marner good to see such a "pictur of a child." But Marner, on the other side of the hearth, saw the neat-featured rosy face as a mere dim round, with two dark spots in it.

"And he's got a voice like a bird—you wouldn't think," Dolly went on; "he can sing a Christmas carril as his father's taught him; and I take it for a token as he'll come to good, as he can learn the good tunes so quick. Come, Aaron, stan' up and sing the carril to Master Marner, come."

Aaron replied by rubbing his forehead against his mother's shoulder.

"Oh, that's naughty," said Dolly gently. "Stan' up, when mother tells you, and let me hold the cake till you've done."

Aaron was not indisposed to display his talents, even to an ogre, under protecting circumstances; and after a few more signs of coyness, consisting chiefly in rubbing the backs of his hands over his eyes, and then peeping between them at Master Marner, to see if he looked anxious for the "carril," he at length allowed his head to be duly adjusted, and standing behind the table, which let him appear above it only as far as his broad frill, so that he looked like a cherubic head untroubled with a body, he began with a clear chirp, and in a melody that had the rhythm of an industrious hammer:

> "God rest you merry, gentlemen,
> Let nothing you dismay,
> For Jesus Christ our Saviour
> Was born on Christmas day."

Dolly listened with a devout look, glancing at Marner in some confidence that this strain would help to allure him to church.

"That's Christmas music," she said, when Aaron had ended, and had secured his piece of cake again. "There's no other music equil to the Christmas music—'Hark the erol angils sing.' And you may judge what it is at church, Master Marner, with the bassoon and the voices, as you can't help thinking you've got to a better place a'ready—for I wouldn't speak ill o' this world, seeing as Them put us in it as knows best; but what wi' the drink, and the quarrelling, and the bad illnesses, and the hard dying, as I've seen times and times, one's thankful to hear of a better. The boy sings pretty, don't he, Master Marner?"

"Yes," said Silas absently, "very pretty."

The Christmas carol, with its hammerlike rhythm, had fallen on his ears as strange music, quite unlike a hymn, and could have none of the effect Dolly contemplated. But he wanted to show her that he was grateful, and the only mode that occurred to him was to offer Aaron a bit more cake.

"Oh, no, thank you, Master Marner," said Dolly, holding down Aaron's willing hands. "We must be going home now. And so I wish you good-bye, Master Marner; and if ever you feel anyways bad in your inside, as you can't fend for yourself, I'll come and clean up for you, and get you a bit o' victual, and willing. But I beg and pray of you to leave off weaving of a Sunday, for it's bad for soul and body—and the money as comes i' that way 'ull be a bad bed to lie down on at the last, if it doesn't fly away, nobody knows where, like the white frost. And you'll excuse me being that free with you, Master Marner, for I wish you well—I do. Make your bow, Aaron."

Silas said "Good-bye, and thank you, kindly," as he opened the door for Dolly, but he couldn't help feeling relieved when she was gone—relieved that he might weave again and moan at his ease. Her simple view of life and its comforts, by which she had tried to cheer him, was only like a report of unknown objects, which his imagination could not fashion. The fountains of human love and divine faith had not yet been unlocked, and his soul was still the shrunken rivulet, with only this difference, that its little groove of sand was blocked up, and it wandered confusedly against dark obstruction.

And so, notwithstanding the honest persuasions of Mr. Macey and Dolly Winthrop, Silas spent his Christmas day in loneliness, eating his meat in sadness of heart, though the meat had come to him as a neighbourly present. In the morning he looked out on the black frost that seemed to press cruelly on every blade of grass, while the half-icy red pool shivered under the bitter wind; but towards evening the snow began to fall, and curtained from him even that dreary outlook, shutting him close up with his narrow grief. And he sat in his robbed home through the livelong evening, not caring to close his shutters or lock his door, pressing his head between his hands and moaning, till the cold grasped him and told him that his fire was grey.

Nobody in this world but himself knew that he was the same Silas Marner who had once loved his fellow with tender love, and trusted in an unseen goodness. Even to himself that past experience had become dim.

But in Raveloe village the bells rang merrily, and the church was fuller than all through the rest of the year, with red faces among the abundant dark-green boughs—faces prepared for a longer service than usual by an odorous breakfast of toast and ale. Those green boughs, the

hymn and anthem never heard but at Christmas—even
the Athanasian Creed, which was discriminated from the
others only as being longer and of exceptional virtue,
since it was only read on rare occasions—brought a vague
exulting sense for which the grown men could as little
have found words as the children, that something great
and mysterious had been done for them in heaven above,
and in earth below, which they were appropriating by
their presence. And then the red faces made their way
through the black, biting frost to their own homes, feeling themselves free for the rest of the day to eat, drink,
and be merry, and using that Christian freedom without
diffidence.

At Squire Cass's family party that day nobody mentioned Dunstan—nobody was sorry for his absence, or
feared it would be too long. The doctor and his wife,
uncle and aunt Kimble, were there, and the annual
Christmas talk was carried through without any omis-
sions, rising to the climax of Mr. Kimble's experience
when he walked the London hospitals thirty years back,
together with striking professional anecdotes then gathered. Whereupon cards followed, with aunt Kimble's annual failure to follow suit, and uncle Kimble's irascibility
concerning the odd trick, which was rarely explicable to
him, when it was not on his side, without a general visitation of tricks to see that they were formed on sound
principles: the whole being accompanied by a strong,
steaming odour of spirits-and-water.

But the party on Christmas day, being a strictly family
party, was not the pre-eminently brilliant celebration of
the season at the Red House. It was the great dance on
New Year's Eve that made the glory of Squire Cass's hospitality, as of his forefather's, time out of mind. This was
the occasion when all the society of Raveloe and Tarley,
whether old acquaintances separated by long rutty dis-
tances, or cooled acquaintances separated by misunder-
standings concerning runaway calves, or acquaintances
founded on intermittent condescension, counted on meeting and on comporting themselves with mutual appropri-
ateness. This was the occasion on which fair dames who
came on pillions sent their bandboxes before them, supplied with more than their evening costume; for the feast

was not to end with a single evening, like a paltry town entertainment, where the whole supply of eatables is put on the table at once, and bedding is scanty. The Red House was provisioned as if for a siege; and as for the spare featherbeds ready to be laid on floors, they were as plentiful as might naturally be expected in a family that had killed its own geese for many generations.

Godfrey Cass was looking forward to this New Year's Eve with a foolish reckless longing, that made him half deaf to his importunate companion, Anxiety.

"Dunsey will be coming home soon: there will be a great blowup, and how will you bribe his spite to silence?" said Anxiety.

"Oh, he won't come home before New Year's Eve, perhaps," said Godfrey; "and I shall sit by Nancy then and dance with her, and get a kind look from her in spite of herself."

"But money is wanted in another quarter," said Anxiety, in a louder voice, "and how will you get it without selling your mother's diamond pin? And if you don't get it . . . ?"

"Well, but something may happen to make things easier. At any rate, there's one pleasure for me close at hand: Nancy is coming."

"Yes, and suppose your father should bring matters to a pass that will oblige you to decline marrying her—and to give your reasons?"

"Hold your tongue, and don't worry me. I can see Nancy's eyes, just as they will look at me, and feel her hand in mine already."

But Anxiety went on, though in noisy Christmas company; refusing to be utterly quieted even by much drinking.

CHAPTER XI

SOME WOMEN, I grant, would not appear to advantage seated on a pillion, and attired in a drab joseph and a drab beaver bonnet, with a crown resembling a small stew pan; for a garment suggesting a coachman's greatcoat, cut out

under an exiguity of cloth that would only allow of minia-
ture capes, is not well adapted to conceal deficiencies of
contour, nor is drab a colour that will throw sallow cheeks
into lively contrast. It was all the greater triumph to Miss
Nancy Lammeter's beauty that she looked thoroughly bewitching in that costume, as seated on the pillion behind
her tall, erect father, she held one arm around him, and
looked down, with open-eyed anxiety, at the treacherous
snow-covered pools and puddles which sent up formidable
splashings of mud under the stamp of Dobbin's foot. A
painter would, perhaps, have preferred her in those moments when she was free from self-consciousness; but certainly the bloom on her cheeks was at its highest point of
contrast with the surrounding drab when she arrived at
the door of the Red House, and saw Mr. Godfrey Cass
ready to lift her from the pillion. She wished her sister
Priscilla had come up at the same time with the servant,
for then she would have contrived that Mr. Godfrey
should have lifted off Priscilla first, and, in the meantime,
she would have persuaded her father to go round to the
horse block instead of alighting at the doorsteps. It was
very painful, when you had made it quite clear to a young
man that you were determined not to marry him, however
much he might wish it, that he would still continue to pay
you marked attentions; besides, why didn't he always
show the same attentions, if he meant them sincerely,
instead of being so strange as Mr. Godfrey Cass was, sometimes behaving as if he didn't want to speak to her, and
taking no notice of her for weeks and weeks, and then, all
on a sudden, almost making love again? Moreover, it was
quite plain that he had no real love for her, else he would
not let people have *that* to say of him which they did say.
Did he suppose that Miss Nancy Lammeter was to be won
by any man, squire or no squire, who led a bad life? That
was not what she had been used to see in her own father,
who was the soberest and best man in that countryside,
only a little hot and hasty now and then, if things were
not done to the minute.

All these thoughts rushed through Miss Nancy's mind,
in their habitual succession, in the moments between her
first sight of Mr. Godfrey Cass standing at the door and
her own arrival there. Happily, the Squire came out too,

and gave a loud greeting to her father, so that, somehow, under cover of this noise, she seemed to find concealment for her confusion and neglect of any suitably formal behaviour, while she was being lifted from the pillion by strong arms, which seemed to find her ridiculously small and light. And there was the best reason for hastening into the house at once, since the snow was beginning to fall again, threatening an unpleasant journey for such guests as were still on the road. These were a small minority; for already the afternoon was beginning to decline, and there would not be too much time for the ladies who came from a distance to attire themselves in readiness for the early tea which was to inspirit them for the dance.

There was a buzz of voices through the house, as Miss Nancy entered, mingled with the scrape of a fiddle preluding in the kitchen; but the Lammeters were guests whose arrival had evidently been thought of so much that it had been watched for from the windows, for Mrs. Kimble, who did the honours at the Red House on these great occasions, came forward to meet Miss Nancy in the hall, and conduct her upstairs. Mrs. Kimble was the Squire's sister, as well as the doctor's wife—a double dignity, with which her diameter was in direct proportion; so that, a journey upstairs being rather fatiguing to her, she did not oppose Miss Nancy's request to be allowed to find her way alone to the Blue Room, where the Miss Lammeters' bandboxes had been deposited on their arrival in the morning.

There was hardly a bedroom in the house where feminine compliments were not passing and feminine toilettes going forward, in various stages, in space made scanty by extra beds spread upon the floor; and Miss Nancy, as she entered the Blue Room, had to make her little formal curtsy to a group of six. On the one hand, there were ladies no less important than the two Miss Gunns, the wine merchant's daughters from Lytherly, dressed in the height of fashion, with the tightest skirts and the shortest waists, and gazed at by Miss Ladbrook (of the Old Pastures) with a shyness not unsustained by inward criticism. Partly, Miss Ladbrook felt that her own skirt must be regarded as unduly lax by the Miss Gunns, and partly, that it was a pity the Miss Gunns did not show that judgment which she herself would show if she were in their place, by stopping a little on this side of the fashion. On the other hand, Mrs. Ladbrook was standing in skullcap and front, with her turban in her hand, curtsying and smiling blandly and saying, "After you, ma'am," to another lady in similar circumstances, who had politely offered the precedence at the looking glass.

But Miss Nancy had no sooner made her curtsy than an elderly lady came forward, whose full white muslin kerchief and mobcap round her curls of smooth grey hair were in daring contrast with the puffed yellow satins and topknotted caps of her neighbours. She approached Miss Nancy with much primness, and said, with a slow, treble suavity:

"Niece, I hope I see you well in health." Miss Nancy kissed her aunt's cheek dutifully, and answered, with the same sort of amiable primness, "Quite well, I thank you, Aunt, and I hope I see you the same."

"Thank you, Niece, I keep my health for the present. And how is my brother-in-law?"

These dutiful questions and answers were continued until it was ascertained in detail that the Lammeters were all as well as usual, and the Osgoods likewise, also that niece Priscilla must certainly arrive shortly, and that travelling on pillions in snowy weather was unpleasant, though a joseph was a great protection. Then Nancy was formally introduced to her aunt's visitors, the Miss Gunns, as being the daughters of a mother known to *their* mother, though now for the first time induced to make a journey into these parts; and these ladies were so taken by surprise at finding such a lovely face and figure in an out-of-the-way country place, that they began to feel some curiosity about the dress she would put on when she took off her joseph. Miss Nancy, whose thoughts were always conducted with the propriety and moderation conspicuous in her manners, remarked to herself that the Miss Gunns were rather hard-featured than otherwise, and that such very low dresses as they wore might have been attributed to vanity if their shoulders had been pretty, but that, being as they were, it was not reasonable to suppose that they showed their necks from a love of display, but rather from some obligation not inconsistent with sense and modesty. She felt convinced, as she opened her box, that this must be her aunt Osgood's opinion, for Miss Nancy's mind resembled her aunt's to a degree that everybody said was surprising, considering the kinship was on Mr. Osgood's side; and though you might not have supposed it from the formality of their greeting, there was a devoted attachment and mutual admiration between aunt and niece. Even Miss Nancy's refusal of her cousin Gilbert Osgood (on the ground solely that he was her cousin), though it had grieved her aunt greatly, had not in the least cooled the preference which had determined her to leave Nancy several of her hereditary ornaments, let Gilbert's future wife be whom she might.

Three of the ladies quickly retired, but the Miss Gunns were quite content that Mrs. Osgood's inclination to remain with her niece gave them also a reason for staying to see the rustic beauty's toilette. And it was really a pleasure—from the first opening of the bandbox, where everything smelt of lavender and rose leaves, to the clasping of the small coral necklace that fitted closely round her little white neck. Everything belonging to Miss Nancy was of delicate purity and nattiness: not a crease was where it had no business to be, not a bit of her linen professed whiteness without fulfilling its profession; the very pins on her pincushion were stuck in after a pattern from which she was careful to allow no aberration; and as for her own person, it gave the same idea of perfect unvarying neatness as the body of a little bird. It is true that her light-brown hair was cropped behind like a boy's, and was dressed in front in a number of flat rings, that lay quite away from her face; but there was no sort of coiffure that could make Miss Nancy's cheek and neck look otherwise than pretty; and when at last she stood complete in her silvery twilled silk, her lace tucker, her coral necklace, and coral ear drops, the Miss Gunns could see nothing to criticise except her hands, which bore the traces of buttermaking, cheese-crushing, and even still coarser work. But Miss Nancy was not ashamed of that, for even while she was dressing she narrated to her aunt how she and Priscilla had packed their boxes yesterday, because this morning was baking morning, and since they were leaving home, it was desirable to make a good supply of meat pies for the kitchen; and as she concluded this judicious remark, she turned to the Miss Gunns that she might not commit the rudeness of not including them in the conversation. The Miss Gunns smiled stiffly, and thought what a pity it was that these rich country people, who could afford to buy such good clothes (really Miss Nancy's lace and silk were very costly), should be brought up in utter ignorance and vulgarity. She actually said "mate" for "meat," "'appen" for "perhaps," and "oss" for "horse," which, to young ladies living in good Lytherly society, who habitually said "'orse," even in domestic privacy, and only said "'appen" on the right occasions, was necessarily shocking. Miss Nancy, indeed, had never been to any school higher than Dame Tedman's: her acquaintance with profane literature hardly went beyond the rhymes she had worked in her large sampler under the lamb and the shepherdess; and in order to balance an account, she was obliged to effect her subtraction by removing visible metallic shillings and sixpences from a visible metallic total. There is hardly a servant maid in these days who is not better informed than Miss Nancy; yet she had the essential attributes of a lady—high veracity, delicate honour in her dealings, deference to others, and refined personal habits—and lest these should not suffice to convince grammatical fair ones that her feelings can at all resemble theirs, I will add that she was slightly proud and exacting, and as constant in her affections towards a baseless opinion as towards an erring lover.

The anxiety about sister Priscilla, which had grown rather active by the time the coral necklace was clasped, was happily ended by the entrance of that cheerful-looking lady herself, with a face made blowsy by cold and damp. After the first questions and greetings, she turned to Nancy, and surveyed her from head to foot—then wheeled her round, to ascertain that the back view was equally faultless.

"What do you think o' *these* gowns, Aunt Osgood?" said Priscilla, while Nancy helped her to unrobe.

"Very handsome indeed, Niece," said Mrs. Osgood, with a slight increase of formality. She always thought Niece Priscilla too rough.

"I'm obliged to have the same as Nancy, you know, for all I'm five years older and it makes me look yallow! for she never *will* have anything without I have mine just like it, because she wants us to look like sisters. And I tell her folks 'ull think it's my weakness makes me fancy as I shall look pretty in what she looks pretty in. For I *am* ugly—there's no denying that: I feature my father's family. But, law! I don't mind, do you?" Priscilla here turned to the Miss Gunns, rattling on in too much preoccupation with the delight of talking to notice that her candour was not appreciated. "The pretty uns do for fly catchers—they keep the men off us. I've no opinion o' the men, Miss Gunn—I don't know what *you* have. And as for fretting and stewing about what *they*'ll think of you from morning till night, and making your life uneasy about what they're doing when they're out o' your sight—as I tell Nancy, it's a folly no woman need be guilty of, if she's got a good father and a good home: let her leave it to them as have got no fortin, and can't help themselves. As I say, Mr. Have-your-own-way is the best husband, and the only one I'd ever promise to obey. I know it isn't pleasant, when you've been used to living in a big way, and managing hogsheads and all that, to go and put your nose in by somebody else's fireside, or to sit down by yourself to a scrag or a knuckle; but, thank God! my father's a sober man and likely to live; and if you've got a man by the chimney corner, it doesn't matter if he's childish—the business needn't be broke up."

The delicate process of getting her narrow gown over her head without injury to her smooth curls obliged Miss Priscilla to pause in this rapid survey of life, and Mrs. Osgood seized the opportunity of rising and saying:

"Well, Niece, you'll follow us. The Miss Gunns will like to go down."

"Sister," said Nancy, when they were alone, "you've offended the Miss Gunns, I'm sure."

"What have I done, child?" said Priscilla, in some alarm.

"Why, you asked them if they minded about being ugly—you're so very blunt."

"Law, did I? Well, it popped out: it's a mercy I said no more, for I'm a bad un to live with folks when they don't like the truth. But as for being ugly, look at me, child, in this silver-coloured silk—I told you how it 'ud be—I look as yellow as a daffadil. Anybody 'ud say you wanted to make a mawkin of me."

"No, Priscy, don't say so. I begged and prayed of you not to let us have this silk if you'd like another better. I was willing to have *your* choice, you know I was," said Nancy, in anxious self-vindication.

"Nonsense, child, you know you'd set your heart on this; and reason good, for you're the colour o' cream. It 'ud be fine doings for you to dress yourself to suit *my* skin. What I find fault with is that notion o' yours as I must dress myself just like you. But you do as you like with me—you always did, from when first you began to walk. If you wanted to go the field's length, the field's length you'd go; and there was no whipping you, for you looked as prim and innicent as a daisy all the while."

"Priscy," said Nancy gently, as she fastened a coral necklace, exactly like her own, round Priscilla's neck, which was very far from being like her own, "I'm sure I'm willing to give way as far as is right, but who shouldn't dress alike if it isn't sisters? Would you have us go about looking as if we were no kin to one another—us that have got no mother and not another sister in the world? I'd do what was right, if I dressed in a gown dyed with cheese colouring; and I'd rather you'd choose, and let me wear what pleases you."

"There you go again! You'd come round to the same thing if one talked to you from Saturday night till Saturday morning. It'll be fine fun to see how you'll master your husband and never raise your voice above the singing o' the kettle all the while. I like to see the men mastered!"

"Don't talk *so*, Priscy," said Nancy, blushing. "You know I don't mean ever to be married."

"Oh, you never mean a fiddlestick's end!" said Priscilla, as she arranged her discarded dress, and closed her bandbox. "Who shall *I* have to work for when Father's gone, if you are to go and take notions in your head and be an old maid, because some folks are no better than they should be? I haven't a bit o' patience with you—sitting on an addled egg forever, as if there was never a fresh un in the world. One old maid's enough out o' two sisters; and I shall do credit to a single life, for God A'mighty meant me for it. Come, we can go down now. I'm as ready as a mawkin *can* be—there's nothing a-wanting to frighten the crows, now I've got my ear droppers in."

As the two Miss Lammeters walked into the large parlour together, anyone who did not know the character of both might certainly have supposed that the reason why the square-shouldered, clumsy, high-featured Priscilla wore a dress the facsimile of her pretty sister's was either the mistaken vanity of the one, or the malicious contrivance of the other in order to set off her own rare beauty. But the good-natured, self-forgetful cheeriness and common sense of Priscilla would soon have dissipated the one suspicion; and the modest calm of Nancy's speech and manners told clearly of a mind free from all disavowed devices.

Places of honour had been kept for the Miss Lammeters near the head of the principal tea table in the wainscoted parlour, now looking fresh and pleasant with handsome branches of holly, yew, and laurel, from the abundant growths of the old garden; and Nancy felt an inward flutter, that no firmness of purpose could prevent, when she saw Mr. Godfrey Cass advancing to lead her to a seat between himself and Mr. Crackenthorp, while Priscilla was called to the opposite side between her father and the Squire. It certainly did make some difference to Nancy that the lover she had given up was the young man of quite the highest consequence in the parish—at home in a venerable and unique parlour, which was the extremity of grandeur in her experience, a parlour where *she* might one day have been mistress, with the consciousness that she was spoken of as "Madam Cass," the Squire's wife. These circumstances exalted her inward drama in her own eyes, and deepened the emphasis with which she declared to herself that not the most dazzling rank should induce her to marry a man whose conduct showed him careless of his character, but that, "love once, love always," was the motto of a true and pure woman, and no man should ever have any right over her which would be a call on her to destroy the dried flowers that she treasured, and always would treasure, for Godfrey Cass's sake. And Nancy was capable of keeping her word to herself under very trying conditions. Nothing but a becoming blush betrayed the moving thoughts that urged themselves upon her as she accepted the seat next to Mr. Crackenthorp; for she was so instinctively neat and adroit in all her actions, and her pretty lips met each other with such quiet firmness, that it would have been difficult for her to appear agitated.

It was not the rector's practice to let a charming blush pass without an appropriate compliment. He was not in the least lofty or aristocratic, but simply a merry-eyed, small-featured, grey-haired man, with his chin propped by an ample, many-creased white neckcloth which seemed to predominate over every other point in his person, and somehow to impress its peculiar character on his remarks; so that to have considered his amenities apart from his cravat would have been a severe, and perhaps a dangerous, effort of abstraction.

"Ha, Miss Nancy," he said, turning his head within his cravat, and smiling down pleasantly upon her, "when anybody pretends this has been a severe winter, I shall tell them I saw the roses blooming on New Year's eve—eh, Godfrey, what do *you* say?"

Godfrey made no reply, and avoided looking at Nancy very markedly; for though these complimentary personalities were held to be in excellent taste in old-fashioned Raveloe society, reverent love has a politeness of its own which it teaches to men otherwise of small schooling. But the Squire was rather impatient at Godfrey's showing himself a dull spark in this way. By this advanced hour of the day, the Squire was always in higher spirits than we have seen him in at the breakfast table, and felt it quite pleasant to fulfil the hereditary duty of being noisily jovial and patronising: the large silver snuff box was in active service, and was offered without fail to all neighbours from time to time, however often they might have declined the favour. At present, the Squire had only given an express welcome to the heads of families as they appeared; but always as the evening deepened, his hospitality rayed out more widely, till he had tapped the youngest guests on the back and shown a peculiar fondness for their presence, in the full belief that they must feel their lives made happy by their belonging to a parish where there was such a hearty man as Squire Cass to invite them and wish them well. Even in this early stage of the jovial mood, it was natural that he should wish to supply his son's deficiencies by looking and speaking for him.

"Ay, ay," he began, offering his snuffbox to Mr. Lammeter, who for the second time bowed his head and waved his hand in stiff rejection of the offer, "us old fellows may wish ourselves young tonight, when we see the mistletoe bough in the White Parlour. It's true, most things are gone back'ard in these last thirty years—the country's going down since the old King fell ill. But when I look at Miss Nancy here, I begin to think the lasses keep up their quality—ding me if I remember a sample to match her, not when I was a fine young fellow, and thought a deal about my pigtail. No offence to you, madam," he added, bending to Mrs. Crackenthorp, who sat by him, "I didn't know *you* when you were as young as Miss Nancy here."

Mrs. Crackenthorp—a small, blinking woman, who fidgeted incessantly with her lace, ribbons, and gold chain, turning her head about and making subdued noises, very much like a guinea pig, that twitches its nose and soliloquises in all company indiscriminately—now blinked and fidgeted towards the Squire, and said, "Oh, no—no offence."

This emphatic compliment of the Squire's to Nancy was felt by others besides Godfrey to have a diplomatic significance; and her father gave a slight additional erectness to his back, as he looked across the table at her with complacent gravity. That grave and orderly senior was not going to bate a jot of his dignity by seeming elated at the notion of a match between his family and the Squire's; he was gratified by any honour paid to his daughter; but he must see an alteration in several ways before his consent would be vouchsafed. His spare but healthy person, and high-featured, firm face, that looked as if it had never been flushed by excess, was in strong contrast, not only with the Squire's, but with the appearance of the Raveloe farmers generally—in accordance with a favourite saying of his own, that "breed was stronger than pasture."

"Miss Nancy's wonderful like what her mother was, though; isn't she, Kimble?" said the stout lady of that name, looking round for her husband.

But Doctor Kimble (country apothecaries in old days

enjoyed that title without authority of diploma), being a
thin and agile man, was flitting about the room with his
hands in his pockets, making himself agreeable to his
feminine patients, with medical impartiality, and being
welcomed everywhere as a doctor by hereditary right—not
one of those miserable apothecaries who canvass for practice in strange neighbourhoods, and spend all their income in starving their one horse, but a man of substance,
able to keep an extravagant table like the best of his
patients. Time out of mind the Raveloe doctor had been
a Kimble; Kimble was inherently a doctor's name; and it
was difficult to contemplate firmly the melancholy fact
that the actual Kimble had no son, so that his practice
might one day be handed over to a successor with the in-
congruous name of Taylor or Johnson. But in that case
the wiser people in Raveloe would employ Dr. Blick of
Flitton—as less unnatural.

"Did you speak to me, my dear?" said the authentic
doctor, coming quickly to his wife's side; but, as if fore-
seeing that she would be too much out of breath to repeat
her remark, he went on immediately, "Ha, Miss Priscilla,
the sight of you revives the taste of that superexcellent
pork pie. I hope the batch isn't near an end."

"Yes, indeed, it is, doctor," said Priscilla; "but I'll
answer for it the next shall be as good. My pork pies don't
turn out well by chance."

"Not as your doctoring does, eh, Kimble?—because
folks forget to take your physic, eh?" said the Squire, who
regarded physic and doctors as many loyal churchmen
regard the church and the clergy—tasting a joke against
them when he was in health, but impatiently eager for
their aid when anything was the matter with him. He
tapped his box, and looked round him with a triumphant
laugh.

"Ah, she has a quick wit, my friend Priscilla has," said
the doctor, choosing to attribute the epigram to a lady
rather than allow a brother-in-law that advantage over
him. "She saves a little pepper to sprinkle over her talk—
that's the reason why she never puts too much into her
pies. There's my wife, now, she never has an answer at
her tongue's end; but if I offend her, she's sure to
scarify my throat with black pepper the next day, or else

give me the colic with watery greens. That's an awful tit-
for-tat." Here the vivacious doctor made a pathetic grimace.

"Did you ever hear the like?" said Mrs. Kimble, laughing above her double chin with much good humour, aside
to Mrs. Crackenthorp, who blinked and nodded, and
seemed to intend a smile, which, by the correlation of
forces, went off in small twitchings and noises.

"I suppose that's the sort of tit-for-tat adopted in your
profession, Kimble, if you've a grudge against a patient,"
said the rector.

"Never do have a grudge against our patients," said Mr.
Kimble, "except when they leave us: and then, you see,
we haven't the chance of prescribing for 'em. Ha, Miss
Nancy," he continued, suddenly skipping to Nancy's side,
"you won't forget your promise? You're to save a dance
for me, you know."

"Come, come, Kimble, don't you be too for'ard," said
the Squire. "Give the young uns fair play. There's my
son Godfrey'll be wanting to have a round with you if you
run off with Miss Nancy. He's bespoke her for the first
dance, I'll be bound. Eh, sir! what do you say?" he continued, throwing himself backward, and looking at Godfrey. "Haven't you asked Miss Nancy to open the dance
with you?"

Godfrey, sorely uncomfortable under this significant
insistence about Nancy, and afraid to think where it
would end by the time his father had set his usual hospitable example of drinking before and after supper, saw
no course open but to turn to Nancy and say, with as little
awkwardness as possible.

"No; I've not asked her yet, but I hope she'll consent—
if somebody else hasn't been before me."

"No, I've not engaged myself," said Nancy quietly,
though blushingly. (If Mr. Godfrey founded any hopes
on her consenting to dance with him, he would soon be
undeceived; but there was no need for her to be uncivil.)

"Then I hope you've no objections to dancing with
me," said Godfrey, beginning to lose the sense that there
was anything uncomfortable in this arrangement.

"No, no objections," said Nancy, in a cold tone.

"Ah, well, you're a lucky fellow, Godfrey," said Uncle

Kimble; "but you're my godson, so I won't stand in your way. Else I'm not so very old, eh, my dear?" he went on, skipping to his wife's side again. "You wouldn't mind my having a second after you were gone—not if I cried a good deal first?"

"Come, come, take a cup o' tea and stop your tongue, do," said good-humoured Mrs. Kimble, feeling some pride in a husband who must be regarded as so clever and amusing by the company generally. If he had only not been irritable at cards!

While safe, well-tested personalities were enlivening the tea in this way, the sound of the fiddle approaching within a distance at which it could be heard distinctly made the young people look at each other with sympathetic impatience for the end of the meal.

"Why, there's Solomon in the hall," said the Squire, "and playing my fav'rite tune, I believe—'The Flaxen-headed Ploughboy'—he's for giving us a hint as we aren't enough in a hurry to hear him play. Bob," he called out to his third, long-legged son, who was at the other end of the room, "open the door, and tell Solomon to come in. He shall give us a tune here."

Bob obeyed, and Solomon walked in, fiddling as he walked, for he would on no account break off in the middle of a tune.

"Here, Solomon," said the Squire, with loud patronage. "Round here, my man. Ah, I knew it was 'The Flaxen-headed Ploughboy': there's no finer tune."

Solomon Macey, a small, hale old man with an abundant crop of long white hair reaching nearly to his shoulders, advanced to the indicated spot, bowing reverently while he fiddled, as much as to say that he respected the company, though he respected the keynote more. As soon as he had repeated the tune and lowered his fiddle, he bowed again to the Squire and the rector, and said, "I hope I see your honour and your reverence well, and wishing you health and long life and a happy New Year. And wishing the same to you, Mr. Lammeter, sir; and to the other gentlemen, and the madams, and the young lasses."

As Solomon uttered the last words, he bowed in all directions solicitously, lest he should be wanting in due respect. But thereupon he immediately began to prelude, and fell into the tune which he knew would be taken as a special compliment by Mr. Lammeter.

"Thank ye, Solomon, thank ye," said Mr. Lammeter when the fiddle paused again. "That's 'Over the Hills and Far Away,' that is. My father used to say to me, whenever we heard that tune, 'Ah, lad, *I* come from over the hills and far away.' There's a many tunes I don't make head or tail of; but that speaks to me like the blackbird's whistle; I suppose it's the name; there's a deal in the name of a tune."

But Solomon was already impatient to prelude again, and presently broke with much spirit into "Sir Roger de Coverley," at which there was a sound of chairs pushed back, and laughing voices.

"Ay, ay, Solomon, we know what that means," said the Squire, rising. "It's time to begin the dance, eh? Lead the way, then, and we'll all follow you."

So Solomon, holding his white head on one side, and playing vigorously, marched forward at the head of the gay procession into the White Parlour, where the mistletoe bough was hung, and multitudinous tallow candles made rather a brilliant effect, gleaming from among the berried holly boughs, and reflected in the old-fashioned oval mirrors fastened in the panels of the white wainscot. A quaint procession! Old Solomon, in his seedy clothes and long white locks, seemed to be luring that decent company by the magic scream of his fiddle—luring discreet matrons in turban-shaped caps, nay, Mrs. Crackenthorp herself, the summit of whose perpendicular feather was on a level with the Squire's shoulder—luring fair lasses complacently conscious of very short waists and skirts blameless of front folds—burly fathers in large variegated waistcoats, and ruddy sons, for the most part shy and sheepish, in short nether garments and very long coattails.

Already, Mr. Macey and a few other privileged villagers, who were allowed to be spectators on these great occasions, were seated on benches placed for them near the door; and great was the admiration and satisfaction in that quarter when the couples had formed themselves for the dance, and the Squire led off with Mrs. Crackenthorp, joining hands with the Rector and Mrs. Osgood. That was as it should be—that was what everybody had been used to—and the charter of Raveloe seemed to be renewed by the ceremony. It was not thought of as an unbecoming levity for the old and middle-aged people to dance a little before sitting down to cards, but rather as part of their social duties. For what were these if not to be merry at appropriate times, interchanging visits and poultry with due frequency, paying each other old-established compliments in sound traditional phrases, passing well-tried personal jokes, urging your guests to eat and drink too much out of hospitality, and eating and drinking too much in your neighbour's house to show that you liked your cheer? And the parson naturally set an example in these social duties. For it would not have been possible for the Raveloe mind, without a peculiar revelation, to know that a clergyman should be a pale-faced memento of solemnities, instead of a reasonably faulty man, whose exclusive authority to read prayers and preach, to christen, marry, and bury you, necessarily coexisted with the right to sell you the ground to be buried in, and to take tithe in kind; on which last point, of course, there was a little grumbling, but not to the extent of irreligion—not beyond the grumbling at the rain, which was by no means accompanied with a spirit of impious defiance, but with a desire that the prayer for fine weather might be read forthwith.

There was no reason, then, why the rector's dancing should not be received as part of the fitness of things quite as much as the Squire's, or why, on the other hand, Mr. Macey's official respect should restrain him from subjecting the parson's performance to that criticism with which minds of extraordinary acuteness must necessarily contemplate the doings of their fallible fellow men.

"The Squire's pretty springe, considering his weight," said Mr. Macey, "and he stamps uncommon well. But Mr. Lammeter beats 'em all for shapes: you see, he holds his head like a sodger, and he isn't so cushiony as most o' the oldish gentlefolks—they run fat in general; and he's got a fine leg. The parson's nimble enough, but he hasn't got much of a leg: it's a bit too thick down'ard, and his knees might be a bit nearer wi'out damage; but he might do worse, he might do worse. Though he hasn't that grand way o' waving his hand as the Squire has."

"Talk o' nimbleness, look at Mrs. Osgood," said Ben Winthrop, who was holding his son Aaron between his knees. "She trips along with her little steps, so as nobody can see how she goes—it's like as if she had little wheels to her feet. She doesn't look a day older nor last year: she's the finest-made woman as is, let the next be where she will."

"I don't heed how the women are made," said Mr. Macey, with some contempt. "They wear nayther coat nor breeches: you can't make much out o' their shapes."

"Fayder," said Aaron, whose feet were busy beating out the tune, "how does that big cock's feather stick in Mrs. Crackenthorp's yead? Is there a little hole for it, like in my shuttlecock?"

"Hush, lad, hush; that's the way the ladies dress theirselves, that is," said the father, adding, however, in an undertone to Mr. Macey, "It does make her look funny, though—partly like a short-necked bottle wi' a long quill in it. Hey, by jingo, there's the young Squire leading off now, wi' Miss Nancy for partners! There's a lass for you! —like a pink-and-white posy—there's nobody 'ud think as anybody could be so pritty. I shouldn't wonder if she's Madam Cass some day, arter all—and nobody more right-fuller, for they'd make a fine match. You can find nothing against Master Godfrey's shapes, Macey, I'll bet a penny."

Mr. Macey screwed up his mouth, leaned his head further on one side, and twirled his thumbs with a presto movement as his eyes followed Godfrey up the dance. At last he summed up his opinion.

"Pretty well down'ard, but a bit too round i' the shoulder blades. And as for them coats as he gets from the Flitton tailor, they're a poor cut to pay double money for."

"Ah, Mr. Macey, you and me are two folks," said Ben, slightly indignant at this carping. "When I've got a pot o' good ale, I like to swaller it, and do my inside good, i'stead o' smelling and staring at it to see if I can't find faut wi' the brewing. I should like you to pick me out a finer-limbed young fellow nor Master Godfrey—one as 'ud knock you down easier, or's more pleasanter-looksed when he's piert and merry."

"Tchuh!" said Mr. Macey, provoked to increased severity, "he isn't come to his right colour yet: he's partly like a slack-baked pie. And I doubt he's got a soft place in his head, else why should he be turned round the finger by that offal Dunsey as nobody's seen o' late, and let him kill that fine hunting hoss as was the talk o' the country? And one while he was allays after Miss Nancy, and then it all went off again, like a smell o' hot porridge, as I may say. That wasn't my way, when *I* went a-coorting."

"Ah, but mayhap Miss Nancy hung off, like, and your lass didn't," said Ben.

"I should say she didn't," said Mr. Macey significantly. "Before I said 'sniff,' I took care to know as she'd say 'snaff,' and pretty quick too. I wasn't a-going to open *my* mouth, like a dog at a fly, and snap it to again, wi' nothing to swaller."

"Well, I think Miss Nancy's a-coming round again," said Ben, "for Master Godfrey doesn't look so downhearted tonight. And I see he's for taking her away to sit down, now they're at the end o' the dance: that looks like sweethearting, that does."

The reason why Godfrey and Nancy had left the dance was not so tender as Ben imagined. In the close press of couples a slight accident had happened to Nancy's dress, which, while it was short enough to show her neat ankle in front, was long enough behind to be caught under the stately stamp of the Squire's foot, so as to rend certain stitches at the waist, and cause much sisterly agitation in Priscilla's mind, as well as serious concern in Nancy's. One's thoughts may be much occupied with love struggles, but hardly so as to be insensible to a disorder in the general framework of things. Nancy had no sooner completed her duty in the figure they were dancing than she said to Godfrey, with a deep blush, that she must go and sit down till Priscilla could come to her; for the sisters had already exchanged a short whisper and an open-eyed glance full of meaning. No reason less urgent than this could have prevailed on Nancy to give Godfrey this opportunity of sitting apart with her. As for Godfrey, he was feeling so happy and oblivious under the long charm of the country dance with Nancy, that he got rather bold on the strength of her confusion, and was capable of leading her straight away, without leave asked, into the adjoining small parlour, where the card tables were set.

"Oh, no, thank you," said Nancy coldly, as soon as she perceived where he was going, "not in there. I'll wait here till Priscilla's ready to come to me. I'm sorry to bring you out of the dance and make myself troublesome."

"Why, you'll be more comfortable here by yourself," said the artful Godfrey; "I'll leave you here till your sister can come." He spoke in an indifferent tone.

That was an agreeable proposition, and just what Nancy desired; why, then, was she a little hurt that Mr. Godfrey should make it? They entered, and she seated herself on a chair against one of the card tables, as the stiffest and most unapproachable position she could choose.

"Thank you, sir," she said immediately. "I needn't give you any more trouble. I'm sorry you've had such an unlucky partner."

"That's very ill-natured of you," said Godfrey, standing by her without any sign of intended departure, "to be sorry you've danced with me."

"Oh, no, sir, I don't mean to say what's ill-natured at all," said Nancy, looking distractingly prim and pretty. "When gentlemen have so many pleasures, one dance can matter but very little."

"You know that isn't true. You know one dance with you matters more to me than all the other pleasures in the world."

It was a long, long while since Godfrey had said anything so direct as that, and Nancy was startled. But her instinctive dignity and repugnance to any show of emotion made her sit perfectly still, and only throw a little more decision into her voice as she said:

"No, indeed, Mr. Godfrey, that's not known to me, and I have very good reasons for thinking different. But if it's true, I don't wish to hear it."

"Would you never forgive me, then, Nancy—never think well of me, let what would happen—would you never think the present made amends for the past? Not if I turned a good fellow, and gave up everything you didn't like?"

Godfrey was half conscious that this sudden opportunity of speaking to Nancy alone had driven him beside himself; but blind feeling had got the mastery of his tongue. Nancy really felt much agitated by the possibility Godfrey's words suggested, but this very pressure of emotion that she was in danger of finding too strong for her roused all her power of self-command.

"I should be glad to see a good change in anybody, Mr. Godfrey," she answered, with the slightest discernible difference of tone, "but it 'ud be better if no change was wanted."

"You're very hardhearted, Nancy," said Godfrey, pettishly. "You might encourage me to be a better fellow. I'm very miserable—but you've no feeling."

"I think those have the least feeling that act wrong to begin with," said Nancy, sending out a flash in spite of herself. Godfrey was delighted with that little flash, and would have liked to go on and make her quarrel with him; Nancy was so exasperatingly quiet and firm. But she was not indifferent to him *yet*, though—

The entrance of Priscilla, bustling forward and saying, "Dear heart alive, child, let us look at this gown," cut off Godfrey's hopes of a quarrel.

"I suppose I must go now," he said to Priscilla.

"It's no matter to me whether you go or stay," said that frank lady, searching for something in her pocket, with a preoccupied brow.

"Do *you* want me to go?" said Godfrey, looking at Nancy, who was now standing up by Priscilla's order.

"As you like," said Nancy, trying to recover all her former coldness, and looking down carefully at the hem of her gown.

"Then I like to stay," said Godfrey, with a reckless determination to get as much of this joy as he could tonight, and think nothing of the morrow.

CHAPTER XII

WHILE GODFREY CASS was taking draughts of forgetfulness from the sweet presence of Nancy, willingly losing all sense of that hidden bond which at other moments galled and fretted him so as to mingle irritation with the very sunshine, Godfrey's wife was walking with slow, uncertain steps through the snow-covered Raveloe lanes, carrying her child in her arms.

This journey on New Year's Eve was a premeditated act of vengeance which she had kept in her heart ever since Godfrey, in a fit of passion, had told her he would sooner die than acknowledge her as his wife. There would be a great party at the Red House on New Year's Eve, she knew: her husband would be smiling and smiled upon, hiding *her* existence in the darkest corner of his heart. But she would mar his pleasure: she would go in her dingy rags, with her faded face, once as handsome as the best, with her little child that had its father's hair and eyes, and disclose herself to the Squire as his eldest son's wife. It is seldom that the miserable can help regarding their misery as a wrong inflicted by those who are less miserable. Molly knew that the cause of her dingy rags was not her husband's neglect, but the demon Opium to whom she was enslaved, body and soul, except in the lingering mother's tenderness that refused to give him her hungry child. She knew this well; and yet, in the moments of wretched, unbenumbed consciousness, the sense of her want and degradation transformed itself continually into bitterness towards Godfrey. *He* was well off; and if she had her rights she would be well off too. The belief that he repented his marriage, and suffered from it, only aggravated her vindictiveness. Just and self-reproving thoughts do not come to us too thickly, even in the purest air, and with the best lessons of heaven and earth; how should those white-winged delicate messengers make their way to Molly's poisoned chamber, inhabited by no higher memories than those of a barmaid's paradise of pink ribbons and gentlemen's jokes?

She had set out at an early hour, but had lingered on the road, inclined by her indolence to believe that if she waited under a warm shed the snow would cease to fall. She had waited longer than she knew, and now that she found herself belated in the snow-hidden ruggedness of the long lanes, even the animation of a vindictive purpose could not keep her spirit from failing. It was seven o'clock, and by this time she was not very far from Raveloe, but she was not familiar enough with those monotonous lanes to know how near she was to her journey's end. She needed comfort, and she knew but one comforter—the familiar demon in her bosom; but she hesitated a moment, after drawing out the black remnant, before she raised it to her lips. In that moment the mother's love pleaded for painful consciousness rather than oblivion—pleaded to be left in aching weariness, rather than to have the encircling arms benumbed so that they could not feel the dear burden. In another moment Molly had flung something away, but it was not the black remnant—it was an empty phial. And she walked on again under the breaking cloud, from which there came now and then the light of a quickly veiled star, for a freezing wind had sprung up since the snowing had ceased. But she walked always more and more drowsily, and clutched more and more automatically the sleeping child at her bosom.

Slowly the demon was working his will, and cold and weariness were his helpers. Soon she felt nothing but a supreme immediate longing that curtained off all futurity —the longing to lie down and sleep. She had arrived at a spot where her footsteps were no longer checked by a hedgerow, and she had wandered vaguely, unable to distinguish any objects, notwithstanding the wide whiteness around her, and the growing starlight. She sank down against a straggling furze bush, an easy pillow enough; and the bed of snow, too, was soft. She did not feel that the bed was cold, and did not heed whether the child would wake and cry for her. But her arms had not yet relaxed their instinctive clutch; and the little one slumbered on as gently as if it had been rocked in a lace-trimmed cradle.

But the complete torpor came at last: the fingers lost

their tension, the arms unbent; then the little head fell away from the bosom, and the blue eyes opened wide on the cold starlight. At first there was a little peevish cry of "Mammy," and an effort to regain the pillowing arm and bosom; but mammy's ear was deaf, and the pillow seemed to be slipping away backward. Suddenly, as the child rolled downward on its mother's knees, all wet with snow, its eyes were caught by a bright glancing light on the white ground, and, with the ready transition of infancy, it was immediately absorbed in watching the bright living thing running towards it, yet never arriving. That bright living thing must be caught; and in an instant the child had slipped on all fours, and held out one little hand to catch the gleam. But the gleam would not be caught in that way, and now the head was held up to see where the cunning gleam came from. It came from a very bright place; and the little one, rising on its legs, toddled through the snow, the old grimy shawl in which it was wrapped trailing behind it, and the queer little bonnet dangling at its back—toddled on to the open door of Silas Marner's cottage, and right up to the warm hearth, where there was a bright fire of logs and sticks, which had thoroughly warmed the old sack (Silas's greatcoat) spread out on the bricks to dry. The little one, accustomed to be left to itself for long hours without notice from its mother, squatted down on the sack, and spread its tiny hands towards the blaze, in perfect contentment, gurgling and making many inarticulate communications to the cheerful fire, like a new-hatched gosling beginning to find itself comfortable. But presently the warmth had a lulling effect, and the little golden head sank down on the old sack, and the blue eyes were veiled by their delicate, half-transparent lids.

But where was Silas Marner while this strange visitor had come to his hearth? He was in the cottage, but he did not see the child. During the last few weeks, since he had lost his money, he had contracted the habit of opening his door and looking out from time to time, as if he thought that his money might be somehow coming back to him, or that some trace, some news of it, might be mysteriously on the road, and be caught by the listening ear or the straining eye. It was chiefly at night, when he was not occupied in his loom, that he fell into this repetition of an act for which he could have assigned no definite purpose, and which can hardly be understood except by those who have undergone a bewildering separation from a supremely loved object. In the evening twilight, and later whenever the night was not dark, Silas looked out on that narrow prospect round the Stone Pits, listening and gazing, not with hope, but with mere yearning and unrest.

This morning he had been told by some of his neighbours that it was New Year's Eve, and that he must sit up and hear the old year rung out and the new rung in, because that was good luck, and might bring his money back again. This was only a friendly Raveloe way of jesting with the half-crazy oddities of a miser, but it had perhaps helped to throw Silas into a more than usually excited state. Since the oncoming of twilight he had opened his door again and again, though only to shut it immediately at seeing all distance veiled by the falling snow. But the last time he opened it the snow had ceased, and the clouds were parting here and there. He stood and listened, and gazed for a long while—there was really something on the road coming towards him then, but he caught no sign of it; and the stillness and the wide trackless snow seemed to narrow his solitude, and touched his yearning with the chill of despair. He went in again, and put his right hand on the latch of the door to close it— but he did not close it: he was arrested, as he had been already since his loss, by the invisible wand of catalepsy, and stood like a graven image, with wide but sightless eyes, holding open his door, powerless to resist either the good or evil that might enter there.

When Marner's sensibility returned, he continued the action which had been arrested, and closed his door, unaware of the chasm in his consciousness, unaware of any intermediate change, except that the light had grown dim, and that he was chilled and faint. He thought he had been too long standing at the door and looking out. Turning towards the hearth, where the two logs had fallen apart, and sent forth only a red, uncertain glimmer, he seated himself on his fireside chair, and was stooping to push his logs together, when, to his blurred vision, it seemed as if there were gold on the floor in front of the hearth. Gold!—his own gold—brought back to him as mysteriously as it had been taken away! He felt his heart begin to beat violently, and for a few moments he was unable to stretch out his hand and grasp the restored treasure. The heap of gold seemed to glow and get larger beneath his agitated gaze. He leaned forward at last, and stretched forth his hand; but instead of the hard coin with the familiar resisting outline, his fingers encountered soft, warm curls. In utter amazement, Silas fell on his knees and bent his head low to examine the marvel: it was a sleeping child—a round, fair thing, with soft yellow rings all over its head. Could this be his little sister come back to him in a dream—his little sister whom he had carried about in his arms for a year before she died, when he was a small boy without shoes or stockings? That was the first thought that darted across Silas's blank wonderment. *Was* it a dream? He rose to his feet again, pushed his logs together, and, throwing on some dried leaves and sticks, raised a flame; but the flame did not disperse the vision—it only lit up more distinctly the little round form of the child and its shabby clothing. It was very much like his little sister. Silas sank into his chair powerless, under the double presence of an inexplicable surprise and a hurrying influx of memories. How and when had the child come in without his knowledge? He had never been beyond the door. But along with that question, and almost thrusting it away, there was a vision of the old home and the old streets leading to Lantern Yard—and within that vision another, of the thoughts which had been present with him in those far-off scenes. The thoughts were strange to him now, like old friendships impossible to revive; and yet he had a dreamy feeling that this child was somehow a message come to him from that far-off life: it stirred fibres that had never been moved in Raveloe—old quiverings of tenderness—old impressions of awe at the presentiment of some Power presiding over his life; for his imagination had not yet extricated itself from the sense of mystery in the child's sudden presence, and had formed no conjectures of ordinary natural means by which the event could have been brought about.

But there was a cry on the hearth: the child had awaked, and Marner stooped to lift it on his knee. It clung round his neck, and burst louder and louder into that mingling of inarticulate cries with "Mammy" by which little children express the bewilderment of waking. Silas pressed it to him, and almost unconsciously uttered sounds of hushing tenderness, while he bethought himself that some of his porridge, which had got cool by the dying fire, would do to feed the child with if it were only warmed up a little.

He had plenty to do through the next hour. The porridge, sweetened with some dry brown sugar from an old store which he had refrained from using for himself, stopped the cries of the little one, and made her lift her blue eyes with a wide quiet gaze at Silas, as he put the spoon into her mouth. Presently she slipped from his knee and began to toddle about, but with a pretty stagger that made Silas jump up and follow her lest she should fall against anything that would hurt her. But she only fell in a sitting posture on the ground, and began to pull at her boots, looking up at him with a crying face as if the boots hurt her. He took her on his knee again, but it was some time before it occurred to Silas's dull bachelor mind that the wet boots were the grievance, pressing on her warm ankles. He got them off with difficulty, and Baby was at once happily occupied with the primary mystery of her own toes, inviting Silas, with much chuckling, to consider the mystery too. But the wet boots had at last suggested to Silas that the child had been walking on the snow, and this roused him from his entire oblivion of any ordinary means by which it could have entered or been brought into his house. Under the prompting of this new idea, and without waiting to form conjectures, he raised the child in his arms, and went to the door. As soon as he had opened it, there was the cry of "Mammy" again, which Silas had not heard since the child's first hungry waking. Bending forward, he could just discern the marks made by the little feet on the virgin snow, and he followed their track to the furze bushes. "Mammy!" the little one cried again and again, stretching itself forward so as almost to escape from Silas's arms, before he himself was aware that there was something more than

the bush before him—that there was a human body,
with the head sunk low in the furze, and half-covered
with the shaken snow.

CHAPTER XIII

IT WAS AFTER the early suppertime at the Red House,
and the entertainment was in that stage when bashfulness itself had passed into easy jollity, when gentlemen,
conscious of unusual accomplishments, could at length be
prevailed on to dance a hornpipe, and when the Squire
preferred talking loudly, scattering snuff, and patting his
visitors' backs, to sitting longer at the whist table—a
choice exasperating to Uncle Kimble, who, being always
volatile in sober business hours, became intense and bitter
over cards and brandy, shuffled before his adversary's deal
with a glare of suspicion, and turned up a mean trump
card with an air of inexpressible disgust, as if in a world
where such things could happen one might as well enter
on a course of reckless profligacy. When the evening had
advanced to this pitch of freedom and enjoyment, it was
usual for the servants, the heavy duties of supper being
well over, to get their share of amusement by coming to
look on at the dancing; so that the back regions of the
house were left in solitude.

There were two doors by which the White Parlour was
entered from the hall, and they were both left standing
open for the sake of air; but the lower one was crowded
with the servants and villagers, and only the upper doorway was left free. Bob Cass was figuring in a hornpipe,
and his father, very proud of this lithe son, whom he
repeatedly declared to be just like himself in his young
days, in a tone that implied this to be the very highest
stamp of juvenile merit, was the centre of a group who
had placed themselves opposite the performer, not far
from the upper door. Godfrey was standing a little way
off, not to admire his brother's dancing, but to keep sight
of Nancy, who was seated in the group near her father.
He stood aloof, because he wished to avoid suggesting
himself as a subject for the Squire's fatherly jokes in con-

nection with matrimony and Miss Nancy Lammeter's beauty, which were likely to become more and more explicit. But he had the prospect of dancing with her again when the hornpipe was concluded, and in the meantime it was very pleasant to get long glances at her quite unobserved.

But when Godfrey was lifting his eyes from one of those long glances, they encountered an object as startling to him at that moment as if it had been an apparition from the dead. It *was* an apparition from that hidden life which lies, like a dark bystreet, behind the goodly orna-mented façade that meets the sunlight and the gaze of respectable admirers. It was his own child, carried in Silas Marner's arms. That was his instantaneous impres-sion, unaccompanied by doubt, though he had not seen the child for months past; and when the hope was rising that he might possibly be mistaken, Mr. Crackenthorp and Mr. Lammeter had already advanced to Silas, in astonishment at this strange advent. Godfrey joined them immediately, unable to rest without hearing every word—trying to control himself, but conscious that if anyone noticed him, they must see that he was white-lipped and trembling.

But now all eyes at that end of the room were bent on Silas Marner; the Squire himself had risen, and asked angrily, "How's this?—what's this?—what do you do coming in here in this way?"

"I'm come for the doctor—I want the doctor," Silas had said, in the first moment, to Mr. Crackenthorp.

"Why, what's the matter, Marner?" said the rector. "The doctor's here; but say quietly what you want him for."

"It's a woman," said Silas, speaking low, and half-breathlessly, just as Godfrey came up. "She's dead, I think—dead in the snow at the Stone Pits—not far from my door."

Godfrey felt a great throb; there was one terror in his mind at that moment: it was that the woman might *not* be dead. That was an evil terror—an ugly inmate to have found a nestling place in Godfrey's kindly disposition; but no disposition is a security from evil wishes to a man whose happiness hangs on duplicity.

"Hush, hush!" said Mr. Crackenthorp. "Go out into the hall there. I'll fetch the doctor to you. Found a woman in the snow—and thinks she's dead," he added, speaking low to the Squire. "Better say as little about it as possible: it will shock the ladies. Just tell them a poor woman is ill from cold and hunger. I'll go and fetch Kimble."

By this time, however, the ladies had pressed forward, curious to know what could have brought the solitary linen weaver there under such strange circumstances, and interested in the pretty child, who, half alarmed and half attracted by the brightness and the numerous company, now frowned and hid her face, now lifted up her head again and looked round placably, until a touch or a coaxing word brought back the frown, and made her bury her face with new determination.

"What child is it?" said several ladies at once, and, among the rest, Nancy Lammeter, addressing Godfrey.

"I don't know—some poor woman's who has been found in the snow, I believe," was the answer Godfrey wrung from himself with a terrible effort. ("After all, *am* I certain?" he hastened to add silently, in anticipation of his own conscience.)

"Why, you'd better leave the child here, then, Master Marner," said good-natured Mrs. Kimble, hesitating, however, to take those dingy clothes into contact with her own ornamented satin bodice. "I'll tell one o' the girls to fetch it."

"No—no—I can't part with it, I can't let it go," said Silas, abruptly. "It's come to me—I've a right to keep it."

The proposition to take the child from him had come to Silas quite unexpectedly; and his speech, uttered under a strong sudden impulse, was almost like a revelation to himself: a minute before, he had no distinct intention about the child.

"Did you hear the like?" said Mrs. Kimble, in mild surprise, to her neighbour.

"Now, ladies, I must trouble you to stand aside," said Mr. Kimble, coming from the card room, in some bitterness at the interruption, but drilled by the long habit of his profession into obedience to unpleasant calls, even when he was hardly sober.

"It's a nasty business turning out now, eh, Kimble?" said the Squire. "He might ha' gone for your young fellow—the 'prentice, there—what's his name?"

"Might? ay—what's the use of talking about might?" growled Uncle Kimble, hastening out with Marner, and followed Mr. Crackenthorp and Godfrey. "Get me a pair of thick boots, Godfrey, will you? And stay, let somebody run to Winthrop's and fetch Dolly—she's the best woman to get. Ben was here himself before supper; is he gone?"

"Yes, sir, I met him," said Marner; "but I couldn't stop to tell him anything, only I said I was going for the doctor, and he said the doctor was at the Squire's. And I made haste and ran, and there was nobody to be seen at the back o' the house, and so I went in to where the company was."

The child, no longer distracted by the bright light and the smiling women's faces, began to cry and call for "Mammy," though always clinging to Marner, who had apparently won her thorough confidence. Godfrey had come back with the boots, and felt the cry as if some fibre were drawn tight within him.

"I'll go," he said hastily, eager for some movement; "I'll go and fetch the woman—Mrs. Winthrop."

"Oh, pooh—send somebody else," said Uncle Kimble, hurrying away with Marner.

"You'll let me know if I can be of any use, Kimble," said Mr. Crackenthorp. But the doctor was out of hearing.

Godfrey, too, had disappeared: he was gone to snatch his hat and coat, having just reflection enough to remember that he must not look like a madman; but he rushed out of the house into the snow without heeding his thin shoes.

In a few minutes he was on his rapid way to the Stone Pits by the side of Dolly, who, though feeling that she was entirely in her place in encountering cold and snow on an errand of mercy, was much concerned at a young gentleman's getting his feet wet under a like impulse.

"You'd a deal better go back, sir," said Dolly, with respectful compassion. "You've no call to catch cold; and I'd ask you if you'd be so good as tell my husband to come, on your way back—he's at the Rainbow, I doubt— if you found him anyway sober enough to be o' use. Or else, there's Mrs. Snell 'ud happen send the boy up to fetch and carry, for there may be things wanted from the doctor's."

"No, I'll stay, now I'm once out—I'll stay outside here," said Godfrey, when they came opposite Marner's cottage. "You can come and tell me if I can do anything."

"Well, sir, you're very good: you've a tender heart," said Dolly, going to the door.

Godfrey was too painfully preoccupied to feel a twinge of self-reproach at this undeserved praise. He walked up and down, unconscious that he was plunging ankle deep in snow, unconscious of everything but trembling suspense about what was going on in the cottage, and the effect of each alternative on his future lot. No, not quite unconscious of everything else. Deeper down, and half-smothered by passionate desire and dread, there was the sense that he ought not to be waiting on these alternatives; that he ought to accept the consequences of his deeds, own the miserable wife, and fulfil the claims of the helpless child. But he had not moral courage enough to contemplate that active renunciation of Nancy as possible for him: he had only conscience and heart enough to make him forever uneasy under the weakness that forbade the renunciation. And at this moment his mind leaped away from all restraint toward the sudden prospect of deliverance from his long bondage.

"Is she dead?" said the voice that predominated over every other within him. "If she is, I may marry Nancy; and then I shall be a good fellow in future, and have no secrets, and the child—shall be taken care of somehow." But across that vision came the other possibility—"She may live, and then it's all up with me."

Godfrey never knew how long it was before the door of the cottage opened and Mr. Kimble came out. He went forward to meet his uncle, prepared to suppress the agitation he must feel, whatever news he was to hear.

"I waited for you, as I'd come so far," he said, speaking first.

"Pooh, it was nonsense for you to come out: why didn't

you send one of the men? There's nothing to be done. She's dead—has been dead for hours, I should say."

"What sort of woman is she?" said Godfrey, feeling the blood rush to his face.

"A young woman, but emaciated, with long black hair. Some vagrant—quite in rags. She's got a wedding ring on, however. They must fetch her away to the work-house tomorrow. Come, come along."

"I want to look at her," said Godfrey. "I think I saw such a woman yesterday. I'll overtake you in a minute or two."

Mr. Kimble went on, and Godfrey turned back to the cottage. He cast only one glance at the dead face on the pillow, which Dolly had smoothed with decent care; but he remembered that last look at his unhappy hated wife so well that at the end of sixteen years every line in the worn face was present to him when he told the full story of this night.

He turned immediately towards the hearth where Silas Marner sat lulling the child. She was perfectly quiet now, but not asleep—only soothed by sweet porridge and warmth into that wide-gazing calm which makes us older human beings, with our inward turmoil, feel a certain awe in the presence of a little child, such as we feel before some quiet majesty or beauty in the earth or sky—before a steady glowing planet, or a full-flowered eglantine, or the bending trees over a silent pathway. The wide-open blue eyes looked up at Godfrey's without any uneasiness or sign of recognition: the child could make no visible audible claim on its father; and the father felt a strange mixture of feelings, a conflict of regret and joy, that the pulse of that little heart had no response for the half-jealous yearning in his own, when the blue eyes turned away from him slowly, and fixed themselves on the weaver's queer face, which was bent low down to look at them, while the small hand began to pull Marner's withered cheek with loving disfiguration.

"You'll take the child to the parish tomorrow?" asked Godfrey, speaking as indifferently as he could.

"Who says so?" said Marner, sharply. "Will they make me take her?"

"Why, you wouldn't like to keep her, should you—an old bachelor like you?"

"Till anybody shows they've a right to take her away from me," said Marner. "The mother's dead, and I reckon it's got no father: it's a lone thing—and I'm a lone thing. My money's gone, I don't know where—and this is come from I don't know where. I know nothing—I'm partly 'mazed."

"Poor little thing!" said Godfrey. "Let me give something towards finding it clothes."

He had put his hand in his pocket and found half-a-guinea, and, thrusting it into Silas's hand, he hurried out of the cottage to overtake Mr. Kimble.

"Ah, I see it's not the same woman I saw," he said, as he came up. "It's a pretty little child: the old fellow seems to want to keep it; that's strange for a miser like him. But I gave him a trifle to help him out: the parish isn't likely to quarrel with him for the right to keep the child."

"No; but I've seen the time when I might have quarrelled with him for it myself. It's too late now, though. If the child ran into the fire, your aunt's too fat to overtake it: she could only sit and grunt like an alarmed sow. But what a fool you are, Godfrey, to come out in your dancing shoes and stockings in this way—and you one of the beaux of the evening, and at your house! What do you mean by such freaks, young fellow: Has Miss Nancy been cruel, and do you want to spite her by spoiling your pumps?"

"Oh, everything has been disagreeable tonight. I was tired to death of jigging and gallanting, and that bother about the hornpipes. And I'd got to dance with the other Miss Gunn," said Godfrey, glad of the subterfuge his uncle had suggested to him.

The prevarication and white lies which a mind that keeps itself ambitiously pure is as uneasy under as a great artist under the false touches that no eye detects but his own, are worn as lightly as mere trimmings when once the actions have become a lie.

Godfrey reappeared in the White Parlour with dry feet, and, since the truth must be told, with a sense of relief and gladness that was too strong for painful thoughts to struggle with. For could he not venture now, whenever opportunity offered, to say the tenderest things to Nancy Lammeter—to promise her and himself that he would always be just what she would desire to see him? There was no danger that his dead wife would be recognized: those were not days of active inquiry and wide report; and as for the registry of their marriage, that was a long way off, buried in unturned pages, away from everyone's interest but his own. Dunsey might betray him if he came back; but Dunsey might be won to silence.

And when events turn out so much better for a man than he has had reason to dread, is it not a proof that his conduct has been less foolish and blameworthy than it might otherwise have appeared? When we are treated well, we naturally begin to think that we are not altogether unmeritorious, and that it is only just we should treat ourselves well, and not mar our own good fortune. Where, after all, would be the use of his confessing the past to Nancy Lammeter, and throwing away his happiness?—nay, hers?—for he felt some confidence that she loved him. As for the child, he would see that it was cared for: he would never forsake it; he would do everything but own it. Perhaps it would be just as happy in life without being owned by its father, seeing that nobody could tell how things would turn out, and that—is there any other reason wanted?—well, then, that the father would be much happier without owning the child.

CHAPTER XIV

THERE WAS a pauper's burial that week in Raveloe, and up Kench Yard at Batherley it was known that the dark-haired woman with the fair child, who had lately come to lodge there, was gone away again. That was all the express note taken that Molly had disappeared from the eyes of men. But the unwept death which, to the general lot, seemed as trivial as the summer-shed leaf was charged with the force of destiny to certain human lives that we know of, shaping their joys and sorrows even to the end.

Silas Marner's determination to keep the "tramp's child" was matter of hardly less surprise and iterated talk in the village than the robbery of his money. That softening of feeling towards him which dated from his misfortune, that merging of suspicion and dislike in a rather contemptuous pity for him as lone and crazy, was now accompanied with a more active sympathy, especially amongst the women. Notable mothers, who knew what it was to keep children "whole and sweet"; lazy mothers, who knew what it was to be interrupted in folding their arms and scratching their elbows by the mischievous propensities of children just firm on their legs, were equally interested in conjecturing how a lone man would manage with a two-year-old child on his hands, and were equally ready with their suggestions: the notable chiefly telling him what he had better do, and the lazy ones being emphatic in telling him what he would never be able to do.

Among the notable mothers, Dolly Winthrop was the one whose neighbourly offices were the most acceptable to Marner, for they were rendered without any show of bustling instruction. Silas had shown her the half-guinea given to him by Godfrey, and had asked her what he should do about getting some clothes for the child.

"Eh, Master Marner," said Dolly, "there's no call to buy, no more nor a pair o' shoes; for I've got the little petticoats as Aaron wore five years ago, and it's ill spending the money on them baby clothes, for the child 'ull grow like grass i' May, bless it—that it will."

And the same day Dolly brought her bundle, and displayed to Marner, one by one, the tiny garments in their due order of succession, most of them patched and darned, but clean and neat as fresh-sprung herbs. This was the introduction to a great ceremony with soap and water, from which Baby came out in new beauty, and sat on Dolly's knee, handling her toes and chuckling and patting her palms together with an air of having made several discoveries about herself, which she communicated by alternate sounds of "gug-gug-gug," and "Mammy." The "Mammy" was not a cry of need or uneasiness; Baby had been used to utter it without expecting either tender sound or touch to follow.

"Anybody 'ud think the angils in heaven couldn't be prettier," said Dolly, rubbing the golden curls and kissing them. "And to think of its being covered wi' them dirty rags—and the poor mother—froze to death; but there's Them as took care of it, and brought it to your door, Master Marner. The door was open, and it walked in over the snow, like as if it had been a little starved robin. Didn't you say the door was open?"

"Yes," said Silas, meditatively. "Yes—the door was open. The money's gone I don't know where, and this is come from I don't know where."

He had not mentioned to anyone his unconsciousness of the child's entrance, shrinking from questions which might lead to the fact he himself suspected—namely, that he had been in one of his trances.

"Ah," said Dolly, with soothing gravity, "it's like the night and the morning, and the sleeping and the waking, and the rain and the harvest—one goes and the other comes, and we know nothing how nor where. We may strive and scrat and fend, but it's little we can do arter all—the big things come and go wi' no striving o' our'n—they do, that they do; and I think you're in the right on it to keep the little un, Master Marner, seeing as it's been sent to you, though there's folks as thinks different. You'll happen be a bit moithered with it while it's so little; but I'll come, and welcome, and see to it for you: I've a bit o' time to spare most days, for when one gets up betimes i' the morning, the clock seems to stan' still tow'rt ten, afore it's time to go about the victual. So, as I say, I'll come and see to the child for you, and welcome."

"Thank you . . . kindly," said Silas, hesitating a little. "I'll be glad if you'll tell me things. But," he added, uneasily, leaning forward to look at Baby with some jealousy, as she was resting her head backward against Dolly's arm, and eyeing him contentedly from a distance, "but I want to do things for it myself, else it may get fond o' somebody else, and not fond o' me. I've been used to fending for myself in the house—I can learn, I can learn."

"Eh, to be sure," said Dolly gently. "I've seen men as are wonderful handy wi' children. The men are awk'ard and contrairy mostly, God help 'em—but when the drink's out of 'em, they aren't unsensible, though they're bad for leeching and bandaging—so fiery and unpatient. You see this goes first, next the skin," proceeded Dolly, taking up the little shirt, and putting it on.

"Yes," said Marner docilely, bringing his eyes very close, that they might be initiated in the mysteries; whereupon Baby seized his head with both her small arms, and put her lips against his face with purring noises.

"See there," said Dolly, with a woman's tender tact, "she's fondest o' you. She wants to go o' your lap, I'll be bound. Go, then: take her, Master Marner; you can put the things on, and then you can say as you've done for her from the first of her coming to you."

Marner took her on his lap, trembling with an emotion mysterious to himself, at something unknown dawning on his life. Thought and feeling were so confused within him, that if he had tried to give them utterance, he could only have said that the child was come instead of the gold—that the gold had turned into the child. He took the garments from Dolly, and put them on under her teaching; interrupted, of course, by Baby's gymnastics.

"There, then! why, you take to it quite easy, Master Marner," said Dolly; "but what shall you do when you're forced to sit in your loom? For she'll get busier and mischievouser every day—she will, bless her. It's lucky as you've got that high hearth i'stead of a grate, for that keeps the fire more out of her reach; but if you've got anything as can be split or broke, or as is fit to cut her fingers off, she'll be at it—and it is but right you should know."

Silas meditated a little while in some perplexity. "I'll tie her to the leg o' the loom," he said at last, "tie her with a good long strip o' something."

"Well, mayhap that'll do, as it's a little gell, for they're easier persuaded to sit i' one place nor the lads. I know what the lads are; for I've had four—four I've had, God knows—and if you was to take and tie 'em up, they'd make a fighting and a crying as if you was ringing pigs. But I'll bring you my little chair, and some bits o' red rag and things for her to play wi'; an' she'll sit and chatter to 'em as if they was alive. Eh, if it wasn't a sin to the lads to wish 'em made different, bless 'em, I should ha' been glad for one of 'em to be a little gell; and to think as I could ha' taught her to scour, and mend, and the knitting, and everything. But I can teach 'em this little un, Master Marner, when she gets old enough."

"But she'll be *my* little un," said Marner rather hastily. "She'll be nobody else's."

"No, to be sure; you'll have a right to her if you're a father to her, and bring her up according. But," added Dolly, coming to a point which she had determined beforehand to touch upon, "you must bring her up like christened folks's children, and take her to church, and let her learn her catechise, as my little Aaron can say off —the 'I believe,' and everything, and 'hurt nobody by word or deed,'—as well as if he was the clerk. That's what you must do, Master Marner, if you'd do the right thing by the orphin child."

Marner's pale face flushed suddenly under a new anxiety. His mind was too busy trying to give some definite bearing to Dolly's words for him to think of answering her.

"And it's my belief," she went on, "as the poor little creatur has never been christened, and it's nothing but right as the parson should be spoke to; and if you was noways unwilling, I'd talk to Mr. Macey about it this very day. For if the child ever went anyways wrong, and you hadn't done your part by it, Master Marner—'noculation, and everything to save it from harm—it 'ud be a thorn i' your bed forever o' this side the grave; and I can't think as it 'ud be easy lying down for anybody when they'd got to another world, if they hadn't done their part by the helpless children as come wi'out their own asking."

Dolly herself was disposed to be silent for some time now, for she had spoken from the depths of her own simple belief, and was much concerned to know whether her words would produce the desired effect on Silas. He was puzzled and anxious, for Dolly's word "christened" conveyed no distinct meaning to him. He had only heard of baptism, and had only seen the baptism of grown-up men and women.

"What is it as you mean by 'christened'?" he said at last, timidly. "Won't folks be good to her without it?"

"Dear, dear! Master Marner," said Dolly, with gentle distress and compassion. "Had you never no father nor mother as taught you to say your prayers, and as there's good words and good things to keep us from harm?"

"Yes," said Silas, in a low voice; "I know a deal about that—used to, used to. But your ways are different: my country was a good way off." He paused a few moments, and then added, more decidedly, "But I want to do everything as can be done for the child. And whatever's right for it i' this country, and you think 'ull do it good, I'll act according, if you'll tell me."

"Well, then, Master Marner," said Dolly, inwardly rejoiced, "I'll ask Mr. Macey to speak to the parson about it; and you fix on a name for it, because it must have a name giv' it when it's christened."

"My mother's name was Hephzibah," said Silas, "and my little sister was named after her."

"Eh, that's a hard name," said Dolly. "I partly think it isn't a christened name."

"It's a Bible name," said Silas, old ideas recurring.

"Then I've no call to speak again' it," said Dolly, rather startled by Silas's knowledge on this head; "but you see I'm no scholard, and I'm slow at catching the words. My husband says I'm allays like as if I was putting the haft for the handle—that's what he says—for he's very sharp, God help him. But it was awk'ard calling your little sister by such a hard name, when you'd got nothing big to say, like—wasn't it, Master Marner?"

"We called her Eppie," said Silas.

"Well, if it was noways wrong to shorten the name, it 'ud be a deal handier. And so I'll go now, Master Marner, and I'll speak about the christening afore dark; and I wish you the best o' luck, and it's my belief as it'll come to you, if you do what's right by the orphin child; and there's the 'noculation to be seen to; and as to washing its bits o' things, you need look to nobody but me, for I can do 'em wi' one hand when I've got my suds about. Eh, the blessed angil! You'll let me bring my Aaron one o' these days, and he'll show her his little cart as his father's made for him, and the black-and-white pup as he's got a-rearing."

Baby *was* christened, the rector deciding that a double

baptism was a lesser risk to incur; and on this occasion
Silas, making himself as clean and tidy as he could,
appeared for the first time within the church, and shared
in the observances held sacred by his neighbours. He was
quite unable, by means of anything he heard or saw, to
identify the Raveloe religion with his old faith; if he
could at any time in his previous life have done so, it must
have been by the aid of a strong feeling ready to vibrate
with sympathy, rather than by a comparison of phrases
and ideas: and now for long years that feeling had been
dormant. He had no distinct idea about the baptism and
the churchgoing, except that Dolly had said it was for the
good of the child; and in this way, as the weeks grew to
months, the child created fresh and fresh links between
his life and the lives from which he had hitherto shrunk
continually into narrower isolation. Unlike the gold
which needed nothing, and must be worshipped in close-
locked solitude—which was hidden away from the daylight, was deaf to the song of birds, and started to no
human tones—Eppie was a creature of endless claims and
ever-growing desires, seeking and loving sunshine, and
living sounds, and living movements; making trial of
everything, with trust in new joy, and stirring the human
kindness in all eyes that looked on her. The gold had
kept his thoughts in an ever-repeated circle, leading to
nothing beyond itself; but Eppie was an object com-
pacted of changes and hopes that forced his thoughts
onward, and carried them far away from their old eager
pacing towards the same blank limit—carried them away
to the new things that would come with the coming years,
when Eppie would have learned to understand how her
father Silas cared for her; and made him look for images
of that time in the ties and charities that bound together
the families of his neighbours. The gold had asked that
he should sit weaving longer and longer, deafened and
blinded more and more to all things except the monotony
of his loom and the repetition of his web; but Eppie
called him away from his weaving, and made him think
all its pauses a holiday, reawakening his senses with her
fresh life, even to the old winter flies that came crawling
forth in the early spring sunshine, and warming him into
joy because *she* had joy.

And when the sunshine grew strong and lasting, so that the buttercups were thick in the meadows, Silas might be seen in the sunny midday, or in the late afternoon when the shadows were lengthening under the hedgerows, strolling out with uncovered head to carry Eppie beyond the Stone Pits to where the flowers grew, till they reached some favourite bank where he could sit down, while Eppie toddled to pluck the flowers, and make remarks to the winged things that murmured happily above the bright petals, calling "Dad-dad's" attention continually by bringing him the flowers. Then she would turn her ear to some sudden bird note, and Silas learned to please her by making signs of hushed stillness, that they might listen for the note to come again: so that when it came, she set up her small back and laughed with gurgling triumph. Sitting on the banks in this way, Silas began to look for the once-familiar herbs again; and as the leaves, with their unchanged outline and markings, lay on his palm, there was a sense of crowding remembrances from which he turned away timidly, taking refuge in Eppie's little world, that lay lightly on his enfeebled spirit.

As the child's mind was growing into knowledge, his mind was growing into memory: as her life unfolded, his soul, long stupefied in a cold, narrow prison, was unfolding too, and trembling gradually into full consciousness.

It was an influence which must gather force with every new year: the tones that stirred Silas's heart grew articulate, and called for more distinct answers; shapes and sounds grew clearer for Eppie's eyes and ears, and there was more that "Dad-dad" was imperatively required to notice and account for. Also, by the time Eppie was three years old, she developed a fine capacity for mischief, and for devising ingenious ways of being troublesome, which found much exercise, not only for Silas's patience, but for his watchfulness and penetration. Sorely was poor Silas puzzled on such occasions by the incompatible demands of love. Dolly Winthrop told him punishment was good for Eppie, and that, as for rearing a child without making it tingle a little in soft and safe places now and then, it was not to be done.

"To be sure, there's another thing you might do, Master Marner," added Dolly, meditatively: "you might shut

her up once i' the coal hole. That was what I did wi'
Aaron; for I was that silly wi' the youngest lad, as I
could never bear to smack him. Not as I could find i'
my heart to let him stay i' the coal hole more nor a minute, but it was enough to colly him all over, so as he must
be new washed and dressed, and it was as good as a rod
to him—that was. But I put it upo' your conscience, Master Marner, as there's one of 'em you must choose—ayther
smacking or the coal hole—else she'll get so masterful,
there'll be no holding her."

Silas was impressed with the melancholy truth of this
last remark; but his force of mind failed before the only
two penal methods open to him, not only because it was
painful to him to hurt Eppie, but because he trembled
at a moment's contention with her, lest she should love
him the less for it. Let even an affectionate Goliath get
himself tied to a small, tender thing, dreading to hurt it
by pulling, and dreading still more to snap the cord,
and which of the two, pray, will be master? It was clear
that Eppie, with her short, toddling steps, must lead father Silas a pretty dance on any fine morning when circumstances favoured mischief.

For example. He had wisely chosen a broad strip of
linen as a means of fastening her to his loom when he
was busy: it made a broad belt round her waist, and was
long enough to allow of her reaching the truckle bed
and sitting down on it, but not long enough for her to
attempt any dangerous climbing. One bright summer's
morning Silas had been more engrossed than usual in
"setting up" a new piece of work, an occasion on which
his scissors were in requisition. These scissors, owing to
an especial warning of Dolly's, had been kept carefully
out of Eppie's reach; but the click of them had had a
peculiar attraction for her ear, and watching the results
of that click, she had derived the philosophic lesson that
the same cause would produce the same effect. Silas had
seated himself in his loom, and the noise of weaving had
begun; but he had left his scissors on a ledge which Eppie's arm was long enough to reach; and now, like a
small mouse, watching her opportunity, she stole quietly
from her corner, secured the scissors, and toddled to the
bed again, setting up her back as a mode of concealing

the fact. She had a distinct intention as to the use of the scissors; and having cut the linen strip in a jagged but effectual manner, in two moments she had run out at the open door where the sunshine was inviting her, while poor Silas believed her to be a better child than usual. It was not until he happened to need his scissors that the terrible fact burst upon him: Eppie had run out by herself—had perhaps fallen into the Stone Pit. Silas, shaken by the worst fear that could have befallen him, rushed out, calling "Eppie!" and ran eagerly about the unenclosed space, exploring the dry cavities into which she might have fallen, and then gazing with questioning dread at the smooth red surface of the water. The cold drops stood on his brow. How long had she been out? There was one hope—that she had crept through the stile and got into the fields where he habitually took her to stroll. But the grass was high in the meadow, and there was no descrying her if she were there, except by a close search that would be a trespass on Mr. Osgood's crop. Still, that misdemeanour must be committed; and poor Silas, after peering all round the hedgerows, traversed the grass, beginning with perturbed vision to see Eppie behind every group of red sorrel, and to see her moving always farther off as he approached. The meadow was searched in vain; and he got over the stile into the next field, looking with dying hope towards a small pond which was now reduced to its summer shallowness, so as to leave a wide margin of good adhesive mud. Here, however, sat Eppie, discoursing cheerfully to her own small boot, which she was using as a bucket to convey the water into a deep hoof mark, while her little naked foot was planted comfortably on a cushion of olive-green mud. A red-headed calf was observing her with alarmed doubt through the opposite hedge.

Here was clearly a case of aberration in a christened child which demanded severe treatment; but Silas, overcome with convulsive joy at finding his treasure again, could do nothing but snatch her up, and cover her with half-sobbing kisses. It was not until he had carried her home, and had begun to think of the necessary washing, that he recollected the need that he should punish Eppie, and "make her remember." The idea that she might run

away again and come to harm gave him unusual resolution, and for the first time he determined to try the coal
hole—a small closet near the hearth.

"Naughty, naughty Eppie," he suddenly began, holding her on his knee, and pointing to her muddy feet and
clothes, "naughty to cut with the scissors and run away.
Eppie must go into the coal hole for being naughty.
Daddy must put her in the coal hole."

He half-expected that this would be shock enough, and
that Eppie would begin to cry. But instead of that, she
began to shake herself on his knee, as if the proposition
opened a pleasing novelty. Seeing that he must proceed
to extremities, he put her into the coal hole, and held the
door closed, with a trembling sense that he was using a
strong measure. For a moment there was silence, but then
came a little cry, "Opy, opy!" and Silas let her out again,
saying, "Now Eppie 'ull never be naughty again, else she
must go in the coal hole—a black, naughty place."

The weaving must stand still a long while this morning, for now Eppie must be washed, and have clean
clothes on; but it was to be hoped that this punishment
would have a lasting effect, and save time in future—
though, perhaps, it would have been better if Eppie had
cried more.

In half an hour she was clean again, and Silas having
turned his back to see what he could do with the linen
band, threw it down again, with the reflection that Eppie
would be good without fastening for the rest of the morning. He turned round again, and was going to place her
in her little chair near the loom, when she peeped out
at him with black face and hands again, and said, "Eppie
in de toal hole!"

This total failure of the coal-hole discipline shook
Silas's belief in the efficacy of punishment. "She'd take it
all for fun," he observed to Dolly, "if I didn't hurt her,
and that I can't do, Mrs. Winthrop. If she makes me a bit
o' trouble, I can bear it. And she's got no tricks but what
she'll grow out of."

"Well, that's partly true, Master Marner," said Dolly
sympathetically, "and if you can't bring your mind to
frighten her off touching things, you must do what you
can to keep 'em out of her way. That's what I do wi' the

pups as the lads are allays a-rearing. They *will* worry and gnaw—worry and gnaw they will, if it was one's Sunday cap as hung anywhere so as they could drag it. They know no difference, God help 'em; it's the pushing o' the teeth as sets 'em on, that's what it is."

So Eppie was reared without punishment, the burden of her misdeeds being borne vicariously by father Silas. The stone hut was made a soft nest for her, lined with downy patience; and also in the world that lay beyond the stone hut for her, she knew nothing of frowns and denials.

Notwithstanding the difficulty of carrying her and his yarn or linen at the same time, Silas took her with him in most of his journeys to the farmhouses, unwilling to leave her behind at Dolly Winthrop's, who was always ready to take care of her; and little curly-headed Eppie, the weaver's child, became an object of interest at several outlying homesteads, as well as in the village. Hitherto he had been treated very much as if he had been a useful gnome or brownie—a queer and unaccountable creature, who must necessarily be looked at with wondering curiosity and repulsion and with whom one would be glad to make all greetings and bargains as brief as possible, but who must be dealt with in a propitiatory way, and occasionally have a present of pork or garden stuff to carry home with him, seeing that without him there was no getting the yarn woven. But now Silas met with open smiling faces and cheerful questioning, as a person whose satisfactions and difficulties could be understood. Everywhere he must sit a little and talk about the child, and words of interest were always ready for him: "Ah, Master Marner, you'll be lucky if she takes the measles soon and easy!"—or, "Why, there isn't many lone men 'ud ha' been wishing to take up with a little un like that: but I reckon the weaving makes you handier than men as do outdoor work—you're partly as handy as a woman, for weaving comes next to spinning." Elderly masters and mistresses, seated observantly in large kitchen armchairs, shook their heads over the difficulties attendant on rearing children, felt Eppie's round arms and legs, and pronounced them remarkably firm, and told Silas that, if she turned out well (which, however, there was

no telling), it would be a fine thing for him to have a
steady lass to do for him when he got helpless. Servant
maidens were fond of carrying her out to look at the
hens and chickens, or to see if any cherries could be
shaken down in the orchard; and the small boys and
girls approached her slowly, with cautious movement
and steady gaze, like little dogs face to face with one of
their own kind, till attraction had reached the point at
which the soft lips were put out for a kiss. No child was
afraid of approaching Silas when Eppie was near him:
there was no repulsion around him now, either for young
or old; for the little child had come to link him once
more with the whole world. There was love between
him and the child that blent them into one, and there
was love between the child and the world—from men and
women with parental looks and tones, to the red lady-
birds and the round pebbles.

Silas began now to think of Raveloe life entirely in
relation to Eppie: she must have everything that was a
good in Raveloe; and he listened docilely, that he might
come to understand better what this life was, from which,
for fifteen years, he had stood aloof as from a strange
thing, with which he could have no communion: as some
man who has a precious plant to which he would give a
nurturing home in a new soil thinks of the rain and sunshine, and all influences, in relation to his nursling, and
asks industriously for all knowledge that will help him
to satisfy the wants of the searching roots, or to guard
leaf and bud from invading harm. The disposition to
hoard had been utterly crushed at the very first by the
loss of his long-stored gold: the coins he earned afterwards seemed as irrelevant as stones brought to complete
a house suddenly buried by an earthquake; the sense of
bereavement was too heavy upon him for the old thrill
of satisfaction to arise again at the touch of the newly
earned coin. And now something had come to replace
his hoard which gave a growing purpose to the earnings,
drawing his hope and joy continually onward beyond the
money.

In old days there were angels who came and took men
by the hand and led them away from the city of destruction. We see no white-winged angels now. But yet men

are led away from threatening destruction; a hand is put into theirs, which leads them forth gently towards a calm and bright land, so that they look no more backward; and the hand may be a little child's.

CHAPTER XV

THERE WAS one person, as you will believe, who watched with keener though more hidden interest than any other the prosperous growth of Eppie under the weaver's care. He dared not do anything that would imply a stronger interest in a poor man's adopted child than could be expected from the kindliness of the young Squire, when a chance meeting suggested a little present to a simple old fellow whom others noticed with good will; but he told himself that the time would come when he might do something towards furthering the welfare of his daughter without incurring suspicions. Was he very uneasy in the meantime at his inability to give his daughter her birthright? I cannot say that he was. The child was being taken care of, and would very likely be happy, as people in humble station often were—happier, perhaps, than those brought up in luxury.

That famous ring that pricked its owner when he forgot duty and followed desire—I wonder if it pricked very hard when he set out on the chase, or whether it pricked but lightly then, and only pierced to the quick when the chase had long been ended, and hope, folding her wings, looked backward and became regret?

Godfrey Cass's cheek and eye were brighter than ever now. He was so undivided in his aims that he seemed like a man of firmness. No Dunsey had come back: people had made up their minds that he was gone for a soldier, or gone "out of the country," and no one cared to be specific in their inquiries on a subject delicate to a respectable family. Godfrey had ceased to see the shadow of Dunsey across his path; and the path now lay straight forward to the accomplishment of his best, longest-cherished wishes. Everybody said Mr. Godfrey had taken the right turn; and it was pretty clear what would be the end of things, for there were not many days in the week that he was not seen riding to the Warrens. Godfrey himself, when he was asked jocosely if the day had been fixed, smiled with the pleasant consciousness of a lover who could say "yes," if he liked. He felt a reformed man, delivered from temptation; and the vision of his future life seemed to him as a promised land for which he had no cause to fight. He saw himself with all his happiness centered on his own hearth, while Nancy would smile on him as he played with the children.

And that other child—not on the hearth—he would not forget it; he would see that it was well provided for. That was a father's duty.

PART TWO

CHAPTER XVI

I T WAS A BRIGHT autumn Sunday, sixteen years after
Silas Marner had found his new treasure on the hearth.
The bells of the old Raveloe church were ringing the
cheerful peal which told that the morning service was
ended; and out of the arched doorway in the tower came
slowly, retarded by friendly greetings and questions, the
richer parishioners who had chosen this bright Sunday
morning as eligible for churchgoing. It was the rural
fashion of that time for the more important members of
the congregation to depart first, while their humbler
neighbours waited and looked on, stroking their bent
heads or dropping their curtsies to any large ratepayer
who turned to notice them.

Foremost among these advancing groups of well-clad
people, there are some whom we shall recognise, in spite
of Time, who has laid his hand on them all. The tall
blond man of forty is not much changed in feature from
the Godfrey Cass of six-and-twenty: he is only fuller in
flesh, and has only lost the indefinable look of youth—a
loss which is marked even when the eye is undulled and
the wrinkles are not yet come. Perhaps the pretty woman,
not much younger than he, who is leaning on his arm,
is more changed than her husband: the lovely bloom that
used to be always on her cheek now comes but fitfully,
with the fresh morning air, or with some strong surprise;
yet to all who love human faces best for what they tell of
human experience, Nancy's beauty has a heightened interest. Often the soul is ripened into fuller goodness while
age has spread an ugly film, so that mere glances can
never divine the preciousness of the fruit. But the years

have not been so cruel to Nancy. The firm yet placid
mouth, the clear veracious glance of the brown eyes,
speak now of a nature that has been tested and has kept
its highest qualities; and even the costume, with its dainty
neatness and purity, has more significance now the co-
quetries of youth can have nothing to do with it.

Mr. and Mrs. Godfrey Cass (any higher title has died
away from Raveloe lips since the old Squire was gathered
to his fathers, and his inheritance was divided) have
turned round to look for the tall aged man and the plainly dressed woman who are a little behind—Nancy having
observed that they must wait for "Father and Priscilla"
—and now they all turn into a narrower path leading
across the churchyard to a small gate opposite the Red
House. We will not follow them now; for may there not
be some others in this departing congregation whom we
should like to see again—some of those who are not likely
to be handsomely clad, and whom we may not recognise
so easily as the master and mistress of the Red House?

But it is impossible to mistake Silas Marner. His large
brown eyes seem to have gathered a longer vision, as is
the way with eyes that have been shortsighted in early
life, and they have a less vague, a more answering look;
but in everything else one sees signs of a frame much enfeebled by the lapse of the sixteen years. The weaver's
bent shoulders and white hair give him almost the look
of advanced age, though he is not more than five-and-
fifty; but there is the freshest blossom of youth close by
his side—a blond, dimpled girl of eighteen, who has vainly tried to chastise her curly auburn hair into smoothness
under her brown bonnet: the hair ripples as obstinately
as a brooklet under the March breeze, and the little ringlets burst away from the restraining comb behind and
show themselves below the bonnet crown. Eppie cannot
help being rather vexed about her hair, for there is no
other girl in Raveloe who has hair at all like it, and she
thinks hair ought to be smooth. She does not like to be
blameworthy even in small things: you see how neatly
her prayer book is folded in her spotted handkerchief.

That good-looking young fellow, in a new fustian suit,
who walks behind her is not quite sure upon the question
of hair in the abstract, when Eppie puts it to him, and

thinks that perhaps straight hair is the best in general, but he doesn't want Eppie's hair to be different. She surely divines that there is someone behind her who is thinking about her very particularly, and mustering courage to come to her side as soon as they are out in the lane, else why should she look rather shy, and take care not to turn away her head from her father Silas, to whom she keeps murmuring little sentences as to who was at church and who was not at church, and how pretty the red mountain ash is over the Rectory wall?

"I wish *we* had a little garden, Father, with double daisies in, like Mrs. Winthrop's," said Eppie, when they were out in the lane; "only they say it 'ud take a deal of digging and bringing fresh soil—and you couldn't do that, could you, Father? Anyhow, I shouldn't like you to do it, for it 'ud be too hard work for you."

"Yes, I could do it, child, if you want a bit o' garden: these long evenings, I could work at taking in a little bit o' the waste, just enough for a root or two o' flowers for you; and again, i' the morning I could have a turn wi' the spade before I sat down to the loom. Why didn't you tell me before as you wanted a bit o' garden?"

"*I* can dig it for you, Master Marner," said the young man in fustian, who was now by Eppie's side, entering into the conversation without the trouble of formalities. "It'll be play to me after I've done my day's work, or any odd bits o' time when the work's slack. And I'll bring you some soil from Mr. Cass's garden—he'll let me, and willing."

"Eh, Aaron, my lad, are you there?" said Silas; "I wasn't aware of you; for when Eppie's talking o' things, I see nothing but what she's a-saying. Well, if you could help me with the digging, we might get her a bit o' garden all the sooner."

"Then, if you think well and good," said Aaron, "I'll come to the Stone Pits this afternoon, and we'll settle what land's to be taken in, and I'll get up an hour earlier i' the morning, and begin on it."

"But not if you don't promise me not to work at the hard digging, Father," said Eppie. "For I shouldn't ha' said anything about it," she added, half-bashfully, halfroguishly, "only Mrs. Winthrop said as Aaron 'ud be so good, and—"

"And you might ha' known it without Mother telling you," said Aaron. "And Master Marner knows too, I hope, as I'm able and willing to do a turn o' work for him, and he won't do me the unkindness to anyways take it out o' my hands."

"There, now, Father, you won't work in it till it's all easy," said Eppie, "and you and me can mark out the beds, and make holes and plant the roots. It'll be a deal livelier at the Stone Pits when we've got some flowers, for I always think the flowers can see us and know what we're talking about. And I'll have a bit o' rosemary, and berga-mot, and thyme, because they're so sweet-smelling; but there's no lavender only in the gentlefolks' gardens, I think."

"That's no reason why you shouldn't have some," said Aaron, "for I can bring you slips of anything; I'm forced to cut no end of 'em when I'm gardening, and throw 'em away mostly. There's a big bed o' lavender at the Red House: the missis is very fond of it."

"Well," said Silas gravely, "so as you don't make free for us, or ask for anything as is worth much at the Red House: for Mr. Cass's been so good to us, and built us up the new end o' the cottage, and given us beds and things, as I couldn't abide to be imposin' for garden stuff or anything else."

"No, no, there's no imposin'," said Aaron; "there's never a garden in all the parish but what there's endless waste in it for want o' somebody as could use everything up. It's what I think to myself sometimes, as there need nobody run short o' victuals if the land was made the most on, and there was never a morsel but what could find its way to a mouth. It sets one thinking o' that— gardening does. But I must go back now, else mother 'ull be in trouble as I aren't there."

"Bring her with you this afternoon, Aaron," said Ep-pie; "I shouldn't like to fix about the garden, and her not know everything from the first—should you, Father?"

"Ay, bring her if you can, Aaron," said Silas; "she's sure to have a word to say as'll help us to set things on their right end."

Aaron turned back up the village, while Silas and Eppie went on up the lonely sheltered lane.

"Oh, Daddy!" she began, when they were in privacy, clasping and squeezing Silas's arm, and skipping round to give him an energetic kiss. "My little old Daddy! I'm so glad. I don't think I shall want anything else when we've got a little garden; and I knew Aaron would dig it for us," she went on with roguish triumph, "I knew that very well."

"You're a deep little puss, you are," said Silas, with the mild, passive happiness of love-crowned age in his face; "but you'll make yourself fine and beholden to Aaron."

"Oh, no, I shan't," said Eppie, laughing and frisking; "he likes it."

"Come, come, let me carry your prayer book, else you'll be dropping it, jumping i' that way."

Eppie was now aware that her behaviour was under observation, but it was only the observation of a friendly donkey, browsing with a log fastened to his foot—a meek donkey, not scornfully critical of human trivialities, but thankful to share in them, if possible, by getting his nose scratched; and Eppie did not fail to gratify him with her usual notice, though it was attended with the inconvenience of his following them, painfully, up to the very door of their home.

But the sound of a sharp bark inside, as Eppie put the key in the door, modified the donkey's views, and he limped away again without bidding. The sharp bark was the sign of an excited welcome that was awaiting them from a knowing brown terrier, who, after dancing at their legs in a hysterical manner, rushed with a worrying noise at a tortoise-shell kitten under the loom, and then rushed back with a sharp bark again, as much as to say, "I have done my duty by this feeble creature, you perceive"; while the lady mother of the kitten sat sunning her white bosom in the window, and looked round with a sleepy air of expecting caresses, though she was not going to take any trouble for them.

The presence of this happy animal life was not the only change which had come over this interior of the stone cottage. There was no bed now in the living room, and the small space was well filled with decent furniture, all

bright and clean enough to satisfy Dolly Winthrop's eye.
The oaken table and three-cornered oaken chair were
hardly what was likely to be seen in so poor a cottage:
they had come, with the beds and other things, from the
Red House, for Mr. Godfrey Cass, as everyone said in the
village, did very kindly by the weaver; and it was nothing
but right a man should be looked on and helped by those
who could afford it, when he had brought up an orphan
child, and been father and mother to her—and had lost
his money too, so as he had nothing but what he worked
for week by week, and when the weaving was going down
too—for there was less and less flax spun—and Master
Marner was none so young. Nobody was jealous of the
weaver, for he was regarded as an exceptional person,
whose claims on neighbourly help were not to be matched
in Raveloe. Any superstition that remained concerning
him had taken an entirely new colour; and Mr. Macey,
now a very feeble old man of fourscore and six, never seen
except in his chimney corner or sitting in the sunshine at
his doorsill, was of opinion that when a man had done
what Silas had done by an orphan child, it was a sign that
his money would come to light again, or leastwise that the
robber would be made to answer for it—for, as Mr. Macey
observed of himself, his faculties were as strong as ever.

Silas sat down and watched Eppie with a satisfied gaze
as she spread the clean cloth, and set on it the potato pie,
warmed up slowly in a safe Sunday fashion, by being put
into a dry pot over a slowly dying fire, as the best substitute for an oven. For Silas would not consent to have a
grate and oven added to his conveniences: he loved the
old brick hearth as he had loved his brown pot—and was
it not there when he had found Eppie? The gods of the
hearth exist for us still; and let all new faith be tolerant
of that fetishism, lest it bruise its own roots.

Silas ate his dinner more silently than usual, soon
laying down his knife and fork, and watching half-ab-
stractedly Eppie's play with Snap and the cat, by which
her own dining was made rather a lengthy business. Yet
it was a sight that might well arrest wandering thoughts:
Eppie, with the rippling radiance of her hair and the
whiteness of her rounded chin and throat set off by the
dark-blue cotton gown, laughing merrily as the kitten

held on with her four claws to one shoulder, like a design for a jug handle, while Snap on the right hand and Puss on the other put up their paws towards a morsel which she held out of the reach of both—Snap occasionally desisting in order to remonstrate with the cat by a cogent worrying growl on the greediness and futility of her conduct; till Eppie relented, caressed them both, and divided the morsel between them.

But at last Eppie, glancing at the clock, checked the play, and said, "Oh, Daddy, you're wanting to go into the sunshine to smoke your pipe. But I must clear away first, so as the house may be tidy when godmother comes. I'll make haste—I won't be long."

Silas had taken to smoking a pipe daily during the last two years, having been strongly urged to it by the sages of Raveloe, as a practice "good for the fits"; and this advice was sanctioned by Dr. Kimble, on the ground that it was as well to try what could do no harm—a principle which was made to answer for a great deal of work in that gentleman's medical practice. Silas did not highly enjoy smoking, and often wondered how his neighbours could be so fond of it; but a humble sort of acquiescence in what was held to be good had become a strong habit of that new self which had been developed in him since he had found Eppie on his hearth: it had been the only clew his bewildered mind could hold by in cherishing this young life that had been sent to him out of the darkness into which his gold had departed. By seeking what was needful for Eppie, by sharing the effect that everything produced on her, he had himself come to appropriate the forms of custom and belief which were the mould of Raveloe life; and as, with reawakening sensibilities, memory also reawakened, he had begun to ponder over the elements of his old faith, and blend them with his new impressions, till he recovered a consciousness of unity between his past and present. The sense of presiding goodness and the human trust which come with all pure peace and joy had given him a dim impression that there had been some error, some mistake, which had thrown that dark shadow over the days of his best years; and as it grew more and more easy to him to open his mind to Dolly Winthrop, he gradually communicated to her all he could describe of his early life. The communication was necessarily a slow and difficult process, for Silas's meagre power of explanation was not aided by any readiness of interpretation in Dolly, whose narrow outward experience gave her no key to strange customs, and made every novelty a source of wonder that arrested them at every step of the narrative. It was only by fragments, and at intervals which left Dolly time to revolve what she had heard till it acquired some familiarity for her, that Silas at last arrived at the climax of the sad story—the drawing of lots, and its false testimony concerning him; and this had to be repeated in several interviews, under new questions on her part as to the nature of this plan for detecting the guilty and clearing the innocent.

"And yourn's the same Bible, you're sure o' that, Master Marner—the Bible as you brought wi' you from that country—it's the same as what they've got at church, and what Eppie's a-learning to read in?"

"Yes," said Silas, "every bit the same; and there's drawing o' lots in the Bible, mind you," he added in a lower tone.

"Oh, dear, dear," said Dolly, in a grieved voice, as if she were hearing an unfavourable report of a sick man's case. She was silent for some minutes; at last she said:

"There's wise folks, happen, as know how it all is; the parson knows, I'll be bound; but it takes big words to tell them things, and such as poor folks can't make much out on. I can never rightly know the meaning o' what I hear at church, only a bit here and there, but I know it's good words—I do. But what lies upo' your mind—it's this, Master Marner: as, if Them above had done the right thing by you, They'd never ha' let you be turned out for a wicked thief when you was innicent."

"Ah!" said Silas, who had now come to understand Dolly's phraseology, "that was what fell on me like as if it had been red-hot iron; because, you see, there was nobody as cared for me or clave to me above nor below. And him as I'd gone out and in wi' for ten year and more, since when we was lads and went halves—mine own famil'ar friend, in whom I trusted, had lifted up his heel again' me, and worked to ruin me."

"Eh, but he was a bad 'un—I can't think as there's another such," said Dolly. "But I'm o'ercome, Master Marner; I'm like as if I'd waked and didn't know whether it was night or morning. I feel somehow as sure as I do when I've laid something up though I can't justly put my hand on it, as there was a rights in what happened to you, if one could but make it out; and you'd no call to lose heart as you did. But we'll talk on it again; for sometimes things come into my head when I'm leeching or poulticing, or such, as I could never think on when I was sitting still."

Dolly was too useful a woman not to have many opportunities of illumination of the kind she alluded to, and she was not long before she recurred to the subject.

"Master Marner," she said, one day that she came to bring home Eppie's washing, "I've been sore puzzled for a good bit wi' that trouble o' yourn and the drawing o' lots; and it got twisted back'ards and for'ards, as I didn't know which end to lay hold on. But it come to me all clear like, that night when I was sitting up wi' poor Bessy Fawkes, as is dead and left her children behind, God help 'em—it come to me as clear as daylight; but whether I've got hold on it now, or can anyways bring it to my tongue's end, that I don't know. For I've often a deal inside me as'll never come out; and for what you talk o' your folks in your old country niver saying prayers by heart nor saying 'em out of a book, they must be wonderful cliver; for if I didn't know 'Our Father,' and little bits o' good words as I can carry out o' church wi' me, I might down o' my knees every night, but nothing could I say."

"But you can mostly say something as I can make sense on, Mrs. Winthrop," said Silas.

"Well, then, Master Marner, it come to me summat like this: I can make nothing o' the drawing o' lots and the answer coming wrong; it 'ud mayhap take the parson to tell that, and he could only tell us i' big words. But what come to me as clear as the daylight, it was when I was troubling over poor Bessy Fawkes, and it allays comes into my head when I'm sorry for folks, and feel as I can't do a power to help 'em, not if I was to get up i' the middle o' the night—it comes into my head as Them above has got a deal tenderer heart nor what I've got—for I can't be anyways better nor Them as made me, and if anything

looks hard to me, it's because there's things I don't know
on; and for the matter o' that, there may be plenty o'
things I don't know on, for it's little as I know—that it is.
And so, while I was thinking o' that, you come into my
mind, Master Marner, and it all come pouring in—if *I*
felt i' my inside what was the right and just thing by
you, and them as prayed and drawed the lots, all but that
wicked un, if *they*'d ha' done the right thing by you if
they could, isn't there Them as was at the making on us,
and knows better and has a better will? And that's all as
ever I can be sure on, and everything else is a big puzzle
to me when I think on it. For there was the fever come
and took off them as were full-growed, and left the helpless children; and there's the breaking o' limbs; and them
as 'ud do right and be sober have to suffer by them as are
contrary—eh, there's trouble i' this world, and there's
things as we can niver make out the rights on. And all
as we've got to do is to trusten, Master Marner—to do the
right thing as fur as we know, and to trusten. For if us as
knows so little can see a bit o' good and rights, we may be
sure as there's a good and a rights bigger nor what we can
know—I feel it i' my own inside as it must be so. And if
you could but ha' gone on trustening, Master Marner, you
wouldn't ha' run away from your fellow creaturs and
been so lone."

"Ah, but that 'ud ha' been hard," said Silas, in an undertone; "it 'ud ha' been hard to trusten then."

"And so it would," said Dolly, almost with compunction; "them things are easier said nor done; and I'm partly ashamed o' talking."

"Nay, nay," said Silas, "you're i' the right, Mrs. Winthrop —you're i' the right. There's good i' this world—I've
a feeling o' that now; and it makes a man feel as there's
a good more nor he can see, i' spite o' the trouble and the
wickedness. That drawing o' the lots is dark; but the
child was sent to me: there's dealings with us—there's
dealings."

This dialogue took place in Eppie's earlier years, when
Silas had to part with her for two hours every day, that
she might learn to read at the dame school, after he had
vainly tried himself to guide her in that first step to learning. Now that she was grown up, Silas had often been

led, in those moments of quiet outpouring which come to people who live together in perfect love, to talk with *her* too of the past, and how and why he had lived a lonely man until she had been sent to him. For it would have been impossible for him to hide from Eppie that she was not his own child: even if the most delicate reticence on the point could have been expected from Raveloe gossips in her presence, her own questions about her mother could not have been parried, as she grew up, without that complete shrouding of the past which would have made a painful barrier between their minds. So Eppie had long known how her mother had died on the snowy ground, and how she herself had been found on the hearth by father Silas, who had taken her golden curls for his lost guineas brought back to him. The tender and peculiar love with which Silas had reared her in almost inseparable companionship with himself, aided by the seclusion of their dwelling, had preserved her from the lowering influences of the village talk and habits, and had kept her mind in that freshness which is sometimes falsely supposed to be an invariable attribute of rusticity. Perfect love has a breath of poetry which can exalt the relations of the least-instructed human beings; and this breath of poetry had surrounded Eppie from the time when she had followed the bright gleam that beckoned her to Silas's hearth: so that it is not surprising if, in other things besides her delicate prettiness, she was not quite a common village maiden, but had a touch of refinement and fervour which came from no other teaching than that of tenderly nurtured, unvitiated feeling. She was too childish and simple for her imagination to rove into questions about her unknown father; for a long while it did not even occur to her that she must have had a father; and the first time that the idea of her mother having had a husband presented itself to her was when Silas showed her the wedding ring which had been taken from the wasted finger, and had been carefully preserved by him in a little lacquered box shaped like a shoe. He delivered this box into Eppie's charge when she had grown up, and she often opened it to look at the ring; but still she thought hardly at all about the father of whom it was the symbol. Had she not a father very close to her, who loved her bet-

ter than any real fathers in the village seemed to love
their daughters? On the contrary, who her mother was,
and how she came to die in that forlornness, were questions that often pressed on Eppie's mind. Her knowledge
of Mrs. Winthrop, who was her nearest friend next to
Silas, made her feel that a mother must be very precious;
and she had again and again asked Silas to tell her how
her mother looked, whom she was like, and how he had
found her against the furze bush, led towards it by the
little footsteps and the outstretched arms. The furze bush
was there still; and this afternoon, when Eppie came out
with Silas into the sunshine, it was the first object that
arrested her eyes and thoughts.

"Father," she said, in a tone of gentle gravity, which
sometimes came like a sadder, slower cadence across her
playfulness, "we shall take the furze bush into the garden; it'll come into the corner, and just against it I'll put
snowdrops and crocuses, 'cause Aaron says they won't die
out, but'll always get more and more."

"Ah, child," said Silas, always ready to talk when he
had his pipe in his hand, apparently enjoying the pauses
more than the puffs, "it wouldn't do to leave out the furze
bush; and there's nothing prettier, to my thinking, when
it's yallow with flowers. But it's just come into my head
what we're to do for a fence—mayhap Aaron can help us
to a thought; but a fence we must have, else the donkeys
and things 'ull come and trample everything down. And
fencing's hard to be got at, by what I can make out."

"Oh! I'll tell you, Daddy," said Eppie, clasping her
hands suddenly, after a minute's thought. "There's lots o'
loose stones about, some of 'em not big, and we might lay
'em atop of one another, and make a wall. You and me
could carry the smallest, and Aaron 'ud carry the rest—I
know he would."

"Eh, my precious 'un," said Silas, "there isn't enough
stones to go all round; and as for you carrying, why, wi'
your little arms you couldn't carry a stone no bigger than
a turnip. You're dillicate made, my dear," he added, with
a tender intonation, "that's what Mrs. Winthrop says."

"Oh, I'm stronger than you think, Daddy," said Eppie;
"and if there wasn't stones enough to go all round, why
they'll go part o' the way, and then it'll be easier to get

sticks and things for the rest. See here, round the big pit, what a many stones!"

She skipped forward to the pit, meaning to lift one of the stones and exhibit her strength, but she started back in surprise.

"Oh, father, just come and look here," she exclaimed, "come and see how the water's gone down since yesterday. Why, yesterday the pit was ever so full!"

"Well, to be sure," said Silas, coming to her side. "Why, that's the draining they've begun on, since harvest, i' Mr. Osgood's fields, I reckon. The foreman said to me the other day, when I passed by 'em, 'Master Marner,' he said, 'I shouldn't wonder if we lay your bit o' waste as dry as a bone.' It was Mr. Godfrey Cass, he said, had gone into the draining: he'd been taking these fields o' Mr. Osgood."

"How odd it'll seem to have the old pit dried up," said Eppie, turning away, and stooping to lift rather a large stone. "See, Daddy, I can carry this quite well," she said, going along with much energy for a few steps, but presently letting it fall.

"Ah, you're fine and strong, aren't you?" said Silas, while Eppie shook her aching arms and laughed. "Come, come, let us go and sit down on the bank against the stile there, and have no more lifting. You might hurt yourself, child. You'd need have somebody to work for you—and my arm isn't overstrong."

Silas uttered the last sentence slowly, as if it implied more than met the ear; and Eppie, when they sat down on the bank, nestled close to his side, and, taking hold caressingly of the arm that was not overstrong, held it on her lap, while Silas puffed again dutifully at the pipe, which occupied his other arm. An ash in the hedgerow behind made a fretted screen from the sun, and threw happy, playful shadows all about them.

"Father," said Eppie, very gently, after they had been sitting in silence a little while, "if I was to be married, ought I to be married with my mother's ring?"

Silas gave an almost imperceptible start, though the question fell in with the undercurrent of thought in his own mind, and then said, in a subdued tone, "Why, Eppie, have you been a-thinking on it?"

"Only this last week, father," said Eppie ingenuously, "since Aaron talked to me about it."

"And what did he say?" said Silas, still in the same subdued way, as if he were anxious lest he should fall into the slightest tone that was not for Eppie's good.

"He said he should like to be married, because he was a-going in four-and-twenty, and had got a deal of gardening work, now Mr. Mott's given up; and he goes twice a week regular to see Mr. Cass's, and once to Mr. Osgood's, and they're going to take him on at the Rectory."

"And who is it as he's wanting to marry?" said Silas, with rather a sad smile.

"Why, me, to be sure, Daddy," said Eppie, with dimpling laughter, kissing her father's cheek; "as if he'd want to marry anybody else!"

"And you mean to have him, do you?" said Silas.

"Yes, sometime," said Eppie. "I don't know when. Everybody's married sometime, Aaron says. But I told him that wasn't true: for, I said, look at father—he's never been married."

"No, child," said Silas, "your father was a lone man till you was sent to him."

"But you'll never be lone again, Father," said Eppie, tenderly. "That was what Aaron said—'I could never never think o' taking you away from Master Marner, Eppie.' And I said, 'It 'ud be no use if you did, Aaron.' And he wants us all to live together, so as you needn't work a bit, Father, only what's for your own pleasure; and he'd be as good as a son to you—that was what he said."

"And should you like that, Eppie?" said Silas, looking at her.

"I shouldn't mind it, Father," said Eppie, quite simply. "And I should like things to be so as you needn't work much. But if it wasn't for that, I'd sooner things didn't change. I'm very happy: I like Aaron to be fond of me and come and see us often, and behave pretty to you—he always *does* behave pretty to you, doesn't he, Father?"

"Yes, child, nobody could behave better," said Silas emphatically. "He's his mother's lad."

"But I don't want any change," said Eppie. "I should like to go on a long, long while, just as we are. Only Aaron does want a change; and he made me cry a bit—

only a bit—because he said I didn't care for him, for if I cared for him I should want us to be married, as he did."

"Eh, my blessed child," said Silas, laying down his pipe as if it were useless to pretend to smoke any longer, "you're o'eryoung to be married. We'll ask Mrs. Winthrop—we'll ask Aaron's mother what *she* thinks: if there's a right thing to do, she'll come at it. But there's this to be thought on, Eppie: things *will* change, whether we like it or not; things won't go on for a long while just as they are and no difference. I shall get older and helplesser, and be a burden on you, belike, if I don't go away from you altogether. Not as I mean you'd think me a burden—I know you wouldn't—but it 'ud be hard upon you; and when I look for'ard to that, I like to think as you'd have somebody else besides me—somebody young and strong, as'll outlast your own life, and take care on you to the end." Silas paused, and, resting his wrists on his knees, lifted his hands up and down meditatively as he looked on the ground.

"Then, would you like me to be married, Father?" said Eppie, with a little trembling in her voice.

"I'll not be the man to say no, Eppie," said Silas emphatically; "but we'll ask your godmother. She'll wish the right thing by you and her son too."

"There they come then," said Eppie. "Let us go and meet 'em. Oh, the pipe! won't you have it lit again, Father?" said Eppie, lifting that medicinal appliance from the ground.

"Nay, child," said Silas. "I've done enough for today. I think, mayhap, a little of it does me more good than so much at once."

CHAPTER XVII

WHILE SILAS AND EPPIE were seated on the bank discoursing in the fleckered shade of the ash tree, Miss Priscilla Lammeter was resisting her sister's arguments that it would be better to take tea at the Red House, and let her father have a long nap, than drive home to the Warrens

so soon after dinner. The family party (of four only)
were seated round the table in the dark wainscoted parlour, with the Sunday dessert before them, of fresh fil-
berts, apples, and pears, duly ornamented with leaves by
Nancy's own hands before the bells had rung for church.

A great change has come over the dark wainscoted
parlour since we saw it in Godfrey's bachelor days, and
under the wifeless reign of the old Squire. Now all is
polish, on which no yesterday's dust is ever allowed to
rest, from the yard's width of oaken boards round the
carpet, to the old Squire's gun and whips and walking
sticks, ranged on the stag's antlers above the mantelpiece.
All other signs of sporting and outdoor occupation Nancy
has removed to another room; but she has brought into
the Red House the habit of filial reverence, and preserves
sacredly in a place of honour these relics of her husband's
departed father. The tankards are on the side table still,
but the bossed silver is undimmed by handling, and there
are no dregs to send forth unpleasant suggestions: the
only prevailing scent is of the lavender and rose leaves
that fill the vases of Derbyshire spar. All is purity and
order in this once dreary room, for, fifteen years ago, it
was entered by a new presiding spirit.

"Now, Father," said Nancy, "*is* there any call for you to
go home to tea? Mayn't you just as well stay with us?—
such a beautiful evening as it's likely to be."

The old gentleman had been talking with Godfrey
about the increasing poor rate and the ruinous times, and
had not heard the dialogue between his daughters.

"My dear, you must ask Priscilla," he said in the once
firm voice, now become rather broken. "She manages me
and the farm too."

"And reason good as I should manage you, Father,"
said Priscilla, "else you'd be giving yourself your death
with rheumatism. And as for the farm, if anything turns
out wrong, as it can't but do in these times, there's nothing kills a man so soon as having nobody to find fault
with but himself. It's a deal best way o' being master,
to let somebody else do the ordering, and keep the blaming in your own hands. It 'ud save many a man a stroke, *I*
believe."

"Well, well, my dear," said her father, with a quiet

laugh, "I didn't say you don't manage for everybody's good."

"Then manage so as you may stay tea, Priscilla," said Nancy, putting her hand on her sister's arm affectionately. "Come now; and we'll go round the garden while Father has his nap."

"My dear child, he'll have a beautiful nap in the gig, for I shall drive. And as for staying tea, I can't hear of it; for there's this dairymaid, now she knows she's to be married, turned Michaelmas, she'd as lieve pour the new milk into the pig trough as into the pans. That's the way with 'em all: it's as if they thought the world 'ud be new-made because they're to be married. So come and let me put my bonnet on, and there'll be time for us to walk round the garden while the horse is being put in."

When the sisters were treading the neatly swept garden walks, between the bright turf that contrasted pleasantly with the dark cones and arches and wall-like hedges of yew, Priscilla said:

"I'm as glad as anything at your husband's making that exchange o' land with cousin Osgood, and beginning the dairying. It's a thousand pities you didn't do it before; for it'll give you something to fill your mind. There's nothing like a dairy if folks want a bit o' worrit to make the days pass. For as for rubbing furniture, when you can once see your face in a table there's nothing else to look for; but there's always something fresh with the dairy; for even in the depths o' winter there's some pleasure in conquering the butter, and making it come whether or no. My dear," added Priscilla, pressing her sister's hand affectionately as they walked side by side, "you'll never be low when you've got a dairy."

"Ah, Priscilla," said Nancy, returning the pressure with a grateful glance of her clear eyes, "but it won't make up to Godfrey: a dairy's not so much to a man. And it's only what he cares for that ever makes me low. I'm contented with the blessings we have, if he could be contented."

"It drives me past patience," said Priscilla impetuously, "that way o' the men—always wanting and wanting, and never easy with what they've got: they can't sit comfortable in their chairs when they've neither ache nor pain, but either they must stick a pipe in their mouths, to make 'em better than well, or else they must be swallowing something strong, though they're forced to make haste before the next meal comes in. But joyful be it spoken, our father was never that sort o' man. And if it had pleased God to make you ugly, like me, so as the men wouldn't ha' run after you, we might have kept to our own family, and had nothing to do with folks as have got uneasy blood in their veins."

"Oh, don't say so, Priscilla," said Nancy, repenting that she had called forth this outburst; "nobody has any occasion to find fault with Godfrey. It's natural he should be disappointed at not having any children: every man likes to have somebody to work for and lay by for, and he always counted so on making a fuss with 'em when they were little. There's many another man 'ud hanker more than he does. He's the best of husbands."

"Oh, I know," said Priscilla, smiling sarcastically, "I know the way o' wives; they set one on to abuse their husbands, and then they turn round on one and praise 'em as if they wanted to sell 'em. But Father'll be waiting for me; we must turn now."

The large gig with the steady old grey was at the front door, and Mr. Lammeter was already on the stone steps, passing the time in recalling to Godfrey what very fine points Speckle had when his master used to ride him.

"I always *would* have a good horse, you know," said the old gentleman, not liking that spirited time to be quite effaced from the memory of his juniors.

"Mind you bring Nancy to the Warrens before the week's out, Mr. Cass," was Priscilla's parting injunction, as she took the reins, and shook them gently, by way of friendly incitement to Speckle.

"I shall just take a turn to the fields against the Stone Pits, Nancy, and look at the draining," said Godfrey.

"You'll be in again by tea time, dear?"

"Oh, yes, I shall be back in an hour."

It was Godfrey's custom on a Sunday afternoon to do a little contemplative farming in a leisurely walk. Nancy seldom accompanied him; for the women of her generation—unless, like Priscilla, they took to outdoor management—were not given to much walking beyond their own house and garden, finding sufficient exercise in domestic duties. So, when Priscilla was not with her, she usually sat with Mant's Bible before her, and after following the text with her eyes for a little while, she would gradually permit them to wander as her thoughts had already insisted on wandering.

But Nancy's Sunday thoughts were rarely quite out of keeping with the devout and reverential intention implied by the book spread open before her. She was not theologically instructed enough to discern very clearly the relation between the sacred documents of the past which she opened without method, and her own obscure, simple life; but the spirit of rectitude, and the sense of responsibility for the effect of her conduct on others, which were strong elements in Nancy's character, had made it a habit with her to scrutinise her past feelings and actions with self-questioning solicitude. Her mind not being courted by a great variety of subjects, she filled the vacant moments by living inwardly, again and again, through all her remembered experience, especially through the fifteen years of her married time, in which her life and its significance had been doubled. She recalled the small details, the words, tones, and looks, in the critical scenes which had opened a new epoch for her, by giving her a deeper insight into the relations and trials of life, or which had called on her for some little effort of forbearance, or of painful adherence to an imagined or real duty —asking herself continually whether she had been in any respect blamable. This excessive rumination and self-questioning is perhaps a morbid habit inevitable to a mind of much moral sensibility when shut out from its due share of outward activity and of practical claims on its affections—inevitable to a noblehearted, childless woman, when her lot is narrow. "I can do so little—have I done it all well?" is the perpetually recurring thought; and there are no voices calling her away from that soliloquy, no peremptory demands to divert energy from vain regret or superfluous scruple.

There was one main thread of painful experience in Nancy's married life, and on it hung certain deeply felt scenes, which were the oftenest revived in retrospect. The short dialogue with Priscilla in the garden had determined the current of retrospect in that frequent direction this particular Sunday afternoon. The first wandering of her thought from the text, which she still attempted dutifully to follow with her eyes and silent lips, was into an imaginary enlargement of the defence she had set up for her husband against Priscilla's implied blame. The vindication of the loved object is the best balm affection can find for its wounds—"A man must have so much on his mind" is the belief by which a wife often supports a cheerful face under rough answers and unfeeling words. And Nancy's deepest wounds had all come from the perception that the absence of children from their hearth was dwelt on in her husband's mind as a privation to which he could not reconcile himself.

Yet sweet Nancy might have been expected to feel still more keenly the denial of a blessing to which she had looked forward with all the varied expectations and preparations, solemn and prettily trivial, which fill the mind of a loving woman when she expects to become a mother. Was there not a drawer filled with the neat work of her hands, all unworn and untouched, just as she had arranged it there fourteen years ago—just but for one little dress, which had been made the burial dress? But under this immediate personal trial Nancy was so firmly unmurmuring, that years ago she had suddenly renounced the habit of visiting this drawer, lest she should in this way be cherishing a longing for what was not given.

Perhaps it was this very severity towards any indulgence of what she held to be sinful regret in herself that made her shrink from applying her own standard to her husband. "It was very different—it was much worse for a man to be disappointed in that way: a woman could always be satisfied with devoting herself to her husband, but a man wanted something that would make him look forward more—and sitting by the fire was so much duller to him than to a woman." And always, when Nancy reached this point in her meditations—trying, with predetermined sympathy, to see everything as Godfrey saw it—there came a renewal of self-questioning. *Had* she done everything in her power to lighten Godfrey's privation? Had she really been right in the resistance which had cost her so much pain six years ago, and again four years ago—the resistance to her husband's wish that they should adopt a child? Adoption was more remote from the ideas and habits of that time than of our own; still Nancy had her opinion on it. It was as necessary to her mind to have an opinion on all topics, not exclusively masculine, that had come under her notice, as for her to have a precisely marked place for every article of her personal property: and her opinions were always principles to be unwaveringly acted on. They were firm, not because of their basis, but because she held them with a tenacity inseparable from her mental action. On all the duties and proprieties of life, from filial behaviour to the arrangements of the evening toilet, pretty Nancy Lammeter, by the time she was three-and-twenty, had her unalterable little code, and had formed every one of her habits in strict accordance with that code. She carried these decided judgments within her in the most unobtrusive way: they rooted themselves in her mind, and grew there as quietly as grass. Years ago, we know, she insisted on dressing like Priscilla, because "it was right for sisters to dress alike," and because "she would do what was right if she wore a gown dyed with cheese colouring." That was a trivial but typical instance of the mode in which Nancy's life was regulated.

It was one of those rigid principles, and no petty egoistic feeling, which had been the ground of Nancy's difficult resistance to her husband's wish. To adopt a child, because children of your own had been denied you, was to try and choose your lot in spite of Providence: the adopted child, she was convinced, would never turn out well, and would be a curse to those who had wilfully and rebelliously sought what it was clear that, for some high reason, they were better without. When you saw a thing was not meant to be, said Nancy, it was a bounden duty to leave off so much as wishing for it. And so far, perhaps, the wisest of men could scarcely make more than a verbal improvement in her principle. But the conditions under which she held it apparent that a thing was not meant to be depended on a more peculiar mode of thinking. She would have given up making a purchase at a particular place if, on three successive times, rain, or some other cause of Heaven's sending, had formed an obstacle; and she would have anticipated a broken limb or other heavy misfortune to anyone who persisted in spite of such indications.

"But why should you think the child would turn out ill?" said Godfrey, in his remonstrances. "She has thriven as well as child can do with the weaver; and *he* adopted her. There isn't such a pretty little girl anywhere else in the parish, or one fitter for the station we could give her. Where can be the likelihood of her being a curse to anybody?"

"Yes, my dear Godfrey," said Nancy, who was sitting with her hands tightly clasped together, and with yearning, regretful affection in her eyes. "The child may not turn out ill with the weaver. But, then, he didn't go to seek her, as we should be doing. It will be wrong: I feel sure it will. Don't you remember what that lady we met at the Royston Baths told us about the child her sister adopted? That was the only adopting I ever heard of: and the child was transported when it was twenty-three. Dear Godfrey, don't ask me to do what is wrong: I should never be happy again. I know it's very hard for *you*—it's easier for me—but it's the will of Providence."

It might seem singular that Nancy—with her religious theory pieced together out of narrow social traditions, fragments of church doctrine imperfectly understood, and girlish reasonings on her small experience—should have arrived by herself at a way of thinking so nearly akin to that of many devout people, whose beliefs are held in the shape of a system quite remote from her knowledge—singular, if we did not know that human beliefs, like all other natural growths, elude the barriers of system.

Godfrey had from the first specified Eppie, then about twelve years old, as a child suitable for them to adopt. It had never occurred to him that Silas would rather part with his life than with Eppie. Surely the weaver would wish the best to the child he had taken so much trouble with, and would be glad that such good fortune should happen to her: she would always be very grateful to him, and he would be well provided for to the end of his life—provided for as the excellent part he had done by the child deserved. Was it not an appropriate thing for people in a higher station to take a charge off the hands of a man in a lower? It seemed an eminently appropriate thing to Godfrey, for reasons that were known only to himself; and by a common fallacy, he imagined the meas- ure would be easy because he had private motives for desiring it. This was rather a coarse mode of estimating Silas's relation to Eppie; but we must remember that many of the impressions which Godfrey was likely to gather concerning the labouring people around him would favour the idea that deep affections can hardly go along with callous palms and scant means; and he had not had the opportunity, even if he had had the power, of entering intimately into all that was exceptional in the weaver's experience. It was only the want of adequate knowledge that could have made it possible for Godfrey deliberately to entertain an unfeeling project: his natural kindness had outlived that blighting time of cruel wishes, and Nancy's praise of him as a husband was not founded entirely on a wilful illusion.

"I was right," she said to herself, when she had recalled all their scenes of discussion; "I feel I was right to say him nay, though it hurt me more than anything; but how good Godfrey has been about it! Many men would have been very angry with me for standing out against their wishes; and they might have thrown out that they'd had ill luck in marrying me; but Godfrey has never been the man to say me an unkind word. It's only what he can't hide: everything seems so blank to him, I know; and the land—what a difference it 'ud make to him, when he goes to see after things, if he'd children growing up that he was doing it all for! But I won't murmur; and perhaps if he'd married a woman who'd have had children, she'd have vexed him in other ways."

This possibility was Nancy's chief comfort; and to give it greater strength, she laboured to make it impossible that any other wife should have had more perfect tender- ness. She had been *forced* to vex him by that one denial. Godfrey was not insensible to her loving effort, and did Nancy no injustice as to the motives of her obstinacy. It was impossible to have lived with her fifteen years and not be aware that an unselfish clinging to the right, and a sincerity clear as the flower-born dew, were her main characteristics; indeed, Godfrey felt this so strongly, that his own more wavering nature, too averse to facing difficulty to be unvaryingly simple and truthful, was kept in a certain awe of this gentle wife who watched his looks with a yearning to obey them. It seemed to him impossible that he should ever confess to her the truth about Eppie: she would never recover from the repulsion the story of his earlier marriage would create, told to her now, after that long concealment. And the child, too, he thought, must become an object of repulsion: the very sight of her would be painful. The shock to Nancy's mingled pride and ignorance of the world's evil might even be too much for her delicate frame. Since he had married her with that secret on his heart, he must keep it there to the last. Whatever else he did, he could not make an irreparable breach between himself and this long-loved wife.

Meanwhile, why could he not make up his mind to the absence of children from a hearth brightened by such a wife? Why did his mind fly uneasily to that void, as if it were the sole reason why life was not thoroughly joyous to him? I suppose it is the way with all men and women who reach middle age without the clear perception that life never *can* be thoroughly joyous: under the vague dulness of the grey hours, dissatisfaction seeks a definite object, and finds it in the privation of an untried good. Dissatisfaction, seated musingly on a childless hearth, thinks with envy of the father whose return is greeted by young voices—seated at the meal where the little heads rise one above another like nursery plants, it sees a black care hovering behind every one of them, and thinks the impulses by which men abandon freedom, and seek for ties, are surely nothing but a brief madness. In Godfrey's case there were further reasons why his thoughts should be continually solicited by this one point in his lot: his conscience, never thoroughly easy about Eppie, now gave his childless home the aspect of a retribution; and as the time passed on, under Nancy's refusal to adopt her, any retrieval of his error became more and more difficult.

On this Sunday afternoon it was already four years since there had been any allusion to the subject between them, and Nancy supposed that it was forever buried.

"I wonder if he'll mind it less or more as he gets older," she thought; "I'm afraid more. Aged people feel the miss of children: what would Father do without Priscilla? And if I die, Godfrey will be very lonely—not holding together with his brothers much. But I won't be overanxious, and trying to make things out beforehand: I must do my best for the present."

With that last thought Nancy roused herself from her reverie, and turned her eyes again towards the forsaken page. It had been forsaken longer than she imagined, for she was presently surprised by the appearance of the servant with the tea things. It was, in fact, a little before the usual time for tea; but Jane had her reasons.

"Is your master come into the yard, Jane?"

"No'm, he isn't," said Jane, with a slight emphasis, of which, however, her mistress took no notice.

"I don't know whether you've seen 'em, 'm," continued Jane, after a pause, "but there's folks making haste all one way, afore the front window. I doubt something's happened. There's niver a man to be seen i' the yard, else I'd send and see. I've been up into the top attic, but there's no seeing anything for trees. I hope nobody's hurt, that's all."

"Oh, no, I daresay there's nothing much the matter," said Nancy. "It's perhaps Mr. Snell's bull got out again, as he did before."

"I wish he mayn't gore anybody, then, that's all," said Jane, not altogether despising a hypothesis which covered a few imaginary calamities.

"That girl is always terrifying me," thought Nancy; "I wish Godfrey would come in."

She went to the front window and looked as far as she could see along the road, with an uneasiness which she felt to be childish, for there were now no such signs of excitement as Jane had spoken of, and Godfrey would not be likely to return by the village road, but by the fields. She continued to stand, however, looking at the placid churchyard with the long shadows of the gravestones across the bright green hillocks, and at the glowing autumn colours of the Rectory trees beyond. Before such calm external beauty the presence of a vague fear is more distinctly felt—like a raven flapping its slow wing across the sunny air. Nancy wished more and more that Godfrey would come in.

CHAPTER XVIII

SOMEONE OPENED the door at the other end of the room, and Nancy felt that it was her husband. She turned from the window with gladness in her eyes, for the wife's chief dread was stilled.

"Dear, I'm so thankful you're come," she said, going towards him. "I began to get . . ."

She paused abruptly, for Godfrey was laying down his hat with trembling hands, and turned towards her with a pale face and a strange, unanswering glance, as if he saw her indeed, but saw her as part of a scene invisible to herself. She laid her hand on his arm, not daring to speak again; but he left the touch unnoticed, and threw himself into his chair.

Jane was already at the door with hissing urn. "Tell her to keep away, will you?" said Godfrey; and when the door was closed again he exerted himself to speak more distinctly.

"Sit down, Nancy—there," he said, pointing to a chair opposite him. "I came back as soon as I could, to hinder anybody's telling you but me. I've had a great shock—but I care most about the shock it'll be to you."

"It isn't father and Priscilla?" said Nancy, with quivering lips, clasping her hands together tightly on her lap.

"No, it's nobody living," said Godfrey, unequal to the considerate skill with which he would have wished to make his revelation. "It's Dunstan—my brother Dunstan, that we lost sight of sixteen years ago. We've found him —found his body—his skeleton."

The deep dread Godfrey's look had created in Nancy made her feel these words a relief. She sat in comparative calmness to hear what else he had to tell. He went on:

"The Stone Pit has gone dry suddenly—from the draining, I suppose; and there he lies—has lain for sixteen years, wedged between two great stones. There's his watch and seals, and there's my gold-handled hunting whip, with my name on: he took it away, without my knowing, the day he went hunting on Wildfire, the last time he was seen."

Godfrey paused: it was not so easy to say what came next. "Do you think he drowned himself?" said Nancy, almost wondering that her husband should be so deeply shaken by what happened all those years ago to an unloved brother, of whom worse things had been augured.

"No, he fell in," said Godfrey, in a low but distinct voice, as if he felt some deep meaning in the fact. Presently he added: "Dunstan was the man that robbed Silas Marner."

The blood rushed to Nancy's face and neck at this surprise and shame, for she had been bred up to regard even a distant kinship with crime as a dishonour.

"Oh, Godfrey!" she said, with compassion in her tone, for she had immediately reflected that the dishonour must be felt still more keenly by her husband.

"There was the money in the pit," he continued, "all the weaver's money. Everything's been gathered up, and they're taking the skeleton to the Rainbow. But I came back to tell you: there was no hindering it; you must know."

He was silent, looking on the ground for two long minutes. Nancy would have said some words of comfort under this disgrace, but she refrained, from an instinctive sense that there was something behind—that Godfrey had something else to tell her. Presently he lifted his eyes to her face, and kept them fixed on her, as he said:

"Everything comes to light, Nancy, sooner or later. When God Almighty wills it, our secrets are found out. I've lived with a secret on my mind, but I'll keep it from you no longer. I wouldn't have you know it by somebody else, and not by me—I wouldn't have you find it out after I'm dead. I'll tell you now. It's been 'I will' and 'I won't' with me all my life—I'll make sure of myself now."

Nancy's utmost dread had returned. The eyes of the

husband and wife met with awe in them, as at a crisis which suspended affection.

"Nancy," said Godfrey slowly, "when I married you, I hid something from you—something I ought to have told you. That woman Marner found dead in the snow —Eppie's mother—that wretched woman—was my wife: Eppie is my child."

He paused, dreading the effect of his confession. But Nancy sat quite still, only that her eyes dropped and ceased to meet his. She was pale and quiet as a meditative statue, clasping her hands on her lap.

"You'll never think the same of me again," said Godfrey, after a little while, with some tremor in his voice.

She was silent.

"I oughtn't to have left the child unowned: I oughtn't to have kept it from you. But I couldn't bear to give you up, Nancy. I was led away into marrying her—I suffered for it."

Still Nancy was silent, looking down; and he almost expected that she would presently get up and say she would go to her father's. How could she have any mercy for faults that must seem so black to her, with her simple, severe notions?

But at last she lifted up her eyes to his again and spoke. There was no indignation in her voice—only deep regret.

"Godfrey, if you had but told me this six years ago, we could have done some of our duty by the child. Do you think I'd have refused to take her in, if I'd known she was yours?"

At that moment Godfrey felt all the bitterness of an error that was not simply futile, but had defeated its own end. He had not measured this wife with whom he had lived so long. But she spoke again, with more agitation.

"And—Oh, Godfrey—if we'd had her from the first, if you'd taken to her as you ought, she'd have loved me for her mother—and you'd have been happier with me: I could better have bore my little baby dying, and our life might have been more like what we used to think it 'ud be."

The tears fell, and Nancy ceased to speak.

"But you wouldn't have married me then, Nancy, if I'd told you," said Godfrey, urged, in the bitterness of his self-reproach, to prove to himself that his conduct had not been utter folly. "You may think you would now, but you wouldn't then. With your pride and your father's, you'd have hated having anything to do with me after the talk there'd have been."

"I can't say what I should have done about that, Godfrey. I should never have married anybody else. But I wasn't worth doing wrong for—nothing is in this world. Nothing is so good as it seems beforehand—not even our marrying wasn't, you see." There was a faint, sad smile on Nancy's face as she said the last words.

"I'm a worse man than you thought I was, Nancy," said Godfrey, rather tremulously. "Can you forgive me ever?"

"The wrong to me is but little, Godfrey: you've made it up to me—you've been good to me for fifteen years. It's another you did the wrong to; and I doubt it can never be all made up for."

"But we can take Eppie now," said Godfrey. "I won't mind the world knowing at last. I'll be plain and open for the rest o' my life."

"It'll be different coming to us, now she's grown up," said Nancy, shaking her head sadly. "But it's your duty to acknowledge her and provide for her; and I'll do my part by her, and pray to God Almighty to make her love me."

"Then we'll go together to Silas Marner's this very night, as soon as everything's quiet at the Stone Pits."

CHAPTER XIX

BETWEEN EIGHT AND NINE o'clock that evening, Eppie and Silas were seated alone in the cottage. After the great excitement the weaver had undergone from the events of the afternoon, he had felt a longing for this quietude, and had even begged Mrs. Winthrop and Aaron, who had naturally lingered behind everyone else, to leave him alone with his child. The excitement had not passed

away: it had only reached that stage when the keenness
of the susceptibility makes external stimulus intolerable
—when there is no sense of weariness, but rather an intensity of inward life, under which sleep is an impossi-
bility. Anyone who has watched such moments in other
men remembers the brightness of the eyes and the strange
definiteness that comes over coarse features from that
transient influence. It is as if a new fineness of ear for all
spiritual voices had sent wonder-working vibrations
through the heavy mortal frame—as if "beauty born of
murmuring sound" had passed into the face of the
listener.

Silas's face showed that sort of transfiguration, as he
sat in his armchair and looked at Eppie. She had drawn
her own chair towards his knees, and leaned forward,
holding both his hands, while she looked up at him. On
the table near them, lit by a candle, lay the recovered
gold—the old, long-loved gold, ranged in orderly heaps,
as Silas used to range it in the days when it was his only
joy. He had been telling her how he used to count it
every night, and how his soul was utterly desolate till
she was sent to him.

"At first, I'd a sort o' feeling come across me now and
then," he was saying in a subdued tone, "as if you might
be changed into the gold again; for sometimes, turn my
head which way I would, I seemed to see the gold; and I
thought I should be glad if I could feel it, and find it
was come back. But that didn't last long. After a bit, I
should have thought it was a curse come again, if it had
drove you from me, for I'd got to feel the need o' your
looks and your voice and the touch o' your little fingers.
You didn't know then, Eppie, when you were such a little
un—you didn't know what your old father Silas felt for
you."

"But I know now, Father," said Eppie. "If it hadn't
been for you, they'd have taken me to the workhouse,
and there'd have been nobody to love me."

"Eh, my precious child, the blessing was mine. If you
hadn't been sent to save me, I should ha' gone to the
grave in my misery. The money was taken from me in
time; and you see it's been kept—kept till it was wanted
for you. It's wonderful—our life is wonderful."

Silas sat in silence a few minutes, looking at the money. "It takes no hold of me now," he said ponderingly, "the money doesn't. I wonder if it ever could again—I doubt it might, if I lost you, Eppie. I might come to think I was forsaken again, and lose the feeling that God was good to me."

At that moment there was a knocking at the door; and Eppie was obliged to rise without answering Silas. Beautiful she looked, with the tenderness of gathering tears in her eyes and a slight flush on her cheeks, as she stepped to open the door. The flush deepened when she saw Mr. and Mrs. Godfrey Cass. She made her little rustic curtsy and held the door wide for them to enter.

"We're disturbing you very late, my dear," said Mrs. Cass, taking Eppie's hand, and looking in her face with an expression of anxious interest and admiration. Nancy herself was pale and tremulous.

Eppie, after placing chairs for Mr. and Mrs. Cass, went to stand against Silas, opposite to them.

"Well, Marner," said Godfrey, trying to speak with perfect firmness, "it's a great comfort to me to see you with your money again, that you've been deprived of so many years. It was one of my family did you the wrong— the more grief to me—and I feel bound to make up to you for it in every way. Whatever I can do for you will be nothing but paying a debt, even if I looked no further than the robbery. But there are other things I'm beholden —shall be beholden to you for, Marner."

Godfrey checked himself. It had been agreed between him and his wife that the subject of his fatherhood should be approached very carefully, and that, if possible, the disclosure should be reserved for the future, so that it might be made to Eppie gradually. Nancy had urged this, because she felt strongly the painful light in which Eppie must inevitably see the relation between her father and mother.

Silas, always ill at ease when he was being spoken to by "betters," such as Mr. Cass—tall, powerful, florid men, seen chiefly on horseback—answered with some constraint:

"Sir, I've a deal to thank you for a'ready. As for the

robbery, I count it no loss to me. And if I did, you couldn't help it: you aren't answerable for it."

"You may look at it in that way, Marner, but I never can; and I hope you'll let me act according to my own feeling of what's just. I know you're easily contented: you've been a hard-working man all your life."

"Yes, sir, yes," said Marner, meditatively. "I should ha' been bad off without my work: it was what I held by when everything else was gone from me."

"Ah," said Godfrey, applying Marner's words simply to his bodily wants, "it was a good trade for you in this country, because there's been a great deal of linen-weaving to be done. But you're getting rather past such close work, Marner: it's time you laid by and had some rest. You look a good deal pulled down, though you're not an old man, *are* you?"

"Fifty-five, as near as I can say, sir," said Silas.

"Oh, why, you may live thirty years longer—look at old Macey! And that money on the table, after all, is but little. It won't go far either way—whether it's put out to interest, or you were to live on it as long as it would last: it wouldn't go far if you'd nobody to keep but yourself, and you've had two to keep for a good many years now."

"Eh, sir," said Silas, unaffected by anything Godfrey was saying, "I am in no fear o' want. We shall do very well—Eppie and me 'ull do well enough. There's few working folks have got so much laid by as that. I don't know what it is to gentlefolks, but I look upon it as a deal—almost too much. And as for us, it's little we want."

"Only the garden, father," said Eppie, blushing up to the ears the moment after.

"You love a garden, do you, my dear?" said Nancy, thinking that this turn in the point of view might help her husband. "We should agree in that: I give a deal of time to the garden."

"Ah, there's plenty of gardening at the Red House," said Godfrey, surprised at the difficulty he found in approaching a proposition which had seemed so easy to him in the distance. "You've done a good part by Eppie, Marner, for sixteen years. It 'ud be a great comfort to you to see her well provided for, wouldn't it? She looks blooming and healthy, but not fit for any hardships: she doesn't look like a strapping girl come of working parents. You'd like to see her taken care of by those who can leave her well off, and make a lady of her; she's more fit for it than for a rough life, such as she might come to have in a few years' time."

A slight flush came over Marner's face, and disappeared, like a passing gleam. Eppie was simply wondering Mr. Cass should talk so about things that seemed to have nothing to do with reality; but Silas was hurt and uneasy.

"I don't take your meaning, sir," he answered, not having words at command to express the mingled feelings with which he had heard Mr. Cass's words.

"Well, my meaning is this, Marner," said Godfrey, determined to come to the point. "Mrs. Cass and I, you know, have no children—nobody to benefit by our good home and everything else we have—more than enough for ourselves. And we should like to have somebody in the place of a daughter to us—we should like to have Eppie, and treat her in every way as our own child. It would be a great comfort to you in your old age, I hope, to see her fortune made in that way, after you've been at the trouble of bringing her up so well. And it's right you should have every reward for that. And Eppie, I'm sure, will always love you and be grateful to you: she'd come and see you very often, and we should all be on the lookout to do everything we could towards making you comfortable."

A plain man like Godfrey Cass, speaking under some embarrassment, necessarily blunders on words that are coarser than his intentions, and that are likely to fall gratingly on susceptible feelings. While he had been speaking, Eppie had quietly passed her arm behind Silas's head, and let her hand rest against it caressingly: she felt him trembling violently. He was silent for some moments when Mr. Cass had ended—powerless under the conflict of emotions, all alike painful. Eppie's heart was swelling at the sense that her father was in distress; and she was just going to lean down and speak to him, when one struggling dread at last gained the mastery over every other in Silas, and he said, faintly:

"Eppie, my child, speak. I won't stand in your way. Thank Mr. and Mrs. Cass."

Eppie took her hand from her father's head, and came forward a step. Her cheeks were flushed, but not with shyness this time: the sense that her father was in doubt and suffering banished that sort of self-consciousness. She dropt a low curtsy, first to Mrs. Cass and then to Mr. Cass, and said:

"Thank you, ma'am—thank you, sir. But I can't leave my father, nor own anybody nearer than him. And I don't want to be a lady—thank you all the same" (here Eppie dropped another curtsy). "I couldn't give up the folks I've been used to."

Eppie's lips began to tremble a little at the last words. She retreated to her father's chair again, and held him round the neck: while Silas, with a subdued sob, put up his hand to grasp hers.

The tears were in Nancy's eyes, but her sympathy with Eppie was, naturally, divided with distress on her husband's account. She dared not speak, wondering what was going on in her husband's mind.

Godfrey felt an irritation inevitable to almost all of us when we encounter an unexpected obstacle. He had been full of his own penitence and resolution to retrieve his error as far as the time was left to him; he was possessed with all-important feelings, that were to lead to a pre-determined course of action which he had fixed on as the right, and he was not prepared to enter with lively appreciation into other people's feelings counteracting his virtuous resolves. The agitation with which he spoke again was not quite unmixed with anger.

"But I've a claim on you, Eppie—the strongest of all claims. It's my duty, Marner, to own Eppie as my child, and provide for her. She is my own child—her mother was my wife. I have a natural claim on her that must stand before every other."

Eppie had given a violent start, and turned quite pale. Silas, on the contrary, who had been relieved, by Eppie's answer, from the dread lest his mind should be in opposition to hers, felt the spirit of resistance in him set free, not without a touch of parental fierceness. "Then, sir," he answered, with an accent of bitterness that had been silent in him since the memorable day when his youthful hope had perished, "then, sir, why didn't you say so sixteen year ago, and claim her before I'd come to love her, i'stead o' coming to take her from me now, when you might as well take the heart out o' my body? God gave her to me because you turned your back upon her, and He looks upon her as mine; you've no right to her! When a man turns a blessing from his door, it falls to them as take it in."

"I know that, Marner. I was wrong. I've repented of my conduct in that matter," said Godfrey, who could not help feeling the edge of Silas's words.

"I am glad to hear it, sir," said Marner, with gathering excitement; "but repentance doesn't alter what's been going on for sixteen year. Your coming now and saying "I'm her father," doesn't alter the feelings inside us. It's me she's been calling her father ever since she could say the word."

"But I think you might look at the thing more reasonably, Marner," said Godfrey, unexpectedly awed by the weaver's direct truth-speaking. "It isn't as if she was to be taken quite away from you, so that you'd never see her again. She'll be very near you, and come to see you very often. She'll feel just the same towards you."

"Just the same?" said Marner, more bitterly than ever. "How'll she feel just the same for me as she does now, when we eat o' the same bit, and drink o' the same cup, and think o' the same things from one day's end to another? Just the same? That's idle talk. You'd cut us i' two."

Godfrey, unqualified by experience to discern the pregnancy of Marner's simple words, felt rather angry again. It seemed to him that the weaver was very selfish (a judgment readily passed by those who have never tested their own power of sacrifice) to oppose what was undoubtedly for Eppie's welfare; and he felt himself called upon, for her sake, to assert his authority.

"I should have thought, Marner," he said severely, "I should have thought your affection for Eppie would have made you rejoice in what was for her good, even if it did call upon you to give up something. You ought to remember your own life's uncertain, and she's at an age now when her lot may soon be fixed in a way very different from what it would be in her father's home: she may

marry some low workingman, and then, whatever I might
do for her, I couldn't make her well-off. You're putting
yourself in the way of her welfare; and though I'm sorry
to hurt you after what you've done, and what I've left
undone, I feel now it's my duty to insist on taking care
of my own daughter. I want to do my duty."

It would be difficult to say whether it were Silas or
Eppie that was most deeply stirred by this last speech of
Godfrey's. Thought had been very busy in Eppie as she
listened to the contest between her old, long-loved father
and this new unfamiliar father who had suddenly come
to fill the place of that black featureless shadow which
had held the ring and placed it on her mother's finger.
Her imagination had darted backward in conjectures, and
forward in previsions, of what this revealed fatherhood
implied; and there were words in Godfrey's last speech
which helped to make the previsions especially definite.
Not that these thoughts, either of past or future, determined her resolution—*that* was determined by the feelings
which vibrated to every word Silas had uttered; but they
raised, even apart from these feelings, a repulsion towards
the offered lot and the newly revealed father.

Silas, on the other hand, was again stricken in conscience, and alarmed lest Godfrey's accusation should be
true—lest he should be raising his own will as an obstacle
to Eppie's good. For many moments he was mute,
struggling for the self-conquest necessary to the uttering
of the difficult words. They came out tremulously.

"I'll say no more. Let it be as you will. Speak to the
child. I'll hinder nothing."

Even Nancy, with all the acute sensibility of her own
affections, shared her husband's view, that Marner was
not justifiable in his wish to retain Eppie, after her real
father had avowed himself. She felt that it was a very
hard trial for the poor weaver, but her code allowed no
question that a father by blood must have a claim above
that of any foster father. Besides, Nancy, used all her life
to plenteous circumstances and the privileges of "respectability," could not enter into the pleasures which early
nurture and habit connect with all the little aims and
efforts of the poor who are born poor: to her mind, Eppie,
in being restored to her birthright, was entering on a too

long withheld but unquestionable good. Hence she heard Silas's last words with relief, and thought, as Godfrey did, that their wish was achieved.

"Eppie, my dear," said Godfrey, looking at his daughter, not without some embarrassment, under the sense that she was old enough to judge him, "it'll always be our wish that you should show your love and gratitude to one who's been a father to you so many years, and we shall want to help you to make him comfortable in every way. But we hope you'll come to love us as well; and though I haven't been what a father should have been to you all these years, I wish to do the utmost in my power for you for the rest of my life, and provide for you as my only child. And you'll have the best of mothers in my wife—that'll be a blessing you haven't known since you were old enough to know it."

"My dear, you'll be a treasure to me," said Nancy, in her gentle voice. "We shall want for nothing when we have our daughter."

Eppie did not come forward and curtsy, as she had done before. She held Silas's hand in hers, and grasped it firmly—it was a weaver's hand, with a palm and fingertips that were sensitive to such pressure—while she spoke with colder decision than before.

"Thank you, ma'am—thank you, sir, for your offers—they're very great, and far above my wish. For I should have no delight i' life any more if I was forced to go away from my father, and knew he was sitting at home, a-thinking of me and feeling lone. We've been used to be happy together every day, and I can't think o' no happiness without him. And he says he'd nobody i' the world till I was sent to him, and he'd have nothing when I was gone. And he's took care of me and loved me from the first, and I'll cleave to him as long as he lives, and nobody shall ever come between him and me."

"But you must make sure, Eppie," said Silas, in a low voice, "you must make sure as you won't ever be sorry, because you've made your choice to stay among poor folks, and with poor clothes and things, when you might ha' had everything o' the best."

His sensitiveness on this point had increased as he listened to Eppie's words of faithful affection.

"I can never be sorry, Father," said Eppie. "I shouldn't know what to think on or to wish for with fine things about me, as I haven't been used to. And it 'ud be poor work for me to put on things, and ride in a gig, and sit in a place at church, as 'ud make them as I'm fond of think me unfitting company for 'em. What could *I* care for then?"

Nancy looked at Godfrey with a pained, questioning glance. But his eyes were fixed on the floor, where he was moving the end of his stick, as if he were pondering on something absently. She thought there was a word which might perhaps come better from her lips than from his.

"What you say is natural, my dear child—it's natural you should cling to those who've brought you up," she said mildly; "but there's a duty you owe to your lawful father. There's perhaps something to be given up on more sides than one. When your father opens his home to you, I think it's right you shouldn't turn your back on it."

"I can't feel as I've got any father but one," said Eppie impetuously, while the tears gathered. "I've always thought of a little home where he'd sit i' the corner, and I should fend and do everything for him: I can't think o' no other home. I wasn't brought up to be a lady, and I can't turn my mind to it. I like the working folks, and their houses, and their ways. And," she ended passionately, while the tears fell, "I'm promised to marry a workingman, as'll live with father, and help me to take care of him."

Godfrey looked up at Nancy with a flushed face and a smarting dilation of the eyes. This frustration of a purpose towards which he had set out under the exalted consciousness that he was about to compensate in some degree for the greatest demerit of his life made him feel the air of the room stifling.

"Let us go," he said, in an undertone.

"We won't talk of this any longer now," said Nancy, rising. "We're your well wishers, my dear—and yours too, Marner. We shall come and see you again. It's getting late now."

In this way she covered her husband's abrupt departure, for Godfrey had gone straight to the door, unable to say more.

CHAPTER XX

NANCY AND GODFREY walked home under the starlight in silence. When they entered the oaken parlour, Godfrey threw himself into his chair, while Nancy laid down her bonnet and shawl, and stood on the hearth near her husband, unwilling to leave him even for a few minutes, and yet fearing to utter any word lest it might jar on his feeling. At last Godfrey turned his head towards her, and their eyes met, dwelling in that meeting without any movement on either side. That quiet mutual gaze of a trusting husband and wife is like the first moment of rest or refuge from a great weariness or a great danger—not to be interfered with by speech or action which would distract the sensations from the fresh enjoyment of repose.

But presently he put out his hand, and as Nancy placed hers within it, he drew her towards him, and said:

"That's ended!"

She bent to kiss him, and then said, as she stood by his side, "Yes, I'm afraid we must give up the hope of having her for a daughter. It wouldn't be right to want to force her to come to us against her will. We can't alter her bringing up and what's come of it."

"No," said Godfrey, with a keen decisiveness of tone, in contrast with his usually careless and unemphatic speech; "there's debts we can't pay like money debts, by paying extra for the years that have slipped by. While I've been putting off and putting off, the trees have been growing—it's too late now. Marner was in the right in what he said about a man's turning away a blessing from his door: it falls to somebody else. I wanted to pass for childless once, Nancy—I shall pass for childless now against my wish."

Nancy did not speak immediately, but after a little while she asked, "You won't make it known, then, about Eppie's being your daughter?"

"No, where would be the good to anybody?—only harm.

I must do what I can for her in the state of life she chooses. I must see who it is she's thinking of marrying."

"If it won't do any good to make the thing known," said Nancy, who thought she might now allow herself the relief of entertaining a feeling which she had tried to silence before, "I should be very thankful for father and Priscilla never to be troubled with knowing what was done in the past, more than about Dunsey: it can't be helped, their knowing that."

"I shall put it in my will—I think I shall put it in my will. I shouldn't like to leave anything to be found out, like this of Dunsey," said Godfrey meditatively. "But I can't see anything but difficulties that 'ud come from telling it now. I must do what I can to make her happy in her own way. I've a notion," he added, after a moment's pause, "it's Aaron Winthrop she meant she was engaged to. I remember seeing him with her and Marner going away from church."

"Well, he's very sober and industrious," said Nancy, trying to view the matter as cheerfully as possible.

Godfrey fell into thoughtfulness again. Presently he looked up at Nancy sorrowfully, and said:

"She's a very pretty, nice girl, isn't she, Nancy?"

"Yes, dear; and with just your hair and eyes: I wondered it had never struck me before."

"I think she took a dislike to me at the thought of my being her father: I could see a change in her manner after that."

"She couldn't bear to think of not looking on Marner as her father," said Nancy, not wishing to confirm her husband's painful impression.

"She thinks I did wrong by her mother as well as by her. She thinks me worse than I am. But she *must* think it: she can never know all. It's part of my punishment, Nancy, for my daughter to dislike me. I should never have got into that trouble if I'd been true to you—if I hadn't been a fool. I'd no right to expect anything but evil could come of that marriage—and when I shirked doing a father's part too."

Nancy was silent: her spirit of rectitude would not let her try to soften the edge of what she felt to be a just compunction. He spoke again after a little while, but the tone was rather changed: there was tenderness mingled with the previous self-reproach.

"And I got *you*, Nancy, in spite of all; and yet I've been grumbling and uneasy because I hadn't something else—as if I deserved it."

"You've never been wanting to me, Godfrey," said Nancy, with quiet sincerity. "My only trouble would be gone if you resigned yourself to the lot that's been given us."

"Well, perhaps it isn't too late to mend a bit there. Though it *is* too late to mend some things, say what they will."

CHAPTER XXI

THE NEXT MORNING, when Silas and Eppie were seated at their breakfast, he said to her:

"Eppie, there's a thing I've had on my mind to do this two year, and now the money's been brought back to us, we can do it. I've been turning it over and over in the night, and I think we'll set out tomorrow, while the fine days last. We'll leave the house and everything for your godmother to take care on, and we'll make a little bundle o' things and set out."

"Where to go, Daddy?" said Eppie, in much surprise.

"To my old country—to the town where I was born— up Lantern Yard. I want to see Mr. Paston, the minister: something may ha' come out to make 'em know I was innicent o' the robbery. And Mr. Paston was a man with a deal o' light—I want to speak to him about the drawing o' the lots. And I should like to talk to him about the religion o' this countryside, for I partly think he doesn't know on it."

Eppie was very joyful, for there was the prospect not only of wonder and delight at seeing a strange country, but also of coming back to tell Aaron all about it. Aaron was so much wiser than she was about most things—it would be rather pleasant to have this little advantage over him. Mrs. Winthrop, though possessed with a dim fear of dangers attendant on so long a journey, and re-

quiring many assurances that it would not take them
out of the region of carriers' carts and slow waggons, was
nevertheless well pleased that Silas should revisit his own
country, and find out if he had been cleared from that
false accusation.

"You'd be easier in your mind for the rest o' your life,
Master Marner," said Dolly, "that you would. And if
there's any light to be got up the yard as you talk on,
we've need of it i' this world, and I'd be glad on it myself,
if you could bring it back."

So on the fourth day from that time, Silas and Eppie,
in their Sunday clothes, with a small bundle tied in a
blue linen handkerchief, were making their way through
the streets of a great manufacturing town. Silas, bewildered by the changes thirty years had brought over his
native place, had stopped several persons in succession to
ask them the name of this town, that he might be sure he
was not under a mistake about it.

"Ask for Lantern Yard, Father—ask this gentleman
with the tassels on his shoulders a-standing at the shop
door; he isn't in a hurry like the rest," said Eppie, in
some distress at her father's bewilderment, and ill at ease,
besides, amidst the noise, the movement, and the multitude of strange, indifferent faces.

"Eh, my child, he won't know anything about it," said
Silas; "gentlefolks didn't ever go up the Yard. But happen
somebody can tell me which is the way to Prison Street,
where the jail is. I know the way out o' that as if I'd seen
it yesterday."

With some difficulty, after many turnings and new
inquiries, they reached Prison Street; and the grim walls
of the jail, the first object that answered to any image in
Silas's memory, cheered him with the certitude, which no
assurance of the town's name had hitherto given him, that
he was in his native place.

"Ah," he said, drawing a long breath, "there's the jail,
Eppie; that's just the same: I aren't afraid now. It's the
third turning on the left hand from the jail doors, that's
the way we must go."

"Oh, what a dark, ugly place!" said Eppie. "How it
hides the sky! It's worse than the workhouse. I'm glad

you don't live in this town now, Father. Is Lantern Yard like this street?"

"My precious child," said Silas, smiling, "it isn't a big street like this. I never was easy i' this street myself, but I was fond o' Lantern Yard. The shops here are all altered, I think—I can't make 'em out; but I shall know the turning, because it's the third.

"Here it is," he said, in a tone of satisfaction, as they came to a narrow alley. "And then we must go to the left again, and then straight for'ard for a bit, up Shoe Lane: and then we shall be at the entry next to the o'er-hanging window, where there's the nick in the road for the water to run. Eh, I can see it all."

"Oh, Father, I'm like as if I was stifled," said Eppie. "I couldn't ha' thought as any folks lived i' this way, so close together. How pretty the Stone Pits 'ull look when we get back!"

"It looks comical to *me,* child, now—and smells bad. I can't think as it usened to smell so."

Here and there a sallow, begrimed face looked out from a gloomy doorway at the strangers, and increased Eppie's uneasiness, so that it was a longed-for relief when they issued from the alleys into Shoe Lane, where there was a broader strip of sky.

"Dear heart!" said Silas, "why, there's people coming out o' the Yard as if they'd been to chapel at this time o' day—a weekday noon!"

Suddenly he started and stood still with a look of distressed amazement that alarmed Eppie. They were before an opening in front of a large factory, from which men and women were streaming for their midday meal.

"Father," said Eppie, clasping his arm, "what's the matter?"

But she had to speak again and again before Silas could answer her.

"It's gone, child," he said, at last, in strong agitation, "Lantern Yard's gone. It must ha' been here, because here's the house with the o'erhanging window—I know that—it's just the same; but they've made this new opening; and see that big factory! It's all gone—chapel and all."

"Come into that little brush shop and sit down, Father

—they'll let you sit down," said Eppie, always on the watch lest one of her father's strange attacks should come on. "Perhaps the people can tell you all about it."

But neither from the brushmaker, who had come to Shoe Lane only ten years ago, when the factory was already built, nor from any other source within his reach, could Silas learn anything of the old Lantern Yard friends, or of Mr. Paston, the minister.

"The old place is all swep' away," Silas said to Dolly Winthrop on the night of his return; "the little graveyard and everything. The old home's gone; I've no home but this now. I shall never know whether they got at the truth o' the robbery, nor whether Mr. Paston could ha' given me any light about the drawing o' the lots. It's dark to me, Mrs. Winthrop, that is; I doubt it'll be dark to the last."

"Well, yes, Master Marner," said Dolly, who sat with a placid, listening face, now bordered by grey hairs; "I doubt it may. It's the will o' Them above as a many things should be dark to us; but there's some things as I've never felt i' the dark about, and they're mostly what comes i' the day's work. You were hard done by that once, Master Marner, and it seems as you'll never know the rights of it; but that doesn't hinder there *being* a rights, Master Marner, for all it's dark to you and me."

"No," said Silas, "no; that doesn't hinder. Since the time the child was sent to me and I've come to love her as myself, I've had light enough to trusten by; and, now she says she'll never leave me, I think I shall trusten till I die."

CONCLUSION

THERE WAS ONE TIME of the year which was held in Raveloe to be especially suitable for a wedding. It was when the great lilacs and laburnums in the old-fashioned gardens showed their golden and purple wealth above the lichen-tinted walls, and when there were calves still young enough to want bucketfuls of fragrant milk. People were not so busy then as they must become when the full cheese-making and the mowing had set in; and besides, it was a time when a light bridal dress could be worn with comfort and seen to advantage.

Happily the sunshine fell more warmly than usual on the lilac tufts the morning that Eppie was married, for her dress was a very light one. She had often thought, though with a feeling of renunciation, that the perfection of a wedding dress would be a white cotton, with the tiniest pink sprig at wide intervals; so that when Mrs. Godfrey Cass begged to provide one, and asked Eppie to choose what it should be, previous meditation had enabled her to give a decided answer at once.

Seen at a little distance as she walked across the churchyard and down the village, she seemed to be attired in pure white, and her hair looked like the dash of gold on a lily. One hand was on her husband's arm, and with the other she clasped the hand of her father Silas.

"You won't be giving me away, father," she had said before they went to church; "you'll only be taking Aaron to be a son to you."

Dolly Winthrop walked behind with her husband; and there ended the little bridal procession.

There were many eyes to look at it, and Miss Priscilla Lammeter was glad that she and her father had happened to drive up to the door of the Red House just in time to see this pretty sight. They had come to keep Nancy company today, because Mr. Cass had had to go away to Lytherley, for special reasons. That seemed to be a pity, for otherwise he might have gone, as Mr. Crackenthorp and Mr. Osgood certainly would, to look on at the wedding feast which he had ordered at the Rainbow, naturally feeling a great interest in the weaver who had been wronged by one of his own family.

"I could ha' wished Nancy had had the luck to find a child like that and bring her up," said Priscilla to her father, as they sat in the gig; "I should ha' had something young to think of then, besides the lambs and the calves."

"Yes, my dear, yes," said Mr. Lammeter; "one feels that as one gets older. Things look dim to old folks: they'd need have some young eyes about 'em, to let 'em know the world's the same as it used to be."

Nancy came out now to welcome her father and sister; and the wedding group had passed on beyond the Red House to the humbler part of the village.

Dolly Winthrop was the first to divine that old Mr. Macey, who had been set in his armchair outside his own door, would expect some special notice as they passed, since he was too old to be at the wedding feast.

"Mr. Macey's looking for a word from us," said Dolly; "he'll be hurt if we pass him and say nothing—and him so racked with rheumatiz."

So they turned aside to shake hands with the old man. He had looked forward to the occasion, and had his premeditated speech.

"Well, Master Marner," he said, in a voice that quavered a good deal, "I've lived to see my words come true. I was the first to say there was no harm in you, though your looks might be again' you; and I was the first to say you'd get your money back. And it's nothing but rightful as you should. And I'd ha' said the 'Amens,' and willing, at the holy matrimony; but Tookey's done it a good while now, and I hope you'll have none the worse luck."

In the open yard before the Rainbow, the party of guests were already assembled, though it was still nearly an hour before the appointed feast time. But by this means they could not only enjoy the slow advent of their pleasures; they had also ample leisure to talk of Silas Marner's strange history, and arrive by due degrees at the conclusion that he had brought a blessing on himself by acting like a father to a lone, motherless child. Even the farrier did not negative this sentiment: on the contrary, he took it up as peculiarly his own, and invited any hardy person present to contradict him. But he met with no contradiction; and all differences among the company were merged in a general agreement with Mr. Snell's sentiment, that when a man had deserved his good luck, it was the part of his neighbours to wish him joy.

As the bridal party approached, a hearty cheer was raised in the Rainbow yard; and Ben Winthrop, whose jokes had retained their acceptable flavour, found it agreeable to turn in there and receive congratulations; not requiring the proposed interval of quiet at the Stone Pits before joining the company.

Eppie had a larger garden than she had ever expected there now; and in other ways there had been alterations at the expense of Mr. Cass, the landlord, to suit Silas's larger family. For he and Eppie had declared that they would rather stay at the Stone Pits than go to any new home. The garden was fenced with stones on two sides, but in front there was an open fence, through which the flowers shone with answering gladness, as the four united people came within sight of them.

"Oh, Father," said Eppie, "what a pretty home ours is! I think nobody could be happier than we are."

SELECTED BIBLIOGRAPHY
Jane Austen

OTHER WORKS BY JANE AUSTEN

LOVE AND FRIENDSHIP, 1790 Novel
MANSFIELD PARK, 1814 Novel (Signet Classic CY886)
EMMA, 1816 Novel (Signet Classic CW1010)
SANDITON, 1817 Fragment of a Novel (Signet J6945)
SENSE & SENSIBILITY, 1811 Novel (Signet Classic CJ1184)
NORTHANGER ABBEY, 1818 Novel (Signet Classic CW1113)
PERSUASION, 1818 Novel (Signet Classic CY887)

SELECTED BIOGRAPHY AND CRITICISM

Austen-Leigh, J. E. *A Memoir of Jane Austen*, ed. by R. W. Chapman. London and New York: Oxford University Press, 1926.
Bush, Douglas. *Jane Austen*. New York: Macmillan, 1975.
Butler, Marilyn. *Jane Austen and the War of Ideas*. New York and London: Oxford University Press, 1975.
Chapman, R. W. *Jane Austen: Facts and Problems*, London and New York: Oxford University Press, 1948.
Jenkins, Elizabeth. *Jane Austen*. New York: Pellegrini and Cudahy, 1949. London: MacDonald and Co., 1956.
Kroeber, Karl. *Styles in Fictional Structure: The Art of Jane Austen, Charlotte Brontë, George Eliot*. Princeton, N.J.: Princeton University Press, 1971.
Lascelles, Mary. *Jane Austen and Her Art*. London and New York: Oxford University Press, 1939.

Mudrick, M. *Jane Austen: Irony As Defense and Discovery.* Princeton, N. J.: Princeton University Press; London: Oxford University Press, 1952.

O'Neil, Judith, ed. *Critics on Jane Austen.* Miami, Fla.: University of Miami Press, 1970.

Rees, Joan. *Jane Austen: Woman & Writer.* New York: St. Martins Press, 1976.

Tave, Stuart M. *Some Words of Jane Austen.* Chicago, Ill.: University of Chicago Press, 1973.

Wright, Andrew H. *Jane Austen's Novels: A Study in Structure.* New York: Oxford University Press; London: Chatto & Windus, Ltd., 1953.

Emily Brontë

Bentley, Phyllis. *The Brontës*. New York: Viking Press, 1972

Gerin, Winifred. *Emily Brontë*. New York and London: Oxford University Press, 1972.

O'Neill, Judith, ed. *Critics on Charlotte and Emily Brontë*. Miami, Fla.: University of Miami Press, 1968.

Volger, T. *Wuthering Heights: Twentieth Century Interpretations*. Englewood Cliffs, N. J.: Prentice Hall, 1968.

Wilson, Romer. *The Life and Private History of Emily Brontë*. Brooklyn, N.Y.: Haskell House. Reprint of 1928 ed.

George Eliot

OTHER WORKS BY GEORGE ELIOT

ADAM BEDE 1859 Novel (Signet CE1015)
SCENES OF CLERICAL LIFE, 1857 Stories
THE MILL ON THE FLOSS, 1860 Novel (Signet CJ1055)
ROMOLA, 1863 Novel
FELIX HOLT THE RADICAL, 1866 Novel
HOW LISA LOVED THE KING, 1867 Poems
THE SPANISH GYPSY, 1868 Poem
MIDDLEMARCH, 1872 Novel (Signet CE1044)
THE LEGEND OF JUBAL, 1874 Poem
DANIEL DERONDA, 1876 Novel (Signet CE1204)
IMPRESSIONS OF THEOPHRASTUS SUCH, 1879 Essays

SELECTED BIOGRAPHY AND CRITICISM

Baker, William, ed. *Critics on George Eliot.* London: Allen Unwin, 1973.

Bennett, Joan. *George Eliot: Her Mind and Her Art.* New York: The Macmillan Company, 1948; London: Cambridge University Press, 1949.

Cecil, Lord David. *Early Victorian Novelists: Essays in Revaluation.* London: Constable & Company, Ltd., 1934; New York: Bobbs-Merrill Company, 1935.

Creeger, George R., ed. *George Eliot: A Collection of Critical Essays.* Englewood Cliffs: Prentice-Hall, 1970.

Fremantle, Anne. *George Eliot.* New York: The Macmillan Company; London: Gerald Duckworth & Company, Ltd., 1933.

Haight, Gordon S. ed. *A Century of George Eliot Criticism.* Boston: Houghton Mifflin, 1965.

Haight, Gordon S. *George Eliot: A Biography*. London and New York: Oxford University Press, 1978.

Hanson, Lawrence and Elizabeth M. *Marian Evans and George Eliot: A Biography*. New York: Oxford University Press, 1952.

Hardy, Barbara. *The Novels of George Eliot: A Study in Form*. Fair Lawn, N.J.: Essential Books, Inc.; London: The Athlone Press, 1959.

Leavis, F. R. *The Great Tradition: George Eliot, Henry James, Joseph Conrad*. New York: George W. Stewart, Publisher, Inc.; London: Chatto & Windus, 1948.

Mintz, Alan. *George Eliot and the Novel of Vocation*. Cambridge, Mass.: Harvard University Press, 1978.

Stang, Richard. *Discussions of George Eliot*. Boston: D. C. Heath & Company, 1960.

Stump, Reva. *Movement and Vision in George Eliot's Novels*. Seattle: University of Washington Press, 1959.

Thale, J. *Novels of George Eliot*. New York: Columbia University Press; London: Oxford University Press, 1959.

Williams, B. C. *George Eliot: A Biography*. New York: The Macmillan Company, 1936.

Woolf, Virginia. "George Eliot," *The Common Reader*. New York: Harcourt, Brace and Company, 1925.

SIGNET and SIGNET CLASSIC NOVELS You'll Enjoy